SLAY

COMPLETE SERIES

paige press

SLAY

COMPLETE SERIES

NEW YORK TIMES BESTSELLING AUTHOR
LAURELIN PAIGE

Paige Press, LLC
Leander, Texas

Ebook ISBN: 978-1-953520-91-3
Paperback ISBN: 978-1-953520-92-0

Editing: Erica Russikoff at Erica Edits

Proofing: Michele Ficht, Kimberly Ruiz

Cover: Laurelin Paige and Melissa Gaston

Beta Readers: Candi Kane, Melissa Gaston, Amy "Vox" Libris, Roxie Madar, and Liz Berry

ALSO BY LAURELIN PAIGE

Visit my website for a more detailed reading order.

The Dirty Universe
Dirty Filthy Rich Boys - READ FREE
Dirty Duet (Donovan Kincaid)
Dirty Filthy Rich Men | Dirty Filthy Rich Love
Kincaid (coming 2022)
Dirty Games Duet (Weston King)
Dirty Sexy Player| Dirty Sexy Games
Dirty Sweet Duet (Dylan Locke)
Sweet Liar | Sweet Fate
(Nate Sinclair) Dirty Filthy Fix (a spinoff novella)
Dirty Wild Trilogy (Cade Warren)
Wild Rebel | Wild War | Wild Heart

Man in Charge Duet
Man in Charge
Man in Love
Man for Me (a spinoff novella)

The Fixed Universe
Fixed Series (Hudson & Alayna)

Fixed on You | Found in You | Forever with You | Hudson | Fixed Forever

Found Duet (Gwen & JC) Free Me | Find Me

(Chandler & Genevieve) Chandler (a spinoff novella)

(Norma & Boyd) Falling Under You (a spinoff novella)

(Nate & Trish) Dirty Filthy Fix (a spinoff novella)

Slay Series (Celia & Edward)

Rivalry | Ruin | Revenge | Rising

(Gwen & JC) The Open Door (a spinoff novella)

(Camilla & Hendrix) Slash (a spinoff novella)

First and Last

First Touch | Last Kiss

Hollywood Standalones

One More Time

Close

Sex Symbol

Star Struck

Dating Season

Tis the Reason for The Season (A Dating Season Prequel) |Bundle 1 (Spring Fling & Summer Rebound) | Bundle 2 (Fall Hard & Winter Bloom) | Bundle 3 (Spring Fever & Summer Lovin)

Also written with Kayti McGee under the name Laurelin McGee

Miss Match | Love Struck | MisTaken | Holiday for Hire

Written with Sierra Simone

Porn Star | Hot Cop

Be sure to **sign up for my newsletter** where you'll receive **a FREE book every month** from bestselling authors, only available to my subscribers, as well as up-to-date information on my latest releases.

PRO TIP: Add laurelin@laurelinpaige.com to your contacts before signing up to be sure the list comes right to your inbox.

DID YOU KNOW...

This book is available in both paperback and audiobook editions at all major online retailers! Links are on my website.

If you'd like to order a signed paperback, my online store is open several times a year here.

RIVALRY: SLAY ONE

Edward Fasbender is a devil.

He's my father's biggest rival. He takes what he wants, and he bows to no one.

And now Edward Fasbender wants me.

I didn't expect to want him back.

Having him is not in the cards, not when a union with him would destroy my father. But that doesn't mean I can't play with him a bit.

Except, I've never played against such a ruthless opponent. Edward is cold and vicious, and my blood has never run hotter.
They say you should choose the devil you know, but I've always preferred long odds.

Even if it'll get me slain.

For Candi and Melissa,
who champion with soothing words
and kindly, but surely,
lured this beast out from inside me.

INTRODUCTION

Long ago, I learned how to be made of nothing.

Trained my body to convert every experience, every encounter, every observation into emptiness before metabolizing and processing them inside of me. I run on nothingness. I feast on void. My fuel is black and cold and nothing, nothing.

Every breath I take in, the oxygen transforms into wisps of oblivion. Feel it as I exhale (feel nothing). Hear the sound of nothing as it exits from my lungs and circles like a fog around me.

Flesh and bone and blood no longer are my makeup. I'm stacks of naught, packed into my being at the molecular level. My skin, my muscles, my organs, my cunt—cells of non-existence, masquerading as bits of human. Touch me, I'll feel nothing. Bruise me, fuck me, love me—nothing, nothing, nothing.

Everything within me has been altered and adapted.

There's nothing real anymore. Nothing solid. Nothing worthy.

Only pieces of limbo. Only nihilism. Only nothing.

Nothing wrapped securely around my core, an impenetrable seal.

Nothing jammed in all my spaces, crammed in tight, protecting the last embers of a once-blazing heart. I'm barely aware of its beat anymore through the layers of vacuity, barely feel the steadiness of its pulse.

I hear it sometimes, muffled by the padding of nothing squeezed around it, tick-tick-ticking like a metronome. Like a faraway clock. Like the click of a turn signal. Like my uncle's pocket watch.

Like a bomb counting down to detonation.

Like a bomb, waiting to explode.

ONE

"YOU REALLY SCREWED this one up, Celia. Hudson is officially out of reach. You let him slip away, and now everything you dreamed of is over."

I rolled my eyes, even though my mother couldn't see my face through the phone. I was tired of this speech. I'd heard a variation of it at least three times a week since my childhood friend had gotten married over two years ago.

As for my dreams being over...well, it had been a long time since I'd imagined myself ending up with Hudson Pierce. That was my mother's aspiration, not mine. Not anymore.

There wasn't any use in arguing with her. She found some sort of comfort in lamenting over her daughter's failures, and this particular lament was one of her favorites.

"From what Sophia says, he's even more devoted now to this marriage than he ever was, and I'm not at all surprised. A man will leave a wife easily enough, but when she gets pregnant, forget it. He's sticking around."

I leaned my head against the window of my Lyft car and sighed. "How is Sophia these days?" It was a manipulative redirection on my part. It disgusted me that she pretended otherwise, but Hudson's mother wasn't exactly on friendly terms with Madge Werner like she once was.

Pity.

That was also my fault. Hudson's fault too, not that either of our mothers would ever concede that fact.

I knew my tactic worked when my mother huffed loudly in my ear.

Just as I'd thought. My mother hadn't directly spoken to Hudson's mother about any of this. Likely, she'd picked it up through the grapevine. A friend of a friend or overheard it at a charity luncheon. What else did the rich bitches do these days to keep themselves entertained?

My own methods of amusement certainly weren't of the popular variety. But they were definitely more fun.

Or they once were, anyway. Even The Game had lost its spark in recent years.

"I don't even know why I bother talking to you about this," my mother droned on. "It's your own fault you're not with Hudson."

There was his name again. *Hudson.* There had been a time when it hurt to hear it. A time when immense agony had wracked through my body at the two simple syllables. That was a lifetime ago now. The bruise he'd left was permanent and yellowed with age, and I pressed at it sometimes, saying his name, recalling everything that had transpired between us, just to see if I could provoke any of those emotions again.

Every time I came up empty.

I owed that to him, I supposed. He'd been the one to teach me The Game. He'd been the one to teach me how to feel nothing. How to *be* nothing. How ironic that his life today was happy and complete and *full.*

Good for you, Hudson. Good for fucking you.

My mother was still yammering when the car pulled up at my destination. "You don't even realize how much you gave up when you let him get away, do you? Don't expect to do better than him. We both know you can't."

Indignation pierced through my hollow cocoon; anger in its varied forms was the one emotion that seemed to slip in now and again. My mother didn't know shit about me, no matter how close she perceived our relationship. Couldn't *do better* than Hudson? God, how I longed to prove her wrong.

But I didn't have any ammunition. I had nothing. I wasn't dating anyone, not really. I had my own interior design company that barely made enough to pay expenses, and I didn't even take a salary for myself. I was a trust fund baby for all intents and purposes, living off my father's business, Werner Media. And while all of my choices were purposeful, I couldn't exactly explain to my mother that the majority of my time and energy was spent on playing The Game. There was no one who would understand that, not even Hudson anymore.

With no comeback, my best bet was to end the call.

"I'm at my meeting. I have to go now, Mom." My tone was clipped, and I brusquely hung up before she could respond.

I gave my driver a digital tip, threw my cell phone in my bag then climbed out of the car. It was hot for early June. Humidity hung like thick cologne, and it clung to me even after I entered the lobby of the St. Regis Hotel. I was running late, but I knew this building from a lifetime of living among the upper crust of New York, and I didn't have to stop to ask for directions. The meeting rooms were a quick elevator ride up one floor to the level that had originally been John Jacob Astor's living quarters. The hotel had been kept in the elegant chic design of his time, and while pompous in its style, I found the luxurious decor both timeless and elegant.

Since I was in too much of a hurry to admire the scenery, I headed straight to my destination. Inside the foyer for the Fontainebleau Room, I paused. The doors were shut. Was I supposed to knock or walk right in?

I was already digging out my phone to text my assistant, Renee, when I noticed a man in a business suit sitting behind a small table at the opposite end of the foyer. He seemed to be deeply focused on the book he was reading and hadn't yet seen me. I didn't know what the man I was meeting with looked like so I couldn't say if this was him or not.

Cursing myself for not being more prepared, I approached him. "Excuse me, I'm Celia Werner, and I'm supposed to—"

The man barely looked up from his reading when he cut me off. "I'll let him know you're here. Have a seat." He propped his book open by placing it face down on the table and then stood and circled around it to the door of the Fontainebleau. He knocked once then opened it, disappearing inside.

Somewhat baffled at the curt greeting, I scanned the foyer and found a bench to sit on. I took out my phone and shot a text to Renee.

Why isn't this guy meeting me at the office again?

I rarely took initial client meetings anywhere else. When Renee had first told me about the appointment, I'd assumed I was being hired by a committee or a board of directors and that they'd requested to interview me as part of a general meeting of some sort. It made sense in that case to go to them rather than the other way around. But something about the vibe of the situation made me start to doubt my first assessment. If there was an entire committee behind the closed doors, why had the man who greeted me said "him"? And wouldn't I have heard voices or people noises when the door had briefly been open?

While I waited for Renee's response, I pulled the client file from my bag and looked over the papers inside. The usual client questionnaire was on top, but unlike usual, it was completely blank. I flipped to the next page, a background report. I ordered these on any client I considered taking on, not so much as a safety precaution, but more out of flagrant curiosity. My best games had been inspired by skeletons of the past, and I never passed up an opportunity to play.

I had no intention of taking on this particular client, however. In fact, I was only meeting with him so I could turn him down. The reason was laid out in bold in the first line of his information sheet: *EDWARD M. FASBENDER, OWNER AND CEO OF ACCELECOM.*

I didn't know much about Accelecom and even less about Edward Fasbender, but what I did know was that the hardball strategies of his London-based company were the primary reason Werner Media had never been able to penetrate the UK market. My father would be livid if I ever worked for his competitor, but he might be delighted to hear me tell him I'd rejected their offer. Proud, even.

At least, I hoped he would be. God only knew why I cared so deeply to please the man, but I did. It was ingrained in me at an early age to cater to the men who held dominion over me. My father was the lord of our household. If I could make him happy, I was sure my mother would stop her eternal lamenting. If I could make him happy, maybe I could *be* happy.

It was a ridiculous notion, but it had deep roots inside me.

I scanned through the rest of the report on Fasbender. Married very young. Divorced for several years. Hadn't remarried. Two nearly grown children. His father had also owned a media company that had been sold when Edward was a teen, just before both his parents had died. He'd built Accelecom from practically nothing, turning it into a multi-billion-dollar company before he'd even turned forty-two, which would be in September. It was all pretty standard information, but with years of experience, it was enough to help me create a solid picture of what kind of man Edward M. Fasbender was. Driven, calculating, strategic, monomaniacal. His dating history was too sparse for him to be attractive. He likely had to pay for his sex and didn't mind doing so. Egocentric and misogynistic probably as well, if I knew this kind of man, and I did. It would be fun rejecting his offer of employment, as shallow as the move might be.

My cell buzzed.

RENEE: **He insisted on meeting at the hotel. You approved that before. Is that still okay?**

I'd been eager to be amenable, I remembered now. The more congenial I was in the outset, the more surprising the rejection.

It's fine. Did he say what the project was going to be?

Something office related, I suspected, since there was a committee involved. Oh, that was going to be even more fun, turning him down in front of people.

RENEE: **He said he'd only discuss it in person.**

I added *controlling* to the list of character traits. And he definitely had a small dick. There was no way this asshole was packing.

Before I could ask Renee anything else, the door to the meeting room opened and the man from before stepped out. "He's ready for you now," he said, again making it sound like Mr. Fasbender was alone.

I shut the file folder, but didn't put it back in my bag, too eager and intrigued to bother with the hassle. I stood up and walked to the door of the Fontainebleau. As soon as I crossed over the threshold, I paused and frowned. Every time I'd been here in the past, the room had been set up with several round tables, banquet style. This time there was only one long boardroom type table, and though there were several chairs lined up around it, no one was sitting at them. My gaze swept the space and knocked into the one other person in the room—a man who appeared to be the same age the report had given for Fasbender.

But if this really was Edward Fasbender, I had grossly fucked up on my assessment of him. Because this man was not just attractive, he was overwhelmingly so. He was tall, just over six feet by my guesstimation. His expensive midnight-blue tailored suit showcased his svelte build, and from the way his jacket sleeves hugged his arms, it was obvious he worked out. He was fair-skinned, as his German name suggested, but his hair was dark and long at the top. While it had been tamed and sculpted in place, I imagined it floppy in its natural state. His brows were thick, but flat and expressionless, his eyes deep-set and piercing, lighter than my own baby blues, though maybe it was his periwinkle tie that brought them out so vibrantly. Whatever the reason, they were mesmeric. They made my knees feel weak. They made me catch my breath.

And his face!

His face was long with prominent cheekbones, his features rugged without being worn. He was clean shaven at the moment, but I was sure he could pull off scruff without looking gritty if he tried. His lips were full and plump with a well-defined v at the top. Two faint creases ran between his eyebrows making him appear intensely focused, and the slight lines that bookended his mouth gave him a permanent smirk, even when his mouth was just at rest.

Though, he might have meant the smirk in the moment. Considering the way I was standing frozen gawking at him, it was highly likely.

I shook my head out of my stupid daze, put on an overly bright smile, and started toward him, my hand outstretched. "Hi, I'm Celia Wern—" Before I could finish my introduction, the heel of my shoe caught on the carpet, and I tripped, spilling the contents of his file all over the floor.

Blood rushed up my neck and into my face as I crouched down to pick up the mess. It was awkward kneeling down in my pencil skirt, but I was more concerned about gathering the papers before he saw them. It only took five seconds before I realized the concern was unnecessary, because, even though I'd dropped the pages at his feet, he was not bending down to help me. I was right about his character, it seemed. Arrogant, egocentric. Asshole.

I shoved the papers back in the file and shot a glare up at him, which turned out to be a mistake, because there he was, peering down at me with that perma-smirk, and something about the position I was in and his exuding dominance sent a shiver through my body. My skin felt like it was on fire, and goosebumps paraded down my arms. His presence was overpowering. Overwhelming. Unsettling.

My mouth dropped open in surprise. Men didn't make me feel this way. *I* made men feel this way. *I* overpowered the men around me. *I* overwhelmed them. *I* unsettled them.

I didn't like it. And yet, I also kind of did. It wasn't only an unusual feeling, but it was a *feeling*. It had been a long time since I'd felt anything, let alone something so startling.

I swallowed and prepared to rise when he surprised me again, finally stooping down to my level.

"Edward Fasbender," he said, holding out his hand.

With a scowl, I took it. My hand felt warm in his tight grip, and I let him hold on past the length of a standard handshake, let him help lift me back to a standing position before I withdrew it sharply.

He smirked at this too—that mouth smirked at everything, but I could feel the smirk in his eyes as well. "I've been looking forward to meeting you, Celia," he said in his distinguished British dialect. "Have a seat, will you?"

If there had been any logic to not taking a seat, I would have continued to stand, simply because I hated conceding any more control to him than I already felt I had. But there wasn't anything practical about standing, so I threw my bag and the file on the table, pulled out a chair and angled it toward the head where, if the laptop and phone sitting there were any indication, I surmised he was going to sit.

"I hadn't realized I'd only be meeting with you, Mr. Fasbender." I purposefully didn't scoot the chair back into the table so he could have a prime view while I crossed one long leg over the other. I had nice legs. They were two of my best weapons.

The bastard didn't even glance down. With his eyes pinned on mine, he unbuttoned his jacket and sat in the seat I'd assumed he'd take. "Edward, please," he said sternly. He'd already made it clear he meant to call me Celia, even without my invitation to do so.

"As I was saying, *Edward*, I would have insisted we met in my office if I'd known you were reserving a meeting room simply for my benefit."

He tilted his head, his stone expression showing nothing. "It wasn't simply for your benefit. I've been using this room as my office while I'm in the States meeting with potential investors. It's unconventional, perhaps, but I'm already staying in the hotel, and so the location has proved convenient. Plus, I rather like the setting, don't you?"

I ignored how much I liked the low timbre of his voice and surveyed my surroundings once more. The Fontainebleau was one of the more lavish meeting rooms in the hotel. With the numerous crystal chandeliers, gold leaf plating, and ornate molding, the decor seemed to have been directly inspired by Versailles. I appreciated the luxurious look, but this was a bit on the abundant side, particularly when being used as an office. The fact that he liked it said more about his character. I added pompous and extravagant to my earlier assessment. He was probably even going to use the room as an example of whatever it was he wanted me to design for him.

No. Just no. Even if I were accepting his job offer, which I wasn't.

Refraining from commenting on the decor, I turned back to my subtle admonishment. "I'm sure this is convenient for you, but our discussion will be limited because of it. I've brought my computer and a portfolio, which will show you some of my work, but this would be much easier if you could see the models in my office. Maybe we can reschedule and meet there at a later time?" It would be even more delightful to reject him after stringing him along.

"That won't be necessary. I'm not interested in your design work."

The hairs on the back of my neck pricked up in warning, and I was suddenly glad for the man outside the door. Not that I couldn't handle myself. I'd been in much more precarious situations than this and survived.

"I'm sorry," I said, my voice cool and steady from practice. "I don't believe I understand." Though, I was beginning to have my suspicions. If I wasn't here about a design project, this meeting could only have to do with my father.

"Of course you don't. I didn't have any intention for you to understand until I was ready to explain."

He was such an arrogant piece of work. If I wasn't completely aroused with curiosity, I would have been out the door at this point.

"Since I'm here now, I'd appreciate it if you'd go ahead and fill me in. What is it you want from me?"

He leaned back in his seat, somehow seeming just as upright with his posture even in the reclined position. "What I want, Celia, is quite simple—I want you to marry me."

TWO

I FELT my jaw go slack, but I refused to let it gape. Refused to let him see the extent of my shock. "Excuse me, what did you say?"

"You heard me." His expression remained unreadable except for the slight twitch of his left eye, which I guessed to be amusement.

Oh. It was a joke, then.

"Ha ha," I said, hating how uncertainty coursed through my body. It was an unfamiliar feeling. It made my breaths come shallow and my ribs feel tight. "Very funny. Do you use this opening a lot with potential new associates?" At least my voice stayed steady. Surprising considering how shaken my nerves were.

"I assure you, Celia, I'm quite serious."

Heat flushed through me. Embarrassment, as the situation became clear. I'd planned to fuck with my father's rival, and here, he'd beaten me to the punch.

I gathered the file and threw it into my bag. "I hope you enjoyed making a spectacle out of me, Mr. Fasbender." Like hell was I calling him by his Christian name now. "I'm sure it's quite the life you lead where playing around with other human beings is merely a means of entertainment."

The words were out of my mouth before I realized the hypocrisy in

them. I knew about such games. I knew about such forms of entertainment.

But he didn't know that, and I wasn't about to clue him in. I could
be an exceptionally good actress when I wanted to be. "Most of us have
to take our jobs seriously. Most of us don't have ample free time to
satisfy such juvenile whims."

I rose to my feet, slung my bag over my shoulder, and spun toward
the door.

"Sit back down, Celia."

He hadn't raised his voice, but it was sharp, and the authority in his
command was indisputable. It stopped me immediately.

Slowly, I turned back toward him. I didn't even think of the action
consciously. In fact, I could hear myself arguing with my body as I
pivoted in his direction. *Don't do it, don't do it, don't do it.*

But it was as though I were a mechanical doll he was controlling by
remote. I couldn't not turn around. I couldn't not give him more of my
attention.

I was able to find enough restraint to not immediately sit down, at
least. With my heart hammering in my chest, I stared at him with bold
determination.

He raised his brows, as though it wasn't often that his demands
were questioned. It might have given me a thread of satisfaction if I
didn't sense the current of fury underneath the surprise. It was strong
and swift and *there,* as clear as any word he'd spoken.

It scared me.

Thrilled me, too. How often did I meet someone as dauntless as I
was? I'd never encountered someone who was more so.

I swallowed, and when his eyes flicked from me to the chair, an
unspoken order, I sank primly back into the seat.

The edges of his lips curled into a faint smile, and as enraged as I
was at his gloating victory, the small gesture also sparked something
warm and strange along my sternum.

"You'll find I hate to repeat myself," he said after a beat. "But let me
say again, I am quite serious about my proposition."

In an attempt to get my bearings, I studied him. I had absolutely no read on him whatsoever. His motives, his mood—all incomprehensible, no matter how hard I tried to stare into him. I did notice he was even more attractive than I'd first thought, despite his stony expression. Maybe even *because* of it. He was completely composed and poised. Still, and that was unbelievably sexy.

But there was something beyond the steadiness of his gaze that said his mind was busy. Calculating. He had the air of a secret agent—cool and collected but constantly scheming. Always five steps ahead. Able to intercept anyone that got in the way of his mission. I could almost imagine a gun holstered on his hip underneath his suit jacket. He felt dangerous. Sinister.

Strangely, that just made him hotter.

Finding no answers in my inspection, I had to ask outright. "Why marriage?"

"You're a smart woman. Surely you can figure it out." He lifted one arm and adjusted his cuff, though it seemed entirely unneeding of adjustment. A show of boredom. As though this conversation and what I demanded from it were tedious.

I was rarely so disregarded. Especially in the midst of a proposal.

I'd have to work on that.

Sitting up a little straighter, I ran my tongue along my lower lip. "I don't suppose it's an attempt to get me to go to bed with you."

Edward chuckled, a demeaning chuckle that could only be meant to belittle me. "Come on now—such a juvenile attempt to discover if I find you attractive is beneath you." He abandoned the pretense of fiddling with his clothing and set his hands in his lap. "If you wanted to know, you could just ask."

Such a conceited asshole. Arrogant. Haughty.

It didn't help that he was also right.

Well, he could be *right*, but I wasn't letting him *win*. He thought he was pulling my strings, but there was no fucking way I was asking him what he so obviously wanted me to ask, likely so he could degrade me in some other dickish way.

I turned my head toward the mirrored French doors and considered the question more seriously—*why me?* It wasn't unheard of for a man like him to arrange his marriages, and I was the kind of match society found ideal. A typical blonde bombshell with good breeding and lineage, I made a perfect trophy wife, but there had to be hundreds of women that fit the profile. Women he already knew. Women who would be more likely to accept such a ridiculous offer.

So why me?

The answer was obvious.

I shifted my focus back to him. "It's because of my father."

"There you go. I knew you were more than just a pretty face." He rewarded me with his first real smile, revealing two crater-like dimples that were so disarming I barely registered his backhanded compliment.

It was with a great deal of concentration that I was able to return to the conversation. "I'm not sure what you think you could achieve by marrying me. My father would insist on a prenup ensuring my spouse would never touch Werner Media, and if he didn't have that assurance, he'd change his will. He might change his will anyway. My father is not as stupid as you seem to think he is."

His expression resumed its natural stoicism. "I don't think Warren Werner is stupid, not by a long shot. He doesn't trust me or my company, which is rather smart on his part. But I am what you'd call an ambitious man. I want to enter the U.S. market and there's no way that your father will allow that to happen, not the way things currently stand between us.

"However, there will be a day when Warren retires. Sooner rather than later, if I were to guess seeing how he seems to spend more time on the golf course these days than in the office. I'd like to take his place as the head of the company."

It was my turn to laugh. "There's no way he'd appoint you as his successor."

"Not right now, he wouldn't. Give the position over to his rival? Of course not. But in a few years' time, pass the title on to the husband of his one and only beloved daughter? That's an entirely different story."

"You overestimate how much my father thinks of me."

"I doubt that. I have a daughter myself. I may seem detached and disinterested in her, but I assure you, there's not much a man like me wouldn't do for his flesh and blood. And I'm pretty certain your father is a *man like me*."

The insane thing was that I could practically hear my father saying something equally as patronizing.

It wouldn't work. There was a myriad of flaws with the scheme, not the least of which being that my father didn't actually have the authority to name his successor.

But that was neither here nor there. I wasn't accepting the offer. It was appalling that Edward thought I'd even consider it.

"Why would I do this for you? You seem to have a lot to gain in this deal, but what would *I* get out of the arrangement?" I only asked out of curiosity.

He leaned in and braced his elbows on the table. "Let's not play games, shall we? We can be honest here, you and I. What exactly do you have going for you at the moment? Your flat is owned in your father's name. You have one degree, in an art field. Your business barely runs in the black, a business that is neither innovative nor necessary. The lack of customers knocking at your door confirms that. You're almost thirty-two years old, unmarried, childless, living off your trust fund. You're not involved in any foundations or clubs, not on any boards. Your good looks might have gotten you through most of your life so far, but how much longer is that going to last? Not forever, I'll tell you that. Surely your parents aren't ecstatic about your current prospects for the future. Bringing home a husband of my caliber would change everything in their eyes, wouldn't it? Even though I come with a competing business, I would imagine they would consider me a major coup, especially when they hear how generous *my* prenup will be. I think when you really look at it, you're really the one getting the better end of the deal."

I felt the color drain from my face.

It wasn't the first time I'd had deprecating words thrown at me. This wasn't even the worst that I'd heard said, not on the surface, anyway. Heaven knew, I'd deserved most of the insults that had been hurled in my direction. They always slid off my back, never touching any part of me that might care. Call me mean or manipulative or a bitch, I could take it. I knew who I was, and I accepted it.

But there was something about Edward's delivery, his stark manner. Usually people said hurtful things out of emotion, and there was none of that here. Conniving as his tactic was, his assessment came only from a place of raw truth. These were truths that faced me every day in the mirror, and yet I found them the hardest to look at. They were the truths I worked the hardest to hide. Truths that, once acknowledged so frankly by someone else, stirred things. Shifted the icebergs drifting inside me.

I couldn't even try to refute it when I still had my mother's voice echoing with our earlier conversation in my head. *Don't expect to do better. We both know you can't.*

"You're an asshole." This time I said it out loud, and with venom.

Edward ticked his head to the side, a barely perceptible nod. "Perhaps."

I stood up and pulled my bag to my shoulder. "I'm leaving now, Mr. Fasbender." My glare dared him to argue.

He didn't even blink. "Without giving me an answer?"

God, he was bold.

"You should be smart enough to figure out my answer is no," I said, whirling away from him.

"Think about it."

"I won't."

I could feel him following as I stormed out of the room. I was midway across the Fontainebleau foyer when he called after me. "Oh, Celia, in case you're still wondering..."

I kept walking, determined not to give him the satisfaction of turning back.

It didn't stop him from saying more. "My answer is yes—I do find you attractive."

"Go to hell," I muttered under my breath. It was certainly where he belonged.

Eager to be out of the building as fast as possible, I took the stairs. I didn't stop walking when I'd made it across the foyer. I kept going until

I was two blocks away, where I slipped into a coffee shop and sank down at a table. My heart didn't settle down to a reasonable pace for long minutes, and only when it did was I able to realize how severely I was overreacting.

Edward Fasbender was an arrogant piece of shit. His assessment of me didn't matter. I was still the woman I was when I'd walked in to his stupid meeting, and I'd been comfortable with myself then. There was no reason to feel any different now.

Really, all in all, it had been a mission accomplished. I'd gone in there expecting a different offer, but I'd rejected the man all the same. It was a victory. Truly.

So why did it feel like I'd walked out with the losing hand?

THREE

OF COURSE I called my father.

After I'd bought a nonfat latte and a spinach salad from the counter, I pulled out my phone and called his cell. It was Tuesday, and as Edward had accurately asserted, my father was more likely to be at the golf club than the office.

"What's up, Ceeley doll?" he answered in his typical manner. The endearment didn't have much commitment behind it. It was how he always addressed me, more a habit than anything else.

Not that I doubted his love for me. I was one of the things he'd created, and he loved all his creations. Some more enthusiastically than others, but that was to be expected, wasn't it? His business—his *empire* —had produced much more notably than I had, and it naturally deserved the accolades and attention he gave it.

"Are you busy, Daddy?" I could hear the distinct call of *fore* in the background.

"Nope. Just getting in the cart to drive to the next hole. Is every-thing all right? You don't usually call out of the blue like this."

"Everything's fine. I just had a question for you." I propped the phone on my shoulder with my chin so I could open up the wrapper on my plastic fork. "What can you tell me about Edward Fasbender?"

"Edward Fasbender?" He was understandably surprised. I'd never shown much interest in Werner Media and it was unlike me to ask about people associated with the business. "Why, he's the owner of Accelecom. That's a company in—"

"Yes, I know what Accelecom is. I wanted to know specifically about Fasbender." With my father mid-game, I knew his attention was limited. I didn't want to waste the time he was willing to give me to get information I already had.

"Well, he's a scoundrel, that one. A real devil. Ruthless, unethical, shady. Corrupt."

Devil. That was a description I could get behind.

That wasn't what stood out the most in my father's answer. Perhaps it was because I'd played my own game so long, but I had a habit of zeroing in on the dirty laundry in a person's background. "What do you mean by corrupt? I get that he's a rival, but does he actually engage in unscrupulous behavior?"

He chortled. "I'd say. Wouldn't trust that man as far as I could throw him. Zero credibility."

My father said the same thing about half the business associates he talked about and every politician. "Like, has he done anything illegal? Has he broken the law?"

"I wouldn't doubt it if he had."

Helpful, Dad. Real helpful.

"Does that mean you don't know of anything specific that he's done or gotten away with?" I needed details. I needed cold hard facts. I needed a lead.

"Of course I know specifics." He was starting to bristle, the way he did anytime someone pushed him in a direction he wasn't interested in going. "He did that...well, for one, he was involved in that... You know what, Ceeley, it's all complicated business stuff. Hard to explain, and you wouldn't understand all the jargon anyway. Leave these sorts of things for the big boys. Just trust me when I say he's not a good guy."

It was strange how I could both feel and *not* feel the sting of his condescension. I knew it was there, sensed the lash of his words and what they meant, what they suggested he thought about me, but they didn't actually hurt me anymore. Not like they once did.

There were benefits to being nothing.

More strongly, I felt the disappointment of having learned absolutely nothing. Whether my father didn't know anything solid about Edward Fasbender or he wasn't willing to tell me, I wasn't sure. Either way, he wasn't useful.

"Why are you asking about this guy?" His tone was suddenly suspicious.

"No reason. Just curious."

"No, no. This guy's name doesn't come up out of nowhere. There has to be something that put him in your head."

I speared my fork in my salad then picked it up and jabbed again. "He wanted to meet with me, is all. To discuss a design project, I think."

"He, *what*?" I'd only had half his attention before, but now he was completely present. "That bastard! Have you met with him yet? Whatever he says, it's a ruse. He's probably trying to get intel about me from you."

"Actually, I don't even think he realized who I was when he called in. And no. I haven't met with him." Lying was my thing, but I didn't necessarily enjoy lying to my parents. They were good enough people, and I'd already lied too much to them over the years. Lies of omission. Outright falsehoods.

So why was I doing it now?

I stabbed again at the spinach.

"Good! Don't. Whatever you do, don't meet with him. Do not have any further contact with him."

"Don't worry, I'm not planning on it." At least that was the truth.

"And I don't believe that crap that he doesn't know who you are. He knows."

"It probably wasn't even him who reached out. More like someone on his staff that had no idea about the connection between the Werner name and Lux Designs." I didn't know why I was defending the devil. He most definitely knew who I was.

"I wouldn't be so sure, honey." Again, his tone was subtly patronizing. "He's very clever. And a menace. I don't like him one bit."

That was why Edward's plan was flawed from the outset. My father considered him an enemy. If I tried to marry the guy, I'd likely be disowned.

Which was fine, because I wasn't considering it.

And I wasn't getting anything useful from my father, which meant it was time to end the call. "I'm sure you're right, Daddy. That's why I called you as soon as I realized who he was. I wasn't about to get involved with one of your competitors. Like I said, I was just curious."

"Smart girl. I'm at the next hole now. If there's anything else you need, we can talk later."

We hung up, but instead of diving into my lunch, I stared at it, thinking. If I were really smart, I would have told my father the truth. I would have detailed my entire encounter with Edward Fasbender, would have told him about the outrageous scheme he'd concocted and how he desperately wanted control of my father's business.

But, for whatever reason—be it that it had ended so humiliatingly or that I didn't want to confess that I'd met with his rival in the first place or some other motive I wasn't ready to admit to—whatever the reason, I didn't want my father to know.

So the lengths Edward was willing to go to get what he wanted remained a secret.

FOUR

EVEN THOUGH I didn't live for my work the way my father did, I loved my office. One thousand square feet on the third floor of a building in Chelsea, it was one of the few things I'd acquired with my own means, and by my own means, I didn't mean with money.

I'd found the place when I'd been hunting for a location to open my business almost seven years ago. The real estate agent had shown me another space, an awkward unit with an extra thousand feet that I had no need for, that backed up to the spot I eventually acquired. My office hadn't been for sale at the time, but we'd been fortunate enough to run into the owner while looking, and he'd been kind enough to show us around.

Kind enough wasn't really the correct term. *Interested* enough, was more like it. Scott Matthews had been a forty-something-year-old accountant who enjoyed flirting with the twenty-five-year-old darling he'd seen poking around on his floor. He'd explained how his own business had grown too big for the small space, but he wasn't yet ready to part with it, in case he needed to downsize one day.

He was married; his ring was firmly lodged on his finger, his skin puffing out around it like he'd gained a few pounds since he'd last taken it off. He gave no indication of wanting to engage in anything that would break his marriage vows. He was simply talking to a pretty lady. No harm in that.

Except I was more than a pretty lady—I was a dangerous lady, even at that young age.

It had been easy enough to dismiss my realtor and then it hadn't taken much persuasion to get Scott to take me out to dinner. I'd been playing The Game by then for a couple of years, and while most of the schemes I'd pulled at the time were with Hudson, I'd decided to conquer Scott all on my own.

The thing was, I'd really loved his unit. It was the perfect size, the perfect location. It had the perfect vibe and wouldn't require much construction to make it what I envisioned. But even more, I'd loved the idea of convincing him that the space should be mine.

It really hadn't been as hard to seduce him as it should have been. After dinner, he'd taken me back to the very unit, and I'd let him fuck me against the front door and again on the counter of the office kitchenette. It was the second time that I'd gotten him to let me take the pictures. Filthy, naughty pictures. Pictures that showed everything and left nothing to the imagination.

If I was to believe him, and in this case, I actually did, this was the first time he'd ever cheated on his wife. That should have been considered a victory in itself, and in another situation, I would have let it go there.

But I'd been ambitious, and I'd wanted that space.

All it took was threatening to show his wife the proof of our infidelity and the place was mine. Oh, he'd cried first, and begged. Even offered large sums of money, which I didn't give a shit about. In the end, when I'd told him I just wanted the office, he'd almost seemed relieved. Especially when he assumed that meant we could keep screwing around. Which, it didn't. Once I was done with a mark, I was done, but he didn't learn that until long after the deal was made.

The surprising part of the whole thing was how long I'd been able to keep the lease. I'd figured I had a year or two before he'd get tired of the looming threat, but he'd been desperate to keep his dirty little secret, and I'd been happy to benefit from the indiscretion.

I couldn't say for sure if I would have actually told his wife or not if Scott hadn't agreed to my terms. The best threats are the ones that will be followed through, but I hadn't planned on really telling her, in the beginning. I'd only set out to see if I *could* do it, if I could get what I wanted with just my body and a few hours of my time. Since I'd only wanted the space, there would have been no use in actually ruining his life, but if it came down to it, I might have. Just for fun. Just to see what would happen next.

I should have felt bad about that. If I still felt things, maybe I would have.

In the meantime, I didn't have to worry about what I would or wouldn't do because the space belonged to me.

It was a simple layout with a reception area, an office for me, the kitchenette, and a consultation room. While the consultation room was intended for clients, I also used it when meeting with Renee. I'd designed it to feel casual with cushy couches and an oversized coffee table that could hold models for presentation.

Then, at the window, I'd installed a seat with plump pillows. I liked to sit here while Renee ran down production schedules and product information for our current projects. I'd lean my back against the curve of the alcove, my body lengthwise along the glass, my knees bent, my feet flat on the seat cushion. Three floors up was high enough to not be particularly noticeable to pedestrians and still be the perfect height for people-watching. I could lose long hours to surveying the passersby below, studying how they moved, how they interacted. Wondering what they thought, what their motives were. Wondering if they saw all the nuances of human behavior that I did.

That man there, does he realize his companion is irritated by him?

Does that young girl notice the businessman leering at her from across the street?

Is the smile on that woman's face genuine? Or is she empty and hollow inside?

Today, though, while Renee gave me a detailed rundown of the quality inspection procedure for a client residence—our only client, at the moment—I wasn't watching the people below the window. Instead, as I had so often in the week and a half since I'd met with him, I was thinking about Edward Fasbender. Thinking about the things he'd said to me.

Your flat is owned in your father's name. You have one degree, in an art field. Your business barely runs in the black... The lack of customers knocking at your door confirms that. You're almost thirty-two years old, unmarried, childless, living off your trust fund... Your good looks might have gotten you through most of your life so far, but how much longer is that going to last?

They were words that carried bite, but the more time that passed, the easier it was to repeat them in my head. I'd said them to myself enough now that it felt like recovering from a sunburn. After the initial sting, the dead skin peeled away, exposing new skin underneath.

It was startling to discover that beneath this particular sting was arousal.

It took awhile to figure out what it was, the feeling was so foreign. That wasn't exactly true—my body got aroused all the time. I actually found sex enjoyable on a very base level. My skin reacted to human touch. My pulse quickened. My pussy got wet. I had orgasms.

But arousal was always confined to physical reactions. My mind and heart remained separate and unaffected. Disinterested. Noncon- cordant.

This time, though, after I got past the harshness of Edward's words, I was turned on. Completely. With every part of me, and I couldn't help but want to examine that more closely. Maybe I had some humilia- tion fetish I hadn't discovered before, a very real possibility that I should possibly explore more thoroughly, but there was more to it than that.

I reacted to him, I realized, because he'd *seen* me.

I couldn't remember the last time someone had truly seen me, the last time anyone had even tried to look behind the pretty face, the well- cared-for physique, the expensive clothes, the prominent name. Those superficial aspects were more than enough for most. That was why it was so easy to play people the way I did.

Edward, though, had looked past all the bullshit, and while it was embarrassing that he'd seen me for the failure that I was, it was also a relief to be acknowledged.

Relieving and arousing.

What would it be like to go to bed with a man like that? To relinquish control, be stripped down bare…

I sat up suddenly. *What about sex?*

Renee broke off her instructions mid-sentence. "Uh, what did you say?"

Shit. I'd said it aloud.

"Nothing. My mind wandered. Go on."

She gave me an inquisitive stare and then went on. We weren't close enough for her to probe further. I wasn't close to anyone.

Later, when I was alone in my office, I rung her desk. "Can you get me Edward Fasbender's contact information?"

"Certainly. Are you following up with him? Would you like me to get him on the line?"

I considered. "No. Just get me his number."

I wrote down the number she provided and hung up. Then I retrieved my cell phone from my purse and dialed from there. I didn't want the company name to show up on the caller ID, and while I knew my cell didn't show my name when I called out, I wanted him to have my number, for some reason I couldn't quite identify.

"Celia," he said when he answered.

My breath caught. He'd saved my number in his phone. I hadn't expected that and it almost threw my train of thought.

But I recovered. "What about sex?" I asked.

"Hmm." The simple sound reverberated low in his chest. I could sense an air of amusement. "Are you asking about sex in our marriage?"

It was hard not to be distracted by his voice. How had I not noticed how bewitching his timbre was? His accent was absolutely panty melting.

I shifted in my seat, crossing one leg over the other to press against the ache that had crept up unexpectedly. "Yes. I wondered. That."

God, I sounded like a complete imbecile.

"A perfectly natural question. I'd planned on discussing it the other day, but you ran out so suddenly."

The reminder of our previous meeting's events was all I needed to snap out of it. "You've got me on the phone. Get to the discussing now, will you?"

"Awfully eager, aren't you?"

Jesus, I didn't need this. "I'm going to hang up..."

"No obligation." It took me a second to register that it was the answer to my question.

No obligation. Oddly, it made me disappointed.

"No obligation, but it might occur?" *Please let that not have sounded as desperate as it felt saying.*

"No obligation because it *won't* occur."

A beat passed.

"Interesting."

"Sounds like you're thinking about it?"

"I'm not," I said quickly. Too quickly, and I wasn't even sure if I meant I wasn't thinking about the silly marriage proposal or wasn't thinking about sex with him. One of those, at least, was a lie.

"I'm not," I said again, more certain.

"That makes one of us." Then we were talking about the marriage, because why would he be thinking about sex with me when he'd just said it wouldn't occur?

I hated this, hated how unbalanced he made me. It was a simple phone call and he still had the ability to shift my world off-kilter.

And that was stupid. I'd been in situations more uncertain than this and managed just fine. I stuck my chin up and channeled that confident persona. "I hope you're used to disappointment, then."

"Quite frankly, Celia, I'm not, and I don't see any reason to plan for it now. You should understand something fundamental about me—I don't accept no as an answer."

I was still stammering for a comeback when he went on. "Good day, Celia. We'll talk soon."

Then the line was dead. And I was, once again, reeling. Once again, rejected.

Once again, aroused.

FIVE

HUDSON HADN'T CALLED it a game—that was my term. He'd called it experiments. He'd been conducting them for years before I learned about them, before he used me as one of his subjects.

I didn't realize until much later that they actually *were* experiments for him. He wasn't out to play people, though that was the ultimate outcome. He was studying behavior, trying to discover what made them work, what made them feel. What made them love. He was attempting to understand fundamental human emotions that he was certain he lacked in himself.

He didn't lack them, of course. He was the Tin Man come to life, searching for a heart that he hadn't realized he'd possessed all along.

Back then, I was just as unaware of his capability to love as he was. I saw him as he'd appeared—callous, cold, and cruel.

I'd envied him.

I'd suffered pain after pain after pain, some of the more recent injuries at his hand, and I'd wanted nothing more than to be numb. I'd wanted to be empty and void. I'd wanted to stop feeling.

And he agreed to teach me how.

I never knew exactly why he chose to let me in on his experiments when he'd let no one in before. Maybe it was because we'd grown up together. Maybe he'd had a sense of responsibility. Maybe he'd thought he owed me—he did, by the way. He'd definitely owed me.

Whatever the reason, he'd taken me under his wing. He'd taught me how to manipulate, how to prey, how to influence and exploit. The first time had been easy. It had been my job to flirt, then to seduce. The affair I'd had with Tim Kerrigan had been free of attachment, but it had empowered me. I'd set my sights on a stranger, and I'd drawn him into my bed, exactly as I'd planned. That had done quite a thing for my self-confidence. It had been so effective, I'd nearly forgotten the goal of the scheme.

Then, when his wife discovered our indiscretion, as had always been the objective of the experiment, my feelings changed. She'd been devastated. Heartbroken. They'd been newlyweds, and I'd destroyed their happiness. At least that's what she'd said to me the one time I'd come face to face with her. It hadn't stopped her from staying with him.

That day, though, when she spewed words of hatred and venom in my direction, I had a moment of anguish. It didn't feel good to be the bitch. It didn't feel pretty to be cruel and destructive. The whole point of playing these games with Hudson had been to feel nothing, not to feel terrible.

But as I'd stood in the wake of her attack, as I turned my focus from concentrating on what I was feeling to observing her, the calmer I'd become. My reality altered. Instead of pain being a thing that lived only inside of me, I discovered it could exist elsewhere. Outside of me. Detached from me. Severed.

And that was why I'd played. Not because I'd wanted to see *what would happen if* but because when someone else cried and fell apart, when someone else's world was sabotaged, my pain diminished. The scars left by Hudson and Charles and all the others would lighten. The deeper wounds, the ones inflicted by the person I should have been able to trust more than almost anyone, wouldn't throb with intensity, wouldn't cripple me with their ache. Every bit of my pain grew smaller and smaller until I'd become numb.

Numb didn't mean gone, though. It was still there, somewhere, invisible and buried inside, waiting for me. I knew that as soon as I stopped playing it would return and take me over. That was how it had become a game in my mind. The objective was them or me. Someone had to hurt, and as long as it wasn't me, I won. As long as I was the one still standing, I won.

It was the only way I knew to survive.

Once upon a time I'd hoped that one day I'd overcome it. That I'd hurt enough people and break enough hearts, and I'd be empty for real. That the scars and the wounds would be magically healed, and I'd be new and pure and whole. I could quit The Game, then, and learn to feel again.

But I'd hurt enough people now. I'd hurt people who'd actually meant something to me. I'd turned The Game on Hudson. I'd hurt him. I'd hurt his wife. Pain very much lived outside of me. I'd seen it close up on the faces of the people I should have cared most for.

And still I felt it waiting for me, lingering in the shadows. A ghost that would always haunt me. A cancer that yearned to spread.

SIX

I WAS antsy after my phone call with Edward. The collar of my shirt felt too tight. I was roasting in my slacks. It was a scorching summer day, but the air conditioning was on in the office, and Renee, who usually complained I liked to run the place like a sweatbox, had her sweater on.

I was hot and bothered and rejected, and that pissed me off.

Too restless to concentrate on work, I opened my laptop and entered Edward's name into my Google search bar. I meant to scour the information that popped up, find his weakness, perhaps, or discover a skeleton in his closet. He had to have one. Everyone I'd ever met who'd held a position of power had something they were ashamed of. Something they were afraid the world would discover.

But instead of looking at the news items, I found myself clicking the images tab.

My screen quickly filled with a grid full of Edward Fasbender. Edward Fasbender at a media summit. Edward Fasbender on *Forbes Magazine*. Edward Fasbender at Accelecom. Edward Fasbender at LinkedIn. Business Insider had him listed as one of the Top Fifty Sexiest CEOs, because duh. *Fortune* called him one of the most innovative corporate leaders of the twenty-first century. There were pictures of him at charity banquets, at tech conventions, at the gym. Half of the images were for publicity only. Most of the rest were candid shots at different events, nearly always he was dressed in a designer bespoke suit. In every one he looked as hard and handsome as he had in person.

And, Jesus, could that man wear a tuxedo. As though it were a second skin. His head usually tilted with the perfect arrogant slant. As though he practiced looking good in a mirror. As though he knew how arrestingly good-looking he was. How uncomfortably attractive he was.

I had to shift several times in my office chair to ease the discomfort of staring at him so intensely.

Why the hell wasn't he interested in sex?

Was he gay? He'd been married, had kids. That didn't mean anything these days. Neither did the several occasions where he sported a beautiful woman on his arm. Were they beards? Was that the real reason he wanted an arranged marriage? Was that his deep dark secret?

For some reason, I didn't think so. There'd been too much heat in his gaze when we'd met in person. And he'd said he was attracted to me.

Hadn't he? Or had I made that up?

He baffled me. He annoyed me. He stirred something inside of me that I didn't recognize or remember noticing before. He was completely maddening.

I clicked an item that looked recent, a group picture of him with several other important-looking people in important-looking clothes. A new tab opened with a headline that said it was an industry awards showcase that had been held at the Hilton in Midtown a couple of weeks before. I skimmed the article and then scanned through the gallery, pausing to examine every image he was featured in. He rarely smiled, I noticed. Not really. Even at what was likely a jovial event. And he knew people that ran in the same circles my father ran in. I could identify several individuals, if not always by name, at least by face.

Then I got to the image that made me momentarily freeze. It wasn't of Edward, but of Hudson and his wife. I hadn't seen any pictures of him in ages, not since I'd curiously sifted through reports on his wedding a couple of years ago. It was startling to see him now, see how he'd changed. How he'd stayed the same. He looked older, but as distinguished as he'd always looked. He looked happy, the glow on his face matching the radiance of his bride. She looked happy too, with a hand resting on the small swell of her belly.

I took a long breath in and blew it out slowly.

I really hadn't been in love with Hudson, not in the end. Hadn't been for a long, long time. I'd been mad at him, yes. Mad that he'd left me. That he'd moved on. But I hadn't been in love with him.

And yet, faced with the image of his happy life, I felt a pang of something, a stray lightning bolt of envy in an otherwise black, emotionless sky. *That was supposed to be me.*

Everything would be different if that had been me.

I closed out of the tab and the brief flash of jealousy vanished with the disappearance of the image.

Voices in the lobby pulled my attention. Renee was talking to someone, another woman. A voice I couldn't quite identify. We weren't expecting anyone that I knew of. God, I hoped I didn't have to see anyone today. I wasn't in the mood.

Leaving my laptop open, I pushed up from my desk and headed to the door to investigate.

"I'm sorry, I don't see you on her appointment book." Renee was studying her computer screen as though she didn't have my schedule memorized.

I peeked cautiously out my door. Fortunately, my viewpoint allowed me to look out on Renee's desk, which meant the woman in front of her couldn't see me.

It also meant I only saw her back. Her hair was shoulder-length auburn, her dress a whimsical style that wouldn't be worn by most of the clients I worked with. Over her shoulder was an oversized portfolio bag, the kind an artist used to carry around small works of art.

"I don't have an appointment," the woman said patiently. "But if I could just have a second of her time..." She gestured toward my office, turning her body enough that I was able to better see her.

Fuck.

I withdrew quickly into my office, pressing my back against the metal frame of the door. I knew the unannounced visitor. Blanche Martin, an artist I'd met at a gallery exhibition a few months back. She'd had an underwhelming showing, as far as I could tell. Not one of her pieces had been purchased, and judging from the dreary amount of interest there was around her, she wasn't going to be selling any in the near future either.

Still, she'd been excited and eager to talk about her work.

It made for a perfect opportunity to pull her into one of my favorite games.

It was an easy setup, which was why I played it so often, even though the payoff wasn't as exhilarating as some of my other games. It was a scenario I could easily walk into. One I could manage while balancing other elements of life.

"I really don't mean to intrude, but I swear she said I could stop by anytime." Blanche was incredibly determined, which was more than could be said for her unremarkable art.

I *had* told her she could stop by anytime. I'd also told her that I was an interior designer, and that a very wealthy, very well-known client of mine was interested in decorating his entire penthouse flat with the work of just one artist. And her work would be perfect for his vibe! But could she please work up some new pieces so that I could show him before we made the deal?

It was all bullshit, of course.

Obviously she was here to show me what she'd come up with. This was where The Game was supposed to get good. This was the part I lived for.

For some reason, I wasn't motivated today.

But I'd put in the work. And she was here...

With a sigh, I put on a smile and emerged from my hiding place. "Blanche! I was just thinking about you! What perfect timing!" I nodded to my assistant. "It's okay, Renee. I have a few minutes for Ms. Martin."

Renee was used to these types of encounters. While she wasn't involved in these conversations, she believed I was always on the lookout for latest art trends. She didn't know any more than that, and didn't need to.

I ushered Blanche into my office and closed the door so Renee wouldn't hear anything that might be off-putting. She was a good assistant. I would have hated losing her.

"Thank you so much for seeing me, Ms. Werner. I should have made an appointment, but I've been so busy working on these pieces you asked for, and as soon as I was convinced they were ready, I didn't even think! I just came straight down here!"

I could practically hear the exclamation points in her speech. Blanche was even more enthusiastic than she'd been when I'd first met her. Even more optimistic.

The easiest kind of person to destroy.

"Now, Blanche, I know I told you to call me Celia. And no worries about stopping in. It's perfectly fine. Want to show me what you have?" The lines came automatically now, having performed them so many times.

"Yes!" She unzipped her bag, babbling on as she pulled out first one canvas then a second.

I moved my laptop to the side to make more room on my desk then pretended to scrutinize the paintings as she laid them out in front of me.

Except, I didn't really pretend. I actually looked at them, something I hadn't done while pulling this scam in, well, maybe ever. There had never been a point. I wasn't ever going to buy any of it, no matter how good the work was.

This time, though, there was something about them that pulled me in. Something that made me have to catch my breath. The first one was of a country garden. A green field of grass sprawled across the canvas, the edges punctuated with flowered bushes. A stone path meandered over the grass and through a white arbor covered with purple blooms.

The next canvas displayed a similar theme, another part of the same garden, maybe, but this time there was an open field of wild-flowers in the background, and instead of an arbor, this one featured a large fruit tree, apples buried in its leaves and scattered on the ground around it. The centerpiece of the painting was a wooden swing, tied with thick rope to a sturdy branch. Both the swing and the ropes were worn, and it was impossible not to imagine the child who had spent her time here. A cheerful, naive girl who'd loved nothing more than to fly through the air and try to touch the clouds with her toes.

My eyes suddenly pricked.

I didn't want to look at her paintings anymore. I didn't want to give her a speech about her work—the art she'd obviously labored over for the last several months—not being a good fit for my client after all. I didn't even want to see her break down and cry.

I just wanted her to go.

"Oh, I know him! That's Edward Fasbender. My, he's such a looker, and even more attractive in person. Those pictures just don't do him justice."

I followed Blanche's gaze to my laptop sitting at the edge of my desk, the screen still displaying the image search from earlier.

My thoughts slid easily away from the uncomfortable place her paintings had taken me to what she'd just said. "Yes, that's him. He's a potential client. You've met him before?"

"I worked for him, actually. I lived in London for a while and had a job in the graphic design department of Accelecom. He was very hands-on with his staff. And quite particular. Hard to please. I hope he's easier to work with as a client than a boss."

My head swirled with intrigue. "Well, I don't know yet, since I haven't agreed to take him on. Your comment definitely gives me pause."

She blushed. "I shouldn't have said anything. It's been a few years now since I worked with him. He may have changed. Or it might have been me! I'm not a graphic designer anymore for a reason."

"Oh, please. You're very talented." It wasn't even that big of a lie. She'd gotten better since I'd seen her in the spring.

I glanced again at her paintings and felt that same stirring of unease. I still didn't want to look at them, but now I was interested in talking with her more about Edward.

I stacked the canvases on top of each other and held them out to her. "How about we do this...I need to speak to my client and see where his current thoughts are on this project. Then maybe we can meet again sometime this weekend and discuss this further."

Blanche's brows momentarily drew close together. She'd had yet to take the paintings from me. "Sure. Sure. I'm free Sunday, if that works for you. Do you want to just keep these to show him?"

I definitely did not. I wanted them as far away from me as possible. "That won't be necessary. I've seen enough to attest to the quality. Could you email me with digital photos of them and any other paintings you propose for this collection? I'll forward them on. And Sunday is perfect! How about a late lunch around two? I'll reply to your email with a restaurant."

Her earlier zeal returned and she finally took the paintings from me. "That sounds great! To be honest, I'm going to be sweating until then, but I can wait. It's only a couple of days."

"I totally understand. But as you said, it's just a couple of days. I have an appointment soon, anyway, and I'd rather not be rushed when we talk." I was already escorting her to the door.

"Of course. Makes total sense."

"I'd love to quiz you some more about Edward Fasbender, too, if you don't mind." I could have kept her longer and drilled her right there, but I'd learned from experience that patience was a good friend. This way she'd have time to think of things she might not have thought of on the spot. Especially if she was as eager to please me as I believed she was.

"Whatever I can do to help! Thank you for all of this. You've really made my day!"

She walked out of my office with hope. The same kind of hope I'd once had about living a life like the one Hudson led with Alayna, a life filled with love and vows and swollen bellies. The kind of hope that was devastating when destroyed. It was the kind of hope I loved seeing in the people I played, and normally, I'd cling onto it, fantasizing about how satisfying it would be to eventually deflate their aspirations.

But an hour later when she sent over an email with her art attached —images I didn't open—I wasn't thinking about the game I'd set up with Blanche Martin. As I replied with the address to a restaurant in Lenox Hill, I was thinking about what kind of game I'd play with Edward.

SEVEN

I DIDN'T OFTEN DREAM, or, at least, I didn't remember if I did. Those had disappeared along with my emotions. Apparently there was no way to spin imaginings of the soul when a person no longer had a soul.

But I did have one recurring dream that visited me as regularly as the seasons. It was always vague, always a bit hazy, as though I were viewing it through a fog.

No, as though I were *in* the fog, because it was a dream about me, I was pretty sure. I could never actually *see* myself there, but I *felt* myself there. Felt myself there in that misty nowhere, a faceless man at my side and a baby in my arms. Every time, the infant was bundled so tightly that I couldn't see its face, couldn't tell if it was a boy or a girl, or how old it was, but I could feel the weight of it, could smell the very distinct baby scent when I lowered my nose toward its head. Could hear its gentle baby sounds as I tried to move the blanket to reveal the form underneath.

But I could never move the blanket. I couldn't move anything at all. My arms were missing, my body invisible, like I wasn't really there. Like I was nothing. Like the man and the baby were real, and I was a ghost clinging to their existence.

I dreamt it that night, and as always when I dreamt it, I woke up sobbing.

Dumb, I thought, as my body shook with grief I couldn't actually feel.

I didn't even like babies.

EIGHT

I ARRIVED EARLY to the restaurant on Sunday. I hadn't planned to; it was just the way traffic worked out.

I'd made reservations, thankfully, but Orsay wasn't the type of establishment that seated guests without all members of their party present.

Usually, anyway. I had ways of making people change their minds about such stifling rules.

After a bit of flirting with the hostess—yes, my charms work as well on women as men—I found myself escorted to a table for two. I asked her not to send a waiter until my guest arrived, then I took the bench side of the arrangement, which allowed me to face the door. I liked having the advantage in these situations.

Unfortunately that meant I couldn't see anyone approaching from behind until they were well on me. Which was why I wasn't prepared when I glanced up at the two men passing by on their way out of the restaurant and locked eyes on none other than Edward Fasbender.

Startled, I felt my mouth fall open. What was *he* doing here? Lenox Hill wasn't exactly near St. Regis. Most importantly, what was he doing here *now*? Minutes before I was supposed to meet with someone to discuss him, no less.

His reaction was decidedly less severe than mine felt. His eyes widened in surprise then a smug smile uncurled across his lips.

"Vincent," he said to the man he was with. "I've just spotted someone I know. Thank you for meeting with me. I'll follow up with you sometime this coming week." He didn't wait for his companion's response before pulling out the chair across from me and taking the liberty of sitting in it.

Vincent nodded in acknowledgment and went on his way while I blinked in astonishment.

"Oh, hell no," I said, when I managed to get my wits about me, a difficult task in the shadow of Edward's presence. It was overpowering. *He* was overpowering. It was hard to think around someone so incredibly assured. So completely captivating. "That seat is not for you. I did not invite you to sit."

He gave me a bored sigh. "Come on, now. You don't want to make a scene."

I hadn't realized how loud my voice had been, but his comment didn't help to calm me down. Who was he to tell me what I did and didn't want to do? I had half a mind to very much make a scene. Whatever it took to get him out of that chair and away from me.

Except, I really didn't want to make a scene. It would please him too much to see me riled. There was no way I was giving him that satisfaction.

I straightened my back and made a deliberate effort to lower my voice. "Five minutes. You get five minutes to say what you need to say and then be gone."

"Fine." He didn't look at his watch to check the time, but I did. It was a nice piece, actually. A Piaget with a steel band and a sapphire face that had to cost a fortune. Worth it for how well he wore it.

Oh, please. It's a luxury watch. It would look good on anyone.

I forced my gaze up to his face. Which wasn't any less stunning. His eyes were so blue, so translucent. Hypnotizing.

Jesus, what was wrong with me? I had to pull myself together.

The waiter chose that moment to come take our drink orders,

giving me a thankful distraction. "Not yet, please. This isn't who I'm expecting to—"

Edward bulldozed over me. "She'll take a Juliet. Nothing for me. And put this ticket on the credit card I just used."

The waiter looked more closely at Edward and, apparently realizing he'd served him once before that afternoon, nodded. "Yes, Mr. Fasbender. I'll be right back with that Juliet." He disappeared into the kitchen.

I was fuming. "I do not need you to order my drinks for me, and I most certainly do not need you to pay for my meal."

"Of course you don't. But I have extremely good taste. It's vodka and lemoncello and something floral. You'll see. You'll like it." His English dialect was so enchanting, even with the added air of haughtiness. It was almost a form of delicious torture. Like being tickled—an ear tickle. "As for paying for your meal...what sort of potential husband would I be if I didn't prove I meant to take care of my wife."

I'd been dead inside for nearly a decade, and yet his use of the word *wife* in relation to me set something blooming deep and hidden inside me.

No, no, no. Close it off. Let it die. Stay numb.

"I hope you don't plan to use your entire five minutes to discuss that ridiculous scheme of yours." The irritation in my tone was directed at myself, but I was fine with him thinking it was all for him.

"Not all my five minutes, no. I have other things to say."

"Well? Get on with it."

Casually, as though he had all the time in the world, he brought his elbows to the table and clasped his hands together, his eyes never leaving mine. "You're stalking me," he said finally.

"No, I'm not!" I was flabbergasted. "How would I even... Why would I ever think you'd be at this restaurant? When there's a million other restaurants in Manhattan."

"That's what I find remarkable about your skills. You found me here, of all places."

Fury rose in me like smoke from a wildfire. What an egotistical, self-centered shithead. I'd done more than my fair share of stalking in my life, but to assume that I'd bother to chase after *him*...!

Never mind that I'd spent several hours researching him on the internet the night before. Or that I'd ordered a deeper background check, and maybe took a route that went by his hotel on my run that morning.

"I am *not* stalking you," I said definitively.

He chuckled as he leaned back into his chair. "I understand. It's all right. You're embarrassed. Honestly. I'm flattered."

"You're so...so..." I couldn't find a word to describe how exasperated he made me.

"*So...what?*" He tilted his head in that conceited way he did in all his online pictures. "Assertive? Potent? Charming? Probably not that. Undeniable?"

"Vexing. I was going to say vexing." I dug my fingernails into my pant legs under the table, afraid I'd reach across the table and claw his beautiful bastard face if I didn't.

He gave a sidewise nod that had the same effect as a shrug. "Could be worse. I believe you called me an asshole the other day."

"I still mean it, too." I lifted my chin as though I'd somehow won, but of course I hadn't. I was nowhere close to winning.

Which meant I was losing, and I hated losing.

I gave him a bristling frown. "What do you want? Why are you bothering me?"

"I'd like to know what you've decided."

"*...what I've decided?*" I found that I was constantly repeating his words back to him in question form because so much of what he said was outright incredible.

"About my proposal. We were just discussing it. You obviously have a faulty memory. Perhaps you should get that checked out."

That pompous little... "You're obviously not a very good listener. I already told you no."

His expression grew serious, and before he even spoke, I had the distinct feeling this was a look he used a lot in the boardroom. When he was about to make a killer move. When he was about to crush his opponent with new terms.

It would have been hot if I weren't currently his opponent.

"Would it make a difference if sex were on the table?" he asked solemnly.

"No?" It sounded like I wasn't certain so I repeated it again, more emphatically. "No."

His brow rose skeptically. "Are you sure?"

"Positive." I *was* positive. Nothing would change my answer, even as his allure tugged on my libido, making the space between my legs ache in a way they hadn't in a long time. In years. In a lifetime.

Still, even with my mind made up, I couldn't help being curious. "But, why isn't it?"

"Why isn't it on the table?" He appeared surprised by the question.

That was a point in my favor. It seemed that very little threw him. What a nice change of pace to be on the other side of the teeter-totter.

"Yes, why wouldn't you expect sex in a marriage?" More specifically, why wouldn't he expect sex *with me*? I was attractive. More than a few men had done really stupid things to get me in their bed. Throw away marriages and change long term goals sort of stupid things.

Why wouldn't Edward want me as well? Why wouldn't he demand it?

The damn waiter came back then, setting my drink—correction, the drink Edward had ordered—in front of me. Miffed at his timing, I shooed him away, telling him I'd flag him down when I was ready to order rather than explaining that the man sitting with me wasn't even the person I planned to eat with.

With the server dealt with, I pushed the drink aside dismissively, and reminded Edward where we were in the conversation. "I asked you a question."

He narrowed his eyes as though thinking it over.

My breath stuttered as I waited for his answer. I was nervous, for some insane reason. His lingering hesitation to respond wasn't helping matters. Each second that passed drew the tension between us tauter and tauter.

He knew exactly what he was doing. He had nothing to think over. He was the kind of man who knew every one of his motives before he said or did anything. It was almost impressive.

God, I hated him.

Just when I thought I couldn't stand it anymore, he spoke. "It's rather simple, actually. I have kids already. I don't need an heir. I don't want a baby with you."

I ignored the sting of his last comment. "Children are hardly the reason most men want sex."

"Yes. I'm well aware, my dear." So patronizing. So impossible.

"I am not your dear," I seethed.

"Not yet."

"Not ever!"

He grinned slowly. That self-satisfied smile of his was a nuclear weapon.

It was going to be my undoing, if I wasn't careful.

I refused to look at him any longer. I couldn't if I wanted to leave this encounter still a whole person, as whole of a person as I was these days, anyway. "You're avoiding the question. If you don't want to answer, then you can just go ahead and leave now. Besides, your time is up, and I have no interest—"

He leaned toward me and cut me off with a low rumble. "If you must know, *Celia*," he used my name pointedly, making sure I was aware he hadn't called me dear again. "I'm not an easy man to please in the bedroom."

"And that's different than any other room...how?"

He laughed, his eyes brightening with sincere amusement. "You learn quickly. I like that in a woman."

How could such a condescending comment make me feel so...*warm*? Heat spread through me like the early sun's rays spread across a new day. With extreme alarm, I realized I liked the thought of trying to please this intolerable man.

Because I liked challenges. That had to be why. No other reason.

Suddenly, it dawned on me what he'd really been saying. "Then you'd be going for sex elsewhere." I hadn't meant to sound disappointed.

"Would it matter?" he challenged.

"It wouldn't." I shook my head and amended. "It doesn't. Because I'm not considering any of this." Here I was again saying no, and still I was sure I was the one who'd been rejected.

I hated it. I hated him. I hated everything about him.

I especially hated the way he regarded me now, his gaze piercing and penetrating, as though he could see beyond the carefully coiffed woman in front of him to my very core, to the ice fields and dark caverns that lay at the heart of me.

Long silent seconds passed, seconds that stretched as tight as the pressure between us. Seconds where I formed a million things to say, and just as quickly dismissed each comment as immature or quaint or lame or just plain desperate.

Eventually, he took the burden off me. "This buttoned-up working girl look is a bit much." He gestured to the pearl buttons that ran below the collar of the peach-colored shell I wore. "It's the weekend. You should wear something more casual. Let your hair down."

"How dare you!" The harsh reaction came out before I could stop myself. "And who are you to talk? You're wearing a suit on Sunday. I'm guessing you didn't just come from church."

"I had a business meeting."

As if there couldn't be any other reasonable answer. As if *I* couldn't possibly work on the weekend.

It had the same tone of superiority that my father frequently used. I'd never been good at talking to him, either.

This conversation exhausted me. I was bored with it. Which was a gentler way of saying I was defeated by it.

I scanned over his shoulder, hoping to see my lunch date, and responded to him halfheartedly. "I doubt your meeting had anything to do with your choice of attire. All you ever wear is suits. I've never seen you in any sort of casual wear. If I hadn't seen proof otherwise, you could have told me you worked out in an Armani three-piece, and I would have believed it."

I knew I'd slipped up as soon as the words were out of my mouth.

"You've been looking, have you? Of course you have. You wouldn't be a very good stalker if you hadn't."

Under the table, my leg bounced furiously with indignation. There wasn't anything I could say that wouldn't make the situation worse.

I attempted to redirect. "You know what *you* should do? You should grow a beard."

"A beard. Really."

I'd made the remark defensively, to criticize his look after he'd criticized mine, but I genuinely meant it. "Not a full beard. Something tamer. A Van Dyke, with your cheeks clean shaven." I could see it clearly. Could picture how it would add to his potency. Could practically feel how the rough stubble would feel under my fingers. Between my thighs.

"That's very specific. As though you've been thinking about me. Fantasizing about me."

My cheeks heated with his acute perception. "Uh, no. Not even a little. I was simply offering you a suggestion that anyone who has met you in person has likely thought but was too scared to tell you."

"I do believe people are afraid of me. Are you?"

"Hardly. I'm annoyed." And aroused. And maybe a little afraid. Or a lot afraid.

He stared at me with that same persistent stare, seeing more than I wanted him to see, I was sure.

I couldn't take it anymore, couldn't stand him looking. Couldn't stand him seeing. I put my elbows on the table and covered my face with my hands. "Your time has been up for..." I peered around my palms to note his watch before hiding again. "For four minutes. Do you think you could leave now?"

"If I grew a beard, would that change your mind about my proposal?"

I dropped my hands and glared at him with incredulity. His perseverance was remarkable.

"Well?"

"No. I'm not changing my mind if you grew a beard. It would just make you look better. Sexier." Oh my God, why did I keep talking?

He never missed an opportunity to humiliate me. "Sexier? Then you already think I'm sexy."

Sexy was an understatement. I thought he was irresistibly attractive and extraordinarily provocative, and if I had to sit across from him one more minute, I wasn't sure I could restrain myself from crawling over the table and demanding he kissed the fuck out of me right then and there.

Not that Edward Fasbender was a man who would ever take demands. He was the kind of man who had to be in charge. The kind of man who would slay me in every way if I let him.

I couldn't give him that opportunity. "It doesn't matter what I think about you, remember?"

For a minute I thought he might argue with me, might change his entire game and say *forget this marriage bullshit, come back to my hotel with me.* Instead, he said, "You're right. It doesn't."

But his eyes...they said something else. I was sure of it. As sure as I'd ever been of anything.

"Celia! Sorry I'm late, I got on the wrong train and then I went the wrong direction when I got on the street and then—" Blanche broke off when she noticed the man sitting in the seat that was supposed to be hers. "Oh."

She blushed, and I felt for sure she was about to spit out an awkward apology of sorts to him as well, but before she could, Edward stood. "Excuse me. I was just leaving." He pushed away from the table. It was then he truly looked at her. "You work for me."

She shook her head, her cheeks growing even redder. "Not anymore, sir."

"That's right." He stepped out of her way, letting her take the seat. "I look forward to hearing from you, Celia. Or you'll be hearing from me. Good day, Ms. Martin."

Like hell, he'd be hearing from me. But I knew it would be ten times worse if he had to come to me.

Fuck, I needed a drink.

As soon as he turned to leave, I grabbed the blasted Juliet and took a long gulp. Fuck him, it was actually a really good cocktail.

I'd drunk too soon, as it was, because not three seconds later he pivoted back toward me. "Oh, and Celia...I recommend the oysters. They're delicious and slippery. Just like you."

I definitely hated him. I definitely wasn't going to marry him.

And I most definitely wasn't ordering the oysters.

NINE

I STARED after Edward for longer than I meant to, my eyes trained on the front doors for thick seconds after his tight backside disappeared into the summer sun.

Blanche looked over her shoulder, following the line of my gaze. "I'm sorry I was late," she said again, "but maybe I should have been even later?"

With a frown, I brought my attention to her. It took another beat before I realized she was insinuating I might have liked to have been alone with the devil longer.

No. Absolutely not. No, no, no.

"No," I said, a much tamer dismissal than the one going on inside my head. "I hadn't meant to... I didn't know he'd be here. He sat himself down. After I'd told him I was expecting someone, even. Then he harassed me. Basically that's what he did, he *harassed* me, and I didn't —" I cut myself off when I noticed the hand holding my glass was shaking.

This wasn't the woman I was. Not the person I'd wanted to meet with Blanche Martin. I was flustered and babbling and off-kilter. I was a million miles from being Celia Werner.

Tossing my napkin on the table, I began to slide across the bench.

"Could you excuse me for just a moment? I need to use the restroom." I was on my feet before she could respond.

Quick, anxious steps carried me to the bathroom where I braced myself with both hands over the sink and sucked in air like I'd been on an oxygen-restricted diet. I confronted my reflection, a hot mess version of my usual self. Stray blonde strands of hair had escaped from the bun that had been perfectly coiffed earlier. My makeup was near perfect, but my skin was pale, my eyes wild. I looked frazzled. Like I was open and on display. Like all of my insides were scattered around me for everyone to see.

"Get yourself together," I scolded the unrecognizable woman in the mirror.

I turned the faucet on cold and wet my palm, then wiped the cool water along the back of my neck. The shock of temperature settled my thoughts. My breaths were coming easier now. My shoulders were less slumped. My expression less agitated. I felt myself come together bit by bit, like a reverse clown car. All the ugly pieces of my nothing-colored interior collected and tucked away neatly where they belonged.

There. Much better.

And now that I was no longer ruffled, a new determination rose up in my sternum. A single-minded resolution to find something on Edward Fasbender. Something small, if that's all there was. *Anything.* Anything I could use to fuck with him the way he fucked with me.

Resolve was empowering.

Resolve was fuel.

Resolve was motivation to go back to the table and endure a tedious lunch with Blanche.

Five minutes later, with my hair fixed and my lipstick reapplied, I returned to the table. I gave my companion my most winning smile. "So. Have you decided what you'd like to order?"

Blanche, it turned out, was a Belgian waffles kind of woman. The kind of woman that wore a bright purple and orange checkered sundress to a fancy French restaurant. The kind of woman that worried not about appearances or waistlines or fitting into a specific box. The kind of woman who chattered like a schoolgirl, her points of conversation spiraling around in circles like a butterfly flitting from one aromatic blossom to the next. The kind of woman who painted gardens and springtime.

She was the kind of woman who felt passionately and wasn't afraid to let everyone around her know.

I was a La Salade de Poulet sort of woman, myself. The sort of woman who ran a wearisome three miles on a treadmill daily and wore her hair up, even on the weekends. The sort of woman who knew what she wanted and was direct about it, and if I ever had the inclination to emote about every colorful object in sight, I was sure that I would keep it to myself.

The contrast in our characters made for a laborious afternoon as Blanche shared whimsical bits of her life from her recent breakup with her girlfriend to the ups and downs of her art career to the promising interest from an art gallery that had landed her in London for a brief spell. If I'd been interested in playing her, I would have hung on every word she shared, collecting details to spin into a game.

As it was, I was only interested in Edward Fasbender, and it was taking a lifetime to arrive at the information I hoped to glean from her.

But I was patient. I'd learned long ago that extricating knowledge from an unsuspecting individual came easiest if the individual felt comfortable and relaxed. Listened to.

So I listened as we dined, calmly waiting for my opportunity.

"Then when the Camden exhibition fell through," Blanche said eventually, dropping her fork and pushing her mostly clean waffle plate away, "I had to decide if I wanted to stay in the UK or come back home, and coming back home seemed like such a dreadful fail, and I couldn't bear for Darcy to say I told you so, even though we'd been broken up for months by then, so I applied for any job posting I was even close to qualified for. Accelecom was the first place that offered something with a decent salary." She propped one elbow on the table, rested her chin on her palm, and wrinkled her brow. "I have to say, I'm surprised that Fasbender remembered me, let alone my last name. I didn't interact with him all that often."

I wasn't surprised. Edward seemed like the kind of man who cataloged everything, a fact I'd do well to remember.

Right now, I wasn't remembering much of anything because here was the opening I'd been waiting for. "What else can you tell me about him?"

"About Fasbender? Hmm. I don't know what's relevant."

"Anything. Everything," I encouraged.

She considered for a moment. "He's a brilliant businessman. Built the whole company on his own, really. I think he excelled because he was a visionary. He's good at determining trends, and he successfully predicted the scope media would take clear back in the early days of the internet."

"Yes, yes." This was all stuff I'd already discovered on my own. "But what kind of *man* is he?"

Blanche fretted, as though she were afraid to be unhelpful. "Dedicated. Innovative. Ambitious. Hot—obviously." She gave a crooked grin.

Very hot. Disturbingly hot.

I fidgeted in my seat, as though movement alone could jostle out thoughts of how wickedly attractive the man was.

"He's extremely wealthy, as I'm sure you know," Blanche went on. "Brilliant. Methodical. A perfectionist."

I tried not to groan. She'd babbled on all afternoon, and now I got little more than one-word answers. Not very helpful in building a character case against him.

I was going to have to spoon-feed her. "What's his personal life like?"

"Well. He doesn't have much of one, I don't think. He's married to his work. I have a hard time picturing him with any sort of family, though he does have one. Or *had* one. He's divorced and his two kids, a son and a daughter, are both grown. Oh, he has a sister too—Camilla. They seem to be really close. She works for the company as well."

I sat forward eagerly. "*Close*...how? *Close* like there's something funny going on?"

"Close like he took care of her after their parents died. After he was out of foster care himself, that is."

"I didn't realize he was orphaned." It was a lie, obviously, because I had known, but I didn't want to seem like I'd been studying him. Or stalking him.

"Yep, an orphan," Blanche said, grimly.

I paused, as though I was letting it sink in, and in that pause, it *did* sink in. Before it had been words on a paper. Now, it pressed heavy on my insides. There was something especially tragic about being left alone in the world, I supposed, and to be so alone that society was the only willing caretaker...

Not that I cared about people's tragedies in the way most others did. For me, these details were useful rather than sad. A man who'd been orphaned would have certain characteristics that would be easy to manipulate. He would possibly be afraid of rejection, afraid of attachment. Afraid of ever being weak.

There was potential there.

But there was also that pressing inside me, pressing like too much bread in my stomach. Like I'd swallowed something too hard and thick and it wouldn't settle in me. This wasn't the kind of way I wanted to fuck with the man. It wasn't the right kind of pain.

Blanche recovered quickly from her morose. "That's what makes him so incredible, though. That's what I mean when I say he became successful all on his own. While raising his sister plus getting married and having children so young... He was only twenty when Hagan was born. He's just in his forties, and both those kids must be in their early twenties now. Genevieve was starting university when I was there. I met her once, at a company event right before the semester started. Real pretty girl. Serious. Smart too. Both she and her brother planned to follow in the family business, though I had the feeling that Edward would prefer his daughter just got married."

"Why's that?"

She paused. "I don't want to go so far as to say that he's a misogynist... Traditionalist is maybe a better term."

I perked at the new potential. "Do you think that his traditional values have hurt him in any way? Maybe they're what led to his divorce?"

"I don't think so. I mean, I wasn't around when he'd been married, but from what people said, it was quite a shock when Marion left him for another man. Everyone thought they'd be together forever. Edward had apparently doted on her like she was the center of the universe. My ex-coworker, Kelly—she's worked for Accelecom since the beginning— she said he was completely devastated when she left."

"Doted? I can't imagine that man doting on anything." And why, when I tried, did that heavy feeling in my stomach dissolve into some-thing sharper, more acute? Something akin to jealousy?

"Me either. But Kelly said he got even more serious and even more driven after that, and she swears it was because of heartbreak. Anyway, if Marion Fasbender thought her first husband was too traditionalist, she sure didn't choose anything different with her second husband. This new guy's a Catholic Spaniard who seems to think women should be kept barefoot and pregnant. Again, this is all from Kelly." She smiled guiltily. "And the internet. I've done my fair share of curious online snooping. I don't know much about any of that personally."

Information I could gather from a Google search wasn't helpful. I hadn't looked up his ex-wife yet but I certainly could, all on my own.

I groaned audibly. "This isn't enough. I need juicier info."

"*Juicier* info?"

"More sensational. Has he had any scandals? Made any ethically harmful business decisions? Ever murdered anyone?"

The questions hung in the air unanswered for several seconds while Blanche's expression grew wary.

Perhaps I'd been a bit jarring. "Of course he hasn't murdered anyone. Just kidding. But also, not really. If he has skeletons, I'd really like to know. Even if it's just water-cooler gossip."

She stared at me cautiously. "You really dig deep with potential clients, don't you?"

I sighed inwardly. She needed more from me, needed a clearer motivation, and I'd been lazy about giving it.

I had to up my game.

"All right, honesty here. This has to be just between you and me, though, okay? Edward isn't just a potential client." I leaned in like I was telling a secret. "He asked me to...to go out with him."

I could feel it was the correct angle the minute I turned into it. The air loosened around us as Blanche visibly relaxed. It was always best to play the truth, or as close to it as possible. I should have gone this route from the beginning.

"Oh!" Understanding dawned across her face. "Ohhhhhh."

Her renewed interest spurred me on, the words now flowing easily. "And since he's a rival of my father's, it becomes really tricky. I have to question his motives. Is he really interested? Or is he trying to get close to my father? I can't just go out with him without truly considering who he is as a person. My dad would kill me if I said yes, which is why I should just say no, but..." I lifted my eyes to appear as though I was staring dreamily in the distance.

Blanche picked up where I'd left off. "But how can you say no to that man? He's got something about him."

"I'll say." My skin tingled thinking about him. Thinking about his penetrating gaze and his plump lips and how it would feel to have both his gaze and his lips doting on me.

I blinked away the insane notion. Doting wasn't what I wanted from Edward. I wanted to see him on his knees, yes, but not adoringly. I wanted to see him writhing.

And I was so close to finding out something useful. Something that might give me what I wanted.

I narrowed in on the prize. "So you can see why I need to know everything I can about him, right? If he has something to be ashamed of...like, if he's really a misogynistic asshole, then I should know and just say no now."

Blanche shook her head cautiously, as though she were afraid she'd give a wrong answer. "Like I said, I'm not sure he really is an asshole, not like that. I didn't exactly see evidence that he was anti-female. He had plenty of women in powerful positions in the company. And he gave Camilla a job, so that doesn't make sense, does it? And I don't know anything that might be considered scandalous. Except..." She bit at her lip hesitantly. "There is one thing I've heard... It's not gospel, but maybe it's a thing?"

"What? Tell me." I was greedy for whatever secrets lay on her tongue.

"Okay, um. Right. Okay, there were rumors he was into..." She glanced around, as if Edward might have returned and was eavesdropping on our conversation.

Satisfied with her surroundings, she leaned in and whispered. "I heard he was into something kinky."

"What kind of kinky?" I wasn't as quiet as Blanche had been.

Her cheeks flushed red. "Something with sex."

I managed not to roll my eyes. "Yes, but what kind of sex kinky? Is he into bondage? Rape play? Golden showers? Cuckolding? Erotic humiliation? Is he a masochist? A crossdresser? A pedophile?"

Edward's own words replayed in my mind. *I'm not an easy man to please in the bedroom.*

Was he a dominant? A sadist?

I shivered at the possibility.

"I don't...I don't know." Blanche's eyes glossed over, overwhelmed. "That's a lot of options, and I don't know anything about most of what you said."

"What *do* you know, Blanche?"

"Well, I know what a pedophile is. And bondage. And crossdressing."

"I mean about *Edward.*" I'd lost my patience. "What do you know about sex and Edward?"

"Oh, right. Just this rumor I heard through the grapevine that someone had seen him at a sex club. On more than one occasion."

Now we were getting somewhere. "Any idea what the name of the club was?"

"I'm afraid not." Her shoulders sank dejectedly. "I'm sorry I'm not more helpful."

"No, you're good. This is good." It was *something*, anyway. A lead. Something I could potentially work with. Something I could potentially hang over his head.

At least, that was the reason I was giving myself for the nature of my interest.

"Any idea how long he's going to be in the States?" I asked, suddenly worried about how much time I had to find out more.

"Not exactly. When you asked about him on Friday, I did email Kelly and ask why he was here, though. Out of my own curiosity. It appears he's been meeting with Visioware—have you heard of them?"

I nodded. Technically, they were another media competitor of my father's. Small potatoes. Probably not even on my father's radar. "What's he want with them?"

"I think he's trying to negotiate a merger. I'm not sure if you're aware, but Accelecom has been trying to enter the U.S. market for quite some time. I think Edward would do almost anything to make it happen."

Like try to marry his rival's daughter.

Something seemed to click in Blanche's head. "Oh, maybe that's why he wants to date you!" As soon as she'd said it, she realized what she said might have been offensive. "I mean, that's *not* why he wants to date you. Look at you! Who wouldn't want to date you? You're perfect." Her face went red again. "I mean, I'm sure he's really interested in you. But I see why you might be worried."

I smiled faintly. Edward had already laid out his real interest in me, of course, so there was no reason to be offended.

But I did like thinking he was attracted to me as well. He'd said as much, so it was easy to think.

But also confusing because then why didn't he want to sleep with me? Why didn't he think to even find out if I was interested in the same kink he was interested in? Was he not really attracted to me? Was he already so sure I couldn't be right for it? Right for *him?*

"Anyway," Blanche interrupted my thoughts. "I don't know how the negotiation is going, but I do know he'll be here for the rest of the month."

"Oh?"

"He's hosting this year's International Media Innovators' Banquet on July twelfth. Kelly mentioned that as well. Is that useful?"

"You know what, Blanche? I think it is." In more ways than one. At the very least, it meant I had three more weeks.

And with this settling in the conversation, I knew where we had to head next, the part that I usually relished most about these types of encounters. The part where I acknowledged the reason she'd met with me in the first place, to discuss her art.

After all the info she'd given, after all the time she'd invested in this afternoon, being let down would be particularly hard on her. Particularly delicious for me.

Delicious and slippery, just like you.

My eye twitched remembering Edward's parting remark.

It was because I hated him being right, because I hated him seeing me so clearly that I changed course. "I'm sure you're eager to hear about my client, if he wants to purchase your work, and I'm sorry to say that he's going to pass." I paused just long enough to let the disappointment sink in before snagging it back away. "But! I'm so certain the pieces you've completed are right for the sorts of projects I work on that I'm willing to buy the two you brought into my office as well as the four others you sent via email. Just tell me the amount, and I'll write a check tomorrow."

I'd maybe even actually look for a place to display what I bought.

Not the painting with the garden swing, though. No, that one would be burned as soon as I had my hands on it.

I wouldn't tell her that. "So what do you think?"

If I weren't so distracted, I might have discovered something counter to my usual M.O. I might have discovered it was just as satisfying to put a smile on someone's face as it was to take it away. Might have discovered it was just as delicious to give as it was to take. To build dreams as it was to tear them apart.

But Blanche's tears of elation were background noise to the tune buzzing at the forefront of my mind—a driving melody of fascination. A hum of intrigue I hadn't felt in years that had nothing to do with her, and everything to do with the man we'd spent the last half hour talking about.

TEN

I DIDN'T USUALLY HAVE to find the game that belonged with the person.

While I didn't experiment in the way Hudson did, his methods had informed the way I played. Schemes presented themselves by the nature of the characters we came across. Like science, the schemes began with a question, not a subject. Here's a pair of newlyweds—would they throw away love for the right distraction?

Here's a man who desperately wants recognition—what would he give to receive it?

Here's a woman recovering from an obsessive personality disorder —what would it take to make her relapse?

The experiments were never conducted out of spite. I'd never had to look for the question hidden in a subject's past.

Which was what made Edward Fasbender a different animal. There wasn't an obvious game about him. There was only my resent-ment. Only my malice. Only my complete dedication to throwing him off balance the way he'd thrown me.

And so I had to dig to find the question. I had to search to find the game.

While lunch with Blanche Martin hadn't been entirely productive, she had given me several leads, and I spent the next few weeks following them, splitting my attention along various paths, hoping that at least one would take me to a scenario that posed an evident ploy.

The easiest trail was the International Media Innovators' Banquet, but it was the one I hated using most for a number of reasons. First, it wasn't a promising lead. Edward was a host, and that meant he'd be present for the banquet, but what would be scandalous about that? What game was there to play there?

Second, it was a lead that would require my presence. I'd found no potential drama through my research of the event. The attendees to be honored were not remarkable beyond the works that had precipitated the invitation. There was a question of why Edward would choose to be involved in such a benevolent affair, but the answer seemed glaring —he was likely sincerely interested in innovations in a field he loved. For me to discover anything more about the event, I'd have to attend in person.

That led to the third reason I was reluctant to pursue this avenue— I'd have to find a way to get invited. It wasn't really a big dilemma, considering my father was also in the media world, and I was sure he could get me there if I wanted, or connect me with the person who could.

That meant that I'd have to involve my father, which was the fourth reason this was not a good plan.

It was the final reason that gave me the most pause—attending the event would mean seeing Edward. It would mean being in his world, on his turf. He was always formidable, always a man who could knock me off my feet, always a man who stole the breath right from my lungs, and if I chose to walk into *his* event, I'd be going in more vulnerable than ever.

Strangely, the prospect of seeing Edward again was also the reason I didn't cross the banquet off my list entirely. There was no denying I was drawn to him. Or drawn to the power he held over me, anyway. I wanted to dissect it. I wanted to open it up and tear it apart and analyze the whys and hows of his control.

Maybe Hudson had made me into a scientist after all.

The other leads were more vague but also held the most potential. His relationship with women and his sister, Camilla. The death of his parents. His divorce. His sex habits.

All but the last required straightforward investigation. It took time, yes, lots of time, and I was thankful that I only had the one client and no current games in the works so I could devote my energy to the project. It was a task that I would normally find monotonous—there was a reason I'd stayed with Hudson's method of choosing subjects rather than employing this new tactic.

Surprisingly, though, I found researching Edward compelling. I realized fairly quickly that he was an onion. Every detail that I discovered, each layer that I peeled away from the story behind the man led to another equally complex and fascinated layer, none of them ever providing any answers, just more questions. One question in particular came up over and over, at each new finding—why? Why did he do what he did? Why, why, why?

It appeared he was indeed close to his sister, who he'd taken custody of after he'd aged out of the foster care system himself, but then he'd also taken care of her more recently, when her husband had died leaving her a pregnant widow. She'd moved in with her brother then, and as far as I could tell, she and her toddler son still lived with him. Why? Why not set her up in her own place? He had enough money for that.

His marriage brought a similar question. His ex-wife Marion had indeed left him for another man, but despite the fact, even though the courts removed any obligation of alimony, he'd given her a settlement of an undisclosed amount as part of the divorce proceedings. Why? Did she have something over him? Was there more to the story? Was he just...nice? That certainly didn't lend credence to the idea that he might despise women.

His parents' deaths were also intriguing, his father's life having ended in suicide when Edward was only thirteen. Why? What would drive a man—a parent of two—to kill himself?

This particular why, however, was one I was able to dismiss after further digging. The same year, Edward's mother had a battle with cancer. His father sold his business, perhaps to focus on his wife's health, but ended up losing her. With his company and his childhood sweetheart gone, he must have seen little reason to keep on living.

That had to do damage to a kid—losing both parents in such a short timeframe, one of them having left by choice. There were definitely wounds there to exploit, but I couldn't see the best ways to use them.

Rather, I didn't want to see them. That begged its own question of why, one I hadn't tried to answer.

Discovering about his sexual proclivities was the trickiest lead to follow. I couldn't just use Google to find what I wanted to know, though I tried in every peripheral way I could imagine. I looked for sex clubs in London that were near his home and near his office. Looked for connections between him and the owners of more prestigious clubs. I found lots of names, lots of possibilities, but nothing definitive.

Once I discovered how long Edward had been in the States—three months already—I started searching for a club he might be visiting locally. Surely he'd be seeking out entertainment while in New York. But there were too many in the city and, short of hiring a detective to follow him, no way to tell if he'd visited any of them.

I put up feelers where I could, joined sex forums, and made several different profiles hoping to bait him out or attract someone who might tell me where to find a man who fit his description. Without knowing what he was into specifically, though, it was hard to actually describe him.

I looked very closely at Marion, his wife, inspected her pictures for bruises, searched for reports of domestic abuse, hunted for gossip about the reasons for her affair. Everything seemed to show they'd had a model marriage, even after an apparent shotgun wedding. If Edward had practiced kink with his wife, it hadn't been a destructive element to their relationship.

Although, she had left him in the end.

Lots of people got divorced. Lots of spouses cheated. Lots of people got left behind.

Still, I couldn't help asking why.

A WEEK BEFORE THE BANQUET, I had nothing, despite the numerous hooks I had out in the ocean. Defeated, I called my father.

"Why do you want to go to that dreary old thing?" he asked. I knew he would. I'd prepared for this.

"Daddy, I want to go for you, of course."

"For *me*?"

I took a deep breath and reminded myself that sticking to as much of the truth as I could was always the safest lie to tell. "Remember that Accelecom guy? The one you said was a devil? Ever since he tried to use me to get close to you, I've been wondering what I could do to turn the tables on him. Then I found out he was hosting this banquet. He's the keynote speaker, even! There's a good chance he's going to talk about some of his own innovative strategies, and since there's no press allowed, and since Werner Media isn't a participating corporation, I thought, wouldn't it be a great idea to have someone on the inside to hear what he has to say?"

I bit my lip as I waited for his reply.

"Oh, honey, that's not something you need to be concerned about." But he was intrigued, and he proved it, entertaining the idea with his next question. "I do know someone who could probably arrange for you to help with the banquet setup. Maybe you could stick around in the background afterward..."

Within the hour I was officially on the committee overseeing the table decorations. I was still high with the victory when Renee walked in carrying a canvas wrapped in brown paper.

"Is that the art for the master bedroom?" We'd been waiting for a piece to show up for my client's penthouse design.

"Actually, it's another piece from Blanche Martin. She had one more in the collection, it appears."

"Huh." I'd already received the first paintings, and while I hadn't yet bothered to destroy the garden swing piece, I hadn't opened it either. They were currently all stacked in the corner of my office.

Without prompting, Renee tore off the packaging of the latest canvas, revealing another landscape, still a garden of sorts, but this one was less traditional. The flowers pictured grew wild intermingled with long grass; the only sign of human touch was the carefully pruned cobblestone path that ran through it, disappearing into the distance.

"That's nice," Renee said, then, before I had time to really study it, she turned toward me, blocking my view of the painting behind her. "Also, I have something to tell you."

"All right." I closed my laptop and gave her my full attention, my curiosity piqued from her hesitant tone.

"I'm giving you notice. I'll work through the end of this project, through the end of the summer, but then I'm...I'm..." She stumbled over the next part. "Then I'm going to do something else," she said finally.

"What? Why? Are you unhappy here?" Granted, I wasn't the most generous employer, but I wasn't terrible.

"I'm not exactly unhappy," she said, seemingly careful about her choice of words. "But I'm not exactly happy, either. It's just not fun anymore. It used to be, back in the beginning. I don't know what's changed. Me, probably. Whatever it is, I need to do something different now."

I could tell her what had changed—me. I'd started my business when I still had passion, when I analyzed personalities in order to design matching decor rather than to find weaknesses to exploit.

It *had* been fun, I remembered now. Where had all that joy gone?

"I'm sorry," Renee said, sincerely. Followed by other words, necessary words, niceties exchanged by both of us before she went back to her desk, leaving me alone.

In a daze, I stared at the painting long after she'd gone, studying the stones that meandered so prominently in the foreground of the wild garden before dissolving into nothing in the background. There weren't any people in the image, but it was clear to me it was a piece about leaving. Someone had walked that path, someone had followed to the only place it led—away.

I had something in common with Blanche Martin after all. She knew, like Edward Fasbender knew, like *I* knew, that eventually everyone leaves.

ELEVEN

THOUGH THE INNOVATORS' Banquet was on Edward's turf, I did have one advantage—I'd come prepared.

I'd planned the conversations I meant to have with him, practicing various reactions in the mirror. I'd dressed provocatively, choosing a red midi dress with cleavage, rather than my usual more conservative attire. I'd worn my hair down, instead of up-knotted.

I'd dressed *for* Edward.

It was counterintuitive, catering to his wishes in order to get the upper hand, but it was all that I had. It was enough to give me a confident air. I walked around the South Salon of the Mandarin Oriental, supervising the setup, like I belonged there. Like I owned the place. With all the authority of a goddess. The fierceness of a dragon.

Bustling around in heels was always risky, however, no matter how well comported I was, and once again my shoes became my downfall. Literally.

It was my fault for being meticulous. I'd noticed the water in one of the decorative bouquets was low, and having no water can available, I'd carried the large glass vase to the restroom outside the salon. After filling it to the appropriate level, I'd set off toward the banquet room in such a hurry that I slipped on the marbled floor, dropping the floral arrangement to the floor with a loud crash.

It was there, with me on my hands and knees, cleaning up broken glass, surrounded by calla lilies and long-stem roses, that Edward found me.

"Shit," I mumbled when I realized he was the owner of the Italian leather shoes standing in front of me. Since it was also the same moment I sliced my palm with a sharp fragment of glass, I was easily able to pretend the cursing had been for the blood dripping from my fresh wound.

"You seem to have trouble with walking," he said, bending down to the ground, where I was firmly pressing two fingers over the bleeding cut. "Let me see it."

"I'm fine," I said with a scowl, pissed off that, after all my attempts at preparation, this was how our encounter would take place.

"Let me see it."

His tone was emphatic and forceful without his voice raising in the least, a tone that said *I do not like repeating myself and you'd best do as I say or else.*

I was more than mildly curious about what that *or else* would entail, but I was also so caught up in his command that I held out my hand immediately, without a second thought.

"This isn't too bad. Probably won't even need a bandage after a minute or two." He traced the cut with a single finger, collecting the droplets along the path.

Mesmerized, I watched as he brought the tip to his mouth and sucked the blood clean. He seemed to suck the air from the room at the same time because all of a sudden I couldn't breathe.

I still hadn't caught my breath when another, thinner, trail of blood formed on my palm, and this time, without any warning, he brought my palm to his mouth and licked the wound clean.

I felt that lick down low, along the lips of my pussy. Felt it on my buzzing clit, as though his face was buried between my thighs instead of inches from my own.

I peered up, and his cerulean eyes trapped mine, and I wondered if a deer, frozen in a lion's sightline, was as sure that its hunter could hear its thudding heart as I was sure that my hunter could hear mine.

I opened my mouth to say something, I wasn't sure what, but whatever I'd planned, it wasn't what came out. "You grew a beard." I'd only just noticed the new facial hair that clung to his chin and above his lip, in exactly the pattern I'd suggested he adopt.

Had he done that for me? He had to have. There was no other option, and something about that knowledge, knowing that he'd changed something about himself *for me,* made me heady and weak. Manipulative, though the move might be, because surely it was meant to...to do *something* to me. Why else would he do it?

It was every bit as sexy as I'd imagined. Sexier. Before he'd been suave and sophisticated. Now, he was also rugged and dangerous.

He's always been dangerous, I reminded myself, just as he blew a fine mist of air across my cut.

"Ow!" I yanked my hand away, then, the spell now broken, raised up to my feet.

Edward stayed crouched, the lower position doing nothing to steal his power. "Did it sting?" he asked, the corner of his lip curling up in a cruel grin.

"Yes, it stung," I retorted, annoyed. And aroused.

Annoyed at being aroused.

With a huff, I spun back toward the bathroom I'd come from, intending to clean my hand before returning for the mess on the floor.

Also intending to get some space from the man who somehow always managed to steal my wits.

Except, before the door could shut all the way behind me, it swung open again, and Edward strode in after me.

"You're a predator," I said, meeting his eyes in the mirror above the sink. They were like magnets for my own, drawing my gaze toward them and locking them in place at every opportunity.

"Your hand was bleeding. I was being a conscientious host."

I'd meant he was a predator for following me into the women's restroom, but he'd obviously thought I was referring to what he'd done in the hall. With his tongue. On my skin.

Yes, he'd been a predator then too. And I'd been willing prey.

Stupid, willing prey.

I didn't know what to say. I had no words. All that planning, and I was dumbstruck.

So I didn't say anything. I simply turned my focus to my hand and let my hatred seethe silently in his direction.

If he was attuned to it, as he was attuned to everything, he didn't let on.

Or he liked it. That was a possibility too.

With seemingly no intention to leave, he leaned his hip against the counter and watched as I ran the faucet over my palm, the water mixing with the blood, making it look like my cut was gushing when, in fact, it was nearly stopped, just as he'd suggested it would soon.

His accuracy about this was like salt on, well, on my fresh wound. Like the sting of his breath across my palm.

I shivered, unable to help myself.

And now I wasn't just annoyed, I was pissed. At myself. At him, too, but mostly myself.

I slammed the faucet off with my elbow and reached past him to tear a towel from the dispenser, which I crinkled up and dabbed at my palm. The rough paper scratched and irritated my sensitive skin, turning it an angry red. Turning *me* angry red.

I let out a frustrated groan, then whirled my exasperation on him. "What are you even doing here?"

One of my pre-planned talking points came rushing back at me in the beat that followed. "You're stalking me," I charged. It was supposed to have been an accusation with weight, meant to have been thrown at him when I innocently discovered he was at the same banquet I was attending, and *how dare he*! Much the way it had come across when he'd said it to me at Orsay.

Now, spat out so sourly, it sounded lame and desperate, probably because I was lame and desperate.

Grinning like a cat that had caught the canary, Edward gently took my hand in one of his and pulled the blue paisley square from his front pocket with the other.

"Am I?" he asked, the raw timbre of his voice oddly soothing. "Stalking you?"

"Yes, you are." Rapt, I stared as he patted my palm dry with the handkerchief. I was shaking. Could he see that? Could he see how his touch seared into me? How it boiled? How it burned?

"That's cute that you think that. I'm not, obviously, as this is my event, which, of course, you already know." He wrapped the printed material around my hand, fashioning it into a bandage. "And if your presence here is an attempt to hint that you expect me to court you, I shan't do that either, so get over yourself and accept my offer."

"You're the one who needs to get over yourself. I'm not interested." I jutted my chin out as if to dot the i of my disinterest.

Or to bring my lips closer to his.

He was already so near, his mouth only inches from mine and so tempting. As tempting as it was off limits, because I was certain it was. Even more tempting *because* it was off limits.

I wasn't conscious of leaning in, wasn't aware of the physical movement that brought my face to his. I only knew that there was this thing that I had to have, had to have badly, and that thing was his mouth pressed to mine. That thing was the taste of him on my tongue. That thing was the aching relief of his kiss.

My lips moved slowly against his with a cautious sort of eagerness, coaxing him open with a hint of my tongue. There wasn't a question— my mouth was there, taking whether he gave or not—and yet, it felt like begging. Felt like I was pleading with the very shell of my soul to let me in. To kiss me back. To kiss me well.

He let me work for it, allowing me to suck and rub and beg and plead for a space of several humiliating and tortured seconds.

Then, abruptly, he twisted one arm—my uninjured arm—behind my waist and spun me so my back was pushed into the tiled wall. Pressing his palm against me, just below my neck, he held me firmly in place while he kissed me hard. Kissed me rough. Devoured me, wrenching my arm to the point of pain as he sucked my tongue and swallowed my cries and bit at my lips until I could taste the faint metallic tang of blood under the distinct flavor of Edward Fasbender.

And, God, that flavor was *everything*. His *kiss* was everything.

Everything that I didn't own, didn't possess. Everything outside of me and unknown to me. Every single thing, and it threatened to fill me, threatened to erase the very nothing that I professed and practiced to be with its substance. With its wholeness. With its entirety.

With its everything.

I wanted it and didn't want it all at once. I wriggled my arm behind me, trying to break his hold, but if I wasn't sure that, if I managed to get free, I wouldn't just use my hand to clutch to him and bring him closer. It was awful and wonderful, I didn't want it to go on, and I hoped it never ended, and if either of those things happened and it destroyed me, then so be it.

The damage was already done. I was already destroyed.

Then, just as suddenly as the assaulting kiss had begun, he broke it off.

"You wouldn't be able to crawl when I was through with you," he said, his face still only an inch away, his palm still crushing against my sternum. "And that would be just one night. You couldn't take a marriage with my demands, and I'm more interested in being married to you than fucking you, so this is off the table." He released me with brutal abruptness, as though he were disgusted by me and my mouth and my body and what he'd done to me and my mouth and my body.

"And so is marriage," I snapped, as if I could have any impact in return.

He chortled. "We'll see."

He was gone before I could deliver any sort of comeback, leaving me mad and turned on and violated and unsatisfied.

And victorious. Because I'd gotten what I'd needed—the beginnings of an idea.

TWELVE

YOU WOULDN'T BE *able to crawl when I was through with you.*

From those words, from the way Edward had wrenched my arm around my back, from the way his eyes had glazed when his breath stung my fresh wound, it seemed safe to assume he was a sadist.

A dominant too, a fact that made my pulse race more than I wanted to admit. I'd never been the submissive in the bedroom. Even when I let a man spank me or rough me up, I always found a way to top from the bottom. The idea of letting someone—letting *Edward*—have true complete control was out of the question, but letting him believe that he had control was a different story all together.

I intended to make that happen.

But first, I had to be sure the plan was genuinely feasible, and to do that, I had to find out the extent he practiced his sadism. That required either seeing him in action or speaking with someone who had. Both options could be dismissed as too difficult to orchestrate, but I was up for the challenge.

And now I had enough information to put out more precise feelers, which gave me a good place to start. Using LadyPrey, one of the profiles I'd set up to do my fishing, I posted in each of the forums I'd joined.

Submissive seeking opportunity to play. Luxurious club environment preferred. No strings. Pain welcome.

Numerous responses arrived, most invitations to private hookups. I deleted all of these. I wanted the clubs. I wanted a place where I could easily talk to a variety of women about their sexual encounters without drawing any attention to myself.

It was a couple of days before I got a reply that was useful, from a profile going by the name FeelslikePAIN.

FeelslikePAIN: **You want a one-on-one thing or a party situation?**

LadyPrey: **Party situation sounds good. As long as it's a big party.**

FeelslikePAIN: **I have something. But it's a hefty membership fee.**

Hefty membership fee was less a deterrent and more a bonus. Edward would likely attend clubs that employed exclusivity.

LadyPrey: **Money isn't an object.**

FeelslikePAIN: **I'll see what I can do. Watch your email.**

Over the next several days, I checked my LadyPrey Gmail account obsessively. I even set up the emails to forward to my regular account so I'd get the notification on my phone when it came in. For four days, there was nothing. Well, nothing beyond spam advertisements for sex toys and strip shows and reminders from Google to finish setting up my profile. Nothing that I didn't immediately delete.

On Sunday, though, the fifth day, there was something different. The subject line was simple and vague: **INVITATION TO JOIN.** A single, bold red word filled the inside of the email: **OPEN.** The word was underlined, indicating a hyperlink.

"Jesus, fuck," I muttered to myself, my pointer hovering over the link. Was this really what I hoped it was? Or was I going to click and quickly lose my laptop to a nasty virus or hackers?

I was too invested to ignore it. Too eager to even move to another computer, preferably one that wasn't mine. Holding my breath, I clicked.

Instantly, a web page opened up displaying a series of questions, each followed by a space to answer. At the bottom of the page was a button that read Submit for Approval.

1. *ARE YOU OVER THE AGE OF 21?*
2. *ARE YOU A NEW YORK NATIVE OR JUST VISITING?*
3. *DESCRIBE YOUR CURRENT RELATIONSHIP STATUS.*
4. *WHO REFERRED YOU?*

I was midway through entering in my answers, taking time to make up the details of my LadyPrey persona as I typed, when a notification from FeelslikePAIN showed up in the bottom corner of my screen.

FEELSLIKEPAIN: **Type the following as your answers and nothing else: 1. Red. 2. Yellow. 3. Green. 4. Black.**

Ah, clever. If an invitation ended up in the wrong email inbox, someone who hadn't legitimately been referred to the club, the admins would know by how the respondent answered the questions. Good thing I'd been slow with my reply.

I erased everything I'd entered in already and replaced my answers with the answers FeelslikePAIN had provided then hit submit. Next came a screen asking for payment information with no indication of the membership fee. The only method of paying was through anonymous bitcoin, a method I'd used a time or two on the dark web for previous games, which was not reassuring. Sure, *I'd* be anonymous, but that made it just as hard to track *them* down, whoever *they* were, when the whole thing ended up being a scheme to get to my bank account.

I sent a message to FeelslikePAIN.

LADYPREY: **This is requiring a lot of trust on my part.**

FeelslikePAIN: **Good sex always does.**

There were so many reasons I shouldn't, so many reasonable objections playing through my head. How many times had I secretly mocked people for being so gullible? So naive? I'd always promised to stay vigilantly aware. This scenario asked me to set aside that promise, and that ate at my conscience on a very base level.

But obsession had a way of undermining wise intentions. It suppressed all reason with its monomaniacal agenda.

Stupidly, I authorized payment from my bitcoin account. Before I had time to regret my decision, a new window popped up on my screen loaded with terms and instructions and dates and locations. With a victorious smile, I trained my eyes on the bold red headline:

Welcome to The Open Door.

THIRTEEN

MY TRIUMPH WAS QUICKLY OVERSHADOWED by the dread of reality. The Open Door was, as FeelslikePAIN had suggested, not an actual club. There was a membership fee, yes, but the weekly Saturday night get-togethers weren't held in one location, but rather was hosted at various private locations, like rotating parties rather than events sponsored by an establishment.

The difference may have been slim in the eyes of most people, but for me, it was distinct. In less than a week, I was attending a sex party.

I'd never been to a sex party.

That wasn't true, though. I had been to a sex party, for all intents and purposes. More than one. Years ago. I'd gone, but not willingly.

Except that wasn't true either. I'd never said no. I'd never tried to get out of it.

Still, I'd been powerless. I'd vowed never to be in that situation, or any even remotely like it, ever again.

That meant that if I was going to follow through with this ridiculous idea, I had to be extremely prepared. I had to find ways to keep the control in my hands. I had to go on my terms, and no one else's.

Six days was almost not enough time to get ready. The physical items I needed were easy enough to gather—underwear, a stunning but sexy dress that would be easy to move in, temporary hair dye and a mask to keep my anonymity.

It was the mental preparation that was more difficult to undertake. Having never been to these particular parties, how could I know what to expect? Would it be formal and structured? Would it be casual and laid back? Would it be a combination of both? Would there be performances or games or icebreakers? Would everyone already know each other? Would I be the only newbie? Would I be put in the spotlight?

Would it be like the sex parties I'd been at in the past?

God, I hoped not. I prayed not.

I thought about asking FeelslikePAIN for more detailed information, but I didn't want to risk the chance of her—him?—trying to take me under her or his wing. I needed autonomy for this. I needed freedom.

Since there was nothing to do with the unknowns, I had to concentrate on the knowns, the things I had complete control over. By Monday, I'd reread The Open Door's terms and bylines so many times I had them memorized, grateful that there were strict policies enforcing consent such as a restriction on liquor. On Tuesday, I scoped out the building for this week's party. Wednesday, I studied the floor plan and researched the listed owners, a couple who'd earned their wealth in dog food. Thursday I left the office early to purchase a new dress and heels, both of a style that Celia Werner would never wear. I fine-tuned my persona as I spent Friday night weaving temporary brunette highlights into my hair.

Early in the day on Saturday, I ventured out to explore local costume shops for a mask.

The website stated a good many members chose to attend the parties in disguise so, conveniently, I wouldn't have to worry about being the only person wearing one. The mask had to be just right, though. While I knew it was a stretch to worry that Edward would be there that night, if he were, I knew he'd be astute enough to recognize me if I didn't really cover my face. There were many designs that only hid the eyes. Masks meant more for fun than concealment. I wanted less Mardi Gras, more Venetian. Full-face masks weren't any better.

While they did the job I wanted, they were uncomfortable and made it hard to breathe. I had a devil of a time finding something in between, and I had to leave several stores empty-handed.

It wasn't until the fourth shop that I found what I was looking for. The mask came down over the nose, but not all the way, leaving plenty of room to breathe comfortably. The eyepiece extended up over the forehead and each side dropped lace along the jowls, almost completely covering my cheeks.

My favorite part, though, was the red and yellow plumes that swept down one entire side of the mask.

"Feathered dragon," the shop owner said behind me as I tried it on in front of a mirror.

"Excuse me?"

"That's the name of the mask. Feathered Dragon."

"I thought dragons had scales, not feathers."

The man shrugged. "Apparently not all of them."

"Huh." It was the right mask, though, the one that felt most like *me*, or who I wanted to believe I was, anyway, and I handed over my money.

That night, I examined myself in the mirror before heading out. My hair was knotted low at my neck in a new style. The red dress I wore had a slit running high up each leg, more provocative than any outfit I'd ever worn. The bodice was pure lace that only barely managed to cover my braless nipples. With the brown highlights and the mask, I looked unrecognizable.

I looked fierce.

I looked formidable.

There was nothing to worry about, nothing that could bring me down. I was ready.

I was a dragon.

FOURTEEN

I TOOK a cab to the party instead of a Lyft. I didn't want any record connecting me to The Open Door. It was bad enough that my IP address had likely been captured during the financial transactions. In hindsight, I should have been more patient and gone to a public computer somewhere, but what was done was done, and considering the type of clientele that was usually associated with these sorts of events, I had to believe my information was private.

Except for the doorman, the lobby was empty when I arrived. I'd waited to come, wanting the party to be in full swing instead of being one of the awkward first guests. As per the website's instructions, I approached the doorman and told him the evening's code word —*exosculation*. In exchange, I was given a key card for the penthouse that would work in any one of the four elevators.

Efficient. The whole process was simple yet organized, and I admired the system as I rode to the top floor, even as I wiped a bead of sweat from underneath my mask. The disguise wasn't necessarily hot or stifling, and I didn't want to say that I was nervous. On edge, perhaps was a more comfortable term. Wary.

Excited?

Yes, that too. But I always felt some level of exhilaration when initiating a new game, and while I hadn't exactly decided I was playing one with Edward Fasbender, my current course felt close enough to arouse that thrill.

The elevator doors opened into a private foyer where I was immediately greeted by two masked women dressed in couture lingerie and high heels.

"Good evening and welcome," one said, a lanky bombshell with red tresses that could only have come from a bottle. She wrapped her arm through mine and I stiffened as she escorted me to a table manned by another scantily clad woman set up in front of the foyer closet. "Please check your phone and purse here."

"Oh." I hadn't been expecting that, and the idea of leaving my personal items with strangers was unnerving.

Seeming to sense my apprehension, the woman behind the table smiled reassuringly and handed me a polyethylene bag with a self-adhesive tape strip at the top and a black Sharpie. "Your privacy is respected here. Write whatever identifying information you'd like to on the label. I'll seal it in your presence and put it in the safe behind me."

Very efficient.

I let out a slow breath and, after drawing a quick sketch from memory of my mask, I dumped my clutch and my phone into the bag. The attendant sealed it and wrote the number two-hundred-nine in the corner, then, with the Sharpie still in hand, asked, "May I have your wrist?"

Cautiously, I held my hand out toward her. She turned it over, and wrote the same number on the inside of my wrist.

"Your claim number," she explained before turning to the safe with my sealed items.

Ignoring my tense reaction, the redhead linked her arm through mine once again and led me out of the foyer and down a short hall. "The games are being played in the main room. There's a demonstration currently in the dining room. All other rooms that are unlocked are for play. Baskets with lube and condoms are located throughout the apartment. Please use them liberally."

We turned the corner and the apartment opened into a spacious great room with twenty-foot-high ceilings. *Spacious* was probably not the right word. The place was gigantic, covering what had to be about three thousand square feet, and it was filled with at least a hundred people.

I felt my eyes go wide to take it all in. Adults of all ages were gathered in bunches like any well-attended party. Most of the men were dressed in tuxedos or suits, though a few had begun to lose pieces of clothing to the floor while the furniture was littered with discarded jackets and bowties. The women were more plentiful and more often naked or stripped down to designer underwear, though enough wore cocktail dresses to make me not feel out of place. A sensual, pulsing beat pumped through the sound system, an undercurrent to the buzz of energized conversation and flirting laughter. Pillows were generously strewn across the space, *so many* pillows, and the air smelled of a combination of expensive perfume and sex. All around me, people were kissing and groping and grinding and fucking in groups of two, three, seven, ten, a libidinous carnival of depravity and debauchery.

It was shocking. And stunning.

Breathtaking in its horror and its beauty.

"Have fun."

I barely heard the redhead as she let go of my arm and disappeared somewhere behind me. I was too fascinated with everything in front of me. Having forgotten for the moment my reason for attending, I walked through the crowd, taking in the details of the scene. In the corner, a woman was erotically spanking an older woman draped across her lap. Next to her was a half-naked man sucking off another man dressed in high tails while he also gave a hand job to a man who had a sign around his neck that read "Touch Me." A woman wearing nothing but metallic pasties and a cat mask crawled across the floor toward a man holding a riding crop. A kissing orgy was taking place on a huge pile of pillows in the center of the room while a smaller orgy was all out fornicating on the couch next to them.

As the redhead had said, there were games being played. Nearest the front of the room, a very handsy game of suck and blow was taking place. One person passed a dollar to the person next to them using only his or her mouth. At closer look, it was a hundred. Of course. How could I expect anything less? Further in the room a group was playing naked Twister, and still further, a wicked game of Truth or Dare was underway.

Everywhere there was touching. Everywhere there was sex. It was intensely erotic, and maybe in another lifetime I would have found it arousing. And I *was* aroused, on one level. I felt flushed. My pulse had quickened. My pussy was wet and swollen.

But my head wasn't in it. My head was never in it. I enjoyed sex, for the most part, on a purely physical level. My body knew how to respond, how to give good orgasms. My head, though, always remained detached and separate, safe behind the ice walls I'd built around me. Just like every other emotion, arousal was one I'd grown numb to, even in this environment, with shameless licentiousness surrounding me.

It was like that all those years ago, too. I'd disassociated then as well. I'd had to in order to survive. Was that where the nothing in me really began? Not with Hudson, but in the depravity of that first sex party way back then?

That night had been nothing like this one. This party was celebratory and empowering and consensual where the other had left menacing shadows over my existence. The difference gave me the last burst of confidence I'd needed, and any traces of my initial anxiety melted away.

Still, I clung to the wall as I made my way through the room. I hadn't seemed to attract much attention, as of yet, and I wanted to keep it that way. While many of the people were wearing masks as I was, others had lost the pretense of disguise. It was a surprise to realize how many faces I recognized, some because they were well-known entertainment, sports, and political figures, others because they ran in the same elite circles of the wealthy that I did. A nude woman bent over in the Twister game with a hand on red and a foot on yellow was a reporter for a major news show. The man fingering her was a Broadway director.

Another woman who called herself Miss T wore a mask, but I could swear she had the exact same jawline as Hudson's secretary.

Though, to be fair, I saw traces of Hudson in all sorts of things that had nothing to do with him. Not as much these days, but at times.

It wasn't until I saw my father's CEO of children's programming going down on a man in drag that I had the jolting realization that I might *really* know some of the people here. Jesus, what if Hudson himself was in attendance? Or his *parents*? Or *my* parents?

That thought was a reminder of my purpose. I needed to get on with this and get out of here. I stopped gawking at the festivities and concentrated on my task, looking for someone who might have interacted with Edward at one of these things. The good thing was I was pretty sure I'd found exactly the kind of place he might attend. Another good thing was there were plenty of women who seemed to enjoy S&M play. Now to find one that wasn't currently occupied...

After making mental notes of all the possible candidates I'd already come across, I decided to leave the game room and scope out the more private areas of the unit. My parents lived in a more than decent size apartment, but this penthouse was one of the largest I'd seen in the city. More than eight thousand square feet total, if I had to guess. And no rooms were off limits to play. That left a lot still to explore.

I slipped through the chef's kitchen where a sextet was having fun with whipped cream and chocolate sauce and into the dining room. This was where the demonstration was supposed to be taking place, and indeed, something seemed to currently be happening on the table, but there were so many people gathered around, I couldn't see exactly what, at first.

But then, a couple in front of me broke away from the assembly, leaving a small window in the crowd for me to slip through and watch. The demonstrator was an older man with gray hair in a tux with a red jacket, his eyes directed at the woman dressed in a schoolgirl outfit who was on her hands and knees on top of the table next to him. Her skirt was flipped up to expose her cotton white panties.

"Who wants to pull them down?" he asked the onlookers. "Who wants to show us what our innocent girl is hiding underneath?"

The crowd roared enthusiastically, volunteers rushing to be the one he called on.

A memory shot through me, through all of me. Through my head, through my bones, through my veins, turning my blood to ice. *How much to touch her here? How much to be the first?*

A wave of tremors came over me, as though it weren't my body itself shuddering, but as if the ice walls around me were actually bars of a cage, and that cage were being rattled. I could feel a scream building inside me with no place to go. It was trapped, stuck in my throat. As much a prisoner as I was in the presence of those memories.

I couldn't be there anymore. I had to leave. If not the party, at least the demonstration.

Shoving through the bodies, I made my way out to the opposite side of the dining area than I'd come in. This fed me into the family room, a quieter space despite the abundance of guests. I looked around absent-mindedly, my eyes scanning past the two men masturbating in the corner and the trio fucking on the sofa and stopped when they came to the woman in a black sparkly wrap dress kneeling at the foot of a man sitting in an armchair.

Then my heart really began to pound.

Not because of the scene I was witnessing—the man stroking the head of the woman at his feet—but because the man was Edward Fasbender.

FIFTEEN

MY FIRST INSTINCT was to run. Dash from the room and get the hell out of there before he spotted me.

But my feet wouldn't move. I could barely even breathe, my entire body frozen like a deer in the sightline of a hunter.

The fear of being caught was real and overwhelming. It clouded my head, which was why it took a few seconds to remember I was in disguise. He wouldn't recognize me behind my mask. Relaxing in the realization, my pulse began to slow. Not completely, but to a more reasonable tempo, at least. I could think clearly again. This was what I'd come for, ultimately. Well, I'd come for someone who'd possibly been with Edward and here was a woman who was with him for sure.

Having Edward here too was actually a bonus. Wasn't it?

I decided to believe it was.

Pressing my back against the column of wall behind me, I took on the role of voyeur, and trained my eyes on the scene. He hadn't noticed me, which gave me even more confidence. My breaths came easier as I studied him. Like most of the men in attendance, he was dressed, but not to the nines as some were. His black suit was tailored, fitting him like it was sewn on, just as the other suits I'd seen him in had been, but this time he wasn't wearing a tie. His white dress shirt was unbuttoned at the collar, and even though he wore a vest over it, this subtle change in his usual attire gave him a casual look. His facial hair had grown in thicker but still looked impeccably groomed.

He was devastating.

Completely, utterly devastating.

So much for getting my breathing under control. My legs were so weak from looking at him, I wasn't even sure I could have stayed standing without the support of the wall. I was suddenly very aware of the slickness between my legs, of the tight beads of my nipples. The hair on my arms stood in the grove of goosebumps that had sprouted over my skin.

How long had it been since a man had affected me like this?

Years. More than a decade.

With seeming disinterest, he stared at the woman on the floor who was practically humping his leg at this point. His impassivity was a ruse, though, judging by the bulge in his pants. And with a bulge like that, there was no way he was wearing underwear.

Devastating.

"Your desperation is embarrassing, Sasha," he said callously. Or I thought he said, it was hard to tell for sure across the low buzz of the room.

I couldn't make out her response, but whatever it was must have pleased him because he yanked her up to straddle his lap, her back to his chest, and now a new sensation gathered inside me. A covetous heat pressing against my lungs, filling up the cavity between my ribs, restricting the beating of my heart. I wanted to be Sasha. I wanted to sit on his lap. I wanted to be the one who pleased him.

It was a sensation that both pissed me off and turned me on. I seethed underneath my mask, not wanting to watch anymore. Unable to look away.

Edward remained stone-faced as he tangled his fingers in her dark brown hair and tugged sharply, so sharply her head touched his shoulder, exposing the long column of her sepia-toned throat. His nose traced the curve or her neck while his free hand clawed across her decolletage, leaving a trail of scratches in its wake.

I remembered his hand on my throat when he'd kissed me, remembered it so vividly that it felt like it was me that his nails scratched now, and I shivered despite my rising body temperature.

I swore I could feel his fingers as they trailed down over her bosom to find the sash of her wrap. With one pull, the dress fell open, and after Edward rearranged the material to his liking, I could see she was completely bare underneath.

My breasts grew heavy, my nipples tighter mirroring the taut, brown tips on the woman before me. And when Edward brought his hand up again to roughly squeeze her tit, I had to bite my lip to stifle a gasp.

I could *feel* it. Could feel the shot of electricity from my own breast to my pussy as though he were fondling me. Could feel it because I wanted so desperately to be feeling it.

He moved to her other breast, handling it just as brutishly, and then, when she moaned with pleasure, his eyes lifted and locked with mine.

The air hitched in my chest. Adrenaline coursed through my veins. He'd seen me, was *seeing* me, and still I couldn't look away. His lips curled up in a self-satisfied smile, and for one terrifying second, I was sure the jig was up, certain that he knew who I was.

But of course he didn't. He'd merely realized he had an audience, and the conceited bastard couldn't help gloating about it. He even appeared to gloat about it to Sasha, whispering in her ear before letting go of her hair and helping her tilt her head up to look at me as well. Her grin was almost as cocky as his, though warmer in its fullness. As though she were welcoming the guest of my gaze.

Again, I wanted to flee, but I was incapable, held in place by the weight of my curiosity. I had to know what happened next. I needed to *see* it. I wanted to *feel* it.

Now with an onlooker to entertain, the show progressed quickly. Edward once more said something in Sasha's ear, likely instructing her because immediately she spread her legs wider, proudly displaying bare mocha lips and a hint of pink skin.

Taking her hand with his, he brought her fingers up along her slit, gathering wetness before settling on her swollen clit. Continuing to guide her, they rubbed at her bud in small tight circles. His other hand came back to pull at a steepled nipple, twisting it so cruelly her torso involuntarily tried to buck away.

And mine arched forward.

And all the while, his eyes never left mine. As though I was the woman he was fucking with his fingers. As though it was me he wanted to take to the brink of pleasure. As though he weren't using my desire to destroy me.

I swallowed. My throat felt too moist. My chest rose and fell with rapid, shallow breaths. My hands felt heavy and useless at my sides. My fingers curled into the material of my dress, half needing an anchor and half wanting to pull up my skirt and relieve the ache of my pussy.

I wondered what my eyes showed. My stare was leashed to his and while his eyes showed almost nothing beyond pupils dilated with lust, I was sure mine gave away much more. Could he see the storms brewing inside me from this distance? Could he see I was on the edge, ready to combust with rage and heat and jealousy? Ready to explode with raw lust. I hadn't even actually been touched, and I could feel an orgasm brimming.

Edward lifted Sasha's hand from her clit and, after bending her pinky and thumb into her palm, moved it down to her gleaming wet entrance. He released his grip on her, letting her thrust her three fingers in and out on her own. She was close, as close as I felt, I could tell from the erratic shift of her hips back and forth, rubbing his erection underneath her.

I pressed my own thighs together, trying to temper the building fury between them.

All it took was Edward pinching her clit, and then she was convulsing with waves of pleasure.

His eyes left mine to glance at the woman writhing on his lap, and with the tether between us cut, I bolted free, taking off in search of somewhere I could be alone, somewhere private. Somewhere away from those piercing, wretched eyes.

The first open door in the hallway led to an empty bathroom. I slammed the door behind me, having enough sense to lock it before I pulled up my skirt and shoved my hand down my panties. My pussy was hot and drenched. My fingers slid easily against my coated clit.

Bracing myself on the sink counter, I rubbed furiously and didn't stop even after the first orgasm ripped through me. I had to get it all out, all of *him* out. Had to get rid of this poison he'd put inside me. My knees buckled as a second wave rolled over me, and still I kept on, rubbing until my skin felt chafed and on fire. Rubbing, rubbing, rubbing until I was shaking and tears were rolling down my cheeks, until I'd let out a loud guttural cry of relief.

Until I'd yanked the last of my pleasure from my cunt and was free of that devil and the dark, agonizing curse of desire.

SIXTEEN

I WAS SWEATING when I'd finished.

I removed my mask and tucked the strays of my hair back into my knot as best as I could. Without my purse, I couldn't fix my makeup. Luckily most of my face was covered by the disguise, but my mouth was still visible and my once-red lips were now pale and blotchy. I dabbed at them with a tissue then stared at my reflection.

I looked wrecked, and I was.

Some dragon.

After all that, I hadn't even gotten what I'd needed. I'd verified that Edward liked things a little bit kinky, but I'd already guessed that. He was a bit of an exhibitionist, a bit of a dom. A bit brutal. So what? None of that was useful.

I'd learned more about me from the experience than I'd learned about him, and what I'd discovered wasn't something I wanted to know —the man had power over me. Real, ruinous power.

Fuck him for that. *Fuck him.*

The handle of the door jiggled next to me, followed by a knock when it didn't open. "There are bedrooms for what you're doing," a female voice called.

Ah, shit. She'd probably heard me.

Whatever. This was a sex party, after all. I couldn't possibly have been the only woman to get herself off in here tonight.

"Just a minute," I called out tersely. With a sigh, I donned my mask and opened the door.

"Oh, it's you," Sasha said when I walked out.

Of all the people who could have been waiting for the bathroom, it had to be her.

She'd put her dress back together, and she looked unfairly more put together than I felt, and she'd been the one who'd actually had an orgasm.

Well, I'd had one now too. Three, actually. Perhaps the unbalance was warranted.

"I bet you needed that," she said with a knowing smile. Friendly. As though we weren't strangers, as though we were close now that she'd come in front of me.

No. We were *not* friends. The only reason she wasn't the enemy was because that title was already taken by her lover.

Thinking of Edward again and the way he'd touched her made my stomach twist. It was definitely time to leave.

Without saying anything, I stepped out of her way so she could get past, but just as she was about to shut the door behind me, I reconsidered. "Sasha," I called to her. I waited until she turned around. "That is your name, isn't it?"

"Yeah." She didn't ask how I knew, possibly realizing I'd overheard it earlier.

"That guy you were with..." I paused, glancing around to be sure he wasn't lurking nearby while trying to decide how to frame my question. "Do you know what he's into?"

"Trying to steal my ride home, are you?" But the smile remained, suggesting she was teasing. "Or are you warning me off? Because if you are, I already know what I'm getting into. I've gone home with him before."

My jaw clenched, and I had a strong urge to claw her eyes out.

At the same time, the back of my neck tingled with excitement. Maybe this night wasn't a waste after all.

I stepped toward her, closing the small gap between us. "What's he *like*? Is he...?"

"Is he *good*?"

That wasn't exactly the word I'd been looking for, but I nodded for her to go on, hoping she'd give me something worthwhile.

"He's real good, actually. If you can take a beating." She smirked. "Fortunately, I can."

Now as I looked at her I saw the signs I'd missed earlier—the fading bruises on her arms, the red marks at her wrists from some type of bondage.

"He *is* a sadist," I said, more to myself than to Sasha.

"You could say that. Roughest time I've ever had. Best time too. So thanks for the warning, if that's what you were about, but also no thanks because I'm good."

For the first time that evening, I gave my own smile. "Good for you. Enjoy yourself." I turned away before she could say anything else. I didn't need any more from her, and I was eager to get out of there in case Edward came looking after her.

With a satisfied buzz, I headed back to the main foyer. Checking out was as efficient as checking in had been. After producing my wrist for inspection, I was given my items, the bag they'd been contained in still sealed.

One of the hostesses that had greeted me called an elevator for me, and by the time I'd gotten my purse and my phone out, it had arrived. I stepped inside feeling smug. I'd gotten what I'd been after, and even with the inconvenience of running into the devil himself, I was leaving undiscovered.

Except, before the doors could close, a familiar voice shouted to hold the elevator. A familiar *British* voice.

Fuck!

I did not want to share a ride down to the lobby with him. What if he talked to me? What if he expected *me* to talk to *him*? What if I did and he recognized my voice?

Panicked, I hit at the door-closed button, but the hostess stuck her arm in, blocking the doors from shutting, and a few seconds later Edward and Sasha joined me in the elevator.

I huddled in the corner, hoping I'd go unnoticed, even though there were only the three of us in the car. Hoping they'd be too wrapped up in each other to pay attention to me.

It was a hope I didn't send into the universe with much energy, though, since I simultaneously wanted him to never look at her again.

Unsurprisingly, his eyes fell on me. I could feel them even with my head turned away.

"Look, Sasha. It's our new friend. I wonder if she enjoyed your performance as much as you did." He was as patronizing with his tone as he ever was. I'd learned that tonight, too, I supposed. That he was this way with everyone. That it wasn't a demeanor he reserved explicitly for me.

I hugged my arms around myself. Maybe I could play shy. Or rude. I didn't care what his impression of me was as long as he didn't know it was indeed me.

Sasha draped her arm over his shoulder possessively. "Oh, she enjoyed it. I heard her in the bathroom rubbing one out."

My entire body flushed with equal measures embarrassment and anger. I had wanted that to belong only to me. It was bad enough that Sasha had witnessed it. I had definitely not wanted Edward to find out. Even with him not knowing who I was behind my mask, it gave him too much of a win. I hated that he had that power over me. It made me sick that he knew it too.

"That's a lovely shade of red your skin turns, little bird. That has quite an effect on me. It's going to be a miserable ride to my hotel, thanks to that."

My head shot in his direction, and I couldn't help but glance at the effect he referred to. He was visibly hard again. This close, I could see the outline of his cock through his slacks. It was big and brutal, just like he was.

My pussy throbbed in response, that traitor, and without thinking, I lashed out in response. "Your misery is *not* my problem, you asshole."

Fuck, I thought too late. *Fuck, fuck, fuck!*

Did he recognize my voice? Could he tell it was me? He stared at me, his eyes narrowing, and I held my breath, waiting for him to call me out.

"Of course it's not your problem," he said, eventually. Harshly. "Considering the kind of party you just left, I thought you'd find the information stimulating. It was certainly stimulating for me to tell you. Pardon me for my erroneous assumption."

My heart thudded wildly against my rib cage, and it took almost all my restraint not to throw a punch. It took just as much strength not to fall down at his knees and beg for him to give me his kiss, his hands, his cock. To take out his misery on me.

How could every word out of his mouth make me hate him more while also turning every cell in my body into a blazing cell of want?

"Don't worry about this," Sasha said, palming his thick bulge. "I'll give you what you need."

I hated her for that, too. Perhaps she was my enemy as well.

He didn't say anything, didn't give Sasha any morsel of his attention, his stare staying planted on me. It should have been unnerving, and it was, but it was also something else. Something warm and electric. Something I couldn't identify.

The elevator doors opened in the lobby, and I rushed out ahead of them, dying to get away from them. Stupid, it turned out, since I had to wait while the doorman hailed a cab. Edward already had a car waiting outside.

I refused to look directly at either of them, but I also couldn't help watching them out of the corner of my eye. He opened the back door of the sedan and let Sasha slide in first. Then, before he got in himself, Edward called to me. "Do you need a ride, little bird?"

I scowled in response.

But just because I had no control where he was concerned, because he made me reckless and insane, I corrected him. "I'm a dragon, not a bird." At least I'd remembered to change my voice this time, making it lower than my usual pitch.

He paused, considering, those wicked eyes boring into me. "No. You might think you're a dragon, but you're definitely a bird."

I shot daggers after him long after his car had pulled away from the curb. He stirred so much inside me, feelings that had been dormant for so long.

They were the kind of emotions that could be burned as fuel, emotions with energy—hatred, vindictiveness, disgust. Spite.

Lust, too, but even that would be beneficial.

I intended to use them all, and now that I had what I needed, there was nothing he could do to stop me.

The game was on.

SEVENTEEN

MOST GAMES DIDN'T TAKE much time to prepare. A few days. A week at the most.

This scheme with Edward was different, though. It was going to take a level of dedication I hadn't pursued before. I would need band-width to commit. My entire life had to be cleared.

Conveniently, I only had the one client, and his project would be wrapped up by the end of summer. Renee would be gone by then too. Her resignation, it seemed, had turned out to be fortuitous. All the dominoes were lining up, and I was motivated by the desire to get to the day I'd see them all knocked down.

The one concern I had was Edward's patience. There were five weeks still before August ended. Would he still be in the country then? Would his offer still stand?

Luck, however, continued to be on my side.

A handful of days after my visit to The Open Door, a Thursday on the last day of July, Renee walked into my office carrying a glass vase filled with the most stunning bouquet of flowers.

"These just arrived," she said as she set the arrangement on the corner of my desk. She handed me a small, sealed rectangular envelope with my name scribbled on the front. "Either you're seeing someone you haven't told me about or you have a secret admirer."

I often received flowers. It was the nature of the games I played. So many times the goal was to make them fall for me, and that led to a myriad of romantic declarations.

While I didn't ever tell Renee the entire truth about these liaisons, I usually fed her a story about whatever current relationship I was pursuing. It had made things easier in the beginning, prompted fewer questions. Over time, though, I'd come to enjoy these narratives as much as the reality. They were pretty stories, fairy tales with potential for beautiful happy endings, and I found something sweet in Renee's belief that they were happening to me, even while I was aware of the lie underneath the prose.

The satisfaction wasn't about that lie, though. As much as I loved playing strangers, I never found it gratifying to deceive the few people close to me, Renee being one of them.

No, it was about the hope. The brief glimpse of what was possible, seen through the eyes of my assistant. It was the closest I'd ever get to my own happy ending, and while I'd given up on that dream a long time ago, there was a nostalgic peace in letting the pretense exist, in letting it hang in the air before it again dropped into the bleak nothing that extended before me.

I didn't currently have a story for her, though, and the arrival of the flowers was as much of a surprise to me as it was to her.

I didn't like surprises. I hated being thrown off guard.

I studied the cursive on the envelope, the hasty scrawl of only my first name—Celia. It wasn't handwriting I'd seen before, and I made a mental list of possible senders. My current client had been in that morning, and his current frustration with a hiccup in his installation didn't lend to sending flowers. A former client seemed unlikely. Blanche, perhaps.

Edward?

Sentiment wasn't his style. On the other hand, the floral arrangement was familiar.

Renee read my hesitation as a sign. "I'll give you your privacy," she said politely, closing the door behind her as she left.

I barely looked up at her departure, and I was already smiling when I tore open the envelope to read the card inside.

I head back to London tomorrow. My offer stands.
– Edward

"What happened to not courting me?" I asked the air.

As if in answer to my question, I found a postscript on the back.

P.S. The flowers are for your secretary.

I laughed out loud. Bullshit they were for my secretary. The bouquet was a near duplicate of the arrangement I'd dropped at the International Media Innovators' Banquet. It was definitely meant for me. He'd picked it out *for me*.

And the message had been handwritten instead of typed like when ordered online. If the handwriting was his, and I believed it was, it meant he'd seen to the transaction personally.

"London, huh?" Again I was talking to an empty room. "I can work with London."

As I sat back in my chair, I halfheartedly gazed at the beautiful display and began to think through altering my plans, all the while pretending that the flutter in my stomach had everything to do with excitement about my scheme and nothing to do with the man it centered around.

EXACTLY FOUR WEEKS LATER, I walked through the empty rooms of my office, turning off lights as I went, looking for anything at all that might have been missed. The space seemed so much bigger now. I'd forgotten how spacious it had been that first night. How weird to realize how filled it had been with a life of nothing.

The nothing made it easy to pack. My apartment had been sorted through over the month. I owned my own condo—well, my father technically owned it, but it had been a gift from my parents when I'd graduated from college. He'd never gotten around to transferring the title, but the point was, there wasn't any need to move anything to storage since no one else would be living there in my place. I'd only had to crate what I couldn't live without. These I labeled and stacked in my living room so they were ready to be shipped when the details of my future life were arranged.

The categorizing of what was essential and what wasn't had been so simple, I realized, because there was very little I was attached to. My extravagantly designed space was filled with high-end furniture and art, my closets overflowing with expensive clothes, and none of it mattered to me in the least. There had been only one item I'd deliberated over, or, one set of items, rather—the diaries I'd kept over the years documenting the details of the games. On the one hand, they represented everything I'd been living for, and I wanted them with me for that. They were comforting. Familiar.

On the other hand, I didn't want them to be found. By anyone, but especially Edward. That made them safer packed up as well, but instead of stacking them by the door for shipment, I hid the crate in the guest room closet.

The office had been even easier to deconstruct. Renee had taken the task on herself, hiring laborers when needed, and even when the client design was finished ahead of schedule, the office space was ready to be emptied the following day.

All that was left was to hand over the keys.

"Where the heck is everything?" Scott Matthews' voice boomed across the vacant rooms.

I retreated from the kitchen and walked out to greet him. "Gone, obviously." There had been snark in my comment, and I chided myself silently. I had meant for this to go peacefully, and this wasn't a good start.

Putting on a smile and a cheerier tone, I tried again. "I'm closing up shop for awhile. Leaving town."

He eyed me warily. "And I'm supposed to hold this until you return?"

"No." I stepped toward him, my hand held out toward his. "I'm giving you my key. The space is yours."

I had debated about keeping it, about holding on to it for whenever I came back, but not only did I have no idea when that would be, I also needed to look like I was truly shutting down my life in New York. I'd miss the place, of course I would. But it was greenery from a season that had passed, and there wasn't any good in clutching to the dead remains. If and when I returned, it would be a new season, and there would be a new space.

Scott was still skeptical, and after everything I'd put him through, who could blame him? "What game are you playing now?" he asked, not taking the key.

I chuckled at his coincidental choice of terminology. I'd never referred to these schemes as games to any of the people I'd played. "No game. Well, not with you, anyway. I'm simply returning what I no longer need."

"Let me guess. You want something else from me. What is it? Money? Another space? Whatever it is, I'm not—"

"Scott, I don't want anything from you. Take the damn key."

He paused a moment longer before snatching the key from my hand. Once it was safely in his pocket, he visibly relaxed. "So," he said, strolling past me to stare out the windows. "You're leaving town? For good?"

I pivoted so I was addressing his back. "For good for now. Unless something changes."

"I guess I got used to you being in my life. I kind of thought I was stuck with you. Like, you'd be a permanent fixture." When he turned around, his eyes were filled with something I hadn't seen in them since the first night we'd met. He took a slow step toward me. "What do you say about visiting that kitchen again? For old times' sake."

I pressed my fingers at the inside of my nose, trying to contain the explosion threatening inside. "Jesus Christ, Scott. I've blackmailed you for seven years, and you still want to fuck me? What is wrong with you?" He deserved what I'd done to him. If I'd ever had any doubts, I didn't now.

He shrugged with one shoulder. "What can I say? You black-mailing me has always been kind of hot."

I rolled my eyes. "You're sick."

But I couldn't really judge him. The games that got me off were just as sick.

He grew serious, anger brewing in his eyes. "Okay, I'll take that as a no. If there's nothing else you need, I'd best be leaving."

His resentment toward me was earned, and it gave me an idea. "Wait. There is something else you could do for me."

"Aw, fuck. I knew it. I knew you'd never just walk away from this."

"No, no. Not like that. It's nothing that will cost you."

He raised a cautious brow and cocked his head, waiting for me to go on.

With my spine straight, I pushed my chin forward. "I want you to slap me."

He laughed. "You've got to be kidding me."

"I'm completely serious." And I was. I'd been punched once, by Hudson's wife when she was still his girlfriend. She'd broken my nose, and it had hurt like hell.

But that was the funny thing about pain—even though I could remember in my head that it had been an excruciating experience, I couldn't remember it in my body. Could I take it on command? Would it make a difference knowing it was coming?

Scott shook his head vehemently. "Nope. No way. I'm not falling for this, this...whatever this is. You're recording this, aren't you? I knew you were setting me up." He scanned the ceiling, searching for a hidden camera.

"I'm not setting you up, you asshole. I'm asking you for a favor." I was annoyed, but not so annoyed that I wanted to give up on my request. My annoyance actually cemented the idea in my head. "Here. Give me your phone." I held my hand out. "And unlock it."

He was reluctant, but he was also curious.

His curiosity won out, and a second later he was giving over his unlocked phone.

I quickly found his camera app and, after setting it to selfie mode, I hit the record button. "I, Celia Werner, am asking Scott Matthews to smack me across the face." I held my arm out to the side so the camera would capture my profile. "There. How could I possibly use this against you now? Just do it, will you? I know you want to. You've wanted to for years. I'll even record it, and you can replay it over and over, whenever you think about all the shit I put you through. How close I almost destroyed your—"

I was cut off by the sharp sting of his palm across my skin. My neck was thrown to the side with the impact, my breath caught by the surprise.

"Fuuuuucccck," I cursed, bringing my hand up to caress the burning skin. "That really hurt."

"You asked me to do it," Scott said defensively. Yet, his eyes were hooded and hungry, and I was sure if I'd asked him to do it again, he would have without hesitation.

"I did. I'm not denying that. It still hurt." With my thumb, I stopped the recording and passed his phone back to him. "You can go now."

He nodded and turned to leave, then spun back toward me. "Actually, *you* can leave now. This isn't your space anymore. Remember?"

Now he had a backbone. Hitting me had given him confidence, that shithead.

There were a thousand ways I could bring him down. They ran through my head, tempting me with the ease of which they could be executed.

But Scott Matthews was small fish. I was angling in bigger waters now.

With a smirk that hurt my inflamed skin more than I wanted to admit, I walked up to him, until I was in his face. "Be careful about getting cocky. I still have that recording from that first night. I still could show your wife. You're right that this isn't my space anymore— that was *my* choice, not yours."

I stepped back. "But I'll leave now. I'm done here."

I was done, and I was leaving with a boost of confidence as well. I'd learned what I'd hoped to learn—pain sucked, but it was endurable. Especially when there was a reward attached, and the reward was worth it.

And, where Edward Fasbender was concerned, the reward would definitely be worth it.

EIGHTEEN

"WAS THE FLIGHT GOOD? Where are you going now? Have you checked into a hotel?"

I stifled a groan and tried to respond in a reasonable tone. "Mom, stop with all the questions, will you?"

Maybe I should have been happy she was so interested, but I'd hardly slept on the red-eye from New York to London, and I needed the little energy I had to calm the nerves that were growing increasingly frayed the closer my cab got to my destination.

"Celia, really, what do you expect? You tell us you've fallen for a client and you're moving to London immediately. You haven't even told us his name! We're your parents! It's our job to ask these questions."

Funny how she always talked in the plural, as if my father cared about the details of my existence.

With a sigh, I stared out the window. It was fall already in London while the New York I'd left had been clinging desperately to summer with its record heatwave and thick humidity index. It was fitting—new colors for a new life. I was ready.

I just wasn't ready to tell my mother.

"You're right," I said, an attempt to make peace. "I haven't been very forthcoming."

"You've been downright secretive," she said, unable to let go of her exasperation just yet. "This isn't like you!"

Well, that wasn't true. It was exactly like me. I was always secretive. I was just usually better about hiding the secrets from my parents.

I shouldn't have mentioned there was a guy. I should have told them I was leaving for a client and left it at that. This was one time where sticking close to the truth had backfired. Hindsight really was twenty-twenty.

I tried again to calm her. "I know, Mom. I said you were right. And I promise I'll tell you more, just not yet, okay? This guy—he's a client, and I'm not sure where any of this is going, and—"

"Oh, God, Ceeley," she cut me off, aghast. "Are you surprising this guy?"

Yes?

She lectured on. "You can't just pick up and move to another country without the guy inviting you!"

But I *had* been invited. Technically.

"Mom." I waited for her to take a breath to try to interject again. "Mom, stop. Please. It's not what you think."

"How can you know what I'm thinking when you *haven't told me anything?*"

I laughed quietly. It really was sort of funny how worked up she was. Funny because, if she knew the whole truth, she'd have real cause to be worked up.

"What's so funny?"

"Nothing. I'm just tired. And no, I'm not showing up uninvited. I'm designing his offices, after all. And I don't want to say anything more yet because I don't want to ruin it. You can understand that, can't you?"

There was a beat of silence where I could practically hear her wrestling with her need to *know* and her desire to see me happy.

It was her turn to sigh. "You have seemed to be in an awfully good mood ever since you announced this little adventure of yours."

I had been cheerier than usual, I realized now. All the past month, as I was planning and preparing, I'd had a steady buzz of low-key exhilaration. The thrill of this game was more emotion I'd experienced in years.

It wasn't just The Game, if I was honest. The bursts of feeling had started even before. I could trace them back to that first meeting with Edward when I'd left pissed and indignant and humiliated, not to mention aroused. It was as though he'd awoken a beast that had been hibernating inside me, and now that beast's appetite drove me to take him down.

When I did, would that beast sleep again, returning me to the ice-cold safety of numbness?

I hoped so.

Though, this giddiness wasn't all that terrible of a feeling. When I didn't overthink it.

"So if you're happy, I won't worry so much," my mother said finally.

It was a chance to reassure her, tell her I was indeed happy. But despite the excitement running through my veins, I couldn't bring myself to say I was *happy*. I didn't know what that felt like anymore. Maybe I never had, and telling her that I was now was too bold of a lie, even for me.

Thankfully, an outburst from my father in the background distracted her. "That's terrible, Warren, and you can tell me all about it as soon as I hang up from talking with our daughter." Her words came out muffled, as though she had pressed the receiver of the home phone into her shoulder. "Okay, I'm back," she said a second later.

"What's Daddy upset about?" I'd rather talk about him than resume our conversation.

"Something at work," she said dismissively, then decided to say more. "He was trying to set up a subsidiary in France, but there's some Fasfender guy who keeps blocking his attempts to expand in Europe."

A tingling ran down my spine. "Do you mean Fasbender?"

"That's it. That guy. He's complained to you, then, too?"

"He has." My stomach twisted into a knot. He was not going to be happy with what I had planned.

But he'd be happy with the final outcome. I knew he would. Maybe he'd even be proud of me. I just had to hope he wouldn't disown me before then.

"This is you, miss. Coming up," the cabbie said from the front seat.

"Mom, I have to go. I'll call you later, okay?" I wished I could leave her with something more reassuring, wished I could tell her I really was happy, wished I could tell my dad I was going to fix his Fasbender problems, but I knew better than to let my hand show early in a game. So, instead, I muttered a quick *I love you* and hung up.

Then I smiled, a real genuine, honest smile, because here I was in front of the Accelecom building. It was finally beginning.

I paid the driver and stepped out of the car onto the sidewalk. The building for the media headquarters was bigger than I'd expected. Even though it had the same population size as New York City, there were far fewer skyscrapers in London, and I'd assumed Accelecom would be housed in something with less vertical expanse. To my surprise, the building before me was one of the tallest I'd seen in the England capital.

I took a deep breath. There was no way security was going to just let me waltz in, and I wondered if I should break down and call Edward now.

I didn't want to. Not yet. It was important for me to walk into this with as much of the upper hand as possible, and that meant throwing him off his guard for once.

Deciding to scope out the situation before I made any rash decisions, I pulled out my props from my purse—a notebook, pen, and measuring tape—and headed in through the main doors. Thank God, I'd stopped at the hotel to drop off my bags before arriving, even though I'd been eager to head straight over. A suitcase would have been a real hindrance.

Inside, the lobby seemed less formidable. There was a cafe, a UPS shop, and an information desk next to a large directory. The elevators were divided into banks. The first two banks were open to the general public. The last was overseen by a security guard.

I was pretty sure the directory wouldn't list Edward's office—he was too important to be that prominently on display. That was fine.

I'd already done my homework, so, not only did I know exactly where his office was located, but I also knew he would be in today. Without getting close enough to see what floors each bank of elevators went to, I was also sure I'd have to go past the guard to get to him.

But it was just the one security guard. That wasn't so bad. I'd feared there would be an entire screening like there was at the airport. My father had that kind of security at his office. It was overkill and ridiculous and completely unnecessary, but he liked the pomp and circumstance. Maybe Edward wasn't as narcissistic as my father after all.

The idea almost made me laugh out loud.

Well, I couldn't stand around gawking all day. If I was going to do this, I should just do it.

Throwing my shoulders back, I beelined toward the final elevators. I walked with purpose, not slowing down when I reached the security guard but strolling past him like I belonged.

It was surprising how many times that had worked for me over the years.

Unfortunately, this wasn't one of those times.

"Pardon, mum. Can I see your pass?"

I blinked at the guard, as though he spoke a foreign language. "A pass? I don't have a pass. I wasn't told I needed a pass."

"Everyone who wants to go to the upper floors requires a pass," he explained. "Who is it you're trying to see?"

"I wasn't told anything about a pass. Edward Fasbender personally hired me for a design job, and he's expecting me in his office right now. If you want to keep him waiting, then you can go ahead and call up and let him know I'm here." I glanced at the huge clock above the elevators and shook my head. "I'm already late. He's not going to be happy."

This was where I expected the guard would go back to his desk, call Edward's secretary, and ask if I had clearance to go up. There would be a bunch of fuss while his office tried to determine if I did indeed have an appointment. That would take time and I planned to use it. As soon as the guard walked away, in fact, I would dash into the nearest elevator. Hopefully, I'd get to his floor before the situation got sorted upstairs.

Only that didn't happen.

Instead, the guard pressed his finger against his ear piece, as if to better hear a message coming through. "You're good, mum. You can go on up."

I scanned the area looking for the cameras. They had to be there. Edward had to have seen me. Why else would I be cleared to go up so easily? I hadn't even given the guard my name.

"Mum?" The guard had called the lift for me and was holding the door open, waiting. "Wouldn't want to keep him waiting. Like you said."

With a scowl, I stepped past him into the elevator. The doors shut, and I cursed silently. *Damn him. Damn him for being so smooth and damn him for always being a step ahead.*

Except, he wasn't exactly a step ahead. So he might know I was on my way up, but I could still create a little chaos before we came face to face.

When the elevator arrived on his floor—the *top* floor—I walked out with determination, headed down the main hall toward the back where I knew his office was located. Once there, I pushed through the glass door, and ignoring his secretary, I went directly to the sitting area in front of her and began measuring the couch.

"Standard size," I muttered, as though disgusted. I nudged the piece of furniture from the wall and pretended to study the backside. "Could possibly be reupholstered."

"Excuse me, madam. You can't do that?" The secretary was on her feet, her hand braced on the phone.

She was curvy and pretty with big doe eyes and, so help me, if she was sleeping with Edward...

"Are these the original cushions?" I asked, forcing myself to maintain my character.

"I don't know," she answered, caught off guard. Immediately she frowned, annoyed that I'd gotten her flustered. "Could you please explain why you want this information?"

"No worries. I can find out." I moved on to measure the side table next to it.

"What is it you think you're doing?" This didn't come from the secretary.

No, it was a very manly, very familiar voice. A voice that sent a delicious shiver down my spine.

There he is. The secretary hadn't even managed to call him yet. He'd definitely known I was coming up. He'd been waiting.

I had to catch my breath before I turned to face him, then I had to catch it again when I saw him. He was leaning against the doorframe, looking as devastatingly handsome as always.

"There you are, Edward. Is that your office through there? I'm going to need to see that as well." It was a miracle that I hadn't stammered.

Before he could answer, I brushed past him and glided into the room beyond.

"This isn't horrible," I said honestly, surveying the dark wood walls, the oversized desk in the center of the room, the chocolate leather of his chair. "This paneling is going to have to go. It's nice, but it makes this space feel like a cave. The patterned ceiling is stunning, though. We're keeping that."

I crossed the room, circling his desk so I could open the curtains. With the light streaming in, the decor took on a whole new appearance. "That's better. This room was designed for the curtains to be open."

I could feel him close behind me, and when I turned again, he was leaning his fists on his desktop. His knuckles were white as though the furniture was the only thing keeping his hands from roughing someone up.

I'd liked that desk initially. Now I suddenly hated it.

"What. Is it. You're doing." He was so terse in his delivery, that it was no longer a question but a demand. A demand he was irritated to have to repeat.

Good. This was good. I liked seeing him this barely restrained. I liked it a whole lot more than I should.

"I'm taking notes so I can put together a design," I explained, as though it was obvious.

He let out an incredulous laugh. "I'm not hiring you to be my decorator."

"You are." I stalked toward him until I bumped up against the desk, the only barrier now between us. "My father already thinks that's how we met, and there's no way I'm telling him the truth. Besides, your office is badly in need of an update. And I'm a *designer*. Not a decorator. Don't make that mistake again."

His lips curled up into a smug smile. A ridiculously sexy smile. "This means you're accepting my offer then."

He still had the beard I'd asked for, and he was so attractive it was almost hard to look at him. It was even harder not to crawl over the bulky piece of furniture in front of me and give him my answer by pressing my mouth against his, but somehow I managed.

Instead, I held my left hand out and wiggled my bare finger. "It means, Edward, that I'm going to need a ring."

NINETEEN

THE DRIVER OPENED the door of the Maybach, and I stepped out onto the carriage driveway and gasped. I'd come from wealth, and the home I'd grown up in had encompassed two penthouse floors in a Fifth Avenue highrise, which perhaps gave me a certain impression about what expensive homes were like in big cities.

Edward's home was nothing like what I'd expected.

Instead of an apartment or a townhouse, the building I stood in front of was a well-known, long string of consecutive mansions called Cornwall Terrace. The architecture was both historical and stunning, and the location was superb, at the edge of Regent's Park, no less. I quickly counted the rows of windows stacked before me. Four floors. Holy luxury! This residence had to cost a fortune. The view across the park alone had to be worth millions.

Once again, Edward had thrown me.

He did that a lot, it seemed. If I had to guess, I would have even said he thrived on it. At the very least, he enjoyed calling the shots. After I'd shown up at his office on Wednesday, I'd hoped we'd sit down and talk about what happened next, made plans for our forthcoming marriage. But Edward had seemingly had enough of being the bystander, and he'd quickly taken the reins in his hand, commanding I go to my hotel, settle in, and recuperate from my travels. He'd escorted me out of the building telling me he'd send a car for me on Saturday. We could "dine over discussions," he'd said, a term that made me bite back a smile.

Three days had been an awful lot of time to sit around. After all the planning I'd done over the last month, the wait had felt like an unnecessary delay, and I'd been more than a little eager and excited when the driver had pulled up in front of my hotel.

Excited because I was ready to get on with The Game, not for any other reason. Certainly not because I wanted to see Edward.

I'd found ways to occupy myself, but standing now in front of his insane mansion, I'd wished I'd used some of that time to do more research on my fiancé. Exactly how rich and powerful was my husband-to-be? Did I really know who I was playing with? What level of game had I entered?

I was still standing in the driveway when the front door swung open and a liveried servant welcomed me with a nod of his head.

With a toss of my hair, I threw aside my self-doubt and walked in with my head held high. The entrance led immediately into a large reception area.

"Master Edward should be with you shortly," the butler said politely. "You may have a seat if you'd like. May I get you something to drink while you wait? Water? Wine? Tea?"

"No, thank you," I said, distracted as I surveyed my surroundings. The room was conventionally furnished, in the vein of a formal living space. There was a sitting area comprised of two black sofas, a white sofa, and two armchairs, all of which were tufted and ornate. The hardwood floors were stained dark chocolate, matching the color of the walls. Long white curtains with black valances draped each of the four windows. Two large filigree mirrors occupied the opposite walls.

It all had a traditional, masculine flavor that was all well and good for a bachelor, but would need to be softened if I were to be expected to live here. Even the very nature of the front room was old-fashioned. With no foyer or front hall, it was truly a receiving room, meant to receive guests, preventing them from needing to journey farther into the home. It was an outdated style of floor plan that I'd had little opportunity to encounter in my design work in New York City. It was fascinating and foreign all at once.

By the time I'd taken in enough to truly be aware of him, the butler had disappeared, leaving me alone. If he'd gone to inform my date that I'd arrived, Edward didn't rush to greet me. At least ten minutes went by with me sitting poised on the edge of an armchair, my nerves getting the better of me with every passing second. The tick-tick of the grandfather clock in the corner filled the quiet space, sounding louder than it actually was. The rhythmic beat magnified the passing time and heightened my anxiety.

He was doing this on purpose, I was sure of it. Making me wait. Like I'd said, he enjoyed unsettling me.

Too restless to sit any longer, I stood and ventured toward one of the mirrors to inspect my makeup for something to do. I'd worn a floral jacquard A-line dress, and though it had a severe plunging neckline, it was more romantic and casual than my usual attire. I'd left my hair down as well, remembering what he'd said earlier in the summer about appearing too uptight. It was a deliberate attempt to try to appeal to Edward, and while I'd frequently dressed for whatever role I was playing in the past, I'd had more of a struggle deciding to do it today, for some strange reason. Maybe because he'd asked specifically for me to be different, and I'd always hated letting anyone take authority over me. Or maybe it was because I wasn't entirely comfortable yet with the woman he wanted me to be.

Most likely it was because it wasn't about The Game at all. I'd dressed this way for him. Because I wanted to *please* him. And that wanting felt dangerous.

As I fluffed the curls I'd spent all afternoon applying to my shoulder-length hair, I caught movement low to the ground in my periphery.

My head shot toward the hall leading into the house. There was nobody there. I stared for long seconds, seeing nothing.

But I could *hear* something. Short, heavy breaths followed by a light giggle.

Curious, I tiptoed toward the doorway, hugging the walls of the room. I was just about to peer around the open door when a little face poked out and peeked at me. The laugh that erupted this time was still light even in its fullness. Light and adorable, making the insides of my chest feel liquid and warm.

"Well, who are you?" I crouched down to better see my new friend, a little boy wearing a dress shirt and vest paired with little boy blue jeans that were too cute for words. Having not spent much time around kids, I couldn't be sure of his age, but I guessed around two. He toddled the way I'd always imagined toddlers toddled, anyway, his steps unsteady as he came out from behind the door and into the room.

"Hi!" he said with another bewitching laugh, his face pinching up as his mouth opened wider with the sound.

And oh that face...

While his laugh was adorable, his face was ten times as precious. It was the cutest thing I'd ever seen in the flesh—brown hair, chubby cheeks, and blue eyes that were reminiscent of the shade belonging to the man I was betrothed to. There was no doubt they were related, a realization that should have set off alarms in my head, but instead had my gut twisting with inexplicable longing.

Was this what a baby Edward would look like?

Why did I suddenly want to find out more than anything I'd ever wanted in my life?

"Come away from there, Fred."

The stern voice drew my gaze down the hall to a woman I recognized from my online searches. I'd seemed to have forgotten Edward's sister lived with him, or at least hadn't expected to see her tonight. She was thin and pale and gorgeous, her dark brown hair and hazel eyes as captivating as her flawless skin. Even though she wore jeans and a simple long-sleeve black shirt, I felt plain in comparison.

She scooped up the toddler, and I stood to introduce myself. "You must be Camilla. I'm Celia."

"I know who you are," she said sourly, ignoring the hand I held out to her as she hugged the child—Fred—closer to her.

Stunned by the hostile greeting, I dropped my hand quickly and gaped.

"Good! You've had a chance to meet."

I glanced behind his sister and saw Edward coming down the stairs. He was arresting as always, but especially so with his laidback look. His hair lacked the usual slick styled appearance, and while he wore black slacks and a white button-down, he had the collar unbuttoned and the sleeves rolled up to his elbows. It was the first time I'd seen him without a jacket, and the tight fit of his shirt showcased an impressive set of pecs underneath.

Damn, Edward wore casual well. Too well for my good.

Camilla turned toward him. "Yes, we've met. Can you and I talk for a moment please?" She walked past the staircase and stopped to wait for him to join her.

He looked from me to her and then back again. "I'll be just a minute," he said to me, his gaze pointing at the receiving room behind me, a not-so-subtle hint that I should retreat there and give them their privacy.

I didn't like being ordered around, but I was on my best behavior, so I did as I was silently told.

Sort of.

I mean, I did go back into the room, but I hovered at the door, the way I had when I'd been looking for the child. Pressing my back to the wall, I listened in.

"You can't expect me to like her, Eddie. That's beyond reasonable." Camilla's voice was tight and filled with animosity.

I stiffened. I didn't need friends, and in general, I wasn't bothered by enemies, but this woman's hatred felt intense without reason.

I strained to hear Edward's response, but his words were hushed in comparison, so all I could hear was a low rumble.

Whatever he'd said, it didn't settle his sister. "Of all people, why does it have to be *her*?"

Apparently my father wasn't going to be the only one upset by the arrangement between me and Edward.

Again, I couldn't hear his response, but his tone had taken on a soothing timbre.

"Fine. But I'm not eating dinner with her."

He said something quick at that and then there was a bustle and footsteps. I jumped away from the door so as not to be caught eavesdropping, but didn't move fast enough, or moved too fast, because when Edward appeared in the room he saw me scurrying in a way that could only indicate what I'd been doing.

He narrowed his eyes and gave me that smug, knowing smile. That smile that seemed to have a direct voltage line to my lower regions since every time he gave it, my pussy buzzed and clenched.

There was no point pretending I hadn't been caught. "Eddie, huh?" I teased.

"Sisters have a way of poking, don't they?"

"I wouldn't know. I'm an only child. *Eddie.*" I prided myself on my ability to poke as well.

"Oh, no. That's not for you to use."

I took a challenging step toward him. "Isn't it?"

"No. It's not." He said it so finally, I didn't dare refute.

He moved then to the wine fridge at the other end of the room and began sifting through bottles.

I stared at his back, clutching and unclutching my hands while I tried not to be hurt that he'd dismissed my attempt to be more familiar, hurt that he hadn't actually greeted me. Hadn't said hello or even looked at me in a way that said he'd seen me.

So much for pleasing the man.

"A Malbec all right?" He was already unscrewing the cork, so I didn't think my answer was really wanted.

"Fine," I said anyway. Feeling defeated, I searched for another way to gain footing. The private conversation in the hall seemed as good a place to step as any. "She doesn't like me."

"Who? Camilla?" He didn't look at me while he dealt with the wine glasses and the pouring. "I'm sure that's not true."

He was condescending me again, and it made my blood boil. I shot daggers at his backside.

His perfectly shaped backside.

Seriously, his pants had to be sewn on the way they showed off that rock-hard ass.

Forcing myself to focus, I pushed once more. "I am definitely sure that's true, and don't say I'm wrong. We both know I'm not."

He paused his task and looked at me, truly looked at me, for the first time that night. After a beat he shrugged. "She doesn't care for Americans." He poured the second glass and held it out toward me.

He could very easily have dismissed her acrimony as a symbol of loyalty. It wasn't like I wasn't aware of the feud between her brother and my father. Why hadn't he just said that's what it was? Was there more to her hostility than that?

I considered other motives as I sauntered toward him, and remembered with an odd stab to my gut the first suspicions I'd had about his relationship with his sister.

"I think it might be a more particular lack of caring, for Americans who are dating her brother." I took the wine glass from his hand, shivering when I "accidentally" touched his finger, despite it not being an accident at all.

His brow furrowed sharply. "Are you suggesting my sister is jealous?"

"You're as rich as God and yet your sister—who is older than me, I might add—still lives with you. It could lead some people to suspect there's more to your relationship than it first seems." I was goading him was all, but the little boy's eyes flashed in my mind, eyes that looked so much like his uncle's. They were so similar, he could have passed for Edward's son.

The thought brought on another stab to my stomach. God, I was the one who was acting jealous.

Edward's expression grew hard and mean. "I'm more than a little disturbed by your implication that my sister and I have anything other than an appropriate sibling relationship. She lives with me because she was going through a difficult time and needed support. I am her only family, so, of course, I endeavor to look out for her and Freddie in any way I can, including offering them my home when they need their loved ones close. I'll ask you kindly to never again suggest anything as crass or depraved or irresponsibly cruel where Camilla is concerned."

I never liked being scolded. Who did? Particularly I hated anyone ever thinking they knew better about who I should or shouldn't be, how I should or shouldn't behave.

But there was something about this scolding that especially stung. It sunk into my pores and stayed with me, the way that menthol cream clings and burns for hours after it's applied.

I wanted to scrub it off of me. Wanted to wash myself from his brusque words and earn words that would soothe instead.

That wasn't like me, though, and I didn't know where to begin.

I sipped from my wine glass, holding the swish in my mouth until the black cherry notes showed themselves before I swallowed. *"Freddie,"* I said suddenly, noticing the child's name's similarity to Camilla's nickname for her brother. "Is he named after you?"

As soon as it was out of my mouth, it hit me that this could be taken as a further attack on his bond with his sister. "I don't mean that like it sounds. I meant..." What did I mean by it? "I heard what you said. I'm trying to understand, not belittle."

I bit the inside of my lip while I waited for him to respond, every muscle tense, my breath held tight within me.

Edward swirled the contents of his glass around once. Twice. Three times.

Finally, he answered. "After me and his father, Frank."

There'd been very little to read online about Camilla's husband, only that he'd died in a fire before her son had been born.

I didn't know anything about that kind of loss, and yet, I did. Somewhere, deep inside me, hidden in a shadow, there was a part of me that did know. A part of me that remembered the kinds of pain that drove a person to search for safety in anyone and anywhere they could find it. I'd found my solace in a questionable friendship and a game that stole every essence of emotion and humanity from my soul.

Perhaps Camilla had found her solace in much kinder forms—a protective brother and an adorable child.

"He's absolutely precious," I said, the very thought of his chubby-cheeked grin putting a smile on my own lips. "I'm sure he brings a lot of joy to your world. I apologize for insinuating anything else was going on." I was even a little bit sincere.

More than a little bit, maybe.

His hard stare showed no signs of forgiveness. To be fair, it showed nothing at all.

I fidgeted under the uncomfortable weight of his gaze. "It's just..." I fumbled with where to go, what to say. "I know very little about you. You've given me so little to go on. It's hard not to let my imagination get carried away."

"Well, try," he said brusquely. He closed his eyes and pinched his fingers along his forehead just above his eyebrows. Then, with a sigh, he dropped his hand and opened his eyes. "Tonight should help. That's what this whole evening is for after all. To get to know each other. To start, anyway."

It sounded like he was trying to convince me, but I wasn't certain he wasn't trying to convince himself.

Either way, he'd given me a hint of where to go from here, and I wasn't about to ignore the path.

I smiled brightly, some of my anxiety releasing just from the act of putting on confidence. "I'm glad to be here for that very reason. Glad to have an opportunity to get to know you better. And I'm glad Camilla isn't joining us for dinner, not because of her apparent ill feelings toward me, but so that we can have that time alone to get acquainted."

It was hard not to think of all the possible ways we could get acquainted.

For the purpose of The Game, of course.

But there was that supercilious expression again, that arrogant smirk returned to his lips. "Oh, we aren't dining alone tonight. Camilla may have bowed out, but Hagan and Genevieve will be here as well."

"What?" I couldn't manage to be subtle about my surprise.

Edward pulled his phone from his trouser pocket and jabbed at the screen with his thumb. "Yes, it seems Hagan picked up Genny about an hour and a half ago, so they should be here any minute now. Didn't I mention that before?"

He *knew* he hadn't mentioned it.

He enjoys this, I seethed to myself. *Loves seeing me rattled. Fucking gets off on it.*

If I wasn't sure before, I was positive now. The goddamned twinkle in his eye gave him away. Not only was he having fun, but he was gloating as well.

"But...but...but..." I stammered. "We don't even have our story straight! What do they know about me? What am I supposed to say about *us*?"

"You'll figure it out. I have a feeling you're quite good at coming up with stories on your feet." He winked, and the contemptuousness of it, of all of it, made him so easy to hate.

Combined with the cocky pose he'd assumed, leaving his hand casually in his pocket after returning his phone, he was also the cruelest, sexiest thing I'd ever witnessed in my life.

My composure was definitely on thin ice.

Before I could collect myself, the front door handle turned and in walked a young man and woman, each so strikingly similar in appearance to their father, it was impossible to mistake them for anyone other than his children.

"Ah, here they are. Just in time. Dinner's about to be served." He set down his wine and crossed to his daughter who kissed him on the cheek.

"We wouldn't think of being late. Believe me, we've learned that lesson." She exchanged a look with her brother, as if they were sharing an inside joke.

Then her eyes fell on me, and I waited to see how she addressed me, hoping to take my lead from there.

Unexpectedly, her expression turned confused. "Oh, hello. Who's this?"

Jesus Christ, he hadn't told his kids I was going to be here for dinner either?!

At least it wasn't just me he liked to unsettle. I should have taken comfort in that. But at the moment, all I could focus on was the growing unease stirring in my belly.

Edward swept in next to me, putting an arm around my waist and wrapping his other hand in mine. I tried to ignore the bolt of electricity that surged through me at his touch, and focused on his mouth as he announced, "Hagan, Genny, Celia Werner and I met this summer. She's the reason I invited you over tonight. I thought you both should meet the woman who's agreed to be my wife."

"Your...*wife?*" Hagan's eyes were as wide as his sister's.

My own shock was startling, and I'd at least had a sense of what was coming. Talk about awkward.

It was definitely going to be a long night.

At this rate, I had a feeling it was going to be a really long marriage.

TWENTY

THERE WAS an uproar of questions from his kids that Edward easily put to silence. "We'll discuss everything over dinner," he said firmly. "It's seven now. I'm sure Gavin is waiting for us to be seated."

With his palm pressed at the small of my back, Edward led us down the hallway toward the formal dining room pointing out the floor plan as we walked. "The staircase, of course. There's the lift. Both go to the lower ground floor as well as all the way to the top. Behind the stairs is the water closet. To the left is the kitchen—the one we use on a daily basis. The catering kitchen is downstairs. Farther down the hall is the salon. And here we are."

He dropped his hand, but I could still feel it there, as though he'd branded it into my skin. It made me dizzy, even when he was no longer touching me. That was how powerful his affect was on me. It lingered. It permeated the membranes of my cells. Got into my bloodstream. Altered my DNA.

I surveyed the room we'd entered. The traditional design had been continued in here in the two crystal chandeliers that hung from the patterned tray ceiling and the elegant dark wood table with intricate apron details and lion claw feet. There was room for twelve fabric padded chairs with cabriole legs, five on each side and one at each head, but only four place settings had been laid out.

Edward moved to the setting at the far head. "You'll sit here to my left, darling. Genny, you can sit by your brother this evening."

My knees buckled at the term of endearment, even though I knew it was likely for show. I was grateful it was only a few steps to my seat. The butler who'd greeted me when I arrived pulled out my chair for me to sit. I assumed he was Gavin, but later was informed his name was Jeremy. Gavin was the personal chef. I'd planned for an intimate dinner, but the level of staff on hand made me feel a little underdressed.

Edward, though, had worn casual, I reminded myself. He apparently liked a formal routine with or without the formal attire.

The next several minutes were spent settling in. Jeremy filled our wine glasses then set out our first course, a blueberry poached pear salad with candied walnuts. He'd barely had time to walk away after setting down the last plate before the inquisition resumed.

"If you're getting married, where's the ring?" Genevieve's sour expression, along with her tone, said she wasn't ready to accept the news of our engagement.

Without being told so, I had a feeling I was expected to help change her mind.

Here goes nothing.

I put on a friendly smile, one I'd carefully practiced for just such occasions. "We haven't picked one out yet."

"I have it," Edward said in contradiction. "I wanted Celia to be sure about us before she put it on." He gazed in my direction as he took my hand in his, the one with the missing ring, and squeezed.

Oh, he was smooth. Real smooth.

And a good liar. I was sure he didn't really have a ring since this was the first I was hearing about it.

Genny wasn't so easily wooed. "And you're sure now? Because we haven't even heard of you before tonight. You can't blame us for thinking this is rather sudden."

Though she included her brother in the use of her plural pronouns,

Hagan's congenial expression suggested he wasn't as suspicious as she was.

Ugh. I hadn't been prepared to deal with the frank grilling of protective offspring.

"I understand," I said, trying to imagine the scenario from her viewpoint. "I can't speak to your father's reasons for not sharing our romantic involvement with you both, but I can assume he didn't want to say anything until I had given him a definite answer. And I have now. And yes, I am sure."

She didn't seem convinced, but before I had to endure another hostile round of interrogation from her, Hagan intervened. "Lay off her, Gen. We haven't even heard yet how they met. It was in New York, yeah?"

I glanced at Edward to see if he might take this one. Frankly, I would have loved to hear what he would have said.

He turned in his seat, fixing his gaze on me. "Why don't you tell them that story, darling?"

He was a cruel man, casually using that *darling* in that British dialect of his like it wasn't a weapon of mass destruction.

The sweep of his thumb along my knuckle wasn't helping my train of thought. "Okay. Sure." I sounded flustered. This wasn't going to cut it.

I could do better. I had this.

Gently, I pulled my hand out from his, which cleared my head immensely. *As close to the truth as possible.* "I've known about your father for years, obviously. His reputation proceeds him, but also I'd heard about him because my own father is in the media business."

Genny perked at this. "What did you say your last name was again?"

"Werner." I waited for her to comment again. When she didn't, I went on. "So, anyway. I'm not personally in the media business. I run an interior design company, and your father asked me to meet with him to discuss redesigning his office."

"Your office here?" Hagan directed this question to his father.

"Mm." Edward nodded, his eyes never leaving me.

"Thank God," Genny said. "That office is in bad need of a redo. It's abrasive and overly masculine and not at all welcoming to the female gender."

Under different circumstances, I had a feeling Genevieve and I might have gotten along splendidly.

Hagan shrugged. "It's not that bad. I sort of like it."

"You would," Genny muttered. She brought her focus to me, her eyes softer than they'd been before. "Was Dad as terrible to work with as I imagine he is?"

"He is," I said smugly. Honestly. "Within five minutes, I'd decided he was an incredible self-centered ass." I peered back at my husband-to-be and was surprised to see I'd amused him.

I liked that. Liked amusing him.

Liked it too much.

"Now, now, confession here." Finally Edward was stepping in. "I didn't really care about her silly office design ideas."

"Dad!" Genny gasped.

He put up a hand to shush her. "I don't really need my office redesigned. It was an excuse. I'd seen Celia at a charity ball, from a distance, and there was no way I could go without seeing her again. Hiring her was an opportunity to spend more time with her."

The ball was a nice touch, and then I remembered I really had attended a charity ball in the weeks before meeting him. "The Building Futures event?"

He nodded slightly, as if not quite sure he wanted to give himself away.

"Oh. I didn't know." I hadn't seen *him* there.

"Her hair was in this soft twist and she was wearing a slinky red gown with a slit up one side and these sheer panels up here and here." He gestured to his neck and then the sides of his torso. "She was absolutely breathtaking."

He was absolutely breathtaking. As in I couldn't currently breathe. He'd definitely seen me. How had I not noticed him?

"So, as I said," he continued, his hand finding mine again. "I made up an excuse to hire her, and after I convinced her that I wasn't the complete ass she thought I was—"

I interjected. "Oh, no, I still think you're a complete ass."

"—after I convinced her that I had some good qualities despite being an ass," he corrected, "she agreed to go out with me. We were inseparable after that."

"Then why didn't you tell us about her?" Genny demanded, and now that the question was specifically directed toward her father, I didn't have to be the one to answer.

"Like Celia said, I wanted to wait until she'd made up her mind about me." His face turned serious. "It was terribly difficult to part with her when my business was over and it was time to come home, but I didn't want to push her. I'd asked her to marry me, because I already knew I wanted to spend the rest of my life with her, but I was asking a lot, expecting her to give up everything she had in New York to come live with me in my house. To fit in with my family. I knew she needed time to think about it, and I also knew if I told you both, I'd only get my hopes up."

He brought my hand to his mouth and kissed the inside of my wrist. "I'm so very glad that you changed your mind."

Warmth rushed up my torso, expanding through my chest and into my ribs. It was all a story, yes. I knew that's what it was. That it was all a fabricated lie. That he hadn't really meant any of the wonderful things he'd said about me. About us.

But there was a camaraderie about the whole thing. A sense of having someone on the same side that I hadn't had since I used to play with Hudson. We'd done this together too—made up stories. Pretended our lives were tangled in ways that they weren't, and that had been fun and exciting and amusing.

This charade with Edward felt like that. Like we were working together for a common end, and we were, actually. For once the goal wasn't to destroy someone else in the process, and I was surprised to find that missing element didn't diminish the experience.

Except, I *was* setting out to destroy someone in the process. I was planning to destroy Edward. I couldn't let myself forget that.

Whether or not Genny was satisfied with our ruse, Hagan was, and he turned conversation to his intern position he was doing at Accelecom in his spare time and then to a project he was involved with at school. Before the end of the meal, I'd learned he was graduating from university in the spring and planned to go work with his dad full-time after that and that I was closer to his age than Edward's, but just barely.

Genevieve was also at university and seemed also to be following in her father's footsteps, much to his chagrin. He insisted it was a terrible pathway for a girl, and wouldn't she be happier getting married and being a socialite?

I barely refrained from kicking him under the table for his sexist attitude. I had a feeling it came from a place of love. My father had encouraged me in the same way when I'd been younger, because he wanted me taken care of, not because he didn't think I was capable. And as much as he ignored me or overlooked me, he had always supported my decision to open a business on my own. Hopefully Edward would come to that place with Genny as well, eventually.

When the meal was over, Edward invited both his children to join us in the salon for an after-dinner drink.

"I can't, Dad," Genny said. "I really have to get back to studies. I have a full load this term, and there's lots of reading." She turned to her brother. "If you can't take me home, I can call for a ride."

"I'll send you in my car," Edward said, looking aghast at the mention of his daughter in an Uber.

Hagan shook his head. "You'll do neither. I can take you. I can't stay either. I'm meeting someone in a bit."

Edward checked his watch. "At this time of night?"

"It's still early, Dad." The way he looked away when he said it told me exactly what kind of meeting he was escaping for.

"Very well. Before you leave, though. I need you to sign that proposal. It's up on my desk. I'll show you."

Edward and Hagan disappeared up the stairs, leaving Genny and me alone. We walked together to the receiving room to wait in thick silence. I had no idea if I'd won her over or not, but if the tension between us was any indication, I was betting the answer was no.

As soon as we'd made it to the front room, my impression was validated. "I know who you are," she said accusingly. "I know why he's really marrying you."

My stomach dropped, but I kept my head high. Edward had never said his children had to be kept in the dark. Maybe it was even better if they knew.

Or maybe that just complicated matters.

I wasn't ready to make a decision about it, so I decided to put the ball back in her court. "And what reason is that?"

"Because you're a Werner. Everyone knows how badly my father wants in with your father's company. I'd never thought he would go to these sorts of means, though."

"You sound as if that bothers you."

She sighed, running a hand through her long brown hair. "I suppose it shouldn't. It's what he wants, it's what you want. You're both adults. I'm assuming it's mutually beneficial."

"But...?"

She met my eyes. "But he was completely heartbroken when my mother left him. In some ways, it destroyed him. He's not the man he was before their divorce, and I guess I thought..." She lowered her gaze to the floor. "I'd hoped that he'd find that again. I'd hoped he could be happy like that with someone new."

Her tone was sad, and sad tones had never had much effect on me.

And yet, I wanted to give her a different story. Because I liked her, maybe. Because I could relate to her, being the daughter of a successful man like she was. Men who didn't give their daughters enough credit or time or attention.

Or because I wanted another story to be true, one different than the one we were living.

Or maybe it was because I simply wanted to see if I could convince her of something else. For the challenge of it.

I couldn't explain my reasons, but the urge was strong to correct her, so I did. "You're right," I said. "You're right that this started purely as a business decision. Edward wanted access to my father's company and I wanted his money and that was all. But that's not the case anymore. It evolved. I've never met someone like Edward. He challenges me. He gives me something that I didn't think I would ever have. He makes me feel things I thought were impossible to feel. He makes me look at the future as a possibility instead of more of the same old thing."

I stopped, stunned by how effortlessly the story had fallen from my lips. As though it were more honest than I'd realized. Honest stories always came the easiest.

"Anyway," I said, remembering that I had an audience. "My decision to marry your father is based on that, not on any mutually beneficial deal. Of course I can't speak for him, but I think..." What did I think? "Just don't give up on him finding happiness because of how we found each other. Your father and I are full of surprises."

She studied me for long seconds before gifting me the first genuine smile I'd seen from her all night. "Thank you for that. I don't know what to think right now, and I don't know how I feel about you, but I'm rooting for him. I hope he surprises me."

I sort of hoped he did too.

No, I didn't. I didn't want to be surprised. I wanted to know exactly where this was going. I wanted it to follow my predictions. I wanted to play Edward the way I'd played so many others and then get out and walk away, untouched as always.

But after Edward and his son had returned, and after we'd said goodbye to the kids and sent them on their way, when we were alone again, just the two of us, the tension I felt strung out between us wasn't the kind of tension that came from the thrill of The Game. It was darker and more taut, yet not too taut. Like it could keep pulling or it could break entirely and the not knowing which would happen made my skin feel prickly and hot and made me feel like I wanted to cry.

With his back against the front door, Edward looked me over, his gaze sweeping up my body with slow intensity, as though he were seeing me for the first time that evening.

Goosebumps broke out along my arms and the space between my legs began to throb.

"Nice work in there tonight," he said, his voice low. "With them. It was impressive."

"Thank you." I could feel the blush run up my chest and cheeks. It was the first time I ever remembered him complimenting me, and I hated that I cared, but I did. I cared. I wanted him to compliment me again and again.

His eyes grew dark and hooded and the tension pulled tighter between us. "There's a lot going on here, I can tell," he said, and I practically sobbed from relief that he was addressing it. "So let's go upstairs and sort it out, shall we?

I didn't hesitate for one second before giving him the only answer I could. "Yes, please."

TWENTY-ONE

"IT SEEMS strange to be discussing our prenup when I'm still not wearing a ring." If I sounded bitter, it was because I was. When Edward had suggested we go upstairs, I'd naively thought he meant his bedroom. I'd certainly been on that page. The energy around us was so fraught and charged, I'd assumed he was there with me.

Instead, "upstairs" had meant up one flight to his den and "sorting it out" seemed to be completely administrative.

The paperwork was necessary for the marriage, I supposed. It was also boring. I didn't want his money. I wanted to ruin him.

I wanted him to ruin me, too. In a completely different way.

I glanced at the document in front of me, then at the still bare ring finger of my left hand.

"You're awfully anxious about that, aren't you?" Edward asked from the other side of the oversized mahogany desk. The formal setup made the whole thing even more tedious.

"What can I say, I like jewelry." A subject I found much more intriguing. I'd even taken the liberty of doing some of my own preliminary engagement ring browsing while I'd been sequestered in my hotel. "I can give you some ideas of what I like and what looks—"

He cut me off brusquely. "I don't need them."

"Oh. Okay." Back to tedium then.

Pretending to care about the prenuptial agreement, I picked it up and skimmed it halfheartedly. I could feel his eyes on me, which made the idea of actually reading even more preposterous. His gaze was too distracting. *He* was too distracting.

"Do you have any questions?" he asked after I'd flipped through several pages.

I couldn't remember a word of what I'd just read. Frankly, I was still thinking about the upstairs I'd believed he'd eluded to. If this level was devoted to his den and home office, where was his bedroom? The next floor? The top?

Then I did have a question for him. A valid one, I thought, considering it mostly concerned my agenda, not his. "You'll want me to live here with you, I assume. How exactly will that work as far as sleeping arrangements? Your children seem to believe we're going to have a real marriage. I'm not sure what your sister thinks or what you want her to think, but I'm imagining you'll want the ruse to be kept with everyone else. It will be hard to keep up that pretense if we're in separate bedrooms."

His lids appeared to grow momentarily heavy, a gesture I'd begun to realize was his version of an eyeroll. "I meant questions about the prenup," he said curtly. "But, since you've asked, I don't see that pretense will be a problem. The master suite is on the next level. Along with the bedroom and two dressing rooms, there's also a flex space for a nursery or a morning room or what have you. It's a decent size and will adequately fit a king bed. We won't even have to share a bathroom.

"Since that floor is completely devoted to the master suite, there's been no reason for anyone to go up there except for me. The guest rooms, including Camilla and Fred's room, are all on the fourth floor, and everyone tends to access that using the lift. No one will have any cause to know what happens—or doesn't happen—in our rooms."

It was almost refreshing to have grown up as wealthy as I had and still be surprised by the extravagant lives of other billionaires. An *entire floor* dedicated to the master suite? *Two* dressing rooms?

That was...wow.

But more than being impressed, I was disappointed. I'd hoped beyond hope that we'd have to share a room.

I wasn't ready to give up on that aspiration. "The house staff will know there's two beds being slept in when they make them up every day. You might think you have a loyal staff, but we both know no one can ever be truly trusted."

"Indeed." His smile, though tight, was agreeable, and for the briefest second I thought I might be on the verge of victory.

He stood up and crossed to the minibar. "However, there's no reason to need them to keep silent in this matter. Plenty of couples sleep in separate beds. It doesn't mean anything about their relationship or, for that matter, their sex life."

Somehow I'd momentarily forgotten how old-fashioned he was. Like, nineteen-fifties old-fashioned.

As if to bolster this stereotype, he began pouring cognac into two tulip glasses without asking if I wanted any. "Marion had her own bedroom when we were together as well, and that was a 'real marriage,' by your definition."

"You slept apart? No wonder that ended," I muttered.

"Pardon?"

Not wanting to discuss his "real" marriage, I looked back at the prenup still in my hand. This time I managed to focus enough that a section caught my eye.

When he came back to the desk and stood over me, holding a glass out for me to take, I ignored the offer and raised a curious brow. "There's a clause here for children."

A clause stating how much I'd get if we had kids when we got divorced. Ten million for each one, which seemed awfully generous.

And suspicious.

We weren't even supposed to be having sex. Was that a ploy? Was he setting me up to have a child with him after all? Was he expecting me to do in vitro, because no way. An heir to the Werner fortune, though—that made more sense than the ridiculous reason Edward had put forth before.

The notion of adding a baby to the bargain should have made me angry, but instead, a warm bubble of hope began making its way up my chest.

Because it would make this game easier, was why. No other reason. Certainly not because I wanted kids with him. Or anyone, for that matter.

But if I could use that excuse to get him into bed...

He still stood next to me, one cognac held in my direction. "My lawyer said it was irresponsible not to include it. You and I will be the only two who know it's there merely for appearances."

And just like that, the bubble popped.

I practically growled in frustration.

"Take the drink, Celia."

I started to shake my head, but his stern frown made me change my mind.

Relenting, I took the glass and brought it up to my mouth for a sip. I wasn't generally a fan of brandy, but I hadn't tasted any with quite as complex of flavor as this. There were so many different notes, I couldn't discern them all. Jasmine. Vanilla. Cigar box. Something earthy. I liked it.

I took another sip. "Are you hoping to liquor me up?"

"Why would I want to do that?" He sounded innocent, but he was far from. Every move he made was purposeful. Every action had a goal.

Maybe this time his goal was to get me in his bed.

A girl could hope. But I'd learned hope works best with action.

"I don't know," I said seductively. "So I'll agree to something not in my best interest."

He chuckled, and admittedly, I liked the sound. I liked that I amused him.

"It's a digestive, Celia. Don't make more of it than it is." He circled to the other side of his desk, but didn't sit. Studying me, he took a swig of his drink, his Adam's apple bobbing as the liquid ran down his throat. "How does the agreement look?"

I blinked, tearing my gaze from his far-too-sexy swallowing action and forced it back to the papers. After a second, I put down my glass so I could fold the document in half. "It looks good to me at first glance. I'd like to have a lawyer look it over as well before I sign, if you don't mind."

"Of course. I'll email you a copy." He took another swallow, his expression saying he knew I would have signed it right then and there if he'd asked.

Tell me to sign it, then. Tell me so we can move on to what's next. I was pretty sure my own expression gave away my thoughts as well.

"I didn't expect your signature tonight," he said, reading me. "We'll do it in front of a notary. Make it legal and all that. I merely thought you should have the opportunity to go over it beforehand."

"How kind." I almost managed a smile.

"Besides, you might not want to sign it once you hear the other terms of our arrangement."

"You really do know how to set a girl up for thinking the worst, Edward. I'm not sure if it's a skill of yours or a flaw."

"Can't it be both?"

I squinted my eyes at him coldly, irritated that once again it seemed he was playing with me.

This was ridiculous. I had to be better about my moves. I could play him just as easily. It was second nature.

Edward was about to learn from the woman who'd practically invented the game.

TWENTY-TWO

RETRIEVING MY DRINK, I stood up and scanned the room. Officially, he'd told me, his office was down the hall, an equally large space with his computer and his file cabinets where he did most of his work when at home.

This room was more relaxed, more like a library. For schmoozing, I assumed. Everything was for show. Shelves lined the room containing books that appeared to have never been read. Collector's editions of classics. The Renaissance paintings on the wall looked familiar, and I guaranteed they were originals. The carpet was plush with a complicated design. The furniture both inviting and expensive.

Knowing he was watching my every move, I sauntered over to the sofa near the fire, which had been roaring before we'd entered the room. I set my glass down on the end table, and I bent down to unbuckle the strap on one of my heels. "Go ahead then. Fill me in on these elusive terms. But don't expect me not to be comfortable for it."

I kicked off that shoe and began working on the next, never taking my eyes off him.

His lips twitched as if fighting a smile, and when he began to cross the room, coming straight toward me, I wondered if it was really that easy.

But he walked past me, stopping in front of the end table. Picking up my drink, he opened a drawer, pulled out a coaster, and set my glass on top.

God, he was more anal than my grandmother had been, and I was pretty sure that woman loved her furnishings more than me.

After kicking off my other shoe, I pulled my feet up under me and exaggeratedly lifted my drink from the coaster as if to say, *I'd only set it down for a minute.*

Edward ignored my pointed gesture and sat in an armchair cater-cornered from me. "I am what some might call a traditionalist," he said, as soon as he was settled. "I'm the man of the house, and as such, I believe my wife's duty is to be by my side, first and foremost. It's her duty to submit to my authority at all times. Her primary focus is on my needs, and in return, I will look after her needs. Certainly you are welcome to entertain yourself with hobbies and trivial pursuits, but I will not allow a wife of mine to have a career of her own."

"Wow." I blinked a few times. I was having trouble digesting all he'd said. No wonder he'd thought I needed the cognac. "That's so patriarchal. I hate to tell you this, but that way of thinking is considered out of vogue these days."

"I've never cared about popular opinion. Nevertheless, I'm aware that it would be an adjustment for you."

"An 'adjustment'?" It was an understatement if I'd ever heard one. "You're asking me to give up my business." I wasn't about to tell him I'd already shut it down. Right now it was a bargaining chip.

"I'm asking you to give up your business for a better opportunity. I assure you the position of my wife comes with more prestige and higher pay."

I had to fight not to gape. "No one can ever say you don't have a big ego."

"I have a realistic sense of self."

He was such a narcissist, it was unreal.

"And the rest of what you said—you expect me to submit to your authority. What exactly does that mean? Because I know you're not talking about the bedroom." But I was sure he'd expect that in the bedroom too, if I ever got him to agree to taking me there.

"It means I'm the one in charge," he said, as though it were obvious. "I expect that you will want to argue with me about a myriad of subjects, and that's your prerogative, as long as you understand never to disagree or disobey me in public and that I will always have the final say. And while you are free to speak your mind in the privacy of our home, I can't assure you that there won't be consequences."

I choked back a laugh. Was he serious? "Consequences? I'm dying to know how you plan to inflict consequences on a grown woman."

"As I will be the sole source of your income, I'm sure you'll see there are plenty of opportunities for punishment."

Everything he said was more flabbergasting than the last, almost as if he were trying to push my limits, but I refused to let him see me react. It helped that I didn't know how to feel about so much of it. It was disgusting what he expected of his wife. It was alarming.

It was also useful. Exposing his values alone would be enough to get him attacked by the Twitter Social Justice Warriors.

And beyond that...it was fascinating. I was utterly rapt with the idea. Surrendering total control to another human being—by choice, not manipulation—what would that be like? What *could* that be like?

It couldn't be at all.

There were flaws with his consequences, for one. "You're forgetting that I come to this marriage with my own money."

He crossed one leg over the other, propped his elbow on the arm of the chair and worried his chin with a single finger. "Ah, yes. But as your husband I will insist on overseeing your spending, whatever the source."

No one had a say in what I did, what I spent. My parents had barely supervised my spending when I was a child. And he wanted me to let him tell me what I could and could not buy?

I took a long swallow of my drink.

He seemed to understand I was near a limit. "You'll find that I'm more than generous beyond these boundaries," he explained, trying to cushion the blow. "I will provide you a monthly allowance of one hundred thousand pounds, which will above and beyond pay for the kind of lifestyle you are accustomed to living. Any expenses over that will require my approval."

So he wasn't a monster. Not entirely.

But mostly.

I tried to fight the inclination to challenge him. Had to remember the goal. If it weren't for The Game, I would have left the room when the conversation started. I wouldn't even be in the room to begin with. There was a point to this, and I had to keep that in mind. Going along with his stupid rules and "expectations" now would make ruining him all the more victorious.

Except, he was maddening. And even with the silent pep talk, I couldn't resist pushing back. "Can you remind me again what it is that *I* get out of this marriage?"

"You get to be my wife," he said, as though there could be nothing clearer in the world.

I clenched my fist at my side, my fingernails digging into my palm.

After a breath, I said, with as much courtesy as I could muster, "As you've explained it, being your wife doesn't sound like much of a reward."

"I believe there are a lot of women who would beg to differ."

"But you're not asking a lot of women. You're asking *this* woman, and this woman wants to know what she gets out of it." There was no doubt I sounded snarly, but what the fuck did he expect?

"Fair enough." While I'd thought my bitterness might earn me a reproval, Edward seemed instead to be impressed. "As my wife, you'll have money, power, and a reputation that you can't earn on your own with your current credentials. You'll have respect from important people who, at the moment, don't even know you exist. Most importantly, you'll finally be able to move out of the shadow of your past, as I believe you want so very much to do."

A chill ran down the back of my neck. There was no way he knew about my past, about the things I'd done to people. The games I'd played.

He was bluffing. He had to be.

I played dumb. "The shadow of my past...? I don't have a shadow on my past."

"I apologize," he said, his gaze digging into me. "The shadow of your father, I should have said." My chest loosened as the breath I'd been holding released. "Wouldn't you like to be known as more than just Celia Werner, daughter of Warren?"

"And you're offering me Celia Fasbender, wife of Edward. Forgive me if I don't see the difference."

"You became a daughter by the luck of the draw. You become a wife by being chosen. My decision to marry you signals to the world that I believe you are worthy of the title. Believe me when I say my approval carries a lot of weight."

It was the first time since he'd proposed his ridiculous plan that I considered that he actually did have something to offer me. I'd grown up believing an important man would want to marry me. Specifically, I'd believed that man would be Hudson Pierce, and when that option was taken away from me, I'd lost a sense of my identity. Even now I wondered what Hudson would think of me marrying Edward, if he'd regret letting me get away. If he'd finally see me as worthy.

Stupid, right? Weren't we past the age when women's lives were valued in relation to a man's?

I knew that, and yet I also didn't. It wasn't something I'd ever been able to explain to anyone, mostly because I couldn't begin to explain it to myself.

Now here, this asshole got it.

It annoyed me. It annoyed me that there was a part of me that still felt that way. It annoyed me that he knew that. It annoyed me most that, even if I acknowledged he was right, I would still never feel validated by this marriage because, even if no one else knew, *I* knew that none of it was real.

"That's so arrogant," I said, turning my irritation toward him. "And patriarchal. And intangible. Especially when you aren't truly offering me the position of wife."

"What do you mean?" He dropped his hand from his chin, and

leaned ever so slightly forward, as though he really cared about my answer.

"I mean…" I had to pause to think about what I meant. Think about how to explain it. The last thing I wanted was for him to think I wanted something like love from him or that I was infatuated with him, which I most certainly was not. "What if I want a baby? I know you said you didn't want any more, but what if I do?"

He cleared his throat, seemingly surprised. "Might I remind you that I said we won't be having sex."

Right, right, that was another thing I planned to address before the night was over. "But I'm certain that you're going to be having sex elsewhere. And if you are, then I should be allowed the same."

He was going to say I wasn't allowed, and that would be a perfect opportunity to demand it from him. He certainly couldn't expect me to live as a celibate.

Except he didn't say that. "Whatever you do, you will be perceived as a faithful wife by everyone around us."

"That's not a no."

"It's not." But his jaw twitched, and I felt somewhat mollified that the idea of me sleeping with someone else might bother him.

Only, now I couldn't use that as a reason to goad him into sex with me.

I went back to my last line of interrogation. "Then, let's say I had a discreet affair and got pregnant?"

"You won't," he said with finality. "Not if you expect to stay living under my roof."

"So you'd make me get an abortion?"

"I'd make you get a *divorce*. And you can be sure that ten million mentioned in the prenup requires a paternity test."

I blinked, astounded by his inflexibility. "You really hate children."

"I won't raise another man's child."

And now I had another angle. "What if *your* mistress got pregnant?"

"They wouldn't."

I tried not to flinch at his reference to plural women. "Of course they wouldn't, because what you say goes, even with biology. Maybe you haven't yet heard that the only reliable method of birth control is abstinence."

"It's not quite the same comparison, though, is it? I could sire a child and no one would ever be the wiser. You, however, couldn't hide a pregnancy. In other words, what happens in this area with me and my mistresses, is really not any of your concern."

This, out of every unreasonable thing he'd said so far, this was the one that not only pinched at my ideals of equality, but also stung.

I didn't have any idea why I cared. I didn't like children. I didn't like him. It shouldn't have mattered what he did. Why was I pushing this when none of it mattered in the grand scheme?

We stared at each other, as though we were at a stalemate.

After several beats of silence, he sat back in his chair. "If you're set on having a child, I think you should consider backing out of this right now."

"I'm not," I answered too quickly. "I'm still young, though. That could change." It wouldn't, but that was beside the point.

And, though he'd closed the door on that protest, I wasn't ready to stop pushing back. "What if I don't think the monthly salary is suitable?"

"It *is* suitable."

"I might not agree."

A knowing smirk played on his lips. "You're just trying to test me. See if I'll budge on anything, and I won't."

We'd see about that. "What if I want to take a trip without you? Go and visit my friends back home."

"Then you'd approach me with the idea, and we'd discuss it."

I spelled out his subtext for him. "And you'd get the final say."

"Yes."

We were going in circles. I changed course. "I want two vacations a year without you. I walk out of this room if we can't agree on that."

"Sure." He'd given in too easily. It couldn't be that simple.

It wasn't. "I encourage you to take vacations, in fact," he went on. "Time for yourself is always a good idea. You decide when and where, and if it doesn't conflict with my schedule or my notions of where a wife should travel or who she should visit, you can take your little trips."

"Maybe I should rephrase—I want two vacations a year *guaranteed*."

"And you'll get two vacations. On my terms."

God, he was impossible. I could just imagine him in a boardroom. No wonder my father hated him. "You were right to assume these conditions would be a hard sell."

"And I'm not even finished." There was that grin again. The one that made my knees knock and my panties damp.

I threw back the rest of my drink and held it out toward him. "You might want to refill my glass before you go on."

He made no move to get up. "I think you've had enough already. I appreciate wanting to soften the punch, but I'd prefer you had a clear mind for this discussion."

It rankled me that he thought my alcoholic intake was his business.

And, also, it didn't. Also it felt natural. It felt nice, even. To have someone care enough about me as a person that he'd think my behavior even mattered.

I set the empty glass on the coaster he'd provided, and stared at the fire as I considered. "Is that an example of what it would be like? Bossing me around about when and how much I drink or what I wear or how I do my hair."

"Mm." The sound rumbled in his throat, and I willed myself not to shiver.

I turned my gaze toward him, finding his eyes already on me, as they so often were. *This is how he'll always be. This is how he'll always watch me.*

This time I did shiver. "I'd have to stop calling myself a feminist."

"That's not what's making you hesitate."

I laughed out loud, glad for an excuse to break the increasing tension. "Oh, really? Then what is?"

"You're ashamed of how much you like it."

The blood drained from my face. I could feel it dropping through my body as fast as my stomach. He had no right. It was one thing to order me around, but he had no right to guess what I was feeling. No right, even if he wasn't wrong.

"Don't fuss because I've called you out. There's no need for that. There's a benefit in both of us being on the same page." As disapproving as his tone was, his scowl was playful, reinforcing my suspicion that he relished my discomfort.

I had nothing to say in response. I didn't want to give him an opportunity to see anything else about me.

He let the silence stretch out for a beat, then asked, "Shall I go on with my expectations now?"

"Sure," I said stiffly.

"We won't have a big wedding. A small ceremony in the salon should be sufficient. There's no need to wait. Sometime before the end of the year will do. We can arrange a date with my secretary. We'll want to be sure my schedule is clear so we can work in a honeymoon."

A small ceremony was fine. This wasn't a real wedding, after all, and I had never been fond of pomp and circumstance. But as sure as I was that he was simply goading me with all his demands, his last sentence was so infuriating, I couldn't let it pass by without remark. "And why exactly would we go on a honeymoon?"

"Again, appearances."

Of course. *Appearances.*

"We'll go to my island in the Caribbean. It's beautiful there. You'll like it."

"I like sunny places." An isolated island in the Caribbean could be a good opportunity for seduction. "Anything else?" I didn't bother to hide my impatience, more than ready for this whole list of stipulations to be done with.

But Edward had more. "Your father..."

Ugh. My father. He didn't have to finish his sentence. "Yes, he is the reason for this marriage after all. I can't promise you anything from my father. He's his own person, and I have very little pull where he's concerned."

It was petty how much I enjoyed not being able to give him reassurances, even though, by lack of doing so, I was potentially ruining the entire arrangement.

Or maybe he'd change his mind and see he needed an heir for this to work out after all.

"I don't expect you to make any commitments on his behalf." He dropped his hand from his chin, punctuating what he intended to say next. "I do, however, expect you to make every effort to endear him to me. Show him that you believe in me and my motivations. Help him build confidence in me so that, when the time comes, he'll see me as the natural person to take over as the head of Werner Media."

I still contended that Edward had serious misconceptions about my influence.

But if all he wanted was for me to play nice, to play like he was a good guy in front of my father, I could do that. It would be hard to deceive him in such a way, not hard like I couldn't do it, but hard because I was eager for the day that I could tell him what all of this had really been about. I couldn't wait to see Dad's face when he realized I'd destroyed his enemy.

That *was* what I couldn't wait for, wasn't it?

"Fine. Sure," I said, not wanting to think about it too hard anymore. "I'll do what I can."

"Excellent." Edward finished off his drink and stood to take both his and my glass back to the bar. I'd thought he had wanted to tidy up and was going to leave them there, but the asshole refilled his glass, leaving mine empty.

Yes, destroying him *was* what I wanted. Maybe I'd even be able to let my parents in on what I was about from the beginning.

"What have you told your parents about us?"

Except I'd forgotten for a second that Edward planned to dictate every aspect of my life. Best to keep them in the dark after all.

"Not a lot," I answered honestly. "I told them I was coming to London for a client whom I was also interested in romantically. I didn't tell them your name. I wanted to build you up anonymously before my father realized who you are."

Edward, having returned with his drink, perched on the arm of his chair. "Good. That's very good."

There was genuine admiration in his eyes, and like a fool, that was all it took to revive the flutters in my belly.

I was keen for more praise. "After this is all decided, I'll tell them I'm engaged so they'll get used to the idea that I'm really with this mysterious guy. But I'll dodge questions about who you are until after we're married."

The other option was to not even tell my parents I was engaged until after it was a done deal, but I'd decided that wouldn't be the best way to win their support for this man I supposedly loved. I'd thought this all through already, and this was the much better plan.

I held my chin up waiting for Edward to agree.

He didn't.

"No," he said with a frown. "That won't work. I want them here for the ceremony. I need Warren Werner to watch as you vow to be mine."

Mine. That word sent a shot of heat through my bloodstream.

It's not real, I reminded myself. I wasn't really going to be his, and why would anyone really want that anyway after hearing all his expectations?

My annoyance was more with myself than with him, but his proposal was pretty dumb. "Uh, keep dreaming there, buddy. There's a whole host of reasons why that's not going to work."

"And they are?"

I swung my feet to the floor and leaned forward. "First, my mother would never let me get by with a small ceremony. As it is, I'm going to have to play along with her about wedding preparations until we tie the knot. Even then she might insist we do a redo just so she can go big. Secondly, if my parents were here before—if my *father* is here before we're married, he will definitely try to put a stop to it."

"Not if he believes you really love me."

"Even then." Surely he had to realize how much my father hated him.

Edward tilted his head, his expression skeptical. "He'd prevent you from marrying your soulmate? The man you've waited for all your life?

I seriously doubt any father can deny his only daughter's happiness, even if it's tied up in his business rival."

"Yes, but..." But Edward *wasn't* my soulmate. He wasn't the man I'd waited for all my life.

"You have to sell it that way," he said, reading my doubts which I was sure were all over my face. "And I trust that you can."

I'd been about to say it was impossible, but his trust in me made me hesitate. Could I really do this? Could I convince my father that Edward made me happy, that I wanted to spend my life with him?

It would be the hardest con I'd ever played. And I did like a challenge.

Still... "I don't know. I don't see how I'll get them here for it. I can put off telling them who you are for a while, but as soon as I tell them the wedding is soon and not a year or more away, they'll start demanding more information and once I say it's you, I'm not sure I'll even be able to keep my father on the phone to discuss it."

Unless...

"Then don't tell them you're getting married until you're face to face."

Edward voiced the very idea I'd just been considering. It had merit.

"Here's a thought," he said. "Tell them you're engaged, and you're in love and very happy, and that rather than tell them anything about your intended, you'd prefer for them to meet me in person. Then invite them to come to London. For your birthday, perhaps, if you need an occasion."

I nodded, seeing where he was going. "Then when they're here, 'Surprise! We're getting married right now.'"

"Exactly."

I sat back and pondered the idea from all angles. They'd be upset, of course, but in person really was the best way to convince them of something so big. "My birthday is November ninth," I said, doing the math. "Two months from now."

"I know."

For fuck's sake, Celia, do not get all giddy because he knows when your birthday is.

His gaze drifted up in thought. "I actually just had a project drop from my calendar in November. I think that will work perfectly. I'll check with Charlotte on Monday."

"Okay." I had to take a deep breath to keep the room from spinning. We had a date. This was happening. This was really happening. "Okay," I said again, steadying myself with the two syllables.

Edward's brows perked up. "Okay? To everything?"

I opened my mouth to answer, and then stopped myself. This was my chance to make my own appeals.

"Yes, okay to everything, but while we're negotiating..." I met his eyes and my heart skipped a beat at the intensity of our connection.

Damn, I really wished I had that second drink.

"Are we? Negotiating?" He was so smooth. So unaffected.

"While you're *demanding*," I said, standing up. I tossed my hair hoping it looked as sultry as it felt. "It seems only fair that I have a chance to make my own requests."

"Just so long as you understand that they are only requests."

The amusement was back in his expression.

I sauntered over to him, stopping directly in front of where he was perched. "Right. Because you have the final say on everything. But only once this arrangement starts, and until there's a ring on this finger," I wiggled the appropriate digit, "I haven't agreed to anything yet."

Sitting like this, on the arm of the chair, his back straight, we were practically the same height. It occurred to me that this was the closest we'd ever been to having equal footing, and somehow that made me both heady and encouraged.

I reached out to rub the collar of his shirt between my thumb and forefinger, my breath stuttering under the thick weight of apprehension, my mouth watering from how close I was to touching his skin. This close, I could smell the liquor on his breath and the musky scent of his cologne and the fainter scent underneath of pure man.

"Tell me your requests." Was it my imagination or did his voice suddenly seem darker? Less steady?

"There's only one." I leaned in until my lips were near his ear. "I want to add sex to the deal."

He made a sound low in his throat, half like a laugh, half like a moan. "What, now?"

He turned his face toward mine, and now our mouths were only inches away from touching. I could feel the warmth of his exhale on my skin, sending a trail of goosebumps down my arms.

"Now, sure." Fuck, I was wet already. "But I meant in the marriage, too."

His lips danced around mine. "You don't know what you're asking for. You want to be humiliated, degraded, and hurt?"

Yes.

Because that was the goal of The Game.

But, also, *YES!*

Because, in that moment, there was nothing more I could imagine wanting than to be all those things, to be humiliated and degraded and hurt, by him. I wanted it so much I ached. Ached in places I hadn't known could feel.

I reached my neck forward, pushing my mouth toward his.

Just when I thought the kiss was inevitable, he leaned back. "You couldn't handle it."

I was frustrated, but he was still here. Still engaged in the conversation. I hadn't lost him completely yet. "How do you know I'm not into what you're into?"

He brought a finger up and traced the tip along my jawline. "If you were into what I'm into, you would settle for what I give and not try to demand more."

Somewhere in the back of my head, I understood what he was saying, that he wanted submission here, too. That he was the one who did the seducing.

But I was too desperate for him, and too scared that he wouldn't do the seducing if I pulled back. "I don't think it's fair to come to that conclusion while we're still in the negotiation stage."

I lifted my hand to cup his cheek, to hold his face still.

He caught my wrist before I reached my destination and brought it down to hold between us. "You still haven't figured it out, have you? This isn't a negotiation stage. There's no bargaining here, Celia. Not with me. There's what I want or there's nothing at all. I don't negotiate."

I studied his face while he spoke, so I didn't see what his other hand was doing until I felt the ring being slid down my finger, slipped past my knuckles, until it was snug at the base.

Surprised, I glanced down to see what I was wearing. Once I saw it, I couldn't look away. It was vintage and white gold and square—a ring I would never have chosen for myself. Nevertheless, it was exquisite. The center stone had to be at least three carats and was surrounded by a double cushion-shaped frame lined with shimmering round accent diamonds. Intricate milgrain details ran along the band. There were so many stones that, no matter which way I turned my hand, they caught the light.

I'd never been given anything as beautiful in my life.

"It's stunning," I said, barely able to speak over the knot in my throat. Where had it even come from? I'd thought he was being a dick when he said he already had something. He must have had it in his pocket all night long.

"It's stunning on your finger." He sounded almost as awed as I felt.

It made me feel beautiful, both his words and the ring itself and suddenly I wanted to do something for him, give him something that made him feel as good as this small object made me feel.

"Will you wear a band as well? I'd like to pick it out, if you'll let me."

He searched my face for several heavy seconds, his eyes flicking more than once to my lips, and I was sure, absolutely sure he was going to kiss me.

I held my breath, waiting.

But he didn't kiss me. Instead, he stood and pushed past me, heading toward his desk. "It came in a set. I have wedding bands for both of us already."

I was still recovering from that rejection when he picked up the cradle on the antique phone I'd thought had been just decoration. "Ms. Werner is ready to go back to her hotel," he barked. "Bring the car around. She'll be down momentarily."

The message was clear. There'd be no kisses, no negotiating, no sex. Edward's word was law.

"I guess I'll be going," I said, as though I had a choice in the matter, fighting like hell to hold back tears. "Thank you for the wonderful evening."

I took off down the stairs, not waiting for him to offer to escort me or even say good night. If I stood around even a minute, I was afraid he'd see into me like he always did. Afraid he'd see truths about me I didn't even know myself.

It wasn't like I was leaving with nothing. We were officially engaged. I had a ring. He'd established the rules of this dark little game of ours. A game I was more committed to playing than ever.

I just couldn't say anymore if I wanted to play to destroy him or to win him.

TWENTY-THREE

"LOOK UP, AND DON'T BLINK," Jodie, my makeup artist, directed.

Don't blink was an easy enough instruction to follow. My problem was fidgeting. I would never admit it out loud, especially not to Edward, but I was nervous. How had two months gone by so quickly?

That was a stupid question. I knew exactly how they'd flown by—I'd been kept extremely busy, that was how. The day after he'd slid the engagement ring on my finger, Edward had thrown me into wedding planning, much to my chagrin. I would have much preferred to hire a professional. The budget I'd been allowed for the event could certainly have paid for one of the best and still had plenty left over.

When I'd run the idea past Edward, though, he'd been vehemently opposed. *"Your parents know you,"* he'd said. *"The ceremony may be small, but they will expect to see your touch in the details. If it's generic and cold, they won't believe your heart is really in this marriage."*

Well, because my heart really wasn't in the marriage.

"Besides," he'd countered when I'd continued my argument. *"You might find you enjoy it."*

I'd laughed in his face then. But the last laugh was his, because, although I'd been pissed to be tasked with the project, I *had* grown to enjoy it. It hadn't really been like planning a wedding—an event I had absolutely zero interest in taking part of—because the guest list for our ceremony was so small. It had been more like organizing a fancy party with flowers and live music and a designer dress and gourmet dessert trays. With a sizable budget and free rein to do whatever I wanted in the salon and dining room, I'd found the process similar to interior designing. The beauty was in the particulars, as Edward had suggested, and I'd gone all out making it feel like it was *mine*.

I was pleased with what I'd come up with, in the end. Proud. Excited, even. Definitely nervous to see it all go off without a hitch.

Between the planning and meetings with lawyers to both review and then sign the prenup, I'd barely had time for anything else, including seducing my husband to be. His schedule had been part of the problem. He had indeed been able to get the time off for a honeymoon, but he'd had to cram a lot of long days into the weeks beforehand. I'd convinced myself it was fine. My scheme required sexing to happen after vows were exchanged, not before.

That reasoning didn't seem to translate to my libido.

I'd spent eight long weeks drowning in want. While I'd stayed at the hotel the whole time, I'd made sure to connect with Edward whenever possible. His desire to be apprised of everything wedding related had made that easy enough, and as annoyed as I'd been with this specific demand, I'd taken advantage of it, using it as an excuse to meet for dinner or drinks. I'd inundate him with details and took every opportunity to brush past him and sit too close and accidentally touch.

But, as much as I'd flirted and prolonged these encounters, I'd left each night more aroused than when I'd arrived. He was good at that, I'd learned. Good at provoking me. Good at pushing the tension. Good at winding me up tighter and tighter and tighter until I didn't think I could stand another second without the crush of his lips against mine. Good at leaving me with the female equivalent of blue balls.

Tonight, though, everything would change. Tonight, we'd be married and instead of sleeping in a room halfway across the city, I'd be in a bed next door to him. This morning I'd checked out of my hotel and had my belongings delivered to my room in the master suite, and now, getting ready for the big event in *his* house—in *his* personal space —I already felt closer to my goal.

If I was honest with myself, that was what had me the most nervous. Not my parents' impending arrival, not the show we'd put on in this farce of a wedding, not the menu or the decor or anything to do with the actual ceremony, but what happened after. What happened tonight, when we were finally alone in the suite. That's what had me twitching and sweating. That's what had the butterflies swarming in my stomach like I was climbing the big hill of a roller coaster.

Jodie put her mascara wand down on the counter and turned back to me. "Okay, look right at me so I can see if your eyes are even."

I did as she asked, fighting the urge to glance at my reflection in the mirror behind her instead.

"You look fab, girl. Now, all we have left is your lips and then we can get those curlers out of—"

A noise downstairs caused me to put up my hand to shush her.

"Did you hear that?" I strained my ears to see what else I could hear. Two floors up, most noise from the ground floor came up muffled or not at all, but I'd left all the doors of the suite open specifically hoping I'd hear the doorbell.

Jodie shook her head, her expression baffled.

"Did it sound like the doorbell? I swear it was the doorbell." I jumped up and ran to the window and peered down at the front step. "Shit! It's my parents! They're early!"

"Actually, uh, we're running a tad late." Jodie smiled guiltily, even though it wasn't entirely her fault we'd gotten behind schedule. A delay in the floral delivery had prevented me from getting started with my hair and makeup at the time I'd originally planned.

It didn't matter whether we were behind or on time—I had to greet my parents. I still had hot rollers in my hair, and I wasn't even dressed, but they still didn't know anything about what was happening today or who my fiancé was, and there was no way I was letting Edward get to them first.

I grabbed my dressing robe and tied it quickly around me. "I'm sorry. I have to go down there. I'll be back up as soon as I can."

Unless my father dragged me out of the house kicking and scream-ing. I hadn't totally ruled that out as a possibility.

Taking them two at a time, I rushed down the stairs, pausing on the next floor down to be sure Edward was still locked away in his office where he'd been sequestered until the ceremony. The doors were only slightly ajar, but I glimpsed a partial view of his backside and blew out a sigh of relief, and not just because of how damned good his ass looked in his suit pants.

While he'd agreed to every other of my suggestions, my parents' arrival had been the one thing the two of us had argued about in the planning process. He'd wanted to be there when I told them who I was marrying. I insisted he wasn't. His presence would only stir my father up before I had a chance to offer any explanation, and even if I managed to get him to stay for the wedding after that, it would greatly reduce the chances of him ever liking Edward.

And there was no good benefit of Edward being there. As far as I could tell, his reasons for wanting to be were sadistic and mean. He wanted to see my father's face when I announced my engagement to his rival, that was all. It was only when I called him out that he backed down, lucky for me, because as he'd promised the night of our "negotia-tions," he really did have the last word on everything. Even then, I hadn't trusted him to not try to undermine the decision when the time came. Hence why I was eager to get downstairs.

When I got to the ground floor, Jeremy was just exiting the receiving room. "Ah, ma'am. I was just coming to inform you of your parents' arrival."

"I heard the doorbell, thank you." I started to move past him then stopped. "Jeremy, would you mind making sure that Edward doesn't come down here?"

I knew it was hardly fair, asking him to try to influence anything his boss did or didn't do, and his expression told me that he wasn't at all comfortable with the idea.

"Because it's our wedding day, and all," I said, hoping he'd buy the excuse. "The groom isn't supposed to see the bride until the cere-mony." It wasn't like we'd purposefully been trying to honor the tradition. With both of us having separate agendas for the day, it had just worked out that way. It was now seven in the evening, and we'd only bumped into each other in the hall once, much earlier in the day.

"I'll do what I can," Jeremy reluctantly acquiesced. It wasn't a guarantee, but I'd take what I could get.

With that issue managed, I slipped into the receiving room. "Mom! Dad! You made it!" They'd actually arrived in London the day before, but this was the first time I'd seen them. Between their jet lag and the last minute preparations, it had seemed easiest for everyone involved to wait until tonight.

"There's the birthday girl," my father said, kissing my cheek as I embraced him. "You're not dressed yet? Are we early?"

"No, it's me. I'm behind."

My hands were both still around my father when my mother exclaimed, "Oh, Celia! That ring!"

I pulled out of his arms to show off the jewel I'd become quite attached to. After she oohed and ahed over it to her satisfaction, I moved to hug her. "You look fabulous, Mom. Is this dress new?" I knew it wasn't. She'd worn the metallic sequin gown for a charity event the previous year, but I figured they both needed as much buttering up as possible.

"This old thing?" she said, her cheeks getting red. "I was afraid I'd overdressed. You did say the party was formal?"

"I did," I said, cringing inwardly at her reference to a party. That was the lie I'd told in order to get them there and dressed appropriately. "I mean, it is. Formal. You both look great."

Okay, perhaps my nervousness extended to telling my parents the truth, too. Because right now my heart felt like it was about to pound out of my chest and my throat felt like I'd swallowed a quart full of sand.

Best to rip the Band-Aid off fast.

"Hey, um, let's sit down for a moment and talk." With my hand on each of their backs, I gestured them gently toward one of the sofas.

"I don't need to sit," my father said.

"Right," my mother agreed. "We're both eager to meet this man of yours. And don't you need to finish getting ready?"

"Yes, yes, I do. And you'll meet, uh, *my man* soon enough. Actually, that's kind of what I want to talk to you about. So could you please, for me, just sit down for a minute?"

"Sure, honey. Sure." My mother exchanged a glance with Dad, a glance that said *oh, no, the engagement's been called off.*

Of course they'd immediately think the worst. Maybe that would be to my benefit. They'd be so happy to find out I hadn't ruined things after all that they wouldn't care who I was marrying.

Yeah, right.

I waited until they were both settled on the sofa then I pulled an ottoman over so I could sit directly in front of them. As soon as I was seated, though, I started to panic. Should I have a drink for this? *They* should probably have a drink for this.

I shot back to my feet. "Can I get you something to drink? Some brandy? Scotch?"

"None for me," my mother said, giving her husband a look that said he'd better say the same thing.

I'd never realized how well the two communicated without words. It was something to aspire to in a relationship, really. If I ever had a real one of those in the future.

With no chance of liquor easing the sting of my confession, I sank back down on the ottoman and took a deep breath. "As I've told both of you already, I am...um, in love with Edward."

Way to sell it, Celia.

I could do better. I had to do better.

"I'm *completely* in love with Edward. Eddie." Eddie sounded like a good pet name, right?

"Edward...Eddie. Is that the name of your fellow?" My father didn't wait for me to answer before diving into his next question. "Is this his house we're at? This is a really expensive house, Madge. Did you notice it's across from Regent's Park?"

My mother nodded, her eyes wide and glimmering. "You didn't tell us this Edward was so well-to-do."

At least Edward's wealth impressed them.

It also gave me something to latch onto as I tried again to emphasize my "feelings" for my husband-to-be. "I guess that's because I don't even notice his money, Mom. That's how much I love him. How much I love Eddie. He's turned my entire world upside down. But in a good way! I can't even remember what life was like before him. He's...just..." What the fuck did women say about the men they loved? I'd gotten in the middle of enough relationships that I should know this.

The truth. Stick to as much of the truth as possible.

"I was numb before Edward. Since I've met him, I've felt things that I haven't felt in ages. He makes me excited. He makes me crazy. He makes me calm, too, strangely enough. Even when he has my stomach fluttering like I swallowed a bunch of bees, I feel anchored."

It was the first time I'd been honest with them about Edward.

It was the first time I'd been honest with myself, too.

My mother reached out to pat my knee. "Well, honey, that's what love is. I'm so happy you've found it, and with such an impressive man. What does he do again? Did you ever tell me?"

"Uh...he owns his own company. I'll tell you more in a minute, but first—"

The front door swung open, cutting me off mid-sentence. "Hello!" Genevieve said, smiling brightly. "Oh. I thought I was late. But you aren't even dressed yet. Is everything all right?"

I wanted to say, *No, everything is not all right,* especially when Hagan came in right behind her, but she'd likely already gotten that from looking at me. All the blood had drained from my face the second she'd walked in the door. I'd been so worried about Edward walking in and ruining my whole confession, I hadn't even considered the possibility his children could do the same thing.

This was fine. If I dealt with it swiftly and carefully, this didn't have to be a big deal at all.

I stood up, and my parents followed suit. "Everything's fine. I'm behind, is all, but I wanted to talk to my parents for a minute before the whole evening started." *Hint, hint, I want to talk to them alone.*

"Ah! These are your parents!" Hagan had no skills at reading subtext, apparently, and instead of rushing along he was now extending a hand out in greeting.

"Mom, Dad, this is Hagan and Genevieve, Edward's children." I turned to the siblings. "Madge and Warren Werner." It was a quick introduction, but adequate, and maybe now they'd get the clue?

Hagan didn't move. "Fantastic to meet you. Are you excited for the big event?" Obviously neither of Edward's kids knew the whole night was a surprise to my parents.

"For the wedding? Or for tonight's—"

I cut my mother off. "I don't want to be rude, but I really need to finish talking to my parents, and I'm sure Camilla could use some help with Freddie while she finishes getting ready."

Genevieve wasn't so obtuse. "Hagan, come on. Dad's probably pacing a hole in the carpet upstairs. Let's go check on him."

Thank the Lord they were leaving.

I'd just gotten my parents sat back down when Genny reappeared. "Whoops. Didn't shut the door. Wouldn't want Dad to see you before it's time."

I held a frazzled smile until the doors were closed, and she was definitely gone.

"What did she mean about her dad not seeing you?" Of course my mother hadn't missed that.

"Nothing. It's nothing." I shook my head profusely, refusing to figure out a better explanation. I needed to just get through this. She'd figure it out soon enough. "Where was I?"

"Those kids of his are adults," my mother said, not caring where I'd been before. "How old is their father?"

"He's a decade older than me, Mom. He had his kids young. Not a big deal." Seriously, if she was going to get worked up about our age difference, I didn't stand a chance with the other information.

"He's established, Madge," my father said. "That's what matters." He turned back to me. "You were telling us about Edward's business, I believe."

That hadn't actually been what I'd been telling them. "Right. But first—"

"Yes, but first..." My mother nodded encouragingly. "That's what you were saying."

"But first, I want to really be sure you understand how happy I am and how much I want to be with Edward."

My mother brought her hand to her heart like an actress in a melodrama. "Honey, you're making me nervous. What's wrong?"

"Are you knocked up?" My father's tone said he might have to kill my fiancé if I was, an almost comical reaction since I was already getting married. To be fair, he'd had the same reaction the one time I had been pregnant. At least he was consistent.

I laughed nervously. "No, no. I'm not pregnant." *That would require us to have had sex first.* "And nothing's wrong. But there are a couple of things you should know. Um." I blinked, the words stuck in my throat. Why was this so hard?

"Just spit it out, Celia." My father never had patience for drawn-out conversations.

"Okay. Right. Okay." I leaned over to take my mother's hand. "Now, don't be mad, Mom, but this isn't really a birthday party."

"Are you saying...?" She trailed off so I couldn't be sure she'd guessed accurately.

"I'm saying, surprise! I'm getting married!" I'd been joking when I'd originally proposed breaking the news like that, but in the moment, that was the way that came out.

"Tonight? You're getting married *tonight*?" My mother was as taken aback by this announcement as I'd thought she would be. She carried on for another ten minutes this way. I was anxious about getting my hair done in time, so I was watching the clock.

My father, on the other hand, was pleased as punch that he wouldn't have to pay for a wedding, the bastard. It wasn't like he couldn't afford it.

"Mom, please," I said finally, wishing I could stop the seconds from ticking by. "I'm getting married tonight because that's the kind of wedding I wanted. Please, please accept that and don't ruin this day for me."

That clammed her up for all of one heartbeat. Then she was crying and hugging me—awkwardly since we were both still sitting—and telling me how happy she was for me and to just be included on my special day.

It was a knife right through the heart. If only I could tell her the truth.

My father fidgeted in his seat, obviously ready to be done with all the emoting. "Well, do we get to meet this Edward before the ceremony or is that going to be a surprise as well?"

I broke away from my mother's embrace and braced myself. "Actually, Dad. You've already met him."

And for all the times I'd considered him a dense old man, my father proved then and there that he was more quick-witted than I gave him credit for. "Oh, no. No, no, no." He stood up and started walking around the room, as if looking for a clue to confirm his suspicions. "An older British man with lots of money named Edward? A man who had been your client? I told you when you asked me about him not to work with him. I forbade you!"

"You didn't actually forbid me," I mumbled.

"It was implied! No way. There is no way in my lifetime that my daughter is marrying that man. No fucking way."

I rose to my feet and lifted my arms defensively, as if the posture could stop his anger. "Hold on. Can we talk about this calmly, please?"

"There is absolutely nothing to talk about." He snapped his fingers at my mother. "Madge, get up. We're leaving. Where did that servant put our coats?"

"Dad, don't leave!" If I hadn't been worried about messing up my makeup, I'd have tried to make myself cry. I knew how to do that.

It wouldn't have been that hard at that particular moment, actually.

My mother hadn't moved from the couch. "What's going on? I don't understand. Who is she marrying?"

My father's face went redder than it already was. "She's not marrying anyone! She's coming with us. Go upstairs and get dressed, Celia. We're leaving."

What was with all the men in my life thinking it was okay to order women around?

At least with Edward I'd gotten to choose it. My father just assumed that since he'd donated half my DNA that it was his right.

Well, fuck that. I wasn't having it. "I'm not going anywhere. I'm getting married."

"To whom?!" My mother was clearly exasperated.

Edward's voice boomed out in answer. "To me."

TWENTY-FOUR

IN ALL THE COMMOTION, I hadn't noticed the hall doors open or Edward walk in, but there was no way anyone could miss the authoritative way he spoke those two words. He commanded all attention, all three of us turning toward him the way daisies turned toward the sun.

"Edward," my father said tersely.

"Edward," I sighed at the same time. Mentally, I reserved the right to get angry later about his intrusion, but for now, in this exact point in time, I was glad he was there. I was relieved to have someone carry this burden with me.

Which was dumb, wasn't it? Because I didn't actually care about my parents' approval. That was *his* goal.

But maybe it wasn't about Edward, in the moment. This was about my father thinking he had a say in my life. This was about my father ignoring what he believed to be my happiness because of a stupid business rivalry.

This was about standing up for me.

And if Edward was going to be on my side, I was grateful for that. I was more than grateful.

As though driven by a force outside of myself, I floated over and sidled into him. He put a possessive arm around my waist, and extended his other hand toward my mother, who had finally managed to make it to her feet.

"I'm Edward Fasbender," he said graciously then kissed the back of her hand. "While I'd hope to best be known as the man who anchors your daughter, I believe your husband prefers to think of me as his main competitor."

Even as it was clear she recognized his name, my mother swooned, and who wouldn't? Edward was one smooth son of a bitch.

A son of a bitch who'd evidently been listening to—watching, even?—our entire conversation.

I reserved the right to be angry about that later too.

"I'm so very glad to meet you, considering what you mean to our daughter," my mother gushed. Legitimately gushed.

My father fumed, his fists curling and uncurling at his side. "Madge, let go of that man's hand. He's a conniving devil."

"It's not catching, Warren." Edward dropped my mother's hand, seemingly humored by the entire situation.

His amusement incited my father further. He pointed an accusing finger in Edward's direction. "You are truly incredible, Fasbender. After everything you've done, blocking my company's advances in the European market at every turn, going out of your way to sabotage the relationships I've worked my entire life to build..." He was so worked up thinking about Edward's supposed deficiencies, that he couldn't continue listing them.

Instead, he turned his finger toward me. "Don't you realize he's using you? He's not in love with you. He's just looking for another way to ruin me. He probably expects you to hand over company secrets. If you do this, Celia, if you go through with this, we're done. You're on your own."

It should have been validating. I knew my father wouldn't react well, and I'd been right. I'd been right about the depth of his hatred for Edward. It was the entire reason I wanted to play this game in the first place, because I knew how happy it would make my father to see Edward destroyed.

But I didn't feel anything like validation. I only felt empty and numb, a feeling I hadn't felt much of since I'd met Edward.

"Warren, that isn't at all true," Edward said calmly, in stark contrast to my father's ranting. "I do sincerely love your daughter. We both knew our pairing was not ideal because of who I am, because of who you are. Believe me when I say we fought our feelings knowing you'd never approve. But the heart wants what the heart wants."

He was lying out of his ass, and still I couldn't help the pinch in my chest at his declaration.

He dropped his hand from my waist, and left me for the mini bar. "I understand, though, that these are all just words. You have no reason to believe anything I say, nor should you. I certainly wouldn't be persuaded by romantic pronouncements if the shoe were on the other foot. I might add that there is a prenup in place protecting your daughter's assets, which should be reassuring, but still not exactly what you need to place your trust in this relationship."

He poured a brandy as he talked, and then crossed to my father, the drink held out in offering. "In light of all that, of the relationship you and I have had in the past, might I present this to you another way. You fear that I might have forged a relationship with your daughter merely for the benefit of my company. I propose that you have as much to gain from that scenario as I would. Perhaps this could be a union that removes the obstacles that have stood between us rather than building them up further."

For the first time since my father realized I was engaged to Edward, his demeanor cooled. His face, though still red, had lost some of its beet color. He actually appeared to be listening.

He still hadn't taken the glass offered to him, though, and now Edward nodded to it. "Take the drink, Warren. You watched me pour it. Clearly it isn't poisoned."

With a scowl, my father snatched the drink from his hand and took a long swallow before asking, "Are you suggesting an alliance of sorts?"

"In the future, yes. It's a possibility. Tonight, I believe our attention would best be spent on giving Celia the wedding she deserves, with both her parents in attendance."

My breath stuttered as it filled my lungs. It was a clever tactic, on Edward's part, making this whole night about a business advantage. On the other hand, he was an asshole for entreating my father this way. For tempting him with the very gold he hoped to get for himself through our nuptials. Especially without telling me about it first.

It was worse when I looked at it from my father's side. The fact that this was what potentially changed his mind, and not my own appeals, made me livid.

I half hoped he'd balk at the vague proposition.

He took another swallow of the brandy. "I'm not unreasonable. I can agree to set this aside for the time being with the potential of discussing it further in the future."

I wasn't the only one, apparently, who saw the sting in my father's response.

"Warren!" my mother exclaimed. She rushed to him so that she could lower her voice, but I could still hear her clearly. "You cannot use your daughter's happiness to negotiate business."

"I'm not," he insisted. "Celia already said this man makes her happy. Right, Ceeley, sweetie?" He didn't wait for me to answer before adding, "She's always been her mother's daughter. Why wouldn't she fall for someone so similar to her old man?"

I rolled my eyes. As if my father were anything like Edward.

Or, I hadn't seen a similarity until tonight. Now, as far as I was concerned, they were both devils. I had half a mind to walk out the door right then and fuck both of them over.

At the very least, I couldn't stand to be in the room with either of them anymore.

Without a word, I spun around and charged for the hall doors.

"Celia, where are you going?" my mother called after me.

I stopped and forced myself to put on a smile before turning back toward them. "I have to finish getting ready since it looks like I'm getting married in half an hour." I didn't wait for anyone's response—I definitely didn't wait for anyone's permission—before fleeing from the room.

So I'd get married. Sure. Fine. I'd go ahead with my plans to ruin

Edward, but instead of doing it to make my father happy, I'd crush his hopes of a business alliance at the same time.

I wasn't doing this for him anymore.

I was doing it for me.

TWENTY-FIVE

I WAS fifteen minutes late getting ready, but I wasn't too concerned about it. There were only six people in attendance for the actual ceremony besides the officiant and the bride and groom, and even though there was a party planned with more guests invited, we'd left ample time between to make up for a delayed start.

I probably could have made it on time, despite the interruption to deal with my parents, but I'd learned in the last two months how firmly Edward was attached to punctuality, and call me a bitch, I wasn't in the mood to capitulate to him.

By the time I walked down the stairs at eight-fifteen, I suspected he was fuming. I was mildly surprised he hadn't come looking for me. I was even more surprised that he wasn't waiting in the hall to lecture me.

While Edward wasn't waiting, my father was. I wasn't any more interested in speaking to him at the moment than I was my husband-to-be, and when I discovered he was hoping to "walk me down the aisle," it was almost with pleasure that I explained to him that there wasn't an actual aisle for him to walk me down.

I wasn't entirely cruel, though. I allowed him to escort me down the hall into the salon, which, honestly, was essentially the same thing.

I'd seen the salon before I'd started getting ready so I knew what I was walking into, but the transformation of the interior still struck me as I entered. Practically a small ballroom, the space was easily a thousand square feet with gorgeous marble floors and a grand fireplace. Huge windows with heavy luxurious drapery wrapped around the outside of the room, alternating with wooden panels that showcased wall-mounted lights that matched the beautiful candle-style chandelier in the center of the ceiling. It was generously furnished with three large sofas, five decorative chairs, four side tables, a dining table, a piano, and several oversized floor vases, but I'd had half of the pieces removed for the event and the rest reconfigured leaving a generous section of the area open for the ceremony.

While romantic decor had never been my style, I did have a fondness for a good floral arrangement, and so when trying to be sure my touch was seen, I'd filled the room with flowers. Two columns with enormous red and white bouquets flanked the fireplace while eight smaller floral pillars were spread around the salon. Garlands sprinkled with red and white roses had been hung on all the lighting and along the window valances. The hearth had a spectacular arrangement of greenery and blooms, and the table, that would later hold decadent dessert trays and champagne, had a gorgeous centerpiece.

The heady fragrance of all these flowers was what hit me as I walked into the salon with my father. It was a soothing aroma, and as upset as I'd been prior, a blanket of calm fell on my shoulders, settling my nerves.

Until I saw Edward, anyway.

He'd had his back to me talking to the officiant, and I hadn't seen him immediately. My attention had first gone to my mother who was sitting on a sofa holding Fred. Camilla and Genny sat with her while Hagan stood off to the side, lost in his phone. No one had noticed us until my father cleared his throat, and then everyone stood and all eyes landed on me, Edward's last of all. He'd waited to finish whatever he was saying before turning, as though refusing to let anyone interrupt him, but then he did, and his gaze slammed into mine with violent force, making my knees shake and my stomach flip.

He pinned me with that gaze, not letting me move until he'd taken all of me in. And I stood there, unable to even breathe, while he did, waiting to see the verdict on his expression. I'd been anxious for this particular moment for weeks—anxious and eager—because the wedding dress I'd shown him, the wedding dress he'd approved when I'd met with him in planning, was not the one I was wearing. It was the same design—a trumpet style floor-length gown with a slit up one leg and a diamond embellished lace overlay that draped off the shoulder and down my arms.

Except, instead of being white, the dress I wore was red.

It had been an outright act of defiance. I'd assumed he'd disapprove, and he did, it was evident in the way the corners of his mouth turned down and the almost indiscernible twitch of his left eyelid. But along with his disapproval was a heated gaze of appreciation. It seared through me. Ignited my skin with its intensity. Lit the space between my legs until my pussy felt like it was a raging fire.

Whether his appreciation was for the way I looked or the act of wearing it, I couldn't be sure. What I did know was I liked that look. I wanted him to look at me like that all the time.

To be fair, I was pretty sure I gave him the same sort of look.

He. Looked. Incredible.

I'd been too distracted to pay much attention when he'd stormed in on me with my parents earlier, and he'd only been partially dressed then, wearing his trousers and dress shirt and nothing else.

Now, with the addition of the slim fit jacket, the double-breasted waistcoat, and the red ascot tie, he was almost too handsome to look at directly. Damn, did this man know how to wear a tux.

I wondered if he knew how to take it off as well. Or if I'd ever find out.

"Well, here she is," he said, his eyes never leaving mine as he crossed the room to me. "I was beginning to wonder if you were a runaway bride, but now it's apparent why you took so long. You look stunning, darling."

The words were for everyone else, playing the part of an amorous groom. I wasn't stupid enough to believe anything else. He'd even gotten the chance to reprimand me for my tardiness, letting everyone know the late start was not on him. The words were definitely for the others.

But the gaze...

The gaze had been for no one but me.

He kissed me on the cheek, another gesture for appearances, and took my hand in his. "Shall we get started, then?"

The ceremony began with no other hitches. The officiant wore a stole and clerical garb, which made my mother happy, even though he wasn't a minister but rather a registered local authority. Good money had been paid to get him to come to the house as well as to approve the location since legally binding weddings in England usually only took place in churches or registry buildings. I'd chosen a minimalist script with only the barebones required to be legitimate. That made the whole thing, not only simple, but fast-paced.

After the officiant greeted everyone, we stated our declaratory words and then went directly to the vows, or the contracting words. Edward said his first, repeating the words he was given.

Then it was my turn. Which is when I learned that my groom had made a switcheroo of his own, because, while the vows I'd agreed to were traditional, they hadn't included the old-fashioned promise for the wife to "obey."

Now they did.

I hesitated when I heard the presider say it, not because I didn't intend to repeat it, but because the sneaky addition was a reminder of who exactly it was I was marrying, and I needed a moment to let it sink in.

Edward's brow rose as I paused, and I could practically hear his thoughts. *I told you my word is law. I told you not to argue with me in public.*

"To love, cherish, and *obey*," I said, feeling even more vindicated in my dress choice. Yes, he'd set submission as an expectation for his wife, but I'd worn red, and there was nothing he could do about it.

Obviously, there were ways to get around him.

Next came the exchange of rings. I hadn't yet seen the bands that

Edward had said went with the one already on my finger, so when he pulled them from his jacket inside pocket and placed them in the palm of the officiant, I leaned in to examine them. My band had diamonds all around it in a delicate ornate setting. Edward's was a beautiful thick platinum with milgrain detailing and a high-polished edge.

They were both exquisite, but it wasn't the rings themselves that caught my breath in my lungs—it was what the presider said about them. "Rings are made of precious metal, but that same metal is also made precious by wearing them. These rings are even more precious as they have been worn before, celebrating the love and union of Edward's parents, Stefan and Amelie Fasbender."

"These were your parents' wedding rings?" I was too shocked to stop myself from saying the thought out loud. We were getting married with the rings that belonged to his *parents*? He'd put his mother's engagement ring on *me*? We didn't have a real relationship. Even if he hated his parents, why would he want to use their wedding set for this? He could certainly afford new ones.

It didn't make any sense.

I'd interrupted, and Edward gave me a stern look. I wasn't getting any answers now. It would have to wait.

"Sorry," I mumbled, turning my attention back to the officiant.

"These rings mark the beginning of your long journey together. They are a seal of the vows you have just taken. May they guard your love as they guarded the love of those who first wore them."

I couldn't wrap my mind around it even as Edward slipped the sparkling band on my finger.

When I picked up the larger band, I held it more delicately than I would have if it had been from a random ring set, and when I said the words that bound us together, "With this ring, I thee wed," a shiver passed through me, as though I could feel the presence of the woman who'd given it to her beloved before me.

After that, we were done. We were married.

The officiant pronounced us legally wed and congratulated us, and while our small gathering of family applauded, Edward put his arm around my waist and pulled me into him.

I'd somehow forgotten about this part.

We hadn't discussed it, and it wasn't written in the official script, but weddings typically ended with a kiss, and this one wasn't any different.

It wasn't the same kind of kiss that we'd shared before. That kiss had been hungry and wild and out of control and a little bit angry. But even while Edward's mouth met mine with purposeful composure, it was still dominating. Still possessive as his tongue slid against mine. Still made me dizzy and swept me off my feet with its intensity, and when he started to pull away, and I chased after him with my lips, he didn't deny me, pressing his lips once more to mine, drawing a small sigh from the back of my throat.

God, the man could kiss.

And I liked it.

And I'd promised to obey.

Boy, was I in trouble.

TWENTY-SIX

SOMEONE OPENED A BOTTLE OF CHAMPAGNE, and a glass was put in my hand, but we barely had time for a toast before people were arriving. First it was the extra staff we'd hired for the evening. Then the pianist and the photographer.

At nine o'clock sharp, the guests began to appear.

There hadn't been many invited, fifty or so in total, mainly people high up in Edward's company and other important people he worked with. He called them friends, but I doubted the man had any of those.

Since I had only been in London a short time, and since my business had been temporarily shut down, I didn't have any "friends" to invite. There were some old acquaintances from school that had been close enough that they might have flown the distance, if I'd asked. But it was a loveless marriage and guests were only coming to the dessert and drinks portion of the night, so what was the point?

Having only my parents there for myself turned out to be a blessing. It made the rest of the evening easier to deal with. Edward expected me to be on his arm, ready to introduce to this person and that person, and then to stand there quietly smiling while he and the person talked about things that had absolutely nothing to do with me, and the photographer snapped candid pics.

It should have been more irritating than it was, to be arm candy. To be decoration. But it gave me an excuse not to have to talk more to my parents. I didn't want to have to lie more about my relationship with Edward, and I didn't want to have to listen to my father daydream about the new relationship *he* hoped to have with Edward.

Beyond the excuse it gave me, accompanying my new husband around the room was almost fun. I'd only gone along with his stupid, old-fashioned ideas about the role of a wife because I didn't plan to be his wife for long. But playing the demure part wasn't as terrible as I'd imagined. I liked listening to the things he had to say. I liked other women looking at me with envy. I liked the men knowing they couldn't flirt with me or talk to me or even look at me without Edward being involved.

It made me feel like I somehow belonged to him. Made it feel like the ring on my finger actually meant something between us. Made me wish it *did* mean something.

We were an hour into the festivities when I finally got a second alone with him.

"You play the hostess very well," he said, his expression untypically warm, and I swear my heart tripped a beat.

It was ridiculous how the littlest compliment from him made me ridiculously giddy.

It also made me brave enough to ask the question that had been burning a hole inside me since the middle of the ceremony. "I didn't know our rings had belonged to your parents. Why...?"

I'd meant to put more after that why, but once I got there, I didn't know exactly how to phrase it without sounding ungrateful. *Why didn't you get new ones? Why would you want to use a family heirloom on me?*

The warmth he'd shown a moment before disappeared instantly. "They weren't using them anymore. Better on our fingers than in a drawer somewhere."

He was scanning the room, and I guessed he was looking for someone he hadn't talked to yet in order to get away from this conversation, which should have been a sign to end it right there.

It only made me want to push him more.

"But why wouldn't you save them for your children? Why didn't you use them when you married your first wife. Or...did you?" The thought made me suddenly ill. "Are you reusing them on me?"

He scowled at me like I was a ridiculous child. "Of course not." It was obvious he didn't want to say more, but after fretting for a few seconds, he went on. "They weren't in my possession when I married Marion. By the time I hunted them down again, she'd already grown attached to the set we'd gotten married with."

He'd had to hunt them down. When his parents had died, he'd been destitute. I'd learned that from my research. The rings must have been sold to help pay outstanding bills. They were probably difficult to find.

Then they had to mean something to him.

People didn't just hunt down old family items unless they meant something.

Edward waved at someone across the room and started towing me toward them.

Still, I took the time of the approach to ask again. "If they were so important, why did you put them on *my* finger?"

"Because I did," he snapped angrily.

And then we were in front of the guest we'd been walking toward and Edward's features were schooled again and the subject was closed.

It was something I could ask about later when we were alone. But considering it was the first time I'd ever seen him lose his composure, I had a feeling I'd never get the real answer from him.

Or it was simpler than that and the answer was he didn't know.

I was still mulling this over, half-listening to him tell a story to his Chief Strategy Officer when I heard my father exclaim, "Ah, Ron's almost here!"

I obviously didn't hear him right, but apprehension flooded through me at the mention of the name.

With my hand still wrapped around Edward's bicep, I craned my neck in my father's direction. He was standing next to my mother typing into his phone, which didn't explain why I'd thought I heard him say my uncle's name. Because there was no way Ron could actually be coming here.

Could he?

Edward patted my hand, a subtle reminder that my focus should be on him, but then the doorbell rang and giving him my attention became impossible. I had to find out what my father had actually said, and who was here.

I politely excused myself then quickly pulled away from my husband. I'd pay for that later, I suspected, but I figured he was so intent on me not challenging him in public that there was no way he'd challenge me right now either.

"What's going on?" I asked when I reached my father's side.

"Ron's here," he said as he tucked his phone back in his pocket. "Wanted to make sure he was at the right place before he got out of the cab, so he texted, but I bet that doorbell was him."

My throat went dry and my stomach dropped to my ankles. "*Uncle Ron?*"

"Of course Uncle Ron. Who else would I mean?" His eyes were pinned on the doors to the salon, expectantly.

"He's in London?" My voice had miraculously sounded steady.

"He's been in Frankfurt," my mom piped in. "We told him we'd be here for your birthday party, and he said he'd try to pop over. We didn't say anything because he wasn't sure he could make it. Isn't it wonderful that he did? He'll be disappointed to have missed your wedding, but he'll be so glad he got to see you on your special day."

Before my mother had finished talking, my father exclaimed, "There he is!" He waved excitedly.

I felt outside of myself, like I was somewhere else watching what was happening instead of being an active participant. My body turned toward the man approaching. I saw him, saw the familiar balding head and smarmy expression. My face even put on a smile, but I didn't feel present in any of the actions.

Then he was standing next to me, reaching out to give me a hug, and I let him, as though it were nothing for him to touch me. As though I were powerless to stop him. As though my insides weren't twisting and churning with horror.

He was still embracing me, his hands a little too low on my backside as he said something congratulatory a little too close to my ear when a third hand, a warmer, heavier hand—*Edward's* hand—pressed possessively between my shoulder blades, and I suddenly came back into myself.

At Edward's appearance, Ron let me go, his gaze lingering when his body no longer did.

"Darling, I believe we haven't been introduced," my husband said, pulling me tightly into his side.

It was only an accidental rescue. As selfish as Edward was, he'd likely only come over because he saw another man touching his wife—a man that he didn't know, no less.

But as inadvertent as it may have been, I clung to him like a lifeline.

"This is my brother, Ron Werner," my father announced excitedly, eager to be the one who made the introduction between them. "I don't know if you recognize him, Ron, but this son of a bitch who married our girl is Edward fucking Fasbender."

"Fasbender?" Ron mused. "From Accelecom, right? How did this pairing happen? Did you set up some sort of arrangement and not tell me, Warren? Brilliant."

I felt like I was going to throw up.

"Well, we're still in discussions," my father began.

But Edward spoke over him. "Certainly not," he said crossly, yet not loud enough to draw the attention of others. "My wife isn't some pawn to use to conduct business. She's a person with thoughts and feelings and free agency, and she chose to marry me, and you'd do well to remember that. Both of you. As for any dealings that might occur between Werner Media and Accelecom, we absolutely will not be discussing them tonight. If getting something out of my company is the only value you see in 'our girl,' I assure you that we won't be having any future discussions either."

If the photographer had taken a picture of us in that moment, I was sure that it would have captured four Werners with their jaws agape.

Correction—three Werners. I was a Fasbender now.

"If you'll excuse us," Edward went on, ignoring the shocked expressions of his audience, "my wife and I have other guests to attend to."

With his hand securely at the small of my back, he steered me away from my family.

Instead of taking me to "other guests" as he'd said, he directed me to the champagne table. There, he poured a glass of bubbly and handed it to me.

"Drink this," he ordered softly.

I did. I drank it all down, wishing it were something a lot harder. Like cognac or Scotch or rubbing alcohol.

By the time I'd finished, I'd gotten my head back. I wasn't even sure exactly what had happened, but I was grateful and humiliated and ashamed and...confused.

Where had all that come from? After Edward had persuaded my father to allow me to marry with the promise of a potential business alliance, he now was the defender of my honor? What the fuck had changed?

Whatever it was, I wasn't sure I trusted his motives. I sure as hell didn't trust him.

"What was that about?" he asked. Strange since I thought *I* was the one who should be asking *him* that.

"What was what about?"

"You. Your uncle. What's going on there?"

Twenty-four years, and he was the first one to ask.

I didn't know how to feel about that. However I felt, I certainly wasn't going to start talking about it now. "I don't know what you mean."

"Cut the bullshit. You were white as a ghost. You were shaking when I touched you."

"I just...I didn't know..." I shook my head, looking for an excuse but my mind was blank.

After all the years of excuses, all the lies, I couldn't think of a goddamned thing, and that, on top of Edward being the one to really see me, on top of everything else that had happened that day, was the final straw.

I was pissed.

"You know what? *You* cut the bullshit," I said, turning on him. "This doesn't involve you. Why do you care?"

Edward reached out and drew his thumb softly against my lower lip, sending a parade of goosebumps down my arms. "It *does* involve me. Everything to do with you involves me. And I care because, my darling, I'm your husband. And not two hours ago, I vowed to protect and care for you. Or have you already forgotten?"

Tears pricked at my eyes, but I refused to let them fall. I refused to feel. Not for this. Not for him.

And I refused to believe he actually meant to honor his vows or this marriage or me any more than I meant to.

And I absolutely refused to believe he might actually care because, if there was one good thing to have come out of Ron's showing up, it was that he reminded me the lesson I'd learned a long time ago—when rich older men say they care, it only goes badly when they try to show you how much.

TWENTY-SEVEN

THE AFTER-PARTY INVITES had stated the evening would be over by eleven, but as happens, guests lingered until almost midnight. Not being night people, my parents had left earlier taking my uncle with them, thank God. I'd originally felt a tad guilty for my plan of bringing them all the way to London on the pretense of spending time with me and then, not only springing a surprise wedding on them, but also deserting them the next day for a honeymoon. Now, knowing they had Ron in town, the guilt was gone.

Emotionally and physically exhausted, I headed up to my bedroom ahead of Edward. I could hear him below as I climbed the last stairs, giving instructions to Jeremy, who I'd learned was more of a house manager than a butler. After spending the majority of the night on his arm, it felt strange to be away from him, like I was missing something. In contrast, I was very aware of the new band on my finger, pressing heavily into the webbing of my hand.

All in all, the evening had turned out acceptable. The goal had been accomplished. I was married to Edward, and my parents were still speaking to me. It may have taken a few bumps to get there, but that was the way with projects that had any worth.

It *would* be worth it, wouldn't it?

I wasn't sure anymore.

At the moment, I could barely remember why I wanted to do this in the first place. Play The Game. Ruin Edward. The reward was the destruction. The reward was the numbness.

Did that reward always feel this abstract in the process?

Looking back over the last dozen years, I couldn't remember feeling...well, this much. Couldn't remember a time that I'd been more than blissfully empty. Right now I felt full. Full of rage and hopelessness and shame and loneliness and a bunch of other emotions I was too unfamiliar with to identify, and I just wanted them all to disappear. Go back to wherever they'd been hiding.

Maybe I was just tired. Tomorrow I'd feel better. Tomorrow I'd feel nothing.

Holding onto that hope, I found the energy to kick off my shoes, tug down my zipper, and shimmy out of the tight-fitting dress. I left it on the floor and trudged into my ensuite to wash the makeup off my face. On the counter, I found the white lingerie set I'd left earlier. I'd bought them intending to seduce my husband on our wedding night, but now the mood was long gone.

Actually, no it wasn't.

Actually the mood was still very present. It was underneath all those other burdensome emotions, laying low but steady. A constant, throbbing undercurrent of need.

And, when I thought about it, I realized the other things I was feeling stemmed from this pulse, tributaries off a raging river of arousal. As if that sexual tension that had wound and wound and wound over the last few months had twined so tight that the strain had triggered other sensations. I probably wouldn't be so mad if it weren't for my fucking libido. I wouldn't be so melancholy. I wouldn't be so unbalanced.

And after all the shit Edward had pulled today—meddling with my parents, using me as bait for my father's business, expecting me to be his attachment while he mingled with friends, rescuing me from Uncle Ron and making me have nice thoughts about him—after all that shit, didn't I deserve to be relieved of this ache?

Fuck yes. I *did* deserve it.

My energy renewed by my resolve, I abandoned the face washing and freshened my makeup instead. Even after the long day, I still looked good. The soft curls had held. My eyes were sultry and expressive. All I needed was another coat of mascara and lipstick, and I looked brand new.

I stripped from my bridal undergarments and put on the sheer lace bralette and panties and the matching gossamer robe then spritzed some perfume and returned to the bedroom. Just as I slipped my foot into one of the red heels I'd worn for the ceremony, I heard Edward opening the door of his room.

Perfect timing.

The suite was laid out so that each of us could get to our rooms from the hallway, but there was also a door that connected us. I'd examined it earlier and discovered it wasn't locked, which meant I, of course, stuck my head in to check the space out. The design was more contemporary than the rest of the house, the colors all in shades of gold and brown, warmer than I'd expected from the man who slept there. The furniture was distinct and substantial without being too heavy. The chocolate brocade cloth headboard ran to the ceiling behind the bed, which was high off the floor, the centerpiece of the space, with two dark wood side tables on either side. In the far corner, a leather loveseat and high-back wing chair curved around a fireplace. I'd considered intruding further—poking around through his dresser, checking out the sturdiness of the mattress, leafing through the stack of books on the nightstand—but I'd already been behind schedule and couldn't spare the time.

Now I paused with my grip on the handle, knowing I should knock first. Knowing Edward would *want* me to knock first.

But I didn't want to knock.

I didn't want to ask permission to enter. I wanted to stride in boldly with confidence and cool composure. I wanted to command the situation.

So fuck knocking. Enough kowtowing to the man. I'd seduced

plenty of men in my lifetime. I was good at it even. I was going to walk in there and slay.

I threw my shoulders back and then charged into his room. He was standing next to the upholstered bench at the bottom of the bed, where he'd lain his jacket, and without it, I could see how well his dress shirt hugged his biceps and the way the waistcoat emphasized his trim torso. His profile was toward me, and when I entered, he only swiveled his head to glance in my direction before returning to his task of unbuttoning his vest.

"*Now* you wear white," he said, his tone half bored.

He was being cheeky, and I almost laughed out loud at his attempt at impertinence. He'd loved the red dress, and even if he wanted to verbally deny it, I knew the truth, and I was sure he knew I knew it.

Undeterred, I stepped further into the room, moving into his sight-lines. "I don't expect to be wearing it for long," I purred.

His jaw ticked, but his face remained otherwise stoic, his gaze refusing to truly look at me. "We've discussed this."

"We never came to a resolution."

"It seemed resolved to me."

I resisted rolling my eyes. "Give a little, Edward." I sat seductively on the bench, my legs stretched out in front of me. "Give a little, and you'll be happy with how much I give in return. You want the picture-perfect wife? *Make* me a picture-perfect wife."

He finished unbuttoning his waistcoat and threw it on the bench beside me, still unwilling to give me his full attention. "I transferred your monthly allowance to your account this morning. Make yourself a picture-perfect wife."

"Money can't buy satisfaction," I replied tightly.

"Can't it?" He raised one brow in question and looked directly at me.

Once he did, he couldn't help but look at *all* of me. His eyes scanned down the length of me, and not only did I watch as he did, I could feel them as they took in each square inch of my body. Could feel them as they passed down my throat, as they slid over the curve of my breasts, as they lingered on the dusky peaks of my nipples, as they continued lower. By the time he'd made it down my legs to the stiletto heel of my studded Alexander Wang's, his pupils were dark and large.

He was interested. He was *so* interested.

And despite being interested, he strolled away from me, removing his watch as he did, and then placing it on his bedside table.

God, he was so difficult.

Seduction alone obviously wasn't going to work with him. I'd have to try another one of my best tactics—manipulation.

I stood up and followed behind him. "Listen, this makes sense. If you want this to look like a real marriage, then we should consummate it. At this point, I could walk away with an annulment. I could say whatever I wanted about my reasons. *Publicly.* 'He couldn't get it up.' 'He wasn't able to satisfy me in the bedroom.' You're seen as an alpha in the businessworld. I'm sure a little impotence wouldn't be *that* concerning to your reputation. It might be harder to woo your mistresses, though, if they're worrying about your need for a Viagra prescription."

He turned then to look at me, amusement on his face.

I'd seen that expression before. Usually, I liked amusing him. Right now I wasn't sure that it was exactly what I was going for, but at least I had his focus. Maybe this approach was working.

I pushed further. "Or maybe your problem isn't getting hard, but..." I wiggled my pinky finger, suggesting he had a little dick.

He didn't have a little dick. I'd seen the outline of that big boy from across the room at The Open Door. I'd felt it against my belly when he'd kissed me in the bathroom at the Mandarin Oriental. It was a cock he should be proud of.

It was a cock I was dying to feel in the flesh.

"That's very funny," he said. "A clever way to try to get what you want. Someone ought to do something about your stubborn relent-lessness."

"Maybe that someone should be you."

Again, his gaze traveled down to the tips of my breasts, which had tightened into hard nubs. "I don't respond well to being challenged, Celia," he said firmly, even though his eyes said differently.

If I could have breathed fire, I would have. "Forgive me for not having yet had a chance to read the Edward Fasbender handbook," I growled. "Have you read mine yet? If you had, you'd know that I *like sex.*" I enunciated the last words to drive home the point.

He began to work on the knot of his tie, his forehead furrowed. "Perhaps I didn't make it clear that I don't expect faithfulness. Discreet indiscretions are completely permissible. Do you need help arranging a boy toy?"

This time I did roll my eyes. "I can get my own fuck boy, thank you very much. I don't want one. I want the convenience of fucking my husband!"

"The *convenience* is what brought you here tonight, then?"

I threw up my hands, exasperated. "Goddammit, Edward, *you* brought me here, okay? Is that what you want me to say? Well, there it is. I admit it. I'm attracted to you. I'm going out of my mind with how much I want you. I'm dizzy and aching and restless, and I swear if you don't touch me soon, I'm going to burn up out of need, and you'll have to explain to everyone that your new wife has left you widowed because she expired from a fatal case of lust. And maybe you think that's stupid and lame or desperate that I can be so into you when you're such an insane asshole, and maybe I am all of those things, but at least I'm owning it. I'm stupid *and* I need you to kiss me. I'm desperate *and* I need you inside me. So please quit being an obstinate jerk and give me something, I'm begging you. Please, please, please!"

I hadn't planned the outburst. The words just fell out, honest and raw, and now having said it, I felt more exposed than if I were standing in front of him completely naked. There was wisdom to telling lies that lay next to the truth, but there was also prudence in sticking to a strategy that kept the cards close to the vest. This confession was the opposite of that. This confession was weakness and vulnerability and a big fat fucking risk.

It was also the first thing I'd said since I'd walked in the room—no, since I'd agreed to this plan, since I'd met him, even—that had earned me the gleam of pride I saw now in his features. And though he hadn't said a single word in response yet, I could feel a change in the energy around him. An aura of invitation rather than rejection.

What had I just learned? Did he simply want to hear me say I wanted him? Was honesty one of his kinks? Or was it the begging that turned him on?

Or was I reading too much into nothing?

Each breath passed in shallow hopeful bursts as I waited apprehensively for him to say something. Say *anything*.

He finished with his tie and threw it onto the nightstand, his eyes locked on mine. Then he turned his wrist up to undo the cufflink. "I'm the boss when I fuck," he said resolutely. "You should know that before we start."

I almost got down on my knees in relief. In gratitude.

Me. On my knees. Because a subject had told me he was going to boss me around while he fucked me. *I* was always the boss when I fucked. I never gave up that control. What the fuck was wrong with me?

Whatever it was, I didn't want to fix it. I wanted this, wanted what he was giving. My pulse was racing with the wanting, but I played it cool. "And that's different from all the rest of the time...how?"

He tossed the cufflink on the table and began on the next one. "I haven't given you enough credit. It seems you do learn."

"Such an asshole," I mumbled, biting back a grin.

Before I even blinked, he'd pulled me to him, his hand wrapped tightly in my hair. "What was that?"

I swallowed, sure he could feel my heart beating through my chest. "You heard me."

He yanked on my hair, and I gasped at the bite of pain. "And that's why you want me. *Because* I'm an asshole."

It wasn't exactly what I'd said, and I didn't know if it was a question or if he thought he was simply repeating what I'd already said, reminding me. I was too busy staring at his mouth to think too long about it. I licked my lips in anticipation for the kiss I hoped was coming.

He jerked again, harder this time, pulling my gaze up to his. "When I ask you a question, I expect you to answer."

"Yes, Edward," I said, automatically, wanting to make him happy. "And yes. That's why I want you. *Because* you're an asshole." The stupid, lame, desperate thing was that I meant this too. I'd said before that I wanted him *even though* he was the shithead jerk that he was, but it was also *because.*

Admitting it made my already hot skin go up another half a degree. And then another half when the admission earned me his drop dead sexy smirk.

Oh, God that smirk.

And would he just fucking kiss me already? I was convinced he was testing me to see if I could really handle letting him have the control. Honestly, I wasn't sure I could. His lips were hovering above mine, taunting me with their nearness. It would be so easy to press up on my tiptoes and close the distance between us.

But I didn't. I held back and waited for him to call the shots, even though it was killing me.

After another beat, he released his grip on my hair. "Take off your knickers. Lay down on the bed, bend your knees, and spread your legs."

Eager to comply, I scooted out of my panties. I considered taking off my robe and shoes as well, but he hadn't asked me to, and I wanted to show him I could follow directions since that seemed important to him. So I got up on the bed, letting the flimsy material of my robe drape around me, and I scooted back just far enough for my heels to perch on the edge. Then I spread my legs, like he'd asked, and felt a sudden rush of warmth from the scorching heat of his gaze.

"Now, play with yourself. Get yourself ready," he said, dropping his second cufflink on the table. "I won't be happy if you're dry when I go in." His tone was indifferent despite the look in his eyes. Despite the thick bulge of contrary evidence pressing at the crotch of his trousers.

I didn't tell him I was already wet. I'd given him enough honesty. He didn't need to see any more of my cards, though I was pretty sure the truth was obvious because, when my fingers worked their way down to my pussy in compliance, my lips were drenched.

Taking some of the moistness with my tips, I dragged my fingers up my slit to the swollen bud of heat above. With only a couple of swirls, my orgasm began to build, which was good since I needed the release, and I had a pretty strong feeling that he wasn't concerned about helping out. His expectation that I take care of all the foreplay by myself was a good indicator.

Or, maybe it wasn't all by myself, because, while it was my hand doing all the physical work, the way he looked at me while I played with myself was pretty damn hot. It was intense and appreciative, even as he meticulously rolled up first one sleeve and then the other to the elbow.

It also made me feel vulnerable, as vulnerable as when I'd confessed to wanting him as badly as I did, and strangely, instead of shutting down my desire, the vulnerability only racheted it up a notch.

Fuck, I was going to come. Just from this. Just from his gaze.

"That's what you call getting ready for me? That pathetic attempt to get off? How disappointing." Edward's voice was harsh and taunting, and as much as I liked pleasing him, it seemed I really did enjoy his cruelty as well, because those words were all the nudge I needed to send me over the edge.

It was a gentle climax, rolling quietly through my body. A soft whimper escaped my throat and my back arched, bending with the pleasure. It definitely felt good, but after the weeks and weeks of tension, I wished it had been more. Though I'd faked several on more than one occasion, I wasn't a multiple O kind of girl. So this subtle serene orgasm was going to have to do.

But then Edward was there, still dressed, leaning over my torso, a hand braced at the base of my throat, the other pushing two long fingers inside me while his thumb rubbed roughly at my clit.

"I suppose I have to do this myself, don't I? Since you can't seem to get it right on your own." He hovered just above me, his breath hot on my skin while he expertly massaged my G-spot with each stroke of his fingers.

And somehow—impossibly—another orgasm racked through me with surprising speed and intensity.

"Yes, yes," I panted as my body shook with the release.

"Pitiable," Edward said, increasing the pressure on my clit. "You can do better than that. I thought you wanted this. I thought you wanted my cock."

"I do, I do!"

"Prove it, then. Show me how good your cunt will treat my cock. As of now, you don't deserve it." He added a third finger, and now he was truly fucking me with his hand, each thrust penetrating deep.

It was more than I could take, another orgasm already brewing low in my belly like a tumultuous storm, and I felt the impulse to push him away. Yet at the same time, my hips bucked up to meet each piercing stab, and the breathy words escaping from my lips were, "More! Please! More!"

Then it was upon me, a hurricane of a climax, whirling through me with violent fury. Black holes spread across my vision while tears leaked from my eyes.

"Ah, fuuuucccck!" I barely recognized the gutteral moan coming from my mouth as mine. My fingers curled desperately into the bedspread at my sides. Sweat poured down my face, and my entire body went stiff, shaking uncontrollably while my pussy pulsed and clenched.

In the back of my head, I was vaguely aware of Edward still there, talking to me with urging words that I was too brainless to understand. One hand still sat heavily across my nape like a collar, but his other hand disappeared and a second later I heard the familiar unzipping sound of a zipper.

I was still vibrating when the head of his cock brushed across my entrance. "I'm not stopping to look for a condom, and I don't trust you with my cum, even if you say you're on birth control, so I'll be pulling out."

Without any other warning, he shoved inside of me on a low grunt.

And, holy shit, he was big.

I'd known he was big, but the visual evidence was much different than the tactile evidence. His girth filled me completely, pressed firmly against my walls. Each stroke in and out massaged places inside of me that had never been touched, and oh my God, I was definitely going to come again.

My heels flew off as my legs and arms went instinctively around him, both to bring him closer and to keep him from going anywhere. Oh, and also to hold on for my own dear life, because he rode me rough with deep, rapid jabs.

Even at his ferocious tempo, he barely broke a sweat. I was breathless and wild underneath him while he seemed almost unaffected.

His eyes, though. His eyes gave him away. I'd closed mine briefly first, and then I'd opened them to find him studying me intently with his heavily lidded blues. I had no idea what he saw in me, but what I saw made my stomach fly into my chest. There was a softness there I'd never seen in him before. A tenderness completely out of character.

Had that look always been there? Hidden by a grave exterior, did that look live beneath in the same way a nuclear core of emotion dwelt concealed inside of me?

I didn't know, but I hoped so. I liked that look. I wanted to hold onto it. I clung to it with my gaze, and brought my hands from his shoulders up to cradle his face.

He flinched at the touch, and growled. His hand moved to tangle in my hair, and he pulled viciously, as he had earlier. The message was clear—he'd fuck me, but he didn't want it to be intimate.

But he'd started it first, with that softness in his eyes, and I wasn't going to be outdone. I refused to remove my hands, even as his thrusts grew more brutal, and he shifted his pelvis to torment and brush against my sensitive clit.

It was a battle, his resolve against mine. His determination to stay cruel and hard versus my insistence to see more of the kindness peeking out from underneath.

And when his mouth crashed down against mine, and his lips kissed hungrily at mine, I claimed victory as mine. Because that kiss —*that kiss*, with its persistent strokes of his tongue and greedy nips of his teeth—that kiss was generous and warm and affectionate. That kiss was kindling, and as I clutched my fingers in his hair and devoured what he gave, another powerful orgasm surged through me.

"No, you don't push me out," he said, as I clamped down around his cock, a ruthless smile on the lips that had just been locked with mine. "You let me in when I want in." He pushed harder, forcing his way through the clenching walls of my pussy.

When he was deeply seated, his cock buried inside me to the root, he leaned his forehead against mine, and in my hazy post-orgasm state, I may have heard wrong, but I swear he whispered, "It wasn't supposed to be like this. You weren't supposed to be like this."

And, for the briefest of moments, I considered abandoning The Game. Considered trying to be an honest wife. Considered trying to win his heart. To win his love.

Then he changed entirely.

Without disconnecting from me, he stood up to his full height, and pulled me closer to the edge of the bed, lifting my hips to meet his. Here, he pounded angrily into me, as though he were mad at me. As though he wanted to annihilate my pussy as punishment.

If that truly was what he wanted, to destroy me, I wasn't going to fight him. I was weak and boneless, and that could have been a decent excuse for letting him handle me in that manner, but it wouldn't have been honest. I let him because I wanted it, wanted his malice as much as I wanted any of him.

And even while I still had him, I wanted him. Wanted more of him. Wanted *all* of him.

After a few minutes of his ruthless driving, he pulled out and with his hand wrapped around his glistening cock, he jerked furiously toward his climax.

Wanting all of him as I did, I sat up and reached for him. I wanted that glorious cock. I wanted to touch it and tug it, and if he wasn't going to release inside my cunt, I wanted his cum on my belly, on my hands. In my mouth.

But he stepped back, away from me, and a second later, he came, spilling milky white liquid over his hand. And if I for one instant thought he hadn't done it purposefully, that he hadn't done it specifically to deny me, his spiteful expression set me straight.

Like I'd said—he was an asshole.

Well, I could be an asshole too. As though I hadn't just come a miraculous four times—a mind-blowing four times—I pouted. "I thought I wasn't supposed to be able to walk afterward."

"Normally, that would be true. Consider this a wedding gift. I hope you enjoyed it because it won't happen again." He pulled up his pants, leaving them unzipped, the crown of his cock peeking out.

"Good. I'm ready for whatever it is you prefer." It was a lie. One thing this experience had taught me was I was not at all prepared for Edward Fasbender.

He smiled condescendingly. "I meant we won't be having sex again at all." Before I could argue, he went on. "I'm going to take a shower. I'll say good night now since you'll be gone by the time I'm done."

It was a hard and clear dismissal.

Fuming, I stared daggers into his backside as he disappeared into his en suite. Then I sat for long minutes, listening to the sound of the water turn on and the change in its spray when the firm body of the man who'd just fucked me stepped into it. Exhaustion had returned, and though the sex had been vanilla, my thighs ached when I stood, and my pussy felt raw and sore.

I snatched my panties and my heels off the floor and retreated into my own room.

The fighting was over for the night. Each of us could claim at least one victory, but this wasn't over. There would be more battles in the future. We were married now.

And this marriage was war.

TWENTY-EIGHT

I AWOKE in the morning ready for our next skirmish.

Edward had risen earlier than me, though, so I was alone when Jeremy took my breakfast order. Camilla showed up just as I'd been served, but as soon as she saw me, she declared she and Freddie would be taking their meal in her suite and marched right back out.

Good for them. It wasn't like I wanted a side of noisy toddler and bitchy sister-in-law with my yogurt parfait.

Afterward, there was only time to finish packing my suitcase before we were to leave for our "honeymoon." Edward spent the entire forty-minute ride to Heathrow conducting last-minute business over the phone, which might have felt like a disappointing opportunity lost to needle him if we weren't about to be alone together for ten hours on a plane.

"I always forget how fast boarding is when flying private carrier," I said as we climbed the steps of Edward's Gulfstream G650.

He'd barely spoken two words to me all morning, and I suspected he wanted to forget yesterday—more specifically, last night—had ever happened, but now he turned to me in surprise. "Your father doesn't have his own jet?"

I shook my head, knowing this admission would only further inflate his ego. It was probably good to give him a win every now and then, especially when it was such a trivial win. "He thinks they're too much hassle. He prefers to fly first-class commercial."

"'*Too much hassle.*' What a lazy bastard." His chin rose smugly as he took one of the front most seats.

I gave my coat to the attendant to hang up then surveyed the plane. There was a seat available facing Edward as well as one across the aisle. There were at least six other places to sit including a sofa and comfy chairs around a dining table.

Naturally, I took the seat across from him. "I've flown private several times, though." I didn't want him to think I was unsophisticated, and it was the truth. Hudson's parents had their own jet that we'd all used to take joint family vacations, back when the Pierces and Werners still got along. Then, later, Hudson had purchased his own plane that we'd used to travel the world.

This plane was admittedly more luxurious. More pretentious, too.

Edward scowled at me. "There are plenty of places to sit. Don't feel obligated to take the seat closest to me."

I couldn't decide if the rejection stung or if it was a sign I was getting under his skin. "Don't be silly. You expect your wife always at your side. Here I am."

"Well. I may not be here long. It's a long flight. I might take a nap." He smiled at the pretty brunette attendant as she handed him the copy of *The Times* he'd requested before we boarded.

Too friendly of a smile, if anyone asked me.

"Oh, good," I said, refusing to let my feathers be ruffled. "I was thinking I'd do the same. There's only one bed it seems, so we'll have to share." I gave him my own too friendly grin.

"That won't be necessary. The sofa folds into a second bed, though I don't think we'll need to use that if we take turns in the bedroom. In fact, why don't you take yours now?" He smirked, then his features softened as his eyes traveled behind us.

"I'm not sleepy, yet. Thank you." I followed the line of his gaze and found it latched on the attendant's backside as she shut the cabin door. "Ah, I see. You'd prefer some alone time with one of your whores."

"I wouldn't call Carlotta a whore. There's never been money exchanged in our...*friendship.*"

I suddenly wondered if the cabin had a knife sharp enough for human mutilation. Surely it did. Now to decide if it would best be used on Carlotta or my husband.

The witch approached us then. "We're ready for takeoff, sir."

I didn't miss how Edward's eyes lit up at the word *sir.* "Tell the pilot we're ready as well, then. That will be all, Carlotta, dear." His tone was thick and sultry and irritating.

I remembered then that words made excellent daggers. "There is one more thing, actually, *Carla, dear.*" I'd totally said her name wrong on purpose. "I'm not sure if Edward has told you or not, but we were married yesterday. Whatever ways you may have served my husband on these flights in the past will no longer be necessary, as I am his wife and can attend to his *needs* myself."

He'd said I had to respect him in public. He'd never said anything about respecting his women.

"Yes, Mrs. Fasbender," the tramp said curtly before taking her seat for lift off.

Edward began unfolding his newspaper, seemingly unruffled. "I must say, Celia, jealousy doesn't look good on you."

But I'd seen the hint of admiration in his features before he'd schooled them, a hint that said he very much liked the look on me, despite himself.

He hid behind his paper then, and I let him read unbothered while we took flight. I was a nervous flier, a fact I'd never admit, and the climb in the beginning always made me particularly anxious. I couldn't deal with Edward while I needed all my bandwidth to keep settled.

Once we were at cruising altitude, though, I could breathe easier, and I turned my attention back to the man across from me. I'd worn a sundress in preparation for the heat at our destination—okay, and because he'd once suggested he liked me in sundresses. Edward, though, had dressed for the cool temperature of London in a cowl neck blue-gray sweater and dark slacks. It was a casual look for him, but somehow he still appeared regal and distinguished. A magnificent savage beast.

It was hard to look at him now without remembering every detail of the night before. The way his touch had consumed me. The way his cock had moved inside me. The way his mouth had tasted. The way he'd let his guard down and shown me a sliver of what he hid inside.

They were sensory memories, and they made me feel hot and restless and desperate to have him again.

Which, apparently wasn't going to happen on the flight to the Caribbean, and even so, I wanted him. Wanted anything he'd give me in the meantime.

"Any news worth sharing?" I asked, hoping to draw him out.

He didn't even move the paper to look at me. "Nope."

I sighed.

"There's no story about Edward Fasbender's wedding? I thought you were too important not to get a mention." That ought to rile him up.

"No, we were mentioned. I didn't consider that news worth sharing since you already knew."

My eyes widened in surprise. "Really? What did it say?"

"You're welcome to read the paper when I'm finished," he said, clearly uninterested in conversation.

Ass.

"When do we arrive again?"

"We should land about four p.m. island time. It's a ten-hour flight. If you're bored already, I highly suggest you find something to do." He bent the corner of his paper down so I could see his face. "Something that doesn't involve me."

"I'm not bored, you jerk. It was a reasonable question." I quieted for a few minutes, staring out the window at the pool of clouds below us.

All right, I *was* bored.

"You know, you haven't told me anything about where we're going. Do we land in Nassau and then take a boat? Are there other people on the island? Will the flight crew be staying with us?" More importantly, would Carlotta also be there?

He shut his paper and folded it once to sit on his lap. "The crew will refuel and return to London tomorrow. There are other people in my company who use the plane to conduct business. The crew will return again in two weeks to pick us up.

"As for the island, it's five hundred and fifty acres located about fourteen miles off the coast of Exuma and has its own airstrip. The entire island belongs exclusively to me, but there are staff members who live there year round. They'll pick us up when we land and take care of all our needs while we're there."

"Any of those staff members part of your tribe of whores?" The possibility hadn't even occurred to me until just then. "Oops. I mean *friends*, not whores."

"Actually..."

My stomach dropped, and it had nothing to do with turbulence.

He chuckled. "No," he said taking pity on me. "They're a family, and while many of them are female, they're all either married, children, or old enough to be my grandmother."

"That's awfully ageist." I wasn't fooling anyone—I was relieved.

"Azariah is a lovely woman who I'm sure you'll get along with quite well. Even retired, she's feisty and bullheaded." He sounded proud, and that made my chest warm, both because I'd rarely heard him speak about another person with such reverence and because he'd equated the woman to me.

"I like her already." I thought about what else he'd said. "You hired a family? How did that work?"

"It sort of fell into place. I wanted to find a Caribbean vacation spot as a birthday present for myself when I turned thirty. So I spent several days in the Bahamas looking for the property I wanted to purchase and became quite fond of the woman that worked at the hotel I was staying in, on New Providence.

"Not *that* kind of fond," he corrected, probably noting the look on my face. "She was a cook. I fell in love with her food. After I found the island, I asked Joette if she'd come back to London with me to be our personal chef. She declined, saying all her family was in Nassau. She went on to say she was the sole caretaker of her mother, and explained what a burden that had been since her husband had died the year before and she now had to both look after Azariah and work a full-time job. The hotel had also recently laid off a bunch of employees for the off-season including two of her sons. She still had a daughter working there with her, but their hours had been cut."

He paused a moment, remembering. "I knew what it was like to have to unexpectedly care for a family member and to not have the income to do so, and I suppose that's what gave me the idea to ask her if she and the children working with her would like to work for me, taking care of the island. She was delighted, and in the end, all five of her children moved over with her, as well as their spouses."

"And her mother," I added, assumingly. "That's an awfully generous offer. Especially coming from you. I never took you as a philanthropist."

"I'm not," he said sharply, as though the compliment had offended him. I suspected that it wasn't so much that he felt insulted as it was that he didn't like anyone knowing he had a kind bone in his body. "There is more than enough work for all of them, and it's a comfort to me to know that Amelie is being taken care of while I'm away."

"Amelie?" The name was familiar. "You named the island after your mother?"

"Yes. After my mother. Now, if you don't mind..." He took up his paper again and opened it up, putting the barrier back in between us.

I didn't mind. He'd revealed something, and not just that he wasn't completely heartless. Something that I'd been curious about.

He'd revealed that he truly did have fond feelings for his mother, fond enough to name a paradise island in her memory.

I closed my eyes and leaned back against the headrest, a smile on my lips, and fell asleep twisting Amelie's rings around my finger.

TWENTY-NINE

WE LANDED late afternoon to an eighty-degree temperature and a balmy breeze that smelled like fresh seawater. I'd watched from the plane as we descended, realizing how small the stingray-shaped island looked from the sky. Even down on the ground, it was small, less than a square mile of land. It was nice that Edward had permanent residents to care for Amelie, but man, didn't they get stir-crazy?

It would be a fantastic vacation spot, though, with its long stretches of white sand and the crystal clear, turquoise waters on all sides. Very romantic, and not much room for Edward to escape. Perfect for my seduction plans.

The airstrip was on the side of the island opposite to where the main living quarters were located. Mateo and Louvens, Joette's two oldest sons, met our plane with two jeeps—one for me and Edward and the other for the small flight crew. I was happy to find we wouldn't be riding with Carlotta, and even more delighted to discover that Louvens was taking the crew directly to the guest houses, almost a quarter of a mile away from the main house. They also had their own kitchens there, which meant I wouldn't have to see the woman again until we went home in two weeks.

It took only five minutes to drive along the perimeter of the island to the house, a stunning two-story Mediterranean style structure with exquisite columns, arches, balconies, and iron detailing as well as a cobblestone courtyard in front of it. I learned from Mateo on the drive over that it had been rebuilt when Edward bought the island, replacing an imposing castle that had stood there before. He'd left the almost two-mile network of paths that stretched south and west, though, making the island easy to get around by foot. The road didn't go as far, only extending along half of the perimeter.

The inside of the house was as spectacular as the outside, encompassing over ten thousand square feet of space. The ceilings were high, and the floorplan was original and open, connecting the living spaces without doors in between them. The gorgeous arches and columns from the exterior were repeated in here, but the highlight was the pocket glass sliders that ran between the family room and the covered lanai.

No, that wasn't the highlight. The real highlight was the backyard with its outdoor kitchen, hot tub, and a pool that spread across the length of the back of the house. There was only a handful of yards of patio beyond the pool before running into the smoothly raked beach and the cerulean waters of the Caribbean.

It was truly paradise.

My only complaint was the layout of the bedrooms. Unlike the setup at the London house, the two master suites were on opposite sides of the main floor here, with all the shared living spaces in between. They were nearly identical in structure, each with its own en suite, walk-in closet, and sitting room with glass pocket sliders that opened up to the backyard like the family room.

Like both the London house and the Accelecom office, the decor of the Amelie house was traditional, but the style was looser. Edward's bedroom was done in a striking red and gold, and while I would definitely have taken it further if I had the chance, it wasn't a bad design.

My room, on the other hand, left a lot to be desired.

The hardwood floor was covered with a gray shag that matched the bedding. The walls were a boring yellowish brown, the curtains were a plain white, and the furniture was too modern for the rest of the house.

Architecturally, it was charming, but all the interest in the room had been dulled down.

"It was decorated to Marion's specifications," Edward told me later when I complained.

We'd been on the island almost three hours and were eating dinner in the formal dining room at the front of the house. I'd suggested dining in the smaller, radial dinette that overlooked the backyard, but he'd said it wasn't big enough.

It wasn't big enough, I discovered, because, while we weren't joined by the flight crew, we were joined by several of the staff members that lived permanently on the island. It had come as a surprise when, after Joette and Tom, her oldest daughter, finished cooking the food, they carried it out to the table to be served family style and then sat down with us along with Mateo and his wife Sany-jah, Louvens, and Tom's husband, Peter. Jeremy would never have dined with us in England. Edward had a strictly formal relationship with his staff there. Here, he was relaxed and familiar and almost friendly.

"You won't mind if I redecorate it then," I said, hoping his friendlier mood extended to me as well.

"Eh," he finished swallowing the bite of rock lobster he'd just put in his mouth and washed it down with a swallow of chablis. "We really aren't going to be here that long. Can't you live with it for now?"

"Of course I can." I knew the rules and didn't want to argue in front of others.

But there was a difference between arguing and discussing. "I didn't mean right now anyway. I'm sure we'll be back here in the future though. I could take the measurements while we're here and work on it from London. I'd spend my own money, naturally."

His smile was forced. "We can discuss it more later."

We couldn't discuss it later, though, because dinner went long with Mateo and Louvens entertaining us with tales of island life since the last time Edward had been there. Then there were the updates on the family members that hadn't attended dinner and the children—apparently there were fourteen kids under the age of eighteen. Shockingly,

Edward knew the name of every one of them and asked about each of them by name.

So much for the notion that he hated children.

Then after dinner, he disappeared into his library to share a drink with the men, and though I'd meant to stay awake planning to attack him with my feminine wiles, the travel and the time change caught up to me, and I fell asleep in an armchair in my sitting room.

We have two weeks, I told myself as sleep closed in on me. I'd have my chance to be alone with him later.

THIRTY

A WEEK LATER, I still hadn't managed any one-on-one time with my husband.

He was avoiding me.

Mornings he left early for a run around the island. When I asked to go with him, he allowed it, but he didn't alter his pace and there was no way I could keep up with his long stride. Breakfasts he took by himself in his sitting room, and no matter how hard I tried to get him to let me join him, he always refused.

The rest of the day he spent working in the library. If I happened to come by for a book or some paper to write on or even if I decided to lounge on the patio outside the floor-to-ceiling windows of the room, he'd move into his study and lock the door only opening it for Joette when she brought him his lunch.

With nothing else to do, I passed my time walking on the beach, swimming in the pool, and reading while lounging on the lanai. There wasn't much else to do. The internet on the island was spotty at best, and I couldn't even download anything to my ereader. Thank goodness Edward had a pretty extensive collection of books in the library or I would have died of boredom. After only a few days into our honeymoon, I'd finished four full-length novels and gotten a pretty decent tan. I was the picture-perfect trophy wife, exactly what my husband had wanted.

Dinners continued to be spent as a group, though the family members that joined us weren't always the same. I soon met Erris and Dreya, Joette's youngest son and daughter, as well as both of their wives, Marge and Eliana. The kids never came to the house, and neither did Azariah, but I had a feeling Edward snuck away to visit them all during the day when I wasn't aware because of some of the things that were said over supper.

Evenings were always spent divided—the men in the library smoking cigars and drinking cognac and the women not allowed. It was old-fashioned and gross, and though I had a standing invitation to join the ladies on the lanai, I usually retreated to my bedroom.

On day seven, I couldn't take it anymore. I'd come here to seduce my husband. Not only did I need Edward to have sex with me in order to carry out my plan, but I needed him to feel comfortable having *his* kind of sex. Mean and sadistic kind of sex. And it wasn't going to happen as long as we had guests encroaching on our time together.

Determined to kick everyone out, I stood outside the library and took a few deep breaths, trying to get up the nerve. He'd be mad that I made a scene, I was well aware. I could live with that. Maybe it would even lead to some kinky form of punishment.

One could dream.

"You must be furious at that one for spending so much time with them," Tom said, coming up behind me. She spoke in the typical Bahamian dialect, dropping sounds, so what she'd said sounded like *Ya mus be furious a dat one for spendin so much time wit dem.* It had taken me a day or two to get used to it, but now I barely had to ask anyone to repeat anything. "You should do something about it."

"I'm planning to. I was just about to go in there and tell everyone they had to go home." I didn't need anyone's permission to do it, but it was so nice to have someone sympathize with my situation that I couldn't help leaning on her for reassurance.

"Mmm," she said with a frown. "Are you sure that's such a good idea? Edward doesn't seem to take kindly to folks confronting him. Unless it's Azariah. She has that man wrapped around her finger."

I never thought I'd be as jealous of an eighty-five-year-old woman as I was of Azariah.

And now I was doubting myself. "What do you suggest I do? It's our honeymoon, for crying out loud."

"What you need to do is put on something really sexy like and flaunt around in front of those windows. He'll take notice and kick the boys to the curb."

It wasn't a bad idea. I'd tried to do exactly that several times already, putting on a revealing swimsuit and prancing in front of the windows. But since Edward had holed himself off in his study, he'd never been around to see.

I hadn't considered trying it late at night. Now that I had…it was brilliant.

Thanking her, I excused myself and ran to my bedroom to change into my skimpiest bikini—I'd brought one for each day of our trip, all of them pretty risque. Red seemed to be my power color as far as Edward was concerned, and the classic string variety was never a bad choice.

A few minutes later, I strode out onto the lanai from my sitting room wearing nothing but my red string bikini and a strappy pair of Louboutin wedge sandals.

"Look at you!" Tom said, while the other women cat-called.

"I was just thinking I'd take a swim," I said innocently, walking over to join them. They were sitting out of the sightline of the library, but I had to pass them to get there and it would have been rude not to at least talk to them first.

"You're not fooling anyone," Eliana said. "You're here to catch the attention of that beefcake husband of yours."

Everyone laughed—not *at* me in that awkward embarrassing way, but conspiratorially. The kind of laugh that was nice to get.

"Sit down and have a drink with us first," Joette said. "The men are in there drinking brandy, but we have the good stuff—Sky Juice." She held up a white-colored drink that looked like milk with ice. In other words, disgusting.

But the women were friendly, and it had been so long since I'd had companionship... "Sure. I'll take one."

"You can have mine. Just made it," Tom said. "I'll go whip up another for myself."

I sat down on a lounge chair and took a sip of the beverage, which turned out to be a concoction of sweetened condensed milk, gin, and coconut water. Generally, I didn't like sweet alcoholic drinks—and this one was particularly sweet—but, right now, with the sound of the ocean crashing on the nearby shore and the Caribbean breeze carrying the salty garden scent of the island, it seemed fitting.

I drank slowly, chatting with the women while I did. They were very different than the people I usually spent time with, very down-to-earth and unbothered. Back in New York, everyone seemed to always be rushing around doing Important Things and swallowing down Xanax with their Phentermine like they were the secrets to success. Even though I'd been gone from that world for several months now, my brain still operated at the same speed. Talking to the islanders made me slow down, made my thoughts pause. It was nice to have the change of pace.

While we didn't talk about much that was important, I did learn a few things, such as that Eliana was Dreya's second spouse. She'd been married to Louvens previously, but once they'd all moved to the island together, she'd fallen in love with his little sister, which seemed pretty scandalous for such a tight-knit group. The strangest part was that they all still lived here.

"Because of the children," Eliana said. "Louvens is a good father."

"And we'd never want to split up the family," Dreya agreed.

I also learned that the segregated after-dinner arrangement was new. Edward had apparently never employed it in the past.

"When Camilla is here, and when he was married to Marion, everyone usually hangs out together," Joette said.

"If we even stay after dinner," Tom added. "Most times we go straight home."

It was because of me. He was definitely avoiding me.

But it was a relief to know that he wasn't as archaic in his traditions as he'd made me believe.

The women seemed to realize it had to do with me, as well. "He's nervous around such a pretty bride," Dreya said.

"I doubt that's it," I protested.

"Maybe he's forgotten what to do in the bedroom," Joette giggled.

"No, he definitely hasn't forgotten." We'd only been together that one time, but he'd definitely known what he was doing.

At this rate, though, I was going to forget. "Well, ladies, I think it's time to do my thing." I swallowed back the last of my cocktail. I was just starting to feel the buzz—Tom made her drinks strong—and it was exactly the confidence I'd needed for my strutting.

"We'll get ready to go," Joette said. "I have a feeling we're about to be sent home."

I prayed she was right.

Throwing my shoulders back, I paraded along the line of the house, passing the rest of the family room windows, circling along the curve of the dinette, finally ending up at the library.

Here I paused to stretch, exaggeratedly, making sure all my best features were on display. I could feel eyes watching me, which could have been all in my head, because I refused to look. The outside lights were on, though, and the entire backyard was illuminated, so at least I knew I wasn't being swallowed up in the dark of night.

Assuming I had his attention, I sat down on one of the deck chairs and stretched a long leg out and removed first one sandal than the other. When they were off, I stood up again, turning toward the pool so that my backside faced the library windows. I adjusted my bikini bottoms, pulling them out of my butt crack where they'd bunched up when I sat, then strutted to the pool and jumped in.

It was only five minutes later that our guests were gone. I was swimming laps, but I heard Mateo come out and call the ladies inside. A minute later the family room doors slid shut, the lights went off, and the whole middle section of the house was dark.

I finished my lap and only then, did I look for Edward.

I found him immediately, standing at the library window, one hand holding a drink, the other shoved into his trouser pocket, his eyes pinned on me.

Even through the glass and the ten yards that separated us, I could feel his angry, rabid want. It was lasered in my direction like a death ray, ready to obliterate me at a moment's notice.

I was instantly wet, and not just because I was standing chest-deep in the swimming pool.

We stayed like that for what felt like forever, our stares intense, each of us waiting for the other to call chicken. When it was clear he wasn't going to make the next move, I decided that I would. I'd started this, after all. Might as well finish it.

Never taking my eyes off his, I stalked out of the pool. I'd forgotten to bring a towel—*whoops*—so I was wet and dripping as I moved toward him. As I passed the outdoor shower—a single pipe coming out of the ground with two heads—I decided I wasn't done taunting him. I turned on the water and waited for it to heat up before standing beneath it, letting the spray fall over my hair and down my back.

Still, I watched him. Watched him watching me as I reached behind me and pulled the strings of my top and let it fall on the ground in front of me. Next, I untied first one side of the bottoms, then the other, until I was standing naked under the rushing stream.

He'd never seen me completely naked, and if I'd ever thought he never had the interest, that thought was proven entirely false when Edward pulled his hand from his pocket and braced it against the window above him, as if he needed the support to stand.

I understood the feeling. My knees felt weak, too, even as I felt stronger than I had all week. Bolder than I had in months.

I'd gotten him. He'd come to me now. There was no way he could resist.

Relishing in the early satisfaction of victory, I closed my eyes and threw back my head, bringing my hands up to cup my aching breasts then sweep down to rub against the swollen lips between my thighs.

And I waited. Waited for the sound of a door sliding open. Waited for his footsteps across the cement patio.

When a couple of minutes had passed with no sound and no

Edward, I opened my eyes again. The library was dark. No one stood watching me at the glass. I was alone outside.

I scanned the windows looking for him inside. A second later a light turned on his bedroom. Then he was in his sitting room, and I held my breath, waiting for him to open his patio door and summon me inside.

But he only closed the curtains, cutting off my view to his bedroom. Cutting off my view to him.

And I knew without actually trying that, if I went to his patio door on my own, I'd discover that it was locked.

THIRTY-ONE

I WOKE up the next day with new determination. The previous night hadn't played out the way I'd wanted, that was certainly true. But it was the closest I'd been in a week to seeing Edward crack. My behavior had had an effect.

Obviously, that meant I should do more of the same.

I'd set my phone alarm extra early and dressed in short shorts and a sexy sports bra—not one of those ones that squished everything together, but a Brazilian design that resembled a bikini top with black mesh that showed off a whole lot of breast. I gathered my hair into a ponytail, put on my running shoes, and then, instead of asking Edward if I could join him on his morning run, I snuck outside and kept out of sight behind the trees at the end of the courtyard.

I had to wait around almost half an hour until he showed up, but when he did, I slipped out of my hiding spot and jogged up next to him. "Oh, hey. I was just taking my run too. I'll tag along."

He grunted, his eyes sweeping down my body, lingering on my cleavage, then, as I'd predicted, he took off at a sprint I couldn't keep up with.

It was all good. Keeping up wasn't the goal.

I'd only run with him twice since we'd been on the island, and I knew from that, and from watching him, that he went the same way every time, going east along the network of paths and then north until the trail ended. Then he took to the beach and followed the shoreline south until he returned to the house.

I also knew from my conversation with the women the night before that Erris and his wife Marge, were the official gardeners, and today, along with Louvens' help, they planned to cut back some plants that had been damaged in the last big storm on the southwest shores of the island—right along the last quarter of Edward's run.

So, instead of dragging behind Edward, I took my own course, veering west to the beach. I jogged along the coast until I spotted the three working in the brush. I waved at them enthusiastically, so enthusiastically that I "forgot" to watch where I was going and "tripped" over myself. I went down flat on my ass.

Yeah, I totally faked it. I was a pro at this shit.

The three gardners ran over to me immediately, making a big fuss with, "Are you all right?" and, "Do you think you can walk?"

I assured them I could, but Louvens and Erris helped me up anyway, and as soon as I put weight on my right ankle, I pretended to cry out in pain.

"I think I twisted my ankle," I said, grimacing.

"I'll help you back to the house," Louvens volunteered.

Perfection.

He'd already been the one of the three who couldn't take his eyes off my breasts. I mean, they looked good. It wasn't his fault. He was actually a decent guy, and not that I believed that a woman's clothing choice allowed men to do what they want with her, but if I wore something provocative, I certainly expected people to look.

I'd assumed that when he offered to help, Louvens meant that I could lean on him as I hobbled back to the house.

Nope. He lifted me into his arms and proceeded to *carry* me. The man was so much cooler than I'd predicted. Stronger too.

And my timing was impeccable, because when we were just out of sight of the others, about halfway to our destination, Edward came running by, finishing up his course.

"What's going on? What happened?" He was breathless from exercise, genuine concern etched in his features.

"Mrs. Fasbender had a fall and twisted her ankle," Louvens said.

"Oh, Louvens," I said, pouring on the sweetness. "You should really call me Celia." His face happened to already be at chest level, but I pushed my shoulders back so my breasts would be even closer. As a reward for being so heroic, of course.

He really was an attractive guy, I noticed now. Very muscular. The kind of muscular that was earned by good old-fashioned hard work and outdoor sport rather than scheduled exercise.

Edward glowered, and I could see the debate in his eyes. Should he offer to carry me back himself? Should he let his single handyman do it, knowing his scantily dressed wife would flirt with him all the way there?

Edward was a different kind of fit, with a long lean runner's body and tight muscles from regular weight-lifting. He was definitely capable of hauling me himself, and I suspected, that his deep sense of possessiveness would never allow him to let another man so close to me, no matter what he said about letting me sleep with other people.

Or maybe that was just how I wished he felt.

Because the devil only said, "That's very kind of you, Louvens. I would have made her tough it out herself. What's a little pain, after all?" He looked specifically at me when he said that. Then back to Louvens. "Good luck making it all the way back to the house."

He took off, resuming his earlier swift pace.

Fucking asshole.

"I can make it, Mrs—Celia. Don't worry." Louvens proved himself, barely breaking a sweat before he approached the back patio.

Edward, on the other hand, faltered. He belied his detached, cruel facade when I spotted him watching for me at the library window. Just as he had the night before, he kept his eyes pinned on me until I was safely back on the ground and Louvens had said goodbye. Only when he was walking away did Edward disappear back to his desk.

And then I had another idea.

"Who cares for the pool?" I asked Tom later that afternoon.

"Mateo. He does everything with the water. The boats, the pool, the fountains." She was putting away groceries from Eliana's earlier mainland run.

I leaned my hip against the kitchen island. "Boats?"

"Do you want Mateo to take you out?"

Not at the moment, but it would have been nice to at least been told of the option. *Thank you, Edward. Not.*

"No, no. Not today, thanks. But I think the chemical balance is off in the pool. It has a weird odor that it didn't have yesterday."

"I'll call him to come out," she said, pulling out a jar of Blow Pops and placing it on the counter.

"Thanks. Oh, and can I have one of those?" I pointed to the candy.

"Help yourself."

Awesome. I could use a prop.

When Mateo arrived a half an hour later, I walked out wearing designer sunglasses, high-heel sandals, and a strappy white bikini that was so skimpy it could barely be called clothing. The bottoms had the smallest strip of material possible to cover the crotch and the top was only a band along the bottom, two thin straps going up around the neck, and flesh-colored mesh over the breasts with a cutout daisy-shaped flower covering the nipples. To top it all off, I was sucking on a big red Blow Pop.

In other words, I was walking porn.

I pulled the Blow Pop from my mouth and squatted next to Mateo where he was stooped to check the pool's chemical levels. "What does the reader thingy say?" I asked.

I didn't really care about the answer, but he was facing the house, and though I wasn't even sure Edward was currently in the library, I wanted to be seen talking to yet another man if he was.

"It's, uh." He glanced over at my breasts—because breasts—then quickly looked away, his cheeks reddening. "Well, the salinity looks good." He hit a button on the reader. "And the PH level looks okay too. But let me try the manual color tester just to be sure."

"Oh. Is the machine thing not always accurate?" I heard the slide of a glass door, but I forced myself not to look up. For all I knew, it could be Tom bringing out iced tea. She was really thoughtful like that.

But in case it wasn't Tom, I put the Blow Pop back in my mouth. My lips and tongue were already cherry red from the candy. I'd checked before I came out.

Mateo was more modest than Louvens, but always eager to share knowledge. "The digital tester is accurate as long as it's calibrated correctly. The color tester is more work, but a little more reliable. I just need to—"

"Is something wrong with the pool?" Edward's voice boomed from the lanai.

Bingo.

I looked up at my husband but let Mateo answer. "Nah. Just testing the chemicals," he said.

Edward came closer, stopping at the edge of the pool across from us. "I thought you tested it on Friday."

"I did, but Celia..." We were still crouched down, my cleavage still prominently on display so when Mateo glanced over to gesture at me, he once again caught an eye-full.

Quickly, he stood up, his cheeks going brighter than the last time. "Mrs. Fasbender, I mean, noticed a strange scent," he said to his boss.

Edward crossed his arms over his chest. "Oh, did she, now." He was clearly displeased.

Slowly I rose to my full height and pulled the Blow Pop from my mouth. "It's probably just my nose. I think it's clogged or something. I must be getting a cold." I draped a hand on Mateo's shoulder. "I'm so sorry to make you come all the way over here for something so silly."

Edward's eyes narrowed.

Mateo glanced at my hand then to my husband then back at my hand. He swallowed. "It's not a problem. It's my job."

"You'd better come on inside and rest then, darling. Fight that cold before it settles in."

"I guess that's my cue to say goodbye," I said, too quietly for Edward to hear. Leaning in, I placed a sugary kiss on Mateo's cheek then sauntered around the pool toward the other side.

Edward watched me the whole way.

"Are you going to come tuck me in, my dear husband?" I asked when I was closer.

God, the look on his face. He wanted to hurt me.

It was fantastic.

I wished he would.

"The point is rest, not recreation," Edward said, specifically for Mateo. There hadn't been any "recreation" between us since we'd arrived on the island, and no reason for me to think it was happening now, no matter how much I wanted it.

"I don't think there's much of a difference when it comes to us," I said coldly and softly enough that no one heard but him. I was almost to him now. The patio was large enough that there was no need to get this close, but there had also been no need for Mateo to come over and measure the pool chemicals.

Edward said nothing until I brushed past him. Then he grabbed my arm, firmly, and yanked me toward him.

Yes, yes! He was effected. He was cracking. He was losing control, and any minute now he'd have to kiss me.

Would it be now?

I held my breath and waited, my heart thundering in my chest, my skin burning under his grip.

His gaze lowered to my lips, but he didn't lean in. "I thought you twisted your ankle."

"Oh." I lifted my leg and circled my foot around. "I guess it's better now." I held up the Blow Pop and gave it an exaggerated lick with my tongue. Since he hadn't made good use of my mouth, I reminded him what he was missing.

His eye ticked. "Careful, Celia. You're pushing me."

Good. That was the whole idea.

He let go of my arm with a flourish, almost like he was throwing it away. Throwing *me* away.

I shook myself and lifted my shoulders back proudly. Then I popped the sucker back in my mouth and went into the house, letting him watch me walk away.

THIRTY-TWO

I'D GONE BACK to my suite when Edward ordered me there, took off my shoes and sunglasses, and plopped onto the bed, hoping he'd follow in after me, despite what he'd said.

I must have fallen asleep because, next thing I knew, I was having one of the baby dreams I sometimes had. It was different than usual, though. Instead of being hazy and still, it was vivid and full of motion. Normally I only *felt* like I was in it, but this time I could actually see myself.

There was a man, as always, and for the first time, *he* was holding the baby. But he was in front of me so I could only see his backside and the baby bundle over his shoulder, and I wanted to get to him—get to both of them—so I was walking toward them.

But it was one of those dreams, where the more I walked, the farther away he got.

So I started running. And running. And running. And running, never getting closer.

And suddenly the baby was gone, and the man was behind me, and instead of wanting to get *to* him, I wanted to get *away*. I ran faster and faster, as fast as I could go, but he was on my heels, chasing me. Reaching for me.

"*Careful, Celia,*" he said just as his fingers dug into my arm.

I woke with a start. It was dark out, which made sense since the sun had been near setting when I'd been at the pool with Mateo.

But it felt *too* dark. Like I'd slept too long.

I picked up my phone to check the time, the only thing it was good for on the island because I had zero service. *Seven-twenty.*

Dinner was always at seven sharp, and Tom always came to get me if I didn't show up on my own.

I must have missed her knock, and she hadn't wanted to disturb me.

I got up and started toward my closet to look for something suitable to wear to dinner since I was still in my bikini, then changed my mind. If Edward was cracking, this wasn't the time to back down on my game.

As soon as I walked out of my room, I could tell something was wrong, and it wasn't just the weird energy clinging from my bad dream. The whole house was dark. And quiet. There should have been raucous laughter and the scraping of utensils against plates.

I wandered through the kitchen on the way to the dining room. It was empty and clean where usually it was a mess until after Joette and Tom cleaned it up, which always happened after dinner.

There was no way a meal had been prepared in there. The dining room was also empty, as I knew it had to be. I continued past it toward the library, where, at last, there was a light on.

As much as I hated myself for it, I was relieved when I saw Edward. I'd begun to fear everyone had gone somewhere without me.

He was sitting behind his desk, a pair of reading glasses propped on his nose. I hadn't seen him in eyewear before, besides sunglasses, and I had to catch my breath. Was there no look this man couldn't carry off? Not only carry off, but fucking excel at?

"Where is everybody?" I asked, stretching my hands over my head. I actually needed to stretch this time. It wasn't part of my plan to torment him, but hey, it was a nice side effect.

Or it would have been if he would have looked up from his computer. "I told the staff not to come in tonight," he said plainly.

"Really?" Tom hadn't said anything about it when I'd talked to her earlier. "Any particular reason?" Maybe he wanted to dine alone with me.

God, I hope he wanted to dine *on* me.

"Yes, actually. I couldn't continue to bring guests into my house when *my wife*," he emphasized the last two words, "can't seem to keep from flaunting around in scanty swimwear, now could I?" He turned and bent his head to peer at me over his glasses. "Case in point."

His tone had an edge to it, suggesting he was angry and only barely able to restrain himself. Not just angry, but *really* angry.

There wasn't going to be any dining with me *or* on me.

He was such a sore loser, because that's what this was. A loser's move.

"So you just canceled dinner because you're mad at me?" If he was going to be angry, I was too, and I wasn't even going to try to hide it.

"You're welcome to prepare something for yourself. Joette left a couple of sandwiches in the fridge. I'm sorry—I already ate them."

Bullshit.

He was so transparent. So arrogant. So maddening.

I called him on it. "Bullshit."

"Excuse me?"

"You aren't sorry."

He took off his glasses, set them on his desk, then sat back and stared at me smugly. "You're right. I'm not."

His contemptuous response only fueled my anger. "And you didn't tell everyone to stay away because you're worried about your wife parading around inappropriately." I took a step toward him. "You did it because you can't stand how it makes you feel when other people look at me."

"Pfft."

"When other *men* look at me." I was purposefully taunting him, because fuck him.

He shot up from his chair and leaned one fist on the desk, the other hand curled into itself with one sharp finger stabbing at the wood as he made his points. "I told you before we were married that I expected you to be a model wife." *Stab.* "That you were to be perceived as *faithful*."

Stab. "Parading around in next-to-nothing in front of my staff," *stab*, "And flirting with anyone that has a cock," *stab*, "Will not be tolerated."

Fuck. He was really, *really* mad.

I really, really shouldn't keep provoking him.

Why was I never good at doing what I should?

"Won't be tolerated by *you*, you mean." I took another step toward him.

His eye twitched. Twice. "Damn right."

"I should be punished then, shouldn't I?" I asked in a put-on cutesy voice. "For being such a *bad* wife."

I was next to him now, at the side of his desk. So close I could feel the heat of his rage radiating off of him.

He said nothing, but I could see a vein in his neck pushing tautly against his skin.

"For being such a bad girl." I was wicked. I really, really was.

"Celia—" He warned.

I leaned against the desk at this angle, mimicking his position, my breasts thrust out in front of me. My ass high in the air. "You *want* to punish me, don't you? You want to *hurt* me. I can see it in your eyes. I bet you want to bend me over your knee right now and spank the living—"

And then he was behind me, one hand pushing me over the desk, the other furiously pulling my bikini bottoms down before his palm smacked against my skin, hard. Incredibly hard. And fast, six, seven, eight times.

Nine.

Ten.

Each slap got harder, more difficult to tolerate. I'd been spanked by a lover before, sure I had. But it had always been fun. Playful.

This *hurt*.

A lot.

My ass was on fire. Tears ran down my cheeks. I cursed and yelled and wriggled, trying to get away from the next blow, but his hold was too strong, and all I managed to do was wiggle the rest of the way out of my bikini bottoms.

His punishment went on. Fourteen? Fifteen?

I lost track.

"You want to be punished?" he asked between hits, his voice raw and threadbare.

Yes.

I didn't say it out loud. I couldn't. My throat was clenched, choking on my cries. And even if I could talk, I was too in my head for words, too busy trying to shut down the pain, trying to go numb. Trying to deny that I *liked* the pain. That while my ass ached and burned, my pussy was wet and throbbing and begging for more.

"You might regret getting what you asked for," he said then, as if he could read my mind. The slaps stopped, but his hand pressed against my middle back stayed fixed in place, and I could hear the sound of his belt buckle.

Oh my God, he's going to use his belt!

Could I take it? I didn't know. I wasn't sure. I already probably wouldn't be able to sit for a week.

But it wasn't the cool slap of leather that touched me next. It was the tip of his cock, lining up at my entrance. Driving in with one fierce thrust.

A sob broke through my throat, and more tears fell, this time tears of relief. *Yes, yes, yes.*

I chanted it over and over as he pummeled into me from behind, silently at first, then out loud. "Yes. Yes. Yes!"

His hand moved from my back to my head. Seizing a fistful of hair, he pulled me upright and moved his other hand to the front of me, collaring my throat.

"You parade around here," he said, his cock ramming into me with vicious strokes, his pelvis hitting my burning ass with each thrust. "Tempting my staff, tempting *my* men with what belongs to me."

And that was the start of my orgasm. I could feel it like the beginning of a yawn, starting soft and tentative but heading quickly to a point of inevitability.

With one hand still wrapped around my neck, he grabbed onto one cup of my bikini top and snatched it down with one swift swipe.

"These? These magnificent perfect tits?" He crushed my breast in his fist. "These belong to *me*. You hear me?"

"Yes, yes." I wasn't sure if I was answering him or if it was just the only syllable I could say at this point.

He squeezed harder around my breast. "I own *this*. I own your cunt. And you flaunt your body around like it belongs to you? How dare you? How *dare* you?"

I exploded.

Energy released inside me like a nuclear bomb, radiating through my limbs. Fireworks shot through my vision. My body shook violently, and my pussy locked down on Edward's cock, and I knew right then, knew without a doubt, that I was changed. That this man had found something in me and released it, and there was no way I would ever be the same.

I was still trembling through my climax when Edward pushed me forcefully back to the desk then abruptly pulled out of me. I was too weak to protest. Too weak to attempt to claim his cum, and it turned out I didn't have to because the next thing I knew he was letting out a guttural moan and drops of warm fluid were spilling along my lower back.

He'd claimed me. I was his.

And I was happy.

I sighed, a euphoric, satiated kind of sigh. I lay there, unable to move, unable to do anything but breathe. I heard the zip of Edward's pants. Heard him pacing behind me. Heard him curse as he kicked something hard and loud.

I stood up then, and turned toward him, my ass aching with the movement, just in time to catch my swimsuit bottoms when he threw them in my direction.

"Get out," he said with vile detest. "I can't look at you right now."

Apparently the guy wasn't great with after care.

I didn't move. "Edward...if you're worried that you went too far..." I cleared my throat, complete honesty hard for me. "If you think I didn't like it...don't worry. I did."

"I can't listen to your bullshit lies right now. Get the fuck out of here." He stormed past me toward the windows, refusing to look at me.

I pivoted, my gaze following his backside. "It's not bullshit! I mean it, I liked it. I *loved* it."

I wasn't lying either. Not even a little bit. It wasn't about my scheme to ruin him. The Game was the furthest thing from my mind.

"Please do it to me again," I went on. "Not right this second, maybe, but you know. When my ass doesn't feel like it's just been shredded."

He continued to stare out into the night and let out a harsh laugh. "You just don't know when to stop, do you?"

"And you don't know when someone is laying it all out on the line. I'm being one-hundred percent genuine. I am *into* this. That was incredible. I want more of it. Please, please, please, bring it on."

A beat passed.

Then he shook his head. "It won't work, Celia. I know about you. I knew what kind of woman you were when I married you."

I felt that rush of panic I always had when he said cryptic things like that. That punch of dread that made me jump to conclusions and think that he knew something about my games when there was no way he could.

"I don't know what you mean," I said, breathing my way through the alarm.

He turned to face me, his expression stone. "I mean, my dear wife, that I know about your ruse. How you plan to get me to rough you up in the bedroom then go cry abuse to the authorities."

I felt the blood drain from my face.

"Or maybe that's not exactly the scheme, but something along those lines. Am I warm?"

He didn't know. He couldn't. He was fishing. He was making a guess.

I clung to my best line of defense. "I really don't know what you're talking about, Edward. That you would think me capable of—"

"Shut up." He sneered at me. "You're a pathetic liar."

Now I was mad. Because, sure, fine, I'd planned those things, but he couldn't *know* that, and I was abandoning that plot, and I was not lying about wanting more sex like that, and being called a liar the one time I wasn't lying was just fucked up.

"You're crazy, you know that?" I seethed. "You're making shit up. If that were really true, and if you really knew that before we got married, why would you even marry me?"

"Because I want those Werner media shares."

That hurt. More than the spanking, somehow. I knew we weren't married for love, but his greed hadn't been so evident before. I hadn't felt like such a prop.

Layered over the hurt was indignant anger. He'd only said he wanted to helm my father's company. Now he expected to get his shares? What the fuck was the guy smoking?

"You're not getting anything from my father. You aren't getting anything from me, either, for that matter."

"I'll have those shares," he said adamantly.

"Over my dead body."

I knew then what was coming. Somehow, I knew, even though I couldn't possibly know, couldn't possibly even guess, and this inky black foreboding crawled up through me, spreading up my spine and traveling through my limbs in exactly the same way my climax had stretched through me moments before.

And before the words came out of his lips, I already felt their impact, already felt the air slam out of my lungs, and my knees crumple, unable to hold my weight. Felt the snaking cry of terror lodge in my throat before the smirk settled on his mouth.

And in that way I was almost prepared—*almost*—when he said the words that would later haunt me in my nightmares and brought the dream I'd had earlier crashing to the forefront of my mind. "That is precisely why, my little bird, I intend to kill you."

***Edward and Celia's story continues in
Ruin, Slay Two.***

With her heart literally in his hands, Celia will have to try and bargain with a devil.

**Need help recovering from Rivalry?
Join the Recovery Room! See you there!**

**Order signed copies of this book and merchandise
related to Slay on my website or listen to it on audio,
narrated by
Elena Wolfe.**

You can find a timeline of events related to the Fixed series at the back of the book.

RUIN: SLAY TWO

With her heart literally in his hands, Celia will have to try and bargain with a devil.

Edward Fasbender is my captor.

Trapped on this island he owns everything on--including, it seems, me.

He told me he would break me, but I thought he meant in the bedroom. It turns out Edward is playing a completely different game.

And he won't stop until he's ruined me.

For Liz who gives and gives
without ever getting.

INTRODUCTION

EDWARD

I'd never believed in idle threats. When I told someone I intended to harm them in some way, I was always prepared to back it up.

I was prepared to kill Celia.

I just hadn't decided yet that I would.

Rather, I *had* decided, and now I was having second thoughts.

I wasn't a man who had second thoughts. I was a man who honored my commitments, both to myself and to others. Always. That was how I'd climbed out of the depths of poverty, how I'd risen out of nowhere, against all odds. I decided, and I did. Case closed.

There were always obstacles to overcome. Every goal worth achieving had some unaccounted for hindrance along the way, usually showing up at the most inopportune time. That was how progress worked. Steps forward, a step back. The trick was to not get caught up in the stumble. Take a breath, find balance, then proceed.

But Celia Werner wasn't just a rock on the pathway. She hadn't just tripped me up. She hadn't made me simply stumble. She was a ledge, crumbling under my hold, and no matter how I dug my fingernails into the ground at her feet, I was beginning to fear I might fall.

It was possible I already had.

My mistake had been in fucking her. There, in the grip of her orgasm, when she was vulnerable and real, it was impossible not to see what could be between us. I hadn't even topped her that first time, not really. I hadn't probed into her psyche beforehand the way I normally liked, hadn't brought her walls down, hadn't taken her to ruin, and still I'd slipped in somehow. Slipped in behind her facade where she was unguarded and defenseless, and the authenticity of what I found there was overwhelming.

It wasn't supposed to have been like that.

There'd been a plan. A scheme years in the making, an improbable scheme at that, and yet everything had fallen into place, as though even the stars believed in my operation of revenge. She'd accepted my ridiculous proposal. She'd been satisfied with a prenup. She hadn't made a single bit of effort to redraft her will and trust.

It had been too easy. Every obstacle on the way had been met and breached without incident. When she'd shifted, I'd shifted with her. Without effort. It had been a cakewalk. Logistically, anyway. I'd known she'd be sharp and wily and fierce. I'd prepared for that.

What I hadn't known was that I'd like it.

Like *her*.

Did I like her? It was hard to accept if I did, but I couldn't deny there was something there. Something raw and out of control, yet identifiable as its own, unlike so much of what I'd grown accustomed to feeling in the near three decades that had passed since my parents' deaths.

I hesitated to say it was a nice change, only because of what that would mean for the future of my scheme, but it was a change. And if I were honest, I liked the change.

Before her, there'd only been blackness inside. Not because I had felt nothing, but because I felt too much. Too much anger, too much regret, too much heartache, too much love. Too much responsibility.

Too much *everything*.

And it all mixed together, all the individual *too much* of emotion until it was impossible to distinguish one from another, the same way a child's overzealous watercolor project turned into mud with the application of too many colors.

That was how my feelings existed inside me—as mud. Darker than that, though. An inky blob. A black hole. The perception of black holes very often is that they are large areas of nothing, but they're just the opposite. They are the densest objects in the universe. They suck at the life around them. They tear apart any matter that comes close to them because of their massive gravity.

That was what I was inside before her.

My emotions had mass.

My emotions had gravity.

My emotions were capable of tearing a person apart to ruin.

ONE

CELIA

IT WAS BULLSHIT.

I called him on it too. "Bullshit."

As terrifying as the words were coming from Edward's mouth, "*My little bird, I intend to kill you,*" that's all they were—words. He didn't mean to kill me. Of course he didn't. He wanted me off balance, that was all.

He stared at me for a beat, the anger he'd exhibited a moment before easing into something else. Something calmer, more controlled, yet just as vehement.

Without taking his eyes off me, he settled into the chair behind his desk. "I can understand why you'd choose not to believe me."

"Because you're dramatic and full of nonsense threats? Yeah. Pretty unbelievable." Almost as unbelievable as the fact that I was standing before him half-naked, covered in his cum since only a handful of minutes before his ominous declaration, he'd fucked me, wildly, claiming my body as his as he did.

I'd loved it. I'd even loved the painful and intense spanking I'd received that had precipitated the fucking.

He'd loved it too. I had no doubt of that. He might hate himself for loving it, for whatever reason I couldn't know, but there was no faking that he'd been into it.

Which made his stupid threat more hurtful than frightening. "You have regrets about fucking me, fine. But be a grown-up about it. Childish taunts are not your style."

I snagged a fistful of tissues from the box on his desk and reached around my torso to wipe the sticky mess he'd made on my backside as best I could before pulling on my bottoms. Wadding the tissue up in a ball, I threw it into his lap.

So maybe childish taunts were *my* style. Quid pro quo and all that.

With my jaw set, I crossed my arms over my breasts and met his steady gaze.

Edward let the ball of tissue fall from his lap to the floor, barely giving it a glance as he leaned back in his chair. His lips curled slowly. "You continue to fascinate me, little bird. I'll give you that. And you are correct. Childish taunts are not my style. Which is why you should be most assured that I mean what I've said."

So he was going to cling to that then. How immature.

Unless he actually meant it.

A shiver crawled up my spine. I shook it away. He was trying to get under my skin. He'd only win if I let him.

The best move was to ignore his scare tactics and focus on what he'd given me—an admission.

"Why did you call me that?" I knew the answer, but there was a chance I could be wrong. That the nickname was a coincidence.

"I've just told you I plan to kill you, and you're more concerned with the name I've given you. Fascinating indeed." He was good, I had to give him that. I'd often held onto a ruse way past the time it should be surrendered, but never with such commitment.

Never so convincing.

"Just stop. You don't mean it."

Edward cocked his head slightly. "Don't I?"

"You don't. You're trying to scare me." But my mouth felt dry and my hands were sweaty despite the fact that I was only wearing a bikini in an air-conditioned room.

"Is it working?"

Yes.

But what I said was, "No. Now I'm just pissed off."

His grin widened. "That makes two of us."

He didn't need to tell me. He'd been mad before I'd even entered the room, deservedly so, after I'd pushed him all day, openly flirting with his staff. It had gotten me what I'd wanted—him. Inside me. Unleashed and unbridled.

I'd told myself I wanted him so I could win The Game, but it had been a lie. I'd just wanted him, and having had him, I wanted more of him, and for the first time in years—in a decade—I could see a future for myself that didn't center around the games that Hudson had taught me so well to play, that didn't involve lies and manipulation. A future filled *with* instead of the nothing that had lived so long inside of me.

I wanted Edward, but it was painfully clear that, no matter how much he might want me back, he wouldn't allow it.

I was scared, yes, and pissed. But mostly hurt.

I remembered this emotion. I remembered rejection. I remembered this kind of pain.

I'd rather play The Game.

"Why did you call me that?" I asked again, more sternly, as though I had power to make any demands. So he'd made me feel things. I didn't have to acknowledge that. I knew how to be empty. I could be empty again.

Edward rested his ankle on his opposite thigh, a more casual posture than I'd seen him take before, the nonchalant behavior adding to my unease. "Why did I call you that just now or why did I call you that before?"

Before. It was so vague. He'd called me "little bird" twice now in this conversation. His reference to before could simply mean the first time tonight, and not the time he'd said it to me outside The Open Door. It was a clever tactic, refusing to give anything away. Requiring me to be the one to admit that I'd been there that night or let the mention slide.

I considered it for only a handful of seconds. While I hated being backed into a corner as I had been, I wanted answers more. "How did you know it was me?"

My disguise hadn't been perfect the night I'd attended the sex party and seen him there as well, but it was a stretch to think that anyone would have realized who I was. My hair had been dyed. My outfit had been specifically one I'd never wear. I'd worn a mask that fully covered my face. A feathered mask of a dragon that Edward had mistaken for a bird.

More likely it hadn't been a mistake but a deliberate choice meant to knock me back a peg or two.

Still, as he'd demeaned me with the nickname, I'd believed he'd done so as a stranger. To discover that he'd known all along was the real blow to my esteem.

He studied me, his hand rubbing over the scruff of beard on his chin—the Van Dyke that I'd suggested he grow—and for a tense instant, I thought he might deny knowing what I was talking about. That would be just like him, wouldn't it? Get me to confess and then refuse to acknowledge it.

But if the thought had crossed his mind, he didn't go with it. "I think the better question," he said, "is how did we end up at the same party together."

The rhythm of my heart stuttered, two beats coming so fast that I could actually feel them against the inside wall of my chest. He hadn't just known it was me. He'd known I'd be there.

Now that was terrifying.

And exciting.

And impossible. How the hell had he known? I ventured a guess. "You had me followed."

"Did I?" His brows arched inward as though he were trying to recall the details of the event. So fucking performative. "I believe I was there first."

"Then you figured out I was going to be there. Somehow." I threw up my hands, already tired of the tug of war.

Perhaps in response to my impatience, he threw me a bone. A clue. "How did *you* end up at that party?"

"I was invited."

"By whom?"

"By..." *Oh, fuck.*

I quickly went over the circumstances that had led me there that night. Having learned from Blanche that Edward liked kinky parties, I'd gone searching for one he might attend, putting a call out on kink-related forums under an anonymous username for such events.

One person had reached out in response, inviting me to join The Open Door, an underground organization that hosted weekly sex parties. I'd been wary about accepting, worried that the membership fee would be traced to my bank account, but I hadn't for a minute been concerned about the stranger who'd invited me.

Had FeelslikePAIN been Edward?

I needed to sit down.

As soon as I sank into the chair facing his desk, I regretted it. My ass had cooled down, but sitting reignited the sting of his severe spanking.

Not a chance I was letting him know that.

"That's impossible," I said through gritted teeth, bearing down through the pain. "That couldn't have been you. You couldn't have known that username was me."

"Are you sure?"

With my elbow propped on the arm of the chair, I ran my fingers across my forehead. "This is tedious, Edward. Would you just tell me?"

His lips twitched in a way that suggested my impatience amused him, which only made me more irritable. Of course. As he surely knew it would.

Abruptly he sat forward, setting his elbows on the desk and clasping his hands together, tucking all of his fingers in except the two pointers, which he steepled together and aimed in my direction. "How about *you* tell *me* something?" he asked, his expression wicked with curiosity. "How did it feel to watch me that night?"

"What do you mean?" *Sneaky, exhilarating, conniving.* Was that what he was after?

"How did it feel to watch me touching another woman? Making another woman come in front of you."

My stomach dropped as simultaneously the space between my thighs began to buzz. Against my will the memories crashed into the forefront of my mind. He'd sat across from me, his eyes locked with mine as he'd assisted the woman on his lap in masturbating to orgasm.

"Sasha," I said mindlessly. "Her name was Sasha." Because concentrating on that point was safer than answering him. Even the question had heated my face, not because it was humiliating to be asked—though it definitely was—but because both the memory and the forwardness of his inquiry aroused me, much to my annoyance.

"Her name doesn't matter. It only matters that she wasn't you. Tell me how you felt."

She wasn't you. It came off as a deliberate slap in the face.

The pointed comment also brought my emotions from that night into vivid focus. I'd been vulnerable then. I'd felt exposed, and that was with a disguise. A pointless disguise, it turned out, but I hadn't known that at the time.

Just thinking about what he must have seen in me in that moment made my skin crawl.

There was no way I could share those feelings with him. They were too personal. Too real, and here, under the intensity of his gaze, there was nothing I could hide behind.

"I'm not doing this," I said, as I stood up and turned to leave.

"Sit down, Celia."

The command was sharp and sinister, a verbal lasso wrapping around my torso, holding me in place. I was only a handful of strides away from the doorway. So close to escape.

And yet I couldn't go.

I didn't generally have a problem defying him. I could now. Easily.

Only, as blasé as I'd been throughout our conversation, I actually was scared. More than I wanted to admit, even to myself. I didn't believe that he would kill me, necessarily.

Just.

What if I was wrong?

With my chin held high, I returned to my chair, wincing as my ass touched the surface. "There. I sat down. But only because you're going to give me answers. How did you figure out that was me on that forum? And why did you want me to go to that party?"

Edward sat up to his full height, his eyes narrowing as he stared at me. Into me. "Let me be clear," he said with cool authority. "You are not in a position to ask to see my cards. It's your turn to show yours, and if I'm satisfied after I see them, I may choose to show you some of mine."

I swallowed hard.

Though his face remained perfectly composed, his hands were in fists resting on the desk, and I couldn't help but suspect that he was trying very hard to control his rage. "Now, answer my question."

"And if I do you'll give me answers?" My voice sounded weak, and for good reason, since I'd basically just been told he was in charge and stop defying him or else.

I seemed to have a real problem with authority.

Edward appeared to find that problem amusing. His lip twitched as though trying not to smile. "Perhaps. But I'm not answering anything you ask until I'm happy with what I hear from you."

"Nothing," I said stubbornly. "I felt nothing."

"If you're not going to be honest, then you might as well leave, which will not only end the discussion now but any possibility of discussion in the future."

Whether he meant that this was the only time *he'd* be *willing* to talk or that, later, *I* would be *unable* to talk, I didn't know.

Either way, he'd trapped me once again into answering.

"It was hot," I said, with obvious annoyance. "Okay? The way you touched her was hot."

"And?"

Jesus Christ, he was impossible.

"And dirty."

"And?"

"I don't know..." I shook my head, trying to guess what he might want me to say. "Unsettling."

"And...?"

"And mean. And manipulative. And exciting. And if you want something different from me, then I don't know what it is because I haven't read the Guide to Pleasing Edward Fasbender, and I'm going to need the CliffsNotes."

"I want you to be honest." His tone said his patience was wearing thin.

Well, mine was too. And honesty? That wasn't something I'd been good with in a long time, let alone emotions.

At my hesitation, he prodded. "Close your eyes, Celia, and stop trying. Just imagine I'm touching her now. I'm kissing her. My mouth is on her breasts. My hands are on her cunt. Inside her cunt. Now, tell me what you're thinking."

My eyes were closed, and I could see it all like it was happening right then. I could feel the twist in my stomach, the rush of blood in my ears, the pang of envy.

I opened my mouth and let the words fall out. "I wished it were me you were touching."

And with that admission, I knew in my gut that whatever answers he gave me, if any, or whatever move he made next in this stupid fucked-up game, it didn't matter.

I'd already lost.

TWO

I HEARD his chair move before I opened my eyes, and when I did, he wasn't sitting behind the desk anymore. He was easy to find. He'd moved a few feet away to the mini bar. I already knew that the amber-colored liquor that poured out of the carafe into the tumbler was brandy.

When the glass held two fingers of liquor, he brought it over to me. "That was good," he said as he held his offering toward me. "Was that so hard?"

Was it hard to admit that I'd wanted him?

I'd been openly trying to seduce him for weeks. But I'd been able to convince myself that my only reasons for doing so were to win. Now, with my plans exposed and The Game out of my mind, it was different. It *was* hard. It made me weak.

I hated it.

"I hate you," I said, snatching the glass from his hand, pretty sure I meant it, vehemently, even, despite not having felt anything passionate for years. I brought the tumbler to my lips and took a long swallow. My stomach was empty, and I didn't really want the drink, but he'd made a point to pour it and bring it over, which meant he thought I needed it, and I didn't have the energy to argue about it.

And maybe I did need it.

Edward hadn't moved from my side. He lifted his hand and ran his knuckles across my cheek, a gesture so unexpected, I almost flinched.

"Would it make you feel better to know that I wished it had been you I was touching too, my little bird?"

My skin felt hot, and not from the liquor. I hated that too—how my body reacted to him. How it lit up at his touch, how his words sent my stomach fluttering and my heart racing, my organs not caring that he was a controlling asshole or that he (supposedly) wanted me dead.

Well, I wasn't my body.

I leaned away from his hand, wrapping one arm around myself while the other kept the glass near my mouth, a pathetic shield of sorts. "Stop calling me that. I'm not your anything."

"*Au contraire.* You are my wife." He circled back around toward his chair, and I immediately missed the warmth of his skin against mine.

Or my body did.

I wanted him as far from me as possible. Him on the other side of his desk was good. It was the farthest I'd likely get him until this was over. Until he decided he was bored with the conversation and let me leave.

If I was being forced to stay, I damn well meant to take advantage of the situation. "How did you know that was me on the forum?" I repeated my earlier question. "Even if you knew my IP address, it's supposed to be blocked to others on that site."

A loud clap of thunder boomed overhead. I glanced toward the window in time to see the flash of lightning that followed it, showing a thick layer of clouds covering the sky and sheets of pouring rain.

I was so surprised to realize it was storming that I almost missed Edward's response.

"...is blocked. But I had software installed directly on your laptop that captured all your activity."

What?

He had my full attention now. "How the fuck...?" Quickly my mind searched for the answer to my own question. How would he have gotten to my laptop? Who would have...

"Blanche," I said, her name coming out like a curse word. "You used Blanche Martin. She sent that email to me with those pictures that I, stupidly, downloaded. I should have known! It was awfully convenient that she'd shown up at the same time you did." *Stupid, stupid, stupid!*

"That's not a bad guess, but no. Not Blanche. She was a strange coincidence. When I saw you with her at Orsay, I actually thought you'd had the upper hand on me."

It was a relief to know Blanche hadn't been my mistake. And I still needed to know how he'd gotten into my laptop, but now I also had to know what I should have learned from Blanche that I didn't. "What did I miss? She couldn't tell me anything about you, except that she'd heard rumors that you liked kinky parties."

"I was wondering what gave you the idea to go looking for me on those forums."

"A lot of good that did." I realized I'd admitted more than I'd meant to. "And I wasn't looking for you. Who said I was looking for you?"

His expression said he wasn't fooled. "It seems you formulated a whole plan to bring me down based on that little snippet of information. From your internet searches on consensual versus non-consensual sexual practices within marriage and the law surrounding those practices, I surmise you had intended to use what you assumed about my sexual proclivities to your advantage."

I was fucked, and I knew it.

But I'd never been good about letting things go when I should, and I clung to my innocence like he was clinging to his I'm-going-to-kill-you stance. "That's an awfully big assumption. Narcissist much? Not everything is about you."

"What else were you using the information for?"

"Maybe I was researching for a friend. Or writing a dark romance book."

"I'm sure that's what it was." His mouth twitched as though he were trying not to smile. "You weren't at all hoping to get me to, let's see, what exactly did your digital notebook say? 'Wives assaulted through non-consensual sexual practices have a strong case for nullifying prenuptial agreements.'"

Yep. Totally fucked.

My cheeks heated. I took another swallow of my drink, hoping the burn could wash down some of the humiliation of defeat.

"I'm intrigued about just what it is you imagine that I do in the bedroom, Celia. And offended that you think I don't require consent in my relationships."

"Yeah, well." I'd never presumed anything about consent. The truth wasn't what mattered in my games. "Your word against mine."

"Ah. So that's how you intended to play it. I was right on that then."

I mentally kicked myself. I was giving more than I was getting, and that needed to change.

In an attempt to reassert myself, I turned the conversation back to the information I really wanted. "If it wasn't Blanche who got you to my laptop, then who?"

He shook his head. "It's my turn to hear from you."

Cue eye roll. "You already seem to know everything about me. What do you need me for?"

"Which was what started this conversation in the first place, wasn't it?"

A chill ran down my spine. *I intend to kill you.* His words echoed in my brain. He sure knew how to retaliate against a bratty statement. I had to give him that.

And, as ridiculous as it was, his tactic was working. I was afraid of him. More afraid than made me comfortable.

Why was that also a turn-on?

And how the fuck did he get to me?

"Renee." The answer hit me like a ton of bricks, spilling out of my mouth on impact. "Oh my God. You got to Renee."

"You make it sound like I took a hit out on her. It wasn't like that at all." The squint of his eye said he was pleased—either with himself or that I'd guessed right, I wasn't sure.

Whichever it was, it encouraged me to follow down the rabbit hole. "Somehow you got her to upload something on my computer for you."

"No. She simply gave me access to it. I did what I needed to from there."

Dammit. Really? Renee? She'd worked for me for years. We'd never been close, but I'd thought we had a decent boss/employee relationship. "She just handed it over to you? Without any questions? Did she know what you did to it?"

I wasn't so naive as to be surprised by betrayal, but still. This discovery came as a shock.

Edward waved a hand in the air, dismissing my questions. "It's not important."

"Not to you, maybe, but to me, you better believe it is." When he shrugged, I pressed on. "Did you pay her off? Is that why she quit?"

He studied me again as he considered his answer, or whether he would answer at all. "Nothing so nefarious," he said finally. "I offered her a better opportunity, and she took it."

"Did you sleep with her?" It was another thought that left my mouth as soon as it entered my head, and I was surprised by the gnawing in my chest that accompanied it.

He leaned forward abruptly. "Do you care?"

I asked, so of course I cared, and no matter what I tried to say, he knew it. It was a victory for him, but it felt like an even bigger loss for me.

Especially because I still didn't have the answer, and not knowing bothered me. Almost as much as the idea of Edward sharing his hands, his mouth, his cock with Renee.

I pushed down the sudden urge to cry. I wasn't used to losing, and I was pretty sure I had. I didn't even know *how* to lose. How to act, what to say.

And I didn't *want* to lose.

I turned my head toward the windows where the storm pressed on with torrents of rain. "What was even the point of all of it? Why did you want to see what was on my computer? Why did you care? To convince me to accept your proposal?"

I switched my attention back to him for his answer.

"Whatever it took to nudge you in that direction, yes." His eyes hooded. "You should know I'd been prepared to do a lot more."

My breath tripped in my chest. He hadn't meant it to be seductive, he couldn't possibly. And yet I felt the sharp pang of desire low in my belly.

My reaction said more about me than his statement said about him. Said things I didn't want to know.

I forced myself to focus. "All to get to Werner Media? You have your own company. Why does my father's matter so much to you?"

"It just does."

It was my turn to study him. His blue eyes were as set as his jaw. He gave nothing away but determination, no matter how I searched for more.

No matter how I wished he'd give more.

It was beyond stupid that I cared. Stupid and downright irritating.

I crossed one leg over the other and lifted my chin in defiance of him and my feelings. "Well, it was all for nothing because you're crazy if you think I'm suggesting my father let you helm his company now."

"As if you'd ever planned to do that in the first place."

No matter what I had to say, he had to one-up me. No matter what my hand, his was better.

And, frankly, none of his motivations made any sense. "If you didn't think that I would ever convince my father to select you—the whole point of our marriage, according to your proposal—then why did you put so much effort into getting me to marry you?"

"I believe I've already given you that answer." He sat back in his chair again, cool and smooth.

I considered the answer, his threat. I was sure he wasn't serious, because, mainly, who did that? Who schemed to marry a prominent woman and then killed her?

But if he really never believed I could further his chances with my father, and yet he'd gone to all those lengths to make sure I did indeed marry him, then what had he hoped to gain? What had been his plan?

There was only one answer that made logical sense, as impossible as it was to believe.

"You can't kill me," I said, my voice more steady than I felt. "People would notice."

"I expect people to notice." Edward picked up a fountain pen off his desk and twirled it absentmindedly. "I have a first-rate funeral planned. I expect many will attend, even though it will be held in London. I don't have time right now to go to the U.S., which I'm sure your parents would prefer, but that isn't theirs to decide. It will be a nice event, I assure you. I've even saved you the coveted spot in the family plot next to my parents."

No. He didn't mean it. He didn't mean any of it.

But my stomach twisted all the same, and bile rose to the back of my throat, because even if he didn't mean it, it was an awfully deranged scenario he'd painted.

A scenario that I didn't intend entertaining a minute longer.

I stood up and glared down at him. "You're a sick asshole, you know that? A perverted lunatic, and I don't have to listen to this."

I set the brandy tumbler on his desk and spun toward the doors, determined to make it out this time.

"Did I say you could leave?" His voice boomed through the room with as much fury as the thunder outside, and something in his tone, something that he'd only hinted at before, suggested very strongly that he wasn't to be disobeyed.

Frustrated, I whirled back around to face him. "What is it you want from me?"

He was standing now. At his full height, I was very much aware that he was bigger than me. That he was stronger than me. That we were alone in a storm, and I was helpless, if he wanted me to be.

And he very much wanted me to be.

"Sit down," he ordered, the narrow focus of his eyes daring me to defy him.

I took two reluctant steps toward the chair, but stopped when I remembered the tender state of my ass. "I'd rather stand, if you don't mind."

"I do mind." His flash of teeth told me he knew exactly why

standing was my preference. And that, for the same reason, he was determined I sit.

I paused, deciding.

"Sit," he said again, his voice so controlled that it sent dread coursing through my veins.

I sat down, wincing openly this time as I did.

Edward remained standing, peering down at me with a smug smile.

He liked that. Having me uncomfortable. Having me hurt. The glint in his eye paired with his evil smirk gave him away. That's how much he liked it.

From the hint of color in his face, I would even go so far as saying that it turned him on.

I'd maybe have feelings about that if I weren't so rattled. If I weren't so scared.

"You want my father's shares," I said, thinly, stating the obvious so I could have time to think. "That's what this is about. How will killing me get you that? They're his shares. They aren't in my name."

"They weren't. But as of nine days ago, on the date of your marriage, they now belong to you."

My stomach dropped, and I could feel the color drain from my face. I'd forgotten that. How had I forgotten?

"No one knows that." My voice was nearly a whisper.

His knuckles pressed into the desk as he leaned into them. "I've done my research, too, sweetheart."

It was a change my father made to my trust years ago, when he'd thought I'd marry Hudson Pierce. Some stupid loophole he'd found to avoid paying taxes. His shares would be transferred to my name at the time of my marriage. He'd never expected to actually give up control of Werner Media, though, until he retired. That was supposed to be protected by my prenup, and it was.

A prenup didn't do anything, though, in a case of death.

Oh, God.

He wasn't bluffing. He meant what he'd said. He really did mean to kill me.

There was something Edward didn't know, however. If he did, this whole scheme of his would be null and void. He didn't know that Hudson Pierce secretly owned more shares than my father. My father didn't even know it. If Edward was after control of Werner Media, killing me would get him close, but it wouldn't get him where he wanted to be.

If I told him now, would he realize the futility of his plan and let me go?

Possibly.

It would also make me worth nothing. And now that he'd threatened my life, he couldn't let me walk away and not expect repercussions. I was fucked if he didn't know the truth. I was doubly fucked if he did.

I folded my hands in my lap, aware that they were shaking, hoping he didn't see how much. "So...what? You just come back from this honeymoon a single man?"

He paused only for the space of a breath. "It had been the plan."

"And now?"

"Now, I'm willing to renegotiate."

Hope rushed through me before reality set in. "There isn't anything you can offer that will get me to sign those shares over to you. Threaten me all you want. I'm not handing over my father's company to his arch nemesis." My father would kill me if Edward didn't.

"Forget the shares for the moment." He tossed the subject away casually, as though we were talking about bed linens instead of the state of my life. "Let's talk about what you'd planned to do to me. You wanted to convict me of some sexual crime, but to do so, you would have had to endure whatever it is that I prefer in the bedroom. I'm guessing that you still don't know what that is exactly."

"Uh." It was difficult to focus on anything but my predicament, so I focused on the effort. *Bedroom. What he likes there.* In truth I didn't know exactly what he did with his lovers, but wasn't the gist obvious? "I have some thoughts."

"I'm sure you do," he said, patronizingly. "But let me tell you so you know for sure—I like to see a woman broken down."

I shook my head. "Whatever that means, I have no doubt I could have handled it just fine."

He lifted his hands off the table and thrust them in his pockets, once again towering over me at his full height. "Let's find out," he said.

"I don't know what you're saying." I was starting to get a headache and the lack of food was getting to me. I needed things spelled out.

So Edward started spelling. "I'm saying, that's my deal. You want to live? Then let me break you down."

THREE

LIGHTNING FLASHED, and with a loud crack of thunder, the lights went out, underscoring Edward's offer, because even nature was under his command. Why was I not surprised?

The blanket of darkness was a welcome relief. This time, Edward couldn't see the latest shiver that his words precipitated. He couldn't see the new stippling of gooseflesh along my arms. Couldn't see whatever I was sure my expression hadn't managed to conceal.

Break you down.

What the hell was that supposed to mean?

But now wasn't the time to ask, in the dark, with the wind and rain hitting so forcefully against the windows that I wasn't entirely sure they wouldn't break.

I could hear Edward across from me, a drawer of his desk opening and closing before a light shone brightly in my eyes.

I put my hand up to block my vision, my eyes squinting. The light remained there for several seconds then dropped down slightly, settling on my mouth.

"There are emergency lights in the kitchen," Edward said, and I could see now that what he was holding was only his cell phone.

I'd stopped carrying mine since I'd been on the island. The cellular service was too spotty and unreliable. Now the once relied-on gadget was only good for an alarm clock. Flashlight was another notable use, apparently.

The beam dropped from my face to the floor, moving around the desk along with the man holding it.

"Come," he said, and I was on my feet before I even thought of following his order. Once I was standing, his fingertips gripped tightly at my elbow, as though he didn't believe I'd accompany him otherwise.

Honestly, he might not have been wrong. Power out or not, I wasn't keen on letting him be my hero. With his hand tugging me along, I didn't have much choice in the matter.

He led me swiftly through the library doors into the hall. My nipples immediately stiffened as the temperature out here varied significantly from the warmer cocoon of his office space. Again, I was glad that the lights had gone out so that Edward wouldn't see the noticeable peaks through my bikini top. I'd be damned if he thought they were for him.

Funny how less than an hour ago, they had been for him.

His hand had crushed the flesh of my breast while he'd fucked me from behind, and I'd not only welcomed it all but urged him for more.

The memory brought a fresh wave of warmth between my legs. My stupid libido still responded to him. I didn't know who I hated more for that—him or my body.

Besides the effect it had on my nipples, the cool air brought on another shiver, one that Edward wouldn't miss with his hand on my elbow the way it was.

He stopped abruptly, surprising me. I tripped forward, only managing to stay upright because he was already holding me. His other hand, still holding his cell phone, moved to my other arm, as though automatically, steadying me. His touch was hot, and I despised how comforting it felt against my skin.

As soon as I'd found my balance, I jerked away.

He let me, dropping even his hand from my elbow. "Stay," he ordered, and as I watched the light of his cell bounce down the hall in the opposite direction toward his bedroom, as I stayed in the place he'd left me, I wondered if that was how he'd speak to me from now on, with one word commands like I was a dog.

It wouldn't be quite so disgusting if I wasn't compelled to obey.

Curiosity. That was the only reason I was still there. And I needed a light. And even if I found my way to the kitchen on my own, I didn't know where to find supplies and the search would be difficult without him.

Without his cell phone, I corrected mentally. Because like hell was I relying on him for anything.

He returned a short minute later, and as soon as he did, I felt the warmth of a plush robe being wrapped around me. Despite myself, I thrust my arms through one hole then the other before allowing him to tie a knot securely at my waist. Impressive considering he was still holding his phone.

When he'd bundled me up, he lingered, and with the light pointing at me, I had the impression he was studying me, as he had earlier, as he did so often. Not for the first time, I wondered what he saw. What brought him back to look time and time again?

And why did I hope he never stopped?

I pulled away first, tugging the collar of the robe up to my nose to sniff. It smelled ordinary, like laundry detergent. Not like him. Not unlike him.

"Is this yours?" I asked, unable to help myself, when what I really should have said was thank you.

"No." His answer came quickly, and he stirred into action, once again taking me at my elbow and leading me with him.

My lips puckered into a pout that he couldn't see. *Not his robe.* Whose robe, then? Why had it been in his room? Why did my chest burn at the thought that it was some other woman's? A woman who he'd allowed into his bedroom, into his bed. Into his life.

A woman he didn't want to murder.

It wasn't jealousy. I refused to be jealous for the attention of someone who openly despised me. Just more curiosity.

I would tell myself that as long as I had to. Maybe, eventually, I'd mean it.

Once he'd pushed through the swinging door into the kitchen, he let me go and proceeded to the pantry, the light disappearing as he withdrew into the storeroom. There was one window in the room, but the blinds had been drawn leaving the space in near total darkness.

As though reacting to the location, my stomach growled, reminding me of its empty state. There'd be something to snack on in the refrigerator, which wouldn't have had enough time to warm up at this early point in the power outage. It was on the other side of the room, and would be easiest to get to if I waited until Edward returned with the light.

But I was irritated at being abandoned and even more irritated at having to depend on anyone—that man in particular—so fuck waiting. Holding my hands out in front of me, I shuffled in the direction I thought made sense, only to stub my toe on the leg of the kitchen table.

"Goddammit." Even whispered, the curse was audible in the quiet.

The pantry door swung swiftly open and the light found me bent over, rubbing the pain from my injury.

Edward chuckled. "I suppose that's my fault for not telling you to stay."

"Fuck you. I'm not your pet." I let my foot fall with a thump.

"No, a pet would have more sense than to bumble around in the dark." Instead of returning to the pantry, he crossed over to the sink, the light spraying against the stainless steel. There the sound of tin met the counter as he set something down and then opened a drawer. Seconds later, a match was lit and then another, brighter flame, filled the room, the scent of kerosene in the air.

He turned toward me, and now the hurricane lamp he'd found was in my view. "I have one in my bedroom. I can send this one with you when you go to bed. If you'd rather, I can find you a working flashlight. The batteries on the first couple I tried seem to have died. It's been a while since we've needed to use them here. Usually the backup generator kicks in. I'll have Louvens look at it in the morning."

"The lamp is fine," I said, wrapping my arms around myself. The lamp illuminated the room quite well, and having grown accustomed to the safety of the dark, I felt suddenly exposed.

"Fine. Then on to other business, which is..." He didn't finish his sentence, crossing instead toward the refrigerator where he opened the door and pulled out a tray that he set on the counter by the lamp. He turned once more in my direction, gesturing to me with two fingers.

I took an involuntary step toward him before stopping myself. He already thought I was at his beck and call. I most certainly wouldn't respond to a hand gesture.

He laughed again, a sound so quiet it was definitely for himself. "Come here, you obstinate creature," he said, less of an order than anything else he'd said since the power had gone out. "I'm trying to feed you."

Too hungry to resist, I shuffled toward him, nodding at the tray he'd set out. "What is it?"

"A charcuterie. Joette prepared it for our dinner."

Leaning my hip into the counter next to him, I studied the plate of food, my arms still crossed. "I thought you already ate what Joette left."

"I ate the sandwiches. I didn't say that was all she'd left." When I hesitated, he reached for a piece of roquefort. "It's not poisonous. Shall I prove it?"

He brought it to his mouth, and I had to bite back a smile. It was meant to be a joke, but I didn't want to find him humorous. Especially not with a joke about killing me. It was too real.

But I was starving. And the charcuterie looked amazing. And I was pretty sure he wasn't going to kill me right now.

I picked up a bunch of grapes and popped four in my mouth, one after another. Edward reached next for a slice of capicola, using the bamboo spreader to dab mustard on it. After he'd eaten it, he moved over to a cabinet and pulled out two wine glasses. It was my turn to study him as he easily found a corkscrew and a bottle of something burgundy. He had the sleeves of his linen shirt pushed up to his biceps, showing off the muscular landscape of his arms. He was stunning, really, every part of him. The furrow of his brow as he worked open the wine. The determined set of his jaw as he poured. The smooth glide as he returned with the glasses, handing one out to me.

I took it, careful not to touch him as I did, ignoring the way my fingers ached to stretch out toward his. With my glass delivered, he lifted his own, nodding it first in my direction in a subtle toast before bringing it to his lips.

My skin tingled underneath the safety of the robe as I watched the alluring tilt of his head followed by the bob of his throat as he swallowed.

I looked away, taking my own quick sip and then setting the glass down to concentrate on what item I wanted to eat next.

Or to pretend to concentrate.

Absentmindedly, my fingers closed around a slice of manchego while my head swam in confusion. The robe, the lamp, the food, the wine—my husband had actively been caring for me in a way that made my knees weak. It was unlike the man I knew him to be on an ordinary day.

That he was behaving this way so soon after threatening my life was nearly impossible to process.

It felt wrong and surreal. Like the child being fattened up by the witch before she was thrown in the oven, except this time the child knew exactly what was happening from the onset.

And the child was stupid enough to stay.

I shook my head at myself and threw a butter cracker in my mouth. At least he was fattening me up with the good stuff.

"Feeling better?" he asked, and though I'd been determined not to look at him for the last several minutes, I could tell he was watching me.

"No," I answered honestly. My hunger was abating, but my stomach still felt twisted.

"What would make you feel better?"

I couldn't help it—my gaze flew back to his, wanting to see his expression to help read the subtext of his question.

Of course his face gave nothing away.

"Oh, I don't know," I said with dripping sarcasm. "Perhaps knowing my husband really wasn't planning my funeral might be a nice start."

"The only one who can determine that is you." He took another swallow of his wine, his eyes never leaving mine.

"Right, right." My body suddenly felt heavy. I hadn't realized until that moment that I'd hoped the whole caretaking routine was evidence that his murder plan was a ruse. "You said you want to break me down. What the hell does that even mean? You want me to be your submissive? You want to inflict pain on me? What?"

I popped another grape in my mouth and then pushed the tray away, having lost my appetite.

Edward set his glass down but kept his hand on it, his thumb stroking the stem. "It's not really a process that can be explained. There's submission involved, yes. It's often painful. It can be extremely satisfying as well."

"For you, you mean."

"Yes. For me."

I'd expected him to protest and try to convince me that there was pleasure in being dominated, blah blah blah. His answer instead, honest as it was, caused my breath to catch and the hair to lift at my neck. Was that what he wanted from me? Fear?

He had it. Fuck him for that, but there was no use denying he had me scared.

He must have read the apprehension in my face, and clever as he was, knew exactly how to counter it. With a challenge. "You thought you could endure it. Don't you want to see if it's true?"

I did when there was a reward at the end. "What do I get out of it?"

"You get to live." His tone suggested it was stupid to ask. That I wasn't in the place to be bartering. That he'd called this a negotiation, but it was really only an offer and both choices he was giving were shitty.

The insanity of it all suddenly hit me. "This is ridiculous. I'm not playing games with you. As soon as the sun is up, I'm out of here."

"You are?" He mimicked my pose, casually leaning his hip against the counter. "How do you plan to manage that? Can you man a boat? I'm pretty sure you don't know how to fly a plane. Uber doesn't come out here. You'd better think twice if you think any of my staff is going to help you. With this storm and our location, it will be impossible to get cell service."

My insides felt hard and cold, the blood in my veins was ice. I was stuck here. I'd already been trapped into submission. I was helpless. A slave to his whims.

This was real fear.

I scanned the room, looking for a weapon, for something I could use against him.

It was a subtle move of my eyes, but he read me like a book. "Do you know where the knives are kept?" His voice was low and ominous. "I do."

If I went for a drawer it would only be a guess. He'd get a hold of a knife before I did, and even if I managed to find the right drawer on the first try, he'd beat me there. He'd overpower me.

I had no choice.

But maybe I did. If I told Tom and Joette what Edward was doing to me, they'd surely help me.

I wouldn't be able to get to them until tomorrow though. "Can I have time to think?" I asked.

"Think about if you want to live? Sure. I'm in no rush to snap that neck. It really is pretty." He took a step toward me, and now he was close enough to trail his thumb down my neck, making me shudder. "But I doubt you're really looking for reasons to accept my offer and are instead looking for an escape. There isn't any way off my island."

Anger bloomed hot and new inside of me. He thought he knew everything? Thought he could guess every one of my moves? So he'd been right a few times...okay, a bunch of times, but that made me even more pissed off.

Pissed off enough to poke the bear.

"But maybe I'll kill you first," I said, trying to ignore the pad of his thumb at the hollow of my neck. "Did you think about that?"

He laughed, the amusement extending to his eyes. "You really are a pistol, aren't you?"

I swallowed, and he caressed his thumb against the movement, his gaze caught there at my throat for long seconds before moving up to my lips.

Then his hand moved to cup behind my neck, bringing my head up as he stepped into me. His mouth came down toward mine, and my pulse sped up with want.

At the last second, I got my wits together and turned my head away.

His lips landed on my jaw. He kept them there, sighing against my skin. "You were begging for me an hour ago."

"And then you told me you wanted me dead."

"Details."

He kissed along my jawline and up toward my ear, awakening every nerve in my body. My thighs felt slick and hot, and I could feel the steel press of his erection at my belly, and even with all the bullshit and the scare tactics, there was a part of me that wanted him. A part of me that reveled in him wanting me. A part of me that felt validated by the evidence that the chemistry between us wasn't one-sided.

But that part of me was stupid and wrong.

The smart part of me recognized him for the predator he was. A predator who planned to eat me alive.

"You're not touching me again," I said, resolutely, despite the fact that he currently was touching me.

His mouth was at my ear, his breath warm. "You do realize fucking is part of this bargain."

"I haven't accepted this bargain yet."

His grip tightened at my neck, an obvious threat. "You mean you haven't yet accepted this bargain is your only option."

There was nothing to say to that.

Scratch that, there was one thing to say to that which was that I accepted his unfair bargain and would play whatever cruel game he wanted me to play.

I opened my mouth, but the words refused to come out.

And then I didn't need to say them, because Edward kissed the side of my head before dropping his hand and stepping away. "Take a bit of time to think. We have a few days before I need to leave. I can't stay past Sunday, though. I'll need your answer by then."

He pulled his cell from his pocket and turned the light on. He'd made it to the door before he turned back and nodded toward the stove. "By the way, the knives are there. Top drawer to the right."

Then, by the light of his cell phone, he left me, with the lamp, in the kitchen, with a drawer of knives he knew I'd never be brave enough to use.

FOUR

THE POWER WAS BACK in the morning. In the daylight, with the storm over, I could think more clearly. Yes, I was trapped on the island, but only while we were *on the island*. All I had to do was agree to Edward's fucked-up game, and as soon as we were back in London, there would be plenty of opportunities to get away. Not everyone worked for Edward. Not everyone was on his side.

When I woke up, I considered telling him right away, just to get it over with, but as I opened my door to go look for him, I thought better of it. It was Wednesday morning. If I agreed now, that gave him four days to begin "breaking me down" before we left Amelie. If I waited until the last minute, he couldn't do anything until we were back in the UK, and even if he got ambitious and attempted something on the plane, it would be far less abuse for me to suffer than if he got a head start.

So I shut the door and undertook a very different mission than my previous one—avoid my husband.

It shouldn't have come as a surprise, but this mission was much harder than the last. While he'd been nearly impossible to find in the first week of our honeymoon, now he was there at every turn. In the pool, on the beach, reading on the lanai—all the places I'd adopted as my hangouts when he'd locked himself away in his library. Whatever time I arrived at the kitchen for breakfast, he'd show up soon after. The same thing happened at lunch. By Friday, I was taking most of my meals by myself. I was barely leaving my room at all.

Dinner was the one occasion I had to spend in his presence. He'd never said so, exactly, but the staff still gathered for the meal, and my absence would be something he'd have to explain.

Not that I cared much about inconveniencing the man. Just, it didn't feel like I was in a position to piss him off.

Besides, being around the staff felt safe, even if they all were under Edward's employ. And they were nice, too. Fun. The women had lived very different lives than I had and were not the type of friends I'd pick if I were to choose, but in reality, I'd never picked friends well, which was maybe what made their differences refreshing. Tom, Dreya, and Eliana especially fascinated me. They were always in a humorous mood in stark contrast to my constant seriousness. Their jokes were often crude and they teased incessantly, but their intentions were kind, and I enjoyed their company more than I liked to admit.

Joette, whose cooking had attracted Edward in the first place, was a particular favorite. She was about a decade older than my mother, and nothing like the woman who'd raised me, or, rather, the woman who'd paid a full-time nanny to do the work for her. Madge Werner was the quintessential socialite, an elitist, always at the ready with a snide remark and a fake smile. I loved her, of course I did, and we were close in many aspects, but it was never easy spending time with her. My stomach was always knotted in her presence, my back always straight, my mind constantly aware and waiting for her next attack.

Joette was everything Madge wasn't. She was expressive and warm, her smile always wide and genuine. When I retreated to my room, she checked in on me without making me feel like my privacy had been invaded. She was attentive without smothering. Curious but not nosy. And her cooking was absolutely divine. She'd be the thing I missed most when I was free of Edward.

Not the only thing, but I didn't like to think about that enough to name what those other things might be.

After dinner was where things became tricky. Previously, when I'd been desperate for Edward's attention, he'd disappear with the men into the library as soon as the meal was over. Now, everyone remained together. The sliding glass wall would be opened up to the patio, alcohol would be poured, cigars would be brought out, and the socializing would continue well into the night.

Edward was still himself in these instances, still composed and well-bred, but it was a more relaxed version of the man I'd been exposed to. His smile came naturally, meeting his eyes more often than not. He wasn't particularly chatty or entertaining, but he was engaged, and if a stranger had walked into the group, it would be obvious to him that Edward was the most important figure of the bunch. It was in the way the others angled their bodies, the way they looked to him for approval, the way they attended to his drink.

It made sense, of course. He was the one with the money. He was the one who paid the bills and owned the island and everything—everyone?—on it. But I had the feeling that the reaction to him would have been the same even if his name wasn't on the land title. He had a certain air about him, a magnetism, an authority that exuded from his very being, daring anyone to challenge him as king. As the devil.

Sometimes, seeing him like this, recognizing this about him, I was surprised that I'd ever dared to provoke him. That I'd dare to again if given the right opportunity, at the right time.

That time wasn't now. This was his show, and I let it be.

While the rest of the couples intermingled, Edward would invariably find a spot near me. He'd hand me a brandy then rest his arm next to me, his hand casually placed on my knee, and behind the laughs and the camaraderie, no one had any idea that I was a captive. That my husband had issued the gravest of threats. That his hold on me, a sure sign of ownership, had my heart pounding against my chest with trepidation.

Maybe not just trepidation. Maybe his touch did more to me than that. Still. Even now.

I didn't know what to expect after our guests left for their own residences. If his hand would rise higher up my thigh, between my legs, if his mouth would seek again to find mine. The minute someone yawned or initiated cleaning up, I excused myself to my bedroom so I wouldn't be left alone with the man I'd married. I didn't want to know what would happen if I stayed, and thank God, he never followed me to my room.

Until Saturday night, the night before he'd told me he needed to leave.

I'd packed my bags earlier, quietly, careful not to draw his attention. I wanted to be ready to go in the morning, as soon as I gave him my answer about his offer. The luggage was stowed away in my closet, out of sight. The evening had proceeded as usual with the dinner and mingling. As soon as Marge had looked at Erris with that look that said, *Is it time to go?*, I made my own farewells and slipped away to my room. There, I'd showered in my ensuite, then, with a towel on my head and another wrapped around me, I wandered to my bedroom in search of body lotion.

I found Edward instead.

The entire time we'd been on the island, he'd never once entered my rooms, and seeing him there now, sitting in my armchair, his leg nonchalantly crossed at the ankle over the other knee made me startle. Made my stomach flip. Made my knees go weak.

"I wasn't expecting you." Somehow my voice sounded unaffected.

"We have a matter to settle."

"Do we?" I pulled the towel from my head and began patting dry the still-wet ends. There was nothing to gain from acting flippant, but I couldn't help myself. I wanted to be as casual as he was, even if it was all an act.

His blink was heavy and filled with annoyance. "I'd like to get an early start in the morning, but that depends on my agenda for the morning. Have you made a decision?"

He meant it depended on if he had to fit killing his wife into his schedule or not. The pomposity of it made me want to kick something.

I managed to hold my temper. Somewhat. "You haven't really left me much choice."

"No, I haven't."

"Then, there's my answer," I said, tossing the towel I'd used on my hair to the bed.

"Good. I'm pleased." He stood and nodded as if to seal the arrangement. "We'll get started when I get back."

He was almost out of the room when his words sunk in. "You mean when *we* get back. To London." Right?

He paused at the door, turning only his head toward me, one hand bracing the frame. "No, I mean when *I* get back. *From* London." His clarification delivered, he continued out of the room.

The floor felt like it was dropping from beneath me. "No, no, no, hold on." Gripping the towel around me, I scampered after him. "You can't possibly be suggesting that you're going to leave me here."

"No, I'm not *suggesting* that. I'm saying that exactly." He kept walking. Didn't even look back at me as he spoke.

Though he was still moving, I stopped, shocked. "No way. You can't leave me here. How can you leave me here?"

"Very easily. I simply get on my plane and don't allow you to board with me."

He was all the way through the family room and rounding the kitchen by the time I got my feet to move again. "But I agreed to your stupid plan! I gave you what you want! You can take me with you. You won. I lost. It's over."

"It's not over. It's just beginning." Halting, he twisted his body toward me. "And you know why I can't take you with me."

The way his eyes looked into me—looked *through* me, holding me in place—I knew he was a step ahead of me. As always.

"No, actually, I don't," I said, refusing to accept it. As always.

With a sigh, he took two steps toward me. "Celia, we need to be beyond these little lies. If you're really going to submit to letting me break you down, there needs to be honesty between us."

God, he was so patronizing.

He was right about me and my motives, but that he was so sure he was right was infuriating.

It made me more determined than ever to stick to my story.

"Fine," I said, readjusting the towel since it had slipped in my pursuit. "If we're being honest, tell me honestly why I can't go to London with you."

His head cocked slightly, his gaze piercing deeper into my skin, into my bones. His expression was a challenge, as if to say, *Really? You really want me to spell out why you can't be trusted?*

"Whatever you're thinking I'll do, I won't do it. I promise." I'd gotten good at being able to lie while making direct eye contact.

"You won't run away? You won't try to escape the first opportunity you find? Forgive me for not believing you." He didn't give me a chance to refute, turning and walking away once again.

I scurried after him. "What's the point of honesty if you aren't going to believe anything I say?"

"Trust is earned. Once you've been honest for a significant amount of time, once you've proven your honesty over and over, then I will trust you. Until then, you'll remain here." He paused inside his room to toe off his shoes, then threw me a brow-raised glance, as if to reprimand me for entering his private quarters without his permission.

I hesitated, waiting to see if his reprimand would go further, but it didn't. Seeming to decide I wasn't worth the trouble, he pivoted away from me and crossed to his bed where he removed his watch and set it on the nightstand.

Quickly running through my options, I decided to change my tactic. "How long? How long before you come back?" Maybe he'd be back soon. An extra week on the island wasn't worth arguing about.

His forehead creased as he considered. "I need to catch up on work for a bit. Then it's the holidays, which always put things behind. I'll need some time to catch up from that as well. I should be able to get away again by the end of February."

"THE END OF FEBRUARY?" I was officially shouting. "You can't just abandon me here for three months!"

"Can't I?" The twinkle in his eye, that smirk—this clearly entertained him.

But he hadn't thought it all through. There was no way he had. "What will people say? My family? How are you going to explain this to my mother and father? If they haven't heard from me for a while, they'll at least expect a phone call for Christmas."

He wasn't at all fazed.

"I'm sure no one would question why my wife would want to spend the winter in the Caribbean rather than England." He unbuttoned his shirt as he spoke, his attention only half reserved for me. "As for your parents, I won't have to explain anything. You'll explain things just fine."

"I'll explain things?" I tried to guess what he meant. "If you think you're going to get me to lie to them—"

He cut me off sharply. "You seem to have forgotten the information I've accessed on your laptop."

Meaning he had the passwords to my email accounts. He could easily email them as me. He could even look at past correspondence to copy my voice. I could picture what he'd say—*I loved Amelie so much I'm staying until spring. The internet doesn't work so I can't be reached. I'm only able to send this because I took a day trip to Nassau.*

He really did have me trapped. Had me captive in every way possible. And all my scheming, all my calculating was for naught.

Adrenaline coursed through my body as rage took over. All week I'd been a dormant volcano on the brink of turning active, the fire inside me heating up and now I'd reached a boiling point. He wanted me to break? Well, I wanted *him* to break. I wanted him to hurt.

Quickly, I scanned my surroundings and found a ceramic vase on his dresser top, a piece that was probably some antique worth some ungodly amount.

I didn't care.

I picked it up and flung it at him as hard as I could.

Of course he saw it coming and ducked out of the way. The vase exploded against the wall behind him, shattering into several pieces.

The gaze Edward pinned on me then was cool and narrow. "Temper, temper, little bird."

That's all I was to him. Something insignificant. A bird. A broken bird, at that, because he'd clipped my wings.

"Is this part of it? You've already started, haven't you?" If he meant to break me down, he was on his way to succeeding.

He didn't answer, shrugging his shirt off his shoulders as he crossed the room to toss it on the chair against the opposite wall. When he turned back to me, he nodded toward the pottery pieces. "I hope you don't plan on leaving your mess for Sanyjah to clean up."

My hands were balled into fists at my sides, my breath coming fast and shallow in my chest. I already wanted to punch him. Suggesting I get on my knees and straighten up was the last straw.

Bending down, I picked up a shard that had landed nearby. Then, when I found the piece had a sufficiently jagged edge, I didn't hesitate. I didn't think. I just did.

Holding the fragment up in the air, I charged toward him. I lost my towel on the way. I was naked, and I didn't care. The desire to hurt him was too real, too sharp, as sharp as the ceramic in my hand.

He caught me at my forearm, because he was faster and stronger than I was. He gripped the other as well, jerking it behind my back, drawing me near so that the tips of my breasts brushed against his chest. It didn't escape me that this was the closest I'd been to having my bare skin against his. Less than a week ago, I would have considered the position a win, would have fallen willingly into him. Would have given him all of me.

Now he wanted all of me, and I wanted him dead.

And he knew it.

But instead of wrenching the weapon away from me, he moved the tip to his throat. Lifting his chin, exposing his neck, he offered himself. "Do it. Right there. The carotid artery is your best shot at a clean kill. Swipe all the way across to get both branches. It takes more strength than you think it will, so be sure to push deep."

I held my hand still, keeping the point at his skin, and I thought about it. For a second, I really thought about it.

Then, with a sigh that sounded more like a growl, I dropped the shard, letting it fall to the tile floor with a clunk.

"There now, that's more honest. We both know you don't have the stomach for murder." Though it loosened, Edward's grip on my forearms remained. His thumb traced along the inside of my wrist. Up, down, sending goosebumps across my arm, causing my thighs to vibrate.

"I hate you," I seethed.

"That doesn't bother me."

I wrestled out of his hold and took a step back from him. His eyes perused me, scanning up from my toes to my lips, lingering on the parts of my body that interested him most. He was so fucking arrogant. As if he had a right to look at me that way.

Snatching his discarded shirt, I wrapped it around me. "I wouldn't get so cocky if I were you. I might not be a murderer right now, but three months on this island is a long time. A lot could change."

With that, I left him along with the mess I'd made. If he really wanted it cleaned, he could take care of it himself. He wanted me to submit to him, then fine. But if we weren't beginning until he returned, I had three months to do whatever the hell I wanted, and I planned to do just that.

I HARDLY SLEPT. Variations of the dream I'd had during my nap days ago played out throughout the night. Sometimes I was being chased, sometimes I was the one chasing, but it was always me and a man. The anonymous man, who wasn't quite so anonymous anymore. While I could never see his face, I knew in my gut who it was. Who else would I run after?

Who else would make me run?

I gave up hope for sleep around dawn. Then I just lay there waiting, listening for sounds of Edward stirring in the main part of the house.

I finally heard him around eight. After throwing on a sundress and slipping on a pair of flip-flops, I came out to talk to him. A quick look in the hall mirror showed that I looked as bad as I felt—dark circles under my eyes, my face blotchy. I cringed, but the poor appearance would help.

With my arms wrapped around myself and my head bowed, I found him in the living room giving instructions to Mateo regarding his luggage.

"How sweet," he said when he saw me. "You came to say goodbye." With a nod, he ushered Mateo out to the jeep.

"Can I see you to the plane?" I asked, demurely.

"No, but you can see me to the door."

We walked the distance in silence. I could feel the heat of him at my side, but I wouldn't let it warm me. I stayed cold. I stayed focused.

"I need something," I said, turning toward him when we reached the door. "I need some reassurance. When this is all done, you'll let me go? We'll get a divorce and part with no other baggage between us?"

"Yes." His voice was gentle. Soothing almost.

"You mean that?"

"I do."

I searched his eyes while he searched mine, looking for a speck of compassion I could prey on. I was nearly sure I saw it—a flash of something kind behind his cool blue eyes.

I stepped closer to him. "And when you come back, in February, and you begin...your thing," I couldn't force myself to use his words for what he planned to do to me, "how long will I be here after that?"

"As long as it takes."

"I need an expiration. Otherwise I could be here forever."

"Or you could be dead."

That word again. It could have been devastating to hear so many times. If I weren't so fucking pissed.

Knowing this was my last chance, I pulled out all the stops. I laid it on thick. "Please, Edward." I reached out to curl my fingers in his shirt, linen again. Black this time. Fitting for the demon that he was. "I know I was awful to you, that I'm an awful person. I know I deserve whatever you have planned for me, but you're better than that. You're better than me. Please take me with you. I won't survive three months here. I'll do what you want. I'll be the perfect wife, whatever you want, just take me with you."

The words were staged, but I hadn't planned the tears. The tears, I was pretty sure, were real.

His hand came up to settle over mine. "Stop, bird," he said softly. "Stop with the lies."

He had no heart. He was nothing inside.

How well I knew what that was like.

The tears fell harder, and my grip tightened on his shirt as I grew spiteful. "What's going to stop me from going after you when you let me go? I'll tell everyone what you've done, that you've abducted me and forced me into your sick games. You'll be ruined."

"You aren't really helping your case here, Celia."

"There's no way what I'm saying is a revelation. I'm trying to insure that I get out of here alive." I brought my other fist to meet the one already on his chest, and I wasn't sure anymore if I wanted to beat him with them or hold him so tightly that he couldn't possibly leave without dragging me with him.

"You'll get out of here alive. As soon as you're broken down. And when that truly happens, there's no way you'd turn me in to anyone."

"Oh really." I tried to drop my hands, but he clasped them both under his, holding them in place. I could feel his heartbeat under my palm. Steady and strong. Calm.

"You seem to not understand what you'll become when you're broken down," he said, stroking his fingers over my skin. It was a lover's caress.

He was as good at pretending as I was.

It distracted me, but not enough to not ask the question he was leading me to ask. "What's that?"

He leaned forward, his lips ghosting along my forehead. "Mine."

FIVE

AS SOON AS Edward was gone, I began looking for a way to escape.

He'd warned me that his staff was loyal to him, but with eleven adults on the island, there had to be someone who had a conscience. Someone who knew keeping a grown woman captive was wrong. These were good people, too. I'd spent time with them now, and couldn't believe that there wasn't one of them that would try to help me.

I chose who I'd approach carefully. Joette was the matriarch, the woman that Edward had initially befriended. Winning her favor would likely be the hardest, no matter how friendly and doting she'd been. It followed that her children would stand by her in most things, which was why I decided to approach one of the spouses.

Sanyjah, Mateo's wife, was the obvious choice.

Quieter than most of the women, Sanyjah was one of the primary housekeepers and spent a good deal of time around the main house. That meant I saw her more than almost anyone else except Joette and Tom, who did the daily cooking.

I found her later in the morning in Edward's room, cleaning up the ceramic from the vase I'd broken the night before.

"I'll be done in a few minutes," she said when I came in, obviously thinking I wanted use of the room.

"Actually, I came to talk to you."

She stood up straight, leaning on the broom, her expression mildly surprised. "Do you need something? Did Tom forget to stock your cupboards with toilet paper?"

The staff had never acted like servants around Edward. There could only be a handful of reasons why they'd behave differently with me. Either he'd told them to, which seemed unnecessary, and Edward never did anything unnecessarily. Or I hadn't given them any reason to act any other way.

The latter was more likely. I'd been nice enough with all of them but not particularly friendly. Obviously, I'd been a shitty guest.

I hoped that didn't bite me in the ass now. Hopefully, an explanation of my plight would forgive my previous conduct.

"No, nothing like that. Here, let me help." I bent down to pick up the shards I should have cleaned up the night before. When she protested, I dismissed her. "This was my fault, anyway. Only right that I'm the one to clean it up."

"You knocked it over?" The suspicion in her voice was reasonable. The vase had been placed across the room.

"I threw it. I was angry." I tossed the pieces into the garbage bag at Sanyjah's side then stood again. "I was angry because Edward is keeping me captive here. He won't let me leave. But now he's gone, and so I'm begging you to help me. Please, help me?"

Sanyjah peered at me curiously, as though she thought I might be testing her. Then she laughed and went back to sweeping the particles that had been left behind. "Sure I'll help you. I'll help by cleaning up after you."

"I know this sounds ridiculous, but I'm telling the truth. He tricked me into coming here, and now he's left me here."

"Tricked you? You married him, didn't you?"

"Yes, but." Of course anything I said about that would make my credibility worse. "I did willingly marry him," I said, thinking fast. "I didn't know what kind of a man he was when I did. He hid his true colors, and now I'm his prisoner."

She laughed again, shaking her head. Maybe I'd picked the wrong spouse after all.

I tried again. "I know there's a phone somewhere on the island with satellite reception. If you could just get me to it, I can call my father and..."

"I'm sorry, I can't do that," she said, serious now. "Now, if you'll excuse me, I need to finish my work."

She turned her back toward me, ending the discussion.

My attempts with Marge and Peter went similarly. In desperation, I moved onto Joette's children, but trying to plea to Mateo and Dreya was just as fruitless. Either I wasn't taken seriously or I was flatly dismissed. Clearly, they'd been given orders and those orders wouldn't be ignored.

I considered appealing to everyone all at once at dinner. Maybe with all of them together they'd see reason.

But, while we'd had dinner together nightly when Edward was on the island, that evening I was left only with a premade meal in the fridge from Joette.

The next day I tried something more demure with Tom, asking for use of the phone to call Edward. "We're newlyweds and all, and I already miss him."

She winked. "Exactly why he needs some time away from you. Pretty, young wives are distracting. Who's gonna pay the bills if you don't let the man work?"

Escaping was going to be harder than I'd thought.

I waited out the week. Though Joette and Tom and Sanyjah came almost daily, the house was quieter than it had been my entire honeymoon. Thanksgiving came and went, uncelebrated by Bahamian natives.

Whatever. It had never been my favorite holiday anyway. All those calories that had to be sweat off with extra workouts. Not that I didn't have time to exercise. Being stuck on Amelie was the perfect excuse to get in better shape. What else was there to do? It was paradise, but even paradise got boring after a while.

When Edward had been gone a week, I tried another approach, asking Eliana if I could tag along on her trip to Nassau for groceries.

She tilted her head up as if she was considering, and my chest fluttered with hope.

"I don't think that's a good idea," she said after a minute. "It's not safe."

"Not safe?"

"For a woman in your condition."

"A woman in my condition?" I was repeating everything she said in horror. What had Edward said about me? "Did he tell you I was pregnant?"

"No!" she said, her eyes wide. "Congratulations!"

"I'm not pregnant," I said with a frustrated scowl. "I meant, what do you mean about my condition?"

"It's best we not talk about serious things like that," she said mysteriously. "And leave grocery shopping to me. You stay here where you're looked after. Everything will be all right."

No, everything would not be all right. I was trapped, and no one would give me a straight reason for not wanting to help me.

So I tried to hide on the boat. Actually, I first tried to steal the boat. Sure, I'd never driven one before, but it couldn't be that hard.

Except it completely was. I found the steering wheel and where to put a key, but the rest of the buttons were meaningless. And even if I wanted to brave it, I soon learned the keys were locked up in a safe. There was a sailboat as well, but it was chained to the dock and secured with a padlock. That key, I presumed, was also in the safe.

And thus I was forced to try to hide instead. I buried myself under some blankets at the stern of the boat and waited.

Mateo caught me right away.

I tried again the following week. Monday was always grocery day, which meant I didn't have to cause suspicion by asking when the next boat would go out. I hoped that not mentioning wanting to go with Eliana this time would make it seem like it had left my mind. I got to the dock way before the time she usually left and found a better hiding spot on the cruiser.

Again, Mateo discovered me.

The next week it was Louvens who found me. Which meant I still might have a shot. He was the single man of the bunch and his sneaky stares at me in my bikini and on my daily runs had not gone unnoticed.

"We should take a ride to the mainland together," I said, sidling up to him. "Just you and me."

He wasn't unaffected. The quickness in his breathing gave him away.

"Think how much fun we could have," I pressed. My voice was sticky sweet, and the way I smoothed my palm down his chest was borderline inappropriate.

He grabbed my wrist before I could get anywhere interesting. "If you keep this up, I'm going to have to limit your access to just the house."

The island already felt small and claustrophobic. I couldn't survive confined to the house.

Interpreting my frown, he added, "It's for your safety."

For your safety. There was that phrase again.

"What exactly did my husband say to you about me?" I asked, my tone close to pleading.

Lou frowned and looked out over the horizon. "I'm afraid I'm not the one to ask."

There was no question who *was* the one to ask. When I got back to the house, I stormed into the kitchen where I could hear Tom and Joette singing together while they peeled potatoes.

"What did he tell you?" I demanded. "What did Edward tell you that convinced you that keeping me a prisoner was a matter of my safety?"

Tom looked to her mother. Joette sighed and wiped her hands on her apron. "Why don't you sit down?"

I didn't want to sit down.

But it was mid-December. Including the time with Edward, I'd been on the island five weeks, and if I had any hope of leaving, I realized I had to change my tactics.

I sat down.

Joette took my hand in hers, and as much as I wanted to find it patronizing, I didn't. It felt warm and comforting, even as the terrible words crossed her lips.

"Edward confided in us the truth," she said, tenderly. "About your mental health. About your delusions. Of course he isn't keeping you captive here, darling. He's trying to protect you. We all are. What a wonderful husband you have that he devotes such attention to his sick wife, even from afar."

I snatched my hand away from hers and tried to swallow past the lump in my throat. *My word against yours.* That's what I'd said to him. That's what my plan had been in trapping him with my game. He'd beat me to it. Whatever credibility I might have had with his staff was taken away by him simply telling them that I was crazy.

I'd said it before, but I hadn't believed it until right then. Hadn't truly believed it. I was Edward's prisoner. The only way I'd leave the island was if he chose to let me go.

SIX

THE GIFTS BEGAN ARRIVING AS SOON as I stopped trying to leave.

The first was the clothes. I'd already been quite vocal to everyone who would hear it about my limited wardrobe. I'd come to the island expecting to be there for two weeks. Two weeks that I'd planned to do nothing but seduce my husband, which meant I'd brought lots of short dresses and skimpy swimsuits. Though December in the Caribbean was still fairly temperate, the rainy season was in full swing and more than once I'd wished for a pair of yoga pants. And a sweater. And some jeans. A pantsuit.

More than once I'd thought about the monthly stipend Edward had promised me as his wife. More than once I fantasized spending it. One hundred thousand pounds could go a long way on Fifth Avenue.

In the end, I hadn't had to spend my money on clothing at all—if I actually had any money. Because when Eliana returned the following week from her grocery run, she'd come back with boxes and boxes of clothes.

"Thank you for finally listening," I exclaimed as I tore into the first box, noting the designer label on the outside of the package.

"You're welcome, but it wasn't me," she said with a shrug. "This is all thanks to your husband."

I considered taking a pair of scissors to whatever I found inside, but it was too perfect—a red jersey wrap dress that was just my style. They were all perfect, every item. Every outfit was tailored to me, as though I'd been measured, as though I'd personally selected them.

And there was clothing for a range of occasions, from fancy to casual, all of them designer made. With designer shoes to match.

So he'd found a personal shopper and given her a big check. That wasn't hard. I was grateful for the clothes, but I wasn't grateful to *him*.

Except, then I found the notes, handwritten and tucked inside each item. Simple, brief notes that said things such as *Reminds me of the dress you wore to that first dinner at my house* on a floral sundress, and *A casual Sunday look* on a printed jumpsuit, and *White, the color that wedding dresses should be* on a white pair of linen pants.

He'd had a hand in the selection. Even if he hadn't done the shopping himself, he'd chosen with thought and then made sure I knew it.

But he was still my captor.

I crumpled all the notes and threw them into my bathroom wastebasket.

Then, after putting away all my clothes, one hundred pieces in all, I pulled the notes back out of the wastebasket and shoved them into the drawer of my nightstand. I wouldn't read them again; I didn't care about what they said or what they meant, but neither could I bear to let them go.

THE NEXT DAY Dreya invited me to morning yoga.

"I used to lead classes at the resorts in Nassau. Now I teach it to the kids." Dreya, I'd learned, was primarily responsible for homeschooling and caring for the fourteen children that lived on the island. She didn't shoulder the burden completely on her own; the other men and women rotated their duties to assist her, and though the youngest, Marge and Erris's baby, was only four months old, Mateo and Sanyjah's eldest two girls, at fourteen and fifteen years of age, were tasked with a fair amount of childcare as well as grandma watching.

And all of them, including Azariah, Joette's eighty-five-year-old mother, apparently met on the beach near the staff quarters every morning for yoga.

I'd always hated yoga. I hated group exercise in general, but particularly one that had me twisting in silly positions with weird names.

But island life had left me lonely. I had no internet. I had no phone. And most of my interactions with the staff had remained transactional. I ate my meals alone. I took my daily run alone. I spent my time alone.

So I accepted the invitation to yoga. I bent and stretched and laughed when five-year-old Jaden toppled over out of Vrksasana and smiled impressively when Azariah did a full back bend that I was smart enough not to even attempt.

And when the whole sequence was almost done and I lay in Balasana, child's pose, my forehead on the mat that Dreya had provided, the sound of gentle sighs around me mixing with the crash of ocean waves behind us, I realized I could breathe easier and deeper than I had in a very long time.

"Will you join us tomorrow?" Dreya asked when the mats were all cleared up, and I had nothing to do but leave to go back to the main house.

"I'll be here any day you let me," I answered honestly.

"Every weekday then."

I gave her an answering smile. "I'd like that."

"Your husband will be pleased to hear."

I didn't let that final remark ruin it, letting it fall off me as I turned to go on my way, but I knew without being explicitly told that the invitation hadn't really come from Dreya at all.

THE FOLLOWING day was Christmas Eve. I remarked on it, casually, to Tom.

"Perhaps you want to write a letter to your family?"

The suggestion was startling. And exhilarating.

"Can I?" I clarified. "I mean, am I allowed?"

"Why wouldn't you be allowed?"

I could think of several reasons, the most obvious being that I'd tell them I was being held captive and to get the FBI involved in finding me ASAFP.

But Tom was digging out stationery and a pen, and I wasn't about to clue her in on her mistake.

I kept it simple, sticking to facts and details needed to initiate a rescue mission. I addressed it to my father, knowing he was the one who had the power to do things, the man who would make things happen. I didn't tell him he'd been right, that Edward Fasbender was no good, that he was a devil, that I should have avoided him at all costs.

He'd already know that without me saying it.

I sealed the note in the envelope Tom had provided and handed her the letter, feeling more hopeful than I had in weeks.

THE NEXT GIFT came Christmas morning, along with another invitation.

I'd expected to be alone for the day, and that idea had brought on the worst bout of melancholy yet. Though I wasn't emotionally close to my parents, we were close in other ways. We did things together. We went to the ballet, the opera, charity fundraisers. We spent holidays together. We exchanged cliché, meaningless gifts, but we were together.

Except for the year I was in the hospital, I'd always spent Christmas in their condo, snuggled up in my pajamas, watching *It's a Wonderful Life* and *Miracle on 34th Street*. There'd be an early dinner first, with the Pierces, either at our house or at theirs, but classic movies was the evening routine. My father would leave less than halfway through the first one and my mother would drink too much sherry, but it was tradition. It was what I knew, and I missed it more than I thought I could.

I missed them. More than I should. More than they likely missed me.

But I had dealt with those feelings laying in bed on Christmas Eve. And after acknowledging them, I'd made a plan for distraction. I'd spend the day reading something from the library—one of the countless business communication books or one of the worn paperback romances that I assumed belonged to Edward's sister, Camilla, or his ex-wife, Marion. The pickings were slim, but I'd always enjoyed reading. There would be something to occupy my mind, even if I had to reread something I'd already read.

Instead, I awoke to the smell of something delicious baking and the sounds of commotion.

"What's going on?" I asked Tom when I found her in the kitchen pulling cinnamon rolls out of the oven.

"These should do you for breakfast," she said, as if that was an answer. "Sorry this is all I have time for before getting back to my own. We'll have dinner at our quarters at three. Dress casual."

"Okay." I hadn't thought for a moment I'd be welcome at their family Christmas celebrations, and I wasn't about to question the invitation. "I heard noise in the library too. What's going on in there?"

"Oh, that's your Christmas present from Edward. I think you'll be quite delighted with his choices."

Without hesitation, I left to see what she was talking about. There were a few people in the library—Louvens and Peter as well as the two eldest of Peter and Tom's kids. While Lou was breaking down boxes, the rest were loading empty shelves with books. I surveyed the titles. There were a lot of classics but more contemporary reads, titles that I recognized but hadn't yet picked up. Titles that were definitely on my TBR.

Edward had guessed my taste in books as well as he'd guessed my taste in clothes.

Except, guess wasn't the right word for it. He'd studied me. He'd learned me.

My throat felt suddenly tight.

Unwittingly, a memory popped in my mind, one of the last games

I'd played with Hudson. Or I'd thought it was a game. He'd decided it was something different. The subject was Alayna Withers, the woman who would one day become his wife. He'd called me from the Hamptons with a list of books he needed me to purchase and have delivered to his penthouse immediately.

He hadn't told me, but I'd known they were for her. Even then, I'd suspected where things were headed. That he was done with me.

The books he'd chosen had been personal, it was obvious. He'd put care and thought into the selections, and a strange throb had begun in my chest. Like a knocking against my ribcage from deep inside. I wouldn't let the emotion out, wouldn't let it show itself, but I'd recognized it.

It was envy.

What would that feel like, to have a man care about me so much, to have him be that attentive and adoring that he'd fill shelves and shelves with exactly the books I wanted to read?

When Louvens and Peter and Tom left a short while later, I knelt on the library floor, stared at the shelves of new books, and took long, deep breaths until the dizziness went away. Until the tightness loosened in my chest. Until I could make my mind separate the gift from the man who'd given it.

THE GIFTS CONTINUED the next week and into the new year, if gifts were what they were. The allowances. The evidences that I remained on Edward's mind.

First, on the next grocery day, came a beautiful handcrafted wooden chess set and a book on how to play. Which was fine and all, but I knew how to play already, though it had been ages since I had, and who was supposed to oppose me?

I found myself reading the book anyway, learning new moves, brushing up on techniques. I set the board up and played against myself as best I could.

The next week, Eliana began joining me for afternoon games. She beat me most of the time, but I was a quick study, and the company was good.

One day when she came to play, she noticed the copy of *One Hundred Years of Solitude* that I had on the table near the sofa, face down to keep my place.

"If you have specific books you'd like, let me know," she said. "I'll see what I can do to get them."

I wasn't sure if that meant she'd go through Edward or she'd simply pick them up on grocery day. There wasn't much I wanted, at the moment. He'd stocked me up fairly well.

Except, there was a subject I was interested in, a topic I wanted to know more about before my husband returned. "Could you maybe see if you could get me some books about BDSM?"

"Romance books?" she asked, her expression strange.

"No. Nonfiction. About being a submissive. A how-to guide or whatever you can find."

The following week, she brought me three—*Exploring Kink, A Dominant's Guide for Submissives,* and *Sadistic Desires.* I felt powerful with them in my possession. It gave me a guide for my future.

And if Edward knew about them, fine. Perhaps it was good he knew that I was prepared.

The same week, I learned that Marge had been a massage therapist before she'd moved to the island. I discovered it when, after yoga one morning, she announced that I was to follow her to the pool house. It was right outside the main house, but I'd never bothered to go in. Now I discovered I'd been missing out. It was well-equipped with a steam room and boxing ring and, surprise, surprise, a massage room. For two hours, I lay on that table and Marge worked every muscle until I was a noodle.

"See if you can stay that loose until next week," she said when she was done.

"What's next week?"

"Your next massage. Mister Fasbender has decided they'll be weekly."

I knew by now that everything happened at *Mister Fasbender's* request, and still, each declaration to that effect made my stomach drop and flutter all at once.

THAT NIGHT I wrote another letter to my parents. The first one had gone unanswered, and I suspected it had never been sent at all. This one wouldn't reach them either, but it felt good to talk to them. Felt good to open up and say things, honest things. Things I wished I could say to someone. Anyone.

It's beautiful here.

I miss my home. I miss my freedom. But I'm not any more alone here than I was in New York.

Something's changing in me, and I don't know who I am anymore. Tell me who I am.

I sealed the envelope and gave it to Tom, futile as I knew it was.

THE NEXT WEEK a Hispanic beautician came back with Eliana from Nassau. She couldn't speak a lick of English, and I could only speak a handful of words in Spanish, which I was sure was intentional. Language barrier or not, she understood what I wanted with my hair and after three hours of fussing with it, my highlights and length were back to what I preferred.

The following week beauty supplies were sent. High-quality skin care products and makeup, more than one person could ever use with ingredients that almost made me stop jonesing for my Botox.

The next week it was a Korean woman who arrived from Nassau, with perfect eyebrows and full pink lips. She spoke more English than the hairdresser, but it still took me quite a while to understand her. At first, I thought she'd come to do my nails. When she pulled out a wax warmer and applicator sticks, I figured she was there to shape my brows into perfect arches like her own. And she did do that.

But when she was finished, she gestured lower, toward my shorts.

I did usually keep things neat down there. I'd attempted a trim or two while on the island, but I'd pretty much surrendered to letting it turn into a jungle. I could say it didn't matter without having a man around who'd see it, but the truth was I'd always waxed for myself. I liked the feeling of being mostly bare. I liked the way my underwear rubbed against my skin, the way my bikinis smoothed without a tuft of hair underneath.

I should have been appreciative that Edward had thought of this. Of even this.

But this wasn't a gift. This was going too far.

Leaving the beautician in confusion, I stormed out of the pool house where all my beauty procedures had been performed, and into the house to find someone—anyone—who would listen to my complaint.

Unfortunately for her, I found Tom.

"This has gone too far," I said, my tone harsh and louder than necessary. "He's trying to butter me up. Trying to make me forget I'm in captivity by playing nice with all these favors. But I haven't forgotten. And these aren't favors—not really. They're for him. The clothes? The hair? The makeup? A bikini wax? This is for him. This is what he wants from a wife—a perfect, pretty Barbie doll. He has no right demanding this from me. He has no right!"

Tom looked up from the dough she'd been kneading and wiped a bead of sweat from her forehead with her knuckle. "What about the chess? And the massages? What about the books? Are those all for him too?"

The question threw me off guard, but I was too worked up to let it go. I paced the kitchen as I talked. "Yes. Yes! Because he's dictating my life. It doesn't matter that I like it or want it. He's deciding. He's not even here. He's however many hundreds of miles away, and he's still controlling everything. He's choosing what I fill my days with and shaping me in whatever way he likes as though he expects me to follow his commands. As though I'm his fucking submissive. As though I'm—" *His.*

I cut off before the word passed my lips, but it stopped me in my tracks.

Tom rose one expectant brow, waiting for the end of a sentence I would never finish. I couldn't say it out loud, but this was my fate, I realized. This was what I'd agreed to. To break down. To submit. To become his.

Scowling, I spun around and headed back to the pool house where I let the Korean woman wax my pussy. She took everything off, leaving me bare. Usually I left a strip, but it didn't matter what my preference was. This was what Edward wanted, and that's what he'd get.

Later, I sat out on the lanai, my knees cradled to my chest as I stared numbly out at the ocean. Joette stuck her head out, most likely to tell me she was leaving for the day, but seeing me, she came outside completely. She didn't say anything, just stood there, patiently, making herself available.

Without looking at her, I spoke. "I know what you said. I know what he told you about why I'm here and that you believed him. How can you not see what this really is?"

"How can *you* not?"

My head swung sharply in her direction. A frown tugged at my lips, confusion knitted my brow.

She perched on the edge of the deck chair next to me. "I've known Edward for quite some time. He's a man who holds much inside him. Rage, mostly. Destruction. He can be compassionate and thoughtful, but his darkness has always remained at his core, an infection that has no cure.

"Until now. Until you."

I opened my mouth to speak, but no sound came out. I didn't understand what she was saying well enough to protest, and I certainly didn't agree.

"He's different with you," she went on. "It's not something you can see because you've only ever known him as the man who's met you. But he *is* different. He's more the man I think he wants to be. The man he needs to be, even if he doesn't see it yet. It scares him, I'm sure, and perhaps he isn't behaving the way he should with you, and for that I'm sorry. But I can see something coming—for both of you—and that's what I'm holding on for. I hope you can find a way to hold on for the same."

She was loyal, there was no doubt about that. And optimistic. And I wanted to say her rose-colored view was a bold-faced lie.

But she stood up to leave, and I said nothing at all.

THE FOLLOWING FRIDAY, the second week of February, I decided to do something new—I invited everyone to dinner.

Well, not everyone. The main house was big, but not quite big enough to handle twelve adults and fourteen children.

But when Edward had been here, he'd had most of the grown-ups over every night so I did the same. I approached Tom about the idea first thing in the morning, and by noon she'd confirmed that most of them would be there.

"We're looking forward to it," she said with such sincerity that I chose to believe her.

That evening, we gathered. Joette, Mateo and Sanyjah, Tom and Peter, Dreya and Eliana. I'd been told earlier that Erris and Marge had volunteered to stay with the kids, so I hadn't expected them.

"Where's Louvens?" I asked when I looked around the table and noticed him missing.

Dreya and Eliana exchanged a glance that made me regret asking. As easy as they made it seem, they were a broken family of sorts. Louvens and Eliana had been married and had four children together before Eliana had fallen in love with Lou's little sister. They all seemed to get along whenever I saw them, but perhaps there were disagreements that I wasn't party to.

"He'll be here," Joette said dismissively. "How's the plantain?"

The plantain was delicious. The whole meal was delicious, Joette's cooking made better by eating it in the company of others. It was noisy and chaotic and that was wonderful. The conversation engaged me. The private stories of their families held my interest in a way I'd never thought domestic tales would interest me. I laughed—really laughed—for the first time in months. Maybe even longer.

I felt, shockingly, at home.

We were midway through the meal when I heard the front door open, and less than a minute later, I discovered why Louvens had missed dinner, where he had been.

He'd been at the airstrip.

He'd been picking up Edward.

SEVEN

"EDWARD." It felt like I talked about him all the time, like he was always present in my mind, but seeing him in the flesh felt like seeing a stranger. And as much as I hated him, my breath caught in my chest, my heart tripping with elation.

His eyes held mine as he approached me, one hand held behind his back.

I stood automatically. "I didn't know you were... What are you doing here?" I hadn't expected him for another couple of weeks.

"Could I really stay away from my wife this weekend? It's our first Valentine's Day together. I wouldn't miss it for the world."

Valentine's Day. Time lost all meaning on Amelie. I barely knew it was Friday let alone that there was a holiday tomorrow.

Especially when the holiday wasn't important.

Valentine's Day wasn't why Edward was here.

This was for show, as was the bouquet of calla lilies and roses that he presented from behind his back, but the flowers and the tender kiss on the lips did something to me. Dazed me. Made it hard to think.

I swallowed, running my sweaty palms along the front of my dress in a pretense of smoothing my skirt. Tom was already up and taking care of the flowers, finding them a vase, and Mateo had another chair and place set before I could get my wits together.

Edward sat, taking my hand in his so I sat as well. His attention, though, was on those around him, listening and smiling as his staff brought him up to speed on island life.

I picked at my food after that, sipped anxiously at my wine. My stomach was in knots and the press of Edward's fingers laced through mine was distracting. The tug of an unanswered question swirled through my mind, wanting resolution.

When the group was preoccupied with an unimportant family debate, I couldn't take it anymore. I leaned toward him, keeping my voice quiet. "What happens now?"

"We finish dinner." Letting go of my hand and stretching his arm around my chair—a natural move for a husband who'd missed his bride —he bent into me, the warm air of his breath tickling my ear. "Then, tonight, we begin."

WHEN EDWARD HAD BEEN on the island before, the socializing had gone on long after the meal was over. This night, as though everyone had been given orders I wasn't aware of, the group departed as soon as the table was cleared.

Edward must have slipped away during the goodbyes because, immediately after our guests had left, he instructed me. "I've laid out clothes for you on your bed. Wear them and nothing else. Meet me in the library when you're finished."

With tingling fingers and toes, I nodded and left for my room. I hadn't decided if I meant to make this easy for him or not. I was still angry with him—outrageously angry—but two and a half months had made me more comfortable with that anger. It no longer spewed from me. I was able now to hold it, to wait.

Wait for what, I wasn't sure. I'd know when the time was right to draw it out.

Curiosity now dominated my emotions. And nervousness. What

would Edward do to me? Would it hurt too much? Would it not hurt enough?

I was beyond ready to know.

On my bed, I found the items he'd set out. They hadn't been with the clothes he'd sent me, so he must have brought it. I would have tossed them out otherwise. The underwear were plain white cotton briefs. The matching bra had no wire and did nothing in the way of support. The white dress—smock was a better term for it—had no shape. It hung past my knees, accentuating absolutely nothing about my body. White ballet flats accompanied the outfit. The best thing I could say about them was that they fit.

I lingered in front of my bathroom mirror for almost a full minute. I'd given up doing my makeup since I'd been on the island, and while my body had developed a nice tan, sunscreen had kept my face blotchy and uneven. Edward hadn't specified anything about cosmetics, but he seemed to be going for plain, a look that I didn't wear comfortably.

Some foundation and a bit of rouge would make me feel better. I had a feeling that was the reason he wouldn't want me applying them.

I settled for freshening my lipgloss, leaving my lips a natural pink, then headed to the library to find my husband.

"This isn't sexy," I said when I arrived.

He glanced up at me from behind his computer. "I know."

Ouch.

But now I had to wonder—was this plain Jane appearance meant to throw me off balance or keep him from losing his?

The possibility that it was the latter felt warm in my belly.

A few taps of keys and the printer behind Edward woke up, shooting out several pages. "These are for you," he said, gathering the items and handing them to me.

I could feel the crease in my brow as I looked them over. Right away I noticed something very startling—the pages were emails.

"You just printed these. How are you on the internet? The Wi-Fi has never worked." I'd tried an unbelievable amount of times to connect with no success. There was only one server option. No password required. It wasn't like that was the reason I'd been locked out.

"Because I've had the server disconnected. I had it turned back on when I arrived."

"There's been a working server here the whole time?" I didn't know how he continued to surprise me.

He looked at me like I was ridiculous. "How else would I be able to work while I'm here? And don't get any ideas. It's password protected."

Password protected and disconnected server—the man really didn't trust me.

I considered lashing out about it and quickly decided not to. I'd already been confined to the island with no contact with the outside world. It wasn't like this was a new horror, even if it was new to discover the details around it.

With a sigh, I turned my focus back to the papers in my hand. They'd been printed from my email account. I scanned the top, my eyes rushing lower when I realized the top section was in reply to something below. I recognized the words there. They were my words. For the most part. They'd been edited to exclude the main point, which was that my husband had taken me captive, but the little that was left were the words I'd written to my parents in my first letter.

I shot daggers at him, again contemplating giving him my wrath, but really. What had I expected? I'd never really believed that those letters would get through, that he'd let me talk freely to my parents.

It was a pointless argument.

Taking another deep breath, I read through my mother's replies. Each were cordial and succinct. My mother preferred conversing on the phone, and she said as much in one of the emails, *It's too bad you don't have service there so you can call.*

Beyond that, there was nothing overtly warm. Nothing that expressed concern for me or my new marriage beyond the stock *We miss you* at the bottom of each message.

I tossed them down on Edward's desk, dismissively. "Can we start now?"

"They did send you a Christmas gift," he said gesturing to a Tiffany box on the corner of his desk that I'd overlooked. A bracelet, judging from the size. Probably diamonds. Not the most expensive item in the inventory but not the least either.

I didn't need to see it to know almost exactly what it was.

It was devastating that the gift that Edward sent, the books that currently surrounded me, were of more value to me than what my parents had sent.

Not wanting to give any of that away, I simply shrugged. "I'll look at it later, if you don't mind. When I'm alone."

"We gave them tickets to the symphony, by the way. Box seats."

I half chuckled because the gift was so exactly what I would have selected that they wouldn't have thought for a moment that I hadn't. "You're good," I said, flatly. "I have to give you that."

He nodded once as though he already knew. "Then let's go, shall we?"

My curiosity was killing me, but I managed to remain silent while Edward led me out the front doors and across the driveway to the path that ran the circumference of the island. Since I'd only ever walked it at night, I hadn't realized that the way was lit. They were possibly even lights that didn't come on with a timer and that Edward had turned them on tonight so I may have never noticed them. But the lights weren't the interesting thing about our journey.

The interesting thing was that I'd been this way enough in the daylight to know that there was nothing along the path for us to go to. The staff quarters were in the opposite direction, and unless Edward enjoyed a romp out in the jungle, the only reason I could imagine he would take me this way was to lead me to the cliffs that bordered the west side of the island.

Nervousness turned into fear.

"Where are you taking me?" I couldn't manage to keep the apprehension out of my voice.

Edward, who'd been a step ahead the whole time, turned back so he could walk alongside me, his hand pressed at my lower back.

It wasn't more comforting, if that's what he'd intended.

"We have a destination," he said, not sounding at all like a man who was about to kill his wife, but what did a man in that position sound like? "Not too much farther."

"It's not the journey there that concerns me. I'm concerned that I might not be making the journey back."

The walkway was lit only at our feet, but I could still see the hint of a smirk on his lips. "While it would be awfully fun to let that doubt remain, that isn't what tonight is about. Yes, you will be making the journey back."

I was only somewhat mollified. "What is tonight about, exactly?"

"Trust."

Any tension he'd relieved from his answer before returned with bravado. There were a hundred ways he could test my trust, ways I was certain not to like, and I wasn't entirely sure the cliffs weren't part of that, but I kept my mouth clamped shut and focused on holding onto my courage rather than what my courage might be used for.

Five minutes later, Edward directed me off the path toward the fence that bordered the island's edge. Beyond, the rock dropped off to the ocean one hundred feet below. I hadn't wandered over to this particular spot, but I'd pressed my body against the wood barrier at a place farther along the path and smiled over the dramatic expanse of sea beneath me.

My heart sped up to double its speed as we approached.

Once at the fence, he flipped a latch I hadn't known was there, and a portion of it swung out, opening to let us onto a stairway that I'd never known was there, pressed into the side of the mountain, kept hidden from other viewpoints. One flight down, and I could finally see where we were headed—a small, one-story bungalow with its own private beach.

"Is this your dungeon?" I asked at the door as Edward unlocked the front door with a key from his pocket.

He chuckled, a sound that I'd forgotten made my thighs draw up and tighten. "Nothing that nefarious."

"Your playroom?"

"Something like that." The door open, he reached in to flick on a light switch, then stepped aside to let me in.

I walked in and paused to survey my surroundings—the stone tile floor, the bamboo ceiling, the oriental-style windows, the wrap-around white couch with alternating black and gray and brown pillows, the matching love seat across from it, the square mocha coffee table that anchored the room.

Edward stood beside me, the heat of him radiating toward me. "I've brought women to the island before. I prefer to keep them out of the space I share with my children."

I finished where that thought led. "So you bring them here."

"So I've brought them here. Yes."

That felt heavy inside me and light at the same time. I didn't like the idea that I was in a space that he'd shared with others, but in bringing me here, he'd inadvertently told me that he didn't bring women to the main house. And he'd taken me there first.

It was clever, really. A cozy place he could fill with all sorts of sex toys without being afraid of his children stumbling upon them. Not that there were any obvious toys in sight, but there appeared to be at least one bedroom where he could hide away his whips and chains and fetish equipment.

I walked in farther to draw attention away from the shudder that ran through me at the thought. Even after all the time I'd spent preparing myself for whatever tortures he had in store for me, physical pain was still more a turn-off than a turn-on.

Well, *severe* physical pain, anyway. I'd really liked the hard spanking he'd given me, as much as I hated admitting it.

Hopefully he'd start off slow.

"Should we get to this?" I clapped my palms together, ignoring how damp they were.

Looking both amused and smug, he gestured for me to sit on the sofa. "I can make you a drink if you think that will help." He'd already crossed to the bar to make his own.

Liquor was tempting. It would ease the tension in my shoulders, calm my nerves. Lessen my inhibitions.

The last one was exactly the reason I decided to decline. Whatever was about to happen, whatever Edward was going to do to me, I needed my faculties present.

"Very well then." He took his tumbler of cognac and crossed to the love seat across from me, unbuttoning his jacket before he sat. He was wearing a suit, leading me to suspect he'd gone directly from work to the airport. He must be exhausted, but he didn't seem the least bit tired. In fact, he seemed acutely alert. Like the predator he was.

I waited.

He waited.

"This is an interesting setup," I said, beyond the time when it felt something should be said by someone. "Me here. You over there. Do you break me down simply with the power of your mind?"

He crossed one leg over the other and perched his hand holding the glass on his thigh. "This is how this will work," he said, and I had to force myself not to lean forward. "We will sit here, and when you're ready, you will tell me about something in your life, something that affected you deeply. Something not pleasant. Something that required you to rebuild yourself in the aftermath."

That had not been at all what I'd been expecting.

I repeated his words in my head before clarifying. "You want me to tell you a story?"

He shook his head impatiently. "Definitely not a story, at least not in the fictional sense. It will be from your life, and it will be true. You will describe the event and all the relevant circumstances surrounding it in exact detail. I may ask questions as you proceed. I'll expect answers. All of it, every single word that comes from your mouth, must be authentic."

Now I knew why he'd offered the drink.

I crossed my legs, mirroring his position. Already my head was whirring with the tales I could spin, petty, plausible fables from a rich girl's pretty life.

This was the stuff I was good at. This was going to be cake.

"I'll know it's not true, Celia," he warned, reading my mind like he lived inside it.

"How?" I challenged.

"I just will."

"But how?"

"Celia..." He gave me a stern stare that reminded me of the one my grandpa Werner used to terrify me with as a child whenever I was found doing something I wasn't supposed to do. "I'll know."

"What happens if you don't believe me?"

"If you're telling the truth, I *will* believe you."

I debated pushing the issue further because, really. How would he know? Even if I was honest and drudged up some hurt from the past and shared it with him in excruciating detail, he could accuse me of lying.

But just before I opened my mouth to say that, I looked at him again, really looked at him, and the sharp intensity of his gaze reminded me—he'd always seen me.

He'd see me now too.

There was something I was missing, though. None of the books about BDSM had covered anything like this. And I was pretty sure he was a sadist. Where did the pain come in?

"And then what happens?" I asked, no longer caring that I looked desperate in my need to know.

He looked at me plainly, as though the answer was obvious. "Then, depending on how you do, I'll respond."

There it was. What I'd been looking for. Where the pain would come in. "You'll take me to the bedroom, tie me up, and flog me until I'm screaming, you mean."

He tilted his head, his eyes narrowing as he studied me.

I'd gotten something wrong. I tried to guess what. Perhaps the flogger wasn't his instrument of choice. A cane then. Or maybe he was more inventive with his play. Or more hands-on. Choking, perhaps. Or he'd use his fists.

My stomach lurched at the thought of fists.

After what felt like an eternity, he spoke. "You seem to be under the impression that I beat women up."

"Don't you?" He was probably one of those guys who preferred to use words that didn't make his violent side sound so violent.

"Not typically."

I rolled my eyes, tired of this chasing around the bush. "Look, I know you do. Sasha said you did."

He lifted his chin inquisitively. "She did?"

"Yes. She said..." I tried to remember exactly what the woman at The Open Door party had said about Edward. *He's really good...if you can take a beating.* Which obviously meant that...

Oh, God.

It was a figure of speech.

This was the type of beating he meant to give me, not with physical pain, not with implements that weighed down my nipples or made my ass vibrate, but with words. My own words. My own pain used against me.

I swallowed, carefully. "So you just want me to pick some terrible thing that happened in my lifetime and tell you all about it like we're best girlfriends who've had too much wine?"

That smirk again. "I expect you to be vulnerable, yes."

If I hadn't understood the point of the game before, I did now. And in every way I couldn't have imagined, this was worse than I'd prepared for.

I really wished I'd taken that drink.

EIGHT

"TAKE ALL THE TIME YOU NEED," Edward said, stretching his arm across the sofa, settling in. His self-satisfied look told me what my own expression must have given away, and I remembered again why I hated him.

"I have one already," I said flippantly. "I met with this businessman on the pretense that he wanted to hire me. Oh, by the way, sorry I wasn't around to finish your office. Something came up." He'd never really intended for me to redesign his space, but I'd undertaken the task with sincerity. It pissed me off as much as anything else he'd done that I hadn't been able to see it to completion.

"The pieces you ordered came in. It got finished without you." His tone was flat and uninterested.

"And?"

He took a swallow of his cognac before answering. "Everything looks nice."

It looked fan-fucking-tastic, I was sure of it. He knew it too, but there was no way he'd give me anything, even that.

"Anyway." I let my focus drift, as though I was telling something romantic or whimsical. "I gave up my business, moved across an ocean, and married him. Then he told me he wanted to kill me. Now he's keeping me captive on his pleasure island." I brought my gaze back to him, narrowed and piercing.

If he wanted me to talk about something that affected me, then this definitely should count. There were very few moments in my life that had changed the course of my life the way that meeting him had.

His breaths were usually measured, but this one was deep. I saw it in the slight rise of his torso, the one tell he had that I wasn't as easy for him to manage as he liked me to believe.

He took another swallow of his drink then set it down on the side table. With laser focus, he regarded me. "Is this really what you want to talk about?"

Yes. Yes, it really was.

Except...

He'd said he might ask questions. He'd said he wanted me vulnerable. There were so many ways he could poke and prod at me in this arena, and it was an arena that truly did belong to him. I might be a bull, determined and horned, but he was a skilled matador, and no matter how tempting he was with that cape, he'd be sure to sidestep when I charged.

There were other things to tell. Things that were harder to say but impossible for him to subvert.

Needing an escape from his unrelenting stare, I closed my eyes. Without meaning to go there, I found myself at the beginning, in a time when I was still only innocent, in a country garden, on a rope swing with a wooden seat.

Bile burned at the back of my throat. These weren't memories I ever allowed, and I felt their foreignness like an illness. My body fought to remove them. My head ached with their presence.

But the actual beginning came before, in the reason I'd been in that garden in the first place. "I was close to my grandpa Werner," I said, feeling the tremble in my voice. "I spent a month with him every summer, four glorious weeks without my mother and father. It was just me and him, and I was spoiled and loved. When he died—"

"You were six," Edward said cutting me off. "This isn't what I'm looking for, and you know it."

My muscles tensed as though preparing to fight. He thought I was giving him something basic. Too basic. He assumed I was going to tell him how my granddaddy died when I was a kid and how it broke my heart and how I'd never been the same after, and while all of those things were true, it had only been the prologue to the real story.

But it was good he'd stopped me.

This wasn't something I wanted to tell either. Not now. Not ever.

With a soft laugh, I shook my head, surprised with myself for starting down that path. Irritated that he'd been the one to draw me back when it should have been me.

I propped my elbows on my lap and leaned my forehead into my palms. My fingers rubbed into my skin, massaging my brow. I knew what story to tell. It was the one that I told myself meant the most, which was a bold-faced lie, but it was easier to clutch to it as the cause of all my pain than giving acknowledgment to the others.

For one last moment, I let myself contemplate telling a lie instead. I believed I could get away with it, but I also believed that, if I couldn't, the consequences would be significant.

And what would happen if I told the truth? I sort of wanted to find out.

With my mind made, I dropped my hands to my lap and sat back. Composed. "There was a boy I grew up with. A boy who changed everything. And don't stop me this time because this is real."

He nodded for me to continue.

"Our mothers were friends. Our families got together a lot. Holidays, summers, vacations. We probably should have thought of each other as brother and sister, and maybe he did..." I trailed off for a moment, wondering if that had been the case for Hudson. "Anyway, I never did. My mom believed we'd get married one day, and maybe that's why I did too. It had been bred into me to be his bride, and so it was natural to fall in love with him.

"All through high school, I crushed on him, putting myself out there, waiting for him to make a move. Watching as he went through girls like they were tissues."

"Girlfriends?" Edward asked. "Or just lovers?"

The difference was relevant.

"Lovers," I said quickly. "Never a girlfriend. Which was why I held out hope. I mean, I wasn't the only girl fawning over him. He was super attractive, lean and gray-eyed. He came from mega money and everyone knew he was the guy who'd take his inheritance and quadruple it before he was thirty—which he did. He had the serious thing going for him. He was scary smart and controlled and calculating and strategic. Always a step ahead of everyone else."

"So you have a type." His smug smile made me lightheaded while at the same time want to kick him in the balls.

I gritted my teeth. "The type that likes to fuck with my emotions, yeah. I guess I do."

"What's his name?"

I paused, about to give it. But his wanting to know, even if I couldn't guess why, made it valuable information. "It doesn't matter," I said.

"I'll decide if it matters."

"No, actually, you won't. This is my story—" I corrected myself at his brow raise. "A true story, but totally mine, and that means I'm the one who knows what details are significant and which ones aren't. His name is not."

His jaw flexed, and for the first time ever, I felt him warring for control.

"We'll leave it then," he said, handing me this one win. "For now."

It was impossible not to be pleased with myself, and I didn't bother to hide my grin. "As I was saying, he wasn't popular in the way popular kids usually are, but people knew him. Girls knew him. And if they weren't scared of him, they were into him."

"I imagine some were both." *Like you with me,* his tone said clearly.

I ignored the pointed remark and went on. "I didn't care about the other girls, though. Because he was mine. I was the one he grew up with. I was the one who knew him—well, as much as he let anyone know him. I was the one he had a nickname for when he never had one for anyone, including his siblings. By all rights, he was mine."

"What did he call you?"

"Ceeley." That wasn't technically true—Ceeley hadn't been a nickname that Hudson started, my mother had. He'd simply adopted it, probably because he'd heard me called that more than Celia for much of our younger years. It was a relevant detail to omit, but I was who I was and that meant I reveled in slipping in something that Edward would never know to counter.

"Original," he huffed. "I thought you said he was sharp."

"We were *kids*," I reminded him. *Asshole.*

I took a breath, hearing my own words echo in the room, letting them sink in for both of us. "We were kids," I said again, "and it was a kid crush, and by the time I graduated high school I realized that it wasn't going anywhere, and I needed to move on."

I got up, wary that I hadn't been given permission, careful to portray that I didn't believe I needed it, and wandered around the back of the couch to the bar. When Edward made no protest, I crouched down to examine the contents of the wine fridge.

"I wasn't what you'd call studious. I had good grades, and I was smart, but I didn't get into it the way a lot of the preppy kids did, and having spent all my teen years believing I didn't have to grow up and *do* anything except marry my friend, I had no real plan for college." I pulled out a Malbec and stood. "I liked art and literature. I could study those anywhere. So my only real requirement for choosing a school was that it be far from wherever he was going to be. He was staying east, so I went west. UC Berkeley."

I had to rummage through three drawers before finding the corkscrew, which was only annoying because Edward had chosen to watch me search rather than stand up and help me.

"No, no, don't get up," I said sarcastically when I began the awkward job of removing the cork. "I've got it."

I *did* have it, and I didn't actually want him helping me. I especially didn't want him close to me. I preferred him over *there,* with a distance between us. It wasn't something I was willing to give up just so he could open up my wine.

When the struggle was over and the cork had eased from the bottle with a satisfying pop, I plucked a wine glass from the rack and poured. Then I turned back toward Edward, resting my ass on the bar as I took a swallow.

I let the taste register as I decided what to say next. It had a black-cherry flavor, full-bodied with a hint of chili. "Nice," I said, because I wanted to prove I could give a compliment even if he couldn't.

He didn't react except to prompt me. "Berkeley?"

"I met a guy there. Dirk."

"His name was Dirk?" He didn't hide the mockery in his inflection. That had been Hudson's reaction, too, if I remembered correctly.

I really did have a type.

"Dirk Pennington," I said, unfazed. "He was..." I searched for how to describe a man I'd barely thought about in a decade. "I don't know, he was a good guy. He was nice. Genuine. Sweet." I played up the adjectives with my vocalization, throwing them in the face of a man who wouldn't see himself in any of them.

"In other words, boring."

"A lot of women find the good guys more attractive than the bad."

"But not you."

My stomach flipped at his accurate pronouncement. I despised that he saw that about me even more than I despised that it was true, so, of course, I became overly defensive. "I really liked him! We were good together."

"Did you fuck him?"

"Are you jealous?" There'd been no hint of it in his remark, but I couldn't help myself.

Edward said nothing, expressionless and impervious to my charm.

I sighed. "Not that it's relevant, but yes. He wasn't my first either, so don't try to make that into anything it's not."

"So you fucked him, he wasn't your first, and he was nice," he said in summarization.

I took a swallow of my wine. "Right."

"And he made you forget all about the nameless guy."

"That's right," I said cautiously, feeling there was a challenge in his last statement that I couldn't quite pinpoint.

"I see," he said in a way that made me sure he didn't see at all. At least, he didn't see what I wanted him to see. "And then what happened?"

"Then I came home for the summer. Dirk stayed in California because that was where he was from. He invited me to move in with him, which I considered, but I was young, and I missed home."

"You wanted to go back and flaunt Dirk in the nameless guy's face."

"No." It *had* been the first thing I'd told Hudson when I saw him again. My mother had plans for us to go to a garden show that afternoon, and I didn't have much time to visit, but I'd snuck off to his summer house just to tell him. "No, not to flaunt. I wanted him to know I was over him, though, yes."

"Uh-huh," he said, unconvinced.

"Because I didn't want my old crush to be an obstacle in our friendship."

"I don't believe you."

His skepticism was maddening.

"I wasn't trying to make him jealous," I insisted. If that's what he was suggesting. "What I had with Dirk was real. I thought he could have been it for me."

He let that sit for a moment, letting me absorb the truth of what I'd just said, or the untruth, as he believed.

But it *was* true. Wasn't it?

"So then you wanted to see the old crush to test yourself," he said when I didn't say anything else. "To be sure."

My cheeks flamed with guilt. "Okay, maybe a bit of that too." I pushed myself off the bar with my hip and walked back around the couch and sat down. "But I truly didn't have some glorified plan to make him fall for me. I had fond feelings for him, and I wanted to find a new way to be in his life. So I told him all about Dirk, and it worked. I had a boyfriend and wasn't after him anymore so suddenly I wasn't someone he needed to avoid. We were together so much that summer, going to the movies and the beach and parties of people we knew in high school. Except for my parents and my best friend, Christina, I saw him more than anyone else.

"It was all fine until the end of August. We'd gotten close, really close, and sure, I still felt things for him. Those aren't the kinds of feelings that go away easily, but I was okay with what we were and what we weren't, and I had Dirk, who I talked to every day." I checked myself. "Maybe not *every* day. Not at the end."

"Because the boy was seeming interested."

I scowled because I hated how Edward thought he knew everything. But he was right this time. Which I hated even more. "Yeah. He did seem interested."

I took another swallow of the Malbec and ignored the way Edward made me feel with his presence in order to better remember how Hudson had made me feel in the past. Literally manipulated me into feeling, to be truthful, but I wouldn't know that for sure for another several months. "He would brush up against me, accidentally. Or he'd sweep the hair from my face. Touching, he was always touching me, and that had never been like him before. He'd never been a real physical guy. And he was thoughtful about me. I'd lamented to him about not knowing what to major in, and he'd researched my school and gotten all these brochures on interior design and gave me a gorgeous coffee-table book about it."

The memory made me smile. It had seemed utterly romantic to me —a guy going out of his way to help decide what I should do with my life. What I should *be*. It was the best proof of mattering. A guy wouldn't go out of his way like that, wouldn't notice, if I didn't matter. That kind of gesture got me fluttery every time.

Though there hadn't been that many. The last time a man paid that much attention to me...

I glanced quickly at Edward, as if he could read my thoughts, as if he could know I'd almost compared his gifts over the last three months to the gift Hudson had given that had swept me away.

They weren't the same. I refused to think of them as the same.

"Is there something else?" he asked, trying to interpret my train of thought.

"I didn't sleep with him." I couldn't tell from his expression if that had been truly what he'd assumed. "I did kiss him. Or I let him kiss me. I'm not sure which it was anymore. And I wanted him to kiss me."

I'd wanted him to do more than kiss me. I would have let him, if things had gone the way I'd wanted. I'd thought it was inevitable after that kiss. That we'd be together. That we'd be a couple.

I could still feel that wanting, under layers of years and walls and nothing. Like a bruise that never healed but only hurt when I pressed on it. Of all the made-up things there had been between Hudson and me, before and after, that moment was real. That wanting was real.

Wanting that was magnified by believing he felt it too.

I'd thought all that had stood between us was Dirk, a guy who, as Edward had pointed out, was good but bland.

"I wasn't a terrible person." How long had it been since I'd been able to say those words? "Not yet, anyway. So I did the honorable thing, and tried to call Dirk to break up. But he was at work so I had to leave a message and when he called back I was already at this big party Christina was having, which wasn't the place to break up with a guy, and I knew it, but..." My only excuse had been eagerness, and that sounded petty, so I left it there. "He was hurt. I could tell. Even over the phone." *Let's wait and talk this over when we get back for the new semester,* he'd begged. "It hurt more than I'd imagined it would, hurting him like that. I had to leave for a bit to take a drive and get my head together afterward because it hurt so bad. But when I came back, I was better and ready, and I saw...I saw the boy's car, so I knew he was inside, and I looked for him everywhere. Asked everyone. Searched every room, and when someone said he thought he was hanging in Christina's room, I ran up there."

I could still see it like it was happening. Me flinging open the door, and *them*. The image permanently seared into my mind.

"He was fucking her. Fucking my best friend. As if we hadn't kissed the night before. As if we hadn't agreed to talk more about our relationship at the party. As if I hadn't told him I loved him." It sounded so insignificant in the telling compared to how it had felt to witness.

The worst part, though, hadn't even been that moment but after, when I'd confronted Hudson, and he'd pretended there'd been nothing, that all the signs I'd read were mistaken. He'd told me to grow up.

What did you think was going to happen between us? You thought I was going to love you? You thought we were going to ride off into the sunset together?

"And all I could think was how duped I'd been. Because I hadn't thought he was going to love me until he made me believe he would." It was strange how mad I could still be about it, even after everything that followed. How hurt and abused. How raw. "He'd insinuated the only thing holding him back from me was my relationship with Dirk. And so I'd ended that! To be with him! I'd had real feelings for him, and me? I'd been nothing more than something to do. Nothing more than a game."

It was over. I'd said it all. I'd told it the way it happened, in a way I'd never told anyone, and yeah, I felt vulnerable. It was cathartic too. Cleansing.

Edward remained silent for long beats after, as he'd been through much of my wandering through the past, and while I'd never forgotten he was there, he had made it easier to feel like the telling was natural. My parents had always poo-pooed therapy, and I wondered if it was like this—sitting on a couch, uncomfortable, trapped. Waiting for the therapist to speak and declare you sane.

"That must have made you feel very betrayed," he said eventually. Which would have been comforting if he hadn't added more on. "Being someone else's game." His subtext was clear.

Shame pricked at my insides. Maybe this had been the wrong story to tell him after all.

No, it still could be the right story. If I told it to the very end.

I leaned forward. "So you know what I did? I left him at that stupid party and went back to his place. Then I fucked his father in the pool house for two hours. Did I feel betrayed? Yes. And then I got even."

Edward held my stare for a long time. I could tell his thoughts were brewing, but his expression gave nothing away. My heart hammered in my chest as I waited for his response. I'd bared myself. Then I'd reminded him that I was vengeful, but I'd bared myself first.

Finally, after an eternity, he spoke. "This boy betrayed you, so you ruined both his parents' marriage and your mother's friendship by fucking his father. That's what you're saying, isn't it?"

I could feel the color drain from my face. That was what I was saying, but put like that, it sounded...well, it sounded reprehensible.

And it *was* reprehensible.

Even though I'd left out the fact that Jack already cheated on his wife all the time, and that it had been another decade before anyone found out about it, so my mother's friendship had remained intact. Even with those details, what I'd done was fucked up.

Which was the most horrible part of the story, if I was honest with myself.

The pain that still lingered all this time later wasn't from what Hudson had done to me, but what I'd done to Hudson. What kind of messed-up person did that shit? What kind of fucked-up human was I?

I turned my head, afraid that Edward would see that I understood what I was, what I'd done. Because if he saw that, I'd really be exposed.

I couldn't bear being that vulnerable.

He rose then, and I could feel his anger rise with him like fanned flames. "This evening has been a waste of my time," he said, his voice eerily controlled. "This isn't breaking down. This is bragging."

Without giving me another look, he pivoted and headed to the door. Before he disappeared beyond it, he said, "I'll give you my response tomorrow. You're free to do as you please until then."

He shut the door behind him with an uncharacteristic slam.

I sat stunned. And mad. And hurt. And embarrassed. But mostly mad.

I'd done what he'd wanted. I'd given him his stupid-ass story. And now I was free to do as I pleased? Fuck him because that was a lie. I wasn't free to leave the island.

And fuck him for thinking he knew anything about me, about what was and wasn't breaking down. I'd opened up to him. What I'd said was horrible, but it was hard. Sharing what I'd shared had been hard.

I reached for my wine and chugged the rest down in an attempt to push down the emotions building up inside of me. When it was empty, and the feelings remained, I threw the glass against the wall.

Shattering items was becoming a habit.

If only it were just Edward's antique vases and glassware being shattered and not also me.

NINE

AS BITTER AS the night before had ended, I woke up with a tickle of excitement. He was here, on the island, and that meant that no matter what happened, the day would be different than they had been when he was away.

Plus, there was the added expectation of his response. I lay awake in bed for nearly half an hour wondering what it would be, imagining the ways his reaction to my tale could play out. Now that he'd made clear his sadism centered around the psychological rather than the physical, the boundaries of what might happen felt exponentially larger. The possibilities of what would happen next were titillating and unfathomable and frightening, and the dread I'd felt about what he'd do to me when I'd thought pain would be involved had been replaced by intrigue. I wanted to find out. I wanted to know.

Once out of bed, though, the thrill simmered down.

The house was quiet, Edward wasn't around. It was exactly like every other Saturday on Amelie, when Joette and Tom and the staff had the day off and the meals were prepared beforehand and the day belonged to myself. There wasn't even yoga on the weekends. Ideally, the privacy was a good setup for newlyweds who hadn't seen each other in months.

Edward and I had never fit the notion of "ideally."

With no interest in being the one to seek him out, I went about my routine in the ways I normally did, lounging by the pool, reading *An American Marriage* until the story of a black man's twelve-year incarceration for a crime he didn't commit began to diminish the terribleness of my own imprisonment, and I had to set it down. It was hard to complain about my situation in comparison. My jail was a paradise, sure. And it could be argued that I deserved it, since I was far from innocent. It could definitely be worse, *was* worse for other real people.

I saw that, but I didn't want to. I wanted to believe I had it bad. I wanted to be angry. I wanted to be pissed. I wanted to be self-righteous and indignant and full of contempt.

The fact that those emotions weren't as readily accessible as they'd once been was both surprising and surreal, and it was definitely discomforting.

Edward arrived back from wherever he'd been in the early afternoon. I didn't see him come in, but I felt the atmosphere change, felt *him*, and when I looked up, he was at his library window watching me. He saw me notice him and didn't flinch, as though he had every right to be staring at me.

My pulse sped up and my cheeks flushed, and especially perceptible because of all the weeks he'd been away, I realized how much I liked having someone around to look at me. How much I liked him looking at me.

Before I could help it, I smiled.

Immediately, I thought better and scowled, hating myself for getting caught up in his stupid gaze. Hating him for having a gaze worthy of being caught up in.

I'd turned away too quickly to find out his reaction to my mistake, but imagined or not, I felt his smirk on my profile and hated him for that too.

When I finally came in an hour later, the house was buzzing with the makings of a big dinner, the kind we'd had regularly on our honeymoon, and that sent me fuming again, for no reason I could discern. Then, later, as I cleaned up and applied makeup in my bathroom, I realized the reason was because company for dinner very likely meant company *after* dinner. Which meant waiting another day for Edward's response.

It also meant sharing him with others, and I wanted him all to myself. With that awareness, another wave of anger rolled through me.

My mascara applied to one eye only, I leaned back to study the woman in the mirror. My blonde hair was coiffed in a low chignon, sun-kissed highlights giving vibrancy to my appearance. My face—which I kept meticulously protected with sunscreen—was flawless, my foundation seamlessly matching the tanned skin at my décolletage. My yoga-toned shoulders curved pleasingly, my never-nursed-a-baby breasts still as perky as they'd been a decade ago. In every way, I was a portrait of stoic beauty. No one could possibly know that my insides were shaking with fury and shame, that there was a magma chamber of turbulent emotions in the pit of me that only seemed to erupt in my husband's presence.

My appearance was a lie I told without even trying.

What did Edward think he'd find underneath? What would he find if he kept looking?

It scared me that I didn't know the answer to either question.

Having been given no instruction and needing armor, I dressed powerfully for dinner. The dress was ordinary enough—a mid-thigh length black silk slip dress with a racerback. It was a little fancy for our group, but Edward had included it in the wardrobe he'd sent, so that made it appropriate in my mind. The part that gave it power was what I'd put on underneath—sheer black panties, matching garter belt, and thigh-high stockings. Hosiery on the island was completely impractical, even in February, but they made me feel good. Made me feel sexy and potent and charged.

Especially when I added the red satin Casadei plisse high-heel sandals. *Try calling me little bird now, Fasbender.* I was anything but.

Yes, it was a power play, too. An outright opposition to what he'd had me wear the night before. Maybe it was asking for trouble. Maybe I wanted trouble. I didn't really know anymore.

The irony was that he probably wouldn't even notice.

Except that dinner wasn't like the old days.

When I came out, it wasn't the big dining table that was set, but rather the small radial dinette that overlooked the ocean. And it was only set for two. The lights were off, candles were lit. A bottle of champagne sat chilling in a bucket of ice next to a bowl of fresh strawberries.

I heard movement behind me, and without looking, I knew it was Edward. The heat of his presence bounced off the windows and enveloped me. Then his hand was at the small of my back, escorting me to my chair.

"Don't let this get to your head." His breath tickled the hair at my nape. "It's Valentine's Day and Joette has certain notions. It was easier to perpetuate them."

"Easier, yes." As if he'd ever chosen any method because it was easier.

I sat in the seat he offered, placing the linen napkin in my lap as he moved around to take the chair across from me. He was stunning in dark pants and a white dress shirt with black buttons, the top two open. It was a somewhat casual look for him, but not quite as laid back as he usually dressed on the island. And he'd taken the time to style his hair. All to let Joette believe our romance was real?

Maybe.

My breath stuttered when I considered the possibility that it was something more.

Once seated, he leaned across the table to pour the blanc de blanc in my champagne flute. "We can use the opportunity to discuss some rules."

He was so good at plying me with alcohol just before diving into serious subjects. I took a sip of the drink while he poured his own. "Are the rules your response to last night?"

He didn't answer at first, reaching over again to remove the silver cover from my plate, revealing white fish with lemon and capers and green beans with almonds. My mouth watered at the sight. Mateo didn't go out on the boat that often, but all the fish that was served on

Amelie came from his fishing trips. Every dish I'd had so far had been incredible.

I didn't wait for Edward to pick up his own fork before diving in. The fish melted in my mouth. Orgasmic.

Distracted by the divine taste, I almost forgot I'd asked a question until it was answered several minutes later. "The rules are not my response," he said, now several bites into his fish. "But you need to know them before we get to that."

I took another sip of my champagne. "I'm guessing that I don't have a choice in whether or not I follow them."

I'd become quite good at considering rules as a challenge. Without hearing what they were, my mind was already preparing to find ways around them if not outright defy them.

Edward smiled, as though he expected my response. "Of course you have a choice. What choices you make determine how quickly this process goes."

"The process of breaking me down, you mean."

"Yes. That." He put another bite of fish in his mouth, and I watched, mesmerized. The way his jaw worked as he took it from the fork. The way his throat moved as he swallowed. The way these simple actions made my pussy clench and weep.

I was really glad I'd worn the power stockings. I needed them right about now.

He rinsed everything down with a swig from his flute. "Are you amenable to me continuing?"

It seemed strange that he was asking. Usually he just did with no regard for my opinion on matters. I understood his motives, understood that this was a test. I knew what answer he wanted and the test was to see if I'd give him that answer or be defiant.

Defiance was my nature with him. My gut reaction.

I forced myself to think first. I thought about how things had gone so far since my captivity. How the gifts had begun when I'd stopped trying to escape. How the struggling only seemed to prolong whatever he had planned for me. How prey caught in the sightline of a predator often froze or played dead.

If I ever wanted to get out of here, that's what I had to do—play dead. "Okay, then. Go for it. Tell me these rules."

It was almost imperceptible—the slight nod of his head, the gleam in his eyes caught by chance in the candlelight. He was pleased.

And then it was gone, his expression once again stoic. "For now, we will only address the rules for our sessions together. There will be more in the future. Do not assume that this is all."

I forced myself to take a deep breath.

"During these sessions," he went on, "you cede your power to me."

I laughed. "I wasn't aware that I still had power to cede."

"Are you sure about that?" He tilted his head, both brows raised. "I'll tell you now that the most important rule is honesty. I expect you to only speak the truth, or the truth to the best of your knowledge. You will not exaggerate or deflect. Lies will not be tolerated. Withholding information when I ask will be considered a lie."

My body tensed at his bold expectation. He wanted me to lay everything down for him. Everything. I was beginning to understand what that really meant. Was I willing? No. But if I thought about it in terms of a longer game, of me playing into his hand until he let me go, then I could tolerate it more.

The real question wasn't was I willing, but was I able?

That, I didn't know.

All I could do is try. "In that case," I said, pushing my words from my throat where they wanted to stay. "I suppose you want me to say that I am aware that I do have some power." He was affected by me—that was power. I had my body. I knew how to play against his possessive nature. I had the ability to withdraw.

They were my only weapons, and he wanted me to put them down.

A sudden rush of bitterness took over my tongue. "Forgive me if I find the power I have left so miniscule that I didn't think it was worth mentioning."

That earned me a leveled stare and the next rule. "You will show respect. Sarcasm and backtalk are not acceptable forms of communication."

"Well, I'm screwed." I grabbed a small strawberry from the bowl and took a seductive nibble from the tip. "We aren't in a session now, are we?"

"Fortunately for you, we are not." He watched me finish it off, his eyes glued to my mouth as I licked my fingers afterward. His eyes were dark, hooded.

Yeah, this whole ceding power shit was going to take practice.

"Normally, whenever we're alone like we are, we would be in session." He set down his fork and picked up a strawberry himself, dipping it in cream before reaching across the table, offering it to me. "But we are just beginning."

I was suddenly very aware of my blood rushing through my body, at the damp spot between my legs. Leaning forward, I let him trace my mouth with the cream before I took a small bite. My tongue swept slowly across my lips. When I moved in for the next bite, however, he pulled his hand away, popping the rest of the berry in his own mouth.

He sat back then and frowned. "That was a freebie," he said. "Not what you deserved. To receive pleasure, you must earn it."

"Oh, then I'm *not* screwed, you're saying." It was exactly the type of sarcasm he'd said that wouldn't be tolerated.

"Punishments are also mine to dole out as I see fit." The dark expression was back. The idea of punishing me turned him on as much as anything else, I realized.

That was...intriguing/fascinating/scary/hot.

It was a bunch of things all at once that I didn't know how to process.

"No snappy comeback to that one?" He stroked his chin. "Interesting."

"I was thinking."

"Thoughtfulness is good. It shows you're taking this seriously."

Maybe not seriously enough. "Do I get a safe word?"

"You won't need one."

Either that meant he believed his punishments didn't need them or he didn't care if I felt unsafe when he administered them. Both options felt dangerous.

He studied me. "That makes you uncomfortable, doesn't it?"

"You like that it does, don't you?"

He paused then chuckled with a shake of his head. He picked up his fork and resumed eating. It was two full bites later before he said more. "If you feel unsafe, you'll tell me. There doesn't need to be a game about it."

It sounded clear enough. Still, I didn't trust him.

But there was nothing I could say to argue. "I assume that means there won't be restrictions on my speech."

"No restrictions. I do expect you to think carefully before you do—to choose carefully. But no outright restrictions. Half the fun is what you come up with to say."

I rolled my eyes, decidedly disrespectful. It *was* fortunate we weren't *in a session.*

Sessions, he called them. Not scenes like the books I'd read referred to times of kink play. Like he meant them to be therapy.

I frowned realizing that might very well be the case.

I tried not to think about that. "Anything else?"

"Yes. Your birth control shot runs out next month. There will be a nurse brought to the island to administer another."

"Then I *will* be screwed. How fun."

"I did tell you fucking was part of this bargain." He swirled what was left in his glass before taking it back in one swallow, his eyes never leaving mine.

"Just, from everything that's happened so far, it feels like I'm being fucked in a very different way." What was terrifying was how much I still wanted him despite that.

I tossed my napkin on my plate and pushed my plate away, my irritation returning. "Let me guess. This nurse will only speak French."

"Don't be silly. You know French."

"Are you guessing?"

"*Fais-je fausse route?*"

"*Non,*" I said with a sigh. He was *not* wrong. And that irked me more. "Speaking of being fucked over, how is it that you know when my birth control runs out?"

"Your privacy is not a privilege."

"I suppose that shouldn't be a surprise considering the bikini wax." It worried me though, what else he could know. Which of my secrets he could uncover. "Oh," I said, relaxing with my realization. "My doctor sent a reminder email to schedule something, didn't she?"

He ignored me. "My privacy, on the other hand, is assured."

"Of course it is. Is that all?"

He put his elbows on the table, inching his plate away in the process, and clasped his hands together. "Is that all, *sir*."

"What?"

"When we are in a session, you will address me as sir."

This latest rule sent a shudder down my spine, a flinch I couldn't hide. "I'd rather not," I said softly.

His brow raised in satisfaction. "All the more reason that you will."

I swallowed, my hands sweating in my lap. Memories from another time—another man— flooded me bodily.

"What do you say about my gift, Celia?"

"Thank you, Uncle Ron."

"Thank you, sir."

"Thank you, sir."

I couldn't do it. I *wouldn't*.

Except, it was more important not to let Edward know how I felt about it. It was not a weak spot I wanted him to know.

I managed to keep from shaking as I picked up my champagne flute. "We aren't in a session right now."

"We are," he said, placing his napkin next to his plate. "Dinner is finished. It's time to go." He stood and circled behind me to pull out my chair.

I finished my champagne and set it down before standing. "Do I need to change into some terribly drab outfit first?"

His forehead rose in a silent prompt.

I drew my hands into balls at my sides and gritted my teeth. "Do I need to change into some terribly drab outfit, *sir*." I spat the last word out.

His eyes narrowed, and for half a second I thought he'd challenge my tone. But then he looked me over, scanned me from head to toe, as though really looking at me for the first time that night. He couldn't hide that he liked what he saw. "What you're wearing is fine enough," he said, unwilling as ever to give me anything more.

"Careful," I said, smug about my wardrobe choice. "I might mistake that as a compliment." A beat passed before I remembered. "*Sir.*"

TEN

MY TRIUMPH WAS SHORT-LIVED.

As soon as we arrived at the bungalow, he led me into the bedroom. "Take all your clothes off, fold them, and leave them on the chest. Once you're completely stripped, kneel on the floor facing the chair."

Then he disappeared into the front room, leaving me to my task.

He wouldn't see my power stockings after all.

I brushed off my disappointment. It was fine. I'd worn them for me, not him. Mostly.

At least these instructions were familiar. I'd never played the sub before, but I'd prepared for this. The strip and kneel was very basic submissive training. This was something I could do.

I took a moment to scan the room. Again, there were oriental-framed windows looking out to the ocean and bamboo ceilings and tile floors. It was sparsely furnished with only a king size bed, a chest, and a chair. There was no dresser, but there was a closet. There were no apparent kink contraptions. No hooks hanging from the ceiling. No spanking benches.

Not that Edward wasn't creative. He probably didn't need gadgets.

Who had he brought here before? Who had he fucked in that bed? What remnants of other women would I find if I looked?

I'd taken two steps toward the closet hoping to check it out when Edward called out from the other room. "Hurry up about it, please. I expect you ready by the time I come back."

The clink of glassware told me he was fixing himself a drink. That wouldn't take long. I'd have to rush.

Somehow I managed to get the dress off, the garter, panties, stockings, all of it folded on the wood chest, the shoes on the floor next to it, and myself down on my knees just as he walked in.

I kept my eyes lowered, one of the guidelines from my reading, so I could only really see his shoes as he circled around me. Studying me? Whatever he was doing, it made me feel very exposed.

Except when I'd tried to kill him with the shard of glass, I'd never been completely naked this close to him before. I preferred it to the gut-wrenching storytelling from the night before, but on my knees, with my gaze down, felt chillingly different than standing in front of a man, attempting to seduce him. That was a powerful posture. This was pointedly not.

After he'd completed his inspection, Edward sat in the chair. "Eyes on me."

I lifted them and felt my breath speed up when they caught his heated gaze. It was heady, the way he looked at me. Almost intoxicating enough to distract me from the foreign submissive position.

"This might have happened last night," Edward said, sipping his drink casually, as though he wasn't at all stirred by the naked woman in front of him. The bulge in his pants said otherwise. "The second part of the session. We weren't ready to move on, though, so we've divided it."

When he said *we*, I was sure he really meant *me*. But I did recognize it was possible he meant us both.

"I think we should take a moment to recap what occurred last night. Can you tell me succinctly?"

"I believe I can, Edward," I said haughtily, hoping if I "forgot" often enough he wouldn't correct the "sir" slip. "I opened up, told you something personal, became vulnerable like you asked, and you were unappreciative."

The correction he gave was with a glare.

"What?" I asked innocently.

"We won't continue if you won't follow the rules, Celia. And if we don't continue, you'll never get back home." His tone was more matter-of-fact than stern, but it was a clear enough threat. *Obey or else.*

"You were unappreciative, *sir,*" I said, my skin crawling with the simple added syllable.

He nodded. "Because...?"

I had a thousand snappy answers at the ready, but I held back. He'd just given me every reason to play along.

Except, I wasn't so sure of the answer. Wasn't so sure what he wanted to hear. I thought about how my revealing had ended the night before, how, when I'd felt too vulnerable, too raw, I'd tried to counter with my power grab. As he'd so precisely called me on it, I'd been bragging.

I knew the answer. "Because when I was finished, I didn't allow myself to be weak." My eyes lowered automatically, unable to hold his in the admission, then immediately rose again when I remembered he wanted them on him, as hard as it was to keep them there. "I did brag, yes, but if I'd told it differently, if I'd let the truth come out, you would have seen my weakness there too. Sir." I flinched as I added the address.

"Very good. I'm pleased you could recognize your failure. Very pleased."

His praise made me feel sun-touched, like I was glowing in its rays.

"However, as well as you've done now, there must still be consequences for your behavior last night. Let's see what those books have taught you—show me what you can do with that mouth."

He spread his legs, inviting me to fill the space between them.

A mixture of relief and victory and, yes, want, flooded through me. This was my punishment? Sucking him off? This was a cinch. I was good at blow jobs. They were one of the easiest ways to manipulate men, and I'd become an expert. How fucking lucky could I get? How stupid was he not to see that, with his cock in my mouth, I would definitely not be ceding power—I would be claiming it.

And I'd be touching him too, fondling him in all the ways I'd wanted, in all the ways he hadn't let me before now. Moisture pooled between my legs.

Eagerly, I crawled forward and began working on his belt, pausing to stroke my palm along the hard ridge pressing against the pleat of his trousers. He gave a satisfied grunt, and the muscles in my thighs vibrated. Licking my lips, I glanced up at him. I could feel the smile in my eyes. I couldn't help it. I was excited.

He'd seen it, too. The space between his brows creased as though he was just figuring something out, and when I went back to undo his zipper, he caught my hand, stopping me. "I changed my mind," he said, pushing me away. "Get on the bed."

"Uh. Okay." It took me a minute to stand, I was too stunned.

The bed could be good though too. Certainly more comfortable than the ceramic tile.

But if he still had a blow job on the agenda, it was going to be very different from any I'd given before. Because when I got on the bed, he had me lie on my back, my ass at the foot of the bed, my knees bent, my legs spread—a very similar position to the one he'd fucked me in the night we'd married.

Even better.

My stomach flipped expectantly, waiting for him to unsheathe his gorgeous cock. Again, though, he surprised me. He got down on his knees.

I clamped my knees together and sat upright, alarm shooting through my veins. "What are you doing?"

"What does it look like I'm doing? I'm going to eat that pussy."

I shook my head, even as new arousal gushed between my legs.

"Why would you want to do that?" I couldn't help the panic in my voice. He couldn't do that. I wouldn't let him. There was no way.

"Because you don't want me to."

The asshole saw everything, knew everything. He'd made a momentary misstep thinking that getting me down on my knees was the way to punish me, but I'd given myself away. This was true punishment. This was true vulnerability. Having my legs open, letting a man give me pleasure—letting myself relax enough to feel the pleasure—that was truly giving up my power, truly giving up control. I'd been there before and never wanted to be there again. The idea was a nightmare to me, and it was obvious in the way I shooed him off, the way I tried to kick him away. The way the sweat beaded on my forehead.

He knew, he knew, he knew.

He knew, and he was so satisfied he hadn't even mentioned my lapse of sirs, a slip that he couldn't possibly have missed.

He knew, and I still couldn't stop fighting him. "That's stupid. What woman wouldn't want a guy going down on her?"

"Good question." He stood again, and my shoulders sagged with relief. He was abandoning this. *Thank you, God.*

After glancing around the room, Edward strolled over to the chest and picked up one of my abandoned stockings. "Excellent," he said, with an almost-wink in my direction. "This will do nicely. Scoot back on the bed and raise your arms above your head."

I did it. Whatever he was planning would be better than what he'd almost done. He came around one side of the bed and positioned my wrists together. Then, after tying the end of the stocking around them, he stretched the hose out and wrapped the other end around one of the slats of the bed frame before tying it off.

"Kinky," I said, my heart still racing from my near escape of orgasm by cunnilingus. "Sir," I added, because I was calmer now and wanted to get back to keeping him pleased.

But then he was kneeling in front of me, spreading my thighs with his hands, and the panic returned with a tsunami-like force.

"I can manage your legs," he said in explanation, "but it was going to be real hard to concentrate on making you come with your hands pushing me away."

His grip was tight and he'd done a good job with the binding, but I thrashed anyway. "No, please! Edward." I sat up as well as I could. "No. You can't."

He paused. "Is this really where you'd like to stop for the night? Because I will, and then we'll have to start all over again another night. When I come back."

Fuck!

I closed my eyes tight and reasoned through my options. It didn't matter how long he'd be gone. If it was two weeks it would be too long. I did not want to start over. I did not want to be stuck here forever.

And I did want him. As fucked up as that was, I still wanted him touching me, still wanted him inside me. He'd fingered me before, and it had been glorious. Would it really be that different if he used his mouth?

"Okay," I said, trying to steady my breathing. "Okay. It's okay. I'll do it."

"Good girl," he said, stroking his hand up my abdomen to fondle my breast. My nipples stiffened and my back arched into him. "I'm very happy with your decision."

He lowered his head then, and ran his tongue up my seam. "You'll get two."

"Two licks?" I asked, a little delirious from the first swipe.

"Two orgasms."

"Two?!" I yanked involuntarily against the stocking.

"Now it's three."

I clamped my mouth shut, afraid to protest. But three? I was a one orgasm kind of girl. It had been a miracle that he'd managed two from me on our wedding night, and that situation had been entirely different. Then, I'd been in control.

Well, *more* in control.

It wasn't possible. I wouldn't be able to do it.

But I had to let him find that out on his own because there was no way I was going to talk back and get the number upped to four.

He started gently, his tongue teasing my clit with slow, light circles. Then his licking turned more earnest, swiping first this side of my sensitive bud, then the other. I could tell he was reading me, studying my responses. Learning how to give me pleasure, and despite the tension clutching my back and shoulders, I felt oddly moved by this realization. Even when I reminded myself he was learning me to use his knowledge against me, not because he cared, I couldn't help but think it was one and the same. That everything he used against me was because, at some level, he cared.

That was the way with being caught up in pleasure—it messed with the head. Made the lies I told myself easier to believe.

I was wrapped in that particular lie when the first orgasm grew, sprouting from me like a seedling piercing through the earth, stretching its way through my limbs with a roll so gentle, I wondered if he'd even noticed.

"That's one," he said, lifting up only long enough to say the word before returning to his task.

I breathed easier now, the first one having relaxed my tense muscles. It had felt good—Edward knew what he was doing—and it hadn't felt like I had given up too much to get it. Maybe this wasn't going to be so bad after all.

But he was more aggressive after that, sucking my clit into his mouth, using his teeth, his nips sending megawatt jolts of pleasure through my nervous system, and when the second one came, it had me trembling and gasping his name with shallow breaths.

The third, though—that's when he really went to task. His mouth traveled down my pussy, down along my seam to my wet channel where he speared me with frantic thrusts with his tongue. His fingers entered the scene, dancing over my clit until I was squirming and pulling at the stocking.

I couldn't do it. It was so close, and I couldn't get there. I wouldn't.

The defeatist narrative running through my mind wasn't helping. I struggled against it, tensing up when I should have been calming down, thinking too hard about the man between my legs. Who he was. What he'd done to me.

What I wanted him to do to me.

It was a mess inside my brain, my feelings about Edward, and to top off the confusion, he was giving me the best orgasm of my life. Pulling it from me like he owned it. Like he deserved a piece of me, and I fought, afraid that when he took that piece, he'd take all of me with him.

My eyes were already tearing by the time it finally rushed through me, sweeping me up so unexpectedly, I hadn't been appropriately braced for it. The edges of my vision went black and it knocked the air from my lungs as it took over, shooting bliss through my body like I'd just snorted a line of cocaine.

And then they were done. All three. And I could sigh in relief, boneless. Sated. A survivor.

"One more," Edward said from between my thighs.

I bolted up to protest. "That one was three."

He lifted his head, but left his fingers to stroke against the swollen lips of my pussy. "You're arguing with me?"

"No, sir," I said, defensively. "But that was honestly—"

His expression told me what finishing my statement was going to get me, and I couldn't bear another added to my sentence. I couldn't bear the one he was proposing now.

A tear fell, my mouth quivering. "I'm not trying to argue, Edward. I'm not. I don't want to make you mad, but since you won't let me have a safe word, I just want you to know I can't do it. I can't possibly take one more." It was the most honest I'd ever been. The most raw.

"You will," he insisted, sliding two fingers inside of me to graze against my G-spot.

My hips bucked, my body wanting him inside me despite my head knowing I couldn't take anymore. "You said to tell you," I blubbered. "You said when I couldn't take it to tell you. To not play games, and I'm not playing a game right now."

"Yes, and you are very good to tell me. But I never said I'd listen." He bent down to add a series of quick tongue strokes against my clit to the deep thrusts of his fingers.

"Fuck, Edward! No, I can't. I can't!" I pulled against my restraint. I pressed my knees inward trying to shove him off.

"Eyes on me," he said sharply, shutting me up. When he held my gaze in his, he touched the tip of his tongue lightly to my most sensitive spot. "You don't think you can take it, little bird." Another soft press of the tongue. "But you can." This time his mouth lingered. "Keep your eyes on me. Relax. Let me take care of you. Let it feel good."

His words were soft and anchored me along with his intense stare, and there, wrapped in the solid promise of his authority, I let myself go. I let him take care of me. I let it feel good.

The orgasm released through me in stages, as though it had been wrenched out of me, leaving parts of it behind that had to be wrenched out as well. It seized onto my limbs, my muscles tensing slowly, slowly, slowly until they were rigid in its grip, shuddering against its ferocity. The world went completely dark. Then spots appeared, dancing across my vision.

And the sound that came from me was foreign and yawning, a jagged moan that stretched and stretched and stretched until my voice was hashed and my throat felt sore.

I lay there after, whimpering, barely aware of Edward coaxing me down, kissing my thighs, running his hands along the sides of my torso, bringing me back to life.

Then, when I opened my eyes again, reborn, I wanted him with a fierceness that I'd never known. Wanted all of him. Wanted his cock buried inside of me. Wanted him shoving against my limp body. Wanted to make him come as savagely as he'd made me come.

He crawled up my body, and I could feel the stiff weight of his desire at my hip as he kissed me, his tongue plunging into my mouth as deeply as it had plunged into my core, the taste of my pussy mixed with the taste of him.

"Please," I begged, unable to articulate my want. "Please, please, please." He'd know. He always knew.

He ground his hips against mine, his fingers threaded in my hair. "You can't possibly have any idea how much I want to fuck you right now," he said against my lips.

"Yes, yes." I nodded, encouraging. Pleading.

He kissed me again, his arm reaching above me to loosen the tie at my wrists. When my hands were free, they flew to his face, gripping his stubbled cheeks as though to hold him in place, as though to pull him closer.

"I want you," he said again. Then kissed me again. "But we mustn't forget that this was a punishment."

He rose and stood over me, his cock tenting in his trousers as his eyes perused me from head to toe. With what sounded like a reluctant sigh, he turned away. "Get dressed," he said, picking up the drink he'd abandoned in favor of eating me out. "I'll be waiting in the living room to walk you back to the house."

And I knew in that moment, without a doubt, that he'd succeed, that he was halfway there already, that he'd completely and utterly break me down.

THE NEXT MORNING, when I came back from my run, I found him standing beside the jeep while Louvens loaded his suitcase into the back.

"You're leaving? Without even telling me?" I sounded hurt when I meant to sound outraged, because hurt was what I primarily felt.

"Not true," he said coming to me. "I was waiting for you to get back so I could say goodbye." He nodded to Lou. "Give me a minute." Then, with my hand in his, he led me off the driveway to the side of the house where we were out of earshot from his driver.

I pulled my hand away from his, trying to find my sense of balance. He'd wrecked me the night before, and after a fitful sleep with dream after dream of his mouth and his tongue and his words—*You can't possibly have any idea how much I want to fuck you right now*—I had a curious sense of attachment.

Was this Stockholm Syndrome? What had he done to make me feel such an intense need?

I pressed my fingers against my eyes and shook my head, as if to shake off the complex emotions stirring inside. "I can't believe you're leaving already," I said softly when I brought my hands down. How long would he be gone? I couldn't bear to ask. I couldn't bear to know.

He reached out to me again, bringing his knuckles to stroke against my cheek. "I almost think you're going to miss me."

"No," I said too quickly, flinching from his caress that I wanted but couldn't seem to let myself have. "Just. How can you break me down if you're not ever here?"

"Play better, and I'll come back more often."

Ouch.

He must have seen the hurt in my expression. Swiftly, he wrapped an arm around my waist and drew me to him, holding me tightly to his chest. "You did very well last night, little bird," he murmured in my ear. "I was very impressed."

I stayed tense in his embrace for several heartbeats. Then, on an exhale, I relaxed into him, taking in his scent of spice and musk and pure man. "Were you really?"

"Yes, really." He pressed his lips to my temple, holding them there, holding me for several seconds before leaning back to look at me.

It had felt good, if I was being honest with myself. When it was all said and done. Except for one part.

I pulled back and wrapped my hands in his shirt. "Edward, I know it's a rule...I know I'm not in a position to ask. But addressing you as sir... please. Is there anyway it could be something else? Master or Your Holiness. Anything else..."

He studied me for several beats. "Is this something we'll talk about in an upcoming session?"

No. No. I did not want to talk about it.

But if he wanted to find out, he would. I knew that now.

"I need time," I said, letting out a shuddering breath.

He considered. I was the one who had wanted things to speed up. There was no way he couldn't know this was something I truly needed.

He gave a quick jerk of his head. "Very well then. You can address me as Edward."

I was so grateful, I buried my head in his shoulder. "Thank you, Edward." It was a whisper, but he heard it.

"I left you something on your bed," he said, when I pulled away, his fingers once again stroking my face. "A belated Valentine's Day gift. To make the time go by faster."

I nodded. I couldn't speak past the stupid ball in the back of my throat.

"Be good," he said, pressing one more kiss to my forehead then let me go to head back to Louvens waiting in the jeep.

I turned away, and brought my hand to my cheek, pressing my

palm against the spot he'd touched as if that could hold the feel of him there longer.

"And Celia?"

When I looked back, he'd paused, halfway in the passenger's seat. I furrowed my brow in question.

"I'm going to miss you, too."

ELEVEN

EDWARD

"MR. FASBENDER?" Astor's tone suggested it wasn't the first time he'd called my name.

I'd been somewhere else. Nowhere. It was easy to get distracted like that sitting in my office now, looking at walls and curtains that *she*'d chosen. Sitting on furniture that *she*'d picked out.

She'd left the desk at my insistence, a heavy dark wood monstrosity that I loved and refused to part with. But now it was the foreign thing in the room, the only thing not touched by her, and I found myself choosing to work from the sofa more and more because of it.

The sofa where I sat now, holding my daily meeting with my secretary and assistant.

I flicked the thoughts of her away, a habit I'd grown accustomed to in the past year as my thoughts were often with her, and gave my assistant my attention.

"The new line-up in Turkey—you're good to make a statement next Tuesday?"

I'd been vaguely present as he had gone over the bullet points of the announcement regarding the programming changes. These were details that had been discussed by my executives and discussed even more thoroughly by lower-level executives. By the time these matters became of consequence to my direct team, there was little need for my input.

It wouldn't even be me writing the statement that supported the changes. That would be Astor. All he needed was my nod of approval, which I gave him now.

"I'll be sure it's sent immediately to the high-profile media," Charlotte said, making a note on her pad.

"Good, then," Astor said in confirmation. "That's all set."

"Is there anything else?" I was restless, ready to move on with my day. Ready to dive into projects that took more of my bandwidth, left less of my mind free to wander to Amelie and the woman I'd left there. My wife.

The weeks away were agonizing.

I spent every waking minute trying to keep focused. My workouts had doubled in length, pushing myself to the point of distraction. Then I buried myself in business matters, staying at the office later than anyone else, keeping more on my own plate when, in the past, I would have delegated. At home, I drank. More than I'd drunk in years.

It wasn't an entirely successful method of coping, but it got me through the weekdays. Yet, every Friday, as the clock ticked on, and the buzz of work wound down around me, and the long, lonely weekend loomed over me, I'd invariably pick up the phone on my desk and dial the airfield to schedule an impromptu flight to the Caribbean. Every time I'd make it so far as one ring, maybe two, before I slammed the receiver down, wondering what on earth I'd been doing. What I'd been thinking.

I had no sure plan, and that was so unlike me it set a pit of terror in my stomach that grew and grew anytime I allowed myself to ruminate too long. And having no plan, I knew it was better that I stayed away from her. For her as well as for me.

Even though the distance did little to rectify the situation. Wherever I was, I was fucked.

Another flick of the mind, pushing out those thoughts to concentrate on my employees. Charlotte had already begun to gather her things, but Astor sat still, which gave the answer to the question I'd asked without him having to speak.

Whatever he had left to go over was more personal in nature, then. My secretary's presence wouldn't be required.

Charlotte had made it two meters when she stopped. "Oh," she said then sighed. "Warren Werner."

I stretched my neck to the side, trying to work out the permanent kink associated with his name. "He called again?"

"He did. Personally this time. What would you like me to say?"

It might have been less provoking if his calls were regarding his daughter. A handful of short emails sent under her account to his wife seemed to be all he needed to be rest assured Celia was doing well. If it had been my daughter who had wed my business rival, if it had been my daughter who had crossed an ocean and limited her communication, I would not have been satisfied with impersonal messages sent via computer. I would have demanded phone calls. I would have expected a visit over Christmas. If Genevieve had denied those, I would have flown the pond and shown up on her doorstep.

It only proved what I'd always known about Warren, that he was a cruel, heartless bastard.

Because the only reason the man had reached out those several times was to follow-up on the alliance I'd hinted at on the day I'd wed Celia. I'd only dangled the idea to get him calm enough to accept our marriage. It had been an impromptu move on my part. I'd been so desperately close to the end of the plan. I would have said anything at that point, and I did.

And if I'd followed through with the plan as it were, this wouldn't be an issue now. I'd have already buried my wife and any contact from Warren would likely be through lawyers because there was no doubt he'd try to contest the transfer of Werner Media shares to my name. It would be a long and drawn-out process, but he had no leg to stand on, and I'd win. Eventually.

That eventually would never arrive as long as Celia was alive.

"Put him off," I said, rising and buttoning my jacket out of habit. I couldn't be on this couch anymore. I continued as I crossed the room to my desk. "Tell him I've been preoccupied. Long weekends in the islands with my wife. Surely, he remembers we're newly wed."

"Yes, sir," Charlotte said, her mouth set, clearly disapproving. She knew there was something fishy in my marriage. She knew it was odd that my new bride would choose to stay on a small island away from me. She knew how often I flew off to Amelie.

She didn't know how often I thought about it.

I imagined the woman was thoroughly confused. If she'd thought I'd married a woman a decade younger than me for her body, that notion had been dismissed when I'd abandoned her in the Atlantic. If she'd thought I'd married her because of who she was and the connections she'd afford me, then why hadn't I taken a call with Warren yet? If she'd thought I'd married Celia because of love...

Well, bless Charlotte, then, for her ignorance.

It wasn't her job to think anything about me anyway.

I dismissed her now, but she'd worked for me long enough to get away with one more comment. "But I can't put him off forever."

Then she was gone, and Astor was still here to discuss something that would hopefully take my mind off my wife once and for all.

I unbuttoned my jacket and sat behind my desk, motioning for my assistant to join me here. He stood, bringing the chair and his messenger bag with him.

"Mateo has sent over a list of purchase items that need your approval. He says you've authorized a redecorating project?" He set the chair down and sank onto it.

I nearly told him to pick it right back up and put it where it belonged because I was not in the mood for discussing this.

But that wouldn't make the item go away.

"I did," I said, pinching the bridge of my nose. I couldn't even tell myself it had been on a whim because I'd carefully collected the catalogues for her from a variety of stores I knew she liked based on the bookmarks on her computer and then left them on her bed with a note suggesting she fix the room to her liking.

She hadn't mentioned wanting to since we'd first arrived on the island. I'd dismissed it then, convinced that she wouldn't be around long enough for it to matter. Still believing I'd go through with it, that I *could* go through with it, because *that had been the plan.* That had always been the plan.

By giving her this gift, had my mind been made up?

It gave her something to do. It gave her something to keep her mind sharp and her spirits high. It replaced the wreckage from the walls that had begun to break down in our sessions. What was the point if I didn't intend to let her come out of this whole?

The answers weren't at the ready.

"Approve it all," I said, flicking my hand to dismiss the list that Astor had produced. "Whatever she wants, she gets. She has her money." Several months' worth of money that I'd promised her in our marriage negotiations. The cash had been collecting in a bank account, enough to build an entire new building, if she chose. Still I added, "If that's not enough, transfer what else she needs from my account."

"Yes, sir. And the crew that Mateo's asked for? Did you want to bring in islanders?"

At that I shook my head. "Have Mateo find a crew from Mexico. Spanish speaking only." It would take longer to bring one in with that specification, and would cost more too, and I almost second thought the decision. I didn't want to believe that she'd try to escape again, not now. I wanted to believe I'd earned at least the beginnings of what would one day be loyalty if not something else. Something more.

I thought about how her resistance had begun to diminish when I'd been there last. How she looked better than she ever had, her skin supple, her muscles toned. How she'd relaxed enough to let me bring her to climax, not once, but four times. How she'd begged for me to fuck her.

I could still taste her. Could still feel the unrhythmic vibrations of her body as she came against my tongue. Could still hear the catch in her voice when she'd said her parting words—*Thank you, Edward.*

And none of that mattered. I'd imprisoned her. She'd run if she could. Why wouldn't she?

"Yes," I confirmed, for myself rather than Astor. "A Spanish crew."

"Yes, sir." He bent down to reach inside his bag. "Finally, this arrived. The book you ordered. Shall I send it on?"

I took the book he handed me, a scarlet goatskin leather journal with her initials written in gold foil on the bottom. A heart-shaped accompanying gold clasp was a bit more romantic than I'd intended, but it had been the only quality one I'd found that locked.

The lock had been important. I wanted her to feel free to write her soul, to let out what was inside as she had in her second letter to her parents, without worry of what I'd think or do. While I wanted to know with fierce longing every thought of hers, every detail of her imaginings, I preferred that she tell me those things herself. I liked her vulnerable, yes, like I enjoyed all my women, but the point was for her to choose that, not for me to take it.

It didn't mean anything unless she chose.

And if she did choose, then could things be different? Could this really work out another way?

I traced the letters with my finger—CEF. Celia Edyn Fasbender. I'd taken the Werner away from her when I'd put that ring on her finger —my mother's ring, for fuck's sake. I'd made her mine. She belonged to me now.

Didn't she?

I set the journal on my desk. "Not yet. I'll tell you when it's ready to send. What else do you have?"

The next thing on Astor's agenda was interrupted by the chirp of my desk phone. I hit the speaker button. "Yes, Charlotte?"

"Camilla's on the line for you."

My chest tightened. If the anxiety that was Warren Werner lived in my neck, the emotions I felt for my sister resided deep in my torso, complicated and protective in nature.

But things hadn't been easy between us as of late.

"Tell her I'm in a meeting," I said, tapping the button off with my finger.

Immediately, the phone chirped again.

"She says it's urgent," Charlotte said when I answered.

I should have guessed. Charlotte wouldn't have interrupted in the first place if my sister hadn't pressed. Annoyed, I looked to Astor, as though he could save me from the responsibility of family.

He read my expression wrong. Standing, he picked up his bag. "I didn't have much more. I'll come back." He returned the chair to the spot Celia had designed it to sit on his way out.

I hit line one and put the receiver to my ear. "What is it, C?" I asked, using the nickname that came more easily when I was frustrated. "I was in an important meeting."

It was a bit overstated, but I had a feeling her cry of "urgent" was as well.

"There's a delivery," she said, her tone clipped.

"Then accept it." But I already knew it was more. I'd hoped Camilla wouldn't have been there when it arrived, that Jeremy could have taken care of it all, but she'd canceled her planned photography outing when Freddie had woken up with a fever.

"It's from the States," she went on. "An entire moving truck. And it's addressed to Celia Fasbender. Do you want to tell me what I'm supposed to do with an entire moving truck worth of items? The deliverers are asking."

She was exaggerating. It was a small moving truck. I'd read the manifest before I'd approved the shipping.

But I knew the amount of items wasn't really the concern—it was what they were. That I'd had them shipped at all.

"Tell them to take them upstairs to Celia's room." Jeremy would have already said that. Camilla wanted reassurance from me. "I'll take care of them later."

"But what are they, Eddie? They're her things, aren't they? Why are you bringing them here? Do you realize you called it *her* room?"

"Because it *is* her room." I sat forward, my voice sharp. "There's not anyone else using it. And what would you prefer I do with her things? She's my wife. What would you prefer?"

"I'd prefer that you stick to the plan. You said marrying her was simply a door in. That I would never have to deal with her. You led me to believe that you would be leading very separate lives. Moving her things in is not separate. This wasn't the plan we'd discussed."

"No, it wasn't," I said, but I hadn't been completely honest with her. I hadn't wanted her involved with the gritty details. Camilla was too good. She would have rightly objected, even though it was the surest way to where we meant to end.

I felt guilty about that, more than I wanted to admit. About not being honest with her. About the horrible thing I'd planned to do. About changing my strategy midstream. About getting so fucking twisted by Celia's blue eyes and tenacity and the way she opened up when she began to truly give in.

My guilt made me angry. Angry with myself.

But also angry about being challenged. "Let's not forget that it was *my* plan, Camilla. *My* idea. I'm the one who orchestrated it, all of it. And that makes it my plan to change." Then, before she could argue further, "Let Jeremy deal with the deliverers. I'll worry about the rest. Like I always do."

I hung up before she could say another word. I didn't need to hear what else she had to say. I already knew, already felt the anxiety of having lost control of the reins.

What the fuck was I doing bringing her things to my house? As though she wanted them here. As though she meant to live on with me as husband and wife. As though I planned to keep her.

I scrubbed my hands over my face then held them there. Light slipped in through my fingers, gleaming off the band on my left hand. I pulled them down so I could stare at it. My father's wedding ring, now my own. His marriage had been everything to him. His wife had been his very reason for living. The ring was a reminder of my reasons, why I'd pursued vengeance with single-minded dedication.

But I'd put the matching ring on Celia's finger, and that had changed everything.

That was a lie. *She'd* changed everything. It was why I'd put the ring there, not the other way around.

I reached out and slid the journal toward me. Using the tiny key attached, I unlocked the fasten and opened it to the first lined page in the book. I grabbed a pen and wrote the short note.

Little Bird,

I told you privacy is a privilege. This is yours to keep to yourself. Fill the pages or don't, the words belong only to you. You've earned it.

Edward

I read the words again, disgusted with myself. Disgusted by the flood of warmth that filled my body just from writing my pet name for her. Disgusted that I even purchased the gift and more so that I would still send it anyway.

The plan had always been to ruin Celia Werner.

But she was well on her way to ruining me.

TWELVE

CELIA

THE FIRST TIME Edward had left me on the island, I'd been angry. I'd spent the days with him gone trying to smother the fire of rage inside me, or at least trying to tame it down to a manageable simmer. Weeks passed, and by the time he'd returned, the fury had subsided. Still there, but not quite as much of a focal point as it had once been. Still the thing that motivated me, but the flames calm enough that I could concentrate on how to get what I wanted—away from the island—instead of dwelling on the person who had put me there.

It was still what I wanted most. Even as the winter turned to spring and the weather on Amelie blossomed to perfection, even as I felt myself blossoming along with the new season, even as the place felt more like home and less like a vacation spot, I still wanted to leave.

But it wasn't what occupied my thoughts anymore, and the anger had become so distant that I forgot it for days at a stretch.

This time in his absence, my emotions changed. I wondered about him more—what he was doing, what he was thinking, if he was reading before bed or finishing last minute details for work. They were day-dreamy kinds of thoughts for the most part, wistful and curious. Had he gotten a good night's sleep? Was he driving himself to the office or using his driver?

When they threatened to take over, I pushed the thoughts aside by throwing myself into the project he'd left for me—redesigning my bedroom. It had been an unexpected gift, one I should have been allowed to pursue without his permission, but nevertheless I was grateful. It had been a long time since I'd really gotten into my work. It had been an even longer stretch since I'd done something for myself, and it was fun to discover what I liked again and how my tastes had changed. Most importantly, it helped the days pass while also making them remarkable. I began to look forward to what the sun would bring in the mornings. I no longer lingered in bed bemoaning my existence.

It wasn't until I moved out of the room that the jealousy began to trickle in.

The work had gotten to such a point that it was impossible to continue to sleep there. The house had several suitable bedrooms upstairs, and I considered taking one of those for all the obvious reasons, but in the end, it was more practical to stay on the main floor, near the living areas and the pool, and frankly, I liked the idea of invading Edward's bedroom, even if he wasn't there. I'd been surprised when, after I told Lou and Joette that was where I wanted to move, they'd actually complied. I'd expected a bunch of hemming and hawing and stalling until the idea was proposed to their boss, but there had been none of it at all. They'd simply nodded and began the task of packing up my belongings and shuffling them to the opposite side of the house.

Of course the lack of argument insinuated that Edward was already fully aware of what I was doing, that he'd possibly suggested it himself, but I tried not to think about that too much. I was successful too, until I was lying in his bed that first night, smelling the decorative pillows for any trace of his scent, and the wondering about him became much more personal. Was he thinking about me? Did he know where I was sleeping? Did he like thinking about me in his bed?

I liked the way these new thoughts made my heart trip and my stomach flutter. I closed my eyes, letting them take me where they would, expecting them to morph into something sexual in nature, and they did, just not the way I'd hoped. Because, a dose of reality seeped in, and all of a sudden it occurred to me to not just wonder what Edward was doing but who he was with.

Who *was* he with?

Was he sleeping alone like I was?

Was he fucking around?

The idea made me sit up with a start and clutch my stomach while wave after wave of nausea rolled through me.

It wasn't just possible he was with someone else—it was likely. In our negotiations before marriage, he'd assured me he'd be discreet, but that he'd have whatever side action he wanted to and that it was none of my business if he did. I'd been bothered by the arrangement, but I'd been more bothered that it bothered me so I hadn't fought it more. Besides, fighting him at all had proved futile. He'd gotten everything he'd asked for in that discussion.

At the time, I'd been determined to make sure he never had need of a side piece. My game had required his sexual attention, but also, I'd wanted him. More than I had wanted to admit.

I still wanted him. More than I wanted to admit.

And now my game was long over, and I wasn't with him, and he could be fucking anyone and everyone, and I'd never be the wiser.

I tried not to throw up.

After that, a constant ache lived in the pit of my stomach. My mouth tasted permanently bitter, and jealousy shadowed every other emotion that passed through me. I was even more grateful for the design project then, a distraction that I'd come to depend on, but it wasn't enough. So I doubled my time doing yoga. I played more chess. When Eliana wasn't available, I taught Mateo's oldest daughter, Tanya. When Tanya had schoolwork to do, I moved the pieces along the board myself.

Reading was hard. Even when the story engrossed me, there was always something that brought my thoughts back to him, back to who he might be with. Any book with any sort of romantic storyline was impossible to get through, but even the others would catch me off guard —an orphaned character, a misunderstood hero, an asshole of a villian.

Soon, I was as scared to pick up a book as I was to be alone with my own thoughts.

Then, the diary came.

It was the last thing I needed, and I definitely didn't trust it, even with the two keys and the lock and his promise inside not to read it. The lock could be easily picked or busted, and Edward's word felt as unreliable as the wind. Though, he hadn't really lied about anything so far. Tricked me, deceived me, but hadn't quite lied.

But I'd always had a thing for blank lined paper, an itching desire to fill the pages with whatever words came to mind. I'd kept a diary all through my youth for that very reason, and then later, when Hudson had invited me into his experiments, I'd taken over recording the observations. He'd been quite scientific with his journaling before I'd come along, referring to people as subjects and proposing an expected outcome from the beginning. Mine were more story form. While I'd kept Hudson's name out of them, referring to him only as A—because it was the first letter of the alphabet, and he was definitely the alpha of the games—I'd mentioned our victims by name and noted and evaluated their emotions in prose.

I missed that, I realized. Not the playing of the games, though maybe I missed parts of that too, but more, I missed the telling about them.

And so, six weeks after he'd left, when I was bored out of my mind and unable to ignore the thoughts in my head and the journal on my nightstand, I picked it up and began recording him. Began recording everything I'd had planned for him and how my game had come about, sure to include every one of his nasty assholish quips and misogynistic demands. If he picked it up and read it, he could hear about how much I hated him. How terrible he was. How easily I'd schemed against him. I wouldn't care. In fact, I hoped he did.

But the writing morphed as I went on, and I found it impossible to write with the detached voice that I had in the stacks of journals sitting in the closet of my condo back in New York. Edward had stirred too many emotions. They'd leaked through small punctures in the Teflon walls I'd so carefully built inside. Punctures I hadn't known he'd made.

Emotions I hadn't known still existed. I had a lot of feelings about my parents, apparently. I missed them, but not as much as I thought I did. I resented them. I wanted their approval. Their affection. I hated them a little, too.

And there were other feelings, about other people. Hudson, his father, my uncle Ron.

Edward.

So much about Edward.

Most of the emotions were still shapeless blobs, too complicated to call one color or another, but they were there, oozing out of me. They trickled out into my words even as I tried to hold them back, and soon I wasn't just telling about the devil who'd inspired me to play him and then took me into captivity, but the man I'd begun to glimpse underneath. How he affected me. How I longed to affect him.

How I suspected I *did* affect him.

It was cathartic to have a space to pour it all out, a place to line up the stray feelings and examine them properly. It was like he'd chipped away at a big stone wall inside of me, with his demands and his smirk and his *I'm-gonna-break-you* sessions, and now I was collecting the pieces, attempting to figure out the picture they made if they were whole.

It gave my life meaning. Not because it was one of the only activities available to me on the island, but because of how it let me look at myself. It didn't just give meaning to the life I lived here but to the life I lived before. I began to understand things about myself, things I'd never known, things I hadn't wanted to know. Like how much I enjoyed the power struggles. How they made me feel alive, even when it was exactly that type of struggle that had landed me captive on an island by a man who easily dominated me.

I liked that too. Being topped. Being cared for. Being seen.

There was more he brought out in me, and writing about it, I started to become more comfortable with those feelings—the desire, the anger, the longing, the jealousy.

I found myself in the words. Things I'd buried, I wanted to

uncover. Things I'd held back, I wanted to share. Things I'd suppressed, I wanted to feel.

The most shocking part was how much I wanted those things *with* Edward.

Because he'd started this whole journey, probably. Because I associated this self-reformation with him. Because I was lonely and confused, and he'd brainwashed me. That was likely too.

It was part of his plan, I was sure. Little by little, he was breaking me down, like he had been all along, like he was still doing from afar.

Only difference from before was that now, I wasn't just letting it happen.

Now, I wanted it to.

THIRTEEN

I CONSCIOUSLY FOUGHT NOT to hold my breath as I watched Edward move around my bedroom. It was the beginning of May, almost three months since he'd last been on Amelie, which had been just enough time to have the new design of my bedroom implemented. It had been finished so recently, in fact, that I'd only slept in it two nights.

Like before, Edward had shown up without any warning. One minute I was capturing Eliana's queen, and the next, my husband was standing over us, criticizing my winning move.

I was so excited to see him, I hadn't minded. I'd jumped up, given him a kiss that he might have assumed was for our guest, then tugged him out of the library to my bedroom to show off what I'd done. There was a momentary coldness before he accepted my grip around his hand, a split second where he'd felt cut off and callous like he'd been when he'd threatened to kill me instead of the coy and almost charming man who'd said he'd miss me, but it disappeared so quickly, I decided I may have imagined it.

And then I forgot about it entirely because I was too eager for him to see my room.

It didn't make him special. I'd cajoled everyone on the island into coming by and seeing the finished product three days ago. That was half the fun of completing a design project—showing it off.

I hadn't been nearly as nervous when any of the others had checked it out though. Maybe because everyone else had walked around with smiles on their faces, complimenting each and every detail.

Edward strolled through silently, tracing the beading on the plush gold settee as he walked by it, studying the mural behind the bed and the newly plastered walls. His expression was stoic, his lips drawn in a tight line, his eyes guarded.

"The curtains are purposefully heavy," I said, as he lifted a panel from the ground, as though testing the weight. "It adds drama to the room."

He nodded then sauntered over to the antique curtained yellow and filigree cabinet. He fingered the curvature of the cutout without saying a word.

"It's Louis XV period. Some of the metal adornment has tarnished, but I really wanted an authentic piece in the room."

Again he nodded.

The knot in my chest tightened as I thought about the small decorative decisions I'd implemented in his room. Would he hate those too? Would he tear down the tufted wall I'd added behind his bed? Would he get angry when he smelled me in his bedding?

The last one was stupid. He probably wouldn't even recognize my smell, and surely Sanyjah had changed the sheets on his arrival.

Edward continued on to the other authentic piece in the room—the bronze gilded writing desk I'd discovered in one of the antique catalogs he'd left me. It was small and ornate, and it locked and had been exactly what I'd been looking for when I'd found it.

It was quite unlike anything that had been in the room previously.

"I suppose I have different tastes than Marion," I remarked when my husband had almost made a full circle of the area and still hadn't said anything. His last wife had decorated the space, or rather, stuck furniture in the room and called it good. It was possible the changes were a shock.

I stared at his profile as he carefully examined the rope molding I'd added along the top of the walls, expecting to see him nod again.

"Better taste," he said, surprising me.

His voice was even and his posture unremarkable, and the only reason I noticed the subtle twitch of his eye was because I'd been staring, which meant he hadn't wanted it to be seen, but I *had* noticed it.

And I wondered what it meant.

Then I was sure I knew. He'd never talked to me about his former wife, but Blanche Martin, a woman I'd involved in one of my cons who had also once worked for Edward, had told me he'd been heartbroken when Marion left him. Devastated.

I tried to ignore the pinch of envy and concentrated on what this might feel like to him—another woman coming in and changing everything up, ruining fond memories, officially ending an era. "Does it bother you a lot? That I changed it?"

He jolted, swinging his head to look at me, his expression telling me I'd surprised him with the question. Shocked him, even, by thinking to ask it.

Quickly he schooled his features, and I expected him to deny or ignore, but he didn't. He stuck his hands in his suit pockets—he must have flown directly from work again—and stood next to me, gazing out over the room.

"It doesn't bother me as much as I thought it would," he said thoughtfully. "Perhaps because it's as stunning as it is."

His off-hand compliment made my skin as warm as if he'd kissed me.

"Or maybe it's because I was rarely ever in here anyway. There's nothing that I should have been attached to. Still...I thought that I might have been."

It was the most he'd ever shared with me, and the sharing was even better than the compliment. He'd said he would tell me things, that he'd be honest and exposed with me the more that I was with him, but I hadn't yet seen it, and I'd never quite believed it.

And he might not have let this out purposefully, but he *had* let something out, and I was startled to find how much I liked it. How I wanted more. How I wanted to collect his bits of honesty and hold them to myself like I'd collected his notes in my drawer.

"Tell me about her?" I asked with quiet hesitation, afraid to spook him.

For a fraction of a second, he seemed he might say something else, something meaningful.

Then he gave me a sharp, "No," spinning on his dress shoes back toward the door he'd come in. "We'll meet after dinner for a session. I have things to do in the meantime."

It was maddening to be so close to him after so long, more maddening that I cared to be close to him at all, and I told myself firmly to let him go, that this was a reminder of what a shithead he was and to stop romanticizing the goddamn asshole who'd kidnapped me and threatened me with death because wanting anything from the monster was the real definition of insanity.

But I *did* care.

And after weeks of writing about all the ways I cared in the diary that was right this very moment double locked in the writing desk across the room, the intricate details of those feelings were at the surface and ready to launch off my tongue.

"Have there been other women?" I asked, stopping him at the door. If he wouldn't tell me about his past, fine. But I sure as hell deserved to know about his present. Especially if he expected to take me off to his fuckpad later.

God, I hoped I could call it a fuckpad later.

He didn't turn around. "Other women since Marion?"

"Since me." As reasonable as it was for me to need to know, the simple statement felt like I was giving too much away. Revealing too much.

But wasn't that what he wanted from me? For me to expose and reveal while he gloated in my discomfort of the baring?

He swiveled to face me, a smirk dressing his lips. "I believe you said it wouldn't matter if there were."

It was a gut punch. Because I hadn't meant it when I'd said that, and he knew it as well as I did.

But he'd said things too, things that he also hadn't meant.

"See," I took a step toward him, "but you said you wouldn't be fucking me. And now you have. And you've alluded to doing it again. So, if you're going to be putting a cock that's recently been exposed to another woman's pussy anywhere near me, then it does matter."

Before the words were out of my mouth, I could see his next potential move, could see him taking away sex as an option between us all together, and it would kill me if he did. Literally kill me.

But the jealousy that had taken root inside me was on its way to killing me as well, so the words came out and now I had to face the consequences, whatever they may be.

He assessed me for a beat, his gaze brushing over my features with familiar tendrils. "It's not a concern," he said finally.

Which wasn't a fucking answer. He could be saying he hadn't slept with anyone or that he'd been recently checked for STDs or that he always used a condom or that the sex he'd had didn't warrant worry or that he just didn't care about what affect his sex life had on me at all.

"Does that mean—"

He cut me off. "It means it's not a concern. Don't push me further on it right now. I give what and when I'm ready to give. Your job is to give always. Do you understand?"

He expected an answer. He expected respect. "Yes, Edward," I said.

His smile appeared and vanished so quickly I wasn't sure if it had existed at all. "I'm having dinner with Joette and Azariah. I'll set out clothes for our session beforehand. Be ready by the time I return."

This time I let him leave. I didn't want to know that I couldn't stop him again if I tried.

FOURTEEN

"WHENEVER YOU'RE READY," Edward prompted, making himself comfortable on the sofa across from me. He hitched up the leg of his linen pants and crossed his ankle over his knee, draped an arm over the couch back, and took a swallow of his cognac. Except for the more casual attire, he appeared exactly the same as last time.

Everything was the same as last time, actually.

I wore the same white dress, the same boring underwear. He'd walked me down the same path, ushered me into the cabana in the same way. The only difference so far had been that, instead of offering me a drink, he opened a bottle of Petit Verdot and handed me a glass.

It tasted of plums and figs and spice and couldn't have been a better choice if I'd selected it myself.

He was beginning to know me, really know me. I was already so vulnerable with him, and he wanted to crack me open and bleed me more? I wanted it and I didn't all at the same time. Parts of me were ready to pour forward, like water through a sieve, but other parts— larger, bulkier pieces of past pain—strained against the netting, dislodged by the movement of the liquid, but unable to follow the same path.

I pinched the skin of my forehead and tried to find my balance.

"The same as before, Edward?" I asked, when I felt more solid. "Tell you something that makes me feel exposed?"

"I'm surprised you don't have several anecdotes at the ready. You've had nearly three months to prepare."

I couldn't help glaring. "Was that why you stayed away so long? So that I'd have time to decide what to tell you? It would have been nice to know I had homework."

My irritation slid off him like water. "The length of time wasn't meant to be anything but time. Distance, I've learned, can be very valuable. And homework or not, you can't tell me you didn't think about it, that you didn't peel away layers and find more that you could share."

I suddenly felt a strange urge to cry.

I rarely cried. For sure I didn't cry in front of people. Not because I tried not to, but because I just couldn't. There wasn't enough emotion inside of me to need to get out.

Until now. Until Edward.

Just as suddenly, the urge went away. I took a sip of wine. "Yes, I did think of things I could tell you. Some of them even true." I smirked at him like a smartass because I couldn't help myself, but I quickly dropped the expression because it wasn't who I wanted to be all the time anymore. Not with him.

"I thought of things," I said, honestly, "but I didn't prepare them because I figured there was zero chance in hell that your next session would ask the same thing of me precisely because I had three months. You've always preferred to keep me on my toes, Edward."

My breath shuddered through me as I waited for him to respond. Sincerity was foreign to me, and I didn't know how to wear it. It felt as unusual on my tongue as the cotton panties felt against my skin. Both should have been more comfortable than they were. I wondered if either would ever feel natural.

"It seems I've kept you on your toes once again, then, doesn't it?" His tone was authoritative but not malicious. His own brand of sincerity. "Unprepared is exactly as I prefer, but I'm also glad that you've let yourself think about things you could talk about. I'm sure the right account will present itself now."

I already knew which one it was. There was only one that I was even close to being ready to discuss, and it was going to be a bitch to tell. I'd even tried to explore it in my diary, but couldn't get myself to recount the details—the parts that mattered. But I'd wanted to. For the first time ever, I'd wanted to. And I wanted to now.

God, this was exactly like therapy, wasn't it? I supposed it was beyond time.

I pulled my knees up and bent them to the side underneath me as I searched for where to start. "After..." I paused, wondering if it was best to stay far away from the story I'd told last time since he hadn't approved of the ending, but there was no way around it. That ending was this beginning in every way, shape, and form.

I looked Edward directly in the eye. "Okay, it was a shitty thing I did—sleeping with the guy's dad. It was vengeful and disgusting, and I knew it, even as it was happening. It wasn't comfortable or even fun. It definitely didn't make me feel sexy or wanted or like I'd won anything, but I'm not going to expand on that or try to make myself a victim with that part—even though, let's be real here, the guy had been around me my whole life. I'd been friends with his kids. I should have been like a daughter to him, and when I showed up at his door, it did not take one tiny bit of convincing for him to try to get in my pants." In fact, Jack probably even thought he'd been the one who seduced me. "Which is kind of disgusting all on its own level and somewhat predatory, but my point is, I was culpable, and I was of age, so it was what it was."

"Just because you put yourself in the situation doesn't mean that you have to carry all the blame. It certainly doesn't mean that you shouldn't be allowed to have feelings about it."

His words surprised me so much that it had to be written on my face.

Edward dropped his arm from the couch and leaned forward, and I knew it was a cue to listen, to *really* listen to what followed. "Last time, I didn't approve because you told me this only to boast," he explained. "You wanted to shock me. You acted proud, and we both knew that wasn't honest. *This* is honest. This is what I want you to talk about."

Who was this guy?

I stared at him incredulously. "But you think that fucking him made me a slut, right?"

His cheek ticked at the word *slut*. "It doesn't matter what I think. It matters what you think."

Classic. Turn it back on me.

"Did you really want to be a psychologist instead of a businessman?"

"No."

"Could have fooled me." Not for the first time I wondered what he was getting out of all of this. He wanted to break me, sure, but that was as much a part of his rivalry with my father as it was about me, and he'd suggested he liked to do this with other women too. Did it turn him on to watch women examine their wounds? Because he liked being a sort of hero to them? Or because he wanted to use their pain against them later?

There was a possibility it was both.

It made it hard to want to continue on. What if I bared my soul to him, and all he did was hurt me with whatever he learned? I could feel iron walls threatening to close around everything inside of me, pushing him out.

The thing was, I already expected him to use my pain to hurt me. To break me. He'd not only told me he would, but he'd also admitted to being sadistic. And he'd wanted to kill me. This wasn't supposed to be an easy alternative—it was supposed to be terrible.

I expected it, and I'd accepted it. And maybe I was a bit of a masochist, because I wasn't completely opposed to taking the ride.

So, here I was, buckling in, preparing for the roller coaster.

"Well, I did think it made me a slut. I felt dirty and...used...and...stupid." I'd never articulated the words, and they came slowly as I began to understand the blob of feelings that had painted this time in my life. I had a sudden flash of me on my knees, taking Jack's cock in my mouth while he spouted on about my lips and my eyes and my breasts. "Cheap. I felt cheap. But also like I deserved it because I'd done it to myself."

I shook my head, throwing the memories of the night with Jack out of my head. "I carried all of that with me when I went back to Berkeley. Dirk was there, wanting to talk, maybe even get back together, and that just made me feel worse so I—"

"Why?" Edward interrupted.

"Why did it make me feel worse?" It was another blob I had to examine. This one was particularly hard to look at. "Because I didn't deserve that. I'd dumped him. Over the phone. For no reason other than that I thought my old crush liked me. And then, instead of trying to repair my relationship with him, I went and fucked an old guy. He'd been nothing but decent to me. Decent and kind. The first guy who ever had, really. When I was with him, he'd made me think that maybe I was better than the way other people before him had made me feel, and then one summer away from him, I proved that I was exactly what I'd always been told I was—only worth the value of my body."

"That wasn't what the summer proved." He let that sit in the air for a minute. "I'm curious to know why men before him led you to feel that way, though."

"I'm sure you are, but that's not what I'm talking about right now, Edward." It came out more defensive than needed, but he didn't call me out.

I thought about the other thing he'd said. "I guess the summer hadn't proved that. It had been one night, but the baggage from that felt heavy, and I hated it so much—hated myself so much—that I couldn't even look in the mirror anymore. I certainly couldn't put that on someone else, someone good. So I avoided him, and threw myself into things that made the self-loathing more tolerable. Random hookups. Drugs. I did a lot of coke. Some ecstasy. I drank. A shit load. I was smashed all the time that semester. I don't even know how I passed any of my midterms."

Actually, I did know how I'd passed some of them. I'd paid a girl to write my papers for western civ and I'd let my economics teacher masturbate on my breasts. Thinking about it now made me feel nauseated.

"Anyway, it wasn't pretty for a good two months or so. And then..." I could still remember the moment I realized it clearly, walking down the Walgreens aisle to grab some condoms and passing the pregnancy tests and coming to a halt because I hadn't had a period in ages and I knew, I just *knew* that I was pregnant. I'd bought a box and taken the first test in the store. Then, when it turned positive, I'd taken another one right after.

"And then?" Edward prompted, softly as though he were interested, not as demanding as usual.

"Then I found out I was pregnant." There was weight to that statement. It was obvious I didn't have a kid now, and so there'd be assumptions. I imagined Edward was thinking them through, trying to guess —*did she have an abortion? Give it up for adoption? Where was the birth control?* It was impossible for him not to form a judgment, and I ached to know what he was thinking so I could judge him back.

But he sat silent, waiting for my tale to unfold.

"It's funny, I'd imagined saying that before. I don't know when—in my play. In my fantasies. I didn't even want kids necessarily, but the notion of being pregnant always held drama. 'I'm pregnant', I'd say to the imaginary whomever in my head, and damn, did that get the attention I wanted. It's a heavy phrase, you know? 'I'm pregnant.' 'I was pregnant.' You immediately know something intimate about the person —that she's had sex. Sometimes you even know whom with. And when she doesn't have a husband or a boyfriend, you start wondering who the father could be, and then you also know that she was careless. That she was irresponsible. That she's easy."

Edward looked about to say something, but I waved him away. "Whatever you're going to say, it's true. People think those things and sometimes even say them out loud, and it shouldn't matter what other people think, I know, I know, but those things do matter. Especially when the things they were thinking were true. I was careless. I was irresponsible. I was a slut, and sure, power to a woman if she wants to sleep with lots of men. I'm all for that and fuck everyone who puts her down for that, but that wasn't who I was in that moment. In that moment, I had carelessly gotten pregnant from something that had made me feel shitty and slutty, and those words people said mattered. Because I was already saying them about myself."

I'd meandered. None of this was where I'd thought I was headed. The painful part was coming up, but in telling these parts, I remembered they'd been painful too. I remembered it in my muscles, in the way my hip suddenly ached and my shoulders tensed. In the twinge at my neck. These things had lived inside me, stuffed into the fascia of my body, breathing and festering, and all this time I'd thought there was nothing there.

And now? Could I finally let it go?

I'd been silent for several minutes when Edward asked, "Are you sure it was his?"

He didn't need to frame the question any other way. I knew who he meant, and it was obvious that was where I was going.

"Yes. The dates matched up, and when I did the ultrasound at Planned Parenthood, that matched up too. I'd been on birth control, but I wasn't always that diligent about taking it, and he was the only one I hadn't doubled up with a condom." Which was stupid. Which was why the whole thing had left me feeling stupid.

"Stop judging," he said, sternly. Also, ironically since that was exactly what I was silently pleading from him. "Stop judging yourself and just let it be what it is."

"How do you—?"

"It's written all over your face. I'm not judging you either, for the record, though that shouldn't matter."

He'd set his drink down and folded his hands in his lap, and with the way he was angled and the intensity of his stare, I could feel exactly how much of his attention was devoted to me. All of it. Every single speck of focus was on me.

It should have made me feel more exposed.

Somehow it made me feel more safe.

It didn't make sense. None of it. Why he wanted to know, why he cared. Why he was so rapt. "If you're not judging, what are you doing?"

A smattering of seconds passed before he answered. "I'm listening." He startled me with a smile. "Now go on."

"You're really that into this? You want to hear what happens next." I chuckled as I drank my wine.

"I think you want to tell it." He said it so it was clear when he said *think* he meant *know*.

And that knowing made me feel safer too.

I set my glass down. "Well, I immediately got my act together. Stopped the partying, did better in school, took prenatal vitamins. I didn't know what I wanted to do about it yet, but there was only a couple of weeks until Thanksgiving, and I was going home, and I could talk to my parents about it then. I didn't know about timelines for abortion so I figured it would be fine to wait until then."

"Did you expect them to be supportive?"

I shook my head. "It makes me feel guilty to say that when you already detest my father as you do, but it's honest. He didn't expect much from his only daughter, but he certainly expected her to stay classy."

"As fathers do."

I'd forgotten that he was a father. Or, not forgotten, but the fact hadn't seemed relevant, and now I realized how relevant it was. His daughter, Genevieve, was as old now as I'd been then. He had to be thinking about her, comparing us.

It took all my strength not to ask him about that. He'd tell me if he wanted me to know, and he'd been right—I wanted to finish what I was telling.

"It turned out it wasn't as bad as I'd expected."

"It never is."

I started to agree then stopped myself. Experience had told me better. "No, sometimes it is. But this time it wasn't, because I told..." I hesitated. I'd specifically left Hudson's name out of the first story. He was a prominent businessman, someone who Edward would probably work with eventually if he hadn't already, and I owed too much to Hudson to be the one to soil his name and turn his past against him.

So I left his name out again.

"I told the guy before I told my parents. The guy who I'd liked. The one who slept with my friend."

"And you told him the baby was his father's?"

I nodded. "He decided to claim the baby as his own, and that made telling Warren and Madge a whole hell of a lot easier because who the fuck cared what trouble Celia had made because now she was going to have a very wealthy baby! I mean, it hurt. It hurt knowing their reaction was only what it was because of what it gave them, but at least I didn't have to get the tight-lipped, cold-shoulder treatment. So, you know. It was going to be okay."

Edward sat forward, his finger up to stop me. "Hold on a moment—the guy who'd been an ass before now out of the blue decided to claim it was his?"

Up until then, he'd been almost soft—well, soft for Edward—but there was something distinctly biting in his tone.

"He wasn't always an ass," I said defensively, knowing that wasn't the most important part of his question. "But, yes. He stood up for me. We told our parents together."

It had been tense—all four of them and the two of us, half of us knowing that Hudson was definitely not the baby daddy, the other half ecstatic. My mother and his had immediately begun planning the wedding even though we'd made it perfectly clear we were not getting married. Then, while the others were talking about baby names, there'd been the moment between Jack and Hudson, a moment no one else saw but me. An eyebrow raise from the older, a terse statement from his son. *This baby is mine now. I'm doing this, and it's mine.*

That had hurt in its own way. I'd believed Hudson had volunteered to be dad because he'd felt responsible for the position I was in. He also hadn't wanted his mother to find out what his father had done, cheating on his wife with a woman half his age. But his words to Jack felt like they were only protecting my baby, his little brother or sister. Where did I belong in all of it?

"Why did he do that?"

I furrowed my brow, and since Edward couldn't know what I'd been thinking, I didn't know exactly what he was asking.

"Why did he choose to tie his whole life to yours?" His expression was as accusatory as his tone. "He didn't even want to date you for a summer and now he wanted to be linked to you forever?"

"Uh...kind of harsh, don't you think?" It was actually a valid question, though. One I hadn't spent a lot of time thinking about when it had happened. I'd been too relieved and grateful to have him step up and save me.

And maybe I'd hoped it would turn into more. Eventually. If I was honest with myself.

Maybe letting Hudson pretend it was his wasn't one of my finer moments.

"I only meant that it was a fast turnaround. He went from not caring about you to caring enough to make a terrible situation better for you. Why would he do that?" Edward had backed down, but his critical gaze continued to drill into me.

Why *would* he do that? "He didn't want me ruining his parents' marriage, that's for sure. Though, honestly, I was not the reason there were problems in their marriage."

"That's a hell of a sacrifice to save a parents' marriage." He leaned forward, his elbows on his thighs, his hands clasped together. "He didn't think it was his? You didn't *tell* him the baby was his?"

"No. I didn't sleep with him, remember?"

"There could have been a part of the story you'd left out." He ignored the way I bristled at the accusation. "Was he in love with you after all?"

I could feel a muscle in my neck tick. "Were you listening last time? He knew sleeping with my friend would hurt me, and he didn't care. He most certainly didn't secretly love me."

"Did you have something over him? Was it blackmail? Did you trick him?"

A cold chill ran down my spine. I hadn't done any of those things, and the accusations had me seeing red.

But they were too close to things I *had* done to other people, and that made me feel guilt along with the rage. But how did he know? How could he possibly know?

I swallowed hard before responding. "I don't know what you're trying to get at, but no to all of that. He felt responsible, I think. Because he *was* responsible, in a way, and maybe I was the asshole because I let him do it, because I thought he owed me, but I didn't trick him into it. It was all his own choice."

We held each other's stare for several breaths. Finally, he sat back into the sofa. "He stepped up. That's admirable, I suppose." There was no trace of apology on his features, but he was calm again. "I can't imagine Hagan ever doing something like that."

"I can't imagine you getting in the position where he'd have to, especially after you assured me that you knocking up a mistress would never happen." I frowned because now I was remembering that conversation, the same one where he'd declared he would sleep with whomever he wanted, when he wanted.

"You're right. It wouldn't. You may continue."

He was so bossy, so arrogant. It infuriated me. I was opening myself up for him and he could still remain so closed off. I was half tempted to stand up and stomp my foot and demand that he share too, that he open up and become vulnerable, that he give me something. Anything.

But I didn't have the power in the room. Throwing a tantrum would gain me nothing. My only play was submission.

"Thank you, Edward," I said, as politely as I could manage. I'd intended to go on after that, but I'd lost the momentum and couldn't figure out where to pick up the thread.

"You decided to keep it then." He was gentler now. Encouraging. "How did you feel about that decision? About bringing a child into the world."

The prompting helped. All I had to do was answer honestly, and I did. "I was excited, actually. For lots of reasons that weren't just about having a baby. I'd struggled with an identity for so long, and this felt like such a *good* identity to have—mother. Respected. Loved. I think it was the time in my life I was truly happiest."

It was *too* honest, too raw of a thing to say, not just to Edward but to myself, so I rushed past it as if it hadn't been said at all. "But I was worried too. I hadn't spent much time dwelling on it when I figured I'd probably end up having an abortion, but now that I was going to keep it, I had to face the fact that I'd partied hard. Drugs. Alcohol. In the earliest times of development. There was a good chance I'd already fucked it up, and I spent the next month fretting over every terrible thing I'd done. I was truthful with my doctor, who wasn't helpful. She just said we'll have to watch and see. I was so anxious all the time, my nails were bitten to stubs."

Edward's shoulders sagged then, ever so slightly, but it was enough to tell me he knew where this was going, and that he found it disappointing. "How far along were you?"

"Eighteen weeks. It happened just before Christmas." I hadn't told anyone this, not anyone. Every person important enough had lived through it, and there'd been no one to talk to about it after. And I hadn't wanted to, until now.

I wasn't even sure I wanted to talk about it now, but the story poured out as thick as the blood had gushed out from between my legs. "It was more blood than I'd ever had during a period. And the cramps were the worst. The absolute worst. Like something was trying to tear its way out of me. They had to give me morphine because I was screaming in the emergency room.

"And then I went into shock. I was so cold. The nurses brought three microwaved blankets to wrap around me, and I couldn't stop shivering. The cramps kept on and on while my body pushed out this thing inside me, this dead thing that I'd centered my identity around. This thing that I'd killed with my irresponsibility." My throat was tight, and I had to pause to swallow. "It hurt, it fucking hurt physically. It was basically labor, and labor has a bad rep for a reason, but the actual pain eclipsed what it should have been. Every part of my body ached. For days. My muscles, my skin. My face. I didn't want to feel. I didn't want to live. I didn't know what there was to live for."

It was there in my hospital room that I'd begged Hudson to teach me how to be like him, how to bury emotions, how to become cool and aloof and heartless like he was.

He must not have felt completely heartless because my pleading had won him over, and he taught me The Game. And from then on, I worked not just to bottle and suppress my feelings but to dissolve them with acidic behavior. I annihilated every pain that dwelled inside me by giving pain to others. It had worked for so long.

And now...

Now I was realizing I'd been wrong. That it had never worked at all. That everything I thought I'd killed still remained, and when it finally came out of slumber inside me, it could very well destroy me. Especially if it wouldn't let its grip on me go, and this one wasn't letting go. I felt a need to cry, this pressing need against my chest. But it stayed there, tight between my ribs, unwilling to move higher. Unwilling to come out, even though I had the distinct feeling that it would feel so much better if it would.

It would feel validating, too. Tears. It would prove that I really felt this big, terrible pain, that I wasn't faking what it was or what this experience had meant to me.

But there was nothing. My eyes were dry. My nose didn't even run. The pain wouldn't budge from its prison. Was this supposed to have made things better? What was I supposed to do with this now?

I looked to Edward, silently begging him to tell me what to do.

He sighed, a sympathetic, compassionate sigh, and stood up. He moved to me, stopping in front of me, his body slightly offset from mine. He reached down and stroked the back of his hand along my cheek, a gentle caress.

"My children are the joy of my life," he said, softly. "To lose them would be to lose everything. You are human in this moment. This pain is human. But it's not something I can replace. The only way over this is through. Just know you'll be someone different when you get to the other side."

Fuck you.

I wanted to scream it at him. How was that helpful? *Oh, sorry you feel like your heart wants to rip out of your chest, but not really sorry because I'm the one who made you talk about it in the first place.*

If my eyes were weapons, he would have been dead for all the daggers I shot in his back as I watched him cross over to the bar and refill my wine glass.

And what the hell did he mean by "replace"? It seemed obvious that this was his response, that his response was to pat me on the head and move on, but if I'd told him a different sort of story, what had he intended to do to "replace" it?

I was confused and mad and beat up by the time he returned the glass to my hand. I was also tempted to hurl it at him.

But then he cocked his head, bringing his tumbler to his own lips and taking a sip before he asked, "Were you *told* it was your fault?"

The question jarred me. I hadn't expected it. "The miscarriage?"

"Yes. Did anyone tell you that you caused it? Could it have happened anyway? Maybe it was something completely unrelated to your actions. Is that possible?"

The glass dangled from my fingers as I thought about it. "I didn't tell them at the hospital in New York. Didn't tell them about the stuff I'd done. My doctor back in California was the one who knew, and I saw her a month later for follow-up." I tried to remember if she'd ever told me specifically I'd caused the loss of the baby. Tried to remember if I'd ever asked.

She hadn't.

And I hadn't either.

I'd just assumed. I'd always just assumed.

Edward seemed to understand without me saying it. "That's an awful lot of blame to assume without confirmation. Doesn't seem like you."

I almost snapped back that he didn't know me, but I stopped myself. Because he did know me, better than I wanted him to. Maybe better than I knew myself.

But also, he was right—it wasn't like me to assume something big like that at all. I was too practical for that bullshit. Too intellectual.

So why had I let that be a weight I carried around for so long? Didn't I have enough baggage without it? Didn't it feel better to set that particular piece down?

It was a lot to think about, a lot to process, but as we walked back to the main house in silence, even though the emotions of the evening still pressed heavily against my chest, it did seem like they were a bit lighter than they had been before.

FIFTEEN

THE NEXT DAY carried out very similarly to most of the days when Edward was on the island, but there were some noticeable differences. He still left me to myself, as usual, but instead of disappearing, he hung around. He left the library door open while he worked, and I could hear him tapping away on the computer as I ate my breakfast in the radial dinette. Occasionally he'd record a message for himself, a reminder to "*follow up on the numbers from Turkey*" and another to "*see about purchasing that Jan van Bijlert that went up for auction.*"

Later, I caught him looking at me as I returned from a walk to the beach and again as I sat outside by the pool. He met my eyes that time and made no effort to hide that he was indeed spying. Warmth rushed up my neck and into my cheeks. He was distant and aloof, as always, but there was a new weight in his gaze that kept me pinned down, and surprisingly, I liked that feeling. Liked the way it pulled me together and anchored me. I'd needed it and hadn't known it. How had he?

After the session from the night before, I'd woken up somewhat frazzled. This large thing that had happened in my life, this event that held such enormity, had finally been unpacked, and it was impossible to shove it back inside me again. It didn't fit into the box I'd put it in before. I couldn't completely let go of the blame I'd put on myself for my miscarriage, but I couldn't hold it in the same way either. I could breathe around it now when once upon a time it had suffocated me. And I could feel it breaking up further, slowly dissolving into a new shape as I wrote about it in my diary.

I was changing. I was becoming something new, and it scared me, but it felt good too. Thrilling, almost. Especially when Edward looked out across the patio and regarded me with that intense stare. Part of me couldn't believe he could stay so distant after everything I'd said the night before, but a bigger part of me liked that he did. Was grateful. I needed the space to process the revelations. It was almost as though he could see what was happening inside me, the good and the bad, the breaking apart and the pulling together.

And of course he could see it—he'd orchestrated it. I just couldn't figure out why.

After lunch, Marge showed up unexpectedly to give me a massage.

"It's not our usual day," I said, not actually protesting. Honestly, a massage sounded amazing right about then.

"Mr. Fasbender requested it," she said. "He said you'd had a rough night. Let's see if we can get that worked out of you."

Stunned, I followed her out to the pool house, and when I glanced back toward the library and caught Edward watching us at the window, I smiled.

That evening, everyone came for dinner and stayed to socialize after. The men didn't separate like they sometimes did, instead joining the women in the courtyard. A tense game of poker commenced using poker chips in lieu of actual money. Eliana played savagely, which wasn't at all surprising, though Edward won almost every hand, also not surprising. What was somewhat astonishing was the way Joette cursed and swore like a sailor when she got a bad card. The woman had zero poker face and was the source of many laughs. Even my usually stoic husband spent much of the game with a grin on his face.

There was no session with him. I'd barely spoken to him at all, in fact, and yet he was foremost on my mind as I went to sleep that night. He fascinated and intrigued me, and as much as I still hated him, I also didn't. There was chemistry between us that I couldn't deny, and I wanted him, and it wasn't just Stockholm Syndrome or the common situation of falling for my therapist, though it was definitely those too. But it was more than that. It was that unique feeling of being known in a way that no one else knew me. It was the sense of being cared for, actually *cared for* rather than just groomed. It was the interest of someone in me for something other than my body, someone I hadn't manipulated into giving me his attention.

I'd never had a relationship like that with a man. I'd never had that sort of relationship with anyone. I yearned for it to be real and not just one-sided, but like everything with Edward, I knew there was nothing I could do to influence what happened between us. He would feel what he felt, and if I was ever to be privy to what that was or what went on his head, it would only be when he determined to share it.

Of course, I also couldn't forget that I was his prisoner, that he'd told me he'd kill me if I didn't comply to his whims and fancies. Even though he hadn't done anything particularly terrible to me, hadn't hurt me physically or starved me, he had still taken power over me, and I battled with myself over how to feel about that. Could I ever forgive him? Why should I?

And the biggest question, the one that consumed me, made me toss and turn, made me sigh with longing—did he even want my forgiveness?

That answer alone might change everything between us, if I could just figure it out.

The next few days repeated in the same way—the looks from Edward, the writing in my journal, the massage from Marge, the evening gathering. His stare was always on me, always heated, but there was a dark undercurrent of hesitation that I couldn't understand. At times I'd find him near me, reaching out to brush a hair off my face, then dropping his hand, stepping away. Something was holding him back, and the more he pulled away, the more he drew me in. I had to force my own restraint, knowing I was to take my cues from him.

I hated having to give him that, having to hand over my power so completely.

But maybe I didn't hate it that much. Instead of having to stay ahead of the game, constantly scheming and planning, I got to sit back and relax. There was freedom in his control that I never knew could exist. Never knew I could like. Love, even, maybe?

Maybe.

Monday, I was surprised to find he was still around. I was half afraid to ask, sure he'd leave as soon as I voiced any interest in how long he'd stay. The other half of me tried to embrace the anxiety of not knowing. I meditated on it during yoga, opening myself to his whims, letting his power soothe me instead of rattle me. He'd taken care of me so far, hadn't he? Giving me massages and space and yoga and chess games. He'd tell me when he needed me to know, not a minute sooner.

That night was Joette's birthday. Dinner was moved out to the beach. Tents were set up, and tables brought out. The entire family had joined us, even the children and Azariah, and that might have been an excuse for Edward to act more husbandly, to put on the happily married show, but I'd seen that show before and it was different. He'd stand next to me then, touch me a lot to prove his ownership of me.

This wasn't that at all. He sat away from me all night, rarely getting closer than a foot or two, but always, always, his eyes were on me. Every time I glanced at him, there was his gaze. It was so hot and fierce, I could feel it, even when I wasn't looking in his direction. It made me squirm. Made my thighs tense and my pussy clench. Made my dress feel too hot in the cool night air.

After dinner, champagne was opened and a bonfire was lit. Tom made a Bahamian rum cake that was a family favorite, and Joette wore a paper crown that one of her grandkids had made. Louvens lit fireworks, which dazzled the night sky, but scared Marge's nine-month-old baby, Liam. Erris was too busy with their older son who was delighted by the noise and lights, and Marge had spent the entire evening with the baby, so, somehow, I found him snuggled up in my arms.

It was strange holding a child, and such a young child as that. I'd never been around children. I'd never babysat, never had friends with kids. The closest I'd been to a baby was feeling the tiny feather movements of my own before it had bled out of me.

Now, here I was, days after opening myself up to that loss, and a tiny creature was clutching onto the strap of my dress, trying to snuggle in tighter at each loud boom. He was heavy in my arms, heavier than his twenty pounds should have felt. But the smell of him was sweet and precious, and the brush of his tiny fingers against my skin sent warmth down my limbs.

"See how pretty," I cooed to him, turning my body so he could see the spray of colors in the sky. "It's okay to be scared. Just don't be so scared you miss out on the good stuff."

When Marge came a little while later to retrieve her son, my body missed the weight of him, oppressive as it had been only minutes before. I was empty now. Too empty. And alone.

Except, not alone.

As soon as I turned to scan the crowd, Edward's gaze caught mine. The way he looked at me, I could tell he'd been looking for some time. He held me like that, several feet across the sand, just with his eyes.

He broke the connection first. At my husband's bidding, Mateo had brought out a box of cigars. Nice cigars. The kind people spent real money on. I watched as Edward lit one for the birthday girl then stowed two more in his pocket along with a lighter. Next, he grabbed an unopened bottle of champagne, and he walked over to me.

For the first time all night, he touched me, lacing his fingers through mine.

"My wife and I are going to call it a night," he announced. "Please, everyone, continue celebrating as long as you'd like."

My pulse sped up as he led me toward the house. As emotionally draining as sessions were with him, I was curiously keen to have another. I hoped that was where we were headed.

"Do I need to change?" I asked, eagerly, when he took the path around the house instead of going into it.

"No." Reading my surprise, he added, "Just keeping you on your toes, little bird."

At the cabana, he surprised me again, leading me out to the deck overlooking the ocean rather than having us take our usual seats in the main room. He gestured for me to sit on one of the lounge chairs then turned on the gas firepit before sitting on the chair next to me.

"Want one?" he asked, holding up a cigar.

I hesitated. "I've never had one before. But sure."

He bit off the end, puffed on it until it was lit, and handed it over. "Have you ever smoked a cigarette?" he asked as he watched me delicately put it between my lips.

"No. I've smoked a joint, though."

"You don't need to inhale this. Draw it in like you're sucking a straw. Puff every minute or so."

I did as he instructed, coughing a bit until I got the hang of it. When I realized he'd frozen in place, his own cigar hanging loosely from his lips, I became self-conscious. "What?"

"That's extraordinarily sexy." His voice was deep, vibrating in his chest.

My skin felt hot, everywhere. "That's...surprising."

"Please. I've told you on several occasions how attracted I am to you."

He had. I had memorized every mention. While many men had told me I was beautiful, the few times that Edward had said it seemed to hold greater meaning. He was too honest to not mean it and too rich and spoiled for good-looking women to inspire his notice.

Not that his notice had meant much. "You have said it. But actions speak louder than words."

He chuckled. "Yes, they do. I'd never intended to fuck you at all. Remember?"

My breath shuddered as I inhaled. "I think you've shown an admirable amount of restraint. Not that I'm one who admires it."

He grinned. "I'm sure you haven't. But perhaps you have yet to learn the joy of delayed satisfaction."

"Says the man who has a plethora of women at his fingertips back in London." I couldn't just be happy with the confirmation of his attraction, could I? I had to mention his possible trysts.

"Jealousy only makes you look sexier."

"Whatever, I'm not jealous." I was *insanely* jealous.

"We're supposed to be honest here, Celia." The stern reproval didn't help my withering self-confidence.

"All I'm saying is that it's easier to have restraint with me if you're getting it somewhere else. Perhaps I need to jump Louvens the next time he's working in the house without his shirt on."

"Every man—and woman, for that matter—on this island knows the entire family will be fired and banished from Amelie if they touch you. Just remember what you'll be destroying if you go that route."

Before we'd married, he'd encouraged lovers for me, said he'd help me find one if need be. That had obviously changed. So I still didn't know if he'd wandered into other beds, but now at least I knew that jealousy looked good on him too.

He stood and disappeared into the house, coming back a moment later with two champagne flutes. In my periphery, I saw his eyes rake over my body once more. Then he shook his head and sat down.

I stretched my legs out in front of me, reveling in the attention. I didn't know how to get back to the sexy banter, though, not without dwelling too much on the information that he refused to give me about his fidelity, so I dropped the subject and let my mind wander elsewhere.

"My grandfather used to smoke cigars," I said, savoring the taste of cedar and nutmeg. "They always make me think of him."

"The grandfather who died when you were six? You were close to him?" He spoke around his own cigar as he wrestled with the cork of the champagne.

I remembered the way he'd dismissed me the last time I'd tried to talk about my grandpa Werner. I could sense now that he expected me to tell him how much I'd loved him and how it had been my first brush with death and how I'd cried for weeks.

But the profound effect his death had had on me wasn't in the way I'd missed him, but in how my life had changed with his passing. And as much as I was intrigued by this process of breaking down, I wasn't ready to talk about that.

I threw the ball back at him. "I'm sure it's nothing like having your parents die when you were only thirteen."

"I'm sure that's true," he said, offering nothing more.

So much for getting him to share anything.

The cork popped and champagne bubbled out all over the sand, barely missing Edward's sleeve. Looking smug, he filled both glasses, and handed one to me then sank back in his chair, looking out over the ocean as he puffed and sipped.

I relaxed too, following his lead when the ash grew too long at the end of my cigar and knocking it off in the sand. It was nice—the crash of waves on the shore, the nostalgic scent of the cigar. The company.

But after a stretch of silence, I grew antsy. "Should I figure out another woe-is-me story to feed you, Edward?"

He shook his head. "Not this time. Tonight, I'm going to probe one out for myself."

I raised a brow.

"Keeping you on your toes."

"Keeping me on my toes," I repeated, my breath quickening. I wasn't sure if I liked the surprise element of dealing with him. On the other hand, I wasn't sure that the surprises weren't my favorite part. "Just let me know what I'm supposed to do."

"All you have to do is answer my questions. Answer them honestly." He considered momentarily. "What was your first period like?"

"Oh my God!" I couldn't help laughing.

"After everything else between us, that is the last thing I would expect for you to find embarrassing."

"It's not. I don't. But if you're looking for past trauma, that's not where you're going to find it."

He gave a one-shoulder shrug, an uncharacteristically casual gesture for him. "Let me be the judge of that."

"I was fourteen. It started when I was at a friend's house, and that was the best place it could ever have started because Felina had already had hers and she had an older sister who was much more supportive and helpful about it than my mother would have been. She even taught me how to use a tampon."

A glint appeared in Edward's eyes. "Did she demonstrate?"

"No, you pervert." I took a sip of bubbly and remembered the details of that milestone moment, knowing he'd want more. "I hadn't been looking forward to it, honestly. I was one of the last in my friend group to get it, and it seemed like a bunch of fuss and pain and humiliation."

"Hm." He puffed on his cigar. "I was around for both Camilla and Genevieve's first period. Except for the fact that I had to be involved in the purchasing of necessities, both of them seemed rather ecstatic about it."

My skin tingled with his words. There were very few times he shared with me, and these details, tiny as they may be, left me elated. I wanted more, wanted to know everything about him.

I also knew not to push.

So I gave him more of what got me what he'd given. "Yeah. Most of the girls I knew had been excited, too. I guess..." I'd never really examined why I'd felt the way I had, and as I realized the reasons now, I struggled to articulate it in a way that was honest but didn't give too much away. "I wasn't ready to be a woman, I think. There was a burden that came with that. I'd already gotten a lot of attention over my body from leering older men, and I was caught between despising that and how it made me feel and wanting more of it from the boys I liked. If I'd been given a choice, most days I would have wanted to stay a little girl. Having my period meant the decision was made for me."

Edward's head tilted one way then another as he processed this.

"But it wasn't traumatic or unusual to feel that way, I'm sure. Lots of women struggle with not wanting to grow up and wanting to be an adult at the same time."

"Men, too," he remarked, with an empathetic tone.

I studied his profile. He'd been so young when he'd been orphaned. Then he'd lived for years in foster care before he was old enough to care for his sister. He had to know more about becoming an adult too fast than I could even imagine, and I ached for him without even knowing the story behind his simple words.

A beat passed.

"Your first breakup," he said as the moon came out from behind the clouds. "How did that go? That wasn't Dirk, was it?"

I shook my head. "But Dirk was the first bad one. I had a few boyfriends before but none that were really serious. Each time we either drifted apart amicably or—"

"Or you broke their heart before they could break yours?" There was a hint of accusation, that made my gut drop. Isn't that why I'd played people for so long? So their pain would eclipse mine?

"Something like that," I said, hugging my arms around myself.

"How about when you lost your virginity?"

I almost stopped breathing.

"What exactly does that mean these days?" I asked when I found my voice. "The first time I was penetrated? The first time I sucked a dick? The first time I had an orgasm?" Two of those stories were not ones I was prepared to tell.

His eyes were glued on me, as always, and I was halfway sure he knew exactly what I didn't want him to ask, but then he said, "Let's go with the traditional sense."

"That was fine," I answered, relieved. I hadn't thought about it in a long time, but it hadn't been a big deal when it happened. "Over and done quickly. Nothing to tell Dr. Edward about."

"Uh-uh. That's not adequate. Tell me what happened."

"You're a little horny bugger tonight, aren't you?"

"You wish. Stop stalling. Tell."

A breeze blew a strand of hair across my face. I set my flute down in the sand, making sure it was balanced before I gathered my hair in one hand and pulled it over one shoulder, and angled my body to face him. "It's not a grand tale of erotica, so don't get excited or worry about memorizing it for the spank bank. Okay." I took a deep breath, trying to remember just how it had begun. "I was almost seventeen. It was October. In the fall we spent a lot of weekends at the country club upstate. Dad called it father/daughter time, but really, he'd play golf, and I'd hang out at the stables. Which was fine. I didn't have much interest in spending time with him anyway. I mean, I was a teenager."

I was twice that age now and still didn't want to spend time with him.

"Anyway, John was a security guard, and when I came back from riding, he'd often be—"

"Pause a second. He *worked* at the club? How old was this John?" Edward had the tone I'd seen him get with his daughter, protective and possessive. It wasn't a tone I'd heard often from my own father.

"He was twenty-seven," I admitted.

"Celia." Edward looked at me sharply. "He was ten years older than you?"

"You're ten years older than me."

"You're thirty-two now, not seventeen. Not almost seventeen. That's rape."

I waved at him dismissively. "It wasn't rape. It was consen—"

He cut me off again. "It doesn't matter if it was consensual. He knew how old you were, I'm guessing. If you weren't yet seventeen and he was an adult—"

It was my turn to cut him off. "Fine, it was illegal. But I was two weeks away from my birthday. It wasn't ideal, and he knew my age, and yes, that was bad, and I am not at all minimizing the impact of rape on a woman's life, but this did not have that effect on me. He was just a guy, and he'd noticed me, and I wanted to get it over with, and I didn't want it to be stupid and juvenile, so John seemed like a good choice. *Dad.*"

Edward was quiet, his jaw clenched.

I waited to see if he was going to say anything more, if I was going to have to defend the situation further.

Then, in the silence, I wondered why I was trying to defend the situation at all. "Maybe it was a big deal. I don't know. The whole thing was just so anticlimactic. Literally. There was a utility shed that he took me to with cement floors. He took his jacket off and laid it on the ground for me. Then he helped me pull down my riding pants and told me to lie down. He unzipped his slacks and put on a condom that he'd had stashed in his wallet. Then he laid down over me and pushed himself in. It didn't really hurt, and I didn't bleed. I'm pretty sure my hymen had been broken a long time before that. It wasn't comfortable, though. I wasn't wet. He didn't kiss me. He held my hands over my head, which, nowadays I think is pretty hot, but with John I felt...restrained. And then..."

I trailed off, trying to remember the details, the slapping of his belt against the cement floor, the smell of his breath, the strain in my thighs as I tried to keep them open with my pants still wrapped around my ankles. "My brain shut down. I think it went on for a while, but I don't remember much after that. Just, eventually, he was done and tying off the condom. Then he was helping me to my feet and making sure my hair wasn't a mess before sending me out to meet my father. It happened a couple of other times, exactly the same way. I'd thought it would get better, and it didn't so after the third time, I found excuses not to go to the club anymore and that was that."

Edward's features had relaxed, but his expression was still grim. "He didn't force you?"

"No." Though, there had been a part of me that had felt like I hadn't had a choice. Not that I could explain that, because I certainly did have a choice. He hadn't bullied me. There had been plenty of chances to walk away.

"Why did you do it?" he asked, voicing the question I hadn't been able to ask myself.

I shrugged.

"Not good enough, little bird."

I puffed on my cigar a few times, thinking. "I wanted to get it over with. I know I said that already, and it's true. All my friends had boyfriends. Everyone was fucking. Everyone wanted to be fucking. I don't know that I was especially eager to, but it felt like my virginity was more of a liability than an advantage, if that makes sense. When a guy found out I hadn't done it yet, that's all they cared about. I was tired of always having to protect that virtue. Also, when the right guy came along—because yes, I still believed in that whole right guy thing back then—I didn't want to be inexperienced.

"But if you're asking why John...that's harder to answer. He was always around, saying things. Dirty things. About how pretty my cum would look on his dick and how much better I'd feel with him between my thighs than a horse. Maybe if that had been the first time I'd heard a man say those kinds of things to me, I would have run off and told someone. Made a complaint. But it wasn't even the third time I'd heard them. Not even the thirtieth. I'd been told for years by so many men in so many ways that my value was in getting men off. And since I'd never been fucked, I guess it felt like I wasn't even living up to that."

My mouth felt dry after all that. I picked up the champagne and finished it off in one swallow, then returned the glass to the ground and stared out at the ocean, the light of the moon reflecting on the ripples. "So it was fine. It wasn't awesome, but it wasn't the worst. Do I wish it had been different? Yes. I was a sort of romantic girl. I wanted the dream scenario. The boy who loved me, a boy I trusted. There'd be rose petals laid out and candles burning and soft piano music playing, and I'd be so turned on that I'd be wet before his dick got anywhere near me, especially because he'd give me three orgasms before his pants ever came down. But things rarely happen like the dream, and I didn't see any way the dream was going to happen for me, especially when..." *When Hudson hadn't looked at me twice in any way that wasn't sisterly.*

I let the thought fade off in the wind.

Edward didn't let it go, however. "Especially when the boy from the other story wasn't showing any interest."

"Yeah. So what was the point in holding out this false hope? It was better just to kill the dream before it got out of hand." I cringed, visibly. "That sounds way more dramatic than it was. Teenage girls have crushes. Unrequited love isn't unique; it's a fact of life."

"It doesn't mean it didn't hurt to live it."

I sighed. "I suppose."

Abruptly, Edward got up and sat down on my lounge chair, straddling it as he faced me. I pulled my knees up to my chest to make room for him, but he pulled my legs out one at a time to rest on his thighs.

"I'm going to need a day or two to respond," he said, taking my cigar and putting it out on the sand next to where he'd disposed of his. "But I'm very happy with you."

"You are? I didn't do anything special."

"Exactly." He ran his hands up my bare legs, letting his fingers drift under the edges of my dress. "You didn't put on a performance. You were honest. You were vulnerable."

There was pride in his voice, and I felt my chest and cheeks get warm with the praise. Or maybe it was the way he was touching me. That was heating me up awfully quickly too.

"What would you like?"

"A present?" I tried to lessen my smile, make it more seductive and less sloppy grin. "Can I fuck you?"

"Try again." His hands were now massaging my thighs, speaking a very different language than his mouth.

"Will *you* fuck *me*?"

He shook his head, but he smiled at my attempt.

"Can I blow you?" Another head shake. "Watch you jerk off?"

"My cock is staying where it is."

A glance down at his crotch said that was going to be awfully uncomfortable for him.

"So what you're saying is this gift can't be sexual?"

"It can be if you choose to have your pussy eaten." He pushed my skirt up, letting me know it was already decided. This would be the present I got, whether I chose it or not.

I was okay with that.

"Ohhhh," I laughed, my panties now flooded. "That was a punishment last time. Now it's a present?"

"I think you've learned to feel differently about it." His lips came down against the panel of cotton covering my damp heat, and I let out a hiss.

"Yes, yes," I said, arching into him. "I feel very differently about it."

I stretched my hands up over my head and abandoned myself to his mouth and his fingers and his tongue, and it wasn't until three orgasms had passed, when I was boneless and seeing stars that I realized, despite knowing how he'd answer, it hadn't even occurred to me to ask for the gift of going home.

SIXTEEN

"HAVE YOU EVER TRIED ROLE PLAY?" Edward asked as he led
me into the cabana two nights later.

The days between had been lighter than any I'd had since arriving
on the island. While he continued to be stoic and aloof, he did it in
close proximity. He'd invited me into his library while he worked. He'd
dismissed Eliana and played chess with me himself. He accompanied
me on my morning run. Heated glances had turned into subtle caresses,
brushes of skin, a few stolen kisses that I'd given willingly. His moves
still felt calculated, but there was an organic rhythm to the way we
danced around each other, a natural ebb and flow that drew us to each
other for heightened moments before we'd part and drift away.

Always, the drifting felt initiated by him. There was something he
was hiding—*a lot* that he was hiding—and whatever secrets they were,
they held him back. More than once, he seemed to start to say one thing
then said something else instead. It often felt like a question was ready
at the tip of his tongue, waiting for the right moment to be asked.

Was this the question he'd been hesitant to ask?

It didn't seem powerful enough to give him pause, yet, at the same
time, the question felt significant.

"I can't say that I have," I answered. But if role play was what he was after, I was down for it. I could be his naughty secretary, his sassy nurse, his frisky maid, his slutty nun.

Damn, role play sounded like a lot of fun, actually.

"Never? Never put on another persona just to see what it felt like? Just to see if you could pull it off?" He walked behind me, his fingers sweeping across my bare shoulders.

I shivered, but not just from his touch. Everytime he said something that sounded like it could be a veiled reference to The Game, I got cold. I was paranoid, I knew that, but Edward was the kind of man who made it easy to be suspicious.

I considered how to answer. I'd devoted myself to being honest with him and that meant not tiptoeing around truths just because I didn't want to deal with the fallout. The Game, though. Talking about that wouldn't be exposing how others had hurt me, but rather how I'd hurt others, and I wasn't ready to let him see that side of me, not when he seemed to be starting to like the me that he had seen.

I decided to circumvent. "Is that a loaded question? You know I tried to play you. So you already have an answer."

He circled around in front of me, his fingers wandering over my collarbone before skirting the top of my bodice. "This was an excellent choice, by the way. Quite appropriate. You're stunning in it, too."

I glanced down at what I was wearing. It was an Oscar de la Renta strapless gown with metallic leafing and lots of tulle. It was pretty and poofy and made me feel younger than I was, like I was dressed up for the prom. The dress had been one that Edward had sent earlier in the year, one of the items I'd scoffed at because where in the hell was I going to wear something as formal as that on this stupid island?

But tonight, when his instruction for clothing had merely been, "Dress like you want to be seen," I'd decided why not?

When I'd stepped out of my room and found him waiting for me in an extremely well-tailored three-piece suit, I knew I'd chosen right.

I put a palm on his chest and tugged at his tie with my other hand. "You don't look so bad yourself, Mr. Fasbender." Maybe precocious schoolgirl was what he'd like. I could do that. Look at him coyly underneath my lashes and ask for help with my grades.

He continued his circle around me, the tie falling from my grip as he rounded my side. His lips kissed along my shoulder and up the side of my neck. "Here's what we're going to play—young sweethearts. We've been together for quite some time, but you've never let me have my way with you, and believe me, I've tried. Tonight, though, you're finally ready."

"To have sex with you?" My words came out breathy.

"To give me your virginity."

My stomach dropped. At the same time, goosebumps scattered down my arms. How was it possible to feel both excitement and dread at the same time? I didn't know, but that's exactly what I felt.

"This is because of what I told you the other night," I said stiffly. "Are you mocking me?"

He chuckled, which only increased my skepticism. He found pleasure in my discomfort. He'd never tried to keep that a secret, and so what else would I expect from him now but to twist and turn the private admissions I'd shared with him, using my words against me as I feared from the very beginning.

But his laugh died quickly, and then he was sucking on my earlobe, sending sharp bolts of lust to my pussy. "Does it feel like I'm mocking you?"

"No."

"How does it feel?" He swept my hair off my other shoulder so he could give the same attention to that side as he had to the first.

"It feels like you're trying to be nice," I admitted. "But it's hard to trust you. Especially when I don't know what your motives are."

Swiftly, he turned me to face him. "Trust is the one element here I can't reproduce. You'll either believe me or you won't when I tell you that my motives aren't diabolical."

"Then why? Why do you want to do this?" I wasn't even sure what *this* was, if it wasn't mocking.

"Because once upon a time, an asshole who was a decade older than you took something precious from you without acknowledging how beautiful and precious it was. You were honest and open about that. You gave me what I asked for and this is how I'm moved to respond—with a reward."

"And my reward is another decade older asshole who recreates the whole thing?"

He lifted my chin up with two fingers and stroked my jaw with his thumb. "Not recreate. Replace."

The muscles in my shoulders relaxed ever so slightly. There was a nice sentiment there, if I believed it. I wanted to believe it.

Could I?

"I don't know if this is going to work if it's only about me. I need to feel like you want this too." My heart tripped in my chest. Of all the vulnerable moments he'd pulled from me, that confession was one of the most raw.

Instead of answering with words, he bent his head down and kissed me. It was slow, at first, his lips moving, not with caution, but with self-control. I sighed into it, opening my mouth for him, and his tongue slipped in, probing tenderly at first then more aggressively. His hand cupped my jaw, angling my face the way he wanted it while his other arm wrapped around my waist and pulled me flush against him where I was met with a very thick, very hard bulge.

"Does it feel like I don't want this?" he asked, pulling back just far enough to speak.

"No. I can't say that it does." I wanted to say more, something that would make me feel less unguarded, something that would help me gain my footing.

But he was kissing me again, more eagerly than before, and the thoughts and doubts disappeared from my mind replaced by the captivating sensations of his teeth and tongue, nipping and licking along my lips, along my jaw, down my décolletage.

I was dizzy and disoriented when he finally pulled away so he could tug me toward the bedroom. After pushing the door open, he stepped aside for me to pass ahead of him. I walked in and gasped.

The bed had been made up with luxurious satin bedding. Plush pillows were piled at the head. About a dozen candles were lit around the room, champagne sat chilling in a metal ice bucket. There were four separate vases with bouquets of roses, and the best part, red and white petals were scattered across the bed and floor.

Behind me, piano music began playing softly, and when I turned back to Edward I discovered it was coming from his phone. He set it down on a side table and removed his jacket, his eyes never leaving mine.

My breath caught between my ribs. There was gravity in this moment. Romance and affectionate gestures were not his style. Even when someone else had thought of them, he was not the type to carry them out, and seeing him now, witnessing what he'd done for me was both overwhelming and confusing.

I shook my head as he strode toward me, unsure how to process any of it.

When he reached me, his hand once again cradled my face. "Do you want this?"

It was the first time he'd ever made me feel like I had a choice. Four simple words, and for all the ways he'd held me captive, his asking made the entire scene everything that my first time hadn't been. Then, I'd felt trapped. What happened with John had seemed inevitable. Like it was what I was destined for, to lie down and be quiet. To be a good lay.

Now, with Edward, a man who never asked permission, who took what he wanted and gave even less, his offer of a choice was an enormous gift.

And yes. I did want it. More than I could bear.

"I'm going to need you to say it," he prompted when I hesitated too long in answering. "Nothing happens without your consent."

I stepped into him, brushing my lips against his. "Yes, please, Edward. I want this, please."

He devoured me. He worshipped my mouth, his hands raking through my hair, occasionally pulling too hard, the sting of pain making me wetter than I already was. It was a relief to have the rough mixed with the soft, to know that the man I was kissing was still really Edward and not just this persona he'd invented for this game, not just the guy he thought I wanted.

Because that's what I really wanted—him. Only him.

Kissing led to groping, and when I'd managed to wrestle both his tie and his belt from him, he broke away to lead me to the bed. With the flat of his hand at my back, he pushed my torso down to the mattress.

"Stay," he said before dropping to his knees where he took off my shoes, kissing the instep of each foot as he did. Then his hands stroked up my legs, pushing them wider apart as he settled between them under my skirt. My thong was quickly removed, and then his mouth was there, licking my clit.

He teased me with his tongue, spiraling me up with flat brutal passes over my bud, making me pant when he followed with featherlike flicks with just the tip. The first orgasm came quickly, like a gut punch, the full force of it felt on the onset. If I hadn't already been doubled over, the climax would have taken me to that position.

Edward stood and lay his torso on top of mine. I could feel the ridge of his cock pressing against my ass as his breath blew hot at my ear. "I cannot imagine a better taste than your pussy. My favorite flavor."

Heat rose to my cheeks, and my chest tightened, wanting to believe it. Not sure how much of this was an act.

"Do you mean that?" I asked, unable to help myself.

"Only honesty, remember?"

My cheek was still pressed into the mattress, away from him. He couldn't see the doubt on my face as I echoed him. "Only honesty."

Was that really what this was? Honesty? It felt too good to be honest.

His hand worked the zipper of my dress, pulling me to a standing position when it was all the way down so that it would fall to my feet. I'd gone braless, and my muscles tensed with the realization that I was now naked while he was still almost fully clothed. It made me feel off-balanced. Defenseless. Vulnerable.

But that was always the tilt of power between us, whether I was nude or not, and as disarming as it could be, I was beginning to learn that there were benefits too. *Don't be so scared you miss out on the good stuff,* I'd said to baby Liam.

I could have been saying it to myself.

With the next breath, I let the strain release from my body.

"That's it, little bird," Edward said, turning me to face him.

Even his pet name for me made me feel small. Was that really so terrible? To be littler than him? For him to be able to manage me?

As he tossed me swiftly to the bed, I decided maybe it wasn't terrible at all.

He crawled up over me, spreading his body along mine before taking my mouth in his. He tasted like me—his favorite flavor—and another wave of lust rushed between my thighs. Soon, he moved down to suck on a breast, tugging roughly at my nipple until it was a sharp peak.

"These are mine," he said, lifting his head to hover over the neglected breast. "You know that, don't you? These gorgeous tits only belong to me."

"Yes, Edward." He'd told me that specifically as he'd fucked me over his desk, months ago. He'd been in a rage then, but the words were the same. There was something strangely thrilling that his possessiveness remained at his core, no matter what mood he was in.

His fingers moved down to the space between my legs. "And this too. This cunt is mine."

I cried out as he plunged two fingers inside me, demonstrating how much "mine" it was. The second orgasm followed soon after, brought on as much from his claiming words as from his ministrations on my body.

When I came down from that one, I came down impatient. I jerked at the zipper of his pants, wanting access to the big secret he was hiding inside.

"Three orgasms before my pants come down, Celia. I'm trying to do right by you, but you're making it hard. *Very hard.*" He bucked against my hand, his hardness evident.

It took a minute to remember that I'd been the one who'd specified three orgasms when I'd told him my dream virginity-loss scenario.

"That was greedy on my part. Two is more than fine. I need you inside me." The last words came out ragged, too true to be spoken without emotion.

"How about this—you make yourself come again while I'm undressing. Shall we see who can finish first?"

I was no more comfortable playing with myself in front of him than I'd been on our wedding night, but the prospect of seeing him naked was enough to let those inhibitions go. I'd never seen him completely naked. He'd never let me get that close to him before.

God, the thought, the relevance of this one thing, stripping in front of me—I'd come again before he was even halfway done.

"Fuck," he growled when the orgasm ripped through me, my limbs quivering with the ferocity. "You better treat my cock as good as you treat your fingers." There was a warning in his tone, as though he meant to punish me if I didn't come as easily when he was inside me as I had when he was watching.

It was so Edward, so the man I was used to, and seeing him appear, even just the glimpse of him made me deliriously happy.

"I'll treat you better," I said, sitting up as he approached the bed wearing absolutely nothing, his cock jutting out in front of him with pride.

My pussy clenched at the sight of him. He was chiseled and lean, but not too lean. There was a bulk to him, too. His pecs were man pecs with dark hair scattered across them and down his stomach, which was flat, but not concave. His thighs were long and strong.

And his cock...

I hadn't had much of a chance to admire it before. I'd known it was big from the shape of the bulge in his pants and the feel of it inside me. I hadn't known it was also beautiful. Hadn't known there was such a thing as a beautiful cock until there was his, long and fat with a gorgeous smooth head.

I was speechless.

"Do you want to touch me?" He was already touching me, stroking his knuckles along my jaw.

"Yes, Edward." It was a moment of him handing over the reins. Letting me behind the wheel for even the briefest of minutes couldn't be easy for him. I wanted to respect that, so I watched his face as I reached out to grip him, looking for any signs of misgiving.

But then he was in my hand, and I couldn't think about his face because his cock!

"It's so big," I said, mostly to myself. "How the fuck does that fit?"

"You're really good at the virgin routine," he said, his words ending on a moan as I palmed his crown.

"Not a routine. This is honesty. Remember?"

He stared at me for half a beat before he was pushing me back down, kneeling on the bed between my thighs. He lined his head up to my entrance. "I wish I really had been the first person inside you." It was said so low, I wasn't sure I was supposed to hear it. I definitely wasn't supposed to respond, because he thrust inside of me, all the way with one stroke, and I couldn't speak, couldn't think, could only clutch onto his arms and trust I'd come out of this in one piece.

But if I could have spoken, if I'd been able to say the truth right then, I would have told him he *was* the first person inside me, truly inside me. In all the ways that mattered.

It was a good thing, then, that I'd been rendered speechless. Giving away that truth would have been a far more precious gift than my virginity had been.

He wasn't as vicious with his fucking as he'd been in the past, each stroke didn't tear me apart and blind me with sensation like the previous two times, and for that reason, I knew he was still holding back, that he was giving me what he believed was the ideal lover.

Even restrained, he was magic.

He propped my feet up on his shoulders and lifted my hips to meet him as he pumped into me with vigor. When he was sure I was balanced and wouldn't drop my ass to the bed without his support, he stretched one hand up to plump my breast. His blue eyes were eclipsed by his large pupils, and they swept over me, studying every inch of my body, as though memorizing it. Revering it.

I'd never been looked at like that before. There had been plenty of men who'd seemed to worship me, but they'd only honored the idea of me, the brainless, beautiful woman who let them stick their dicks in her hole. When Edward looked at me, he saw everything that went with the pert breasts and flawless skin and narrow waist. He saw the things hidden underneath. And I knew he saw those things because he'd specifically gone looking, needling my secrets out of me in his "break-you-down" sessions.

How could he see me like that, all weak and impotent, and still look at me like I was something to be admired? Still fuck me like I was someone to be enjoyed? How could he ruin me so completely and also be the only person to make me fully whole?

My eyes smarted with tears, and I could feel another orgasm coming, but I wasn't entirely sure that was the source of the weeping. A feeling of desperation gathered inside me like a cyclone as my pussy tightened around him.

"Is this real, Edward?" I needed to know. I needed to know what this was, if it was all an act, if it was everything it seemed to be. If *he* was everything he seemed to be.

His hands rushed back to my hips, holding them in place as he struggled against my impending climax. "Does it feel real, little bird?"

God, yes. For me, yes. It was the realest I'd felt in my entire life.

Stars shot across my vision, blinding me. My body strained and trembled, and then the devastating flood of euphoria spread through my limbs, leaving me slack and exhausted. My legs fell from his shoulders. Edward lowered me to the bed, never disconnecting from me. He stroked into me long and leisurely.

"What do you want, little bird?" he asked, his lips hovering inches above mine. I'd been thoroughly fucked, and he could do whatever he wanted with my limp body, and still he was seeing this fantasy through. Making sure it was everything I needed him to be.

I could easily curl up in a ball and go to sleep, I was so wasted on him. But I wanted to feel him come, and I wanted it to be real for him when he did. I wanted him to let down his walls the way he'd made me let down mine.

What did I want?

"You," I said, not sure he'd understand but unable to articulate it any clearer. "Just you."

He paused for only a moment before he swiftly gathered my wrists together above my head with one hand and pushed my knee up to my shoulder with his other hand, pressing down on my bent leg with his body. In this position, he was so deep inside me, so deep I felt him at the end of me, and still there was the barrier of my leg between our torsos, that last little obstacle he wouldn't allow to be removed.

Without warning, he smacked his hand across my breast, so hard I yelped. Then he began driving into me with brutal blows, pounding without mercy. It hurt and the hurt was wonderful. It was good pain. Pain that made me want to feel more and more. I knew this was him, the real him, fucking me with such cruelty it was hard to believe he was the same man who'd been so reverent only moments before.

But his eyes...his eyes still looked at me the same, and that's what gave him away.

He came inside me, the first time that he ever had, grunting and rutting into me, milking every last drop of his cum before he pulled out and I collapsed in an almost fetal position on my side. He fell behind me, and I could hear his breaths, heavy and fast, evening out as the minutes passed.

I closed my eyes, afraid of what came next. Nothing good, I imagined, since the last two times we'd fucked the aftermath had been shaky at best.

Which was why I jerked when he curled up behind me, wrapping his arm around my waist.

"Were you not expecting cuddling?" The amusement was evident in his tone.

"I never know what to expect with you," I said sincerely.

He nuzzled into my neck and sighed softly. "That's fair," he murmured. He fell quiet, and I wondered if he was going to sleep.

"I was thirteen," he said, his voice startling in the silence.

I didn't move, not sure where he was going with this beginning, but somehow sensing that it was meaningful.

"My parents were both dead, and I was angry and destructive, particularly to myself, but also to those around me. Pilar was my foster sister. She was not a virgin and was seventeen, and before you ask, yes, that's illegal in the UK, but honestly, she probably left the situation feeling more violated than I did. I'd bullied her into it, though technically it was consensual, and she was good about taking care of herself so she had more than one orgasm. But we went for a long time, and I hadn't come. Couldn't come. It felt good, certainly better than jerking into my own hand, but it wasn't happening, and I really needed it to happen. Being with an actual person, I realized, wasn't the same as doing it on my own. By myself, I'd imagine one of a thousand discomforting situations, and I'd release, no problem. Pilar underneath me, grinning with the delirium of her own orgasms, that wasn't inspiring. It was too easy. I wanted her to be nervous like she had been when I'd come on to her. That's what had been attractive. Her unease.

"So I bent down close to her and whispered in her ear, told her that I had a camera secretly filming us and when I showed it to our foster parents she'd be kicked out. She might even be arrested. None of it was true, but she became quite upset, squirming and struggling to get away. Panic was written all over her face.

"That did it. I came, and it was everything everyone said sex was—amazing and overwhelming and powerful. And from then on I knew who I was, who I am. What kind of a man I am."

A *devil*. He didn't need to say it for the meaning to be clear. There wasn't any apology about it, no shame. It was just fact.

My stomach felt heavy. His story had been dreadful, but along with that heavy feeling there was something else, a warmth in my chest, growing and spreading through my torso. I was drawn to the devil in him. Edward Fasbender fascinated me and captivated me and it certainly wasn't because he was an angel.

But more important than his confession itself, was that he'd confessed anything at all. He'd shared something with me, something I had a feeling he didn't tell many people. He'd opened up. He'd let me in. After everything he'd done that night, this was the thing that held the most meaning.

I turned toward him, needing to see his face. "Why did you tell me that, Edward?"

He traced his finger along the line of my lip. "You told me something honest. I told you something honest in return."

"Why do you care about my honesty? Why do you want to know

all of my secrets? Why does it matter what I have locked up inside of me?" They were the questions that had troubled me for months. His motives. His reasons. It was killing me not knowing, and I doubted he'd tell me now, but if there was any chance at all, I had to ask.

His brows furrowed as though he was confused why I'd even have to ask. "It's the only way to have you," he said.

I held onto those words, let their meaning seep into me well after he'd blown out the candles, pulled the covers up over us, and fallen into the rhythmic breathing of deep sleep. If my vulnerability was all he needed to own me then he owned me, full and clear.

But he'd shared too, he'd been vulnerable as well.

Did that mean he wanted me to have him too?

SEVENTEEN

I WOKE up in the cabana, and before I even opened my eyes, I knew I was alone. I lay there for a long moment, letting the lingering memories of the night before to fully absorb before I officially woke up and let them go. I'd never had such an incredible sexual experience, one where I'd been pampered and adored, made love to. As it was happening, I'd known it wasn't real. Edward had clearly said we were role-playing, and yet there'd been a sliver of myself that had believed it could be something more.

He was good with his games, that way. He had pried into my head and then twisted what he'd found, made it physical, planted his "replacement" deep in my body and my soul. There were pieces of me that belonged to him now, and the longer it continued, the more of me he'd own, just like he'd said.

The worst part was that I loved it as it occurred.

But after...

Today was after, and I was alone, naked and sore, in a room that smelled of sex and vanilla candles, and I couldn't begin to fathom how I felt beyond confused.

And well-fucked. At least there'd been that.

I finally opened my eyes and stretched, squinting against the sun streaming in through the windows. I turned away to look at the empty bed behind me. The sheets were still tangled from where he must have thrown them off of him. Had he spent the night? I'd gone to sleep in his arms. Whenever he'd left, it had been after that.

I rolled over and buried my nose in his pillow, dawdling in his scent before throwing my legs over the side of the bed. I paused then, my eyes catching on the robe laid out on the armchair. *My* robe. A comfortable yet luxurious piece that Edward had sent earlier in the year. A scan around the room said my clothes and shoes from the previous evening were gone. He—or someone—had been to my closet and brought the robe and a pair of flip-flops to wear instead.

Still confusing, but the disappointment I'd felt at my husband's absence lifted ever so slightly. Whatever he was thinking, wherever he was, he'd at least had a passing thought about me, even if it was just to tell Tom to bring the items for me.

God, I was hopeless. Clinging to the scraps given by a man who'd imprisoned me. Making me feel a sense of romance about him. Making me want more.

I'd said it before, I'd say it again—he was good.

The layout of the clothes, besides being a thoughtful and practical touch, also seemed to be an order of sorts. *Put these on, come find me.* The unspoken command was clear in the appearance of flip-flops instead of slippers. The shoes were meant for walking. For that matter, if he'd wanted me to stay put, he'd probably have taken everything and left me naked.

Or maybe I was reading too much into it.

But this was Edward—was there anything he did or said that wasn't calculated and precise?

A stubborn bit of me wanted to rebel. Maybe walk to the main house naked, or not return at all until he came looking for me, but I forced myself to behave. I was adjusting to the man who kept me, learning to acquiesce to his demands. Bowing down to someone else's authority, though, had always been tough for me, and the tendency to force against it came naturally. In some ways, that made the giving into it all the more freeing.

I let that feeling of unconstraint envelop me as I wrapped the robe around my body, momentarily letting go of my worries and fears. I was confused and didn't know what today would bring, but I'd had a wonderful, memorable night, and Edward had thought of me, and wasn't that worth holding onto for a little longer? As unreal as all of it had been to him, it sat real in me, and for now, that felt good. So fantastically good, that by the time I arrived at the main house, I had a smile and a hum on my lips.

"Someone had a good night's sleep."

I stopped, stunned out of my daze by Edward's uncharacteristically charming timbre. My heart beat a little faster at the sight of him, fully dressed and sitting at the small dining area, two settings placed, as though he'd been waiting for me.

"I did, actually. Slept very well. And you?" I felt my breath still as I waited for his response. Whatever he said next would set the tone of whatever followed, and I was eager to know what that tone would be.

He considered quickly, his expression telling me his answer surprised him before his words did. "Despite being unused to sharing my bed space, yes, I did sleep quite well."

So he had spent the night!

My smile grew as I pulled my robe tighter, suddenly bashful. "Good to hear, Edward."

His eyes glinted at my use of his name, and when I started over to the chair opposite him, he shook his head. "Come here." He scooted out from the table, making space for me to sit on his lap.

Years ago, there was a moment, when Hudson's lips met mine, when it seemed like this man I'd been wanting and wishing for so long had finally opened the door for us to be more than what we were. That moment had felt like blossoming. Like being a flower left in the dark for so long that it had stopped believing in the sun, and then, when the rays fell from the sky and nature awoke, that flower opened up and became the beautiful thing it had always meant to be.

I'd felt like that, blissful and fervent and exuberant in my skin until Hudson revealed I'd just been his test subject, and I never let myself blossom like that for anyone again.

Until now.

Now was like that moment, and as I sat on Edward's lap and he wrapped his arms around me, I lifted my petals toward the man I'd married and woke up. The world became vibrant. The colors of the greenery out the window, the blue of the ocean meeting the horizon in the distance, the aroma of roasted coffee, and the warm wall of man at my back—my senses were flooded with an effervescence that had gone unnoticed. Was this what normal people experienced all the time? Was this what it felt like to be alive?

He nuzzled into my shoulder, sending a zing of pleasure through my limbs. "You've been such a good little bird, sharing everything I've asked from you."

The praise brought on a sort of orgasm, my entire being lighting up with euphoria.

His mouth moved up to suck on my neck. "We have a trust between us now, don't we? You've learned the reward of confessing your secrets, haven't you?"

"Mm hm."

His lips continued up to nibble on my earlobe. I could feel the pleasure sting of his teeth rumble between my legs, and I was suddenly very aware of how naked I was below my robe. "Now," he said, his breath hot on my skin. "Tell me about The Game."

Darkness fell like a veil over my vision, a darkness thick enough to permeate all my senses. I clawed my fingernails through the cotton material until I felt them dig into my thighs, bracing myself. Holding myself together.

Then I took a breath, and the haze began to clear.

I was overreacting, like I always did when I heard the term. He hadn't actually made the capital T and the capital G. I was sensitive to the phrase and tended to hear what I feared most.

"What game?" I asked when I had my voice, certain he meant my latest chess match with Eliana or some other benign activity.

But he brought his hand up to grip my chin, hard, holding it in place. "Don't do that," he fumed at my ear. "Don't pretend you don't know what I'm talking about."

The hair on the back of my neck stood up, straightening my spine. Embracing the lie was the best way to pass it off, a lesson I'd learned quite well, though for half a second, the tiniest fraction of time, I considered laying everything out and giving this to Edward too.

Then the second passed. "That would be easier if I actually did know what you were talking about. And I don't."

"You don't." It sounded less like a question and more like an incredulous clarification of my last words.

Still, I answered it. "No, I most definitely do not." Then I held still, my breaths shallow as I waited out his skepticism.

He dropped his hand from my face. "Your determination is almost admirable. I'd be impressed if you weren't such a bold-faced liar. And there's nothing I hate more than a liar."

My stomach plummeted. A minute ago, I'd been glowing in his praise, and now I wanted to crawl under the dining table where I could hide under the long tablecloth.

At the same time, my feathers were ruffled. Being called out irked me, even when it was deserved, because he couldn't *know*. It was impossible. He would have confronted me with it long before, and while he'd acted somewhat guarded around me on this visit to the island, what could have happened while he was gone that would fill him in on the truth?

Nothing. There was nothing.

He couldn't know. He *didn't* know, and I wouldn't stand to be accused. I started to get up so I could face him with my indignation, but his arm around my waist tightened, holding me to him.

"Shall we go about this a different way then?" his voice was controlled and confident. "Who's *A*?"

And then my stomach dropped again, hitting the floor this time. Dropping lower still. That simple question proved he *did* know, as well as told me exactly *how* he knew.

"You read my journals." It was the only place I'd referred to Hudson as A, afraid someone would find them accidentally and discover who they were about. There was nothing to protect me, though, when they'd been found in my own possession.

Fuck, if he'd read those…he knew everything. Every terrible thing.

"I read some notebooks, yes," he confirmed. "Filled with some very interesting things, I might add."

And this was what had bothered him over the last few days. He'd been waiting to bring this up, looking for the best moment to destroy me with the information.

"Things that weren't for you to see." I cursed silently. Then I cursed out loud. "How the fuck did you even get them?" I'd left them in the closet of my condo back home, boxed up so no one would find them.

"I had my wife's belongings sent from her residence in New York to the one we share in London." His breath at my neck had been arousing before. Now it felt menacing, as he surely meant it to.

"Oh, fuck you. The house we share in London?" The house I'd never lived in with him as husband and wife. The house he didn't seem to ever intend to bring me back to. "Fuck you."

I pushed my elbow back into his torso, hoping to throw him long enough to loosen his clutch on me, but my jab didn't even make him wince, and he moved his hands to hold me at my forearms.

"You're welcome," he said with no hint of exertion despite wrestling with me. "It was rather thoughtful on my part. When I was unpacking your items, I came across a box full of notebooks. I had to see what they were to decide where they should be kept."

"Sure, sure. That was why. Not because you're a nosy asshole who doesn't know how to mind his own business."

He brought his face forward so his cheek was next to mine. "You are my business, Celia. Don't ever doubt that."

His words and inflection were so chilling, yet, also, somehow inviting. There was a part of me that wanted to tell him. Wanted to finally confess everything and maybe, *maybe* then I could begin to pay penance.

But I didn't know how to say it. Didn't know where to start, even when he'd given me the opening.

I shook my head, denying him once again. "They were fiction. Stories I made up. That's all. No one was ever meant to see them."

"They weren't fiction. They were real."

"Bullshit. You're guessing. And you're guessing wrong."

"I can tell when you're lying and these were honest. I don't have to ask how long you've been doing this manipulation of innocent people—the dates were clearly written, which I found particularly helpful." He barely hesitated, but when he spoke again, his words were raw. "Was that what I was to you? Another game?"

My eyes pricked. It was the first hint he'd ever given that he might have some sort of feeling for me, and it was revealed in an accusation of betrayal.

This couldn't be happening like this. There was no way this could be how last night ended up.

"You already know what you were." A tear fell down my cheek. I didn't try to wipe it away.

"No." The word was sharp and enraged. "I had a perception of the situation based on your deceit being a singular incident. These journals note that I was only one of a long list of lies."

I craned my neck, turning toward him as much as I was able. "Is that what bothers you, Edward? That you weren't unique?"

The eyes that met mine were hard and mean. "There is a hell of a lot that bothers me, and that's not anywhere near the top. If you start explaining your gross form of amusement, perhaps I can point out my grievances as you go."

I ground my teeth. He'd already judged me. Of course he had, and why shouldn't he? I would have told him eventually, probably. Possibly. If things had continued the way they were. But not like this. I didn't want him to know like this.

I looked forward again, unable to stare at those vacant eyes another second. "Is this a session? I'm supposed to tell you things freely in my own time. This is coercion."

"You get to tell me your vulnerabilities when you're ready. What I read aren't accounts of your vulnerability—they are accounts of your cruelty."

Every pore in my body oozed of shame. And that's why he was wrong. This was the *most* vulnerable thing about me. It was the worst part of me, the worst things I'd done, the actions that no one would ever forgive. The reason I would never be loved.

How could I not be more exposed than that?

With a sudden surge of adrenaline, I yanked myself out of his grasp and stumbled to my feet.

Throwing my shoulders back, I threw him a bitter, forsaken scowl, and started to my room.

He was on his feet in a heartbeat. "Don't you dare walk away from me. We are discussing this now."

I swung back around. "This isn't yours to have! We never bargained for this."

"Clearly you weren't paying attention because my bargain demanded everything."

He'd told me he would break me down and that I would be his, and if for a second I thought that hadn't meant giving him everything, I couldn't doubt it now.

But what was it all for? Give him everything so he could hate me? I already hated myself enough for both of us.

"Who's A?" He was relentless.

I shook my head. "It doesn't matter."

"He sure seems to matter, considering how long the two of you played this game of yours. Did he know about this one? Is he waiting in the wings for an update?"

Oh, the irony of that accusation. Hudson had been the one to leave The Game—The Game that *he'd taught me*—and found the incredibly impossible person who could love him despite everything he'd done. Then, in a fit of envy and disgust and loneliness, I'd obliterated any future for our friendship by playing a scheme on him.

And what exactly was it that Edward was doing with me?

I pointed an angry finger at him. "What about *your* games? This shit you do to my head. The way you pretend you care and that these sessions mean something to you and then pull the rug out from me when I react to that. What about those fucking games?"

"This is not the same."

He began to slowly circle around me, and I moved with him,

keeping him in front of me. "Right, right, because you're above scrutiny."

Abruptly, I was caged against the table, his arms on either side of me. "This isn't a game between us." His mouth was so close I could kiss him with only a tilt of my chin.

My heart pounded so loud, I could hear it in my ears. "Are you certain about that? It sure feels like a game, and believe me, I ought to know."

His eye twitched as it glanced quickly at my lips then back again. "Tell me, or I'm leaving."

He thought I was cruel? That threat was the cruelest of them all.

It was tempting. I wanted my freedom so badly that at times I was tempted to do anything to get it.

But the truth was, my telling him what he wanted to know wouldn't change anything. He might even leave faster if I did. "You're leaving anyway. Eventually."

His lips pressed together in a tight line. A beat passed, and I could hear the gears whirring in his head, deciding his next move.

Finally, he stepped away. "You're right."

He turned around calling Tom out of the kitchen where she likely heard much of our argument, but showed no sign of it when she appeared. "Tell Lou to arrange my flight out today," he told her, then, without giving me another glance, he strode toward his office.

With the decision made and announced, I felt the sharp sense of loss. What if he never came back? What if we never got past this? What if he never tried to have me again?

I tripped after him. "This wasn't a session. You said so yourself. You can't hold this against me."

"Can't I?" He didn't turn around.

"No. You put out the rules, and I followed them. It's not fair for you to change them on me just because you don't like something you found out. You have to still play." *Please, please still play. Please come back for me.*

He spun around then, so quickly, I nearly collided with him. "There is no fairness here, Celia. You still think this is a game? That one of us is going to lose and one of us is going to win? That's not how this will go. I will win. I will win, no matter what you do or say or don't say. The only thing yet to be determined is how badly you lose."

A chill ran down my spine, and this time when he stalked away, I didn't follow.

EIGHTEEN

"WHAT'S ALL THE ACTIVITY ABOUT?" I asked Tom as I came back from my weekly massage in the pool house. Usually it was just her and Joette in the main house on a Thursday, unless Eliana was over to play chess or Lou was there to do some repairs.

Peter and Sanyjah usually only cleaned on Monday, Wednesday, and Friday, but here they were, bustling around with the vacuum and duster, and Erris and Marge were trimming the bushes in the back, something they typically only did in the mornings when it was cooler.

Joette stepped out of the kitchen at the sound of my voice, and Tom turned her eyes toward her, questioning.

All the walking on eggshells made the answer clear before Joette said anything. "Edward arrives today. I wanted to tell you, but..."

She trailed off, so I finished for her. "But you aren't supposed to give me a heads-up on these things, are you?"

Her smile was apologetic. "His plane is landing shortly. Mateo just left to pick him up at the airstrip."

That was more warning than I'd gotten any other time, and for that, I tried to be grateful. It wasn't Joette's fault I was married to an asshole. No, that blame lay solely on me.

"Thank you for telling me." I forced the words out, hoping that she'd try to share more in the future if I were appreciative. Then I took off for my bedroom to change into something less grungy.

After tearing off my shorts and tank, I hesitated at my closet door, deciding I needed a quick shower since I was covered in massage oil and sweat from my earlier workout. Once that was taken care of, I put on a simple sundress, threw my hair in a bun, and applied a swift coat of lipgloss.

"He doesn't deserve this," I told my reflection. Because he didn't. After the way he'd left last time, he didn't deserve my dressing up for him at all. Especially when he'd stayed gone for three months. Three goddamn months. He'd sent gifts as he had before, nothing personalized, things that helped keep my mind occupied, the biggest being permission to redecorate the upstairs rooms and remodel the pool house, a task I'd undertaken with gusto. I loved the work. It was invigorating to have something to do, something I was passionate about.

But no matter how much I enjoyed it or how much mental energy it required, it hadn't taken my thoughts off Edward entirely. He'd left, and I was pissed. He'd told me I couldn't walk away, and then he had. He'd told me if I opened up to him he'd come back sooner, and then he stayed away three fucking months.

I'd been so angered by his absence, I'd mentally given him ninety days. If he wasn't back by August fourteenth, I'd told myself, I was done. I was going to get myself off the island, whatever it took, even if it meant taking a rowboat out on the ocean alone.

But here he was on August thirteenth, as though he could read into my mind, and I was both relieved and devastated.

More relieved than devastated, if I were being honest.

And because he'd shown up within the time frame, I planned to be exactly that—honest. With myself, and also with him. I'd had plenty of time to think about what I wanted to say to him, what our next session would entail, and by God, he was going to hear it, whether he wanted to or not.

Now *that*, he deserved.

I made it to the front of the house where Joette and Tom had gathered to greet Edward just as Mateo pulled the jeep into the driveway.

My pulse picked up, and I suddenly wished I'd had more time to do makeup, that I'd picked something less plain to wear. Despite his unworthiness, I had a sick desire to please my husband.

Even more base than that, I wanted him to notice me, which felt ridiculous under the circumstances.

Still, standing with the two other women who'd become my family over the better part of a year, I suddenly felt like I was the stranger. It wasn't an unreasonable feeling considering his close relationship with Joette's family, but it was hard to grapple with all the same.

Mateo had parked with the passenger side toward us, so it was Edward's long, lean body and devilishly handsome face that I saw first. My breath caught—every time, he stole it from me. It was impossible to get used to how attractive he was, even dressed down in a polo shirt and white jeans. His hair was longer than when I'd last seen him, and a bit unruly from traveling. He still wore the facial hair I'd suggested he grow, and my fingers itched to touch it. His blue eyes were hidden behind his sunglasses, but I could feel them sharp and focused as he scanned his welcome committee. As they landed on me.

Just as quickly, they were gone, and he was opening the door behind his, reaching in. From around the back of the vehicle, a figure appeared. A brunette woman also in sunglasses wearing linen pants, a large brim hat, and a long-sleeved sweater over her camisole.

My body felt immensely heavy, like it was being pulled into the earth, and my ribs felt tight like they were being crushed.

He'd brought a woman. A gorgeous, sophisticated woman to the island where he kept his captive wife.

If I weren't so heartbroken, I'd be seeing red.

But then Edward pulled something out of the back seat—some*one* —and I realized I hadn't looked closely enough at the woman. It was his sister, Camilla, and the small boy he'd lifted into his arms was his nephew.

Damn, he looked good holding a child.

I'd seen him before with the kids on the island, seen him tease them and sneak them cookies behind Joette's back, but this was different. He'd pushed up his aviators, and I could see the pure devotion in his expression as he looked at Freddie. It was knee-weakening. Panty-melting. Ovary-exploding. Men didn't look at kids like that, not generally, and seeing it from Edward was especially astonishing. And poignant. And overwhelming.

It didn't help that the little boy resembled his uncle so entirely with the dark hair and deep-set blue eyes. I could imagine it then, what he must have been like as a father when his children were young. What he'd be like with a baby. What it would be like to have a baby with him. The power of those images was so startling and compelling, I almost forgot I hated him because of how badly I wanted to love him.

They started toward us, Camilla smiling at Joette and Tom, which threw me momentarily. They were *my* people, not *hers*, but of course she'd known them first. The master upstairs was clearly the one she stayed in when she visited, a crib and play area set up in the adjoining suite. I'd just never thought about her actually being in the space that I'd come to think of as mine.

I slunk back in the shadows as she removed her sunglasses and greeted the women, watching as they embraced and gave cheek kisses before they moved past her to help Mateo with their bags.

Which was when she finally laid eyes on me.

Her brows rose, clearly startled by my presence, and for half a beat I wondered if she hadn't known I was there. What on earth had Edward told his sister about me? Surely not the truth.

She turned to face her brother as he strode up next to her. "She's staying in the *main* house? Are you kidding me?"

Somehow I'd forgotten she disliked me.

"Where else would I stay? I'm his wife." She'd had plenty of time to get used to the idea. I had zero patience for her ire.

"You're a *Werner*," she said with such disgust I could feel how sour the name felt in her mouth. "Anything else you are bears no meaning next to that."

So maybe disliked hadn't been a harsh enough word. She detested me. Because of the rivalry my father had with her brother? It was beyond ridiculous.

I shot a look at my husband who hadn't spared me more than the first initial sweep of a glance. He didn't return my look now either, remaining focused on his sister. "She'll stay out of the way," he promised, as though he had any power over that.

My lips flattened into a thin line, my hands curling at fists at my side. Every rage he'd inspired in me over the last year was newly ignited. He'd put me on this goddamn island. It was mine now. He'd forced it on me. Like hell was I changing my routines for his sister who had the freedom to come and go as she pleased. Like hell was I going to be swept under the rug.

But I wasn't going to throw a fit in front of a two-year-old. Three-year-old now, likely, though I hadn't been aware of his birthdate.

Keeping my teeth gritted, I stalked several feet behind them. I continued to hang back as more greetings were exchanged. The staff was just as warm and casual with Camilla as they had always been with Edward, sharing private jokes and knowing what to inquire about back home. Apparently the "August holiday" was an annual event, which meant everyone had known their arrival was on the schedule for some time. Everyone but me, that was.

I shoved every pang of irritation and jealousy into the pocket of anger I intended for Edward. Not that I needed any more fuel than I already had.

Eventually, Freddie became restless and Camilla announced that she was taking him upstairs so they could both have a "bit of a nap." With her disappearance, the staff scattered, and Edward headed, as typical, to the library.

I was right on his heels.

"When I said you'd stay out of the way," he said callously, "I had meant you'd stay out of my way as well."

They were the first words he'd said to me, the first real acknowledgment he'd given to my presence, and I was fuming. So much so that I was momentarily speechless.

"Go on then. What is it you need? Don't be all day about it." He leaned against his desk and gave me a bored stare.

I took a beat to steady myself before responding. "I was going to ask you why your sister hated me so much, but now I think the better question is why do you?"

"I am not in the mood for one of your tantrums, Celia."

"Well, that's too bad, because I'm throwing a big one. Unless you want to be a decent person and sit down and have a civilized conversation, in which case I am perfectly willing to calm down and do so."

"Please. As if a civilized conversation would get us anywhere. We both know that nothing that comes out of your mouth is to be trusted."

There it was. The reason he'd been so angry with me before. I'd wondered many times over the summer what exactly had infuriated him so much about the games I'd played in the past. They hadn't affected him, and he certainly hadn't shown himself to be some moral pillar that couldn't stand unscrupulous behavior, but now, with these words, I understood. Part of it, anyway. All the time he'd spent "breaking me down" had also been about earning his trust, and when he'd realized how easily I lied, he'd doubted his tactics.

Another me, a before-Edward me, would have considered that the very definition of victory.

But I wasn't that me anymore. Whenever it had changed, I wasn't sure. Incrementally, most likely, bit by bit as I'd lived on Amelie and formed real relationships. Most of it, though, because Edward had forced me to knock down walls, not only did he see what was behind them, but so had I, and what I'd found had altered me so much that I couldn't be who I'd been before. I honestly believed that.

Now, the only victory I could imagine would be one where Edward believed that about me too.

There was only one way to fix it. "You know what? You're stuck on what I didn't give you last time so let's just get past that." I stomped over to his wet bar and poured cognac into a tumbler then brought it back, shoving it into his hand before sitting in the chair facing him.

"What are you doing?" His tone was more annoyed than curious.

"We're having a session. I meant for this to all be said later, but if this is the only way you'll hear me, then this is where it will have to be said, so sit your ass down and listen."

"Sessions aren't on the agenda for this visit. Go and—"

I popped to my feet with fury, cutting him off before he told me what I could "go and" do. "No, no. You don't get to say that. You do not get to cut me off from this arrangement." My anger crescendoed, and I pointed an accusing finger at him. "You said that if I played well you'd come back sooner. I played well, and you stayed away. You say you want honesty? Then be honest with your negotiations. Sit down and give me what I deserve, Edward."

His expression guarded, he straightened. His eyes were on me, and behind them I could see him considering. Deciding. After several heavy seconds, he crossed around his desk and took the seat I'd demanded he take.

I managed to sit back down too, though I felt a bit like I was floating.

He swirled his drink and threw back a swallow. Then clapped the glass down on the desk. "Whenever you're ready." He was taking charge.

Or he wanted me to believe he was in charge. But now I knew one of his secrets—that my confessions made him vulnerable too, and that gave me power. A lot of power.

It wasn't power I intended to wield lightly.

"I played games," I began, prepared for this. "I've played them for almost fourteen years. I began playing them when I was in a dark place, right after my miscarriage—you know who I was then. I needed an outlet. I needed something else to occupy my mind, something that wasn't centered on my pain, and someone I knew stepped up and gave me a tool."

I paused only long enough to be sure I had his attention. The slight tensing of his jaw said I did.

"They were never just games, but I told myself they were. It was easier to justify the entertainment value, I think, when I called them that. And they were games, in a way. They required strategy and fore-sight. I don't need to tell you what kinds of situations we set up—you read the journals. You know they involved manipulating other people's emotions. That they were centered around guessing how people would behave when they were forced into crisis situations. We got good at predicting. I got very good, and when the other guy decided to abandon the games, I kept at it. Because it was the only thing I had, okay? There wasn't anything else in my life but this."

I closed my eyes, forcing myself back from the path of justification. That wasn't what I wanted this to be. I was not the victim here, and I wanted to own that. For myself, as much as for Edward.

I really should have poured a drink for myself as well.

Or maybe it was appropriate to face this completely sober.

Taking a deep breath, I opened my eyes. "The things we did were terrible, I admit that. I've never not known they were cruel and devastating. That was the appeal. In no way is this an attempt to validate, but I want you to know my reasons, which, to be honest, I'm still trying to figure out myself. I was so consumed with not feeling all the things that I was feeling—I didn't want to feel anything at all—and I realized that other people's pain was quite distracting from that.

"Having learned that, what I should have done, was volunteer for a homeless shelter or a soup kitchen or a crises center, but I don't know." This was the newest discovery I'd made, the part I was still sorting through. "I was immature, maybe. Self-centered, definitely. My family has always been involved with charity organizations, but the motivation was always about status, not actual giving, and the idea of helping other people was not one that came naturally, and also, I didn't want to think for myself. I couldn't, at the time. I needed someone to hold out a hand and invite me in, and the only hand I saw to grab pulled me in this direction, and *it worked*. Little by little, I stopped feeling. I went numb, and the only emotions that existed were outside of me, in these people's lives I destroyed. It was quite habit-forming—watching the world blow up outside of me instead of inside. Maybe that's why so many angry people are drawn to destruction, because the ruin of others minimizes the ruin going on in your body. It's a distraction.

"Perhaps that's why people bully too." I gave him a hard stare, in case that resonated. "You want to destroy me. That's what you've said, not in those words, but similar, and I can't begin to know your motives since you've never shared them with me. All I can do is compare it to what I know from my own life, and I can't help but wonder if your reasons aren't the same as mine."

He started to open his mouth, but I put my hand up to stop him. "I don't want to talk about that right now. This is about me. This is about my truth, not yours. You were a game too. You know that you were, and yes, you were at the end of a long list, and maybe that offends you to not be a singular incident, but if you were hoping to be unique, then you got your wish, because you are the only person who has ever given me a reason not to play anymore. The only person who has made me feel my own feelings without wanting to demolish everything and everyone around me.

"You want to know why I didn't want to tell you about the games? Because I actually care what you think of me, for some insane reason. I care that you know that I've done terrible things and that I'm a shitstain on the foot of human existence, because you are the first person who has truly looked at me in a lifetime and made me feel like I wasn't those awful things, and I knew that telling you about this would take all that away. You want vulnerability? You want honesty? This is me being honest. This is me being completely exposed.

"And here's where this is also about you." I sat forward, needing him to listen particularly close to what I said next. "This is about you because you made this happen. You reached out your hand and said 'break down for me,' and I grabbed it, because maybe I need someone to lead me more than I like to admit, or maybe just because I was so fucking tired of being alone. Or maybe because you didn't leave me a choice, but here's the thing. I *do* have a choice. I could lie to you and feed you whatever bullshit you wanted to hear, or I could clam up and say nothing no matter what you did to me, but *I'm here for this.* I am all in. I committed to your fucked-up offer, and I know I have no rights as far as you're concerned and that there is no such thing as fairness, but if you don't show up and commit to this as well, then you might as well just kill me like you planned in the first place. You say I'm going to lose, then let me lose. Give me that chance to lose everything. You might even realize I already have. Because I have nothing except what you give me. If you're going to give me nothing more, then I might as well already be dead."

He was silent, his gaze unwavering, his face hard. He'd never let me say so much without interrupting with questions, possibly because he wasn't actually giving what I said a chance, but he'd heard it. I knew he'd heard it. He'd sat and listened and now the next move was on him.

I'd learned a thing or two from him about processing time, though, and I didn't want his response to be rash. I stood. "I'm asking Tom to help me move my things to the cabana for the week. I'll take all my meals there. I will stay out of your way. I am not moving out for your sister, though you're welcome to tell her that's the reason. God knows you'll tell her what you want to anyway. But between you and me, let's just be clear that the reason I'm moving out is one hundred percent because of you.

"When you're ready—if you're ever ready—you know exactly where you can find me, Edward." I turned and walked away then, without looking back, with all my cards laid out on the table. I should have felt powerless, but for the first time since I'd met him, I believed I held the upper hand.

NINETEEN

EDWARD

SHE WASN'T SUPPOSED *to be like this.*

The thought repeated in my head over and over as my eyes followed the line of the beach, wishing I could see past the outcrop that met the rock wall above and hid the cove where the cabana was neatly tucked away.

As my wife had promised, after sufficiently chiding me, she'd stayed out of the way. Thirteen days had passed, and I'd only caught glimpses of her from a distance. When she emerged to attend yoga or walk around the island, she'd avoided the main house. Tom and Peter brought her all her meals, remaining with her in the evenings when everyone else gathered for dinner. She was being looked after, even without my directive. Which was as it should be.

And I missed her.

How the fuck was it possible to miss her? To have gotten close enough to her to regret her absence? It hardly seemed feasible.

The plan had been simple enough. I had never expected it to be easy to execute, but it had been straightforward. There was a clear path to those shares, and while that route required hideous action, I knew I was a man worthy of the task. I'd proven it before, hadn't I?

That plan had assumed Celia was either a shallow rich girl princess or a knock-off of her malevolent father. Both versions of character had their challenges. I'd mapped out all the possibilities, drew up contingencies. I'd been prepared to handle whichever woman it was that I met the day I'd asked for the meeting. Initially, she'd seemed like a mash-up of both.

She had been neither of those things in the end.

Yes, she was calculating and manipulative, more so than I'd even guessed until reading those journals, and she was very spoiled about getting her way, but that was all surface. She was an onion. There were layers and layers underneath, parts of her that she held away. Parts she showed no one. For whatever reason, I'd caught sight of what she kept hidden, whether she'd meant for that to happen or not, I couldn't be sure. Regardless, I was captivated. There was so much to see there, so much to take down. So much of her to know and own and destroy and redesign, and like an old habit, I couldn't break away.

She was an addiction, and I wanted to feed on it. She wasn't supposed to be like that.

She wasn't supposed to want to bend to my whims. She wasn't supposed to open up and give what I asked for. She wasn't supposed to be so eager to take what I gave her. She certainly wasn't supposed to see past my own curtain, wasn't supposed to ask to see more.

I'm here for this, she'd said.

And for thirteen days, all I could think about was how much I wanted to be *here for this* too.

So why was she still there, and I, standing here, hoping for impossible glimpses of her in the distance?

"I have to admit, I like this. Love it, actually." Camilla's voice behind me pulled my focus from the woman hidden in the horizon to closer surroundings. "This was all *her*?"

My sister was referring to the newly remodeled deck on top of the pool house. It had been nonexistent on my previous trip to Amelie. Now it was the highlight of the building. Celia had kept the design minimal with only a four-piece furniture set and a granite fire table, but the stone tile flooring and the ability to see so far along the coast made it a spectacular addition. It was a compliment I knew I should deliver myself.

I also knew I wouldn't.

"It was," I confirmed, wondering if my tone sounded with the pride I unexpectedly felt.

"Hm." The reverberation came out tight behind pursed lips. She wrapped her arms around herself, despite the unusual heat. The long-sleeved shirt had to be a burden on days such as this, but Camilla was more tied to her secrets than to comfort.

I loathed what she hid underneath. I despised how her secrets had come about. I wanted to protect and avenge her more than I wanted to exist.

Or I *had* wanted that. I'd wanted it for so long, I didn't know what it felt like to want something different. And I still *did* want it.

Only, I wasn't sure it was all I wanted anymore.

I turned so my entire body was facing her, annoyance at my inability to stay the course bleeding into my words. "If you love it so much, why have that tone?"

"Because you let her do it in the first place. And I can't begin to understand why." She was frustrated and it showed in both her posture and her expression.

She had a right to be frustrated. She couldn't understand because I hadn't told her much about my plot with Celia at all. It wasn't the first time I'd kept her in the dark. I was almost more father figure to her than brother, and I took that responsibility gravely. I tried to shield her as much as possible, never bothering her with the darker details. She'd had enough darkness to last several lifetimes. She didn't need more.

But now she was asking for more, and I rarely denied her when she asked.

When I didn't say anything, Camilla prodded me. "Are you going to let it sit like that or are you even going to try to explain?"

I couldn't. That was the problem. I couldn't even explain to myself why I'd deviated from my plans, why I'd kept Celia on this island, why I'd taken to giving her gifts and wheedling out her demons and caring.

I had nothing for my sister. I turned my gaze back to the ocean.

Camilla sat down on the wicker love seat, the furniture scratching as it adjusted to her weight, informing me of the action. "What I've been wondering most is what does she get out of this? You married her to get access to her father's company. I didn't approve, but I can understand that. I see the logic, though how *her* shares give you access, I can't quite fathom. I'm not the business-minded of the two of us. But why did she agree to marry you? And why is she living out here? Why is she redecorating and remodeling and making herself comfortable on your island? I can only think that...that..."

"Think what?" I swiveled my head toward her, pressing when she didn't continue.

"Either you've trapped her into this arrangement by some dubious means or you've fallen in love with her."

Camilla was more perceptive than I'd given her credit for.

"Which would be worse, in your opinion?"

"If you didn't already know, you wouldn't have asked."

And that was why I was still standing on this rooftop after thirteen days of wanting to be elsewhere. Because I *did* already know which Camilla felt was the worse of the two options.

I almost believed she'd feel the same if she knew the original plans for my wife had included murder.

"Have you even made any move yet to infiltrate Werner Media?"

She knew the answer. What she wanted to know was why I hadn't.

"It's not the right time," I said with finality.

"Bullshit."

She was right, but I started to defend the decision anyway, only to be cut off. "I've never needed this like you have, Eddie. What's been done has been done, and I don't believe seeking retribution will change any of the ways I've been damaged, but you have. It's been the only thing in your sightline since you took me in. And now? What's going on with you?"

I felt the scowl pulling my lips downward despite intending to remain emotionless. "Nothing's going on with me. My goals haven't changed."

"Then why take this detour?" She sat forward, her hazel eyes pinning me in place the way our mother's used to. "Look, I'm not going to hold anything against you if you abandon your plan. If you were doing any of it for me, it's not necessary. I don't need that. That said, I'm not able to sit back and watch you get in bed with the enemy. Either she's part of your plot or you have nothing to do with her."

"Is that some sort of ultimatum?" I could feel the thrum of my pulse in my veins.

"I suffered, Eddie. I wear the scars like tattoos. Scars in the shape of cigarette butts and hot pokers."

"She's not the one who put them there."

"I wouldn't have been put in that situation if it weren't for—"

"Weren't for *him*," I finished for her, in case she was going anywhere other than the truth with the statement. "Not *her*. She's not who we want to ruin." The words surprised myself because the plan all along had been to ruin *him* by ruining *her*.

Had that changed?

Camilla stood up and crossed the short distance between us. "I can't separate them like that," she said, her shoulder practically touching mine as her gaze drifted over the ocean. "I'm astonished that you can. 'We inherit what's been done to those before us.' Those are your words. If that's true then it stands to reason that we inherit the sins of our ancestors as well."

Did we really, though? Weren't we flawed enough carrying our own sins, and we had to answer for others as well?

"I'm not sure I want to believe that." But I'd been carrying the weight of my father's wrongs for more years than I hadn't.

"You might not *want* to believe it, but you do," she said, echoing my thoughts.

A squeal of laughter drew my eyes over the roof wall to the patio where Freddie played with Joette. She dragged him around, pretending to not be able to find him, with him clutching onto the back of her leg. She'd filled the role of grandmother, a role he'd desperately needed. I smiled despite myself, glad he was here. It was good for him to be here.

"Divorce her," Camilla said, a thick cloud covering a lone ray of sun. "Walk away. From all of it, even your revenge scheme. We win if we're still standing, and we are right now. I'm not sure you will be if you pursue this further."

I couldn't tell her that it was too late, that I'd already said and done too much to be able to divorce my wife without repercussions. Celia would never let me walk away now.

I definitely couldn't tell her that I wasn't sure I wanted to, even if I could.

IT WAS LESS than twenty-four hours later that I made my way down to the cabana. The flight crew had already arrived, and the plane was being prepped for take-off. This couldn't be delayed any longer, whatever this was. I'd spent half the night tossing and turning, trying to figure it out.

I felt caught.

Caught between Celia's lies and her brutal truths. Caught between my sister and my wife. Caught between a past that deserved retribution and a woman who could be...

Could be...*what*? A future?

It wasn't as laughable as I would have once thought.

But there was too much to be sorted in the present to think about anything beyond, and the only way to sort through the present was to speak to Celia.

I hesitated at the door, wondering if I should knock. Then, reminding myself that it was *my* property and that I was the one in charge, I walked in.

She was stretched out on the sofa, her hair up in a ratty ponytail, wearing only a thin camisole that highlighted the beads of her nipples and shorts that made her legs go on for miles. Even lounging around, she was the most beautiful thing I'd ever seen.

Someone had given in and brought her one of the kids' portable DVD players, or she'd stolen it on her own. I'd left specific instructions that her entertainment be restricted to not include screens, and my orders were generally followed, but even Joette had made her disapproval of my treatment of Celia known over the last two weeks, so anything was possible.

The small player sat balanced on her stomach, and I watched silently over her shoulder as Moana sang about how far she'd go, the movie only recognizable because of the countless times Camilla had played it for Freddie. Celia gave no indication of having heard me come in, until, without turning her head, she said, "If you came to tell me you're leaving, that was unnecessary. Tom already told me you'd be gone today."

"That isn't what I came to say." Though it had been the excuse I'd planned to tell her for coming over in the first place.

She paused the show, and spun her head toward me. "You're not leaving?"

The note in her voice was so purely recognizable as hope, I hardly dared to answer.

"I am," I said, after a beat, and before I could say more, she turned her focus back to the movie, hitting a button to resume play.

"What I meant..." I trailed away when it was obvious she wasn't going to pause the show again.

Stalking behind the couch, I pulled the plug from the wall, praying the machine didn't have batteries. Instantly, the picture disappeared from the screen, and she glared in my direction.

At least I had her attention.

"What I meant is that's not all I came to say."

She pulled her knees up and crossed her arms over herself. "Go on then. What is it you need? Don't be all day about it."

They were the same prickish words I'd said to her two weeks ago, said in what she must have thought was a British dialect.

I had to fight a grin at her paltry attempt.

And then I remembered that I hadn't yet worked out what I meant to tell her, and the urge to grin disappeared entirely. "I came to tell you that I heard you," I said, managing to sound sure of myself through the earnestness of the words.

Her arms relaxed and her expression softened, urging me on. "I heard what you said, and I want you to know that I'm willing as well. I commit to this. I'm determined to give you..." *Everything*. I bit back the word, surprised it had even entered my head. "More," I said instead.

Fuck, even that...what was I intending with her?

Celia's eyes glossed over, but she quickly blinked the hint of emotion away. "But you're not staying."

"No, little bird. But I'll be back."

She shook her head dismissively and put the DVD player down on the couch before standing up and spinning to face me. "Your words have zero bearing without something to back it up, Edward. I put myself out there. I waited for you for three months. Add two more weeks on top of that, two weeks where you were five minutes away, and you couldn't bother to stop by, not once."

Her hurt was evident, and I was torn between shame for inflicting it and awe at her willingness to let me see it. I also wanted to touch her, more than I'd ever wanted to touch anyone in my entire life.

"I don't have energy to give you another three months on top of that," she went on. "I deserve more for what I've put into this."

"You do," I agreed, wishing that there wasn't a couch between us or a sister waiting at the house or a business to be run across the ocean. "I'll make up for it. I promise. But I can't right now. This visit has been what it's been, and it's done now. I can't change that, and I have to be on that plane in thirty minutes. All I can do is promise that next time will be different."

Her thigh bounced as she considered, her brows knit tightly together. "Thirty days," she said finally.

"Excuse me?"

"You have thirty days to come back."

I nearly laughed. "Thirty days isn't possible."

"I have nothing left to say to you then." She picked up the player, pulling the cord with it and turned as if to find another outlet to plug it in.

"Two months," I said, refusing to let her shut me out. I'd booked my calendar months ago with quarterly visits worked in. Two months would be difficult, but I'd make a weekend happen.

"Thirty days."

"Six weeks."

"Thirty days."

"Two months, and I'll give you an entire week." I could see my schedule in my head, see how impossible it would be, even as I offered it.

She wasn't budging. "Thirty days."

"I'll give you two weeks." And I smiled, because in all our previous negotiations, she'd been easy to bulldoze. She'd stood up for herself, certainly, but always stepped away when I pushed.

She *had* changed. And it was a good part because of me.

"Thirty days," she repeated. "One day longer, and this whole deal is off."

There were too many important meetings on the books. A gala and a wedding and a critical trip planned to Turkey. "I'll see what I can do," I said, knowing that I'd just agreed.

Knowing it too, she beamed.

There was a field of energy between us, a magnetic pull that wanted me to go to her and draw her into my arms and scandalize her lips.

But there was another force, equally strong, holding me back. A force comprised of promises and blood loyalties and stubbornness and habit and the matter of the sofa between her body and mine. And I was still who I was, and she was still who she was, and the only thing that had been sorted was that there would be more between us, and that was enough to send a flood of relief coursing through my veins.

It was with a lighter step that I started toward the door. "But when I return, you participate," I said, turning back. Needing to have another word. The last word. "No passive-aggressive punishment for wrongs you think I've committed against you. No hiding. No petty stories. No games."

Her body had rotated as I had, and while she still stayed standing in the same spot, she also still faced me entirely. "We aren't a game," she said fervently.

In three strides, I was in front of her. I grazed my knuckles against the side of her cheek and pulled her in with my other arm. My lips hovered above hers. "No, we aren't," I agreed.

Then I kissed her, and while the kiss on our wedding day had been sincere, this one sealed us in a way that one hadn't, and for the first time since we'd married, when the plane took off over the island, I ached. No matter what my sister understood, I wasn't leaving behind Celia Werner.

I was leaving behind my wife.

TWENTY

CELIA

HIS SHADOW HIT ME FIRST, the shade stretching over the catalog full of baby decor that I'd been perusing. Marge's baby Liam was only just over one, and she was already four months along with another one. She'd returned from the doctor in Nassau only the week before with the news that it was a girl this time.

Of course I'd offered to design the nursery. Though I'd never designed anything for children of any kind, it would be something new and the challenge was welcome.

Right now, however, with the fall of his shadow, my interest in the task was eclipsed. My heart all of a sudden felt like it was in my throat, beating a thousand times per minute, and I couldn't look up at him for fear of what my expression would show.

I threw the catalog on the table in front of me and glanced, instead, at the sky. The sun wasn't even directly overhead yet. My guess was closer to eleven a.m.

"You must have left at the crack of dawn," I said, still not able to look directly at him.

"I would have left last night at the end of the business day, but I wanted to cut it close."

And close it was. In two hours it would be thirty days exactly since I'd last seen him.

My gaze shot to his, and I caught the gleam in his eyes. He was teasing, but not really. He wanted me to know his position in this relationship still stood, that even though I'd been granted a moment of strength with his adherence to my demands, he still held the power.

As if I could forget.

As if I wanted it any other way.

"You're a dick," I said, fighting the smile that wanted to burst out on my lips.

"But I'm here."

He was here and I felt all sorts of things about that. I'd believed he'd come back in the time frame I'd given him. Our last encounter had felt too real for him to not. Then, as the days had passed and got closer to the thirty-day mark, I began to doubt. I'd expected him to reach out with some confirmation that he was returning, not that he'd ever shared his plans before. Just, he'd said he committed, and that was new, and because it was new I'd thought everything would be different.

And then everything was exactly the same, and I wasn't so sure about what had occurred between us anymore. It was possible he'd been fucking with my head. It was *likely*, even. Wasn't that the best way to destroy me? Let me believe what was going on between us was genuine, and then pull the rug out from under me. Wasn't that how I would have chosen to do it?

It would have been a fitting sort of karma.

So even as I believed he'd come back by today, I'd held space inside for the possibility that he wouldn't.

Now, with him here in front of me and two hours to spare before the deadline, I could let that space go and all the emotions I'd crammed into a dark corner now had room to stretch and show themselves and there were so many. Apprehensiveness and happiness and desire and disbelief and gratitude and humility and a little bit of suspicion and panic.

Mostly, though, what I felt was relief.

He pulled out a chair next to me and sat, and I hurried to gather up the notepads and catalogs that had been strewn over the table, both an anxious gesture and a show that I was ready to give all my attention to him.

The movement, though, caught his interest. "What are you working on?" he asked, his eyes already scanning the catalogs and notepads.

"Nothing important."

"I say what's important. If I ask, I want to know."

Another display of his dominance, and my skin vibrated in tune with the show. His authoritarian arrogance was annoying on many levels, but there was something soothing about it too. And arousing.

Still, I always had to take a beat and decide if I wanted to fight him or submit.

I decided to lean in. "Marge asked me to design a nursery for her," I said, bending the truth a bit. I assumed he knew about her pregnancy, since he knew everything. He didn't communicate with me during his absences, but he sure communicated with someone, telling staff what gifts and allowances to bring me and how to orchestrate my days.

"She asked or you offered?"

He nodded and reached for my sketch pad, and I forced myself not to make excuses about the rush the drawings had been made in or the quality of the ideas. As if I weren't already nervous.

After he flipped through all I'd drawn so far, he made a low rumble of appreciation in his throat that echoed between my legs, then put the pad carefully back where he'd taken it from. "I'm glad you're doing this. I like to see you using your talents."

I was simultaneously giddy over his approval and indignant that he didn't deliver more effusive praise. Brusqueness won out, as I recalled the negotiations we'd had over our marriage. "Oh, yes, hobbies are fine as long as it isn't a career. I remember now."

"Did I say that?"

"You did."

"And you agreed to it." His smirk was so charming, he was nearly forgivable.

"I wasn't planning to be married to you for long."

"Neither was I." The smirk disappeared with the gravity of his admission.

It hit me in the gut, the severity of who he was and what he'd planned. My little game seemed petty in contrast, and a wave of bitterness swept through me, threatening to sour all the pleasant feelings his arrival had unleashed.

"Wow." I put a hand on my chest, as though to keep my heart from pounding out of my ribcage. "This is a lot of honesty right off the bat."

"It's what we agreed to, wasn't it? Are you still here for it?" He looked down at my other hand, resting on the table. Then he placed his palm on the surface and swept it toward me until the tip of his pinkie finger was nudging mine.

That simple touch was enough to ignite a nuclear explosion inside me.

"Yes," I said, breathless from the effort. Definitely yes. I twisted my hand and pushed it closer so that our little fingers rested against each other entirely.

I studied them together, the way his dwarfed mine, the variances in our skin tone, the heat that emitted from his. I'd never studied his physical characteristics with such depth, and suddenly there wasn't anything I wanted to do but examine all of him, from head to toe, leaving none of his body unexplored.

"How long do I have you this time?" However long it was, it wouldn't be enough.

He paused, and the pause was enough to draw my eyes back to his. "Let's not ruin the beginning by worrying about the end."

"That long, huh?" I was sure he could hear the ache in my voice.

I swallowed it away. "I suppose we shouldn't waste a single minute then." There were things I had to say, things I'd held in too long. In the month he'd been away, I'd come to terms with the fact that, if I really wanted to be in this with him—whatever this was—there were things he had to know.

Things that could end whatever this was.

Things that could get me killed.

"We should go inside," he said, seeming to understand.

"Can we only do this in the cabana?"

"Sessions? No. We can have one anytime, anywhere, but a session wasn't what I've been thinking about nonstop since I left, and I'm not about to let our staff witness the things I want to do to you."

A shiver of want ran through me, and I blushed. "I haven't earned anything yet. How are you so sure I'll deliver?"

"I'm sure." He beckoned me with a jerk of his head. "Come here."

God, I wanted to. I wanted to crawl over the table and straddle his lap and let him carry me inside to show me all the things he'd thought about doing to me. Without even knowing what they all were, I was sure I wanted them twice.

But that secret that pressed heavy on my back had to be set down first.

"I can't, Edward."

His brow raised at what he could only assume was a challenge. "You seem to have forgotten who's in charge here, little bird."

"I haven't at all. You've demanded honesty, though, and I don't think you'll be happy with me if I let anything else go on between us without giving you some truth."

"That sounds ominous."

"I was going for transparent."

"I approve of transparent." But his hand had moved away from mine, and his guard was up, and I couldn't blame him because what I had to say to him was going to be the worst. Not the worst thing for me —those things would come out too, eventually—but the worst thing for him.

He leaned back and crossed his ankle on the opposite knee, pushing his chair back a bit as he did. It could have been accidental, but I was certain it was purposeful, an attempt to mimic the parameters that typically accompanied our sessions. The distance between us. The space to lay out my confessions and for him to process what I said.

I took the cue and withdrew as well, dropping my hands in my lap where I could wring them out of sight under the table. "I know you've done your research, and some of this might be old news to you, but since I don't know what you know and what you don't, I'm going to say it all."

I'd had a script planned, and already I wanted to jump from it. So I did. "First, though, I need you to know—I could have told you this earlier. Maybe I *should* have, but..." I shook my head. "Well, you'll understand when I'm done. I just need you to know what it means that I'm telling you now."

I wanted him to realize how defenseless this made me. I needed him to see that by telling him now, it proved how committed I really was to this. To being his.

"Go on," was all he said, refusing to give me the acknowledgment I wanted until he heard for himself what it was.

Leaving me even more vulnerable.

That seemed about right.

I took a breath and plunged in, beginning with a history lesson. "Werner Media was founded in nineteen thirty-five by my father's father—Jessop Werner. There were some friends involved in the actual work of it, but it really all belonged to Jessop because he had the start-up money. It was old money that had dwindled a lot when the stock market crashed. He seemed to realize what he had wasn't going to last without turning it into something big, so he went all in on the newspaper business, and obviously the gamble worked. The company grew and expanded to magazines. Then TV stations. Then TV programming. I'm sure you know all that better than I do.

"Anyway, when Jessop died, he gave fifty percent of the business to my father, who was the oldest of his two sons, and the one most interested in running things. The one most capable. He left my uncle Ron with thirty percent, which was overly generous considering that his only interest in the business was flaunting the wealth and power it gave him. The remaining twenty percent of the business was divided in two percent increments between Jessop's extended relatives."

"And then those extra shares got sold and bought a bunch of times and divided and diluted," Edward said, almost bored. "And Ron sold his thirty percent to Glam Play and your father sold ten percent to Pierce Industries so now Warren owns only forty percent, which he put in a trust for you to inherit at the date of your marriage. They've already been transferred to your name. I've checked."

"I'm sure you have." I wasn't so sure he meant the threat in the subtext, but it was there all the same. "Did you also know about the conditions Ron sold his shares? He wanted the money, but he also wanted stability, so in exchange for a secure top position in the company, my father required Ron to include certain terms in the sale to Glam Play."

"Ah." His eyes lit up, and finally I'd told him something new. "So that's why they're required to vote along with the majority. It kept your father in control of the company, even with less than fifty percent of the shares."

"Right."

"I'd wondered how that occurred. It's a good strategy."

"Until Glam Play gets sold. And then the terms are null and void." I carefully studied his reaction, trying to feel him out before getting to the blow.

But his response was dismissive. "They aren't selling."

"You've tried to buy them?" I almost chuckled, because of course he had. Of course marrying me wasn't his first scheme to get into Werner Media.

"Yes," he said, slowly, aware of what he'd given away. "I've tried to purchase from them numerous times."

"Because they've already been sold." There. It was said. Easy as that.

But the burden wasn't in the actual saying—it was in surviving whatever he said next.

I watched him as the words sank in, as he absorbed the meaning. If Glam Play wasn't required to vote with Werner Media, then forty percent of the shares wasn't enough to hold a true majority.

His body stiffened, his eyes grew cold. "You're lying."

"You know I'm not." He'd told me he knew the difference between when I was and when I wasn't, and maybe it was naive to actually believe that, but I did.

He didn't refute it, but he was still unsure. "How is there no record of a sale?"

"That was part of the terms of the new deal. The sale happened in complete darkness. No one knows it's been purchased, not even my father. The shareholder votes are to continue to align with the majority unless..." I trailed away. This part was hardest to tell, because the entire strategy had been executed because of me. Because Hudson had needed something to hold over me, and this was what he'd found.

"Unless what?" Edward prodded.

Unless I tried to interfere with Hudson's life again. If I did, he'd destroy Werner Media.

But that wasn't the most important part of this confession. "I guess unless the new owner decides otherwise."

Edward dropped his foot to the ground and pulled at his chin, thinking. Calculating. "That's only thirty percent. Pierce Industries always votes with your father. There's no reason to be concerned about losing Glam Play." The assurance was for himself, not for me.

"Except that Pierce Industries is who bought Glam Play. They also managed to buy out two percent from another shareholder along the way. Technically, Hudson Pierce owns forty-two percent of Werner Media."

I'd held the secret for so long now, carried the weight of it alone, and even though the reality of it was awful and hard to look at, I could breathe deeper than I had in years from the sharing.

But after that breath, I had to face the facts. My father had been usurped of his legacy, and it was my fault. He never had to know for me to feel the shame of that. It was overwhelming.

"How do you know all this?" Edward asked, still unaware of how humiliating this was for me.

He would though. Before this was all over, he'd know.

"Hudson told me," I answered softly.

"Why would he tell you this? Why does he want to own a controlling interest and yet do nothing with it?"

"He wanted power over me."

A beat passed, and his face hardened, and he knew. I could see that he knew.

"What did you do to him?" he asked, crudely.

The disgust in his voice made me shrink inside myself. The sun was beating down as it approached mid-sky, and I was so very cold.

"Does it matter?" I asked, blinking back tears.

"You played him." It wasn't a question. "His names weren't in the journals."

"I didn't record what I did to him."

"Why not?"

Because it hadn't been a game. It had been my reaction to what I had perceived as betrayal. It had been unhealthy and destructive and unplanned, and a million times I'd wished I could take it back. Wished that I had been someone different than I'd been.

Than I was.

Again I shook my head, searching for a simpler answer. "It was a confusing time for me. It was the first time I was playing on my own."

"What did you do to him?" he asked again.

This time I answered. "I tried to break up his relationship with his girlfriend. His wife, now. Obviously, I failed."

"You failed, and he wanted insurance that you wouldn't fuck with him again."

I nodded.

"You'd think you would have learned your lesson about playing powerful men." There was no hint of teasing in his statement.

"You'd think."

He held my stare for several heartbeats, hostility radiating off him as hot as if he were a furnace. It hurt to have him look at me this way, but I forced myself to bear it.

It was he who broke away first to stare vaguely into the distance. "You knew that this undermines my entire strategy of controlling Werner Media through your shares."

I did.

But I searched for optimism all the same. "It doesn't have to mean that. Glam Play could still continue to vote along with you. Unless you tried to do something that would destroy the company from within."

His eyes came back to mine, as though to stare down my naivete. What else had he been planning to do with my shares but destroy the company within? If I'd thought his motive was simply to move his own company into the U.S., I was wrong. He meant to bring my father down.

"Why do you hate him so much?" This was beyond business. This rivalry was personal.

He ignored the question. "You didn't tell me because you saw it as a worst-case scenario way to make sure I still got fucked over in the end, even if you weren't around to see it. You were hoping if I did anything detrimental with those share votes, Hudson Pierce would use his control against me."

After everything, the accusation still stung. "I couldn't possibly have been looking to protect my father," I threw back sarcastically. "You might hate him, but he's still my family."

"So it was still a game. All along."

I slammed my palm on the table so hard it stung. "No, goddammit. It wasn't a game, because that wasn't the reason I didn't tell you, you condescending asshole. I hadn't even thought of that, which is stupid, because I clearly *should* have thought of that. Maybe it was the threat of death that threw me off my game."

I cringed as soon as it was out of my mouth. Not the best choice of words in the moment. Not when Edward had already decided that was what this was all along.

"Look," I said sitting forward, taking a breath to make sure my next words came out clear. "I didn't tell you because it was obvious you were after controlling interest, and this information would let you know that this plot of yours was futile."

"That makes no sense. If you'd told me that your shares wouldn't get me control, what would be the point in killing you for them?"

I flinched at his openness.

"You'd already told me that was your plan," I said, avoiding words like *kill* and *murder*. "Like you were just going to let me go after that.

'Oh, I guess that's not going to work, you can go home now.' Yeah, right."

I gave him a second to face the validity of that before going on. "Letting you believe I still had something to give you was the only thing that kept me valuable."

His features softened momentarily, and I almost believed he was going to deny it, that he was going to say I had value beyond what I knew or who was my father.

But the moment passed, and he went back to glaring into the distance. "Warren doesn't know your family no longer holds control of the company," he said, as though he had to say it again to believe it.

"He doesn't." It would kill him if he found out. Edward could destroy my father with that information alone. Did he realize that?

Apparently not because his next words were, "This entire scheme was all for naught."

I nodded, too unsure of the menace in his tone to say anything else.

His serious expression vanished abruptly as he broke into laughter. Deep, bellowing laughter. It stunned me. He rarely laughed at all, and I'd never seen him laugh so heartily. It was almost frightening in its intensity. I wasn't sure if he'd truly found the humor in the situation or if he was going mad.

It *was* kind of funny, actually. How much work he had done for nothing. Maybe the only option was to laugh.

Then, just as suddenly, he was done.

He shot up from his chair and held his hand out in my direction, his face again solemn. "Come with me."

I hesitated. Despite the moment of humor, he was angry. That was apparent. And maybe a little crazy too. "Where are we going?" I asked, trying to decide if it was really a good idea to be with him right now.

The smirk was back. "Wherever I say. Do you not trust me?"

"Should I?"

"I'm not entirely sure."

It was the most honest he'd ever been with me. And for that reason, because in this moment he was *all in*, I reached out and put my hand in his.

TWENTY-ONE

A LITTLE OVER AN HOUR LATER, with a cooler filled with bottled water and a lunch packed from Joette, I found myself in the middle of the ocean on a boat manned only by my husband.

Sailboats made me nervous anyway. Alone with a man I didn't trust brought an entirely new level of unease. My hands ached from the constant wringing, and my sundress was wrinkled from the amount of times I'd balled it into my fists, only to smooth it out a moment later with my sweat-soaked palms.

It didn't help that the boat's name was *Vengeance*.

"When you said we were going somewhere, I thought you meant to the bedroom or the cabana. I would have changed my shoes if I'd known we were doing something sporty." Not that I was doing any of the work. Honestly, if he'd told me, I might have fought him on it, and fighting him was nearly always a losing battle.

This time I had a deep fear that not fighting him may have meant I'd lost the battle as well. Alone on the ocean...what did he have planned for me?

I shivered at the possibilities.

"What you're wearing is fine," he said without looking at me. "Slip them off if you'd prefer to go barefoot."

I kept them on, not wanting to get too comfortable.

"I thought all sailboats this size had motors," I said, subtly expressing more of my concern. "How do you even manage this thing out here without one?"

"Are you worried about it?" He turned his eyes from the sail to tack me with his gaze.

Yes. I was very worried about it. And for so many reasons, the most concerning being that my skipper had shared his nefarious plans for me on more than one occasion.

But I was trying to play it cool, so I pressed a smile to my lips. "Just curious."

His expression said he didn't buy the act, but he answered all the same. "Purists prefer to sail without an engine. It makes the experience more authentic."

That was Edward—always concerned with authenticity.

I studied him as he fiddled with the boom and jib, terms I'd only just learned. His chambray shirt, in a color that could only be referred to as pink but was too masculine to say out loud, was rolled up to his elbows, showcasing the sculpted muscles of his forearms. When he lunged to get a better angle, his thigh pressed taut against his white linen pants, and I had to swallow and look away.

Even with dread nestled in the center of my belly, the man was still the sexiest thing I'd ever come in contact with. Watching him use his hands and body to steer our boat only made him hotter. And our chemistry wasn't one-sided. There was a blanket of tension that stretched and pulled in waves as unpredictable as the water beneath us.

Once happy with the direction we were headed—how he could even know since there weren't any maps around, I had no clue—he took a seat on the bench across from me and retrieved a container of cold roast chicken from the cooler.

"No, thanks," I said, when he handed it out to me. My stomach was already complaining, either from the motion of the boat or anxiety, I wasn't sure.

He reached again into the cooler and brought out a bottle of water and a loaf of french bread. "Nibble on this. It will help."

Reluctantly, I took both from him, setting the water to my side and tearing off a piece of bread that I ate in morsels.

We were quiet for a while as he ate and I pecked, and the sun moved farther west in the sky and the boat sailed farther from land. I kept reminding myself to relax my shoulders and breathe. There was definitely an aura of calm out here with the rhythmic lull of the sea and the wet, salty air. Serenity rolled lazily underneath the apprehension, and I could almost give into it. But not quite.

Eventually, Edward put away his meal and sat back with a bottle of water, his foot resting on the cooler. "Tell me about your relationship with your father," he said, his attention solely on me.

The tension that I'd managed to release came back in a rush. "Is this a session?"

"No. Just talking." He brought the bottle up to swig, his throat stretched and exposed as he swallowed.

The casualness of it felt dangerous. Staged.

But also not. Also it just felt genuine. Like a question someone you'd known for a while— had sex with, married—might ask.

Whatever was going on out here, whatever this sailing trip was about, there wasn't any benefit in me going backwards.

So I went forward and stayed honest. "We're good, I suppose. Not particularly close, but most of the kids I grew up with weren't close to their fathers either. They all worked too much. Had too many affairs. Weren't around. Mine wasn't any different than the others, except I think the only mistress he had was golf. I'm his only child, and that matters to him. He loves me as much as I think he loves anyone, though he doesn't really know me. At all. Doesn't even try. I don't really try with him either, anymore."

I considered the distance between my father and me, how it hadn't been there when I was young. How we'd grown apart when I was a teenager and why. The afternoon that had changed it all.

The story of it pressed at the back of my throat until it was snaking through my mouth and out my lips. "He was never a corporal punishment kind of guy. That was his father's style, and whenever I was in trouble as a kid, he made sure that I knew that if he'd been *his* father, I would have had my ass whipped.

"I'm not even sure he knew most of the times I got in trouble. That sort of stuff was usually handled by the nanny or, on rare occasions, my mother. But sometimes it was bad enough for him to get involved."

"You were a naughty little girl?" The gleam in Edward's eye caused goosebumps to chase down my skin.

"Not particularly," I said, smiling. "That came later. But there was this one time, when I was thirteen. Almost fourteen. I'd told him..." I paused, deliberating how much of this I wanted to share in the moment, deciding on sticking to the tale on hand and not branching off to the other. "I'd told him something he didn't believe, and it made him very angry. He accused me of lying. Told me to take it back, and I considered it. He was so mad, I actually considered it.

"But I'd been telling the truth, and—don't laugh—that was important to me back then. So I stuck by it. And then, at thirteen flipping years old, he turned me around, pulled down my leggings and spanked me raw. It hurt, I mean it really hurt. I can still remember spending the rest of that weekend on my stomach with ice packs on my ass, but the physical pain was nothing compared to how much it hurt to not have him believe me. I don't think our relationship ever recovered after that.

"I think that was also when I began to realize that there wasn't much value in honesty. If truth was so hard to believe, what was the purpose in it?"

The edges of Edward's mouth turned down. "The lessons from our parents are the hardest to unlearn, aren't they?"

"Yeah. I think they are." My body felt lighter, and even as I wondered what hard lessons his parents had taught him, the tranquility of the sea beckoned me to embrace it and I found I was closer than I'd been before. Closer to peace.

"There is purpose to honesty, you know," Edward said after a beat. "With the right person. A person who will acknowledge and support your truth instead of admonish it."

"Yes. I've been learning that. New teacher."

"*Better* teacher?" He almost smiled, and I wondered if we were flirting.

"Much better teacher." I leaned my elbows back onto the hull of the boat and stretched my legs out in front of me, the knot in my stomach finally uncoiling.

"If this were a session, I'd respond to this tale with a lesson in a different kind of spanking."

"I think you've already taught me that lesson." My core clenched at remembering being bent over his desk, at the heat of his hand against my ass, at the delicious pleasure of his pelvis thrusting against the raw skin as he thrust his cock inside me over and over. I hadn't even thought of my father's punishment while Edward had been spanking me, I'd been too entirely wrapped up in the moment. In him.

Now I'd go so far as saying I liked being spanked hard. It was possible I only liked being spanked hard by Edward.

"That was a good lesson," he said, his eyes shining like he could read my thoughts, and this time he was definitely smiling. "I wouldn't mind giving it again sometime."

A promise of a future? I wouldn't let myself get too snagged up on the thought.

Another silent spell passed.

"What was it your father hadn't believed?"

I sighed, scanning out into the distance where the ocean met the sky. I'd known he wouldn't let that slip when I chose to say it, and yet, briefly, I'd thought he had.

"I'll tell you," I said, sincerely. "But I'd rather it not be here. My stomach's already fighting the waves. I don't want to push it."

When I returned my gaze to him, he was staring, and I could sense how badly he wanted to press. If he did, I'd probably tell him, though I really didn't want to.

"What about *your* relationship with your father?" I asked, hoping the change of subject would force him to move on.

It took a minute, but then he followed where I'd steered. "He's the reason I like sailing."

"He taught you?"

"Some. I was still young when he died. Thirteen." The nod of his head acknowledged it was the same age I'd been in the story I'd just told.

Thirteen had been such a transformative year for both of us. It wasn't significant, necessarily, but it felt binding. Like, I could see him a little more clearly for it, for what had happened to him and what had happened to me.

"He never set out to really teach me, he just liked it. We spent several vacations on the water. We sailed everywhere—the Lake District, the Channel. The Mediterranean. It was the only downtime he took, because my mother liked it so much, I think, and he wanted his leisure to be completely wrapped up in her, and sailing was something we could all do together.

"I had good memories of it, and so, when I had the means, I learned officially. Marion and I sailed a fair amount when Hagan and Genevieve were young."

My jaw went rigid. "You sailed with Marion?"

"Are you jealous?"

He was so handsome and so smug and so right, I had to look away. I wasn't used to being jealous. It prickled inside me like I'd swallowed a porcupine, and the only thing that would make it worse would be to admit it.

"Just trying to understand your relationship," I said, nonchalantly.

"I've gone sailing now with you, too."

I fought a smile that he couldn't see, sure that he'd know even though I wasn't looking at him. He was trying to comfort me, and that did all sorts of delicious and strange things to my insides.

And it did comfort me, because I was out here on the ocean with him, and where was she?

Still, the reality of why and how I was with Edward was unsettling. "I'm not really sailing. You're sailing, and I'm trying to survive it."

"You're surviving just fine from where I'm sitting. So far."

His addendum set off another roll of nausea. I studied the water, trying to convince myself he meant I'd managed to not throw up as of yet, which was accurate, and there was still a possibility that I might.

But maybe that hadn't been what he meant at all.

The poke of a fin above the surface just then sent a chill down my spine. Was it a dolphin or a shark? Was this a safe venture or a dangerous one?

"My relationship with Marion seemed complicated from the outside," he said, drawing my attention back to him. "But very simple on the inside. She was a submissive—a true submissive. She lived to bend and serve and please me. With my help, her entire life was orchestrated so that she could immerse herself in that lifestyle, that's how much she enjoyed it."

The porcupine was back, wriggling in my insides, loosing needles into my ribs. "I enjoy it, too," I said with a pout. "Sometimes."

He laughed, not as deep as he had back at the house, but a sizable laugh at that. "You like it when you finally surrender to it. I'll give you that. You just fight tooth and nail to get there."

"That doesn't mean I don't like it."

The stare he fixed on me was so heated, I was almost sure he would climb across the cockpit and...I wasn't sure what would happen when he got to me, but I was ready to find out.

But he didn't.

The heat slipped away from his expression, his jaw jutting out as he turned to fuss with the rudder. "There were benefits to such a relation-ship. Trust was imperative for it to work, and we had that through and through. When she said something, she meant it. Every word that came out of her mouth was the truth, unless she was teasing me into play. It was very hard to make her uncomfortable, which was bothersome for me, but she never lied or played me or manipulated me in any way. She never kept crucial information from me for her own benefit."

There it was—his anger from earlier resurfaced. I'd been waiting for it.

"Sounds like a boring marriage," I said. It probably wasn't the best time to sass him. Marion probably never would have. But as he'd not so subtly pointed out, I was not Marion.

He didn't find my teasing amusing, or, if he did, he didn't let on. "She was the one who left me, you know."

I did know, but I'd never heard it from him, and now that I had, it was a wake-up call. His heart had belonged to someone else—might still belong to her, for all I knew. I couldn't tell if that was the point he'd meant to make, but if he'd wanted to hurt me, he had.

"Why?" I asked, taking the bait. "You weren't bossy enough for her?" Hell, if I didn't amuse him, I sure amused myself.

His cheek twitched as he considered his response. "She wanted to be my whole world. She submitted everything, hoping to earn that spot, and she never did."

"You had other women?"

"I never cheated on my wife. On either of my wives."

Just like that, the knife he'd pierced through me only a moment before was gone and his words were a salve in its place. He hadn't been with another woman since he'd married me. That confession tilted my world even more than the rocking of the boat.

"At least not with a woman," he clarified. "Marion took second place to my other ambitions."

His career? It seemed the obvious answer, especially knowing what I knew about what it took to be a successful leader of an international business such as his.

Then the real answer struck me, and maybe it was also about his career, but I was nearly convinced there was something more to it. "Ambitions like destroying my father, you mean."

He didn't answer, and a minute later he stood to adjust the boom, slowing down our speed. Then he walked around the steering wheel to peer off the stern of the boat.

I stood too, gazing over his shoulder, wondering what he saw out there in that great expanse of nothing. Wondering what he was thinking. Wondering his motives for taking me out here and saying these things—these earth-shattering things that were too real and precious and enormous to have put on me and not have to adjust my stance.

"This is where I was going to do it." His voice was low, almost a hum, but in the stillness of our surroundings, he was easily heard. "This was how. I'd push you off out here, in a spot just like this. I imagined it a lot—the ride out here, the time of day, the surrounding circumstances.

But in my head, no matter how well I tried to plan it, I could never get to that moment, the moment where we stood here, and I did the thing that was supposed to happen next."

My breath shuddered in my lungs.

He was safe, I told myself. He wouldn't be telling me any of this if he wasn't safe. He was being honest with me now, the same way I'd been honest with him.

At least, I thought so.

There was the possibility that I was wrong.

With shaking limbs, I stepped up beside him so my arm brushed against his. At his side, I looked out at the same emptiness that had stolen his focus. "I've been on yachts plenty, but I've only been sailing a handful of times. Definitely never been sailing without a motor and if anyone had ever invited me to do so, on an ocean no less, that would have been a 'hell, no.' Lakes are okay. Bays are okay. There are borders there. Land corralling the water, and even on the big lakes where you can't see the land, you know it's there. Your head knows that wherever the wind blows, you're still contained.

"Sailing like this, out here on the open water, it's an entirely different thing, isn't it? The breeze could pick up and next thing you know, you're miles and miles from any shore. Completely a slave to the whims of the wind. That's why I never came out on the ocean like this with anyone before. I've been asked—trust me, I've been asked. The idea was always too terrifying."

I could feel his gaze on my profile, and I turned to meet it. "It's validating to find the real experience is as terrifying as I'd imagined."

Because I was scared. I wanted him to know I was scared.

But I was still here. Not entirely at my will, but I was here. I was in this with him.

His lips turned up into a smirk. "And exciting too?"

"Yes. That too."

The breeze sent my hair blowing, leaving a strand across my face. He reached out to brush it back behind my ear, his fingers igniting my skin as they grazed my cheek. "At the whims of the wind doesn't mean helpless," he said. "The only reason you're frightened is because you don't know how to sail a boat."

Then, he expertly demonstrated how very much in control of the *Vengeance* he was, deftly steering us across the ocean, safely bringing us back into port at Amelie.

TWENTY-TWO

THE SUN WAS SETTING when we got back to the house. I walked in ahead of Edward, my shoes in my hand, having finally succumbed to taking them off. The house was empty, which I'd expected since my husband had informed the staff not to plan on us for dinner, and for Joette to leave plates for us in the fridge.

Despite how little I'd eaten, food wasn't of interest. Nor was the hot shower that I'd told Edward I wanted to take when we got back. The orange and pink streaked across the scene outside the window didn't have my attention either. As I stood behind the couch gazing out at the spectacular display of light, it was the man behind me that held my awareness.

He was complicated and terrible. A devil and a jackass.

And I was falling for him.

Spiraling, actually, in all the good ways and all the bad. He made me dizzy and overwhelmed and alive, even when he terrified me, which was almost all the time. I was pretty certain there was no happy ending with a man like him, not coming from a situation like ours, and it didn't matter. It couldn't stop my motion. I was still already tumbling down into whatever mess lay at the end, and if I were honest with myself—

something I was being more often than not these days—I wouldn't try to stop even if I could. I wanted this.

I wanted him.

I wanted him to want me with as much intensity, with no regard to reason. I wanted it so badly, I could taste it. I could feel it. The wanting was as real to my senses as the sunset ahead of me.

I didn't look back when he came in, but I heard the door open and then there was the sound of the cooler set down on the ceramic floor. In the glass, I could just make out the hint of his reflection, frozen in place, his eyes seemingly pinned on me.

"Celia?" His voice lilted up slightly like it were a question or possibly an invitation, but all I heard was my name on his lips spoken with the husk of desire.

Turning around, I let my shoes drop to the floor, and within the space of a breath, I was in his arms. I had no idea who'd moved first, who had made the first step, who started the kiss. One minute I'd been wishing and wanting. The next, my body was crashed into his, my mouth desperately trying to keep up with his frantic lips. His tongue felt hot and thick as it tangled with mine, each stroke feeling like a promise, each swipe awakening every nerve ending in my body, making my pussy swell and sob.

His hands mimicked his kiss, furiously running over my body, through my hair, grabbing my ass, as if to leave their prints on all of me. As if to leave no part of me untouched.

I curled my fingers in his shirt, taking what he gave, hanging on for dear life.

My knees were weak and my lungs empty of air when he drew back, bringing his palms to cradle my face. His expression was unsure as he studied me, searching for something in my eyes.

I held on and let him look, not knowing what he wanted to see there. I only hoped he found it or something close because what *I* wanted to see was in *his* eyes—desire and concern and interest—and I'd do anything for him to keep looking at me like that. Anything for him to keep touching me. For him to kiss me again.

And then he *was* kissing me again, his mouth greedy and demanding as he pushed me backwards until my legs met the sofa. There, he turned me around and pressed my head down until I was bent over the back of the couch.

"Spread your legs," he ordered, though he was already spreading them for me, his shoe nudging my feet until they were wide enough.

His hand traveled from the back of my head and down my spine, a long, possessive caress. Then it disappeared, only to reappear a moment later with his other hand under my dress. He flipped my skirt up then swiftly removed my panties, kneeling in the process. Both of his hands palmed my ass cheeks, his fingernails digging into my skin as his tongue licked along my slit, rimming my wet channel before swiping up to my asshole.

I gasped at the invasion. Shocks of pleasure jolted through my body as he did it again, and again, licking me with fierce, predatory enthusiasm. I was quivering within minutes, and he hadn't even touched my clit.

"Rub yourself, little bird. I want you to come on my tongue."

I shook my head, even though I wasn't sure he could see the movement with me bent over the couch like I was and his head between my thighs. My fingertips were pressed hard into the sofa cushion. They were the only thing holding me up. They couldn't be spared for other activities.

"Do it," he demanded, when I hadn't moved. His tongue speared inside me, prompting me in ways his words hadn't.

"I'm going to come anyway," I moaned. The knot of sensation pulsed low in my belly, each throb bigger than the last. I'd never come so quickly, and I was more than halfway there without clitoral stimulation.

Three sharp smacks fell in rapid succession against my right asscheek, the sting making me cry out. Automatically, my body jerked, trying to pull away from the assault.

Edward pulled his mouth from my body and gripped my hips, anchoring me in place. "I didn't ask, Celia. Put your fingers on your pussy or I'll put mine, and believe me when I say you won't find that as pleasant."

He waited this time, denying me his mouth until I responded.

Having learned how "unpleasant" he could be when he went down on me, I hesitated to obey.

But I didn't want a dozen orgasms this way. I wanted his cock inside me, and it seemed I had a better shot at that if I did what he said.

Lifting my belly from the sofa enough to get access, I slipped my hand down between my legs to the sensitive bud buried in between the folds of skin. I set the tip of my finger to it, scared that any more would set me off, and I wanted to wait to explode on his tongue like he'd asked.

His breath scorched across my aroused cunt, and that alone nearly devastated me. "Rub it like you mean it, Celia, or I can send you to your room like this, alone."

"Don't you dare," I panted, but I swirled my finger across my clit, drawing the edges of my climax in closer.

Another biting thwack sang against my skin, a punishment for the sass, I assumed because his next words were a soft purr. "Good girl."

Then his mouth returned to my hole, his tongue thrusting into my heat with determined drive.

I lasted all of three seconds before my orgasm had seized me. My legs shook aggressively, my knees knocking against the sofa. "Oh, my Godddddd," I roared, the pleasure blinding me with flashes of white.

I was still shuddering when I was snatched up by the hair and spun around to face my husband.

"When it's my face between your thighs, it's my name out of your lips," he scolded.

"Yes, Edward," I said, only to have the words swallowed by his tongue as it shoved into my mouth. He tasted like me, which made me all kinds of hot, especially when he kissed me like it was a punishment, like I'd been bad. Like I deserved to be suffocated with the wrath of his desire.

When I was completely breathless, he abruptly pushed away, only to swing me into his arms. He carried me to his bedroom, bride style, kissing me the entire way. When he got to his closed door, he set me down so he could open it and usher me in.

It was the first time I'd been to his room when I'd been invited. The significance of the moment wasn't lost on me, despite the distraction of my lust.

We hadn't made it past more than the threshold when he tugged on my clothing. "Take this off," he ordered.

I worked the dress over my head while he kicked off his loafers. I couldn't remember having ever seen his feet bare, and the sight was entirely too sexy for what it was. They were long and pedicured and manly. How was it possible that was such a turn-on? I didn't even like feet.

"And the bra," he said, as he began to undo his pants.

I watched him as I threw off the last piece of my clothing, watched as his greedy eyes skimmed across my naked body. Eagerly, I waited to be able to do the same to him, but he'd only gotten his cock out when he lifted me up, letting my legs wrap around him before he pressed me against the wall across from his door.

"I want to be inside you." He rubbed the length of his cock, hard and hot, against my throbbing pussy.

"Yes. Yes, Edward, yes!" I bucked my hips up, inviting him to slide inside. Begging him.

His crown notched at my hole, and I reached down to help guide him in, but he yanked my arm away and pinned it with the other above my head. He held them there with one hand as his other stroked the underside of my breast.

"You know what I mean when I say that. Tell me you know what I mean."

I paused, wanting to be connected with him like this—with under-standing—even more than I wanted to be connected with him with my body. I replayed his words in my head. He wanted to be *inside me*. Inside all the way. Not just physically, but in *every* way. Mentally, emotionally.

Didn't he know that he already was? Hadn't that been his goal all along?

Yes, it had. So he did know. Or he guessed. Maybe what he needed was to know that I knew too.

"I know," I said earnestly. "I know who you are."

He closed his eyes and growled at that, tilting his pelvis to slide his cock through my folds. Still, he didn't enter me, keeping his lids squeezed shut as if trying to hold onto control.

When he opened them again, he brought his hand from my breast up to grip my chin. "You have to choose this. I'm not deciding this for you. You choose if I put you down and let you walk away. Really walk away. Or you choose to keep put. But as soon as I'm inside you, that's where I'm going to stay. You will be mine. Tell me you understand."

I don't know why I hesitated. I understood what he was saying, and I'd already made my choice. Months ago, when I'd first shared anything real with him, the decision had been made. Maybe even before that. When I'd let him put a ring on my finger. When I followed him to Europe.

When I'd taken that goddamned meeting with a stranger, and he'd seen me for who I was. Maybe all the way back then.

Now he was giving me a chance to walk away? To *really* walk away? From this house, from this island, from this marriage. From his threats and his ruin.

A smart woman wouldn't believe him.

Maybe I didn't either.

It was a serious ultimatum, too important to be discussed in the midst of orgasms and the temptation of his beautiful cock. He could very well have said it only to make me uncomfortable. To turn himself on.

Not that the steel rod pressing against my pelvis needed it. The bead of pre-cum at his tip certainly seemed to indicate he was fully aroused.

Still, it could have been just words.

But the possibility that they weren't words, the possibility that he truly meant the rest—that I'd be his, that he'd be inside me permanently? It somehow seemed worth the risk.

"I understand, Edward," I said, sure of the decision if not sure of him. "And I'm not going anywhere. I choose to stay."

I hadn't even finished speaking when his mouth claimed me, simultaneously shoving his cock into me with a vigorous thrust. Over and over he drove into me, his pace rapid and controlled. He released my hands, needing to use his to hold my thighs around him, and I threw them around his neck, winding my fingers through the back of his hair.

He kissed me as he fucked me, his mouth straying occasionally to suck on my neck or pull at my nipple with his teeth until I was squirming from the pain. Then he'd pound into me with even more force, plunging into the deepest parts of me.

It was rough and uncomfortable. My back was going to have bruises from the edge of the closet door frame that slammed into me with each of his thrusts. My breasts were already tender from his bites, my legs ached from how tightly I was wrapped around him, and still it was more pleasurable than any sex I'd ever had. Another orgasm was already gathering, fueled by his frantic tempo, the tilt of his pelvis against my clit, and the skillfully angled stabs of his cock.

And I knew then, if this was as far inside of him that I ever got—him fully dressed, barely in his room, his secrets never to cross the threshold of his lips—it would be enough. I could be the exposed one of us. I could be the one who was opened up and put on display. I could be raw and pulverized and broken down. For him. I could be that for him, and he would never have to give me anything more than he'd given me so far.

Because I was already more loved than I'd ever been, and I could die happy in that.

With this realization, I came, my pussy clenching around Edward's cock so hard I pushed him out of me.

He let go of me so quickly I almost fell. Thank goodness for the wall. I stepped toward him, lifting my mouth for his, but he stepped away, a smirk on his lips.

"I'm going to have to fuck you twice as hard for that," he said, sweat beaded on his brow. "On the bed."

As I walked by, he changed his mind and grabbed my ass with one hand to pull me into him. He assaulted me with a kiss, his chest pressing against the bullet tips of my breasts as he walked me to his bed. As soon as the back of my calves felt the frame behind them, he pushed me to the mattress.

I crawled backward up the bed to make room for us, my eyes never leaving him as he shoved his pants to the floor and worked the buttons of his shirt.

He was always so magnificent to look at. Naked, he was other-worldly. Too perfectly chiseled to be a man. Too manipulative and deviant to be a god. More of a devil in bare flesh than he ever had been in a suit.

Jesus, I thought, dizzy at the sight of him.

But what I said was, "Edward," my tone threadbare, even to my own ears.

"I'm here," he said, stepping up to the mattress, his cock drenched from my juices, jutting out in front of him. He took it in his hand and jerked it up and down, wielding it as confidently as he wielded any other aspects of his power.

He still had a grip on it as he crawled up the mattress beside me, letting it go only to cradle my face when I reached my mouth toward his. He took my lips this time, kissing me even more zealously than he had when he'd had me against the wall. I tried to turn my entire body toward him, wanting my chest against him, but he had other ideas, snaking his hand around my waist and twisting me to my side before pulling my ass up to meet his pelvis. His hand at my face slipped under my head and around so he could hold my chin in place.

While his tongue continued to fuck my mouth, he nudged his cock between my thighs, easily sliding into my soaking pussy.

There was something more romantic about this position, even though he was fucking me from behind. Everywhere we were skin to skin, the contact so intense I felt it on the insides of my entire body. His kiss was deeper. His cock, too, his languid thrusts hitting the most sensitive parts of my pussy.

And even when his hand at my face found its way to my neck, even when his fingers scratched at my throat, pressing against my windpipe, making it hard to get a good breath, even then being in his arms felt good. He was dangerous, yes. He wasn't trustworthy. He was as cruel as he was beautiful.

He was still a devil, but now he was the devil I knew.

And I'd never in my life felt so safe.

TWENTY-THREE

I WOKE up in the dark, the sheets tangled around me, the bed empty. It took a minute for me to remember where I was, how I'd fallen asleep in Edward's arms after marathon sex. My eyes were still heavy, and it would be easy to curl into the pillow that smelled like him and go back to sleep, but his absence nagged at me. Our relationship, strange and fragile and unformed as it was, captivated me. I wanted it to be as big as it might be, wanted to allow it to swell and grow, and shutting my eyes to it now didn't seem like the best move.

With a groan, I threw my arms overhead and stretched, feeling every delicious way my body had been used before climbing out of the comfortable bed. Snatching his discarded shirt to wrap around me, I went to the bathroom then set out on a search for my husband.

I crept into the dark hall, straining for any sound of movement, finding only thick silence. With no light, I fumbled to the library and found it also dark, but a faint flicker drew my attention out the library window. It was coming from the top of the pool house at the back of the yard. The firewall was lit. I'd found him.

I pushed out the side door and stepped barefoot into the breezy night, circling around the pool to get to the stairs beyond it that led up to the sanctuary I'd built. It gave me a prideful thrill to know

Edward was up there. Beyond signing off on the plans, he'd never acknowledged the finished work, which had been fine enough. I'd made the space for me. Still it was nice to know he appreciated it as well.

At the top of the stairs, I paused to take in his profile. He was sitting on the sectional, dressed only in his linen pants, his expression tight as he stared out at the nearly full moon reflecting on the ocean. A bottle of amber liquid sat in his lap, half empty. While I watched, he brought it up to his mouth, taking a swig. From the shape of the container, it looked like Hennessy, which meant it probably hadn't been a full bottle when he'd come out since there had already been one open in his bar, so I couldn't know for sure how much he'd drunk. My guess was enough, since the bed had been cold on his side, and his usually straight posture was slouched.

I'd been quiet, and with the crash of the waves, I wasn't sure he'd heard me approach so I cleared my throat before emerging from the shadows, not wanting to startle him.

He didn't look over until I was standing at the other end of the sectional, and even then it was only a quick glance.

It wasn't like I didn't expect it. Every time we'd fucked, he'd pushed me away after. Why should tonight be any different?

This time, though, when he pushed, I didn't intend to budge.

"May I join you, Edward?" It was a question, but my tone was clear that I meant to sit whether he said I could or not. That was a trick I'd learned from him. How to command even while maintaining a polite appearance.

"You may," he said, and whatever notion I had that I might be able to dominate this moment fell away because his tone clearly said he was still in charge.

I sighed as I plopped down in the corner spot, three cushions away from him. *Too far* away from him. But I didn't know how to be closer, not with the invisible shield I could feel present around him. Not with the distance he'd already created by sneaking out here in the night. Not with the bottle he held as tightly as I wished he were holding me.

I curled my feet underneath me and waited in case he had something he wanted to say. If he was in charge, he had the first rights of conversation. He had the ability to take this anywhere he wanted.

But he remained silent, wrapped up in his thoughts and his cognac, and maybe it was an obvious message that he wanted to be left alone.

I was tired of being alone, though. Tired of being alone on this island, but also tired of being alone in my whole life, and something about the chemistry that clearly existed between us made me think he might actually be tired of being alone too.

He appreciated honesty, anyway. And honesty for me at the moment was being here with him, telling him my thoughts, even if they disrupted his own.

"I don't know what's going on between us," I said, hesitantly.

If he knew, it would be fanfuckingtastic if he clued me in.

When he said nothing, I gave him more rope. "Or if you even think anything is going on between us." My skin prickled with that nervous excitement that comes from putting something brave out there. He could cut me down now. Dash all the hopes I had for us with only a glare.

Or he could surprise me and tell me something wonderful.

I waited in case it was the latter.

His only response was to take another swig of brandy.

Guess I was talking to myself then. "It sure feels like something to me," I muttered, turning my gaze from him to the lone bird circling the edge of the water, his wings caught in the gleam of moonlight.

"What kind of something does it feel like?"

My head shot back toward Edward who was peering at me with a curious gaze.

Well, shit, that backfired. I'd wanted him to tell me what it was, not the other way around.

But that was the way with us. I kept the truth hidden inside me, and he tugged and pulled until it was outside of me, a living thing, wriggling in his hands. Like I was giving birth out of my mouth, and he was the proud doctor who took all the credit.

And I liked that way about us, for the most part. It had gotten us this far, anyway. So I resumed my role. "It's confusing," I admitted.

"You told me you were going to kill me. You alluded to it again today. You keep me trapped as your prisoner on this island, and yet..." And yet I felt things. Enormous things. About him.

Saying that felt too big. Like I wasn't dilated enough for that. I needed some sort of epidural.

I leaned forward and reached my hand out toward the cognac.

"Oh, come on," he said, relinquishing the bottle to me. "How trapped have you been really?"

I practically choked on the swallow I'd just thrown back. I wiped at my mouth, coughing.

"Uh. Pretty trapped."

"How hard did you try to get away?" He stared intensely at me, forcing me to really think about the answer.

I had tried in the beginning. But I certainly hadn't exhausted my avenues. After learning what Edward had told the islanders, I hadn't attempted to talk to anyone besides Joette about the real circumstances of my confinement. I hadn't tried to seduce any of the Spanish-speaking workers who'd helped with my redesigns. I hadn't tried to steal a boat in the middle of the night. I hadn't tried to hack Edward's computer to get to the internet or even searched the staff's quarters for a laptop or a satellite phone, both of which surely existed.

I couldn't begin to say why I hadn't tried harder. It hadn't been because I was scared. It might have been a little because I was lazy. The truth was, though, when I really thought about it now, there hadn't been enough reason to want to leave. What did I have waiting for me beyond Amelie? What did I have waiting for me beyond Edward?

The revelation threatened to knock me off balance.

Then the look in Edward's eyes definitely threw me off balance. It said, *See? Not so easy to define what's going on now, is it?* Because what must he have been thinking leaving me here? Had he expected me to be gone when he came back? Each time he arrived, was my presence a surprise? Had he wanted me to escape?

Had he been glad when I hadn't?

I shook my head, more confused than I'd been before. "If I'm not your prisoner, Edward, then what am I?"

It was his turn to sigh and reach out for the bottle, which I passed without comment. He took a slow draw off the neck then settled it back in the crook of his arm, his brow furrowed as though searching for what he wanted to say.

I brought my knees up to the sectional and hugged my arms around them, letting him take his time, the same way he'd coaxed me with patience in all of his sessions.

Finally, he spoke. "You asked me earlier today what sort of relationship I had with my father."

I blinked, caught off guard by the apparent change of subject. "Sure. Yeah. I did," I said, curious where he was going.

"We weren't close, exactly. Stefan Fasbender wasn't a mean man or cruel in anyway, but like your father, he worked all the time. He did make quite an appearance of being a family man—everyone said he lived for his company and us—but both Camilla and I knew that what he really loved besides his job was our mother."

"Amelie." I twisted the ring on my finger, the one that had belonged to her. It had felt significant that he'd given it to me. Even more so now that I knew it represented a deep love.

"She really was a lovely woman. It was easy to see why he was so enraptured by her. She was physically beautiful, something you can tell just by looking at photographs—dark hair, pale skin, plump lips. But all that was magnified when you were actually in her presence. She radiated joy, and if you've never seen that on a person, it's incredibly attractive. She made everyone around her feel it with her. It was infectious, and the three people most infected were my father, Camilla, and me. She doted on us. Spoiled us with love and affection. She was better than Father Christmas. She was magic like that."

I smiled at the image. "No wonder you named the island after her. It's magic here too."

"Yes." He gave a respectful nod. "You can imagine how devastating it was for all of us to discover she was terminally ill. I was almost eleven. Old enough to understand that what was happening was not normal, but not quite old enough to understand the intricacies of something as complicated as ovarian cancer.

"The real indicator that it was serious was how my father behaved. He stepped away from his job for weeks at a time, desperate to be at her side through every treatment, through every bout of nausea, through every crying jag. I remember making a huge effort to protect Camilla from it all. She was only six, and I'd ignore homework to keep her entertained so that she wouldn't go searching for my mother's attention. But then, when she was asleep or busy with the nanny, I'd sneak up to my parents' room and watch from the door frame as he tended to her, unnoticed by her because of the fog of medication. Unnoticed by him because of his preoccupation with her."

My throat ached with sympathy, and I wanted to say something, but the cadence of his words indicated he was getting to a point, and my condolences weren't it. So I took my cue from the way he always behaved in his sessions with me, holding back and just listening.

"Understandably, the business suffered from my father's absence. Accelerate, was the name of his company. Not impressive compared to Werner, by any means, but it was substantial. A handful of television stations and some newspapers. He'd inherited a lot of money and bought into media at the right time. He'd built most of it before he'd even met my mother. (He was forty-two when they met, a dozen years her senior. I came along three years later.) He was so blinded by his devastation with what was going on with my mother that he didn't take the time to take proper measures at Accelerate. He should have stepped down as CEO. He should have pulled himself from operations, but he didn't. Which made the company vulnerable, and soon it was ripe for takeover.

"When he realized what was happening, he tried to retaliate. Tried to buy stock in the company that was purchasing, but stock options weren't available. Tried to get his entire team to resign—a tactic known as a poison pill—but the purchasing company didn't care to retain the management team. There's probably more to the back and forth of the negotiations—I was only thirteen by the time this came to a head, so my knowledge has been only pieced together from accounts from other board members years later. The point is, he lost Accelerate.

"And two months later, he lost his wife."

My inhale was sharp and audible, despite having already known the bare bones of the story. The sound brought his eyes to me as I covered my mouth with my hand.

"We weren't completely destitute, mind you. We hadn't lost everything. Money was exchanged in the takeover, though a lot of that went to pay the medical bills. My father had gone all out in search of experimental treatments, each of which were costly and didn't work in the end. There was money in a trust, still, but it wasn't going to last forever. He tried to return to Accelerate as a high-level employee, but the new company had no need for his expertise, since all they planned to do was tear the company apart and sell it piece by piece. Which they did, rather quickly, I might add. He was devastated watching his life's work be demolished, and after the death of my mother, his two reasons for living were gone."

"He killed himself." The words came out of my mouth before I meant to say them. I'd read this too, but it hadn't been quite so shocking without the details.

"Yes, he did." Edward's eyes were dark and unreadable. "The trust was left to me and my sister, and our care was put in the hands of a cousin we'd only met once before. She and her husband were the trustees and with no one monitoring them except each other, they sent us to foster care and spent all the money. What money there was after the fall of all the Accelerate stocks, which were worthless after the company was torn apart."

He looked at the bottle in his lap, but instead of taking another swallow, he put the cap on it and set it on the ground. Then he leaned forward, bracing his elbows on his thighs. "The foster system separated us, and Camilla ended up in an abusive family. Burned and beaten for years, until I could get her out of the clutches of that man. The damage had already been done. My situation wasn't nearly as bad. I was moved around a few times, no one wanting an angry, maladjusted teenage boy—and I was certainly both. The homes that took me in along the way were hardly stable. The neglect and lack of supervisory attention did give me time to plan, though, and even before I knew about Camilla, even before I discovered all the money was gone,

I knew that one day I'd get my revenge. One day I'd take back what was owed."

He turned his head toward me, his eyes searing into my skin. "I've been living and planning and working for vengeance since I was thirteen, Celia. Before you were even in preschool. It's taken years to find the right path. So many times I've been close, but never as close as now. Do you understand what I'm saying?"

My stomach dropped like there was an anchor in its place and it had been thrown out to sea, taking all of me with it. Because suddenly I did understand what he was saying. "The company that took over—it was Werner Media, wasn't it?"

He didn't have to answer for me to know I was right, and he didn't. He just kept his gaze pinned in place, watching me react. The brandy on an empty stomach suddenly seemed like it had been a very bad idea.

"But...but...but that's just business!" I exclaimed. Though, I knew that there were ethical business practices and less ethical ones, and from his description of the situation, I guessed this had been the latter. "And what about the cousin? The one who took all the money? Or the foster dad who hurt Camilla? Things turned out shitty, but it wasn't all my father's fault. There were other demons in this story, too."

"And those demons have already been taken care of."

A chill shuddered up my spine at the ominous pronouncement.

"For that matter, my father is also to blame, and I acknowledge that. He was a pathetic coward, taking his own life instead of caring for his children, and believe me, if I could kill him again for it, I wouldn't hesitate."

His tone was as vicious as his words, his demeanor as cruel as his intentions, and if I'd ever forgotten, here was the reminder—Edward Fasbender was a devil.

And I'd fallen in love with him. Crashed into love with him. There wasn't a part of me that wasn't mangled and damaged from the impact. The best I could hope was that he'd crashed into love with me, but now that I'd heard his story, I could see why that outcome was unlikely.

I swallowed back the ball at the back of my throat and blinked away tears. "I've only ever been a tool. A means to get to him. To ruin his life the way he ruined yours."

The slight sag in his shoulders said everything.

It was stupid to be so surprised. He'd outright told me he wanted my father's shares. But I hadn't truly understood. I'd thought he wanted to move into the U.S. market because he was a ruthless businessman. That felt somehow easier to handle than being the means to execute a plan that was emotionally motivated. Especially after knowing the details of his story. If I'd lived through something so brutal and painful, I'd want revenge too.

Except, the man he wanted revenge against was my father. A man I loved, despite his flaws. "You still want to take him down, don't you? Even now. Even after us."

He didn't bother to deny it. "I won't let you get taken down with him."

I bit my lip, holding in a sob. "Really? You've already taken me down. Broken me. All this time you were doing that—you were only ever interested in finding out things you could use to get to my father, weren't you? Hoping to make me 'yours' so I could manipulate him for you somehow. Was that the reason you kept me alive?"

He scowled. "Don't be ridiculous. I wanted you to be mine because you belong with me. I wanted you to be mine so that I could justify—to myself, at least—not going through with plans I've worked a fucking lifetime to implement."

He was still torn, the evidence in the frayed pitch of his words. Still divided between wanting me and a revenge scheme that consumed him as thoroughly as any of my games had consumed me.

Or maybe he was just angry about the situation. About the cost that came with keeping me alive and giving up access to my shares. Fuck, I'd give them to him if he asked me to. If he'd just say he didn't need his revenge anymore because he had me. If he'd just say he loved me.

But I'd never been anyone's first choice, not even my parents'. My mother preferred her gossip and social hour to time with me. My father preferred his golf and his empire. Hudson preferred The Game and then Alayna. Edward preferred his revenge.

"I guess I understand what it must have felt like for you as a kid, not being the priority of your father's affections. Of anyone's affections." It was childish and passive-aggressive, and now he knew how hurt I was, and even without outright telling him that I was in love with him, he would be stupid not to have figured it out.

"Bird..." he said, his arms starting to reach out before thinking better of it and retreating into his body.

I shook my head, denying the term of affection. "It's not your style to pretend like you're worried about my feelings. You don't need to start now. I know what my value is in this world. I'm practiced at being the one who matters less."

The memory of my father spanking me flashed in my head. He'd put me in second place then too. Believing someone else's word over mine.

Edward started to say something, something I heard nothing of because of where my thoughts had led me.

"Wait. Accelerate was a London company." I did the math in my head to be sure I was right. "That wasn't my father who screwed your dad over. He didn't run that branch of the company back then." It had been Werner Media's brief venture into the European market, a disastrous one from what my mother had told me in later years.

"Don't try to protect him," Edward said.

"I'm not trying to protect him. Lord knows he's failed at trying to protect me."

He put a finger up, as if bookmarking the topic. "We're going to revisit that."

Despite the course the evening's conversation had taken, with the promise of a future session, of Edward wanting to know about a pain I had yet to tell him, a bud of hope sprung inside me.

"But tell me who you think I should be blaming if not Warren. It was a subsidiary of Werner, yes, but your father was the CEO. He oversaw everything that happened under him."

"He did, and he didn't. Not back then. The branch that went into England had autonomy."

"Then who was behind the decision?"

The hope bud inside of me blossomed into something bigger, fed by an odd combination of relief and exhilaration. See, I understood the want for revenge, too. I just had never been ambitious enough to try to go after it. Not when my father had shot down my first attempt.

Now, though, with Edward, perhaps it was time to think bigger.

I almost smiled when I gave him my answer. "A man I'd fully get behind you hurting—my uncle, Ron."

TWENTY-FOUR

EDWARD

SHE'D CHANGED EVERYTHING.

From the moment she walked into that conference room at the St. Regis Hotel, my course had veered. Her eyes. The tilt of her chin. The way her lips formed into a natural pout. I'd been transfixed.

Then, little by little, she altered me. Changing the very nature of who I was. I'd been a vessel, a piece of stemware full with the wine of revenge, and she'd shattered me into a thousand shards of glass, and now I didn't even recognize myself.

Discovering Warren Werner might not be the enemy I thought he was, brought the biggest change of all. A death of sorts. If what she said was true, if there was another villain behind the destruction of my family, then I couldn't be the man I'd been anymore. I'd have to become someone new, someone who didn't live and breathe to bring down Werner Media. I didn't know who that man was. I didn't know how to be him.

She thought I'd ruined her?

She'd ruined me. In every dangerous and noble way.

I needed time to process it. Long hours of examination and research, but I couldn't do that yet because of her. Because she was sitting three cushions away from me, on the verge of shedding another layer of skin, and I needed to devote all my thoughts and energy to her. To whatever pain this was that had her tense and snarling.

I didn't just need to—I *wanted* to.

I wanted to know everything about her, the good and the bad, but especially the bad. I knew what it felt like to carry agony, how it corrupted and controlled. How it turned into poison. Without someone willing to burrow and excavate and scrape out the heartache, it grew into a cancer that compelled actions of evil. It was too late for me, but for her—I wanted to replace those pains in her, wanted to weed them out and take them on myself. She didn't have to be the angry, destructive woman she'd been inhabiting for years. I would be her wrath for her.

Starting with Ronald Werner.

"When did it start?" I asked, making my question too direct for her to sidestep.

Her eyes widened, startled. Then she settled into a frown. "Are you guessing?"

"Am I wrong?" I knew I wasn't. As soon as I'd seen her reaction to the man when he'd shown up at our wedding reception, I'd known he'd hurt her in some contemptible way.

And there was only one usual way that men like that hurt younger women.

Even without her confirmation, I wanted to rip his balls off and shove them down his throat so he couldn't scream out while I raped his ass with my fist. It still wouldn't make up for however he'd touched her, however he'd harmed her. But it would be a good start.

Her body sagged as she looked out to the ocean, then toward the fire, the light catching the moisture in her eyes. Finally she turned her gaze back to me. "He didn't rape me, if that's what you assume."

My jaw clenched. If it wasn't rape...

"Would rape have been worse?" I asked, my mind already taking me to darker places. Scenes informed by the terrible things I'd witnessed other powerful, depraved men do. Images I could barely stand to imagine let alone discover they were real.

I was prepared when she shook her head, her chin trembling. "No. It wouldn't have."

She curled her legs into her chest and wrapped her arms tightly around them. I ached to pull her into my arms instead, to wrap myself tightly around her, but I resisted the urge. That would only be sealing the cap on the poison. She needed to let it out before I could fill her with something new.

"When did it start?" I asked again, giving her a place to begin.

Her lips pursed. "Is this a session now?"

"Do you need it to be?"

She started to say no. I could feel her dismissal of the subject in the air, firm and resolute.

But before the word made it out of her mouth, she reconsidered, her eyes drooping with the honesty of her realization. "Yes, Edward. I think I do."

"Have you told anyone before? Your parents? A counselor? A friend?"

The shake of her head was barely perceptible. "Just my father."

"The time he spanked you. When he didn't believe you." It wasn't a question because I already knew. It was only said to let her know that I did.

A nod. "After that it seemed like too much work to talk about it. And pointless. So I just..." She took a deep breath, her eyes searching the horizon as if that would give her the answer.

"You pushed it down inside you. Tried to forget it. Hoped it would disintegrate with neglect, but instead it rotted and splintered until it was jabbing into everything else in your life."

"Yeah, that." She almost smiled. "Maybe you should do this for me."

Ah, little bird, I would that I could.

I reached down for the bottle at my side, feeling the need to guzzle the whole thing down. As much as I needed it, I knew she needed it more. I unscrewed the cap and offered it over without bringing it to my own lips.

Her face paled. "No. Thank you. My stomach can't handle it."

I regretted not having more for her out here—a plate of food, crackers. A bottle of water. The temptation to pick her up and carry her inside where I could properly care for her was hard to resist, but I feared the momentum would be lost, and we had so little already.

I recapped the bottle but kept it in my lap, simulating our usual sessions with the routine of a drink in my hand. "Whenever you're ready."

Her sigh was heavy as she brought her hand up to absentmindedly caress her throat, as though there were an invisible talisman strung around her neck. It was the very spot where my fingers had grazed only hours ago as I'd buried myself inside her. Could she still feel me there? Clinging to every part of her?

I hoped she did. I hoped it helped.

"My grandfather and I were close," she began, and my pulse turned sluggish, realizing she'd tried to tell this story to me before. "I spent a month with him every summer at his country home from the time I was two until he died, which was when I was six. Ron inherited that home, and I guess because my parents thought I was attached to the routine—or, more likely, because they liked the freedom without me around—they decided to keep up the annual trips when my uncle offered to continue them.

"So I guess it started when I was seven, though it didn't necessarily feel like it started then. It was gradual, so gradual that it was impossible to pinpoint a beginning. I was a frog in a hot pot and when I first got in, the water wasn't even warm. I have no idea when it started boiling."

Seven years old. Bile formed in the back of my throat. I could remember Genevieve at seven, still a small child. Practically a baby.

"Did he touch you?"

Her brow furrowed in confusion. "Yes, he touched me. There was always touching. But it didn't feel nefarious, not back then. It felt like love is what it felt like. He adored me. He pampered me. He gave me pretty dresses and brought people in to do my hair and nails. I was a princess when I was with him. He made me feel special, and our relationship was special because of that. So, you know, it wasn't really a big deal when he would bring out his camera. It was fun, honestly. I'd pretend I was a model, posing for him in all sorts of goofy ways. Pretending I was older than I was.

"Or he'd take me out to the garden. He'd put up a wooden swing on one of the trees—a great big wooden swing, big enough to seat an adult. Never mind that there was an entire playscape on the other side of the house that my grandfather had installed for me. Ron said the swing was *our* place. He'd let me on it when I was all dressed up—my mother would have made me change into play clothes, but Ron didn't. And he'd push me so high, it felt like I was flying. And I'd laugh and laugh, and he'd laugh too, and it felt really good to make someone that happy. Because that was new to me. I'd never made anyone happy. Not like that.

"After he pushed me for a while, he would say it was his turn, and he'd sit down in my place, and I'd try to push him for all of two seconds, and he wouldn't budge, of course, because he was so much bigger than me, so then he'd laugh and pull me into his lap with him, and he'd hold me while we rocked back and forth, back and forth. And if he held me a little too tight and a little too long, and if his pants would get rigid underneath me—well, that was just part of it."

I bit down so hard on my tongue that I tasted blood. Castration wouldn't be enough. His punishment would have to be prolonged.

"You didn't tell anyone?" I could barely keep the disgust out of my voice.

"It never occurred to me that I should. Not early on. My parents didn't ask enough about my vacation for it to come up, and I was brought up in one of those *children should be seen, not heard* environments so it wasn't like there was an opportunity for me to spout out the details. And like I said, it had been fun, and Ron made me feel good, so there was no reason to protest when they sent me again the next summer.

"It escalated from there. The touching grew more intimate. The lap sitting happened more often, and not just on the swing. Squirming, I discovered early on, made it last longer. He liked it too much. So I learned to sit very still. The whole time he'd say lots of nice things in my ear. He'd tell me how pretty I was, how beautiful my body was.

How good I was. How *special* I was. He'd tell me he loved me. In detail. Then he'd urge me to tell him I loved him, and after I did, he'd make me promise not to tell anyone about our love because it was so special, it had to be a secret. No one would understand our 'special love.' And it was weird, but it was all right."

"He was grooming you." In general, I tried not to interrupt her monologues with commentary, but I wasn't sure how much she understood of the situation. She'd been a child when it all occurred, and if she hadn't looked back at it very often, she might not have had a chance to apply adult wisdom to the memories.

My suspicion was confirmed when her head jerked toward me, her expression startled. "That's right. He was."

Quietly, she chewed on her lip, her eyes dazed as she likely put pieces together, looked at past memories with this new light. There would be a lot to unpack from this, and I'd do it with her, when she was ready. Right now, though, she had to just get to the end, to the moment that finally pushed her to tell her father. To the place where the water was boiling.

I searched for the right question to ask, the right bait to draw more of the poison from her. Before I could find one I was happy with, she spoke on her own.

"He was very clever about it. About how he trained me. How he *groomed* me." She over enunciated the word, tying it firmly to the situation that had played out with her uncle. "It was subtle and very focused on me. On *my* pleasure."

It was hard to note the color of her cheeks in the weak light of the fire, but I could tell she was embarrassed, and my chest tightened.

"He, uh, he'd put some sort of stimulants in my baths. They made my body feel...relaxed. And fuzzy. Then he'd turn on the jets and show me how to sit so they'd, uh, hit me in the right place. And I'd sit there like that, feeling good while he read me erotic stories. Twisted fairy tales where Red Riding Hood got devoured by the wolf in a carnal way and where Sleeping Beauty was woken up with kisses in obscene places.

"His touch wandered too. Beneath my dresses, into my panties.

Never going all the way inside me, but stimulating all the areas around it. He trained my body to his touch. Before I'd even had a period, he taught me how to respond. I thought I was made for him."

"Celia..." *You were made for* me. The words caught in my mouth, not wanting my devotion confused with her repugnant uncle, but feeling the need to say *something*. Anything.

She waved me away with her hand, knowing better than I did that it wasn't the right time. "He didn't make me call him sir until I was ten," she said. "From then on, it was always, 'Yes, sir.' 'No, sir.' 'What should I do for you, sir?' That was when I first remember being really unhappy about our relationship. It took that long. Isn't that stupid?"

"No," I said harshly, even though I knew the question wasn't for me.

She ignored me. "It started to feel like a chore then. The special princess feeling was still there, but it took more and more effort to get his love. And that was *my* fault, or so I believed. He'd done all these nice things for me and spent all this time with me, and I couldn't understand why I was so resentful about it all. Why I didn't appreciate it. I figured I was spoiled and ungrateful, just like my mother liked to say when I was acting out."

I brought a fist up to my mouth, a reminder to keep it shut. There were so many things I wanted to say to her, and none of them were important. She barely even acknowledged my presence anymore. She was in it, regurgitating the memories without any need of prompting.

"Then the parties started when I was eleven. And that's when I began to hate him. The first one was innocent enough—a bunch of men drinking and smoking cigars while my uncle paraded me around in a fancy dress. Several fancy dresses." She let out a disgusted chuckle. "He told me to pretend it was a fashion show, and then afterward, I was to mingle with 'my fans.' Nothing salacious really, but it felt creepy all the same. How they'd reach out and pet me like I was a dog or a doll. Passing me around to sit on their laps. Twirling their fingers through my hair.

"The next year was..." She shook her head slowly, her eyes closed, and I could only imagine the horrors that she relived behind her lids.

When she opened them again, she let out a long breath before speaking. "I don't know why I didn't tell my parents that year. I knew it was wrong, and I didn't want to go back, but I felt trapped. I felt like I'd agreed to it all, somehow, sometime, and of all the things he taught me, he'd never taught me how to back out.

"So, when I was thirteen, I returned. And I was nervous about it already, especially after...after the last time."

She'd tell me about that too, eventually. She needed to expel it more than I needed to hear it, but I needed to hear it too. I needed to hear every evil thing that had been done to her so that I could properly make up for it.

Later, though. When she was ready.

"I'd already decided that if he had another party, I was going to find some way out of it. I'd pretend I was sick. I'd make myself sick, if I had to. I'd even brought a bottle of Ipecac syrup I'd stolen from the medicine cabinet back home, planning to use that to prove my illness, but the fucker didn't warn me this time. He'd sent me to bed for the night early, and I'd thought that got me off the hook.

"It must have been after midnight when he came and woke me. He gave me a sheer nightie to put on—it was a rule that I slept naked when I was at his house, then he took me down to the conservatory, the room where he entertained. There were fifteen men there. Maybe a few more. The room had a level change, a couple steps up to a stage-like area, you know, for, like, a band. He led me up there and then he..." She swallowed then cleared her throat. "He untied the straps of the gown and let them fall so I was naked. I tried to put my arms around me, to cover up, but he batted my hands down, and made me stand there like that. Everything on display. I mean, really on display. He showed me off like I was merchandise. 'Look at how pert her nipples are.' Then he'd turn me around and spread my cheeks apart. 'Look at her virgin ass.' 'See how pretty her virgin pussy is.'

"Then he auctioned me off."

She stopped, and I was relieved, unable to take another second of her story, but also desperate to hear every last word. I warred between the choice of telling her it was enough and pushing her on.

Because it was about her, because she was so close to the finish line, I prodded her on. "He *sold* you?" When I'd asked how she'd lost her virginity, she'd wanted to know what I'd meant exactly. She hadn't had her cunt penetrated, but there were a lot of other ways she could have been violated. I could picture the scene in my head and still couldn't wrap my head around it.

"Yeah. Basically. He was decent enough to stipulate that no one could actually fuck me. No dicks could come in contact with any part of me, but that was the only rule. They could touch me anywhere without penetration, and no one was to touch my ass—still a virgin there, thank God. They were allowed to come on me. They could use a vibrator for stimulation. They just had to pay for it."

"*Jesus*," I muttered, under my breath. I gripped the bottle in my lap, wanting to throw it. Wanting to destroy something as badly as this monster had destroyed Celia. It took everything in me just to bring it to my lips instead, letting the burn temper my rage. How dare a man do this to a child? To his own flesh and blood?

"Five of them offered the right price. They took turns, right there, in front of everyone else. Two of them helped Ron lift the chaise up to the stage so they could prop me how they wanted me. They touched me everywhere they were allowed. All five of them came on me. On my back, on my belly. On my tits. Two of them on my face. It was in my hair. I accidentally tasted some that was on my lips. The worst were the vibrators, though. Ron had several for them to choose from and they used them all at least once. They loved making me come. Over and over. That was the most humiliating and confusing part, because it made me feel like I must be enjoying it, while I was dying inside. *Dying.*"

I cringed, thinking of how I'd used her orgasms as a punishment, justifying it at the same time because I hadn't used a vibrator. And then wishing I had so that that memory might replace this terrible one.

"You know, I don't even know what any of them paid because the offers were whispered into Ron's ear. He'd either nod or give a thumbs up to indicate he wanted more. Sometimes I imagine they paid very little because that would serve him right. Other times I imagine they paid a fuck-ton because those fucking bastards deserved to pay up.

"It was after that, I told my father. He didn't believe me, and eventually I shut up about it, and the next summer, I was prepared to convince my best friend to invite me to her churchy camp so that I wouldn't have to go stay with Ron, but I didn't have to. My parents took me to Europe with them instead. And then they never mentioned going to Ron's again, and I don't know if it's because my father secretly believed me or if he just decided that he didn't want to deal with my protests, but it was over, and I was so relieved.

"But I was also only ordinary after that. And maybe that was the most horrible part of all of it. As glad as I was to never go back there, I've spent my life since wondering if anyone will ever give me the time and attention and adoration that Ron did. Sick, huh? No wonder I fell for my captor." Immediately, she brought her hands up to her forehead, shielding her eyes, as if she regretted saying the last part.

What was sick was how my entire being lit up at the admission, even in the midst of her horrible tale. She'd fallen for me, and I didn't deserve it, and I wasn't noble enough to try to convince her of that truth.

I couldn't be away from her a second longer, whether she had more to say or not. I was breaking for her and dying to hold her. I needed her touch as much as I was sure she needed mine.

I moved to kneel in front of her and grasped her wrists, peeling her hands away from her face so I could look her in the eyes. "None of this is your fault, bird. None of your reactions are wrong. Your uncle is a fucked-up psychopath and deserves to face severe repercussions for what he did, and none of this is your fault."

She shook her head vehemently, and so I said it again. Slower. "None of this is your fault, and you don't have to be brave about it anymore."

Her expression faltered, and I thought she was going to go there, was going to release herself to the pain, but the moment passed and her face turned hard.

"What, Edward? You think you understand me now?" She tried to yank away from me, but I held my grip.

"I know I do," I said solemnly, never moving my eyes from hers.

"You don't understand anything."

"I do. I understood you before too. This just gives clarity."

She was quiet for a beat, and I let go of her so I could move up beside her, intending to pull her into my lap.

But as soon as I was sitting on the sectional, she jumped to her feet. "It confirms my worth, doesn't it?" She began rapidly unbuttoning her shirt—*my* shirt. "I told you I knew what I was good for. Now you know too."

When she had the shirt loose, she dropped it to the ground and climbed onto me, straddling my lap.

This was all wrong. She was hiding behind this seduction routine. Building walls, trying to distract herself from the emotions she still hadn't let herself really feel. "Celia...what are you doing, bird?"

She began gyrating against me. "What I've been trained to do. What I'm best at."

"Don't." I sat back, bracing my arms on the back of the sectional so I wouldn't be tempted to touch her. It was harder to convince my cock not to react, but somehow I did.

"Am I too damaged for you now? Too used?"

My chest pinched. "Never."

"Then fuck me. I need to feel good. Make me feel good."

Her plea was desperate and heart wrenching, and I wrestled with the lure of her body, the smell of her arousal, the nearness of her mouth.

"Stop," I said, the word coming out tight and gritted.

Her lips pressed against my jaw. "What's wrong? You have to be the aggressor? Are those the rules between us? Just let me know because I'm good at rules, but only if I know them."

She was intoxicating. Hard to resist.

But the revulsion of her tale still hung in the air around us, and there was no way I could let this moment turn lustful. No matter how much she thought she wanted it now. She'd appreciate my restraint later, when she was thinking straight.

Abruptly, I flipped her to the cushion, pinning her wrists over her head. "I said stop."

"Not good enough for you to fuck now, am I?" Her chest heaved with each breath, her fury wrapped up in the movement of air through her lungs.

There wasn't anything I wouldn't do to take her pain from her, if I could. But since I couldn't, she had to actually *feel* it. It was the only way to get through it, and I'd be there for her every step of the way if she let me.

Just not like this. "I don't want fucking me to be associated with this place you're in right now."

"You're supposed to replace it."

"And I will. But not yet. Not this way."

She wrestled away from me, and I let her go, deciding that her retreat was progress, especially when she snatched the shirt off the ground and secured it around herself with two buttons.

But she was angry at me. Some of it misplaced anger, some of it masking other emotions. "What good are you then? Fuck you."

She started to walk toward the stairs, and I jumped up to block her. "You shouldn't be alone right now. If you want to go someplace else, that's fine, but I'm going with you."

"Confining me to this island isn't enough? Now I'm a prisoner in this house too?"

"We can argue about your prisoner status at a later time. Right now I care that you're my wife, and I'm not leaving you alone in this state."

"Your wife?" She balled her hands into fists and threw them against my chest. "Fuck you." When I didn't budge, she hit me again. "Fuck you!"

I stood my ground, then, when she veered around me, I stepped in front of her and held her at her upper arms.

She struggled against my hold, the tears finally reaching her eyes with her frustration. "This isn't fair. If you aren't going to make it better then let me go. Just let me go!"

I pulled her closer, and spoke calmly at her ear. "I am going to make it better, but being alone is not what you need right now. And neither is sex."

"It's exactly what I need right now," she said, wrestling against my grip. When she realized I wasn't letting her go, she shoved at me with her palms. "Asshole." Another shove. "Devil." She pushed harder this time. "Fuck you, Edward. Fuck you for making me talk about this." Her voice cracked, the dam about to break.

"Keep going. I can take it." I braced myself for an onslaught.

Her next shove felt more like a punch. "Fuck you for thinking this would be good for me," she said, the tears flowing freely now. Another punch followed. "Fuck you for making me feel special." And another. "Fuck you for making me feel good. Fuck you for using me like that. Fuck you for breaking me down. Fuck you!"

I wasn't sure anymore if her curses were meant for me or for the uncle who had damaged her so reprehensibly. Possibly she meant them for us both, it didn't matter. I deserved her hatred and her pain, whomever the target was. I wanted to carry it all. It would fuel me in the future when I needed it. When my wrath was carried out appropriately.

For now, I tucked it away.

And when her bellows morphed into weeping, when her body convulsed with gut-wrenching sobs, I picked her up and cradled her in my arms, whispering sweet, soothing words while her tears soaked my skin, and she finally found release.

TWENTY-FIVE

CELIA

I SWEPT my hair to one side, and held it out of the way so that Edward could fasten the chain at my neck. "Is this for my birthday or our anniversary?" I asked, watching him in the mirror.

With deft fingers, he worked the clasp, then trailed the tips along my nape sending a delicious shiver through my body before moving his hands down to grip my hips. He met my eyes in our reflection. "The necklace is for your birthday." He pressed a kiss at the side of my throat. "The night out is for our anniversary."

I fiddled with the bird charm, a pretentious showcase of colored gemstones and diamonds, normally too gaudy for my taste, but the most perfect gift because of its symbolism. "By wearing this, I feel like I'm giving in to something. I was supposed to be a dragon that night, not a bird."

He chuckled. "It's always the tiniest dogs with the biggest barks."

I turned to face him directly, his man and musk scent smacking me so abruptly my thighs clenched automatically. "What's that supposed to mean?"

"That the smallest creatures always think they're scarier than they are."

He leaned in for a kiss, and I leaned away. "You think you can just kiss me after you belittle me like that?" I teased.

His hand came to hold my chin in place. "I think I can do whatever I want with what belongs to me, so yes."

I didn't fight when his mouth took mine, eager for his lips despite my taunting. It was a thorough kiss, one I felt down to my toes, and I wondered briefly how hard it would be to convince Edward to celebrate at home.

Then I remembered our date was taking me off the island, for the first time in a year, and I wasn't missing that for the world. I put my hands up to his satin lapels and pressed slightly, trying to keep some distance from him before he swallowed me up whole. As if he hadn't already.

He took the hint and, after another deep swipe of his tongue, he pulled away. "Anyway, it wasn't an insult. It was an observation." He rubbed at the spot below my lower lip where my makeup had smeared. "This lipstick isn't going to cut it. I plan on doing that a lot tonight, and you won't be given the opportunity to fix it every time I do."

"This lipstick will be fine," I said, shooing him away. "You just need to give it time to dry before you do that again."

He twisted his wrist to glance at his watch. "You get five minutes. Then we're off." In a rare show of consideration, he left me so I could touch-up what he'd ruined without interference.

I took a deep breath, an attempt to settle the nerves he'd riled up, and turned back to the mirror. After fixing the lipstick, I studied my appearance. The dress he'd chosen was black with gold touches on the arms and at the waist. Though it was floor-length and long-sleeved, it was definitely one of the most revealing outfits I'd ever worn, the neckline plunging all the way to my waist. A slit up the front of one leg went all the way to my upper thigh, and Edward's refusal to let me wear panties made my pussy dangerously vulnerable to exposure.

"*Better access,*" he'd said, when I'd questioned him about the choice earlier.

"*Does that mean you're planning on taking advantage of that access?*"

"We'll have to see how the night plays out, won't we?"

My cheeks reddened remembering the conversation, but even without the blush, my pallor was better than it had been in more than a month. Our session of confessions on the rooftop lounge had lanced open deep wounds. I'd been a wreck of myself afterward. Emotions that I'd smothered and ignored grew to vibrant life in the air, emotions that were toxic and corrupt and needed to be felt. Memories I'd buried resurfaced in waves. I spent days at a time crying, releasing the pain of a childhood I'd never been allowed to lament.

Edward had been at my side through the worst of it, holding me. Touching me. Forcing me to eat and move. Refusing to let me stay in bed and sleep away the agony. I'd tried more than once to make it physical, wanting his cock to distract me from my suffering, but he'd remained as chaste as he had in the earlier days of our marriage, insisting that sex would only confuse the things I was working through.

He'd been right, admittedly. Not that I'd wanted to see that at the time.

After a week of sobbing, I'd woken up with a new energy. Not better—not by a long shot—but determined to start moving forward. And that required something that Edward couldn't directly provide. I needed therapy, and I needed time. He arranged the first without a debate, flying in a psychiatrist to stay at Amelie and give me one-on-one counseling.

The second, took more convincing. He'd insisted on staying with me, and I'd insisted that he leave. When I had pointed out that ignoring his business in favor of walking me through my mental health wasn't any different than his father's choice to abandon his career during his wife's illness, Edward had finally seen reason. He'd been gone for almost four weeks, and while my therapist had pressed for it to be longer, my husband refused to stay away for my thirty-third birthday, which fell on our one-year anniversary.

Though we hadn't talked about it, things had definitely changed between us. It was most evident in the lax of the rules that had surrounded my captivity before. Besides bringing in a doctor who spoke my language, I was now allowed on the internet, and Edward and I had spoken by phone several times a week. The conversations were always short, mostly perfunctory, but they'd made me feel cared for all the same. Never once had we discussed the nature of our relationship. He hadn't given me rules of what to say or who not to contact. There had been an agreement of trust when I hadn't taken his offer to walk away, and maybe I appreciated it too much to defy it or I was too absorbed in my PTSD, but I hadn't once thought to use my privileges to "escape." There wasn't anything I wanted to escape from, except the scars that the past had inflicted upon me, and I truly felt I had the best shot at that right where I was.

Even so, I was beyond excited for the outing he'd planned.

"You're really not going to tell me where we're going?" I asked after we'd been in the air for an hour. I'd been surprised when he'd taken me to the airstrip instead of the dock, assuming he'd meant to take me to Nassau for a fancy dinner. Apparently, his plans were grander than that.

Though I was fully aware of the bedroom in the back of the plane, we'd spent the flight talking, mostly about my therapy sessions, which had been uncomfortable, at first, then better as we'd talked on. I'd told him a lot of the most terrible things my uncle had done to me that night on the roof, and the initial telling of it should have been the worst part, but in my game-playing I'd learned there was a human tendency to feel the shame after the words were out, and my reaction had been exactly that. It was easier to try to forget I'd said those things, forget that he'd heard them, but he refused to let me, digging in and picking up the burden of those confessions as if they were his own. He wanted to know it all, every detail of the horrors, every memory as I uncovered it, and I found myself wanting to tell him all of it as well. There was still so much to go through, so many parts to remember and process.

But now, the plane had begun its descent, and I wanted to put aside the awful and focus on our anniversary night.

"It was never a secret," he said, linking his fingers through mine. "You just never asked. We're going to Exceso, a private island between Cuba and Haiti. It's owned by a wealthy man I'm acquainted with who knows how to throw a certain kind of party."

I didn't know much Spanish, but I took a guess anyway. "Exceso —*excess*? As in extravagant?"

"Muy bien, pajarita," his Spanish accent doing things to my lower regions. When I frowned, he translated. "Very good, little bird. Esteban touts the island as a place for men with questionable ethics to negotiate business deals. While there is a fair amount of that occurring, it's mostly a hedonistic pleasure resort."

My stomach tightened. "Like The Open Door?"

"Yes. With fewer rules and more dubious consent."

"Oh." I withdrew my hand from Edward's so I could wrench it with the other in my lap. Anxiety bubbled up through my chest and my mouth suddenly tasted sour. It had taken a lot for me to convince myself to go to the party in New York, and that had been knowing the club was well-monitored and safe. And now, after all the focus on the ones Ron had forced me to attend, an unstructured sex party felt especially disarming.

No wonder Edward hadn't volunteered the information sooner.

He reached over to my lap and took both hands in his, putting a halt to my fidgeting. "You'll be with me, Celia, and that means you'll be safe. Do you trust me?"

He'd shown over the past month that he trusted me. It felt ungrateful not to offer him the same.

And I did trust him. Didn't I?

I mostly did, but that didn't mean I didn't question his judgment. "Is there a reason why you chose this event for our date?"

"Several reasons. First, some of the men who go to Exceso own the women they bring with them."

"As in slavery?" My heart felt like it was beating through mud. My captivity had been nothing like the horrific situations so many other women were in. Situations where they were beaten and abused and forced into all sorts of sick, depraved sexual acts. "How can you be friends with a man who allows such a thing? Why don't you do something?"

"I never said we were friends. Going against Esteban Merrado is not something a person does haphazardly. Besides, it's difficult to differentiate those women who are willing to be owned and those who aren't. It's merely my suspicion that some may not be there of their own volition. If I ever witnessed any abuses that I was assured were real, I would most likely involve authorities—if I could safely—but I have not as of yet. The situation does give me an advantage, however. No one at Exceso pays too much attention when a woman cries kidnapped. In other words, it's a place I can take you and not have to worry about you trying to get away."

So much for having gained his trust.

I tried to remove my hands from his grasp, but he kept them pinned in place.

"Secondly," he continued, "I owe you a response to your last session. It's time I gave it."

My eyes shot up to his, my spine tingling. I'd forgotten about the second part of those sessions. His responses, it seemed, were meant to replace the bad experiences from my past. Did he want to take me to a sex party where I had fun instead? So I wouldn't remember the ones with Ron?

I didn't know that it was as simple as that.

But it was a sweet gesture. And a sex party with Edward wasn't entirely off-putting. Not at all, actually.

"Third, I enjoy seeing you uncomfortable, as you are well aware." He gave me a smug smile. "It's my anniversary, too. You shouldn't get all the fun."

I scowled at him, but it was hard to hold it. He was too charming, and though his charm was far from innocent, I liked the way he used it on me.

He was my husband. And I was in love with him, and for good or bad, that meant I would follow willingly where he led.

"Fine. I'll go." As though he'd given me a choice.

"Somehow I knew you'd come around. I brought you something that might make it easier." He released my hands and reached down into the cabinet at the side of the couch where we sat and pulled out a familiar-looking box, which he handed to me.

"Another present?"

"Not quite. It's already yours."

Puzzled, I opened it up to find my red feathered mask, the one I'd worn at The Open Door. "My dragon mask!" I lifted it to my face and slipped it on.

"Pajarita," he corrected, but I was too touched with the gifts and the moment to even pretend to be offended.

We landed soon after, onto an island that was probably twice the size of Amelie, from what I could see on the descent, and was a lot more built up with various structures. Edward had called it a resort, and I could see why. I counted no less than four swimming pools, and dozens of cabanas lined the beaches.

From the airstrip, a planked path flanked with tiki torches led a short way through forest to an outdoor entertainment area. Evening was upon us, and the festivities were already in full swing. Spanish music played through speakers attached on pillars surrounding the space. Two open bars bookended a large wooden floor. Hammocks were hung at the perimeters and various seating arrangements dotted the expanse. Men in tuxes and women in cocktail attire were spread around, conversing and drinking the way people did at parties my parents hosted back home. There was no signs of debauchery. No signs of dubious consent. Innocent, by all appearances.

I relaxed, doubting suddenly the need for my mask.

Before I could reach to remove it, Edward had his hand at my back, guiding me toward a silver-haired man who was approaching us.

"Edward Fasbender!" the man exclaimed with a heavy accent, followed by some Spanish words that I surmised was a question of how my husband was doing based on the answer he provided.

"I've been well, Esteban. Busy, but well."

"And your little project? How is that going?"

I shot questioning eyes at Edward.

"It's, uh...delayed," he said, his eyes darting toward me making me wonder exactly how much of his Werner revenge scheme he had shared with his acquaintance. "I'm preoccupied with other things, at the moment. Allow me to introduce you to my wife, Celia."

He hadn't included my maiden name in my introduction, making me suspect it was on purpose.

"Ah!" Esteban said, his eyes lingering too long on my very exposed cleavage. "Quite exquisite, I must say. Hard to tell with the mask, but it seems you've gone with a younger model."

I already hated the man. He was smarmy and vile, and that could be gleaned just from his leer. If I spent more time with him, I could imagine how much more of his personality I would find I loathed.

"A younger model, yes. A better model, definitely." Edward's charm wasn't enough to counteract the repugnant stranger, but I held my tongue, gritting my teeth.

Since I hadn't been directly spoken to, there was no reason for me to speak.

Esteban moved closer, his eyes leaving foul stains on my skin. "Tell me, does she like to play the way your last one does? Should I have you escorted to the Resistance Room?" He reached out to run his knuckles across my jaw, and I flinched.

I didn't even want to know what the Resistance Room was. The name alone made me shudder. Though the suggestion that Marion had been there with Edward in the past spiked a curious jealousy.

Edward wrapped his arm around my waist, subtly pulling me into his side and out of Esteban's reach. "We're still learning what we like, at the moment. Tonight, we have something specific planned, however. The Base is open, isn't it?"

The man tsked. "Never any time for fun with you, is there? Yes. There are a handful of other workaholics already down there. Just a moment, and I'll summon one of my angels to take you there."

I followed his eyes as they landed on a woman I hadn't noticed before, wearing a white bikini and kneeling on the rough wood floor near the bar. Her head was down, but as Esteban clapped a syncopated rhythm, she looked up, then stood when she saw him gesture her over.

The whole interaction gave me the creeps. I'd studied the submissive thing, of course, seen it played out at The Open Door, and I could admit to seeing an appeal. But after Edward's hint that some of the women here might not just be submissive, but rather, slaves, I didn't have the stomach for it.

My expression must have given me away because Edward shook his head. "No need. I well know the way. Take care, if we don't see you again on the way out."

Esteban flicked his hand, dismissing his angel with a glower before beaming again at my husband. "That's too bad you don't have time to stay awhile. It would be a delight to watch you break your bride in. The learning phase is definitely the most fun."

His lecherous stare made my hand fly up to fiddle with my necklace, covering myself with my arm.

Edward understood, already steering me away as he gave his parting words. "Yes, indeed. Still, you know I prefer to do the learning in private."

"Forgive me for hoping you'd changed," Esteban called back, followed by more words in Spanish.

Then we were walking out of the arena down another planked path, and I let out an audible sigh of relief. "That man is disgusting."

"He is," Edward agreed. "Which is why I try to come here only when I need to."

"When you 'need' to?" His response had a thousand reactions warring in my head. What kind of business did Edward *need* to do with men that associated with Esteban? And what kind of playing had my husband done here in the past? "I'm sure you *needed* to bring Marion here," I said, the most petty of my thoughts making it to my lips first.

"I didn't need to bring Marion here as much as she needed to be brought here. For very different reasons than you need to be here. The needs that I've had met here have not been sexual, though I have enjoyed those activities here on occasion." The path wound through more forest, breaking off here and there to lead to one structure or another. Signs indicated where the routes led with names that had my head spinning such as Mistreatment Room and Sharing Sector and Recovery Center.

I tried to ignore the distractions of my surroundings and concentrated on what Edward had said. There were questions I should be asking, questions about what he thought I needed here and what needs he had met. I was terrified of what his answers might be, but that wasn't why I didn't ask. My preoccupation with his former wife held too much power over me.

"You said Marion was submissive. Like that woman back there? Esteban's angel?"

"Mm."

"Did she kneel like that for you? Would she come when you summoned her with just a snap of your fingers?"

He studied me as we walked, looking for what, I wished I knew so I could be careful not to show him. Not that he could see much behind the mask, but hiding from Edward was never truly possible.

"She did," he said after several silent steps. "When it fit appropriately into our lives. Which wasn't as often as she would have liked."

"What about you? Did you like it when she obeyed?"

"Very much."

My chest burned, and I blinked away the white spots in front of my eyes. I didn't have to dissect myself too much to understand my anger was with myself, not Marion. As much as I admittedly liked the times that Edward took control and dominated me, I could never be so docile as to kneel in a corner waiting to be summoned. I could never be completely obedient. And because Edward liked it, I wished I could be that. Longed for that nature with a desperation that ached as it rattled against my ribs.

"Is that what you want with me?" My voice was barely over a whisper. We hadn't even discussed what kind of future we might have, if we had one at all, and here I was asking like we'd decided we'd try.

But this answer felt important, like it might decide whether or not a future was something we *should* even discuss.

"Complete submission?" he asked, seeming to consider his response carefully. "I don't believe that's what you want to give me."

His ability to always see me usually made me feel divine. Right now, it made me feel like a bug on a windshield. I'd been flying high in our relationship until this topic smacked me in the face.

I pulled away from his hand at my back and stopped walking. "I'm not asking what you believe I want. I'm asking what *you* want."

He went another couple of steps before he realized I'd halted. When he turned back, his brow was furrowed, his expression impatient. "This wasn't exactly the place I planned to have this conversation, nor the time. But if you need to hear something, I'll make it simple. I want to own you. Does that mean I want you kneeling at my feet like a well-trained dog? No, it absolutely does not. It does mean I want respect and deference, and yes, obedience, in measures that I believe you'd like to give, even if you don't know that you would. I definitely think you're capable. Most primarily, though, I need there to be honesty and trust between us. You didn't answer before—do you trust me?"

It was my turn to wear furrowed brows. His words made me feel warm and hopeful, but also hesitant, because what if he was wrong about what I could give? What if he was wrong about who I really was?

And because I had those doubts, it was hard to say that I exactly trusted him.

Honesty. He wanted honesty.

"I trust you, Edward, as well as I can right now. With as much as I can."

His eyes flashed with disappointment, so fast I almost was unsure I'd seen it. "That's a start. Let me ask you something smaller, then. Do you trust me with you here tonight? Do you trust that I have only your best interests in mind? Do you trust that I know what you can and can't handle, that I will care for you body and soul until we leave this island?"

I bit my lip, considering. It was a fair question. We were at a sex club, a place where trust was important, and I wanted to be here with him, even though he still scared me.

He scared me, but he'd never truly hurt me. And more than once he'd understood what I wanted and needed better than I did myself.

"Yes, I trust you," I finally answered. "But it doesn't mean that I'm not worried too."

He smiled slyly as he crossed the few steps back to me. Tipping my chin up with the knuckle of a crooked finger, he said, "I enjoy your apprehension as much as I enjoy your submission. I think this will work out just fine."

"Okay," I said tentatively. But there were still so many questions about what he wanted from me, what respect and deference and obedience looked like. What he expected out of our marriage. What he expected from me. "What about—?"

He cut me off. "The rest can wait." He nodded to the sign at the path that veered behind him. *The Base.* "We're here."

TWENTY-SIX

MY KNEES WERE SHAKING as we approached the unassuming building before us. There were no windows, which made it all the more intimidating. The only kind of buildings I could think of without windows were the scary kind—prisons, dungeons. I shivered at the possibilities.

A security guard stood outside the two large wooden doors, which didn't help my trepidation. Especially when he scanned us both with a wand before we were allowed to enter. So Esteban didn't want weapons in his play spaces. Did he prefer to provide them himself?

As soon as the guard had cleared us for entry, I stopped Edward, grabbing him by the arm. "I know what I said to you about being able to take anything that you could dish, but I gotta tell you—I was all talk. I really don't like pain. Not real pain. I mean, the spankings are nice, but whips and floggers and other torture devices just aren't my thing. If you're really into them, I'll try. I really will, but I already know I'm not going to be very good at it because even the idea has me sweating and scared, and please don't make me do it. Please, Edward, please."

The guard laughed out loud behind me. "Newbie?"

Edward, at least, tried to hide his amusement. "I think it's obvious," he answered, then focused on me. "Why don't you step inside and take a look around before you work yourself into a panic?"

I pursed my lips. It was bad enough that I was terrified. Worse to be laughed at.

But Edward's voice was calm and his hand at my back, soothing. "Fine," I agreed, hoping my heart didn't beat out of my chest.

With a small smile, he wrapped his hand around the large metal handle and pulled the door open, stepping aside so I could go in ahead of him.

I took two steps and then froze, surprised by what I saw. I'd forgotten another type of building that didn't have windows, the kind of building that held objects that could be damaged by the light—a library.

The Base was the largest private library I'd ever been in. Bookcases wrapped around the walls of the massive room. On top of that, a wooden spiral staircase led to a second level housing more shelves. So many books. I felt dizzy from the sight. I'd been ecstatic with the collection Edward had given me the previous Christmas, but that gift was minuscule compared to what lay before me. My fingers itched to circle the perimeter, to drag their tips along the spines, to pick up each precious volume and hug it to my chest. I could live in a room like this without complaints. I could die here, and I'd be happy.

"I didn't realize it was so easy to make you orgasm," Edward said at my ear. "I've been doing it wrong."

I laughed, the sound more boisterous than intended as my wound-up nerves released into it. "I do like my books. But believe me, you haven't been doing anything wrong."

"I'm relieved." His tone, though, suggested he'd never been too concerned in the first place. "Let's go get a drink, shall we?"

I blinked, taking in the other aspects of the room I'd originally over-looked, too blinded by the array of books. The room wasn't quite a library, but more like a den. Couches and recliners were set up in various tableaus. There were also conference tables and more than one area set up with computers. And there was a full bar tucked neatly next to one of the fireplaces.

"Smoke and alcohol around books? Disgusting." It was the same with most private libraries I'd been in, but it didn't make me any less appalled.

"Francesco hasn't even brought out the cigars yet," Edward said, leading me toward the bar with his hand at the center of my back.

It was then that I truly noticed the people surrounding us. Twenty or so of them divided in groups throughout the space, mostly men in tuxes. The few women in attendance appeared to be accessories. Toys, rather, considering the lady giving a blow job underneath a table while her partner sipped his amber-colored beverage and spoke nonchalantly with his peers.

While Edward ordered our drinks, I scanned the room again, noticing more sexual play that I'd missed at first look. A woman in a white bikini—another of Esteban's angels, likely—knelt at the feet of one of the men in an armchair. Across the room, the man dressed in traditional Middle Eastern garb was fingering the woman on his lap, even though he was engaged in an intense discussion with the balding gentleman sitting across from him.

"He's a sheikh," Edward said as he handed me the tumbler. "Believe it or not. The man next to him is in oil. The man he's arguing with is an arms dealer."

I took a sip of the brandy, suddenly understanding why there'd been a security check. "Legal arms dealer?" I asked optimistically.

"Very little of what happens here is legal, bird."

My insides felt cold. "What is this place?"

Edward brought his tumbler to his lips, taking a swallow before answering. "It's a negotiation room. I told you before that Esteban touts the island as a place for men with few ethics to do business. This is where that business occurs, in this room. It's neutral territory. Many powerful enemies meet here to discuss nefarious deals."

"And this is the part of the island that meets your needs." I couldn't decide if it was thrilling or despicable to realize that. "What am I doing here, Edward?"

"You like the books, don't you?" It was less of an answer and more of a distraction, and I wasn't dumb enough to think anything else.

"Why don't you finish your drink while you look around? Esteban will have small plates brought out soon, if you're hungry."

I looked at him with narrowed eyes. "And what will you be doing?"

"Conversing with old friends. Catching up. Nothing you should worry about."

I could feel the corners of my mouth turning down, but I was determined not to pout. I'd already known Edward was a devil. My father had even warned me that he was a man with questionable ethics. This sort of scene was part of that. Part of him. I should be grateful not to know the details, keep my head down, and my mouth shut.

It wasn't in my nature, but it was our anniversary. Behaving could be the gift I gave him. Absentmindedly, I rubbed the bird charm between my fingers. "Fine. I'll be perusing. But don't you dare think I'll be summoned with a clap of your hands."

He smiled. "Never."

I spent the next three hours combing through the stacks, breaking once when the food was brought out to cushion my stomach before refilling my brandy. Despite the pleasure the sight of all the books gave me, there were fewer treasures than I would have hoped for. Most everything was nonfiction, many were books on law and tax codes on various countries in various languages. There was also a large section devoted to business strategy as well as war strategy, and another larger section on the history of almost every nation.

Upstairs, though, I found some items worth savoring. First editions of a few of my favorite classics as well as a very impressive wall of rare books. I took my mask off for these, carefully inspecting fragile bindings, noting the strange typesets and languages inside. It was enough to keep me preoccupied, and I only found myself looking for Edward once or twice. I felt his eyes on me, however, constantly.

Eventually, when my eyes started to grow weary and raw—apparently Francesco had brought out the cigars by this time—I put my mask back on and went back down the stairs in search of my husband. Attendance had grown over the evening, doubling in size. A few more women had arrived, most wearing little or nothing at all. The hair at the nape of my neck stood up as the scene reminded me less of a party at The Open Door and more of the kinds hosted by my uncle.

I was ready to leave.

Hopefully, Edward was as well.

He was easy to find, tucked comfortably into the corner of one of the sofas, a cigar in one hand, a tumbler in the other, his expression carefully guarded. When he caught sight of me, he set down his cigar in a nearby ashtray and stood to meet me.

"Hello, my dragon," he said after thoroughly kissing me. The endearment and the taste of him suggested he might have had more than a couple brandies while I'd been away. Especially when his hand wandered inside my dress to roughly fondle my breast.

"Edward," I admonished with a blush, my eyes darting to the crowd.

"Yes, yes, you're right. I must make introductions." Apparently he hadn't correctly interpreted my reprimand, but he moved away to set down his drink and now his hands were off me, and I missed his touch more than I wanted to admit.

I needn't have worried. A moment later, his arm was around me again, settling at my waist as he turned to face the group closest to us.

"Gentlemen—and ladies, but mostly gentlemen," he said, his voice loud enough to reach those seated farther away as well. He paused to chuckle with those who laughed. "Allow me to introduce you to my wife, Celia. She's new to Exceso, and it's our anniversary. I promised her a good time."

Eyebrows rose and glances exchanged. Some hoots and hollers filled the air. Whispers could be heard but not made out. The weight of several leering gazes hit me at once.

It wasn't that I didn't like to be watched. There were situations where I found the notion quite appealing. Watching Edward with Sasha at The Open Door had been arousing, and I could only imagine how much more arousing I would have found it if I'd been the one being played with.

But this audience was not that audience. These men were not good men. These men were the kind that had my skin crawling and my stomach churning.

I coiled into my husband. "Edward, can we go?" I asked quietly.

"Not yet, bird. Patience." His hand made its way back to my breast, this time pulling on my nipple until it was fully erect.

It was impossible not to react to his touch, uncomfortable as I was with the surroundings. He knew how to manipulate my body, how to make me erupt in birdsong.

"She's remarkable, Edward," said a man nearby.

"Flawless," said another.

"Obscenely beautiful," said a third.

Edward basked in the compliments as though they'd been about him, and of course, in a way they were, since this was an environment where women were nothing but mere possessions, and I belonged to him. It was to be expected, considering.

What I hadn't expected was Edward's response. "You should see her when she comes."

I could feel the heat spread down my neck. I was mortified.

"Does she come on command?" a thin, pale-skinned man asked, the woman accompanying him turning her head, but not before I caught her frown.

Yeah, lady, I know how you feel.

"She's more work than that." He pulled me tighter to him with one hand, the other reaching down to stroke my pussy through my dress. "Aren't you, my dragon?"

I gasped from the contact as well as the conversation. "Edward," I whispered. "I'm really uncomfortable right now."

"But she's worth it," he went on, not hearing me, perhaps. "The taste of her pussy alone is worth it."

Despite myself, I got wet. My pussy liked being talked about. Liked being talked about by Edward, anyway, even in shady company.

"That's not fair to taunt like that unless you're willing to share." The accent was South African, but I'd missed who said it.

"I could be willing," Edward said, and my stomach dropped. "What's your offer?"

"What are you doing?" I hissed. Was he drunk? Did he think this was fun?

"Ten large to lick her cunt," the South African replied.

A wave of nausea roiled through me. I was going to be sick. This was too much like that night at Ron's. I couldn't do this again.

I tugged at Edward's jacket sleeve. "We need to go."

He pulled my hand from his arm and held it tightly in his grasp, his eyes remaining on the man who'd spoken. "Ten thousand? That's all you have to offer for the taste of the divine?"

"I'd give you twenty to let me come on her tits," said someone else.

"I'm not even going to respond to that. I'm insulted."

This was his response, I realized. This was his way of replacing what Ron had done. But this didn't feel good. It felt just as wrong, just as dirty. It made me feel as much like a whore as my uncle had ever made me feel.

"Edward," I pleaded. "Whatever you think you're doing, this isn't helping. Okay? It's not helping. Please, stop."

"A brick then," the last negotiator countered. "Still insulted?"

Edward glanced at me and for a moment I thought he'd heard me—finally heard me.

But then he turned back to the man. "Look at her, really look at her. A brick for these?" He let go of my wrist so he could once again slip his hand inside my dress. He lifted my breast up and squeezed. "Her tits are perfection."

A tear slid down my cheek behind the mask. "Is this all staged?" I asked, with sudden optimism. He'd been alone down here for so long. Maybe this was all a setup. Maybe these men weren't really bidding for me. "Did you tell them to say these things?"

"Don't be ludicrous," he said.

"You're genuinely worth paying to touch, sweetheart." The oil man winked as he rubbed the crotch of his pants.

I turned my body so I couldn't see him, but Edward, seeming to think I meant to leave, tightened his grasp at my waist, drawing me back into him. My panic escalated with being pinned, and I struggled to get free, only to be overpowered when he brought his other arm into the battle.

"One million to fuck her." This from the arms dealer.

Edward perked up. "One million?"

"I'd want her all night."

"I've seen what you do to women," Edward scoffed. "She's no good to me broken."

The tears started in earnest. This wasn't staged. This was real, and I realized with dread that I didn't really know the man I'd married. How had I been so drawn in to him? I'd let him pull the wool over my eyes. Let myself believe he cared for me, when he was really just as vile as anyone else in the room.

He'd never professed to being a good man. He'd been clear he was a sadist, turned on by the discomfort of others. Just as I'd feared, he'd taken my past and was using it against me. He was really doing this, not for the money, but for fun.

"Two million," someone else offered now. "All night, comes back the way she came. Except happier." Laughter scattered throughout the room, a menacing contrast to the terror happening inside me.

"Fucking let me go, right now." I yanked harder, determined to run.

With an annoyed grunt, Edward twisted his body around mine to get a better hold.

"She doesn't seem to be interested in you, Juri," a man with a French accent laughed.

Juri harrumphed. "She doesn't seem to be interested in being shared at all."

"Half the fun, right?" Edward said with a sneer.

"Please, stop this," I sobbed. "Please. Why are you doing this?" My knees had lost all ability to hold me up. The only reason I wasn't in a pile on the floor was because Edward had me constrained.

And no one would help me! Everyone sat and watched, amused by the entertainment, not caring that my husband was offering to sell my body against my will. They had to know I was upset, despite my covered face. My entire being shook from the force of my crying.

"Has she been fucked in the ass?" a voice came from the back.

"Virgin," Edward responded, and I gasped in horror.

The bids came out faster and higher after that.

"Four million."

"Five."

"Ten and you can watch. All of you can watch."

The world went dark at the edges, my heartbeat whooshing in my ears. The sounds around me became muffled and I retreated into myself. I'd managed to live through what happened in my past, but I wouldn't live through this. I couldn't survive a night forced in a stranger's bed. Edward's betrayal alone was enough to kill me.

But what if it wasn't betrayal? He'd always seen me as I was, even when I couldn't. Maybe he saw what my uncle had seen in me because that was what I really was—nothing. Useless. Only worth my physical appearance and my body. What could be done with my body.

Only honesty between us, he'd said. Then his honest message was that I had no value, and as hard as it was to accept it, it didn't make it any less the truth.

Then, through the din and darkness, Edward let go of me. My knees buckled, taking me to the floor as he exploded with a roar. "She's not for sale! Do you hear me? No one here can have her."

The room went abruptly quiet, stunned into silence, and I lifted my head, blinking away tears to look at my husband.

His expression was furious and intense, his face red, his teeth bared. He scanned the room, making sure everyone saw his anger. "There's not enough money to let any one of you come near her let alone touch her. A single breath from her body is worth more than any of your entire lives."

I couldn't move. I couldn't get air into my lungs. My jaw hung open. I felt dizzy and cold.

"Fuck, Edward that was a good one. Next time I'll kill you for it, so enjoy this one for a while."

Vaguely, I was aware of similar chattering amongst the crowd before people returned to their former conversations. Then Edward was kneeling in front of me, peeling off my mask so he could dab at my eyes with his handkerchief.

"Do you hear me?" he said, tenderly. "Your value cannot be named. You are priceless."

I didn't realize I was shaking my head until he spoke again.

"Listen to me, Celia. You are worth more than anything. There is no amount that would be enough to let anyone use you. No amount in the world."

Another tear slipped down my face. "But I'm nothing."

He gripped my chin between his fingers and held me tight, but not to the point of pain. "You are not nothing," he rasped, sternly. "If you were nothing, my world would not be completely changed by your existence. If you were nothing, I could give you up, I could walk away. If you were nothing, I would not have been moved from the trajectory that I've been on since my father took his own life. You are a planet of an obstacle, and as hard as I've tried to fight it, I am in your orbit now. You are not nothing. You are *everything*."

There was no refuting him. His tone was adamant and final, and I believed him, not just because I wanted to, but because his constant insistence on honesty made it impossible to believe he'd tell this lie.

But this truth was so enormous, so overwhelming that I was left speechless. With my lip quivering, I could only respond with a single nod.

Then he stood and lifted me into his arms, and I clung to him as he carried me out of the hedonistic den and into the light of the dark black night.

TWENTY-SEVEN

OUTSIDE, Edward put me on my feet and escorted me on a path back to the airstrip that bypassed the welcome arena where we'd met Esteban. We walked in silence, my hand clutched in his, my head too dazed to do anything but follow.

Once we reached the plane, however, I found myself. It was like coming out of a fog how one minute I was content to be led and the next, I wanted the reins for myself. I was in love with this man, so deeply and recklessly in love, and he'd said some pretty noble things to me back at The Base, things that were planted in me like little seeds that I intended to help grow.

But he'd also been one-hundred percent a dick.

I came to a halt at the foot of the stairs, snatching my hand away from his. When Edward turned back in question, I pressed my palms against his chest and pushed, catching him off guard.

"You fucking asshole," I spit. "How could you do that to me?"

He put his hands up in surrender. "Hold on, now. Let's not overreact."

I pushed at him again, putting more of my body into it. "Overreact? Are you kidding me? You fucking tried to *sell me!*"

"I would never have really sold you, and you know that."

"I don't know that! I definitely didn't know it when it was happening. And after my past...! Do you know how traumatic that was for me? Do you? *Do you?*" I pressed forward, twisting to shove him with my shoulder.

This time he caught me at the upper arms, his eyes meeting mine with a stern gaze, but when he opened his mouth to speak, I lunged forward and kissed him.

His grip on me loosened in surprise. Then, when I threw my arms around his neck, he pulled me in closer, meeting the thrust of my tongue with a slide of his own. There was still anger in the way my mouth worked his, but also gratitude. A lot of gratitude.

We were both breathless when we drifted apart. He rested his forehead on mine. "Ah, bird," he sighed into me. "I do know how traumatic it was. That was the point. If it was unremarkable, the new ending wouldn't be remembered. It had to be significant enough to replace the old."

A tear slid down my cheek. All the years of never crying, and lately I'd been doing it a lot.

"Why are you doing this for me?" My voice was a whimper. His motives were beyond my grasp, and the confusion left me as raw as his kindness.

Edward swiped my tear away with the pad of his thumb. "You're a smart girl. Can't you figure it out?"

I wanted to make a guess, but I wasn't brave enough. I wanted him to say it.

This wouldn't be the moment for those words, however. Instead of a declaration, he let his hands fall and took a step back, away from me.

"Celia." His tone was formal, only a hint of the affection he'd shown only a second before. "I need you to listen to me, now."

I frowned, afraid of what he would say next. "I'm listening."

"The plane is fully fueled. Igritte and Marco are prepared for a longer flight, if..." He trailed off, seemingly unsure how to proceed. "They'll go anywhere you want them to. You can board right now and tell them where you want to go, and they'll take you."

Confusion transformed to disbelief. "You mean, go without you?"

"I can easily get back to the island later. Don't concern yourself with that. Your passport is in the cabinet inside, where I'd had your mask. You shouldn't have any problem at customs."

The tears were back. The anger fueled. The hurt, unbearable. "After all that? After what you just did to me, *what you said to me,* you're going to leave me?" I rushed at him again, ready to beat him to a pulp, never mind the fact that he could easily overpower me. "Fuck you, Edward! How can you do this to me? How can you be such a monster? After everything, how can you expect me to live without you?"

I pummeled him with my fists, getting a few good hits in before he seized my wrists. "Shh. Shh." When I met his hushing with a string of curse words, he changed tactics. "Hold on, now. Listen to me. I am not leaving you, do you hear me?"

I paused my wriggling, waiting for him to expand.

"I'm not leaving you," he said again. "I'm giving you a chance to leave me."

He let that sink in.

He was giving me the option to walk away, unharmed. No longer his captive. It had been weeks since I'd considered myself a prisoner. I'd somehow forgotten that I still technically was.

Edward released one of my hands so he could sweep my hair behind my ear. "I'm giving you a chance to go, even though it is absolutely ruining me to say those words, and every second we continue to stand here, my resolve to let you do so slips away. So, hear me—take this chance. Get on that plane. I won't bear to be able to give you this opportunity again."

My breath shuddered through my lungs. "You've given me this option before. I already made this choice that night in your bedroom on Amelie."

"It wasn't fair to force that decision from you in the midst of sex. Right here, right now. This is the real choice."

I didn't hesitate. "I don't want to get on that plane alone. The only place I want to be is with you."

A spark of light flashed in his eyes. "If we board together, you understand what that means? You understand that you're accepting that you're mine?"

Mine.

He'd said it so many times and in such cruel ways that I hadn't ever really heard it for what it was. Possessiveness, yes. A claiming. But with the whole heart.

A kind of euphoria winded its way through my body, twining around my limbs, coiling in my chest, pressing against the steady beat of my heart. Our wedding had been a sham, our vows spoken under false pretenses.

Here, in this moment, this was where our marriage really began, and as the script is for all brides, I gave him an earnest answer. "I do."

The kiss that followed was rushed, both of us eager to get on the plane and off the island. Edward insisted that we buckle up for take-off, and somehow we managed to sit in our seats until we reached cruising altitude, our hands clasped together, a lightning storm of energy between us.

As soon as the pilot gave the indication that we'd reached altitude, Edward was on the ground, kneeling in front of me. I hadn't even undone my belt before he'd pushed my dress up my thighs, pulling me to the edge of the seat. He threw a leg over his shoulder, spread me wide and then his mouth found my pussy, greedy and weeping for him.

He easily drew two wicked orgasms from me before abruptly standing and yanking me to my feet. With our lips wrapped around one another, we stumbled to the bedroom where I eagerly worked his jacket off. Then his tie. Then began on his shirt buttons, my mouth never leaving his. He tasted like me and cognac and secrets and desire, and I wanted to lick every flavor out of him, until it was mine as well. Until our taste was the same.

His hands were busy as well, one wrapped around me to keep me steady while the other thrust two wicked fingers inside me, rubbing at my G-spot and coaxing another climax to take me over. When I was gasping his name, lost in another reeling whirlwind of pleasure, he pushed me backward to the bed. He found the top of the slit in my dress, now pushed up around my waist, and with an impressive show of determination, he split the material up the seam, all the way to where it dipped at my cleavage.

I wrestled out of the sleeves, leaving the tattered gown beneath me. He stared down at me with heated intensity, his gaze taking in every inch of my bare skin. I flushed from the warmth, and I distinctly thought that I would never get used to the way he looked at me. The way he opened me up and really saw me.

"Spread your legs," he said as he furiously stripped his shirt.

I did, bending my knees and resting the heel of my shoes on the edge of the bed so he could really see me. His eyes grew dark and hooded, and even next to a man with such fierce command, I felt powerful.

"Pinch those pretty nipples," he ordered next. "Pretend they're my fingers, and make them hurt."

I pinched hard, digging my nails in until I winced, and by the time he was naked and crawling over me, I was ready for his mouth to take over the work. He licked one steepled nipple, soothing the sensitive skin before his teeth nipped sharply.

My cry was lost to the jagged moan that erupted from my mouth as his cock plunged into me. His thrusts were deep and savage, each stab winding me tighter and tighter. He bent me in half, draping my heels over his shoulders and moving his knees to the outside of my hips, hitting me at an angle that found places inside me I'd never known. We were an orchestra of sound, my gasps and whimpers harmonizing with his primal grunts, the slap of his thighs against the back of my legs, a driving percussive beat.

And when we came, it was nearly together, his climax only a half-step behind mine, and I spiraled somewhere higher than I'd ever been, higher than the number displayed on the altimeter in the cockpit, and for the first time in my life, I found I wasn't afraid of flying.

Afterward, he collapsed at my side, only the edge of his body touching mine, but when his breathing returned to normal, he turned to his side and gathered me close to him, his legs twining with mine.

And then my heel dug into his calf, and he untangled himself only long enough to remove the dangerous items before wrapping back around me.

We lay quiet and content, me stroking the length of his torso while he caressed the side of my face. There was nothing awkward about the silence, but words bubbled inside me, loosened by the events of the night, and for once, I wasn't too intimidated to let them be said.

"Once upon a time," I said, trying to remember the way I phrased it the first time I'd begun this story. "I met with a businessman because I thought he wanted to hire me. I gave up my career, moved to London, and married him." I brought my hand up to his cheek. "Then he took me captive and threatened to kill me. Which he did. Slowly, but surely, he killed the worst parts of me, and I'll never be the same, and I wouldn't have it any other way."

He kissed me, tenderly, and I felt it then, how I truly did belong to him. Why else would he care so much about healing me? Why else would he sit patiently through sessions, responding to them thoughtfully?

"You didn't reveal anything about yourself this time," I said, missing that traditional component of his response.

His knuckles brushed along my cheek. "Didn't I?"

I thought about it. Thought about the things he said at The Base, then the words he'd said outside the plane. *"You're a smart girl. Can't you figure it out?"*

"You told me how you feel," I said, my chest blooming with the revelation.

"Go on."

I hesitated, nervousness creeping in like an old friend. "It's..." I hesitated. "It's the same way I feel about you."

"Which is?" A smile played on his lips.

I could feel his cock thickening at my thigh, and even now it was astonishing to see how my discomfort made him react. "You're turned on by this."

"Quite." His expression grew serious and stern. "Tell me."

Only honesty between us.

I took a deep breath. "I love you."

"Yes," he rasped, the evident weight of the syllable on his tongue, as raw as if he'd said the words instead.

He kissed me then, and as other kisses we'd shared had shown me what he wanted to do to my body, this one showed me what he wanted to do to my heart. Protect it, cherish it. Heal it. Love it.

I was bubbling and bouncing and overwhelmed and the unknown future that loomed over us was daunting but thrilling, and I couldn't wait for it. Couldn't wait to be with Edward in it, whoever I was anymore.

"You won," I sighed, realizing suddenly that I'd lost, and that it was wonderful. "You won, I'm yours. You've ruined me. You've broken me down. Now what?"

His gaze touched every part of my face—my swollen lips, my tilted chin, my flushed cheeks, my questioning eyes.

And when he answered, I knew it was the beginning of the next chapter, the beginning of something so much bigger than I could imagine.

"Now, I build you back up again."

The story continues in Slay Three: Revenge.

Edward and Celia's relationship changes once again when his focus for the future includes a past she wants to leave behind.

Need help recovering from Ruin?
Join the Recovery Room! See you there!

Order signed copies of this book and merchandise related to Slay on my website or listen to it on audio, narrated by

Elena Wolfe and Shane East.

You can find a timeline of events related to the Fixed series at the back of the book.

REVENGE: SLAY THREE

Their relationship changes again when Celia learns the devil takes care of his own.

Edward Fasbender is my savior.

From the ashes of who I once was, he is helping me to rise.

He has a list of people who have wronged him. And now he's adding names to that list. Names that I gave him.

And we will have our revenge.

*For Roxie who said
this was the best one yet
when I needed to hear it most.*

PROLOGUE

THEN: EDWARD

I CUPPED my hand over the end of the cigarette, blocking it from the wind as I lit it. My eyes closed, relishing the first draw in. It was like sucking instant Xanax. Exactly what I'd needed. My exhale released, the cloud thicker than when it had just been CO_2 mixing in the January air, and with it my anxiety shrank to something more manageable.

It was a nasty habit, one I fully intended on kicking soon, but the foster home where I'd spent the better part of the prior year had been full of smokers. It was easy to become addicted. Four months out of the environment, and I was still spending more than I liked to admit on cancer sticks. New Year's wasn't far behind us. Quitting had been among my list of resolutions. I planned on revisiting that tomorrow.

Today, I was grateful I still had the crutch.

I peered down the row of graves until my eyes landed on Camilla, kneeling on the cold ground, her hands clearing the leaves that had gathered over the base of the headstone. Even after spending the last several weeks with her, I still hadn't gotten used to how much she'd grown.

Or how young she still was.

She'd been seven when we'd been separated. In my mind, she'd stayed seven as I'd grown. I'd filed for custody as soon as I'd been old enough, on my birthday in September, but the paperwork had been slow, as everything government run was, and it had been late December when she'd finally been released into my care, a present just in time for Christmas.

I hadn't recognized her at first. All the same characteristics were there—her deep-set hazel eyes, her sharp nose—but they were on a girl who was nearly thirteen years of age. A girl who didn't beam like a ray of light the way my sister had. A girl who'd had that light beaten and burned out of her.

It had taken everything I had in me not to go to the man who'd abused her and kill him right then and there. I could have strangled him with my bare hands. And those who put her in that environment—I could have killed them too, without an ounce of remorse. My cousin and her husband. My father, if he weren't already dead. The man responsible for my father's death as well. All I needed was the opportunity, and I would fill a graveyard with their bodies.

But there had to be an order to these things. Roman Moore had taught me that. It was a vital lesson for someone as eager as I was for outcomes. A lesson I had to remind myself of repeatedly.

And so Camilla's foster father would wait. They would all wait. Dealing with them made up the bulk of my resolutions, resolutions I would not break.

I took another puff before flicking the growing column of ash on the ground and glanced at my watch. It was twenty minutes to Victoria Station from Kensal Green Cemetery. We'd need to leave soon if we were to make Camilla's train.

My chest tightened at the thought of parting with her so soon. Was it the right thing to do?

This wasn't the time for doubts. I'd made my decision. I'd started down this path, and I wouldn't look back.

With a burst of resolve, I stalked over to her. She didn't look up when I reached her, but the stiffening of her back said she was aware of my presence.

I gave her a beat to finish up her farewells, taking a long drag on my cigarette while I waited. I flicked again and the ash fell at her side.

She glanced up, her expression smug. "You could show some respect, you know."

Her bitter tone wasn't new. It had cycled in and out over the last several weeks, then had remained permanently the last day, as her departure time neared.

I wouldn't let it change my mind.

"Sorry," I said, unapologetically before grounding the butt out on the left side of the headstone. "That's father's half of the grave," I explained when she peered at me in horror. "He doesn't deserve my respect."

Her frown deepened. "He was still your father. You can't know all the reasons he did what he did. Are you going to hate him for it forever?"

"Probably," I said with a shrug. "And I know all I need to know. He chose her over us. He chose death. Over us. Whatever his reasons are doesn't matter." I shifted restlessly from one foot to the other, and I had to shove my hands in my pockets so I wouldn't be tempted to light another cigarette. "Come on. We're going to be late."

She sighed, a long expelling of air that made my insides feel hollow just observing. She stood, brushing the wet leaves from her knees, her eyes never leaving the grave. "I don't understand why I have to go."

"Fuck, Camilla..." My head throbbed. "We've been over this."

"Go over it again, then, because I still don't get how you abandoning me is any different from him abandoning us."

Zing. Right to my heart.

She was good at that already, at knowing where to hit. It was possible she could be as ruthless as I needed to be, possible that she could be an ally on the journey I had to take.

But I didn't want that for her. I wanted her to be warm and whole and good, and maybe it was too late for that, but if there was any hope for her, it wasn't with me.

This was how it had to be. There was no other way.

"Hampstead Collegiate is the finest boarding school around. It's a privilege that they've accepted you. They don't have to take all legacy students, and on scholarship, at that."

"Ya da ya da ya," she said, rolling her eyes at the spiel she'd heard enough to have memorized at this point.

"You know we can't afford anything else."

"I'd be perfectly happy in a state school."

"A state school doesn't cover your room and board. I would have to feed you and clothe you. Hampstead will even cover the cost of your therapy. It's the best option for you right now." I delivered the speech as if it were the truth, and it was, but it wasn't all of it. I wasn't concerned about the money. Roman would help with that until I got back our family fortune, which would be soon enough.

And that was why she had to be gone. I couldn't have a little girl with me on that road. This wasn't her burden to carry. Resent me if she must, but I had to take this on alone. This was *for* her. This was for both of us.

"Therapy is fine and all, but have you considered that what I really need is a family?"

I had considered it. But what the fuck did I know about family? She didn't need an angry single-minded brother. She needed a parent. How could I be a father when I didn't even know what a father was?

"I have my own schooling to pursue, Camilla," I said firmly, doubling down on my decision. "I don't need to be saddled with an unstable pre-teen with obvious daddy issues."

I knew where to hit too. I saw the blow land in the flinch of her eyes.

"I know what you're doing. You're being cruel on purpose. You're trying to push me away." She met my stare. Held it for several long seconds. "Fine. If you can't handle the responsibility, then send me away. I don't really have a choice in the matter."

I closed my eyes for a long blink, wishing I could change who I was. What I wanted. What fueled my blood and filled me.

But I couldn't.

And when I opened my eyes again, she must have seen the situation for what it was because she shook her head in resignation and turned her gaze back to the grave.

I scanned the names along with her. *Stefan Fasbender and Amelie Fasbender.* He'd died so soon after her that there had still been time to change the engraving. According to Roman, anyway.

"I don't remember much about her," Camilla said, softly. "I only know what she looked like from pictures, and beyond that, it's snatches of memories that have no order. She was always humming. I remember that. And she'd let me brush her hair sometimes. I can't recall the last time I spoke to her or hugged her or anything important she said to me. It's all just vague."

I didn't need to check my watch to know that we didn't have time for this. But I owed her something, didn't I? Something real. Something honest.

I inched closer so that our shoulders were touching. "I don't know if it was the last conversation we had, but I remember one of the last things she said to me very clearly." She'd been riddled with cancer, hooked up to machines. Her shoulder-length beautiful hair long gone, her cheeks sallow, her bones thin. "She said, 'When I'm gone, you'll have a hole in your life, Eddie. You have to find something to fill it.' She made me promise I would." Thirteen years old, and I hadn't had any idea what I was promising, but I'd made the vow all the same.

And if there was anything that I believed in firmly, it was that a man had nothing without his word. Honesty. Authenticity. Truth. What else did I have that was meaningful after losing everything?

I made another promise now, silently at my sister's side. *I'll bring you home soon, Camilla. As soon as I establish a home to bring you back to. As soon as the wheels for our future are in motion.*

"And have you?" she implored. "Have you found something to fill your life with instead?"

I nodded once.

"What is it?"

She was young and it was impulsive, but if this was for her as well as for me, then she deserved to know. Or maybe I was just tired of being completely alone.

Whatever the motive, I answered sincerely. "Revenge."

ONE

NOW: CELIA

"WAIT!" I stopped suddenly, forcing Edward to halt as well since his hand was laced in mine. "I need a minute. I'm not ready."

"You're not ready to go into your own home?" he asked with more than a hint of impatience.

He wasn't the only one who was frustrated with me. I was too. Weeks of preparation and hours of therapy should have made this easier, yet here I was, stalled at the garage entrance to the house, my heart pounding like it was going to burst from my rib cage.

"It's not my home," I said, voicing the anxious thoughts racing through my head.

"Yes, it is."

"It's not." I hadn't lived in Edward's London house in more than a year, and in the handful of months I'd spent there prior to that, I had never considered it a place I would one day actually live. I'd been there under false pretenses. The situation had been a ruse.

"Celia," Edward said sternly, the subtext in the simple utterance clear. He'd already given me time. He'd given me six weeks. He'd wanted to bring me here immediately after leaving Exceso, but I'd insisted on going back to Amelie. I'd needed to work through the avalanche of emotions he'd released in me before I could return to a normal life, and though he'd hated leaving me again, I'd convinced him it was the best thing for me.

And it had been. I'd needed the space to process. I'd changed fundamentally when he'd broken me down. I was no longer the strong, confident woman I'd once been. I'd never been that woman, to be honest. That woman had been built on lies and secrets. Who I was now was authentic and new, and just like a baby, my skin was delicate and thin, and I had to learn all over again how to function in the world.

It fucking sucked.

I loved the freedom that my new identity had brought me, but I hated being weak and vulnerable. I hated being unsure. I hated not knowing how to be real.

"I don't know how to do it, Edward," I said earnestly. "I don't know how to belong. I don't know who to be here." It wasn't the house itself that had me apprehensive, but everything associated with it. Edward's sister, Camilla, who'd been living here for several years, hadn't approved of my presence, though hopefully that had changed, and the servants had never looked to me as their employer. The expectations of my role as the woman of the Fasbender home were still unclear. I didn't have a job. I didn't have a purpose. On the island, my days had been prescribed by my husband, and that had made living manageable. My relationships with the islanders, which I'd grown to cherish, had been chosen for me.

And there was my relationship with Edward. In many ways, he was still a stranger to me, and yet he was the man who ruled my world. What sort of wife did he expect me to be? Could I be the woman he wanted? Did I want to be?

His features softened, though his eyes remained hard. He took my free hand and brought both together in between us. "You belong here, bird. You don't have to do anything to belong because this is your home, and you are my wife, and you are mine. That's all you have to be for now."

"But..."

"The rest we'll figure out in time," he said, cutting in before I spoke one of the dozen objections on the tip of my tongue. He stepped in to me, forcing my chin to tilt up to keep his gaze. "I know you think you aren't ready, but you are. *You are.*"

"You just wanted me here for the holidays because of appearances," I said baiting him for more reassurance.

"That too," he admitted with a smirk. "What would people think if my wife spent another Christmas without me?" His expression grew serious as his eyes traveled to my lips. "I want you with me, Celia. Come inside and be with me in our home."

I managed a single nod before his mouth claimed mine. It was a comforting kiss, though relatively chaste and much too short, interrupted by the opening of the door. It was Edward's house manager. *Our* house manager.

"Pardon me, Sir. Madame," he said, averting his eyes. "I came to get the luggage. I can return later."

Edward's sharp raise of an eyebrow was my cue. "Of course not, Jeremy. We were just headed inside," I said, feeling somewhat bolstered by taking command. "You can have our bags delivered to our rooms, please. I'll see to my own unpacking."

"As will I," Edward added.

"Very well. May I take your coats?"

I turned to let Jeremy help me with mine. Edward had brought it to the island for me, thankfully, as the weather in London had been quite rainy and cold when we arrived, much different from what I'd left behind. I'd boarded the plane the night before wearing a light sundress, an outfit that had been quickly shed once my husband and I were in the air. When I'd woken this morning, he'd already left the bed for the main cabin, but in his place, I found leggings, boots, and a sweater laid out for me to dress in. The clothes were a bit more casual than my usual taste, but they were comfortable, and comfortable was what I'd needed today.

He'd known that. Better than I had known it for myself. As he always did.

No wonder I loved him. We might still have a lot to negotiate, but that was one thing that was sure.

"We'll need nothing else until lunch is served," my husband said when our coats had been taken, his own command much more natural than mine. "Thank you, Jeremy."

Without letting me think about it another second, he pushed past the servant, pulling me along with him through the mud room to the back staircase. "See? You know your place," he said, his hand squeezing mine as we climbed the steps. "You fit here like a long-missing, last piece of a puzzle."

"Is that your way of saying I complete you?" I asked, as we reached the main floor.

He hesitated, turning to look at me, his mouth half open, his tongue silent.

The pause was bothersome. Why was there a pause? Sure, he hadn't ever come out and directly said he loved me, but he'd inferred it in a myriad of ways. He left little doubt of his feelings for me. This should have been an easy comeback. What else was there to say but yes? *Yes, Celia, you do complete me.*

Though...could I say that about him?

The oncoming rush of something small and boy distracted either of us from having to answer.

"Uncky!" Freddie said, throwing his arms around my husband's legs.

Edward swooped his three-and-a-half-year-old nephew up in the air, causing the boy to erupt in laughter.

It was impossible not to break into a smile at the sound. At the sight. Though deep inside, at the core of me, my womb pulsed with its emptiness. It was an ache that had become recurrent. One that knew I had to learn to ignore. Edward was already in his forties, a decade older than me with two grown children of his own. He'd told me before we married that he didn't want more children. That he *wouldn't* have more. It hadn't been an issue when I hadn't planned to stay married to him.

But now?

The rest we'll figure out in time, he'd said. It wasn't something I had to address today.

Camilla Fasbender Dougherty, however, was something I had to address today.

"Oh, for fuck's sake. Really, Eddie? You brought her back here?" She stood at the door to the salon, her arms crossed indignantly. Apparently she wasn't any more tolerable of me than she had been the last time we'd been face to face.

It probably didn't help that she hadn't known I'd be here. Which was as much of a surprise to me as my appearance seemed to be to her.

I turned to stare down my husband. "You didn't tell her I was coming back with you?"

"And no wonder that he didn't since he knew how I'd feel about it." The remark was addressed to me, but it was meant for Edward.

Suddenly it was clear that he'd kept more from her than just my arrival.

"You didn't tell her about my uncle, either?" I was incredulous. Maybe it was my fault for assuming he would have told her already, but it was an important tidbit of information. Why wouldn't he have cleared that up with her before now?

Because he was a sadist, that was why. Because he got off on others' discomfort, and while I couldn't speak to how Camilla felt, I definitely wasn't comfortable right now.

Edward's sly smile seemed to affirm my suspicions. His eyes danced gleefully from the venomous gaze of his sister to the equally venomous gaze of his wife. "I thought it would be a better conversation had with the three of us together."

"Then you should have told that to *me*," I said, angrily. "Edward," I added, using his name as he preferred, but with contempt.

His eyes narrowed and his lips drew into a firm line. He'd told me more than once that he wouldn't tolerate disrespect in front of others, and for the most part, I found a certain satisfaction in obeying that rule.

But bringing me into this situation without any warning was disrespectful to me, and he needed to know how I felt about it.

"Sheri," he called out, flagging down a member of the household staff as she walked by. "Could you please take Freddie to Anwar?"

Once he'd passed off his nephew, he wrapped his hand possessively around my waist and drew me tightly to his side. "Camilla, let's go sit, shall we?"

She sighed reluctantly, then turned toward the salon. Though the invitation had only been extended to his sister, Edward guided me behind her, directing me to sit on the sofa across from the one Camilla sat in. I expected him to sit next to me, but he put distance between us, perching on the arm.

I didn't know if the distance was for Camilla's sake or his own, but it was probably a wise choice. There was a good chance I would have clawed his thigh with my fingernails if he'd chosen to be by me. He definitely deserved it.

"So...?" Camilla's eyes darted from me to her brother, her expression pointed. It was obvious she preferred to have this conversation without me present. It was also obvious that she expected him to be the one filling her in.

It was probably most respectful for me to let him do just that.

But he'd had his chance to tell her, and he hadn't, and since he'd chosen to leave it for my attendance, then, as far as I was concerned, that meant I had permission to step in.

More accurately, I didn't *need* to have permission. I was his wife. I wasn't his submissive.

Was I?

Another thing we had to work out later.

"I'm just going to dive right in and say I'm truly sorry to be sprung on you like this, Camilla. It wasn't fair to either of us." I glared at my husband whose expression was unreadable. "But it particularly wasn't kind to you."

"Don't be insolent, Celia," he warned. "That isn't called for."

I scowled at his rebuke, but he was right. Passive-aggressive digs in his direction weren't going to help my relationship with either of them.

I got to the point. "Edward has told me the circumstances surrounding your parents' deaths, and I understand completely why you harbor such animosity toward the Werner name. You've both been through a lot, and I'm sure that I would feel the same way if I'd been in your shoes."

It was bad enough to have a parent die from cancer. To have the other commit suicide right after was unimaginable. Edward's father had taken his own life, not only because he'd lost his partner, but also because he'd lost his company in a hostile takeover. To a company my father owned.

"That said," I continued, choosing my words carefully. I didn't want to diminish her history, but it was important she knew the truth. "My father is not the Werner that was responsible for Accelerate being bought out from under your father. Yes, he was the head of the company at the time, but it was my uncle Ron who ran everything that happened in the UK. He took over several media businesses here, dismantling all of them. He had one hundred percent autonomy at the time and was later kicked out of his position because of the poor decisions he made and the direction he'd taken that branch of the company, which was in no way retribution for the things he's done, but the fact is, it wasn't my father. Warren Werner had nothing to do with the fall of your family."

She'd listened stoically as I'd spoken, her attention solely on me. But now Camilla's focus flew to her brother. "Is it true?"

"Yes," I said, though I knew it wasn't me she was asking.

"It's all true," Edward confirmed. "I verified it."

I swung toward him. "You verified it? You didn't trust me?" He hadn't given me any indication that he'd doubted me when I'd told him. It bothered me to hear now that he had.

He shook his head. "It wasn't about trust. It was about needing to see the proof."

If there was a difference, I couldn't see it.

"How do you feel about discovering this, Ed?" Camilla asked. The tone of the question was personal, and it made me feel like an intruder. Like maybe the conversation would have been better without me.

Worse, it felt like this was a question I should have asked myself and before now. He may still have been a stranger, but I knew how important his vengeance had been. Changing course this far into his plans had to have been a huge loss. It had to feel devastating, and I hadn't acknowledged that.

"Honestly?" He aimed his response at the person who asked. "I feel relieved."

I blinked in surprise.

"Yes," Camilla said, looking us both over. "I see."

What did she see? I didn't see. What was there to see?

"Then the two of you are...?" She trailed off, and thank God she wasn't asking me, because I wasn't sure I knew the right answer.

But Edward did. "We're married, Camilla. We intend to stay that way. Happily."

Ah, now I saw. He was relieved because, now that my father wasn't the bad guy, I wasn't either. Which meant he no longer had to resist the pull between us.

I was relieved about that too.

"You should know we have no secrets between us," he continued. "Celia knows what my goals are and what lengths I'll go to in order to see them to the end." Lengths like marrying a woman with the intention of killing her to get the shares she owned of her father's company. I wasn't convinced that he would have been able to see that to its end, the evidence being that I was still very much alive even before he'd found out the truth about my uncle.

But Edward wanted to believe he would have done anything, and it wasn't the worst thing to let him have that.

"And you're still with him," she said, finally acknowledging me.

I looked to my husband with my answer. "Very much so."

"She also supports whatever actions we need to take next," he said. "Or so I believe."

"I do," I said. It was the first time we'd made our declarations of devotion in front of another person, even though we had made similar ones to each other in this very room, when we'd exchanged rings.

This time we knew we meant them, and the difference sent a bolt of warmth through my chest and heat down between my legs.

The moment wasn't appreciated by my sister-in-law. "Your family loyalty runs thin," she scoffed.

"No, no. It's not like that." I scanned her over quickly, trying to picture how she must see me. How she must see herself in comparison.

Though she was the one sitting in a designer jumpsuit, I'd grown up far more privileged than she had. I hadn't seen them personally, but from what I had been told, I was sure there were burn marks on her skin under her long sleeves, permanent tattoos from an abusive foster father. After surviving that, she'd gone on to lose her husband quite young. Besides her son, Edward was the only family she had, and he had bent over backwards to care for her, not only raising her after he'd been old enough but also taking her in again after she'd been widowed.

That sort of bond bred loyalty I likely couldn't understand.

But it didn't mean I didn't feel my own version of devotion. As misguided as it often was.

"I'm loyal to my parents," I went on. "And Edward knows the lengths I'd go to—*have* gone to—for them." My own lengths included marrying my father's rival with the intent of ruining him in order to win my father's love. Not a healthy loyalty by any means, but I wasn't sure any of us in the room knew what a healthy relationship was.

"Ron is another situation entirely. He's..." I searched for the words to describe his sins, how he'd groomed me and treated me like his doll. How he'd sold parts of my innocence to his rich friends. "Let's just say he's not a good person. And whatever wrath Edward plans on unleashing on him, it is likely only a portion of what he deserves."

Camilla met my eyes, and though it was tempting to put up my guard, I forced myself not to. She kept my gaze for several beats until her features eased and her head nodded, and I wondered if she saw what I had wanted her to see. Wondered if she understood how much we had in common. How we'd both been hurt by the very people who had been tasked to care for us. How we both loved a man who had tended to us in unorthodox ways.

"It's a shift in the narrative, I know," Edward said, the tenderness in his voice wrapping tendrils around both me and his sister.

"It's a huge shift," she agreed. "Forgive me if it takes me a minute to get my bearings."

"Take your time. But understand that Celia is part of my life now. She is my wife. This is her home, and I expect that to be appreciated."

"I know how to be respectful, Eddie." Her retort was soft, full of affection despite her words. "I never interfered with the arrangement you had with Marion. I can behave. As long as you can assure me this relationship is in your best interest."

"She's not Marion," he said firmly, and though I didn't understand the meaning of the remark, it whipped into my new baby skin. "But she's not Frank either. And neither am I."

The next few comments whizzed by me as I tried to find a thread I could follow.

"Glad to hear it, but I've never thought you were," Camilla said.

"You haven't?"

"I don't know. Maybe I did."

"I'm that despicable, perhaps, but the malice I feel is always earned."

They shared a smile. Whatever had transpired in the exchange, they'd reached some understanding. An understanding that I felt very much left out of.

"Who's Frank?" I asked, hoping one of them would loop me in.

"It doesn't matter," Camilla said, her head turning to peer out of the salon and down the hall toward the bustle at the front door. It sounded like someone arriving or a delivery maybe. Nothing half as interesting as the conversation she'd dismissed.

Before I could make another attempt to pursue it, she stood. Her height when standing was intimidating, to the point that I rose too. "As I said before," she stated, "this is a big alteration in my thinking. Since Eddie took me in, hatred of the Werner name has been drilled into me."

She'd spoken to me directly this time, and the words lashed as harshly as the mention of Marion. I knew and understood where she came from, but I was still who I was.

Or maybe I wasn't anymore.

Because Edward really had torn me down to nothing, and what was left in my place was still unknown.

But this newbie did have a name. And it wasn't the one I'd grown up with.

"Good thing I'm not a Werner then, isn't it?" I said, the comeback a beat late but true enough that the hit landed.

"Yes. Exactly right." She smiled earnestly and held out her hand, which I took without pause. "Welcome to the family, Celia. I look forward to the new war ahead of us. I hope you don't find the burden of being a Fasbender as heavy as those before you."

It was a strange thing she'd said, and I opened my mouth to ask what she meant, but before I could say anything, Edward's children were in the room, greeting us enthusiastically.

"We're not too early, are we?" Genny asked as she hugged her father. "You didn't say what time to be here for lunch, and we wanted you to have time to settle."

"No, not too early." Edward beamed at her.

I smiled as well, despite wanting to kick the man. If I'd known he'd invited his kids over, I would have insisted on changing into something more presentable as soon as we had arrived. Had that been his plan with the clothing he'd laid out? I'd thought he'd chosen my outfit so I'd feel good in my surroundings. Now I wondered if he'd intended just the opposite.

"It's good to have you home," Genny said when she turned her greeting to me. "Father's been miserable without you." She embraced me and I was surprised both by her words and the warmth of her welcome.

"I'm not sure he isn't just as miserable when I'm around."

"Well, that's true enough," she agreed with a laugh that both Hagan and Camilla shared with her.

When their amusement died down, I excused myself to change, though somewhat reluctantly. There was a pleasant aura in the presence of Edward with his children. It was an aura I wanted to feed on like a vampire, as though their bonds could nourish the empty parts of my existence. As though it could complete me like I longed to be completed.

But it was a false completion. It was a puzzle piece that looked like it fit, but didn't quite, and as I paused at the foot of the stairs to gaze back at the bunch, I ached for what they had. Could I ever truly belong to that? Would Edward ever truly let me in?

I wasn't sure.

I wasn't sure I should even accept it if he did. There was too much lacking between us that I wasn't convinced would be fixed with time. Too much uncertainty.

It wasn't just the clothing or the way he could never say outright how he felt. It was also the way he'd set me up with Camilla. The way he hadn't prepared me for his children's visit. The way he said I fit in but continually made me feel like I stuck out. Was his behavior natural hesitation around a new relationship or was it part of his constant need to keep me on edge?

That was the thing with Edward—it was impossible to know if the way he manipulated my life was for my benefit, or his. I suspected it was often a combination, but how could I be sure? To borrow Camilla's concern, how did I know what he did was always in my best interest?

I loved him, no bones about it. I was his, and he owned my heart entirely. That flag was planted as firmly as my feet were planted on the bottom stair.

My trust, however, was still up in the air.

TWO

EDWARD

IT WASN'T that late when I retired for the night, but with the jet lag and the time change it felt late. Celia had managed to sneak in a nap after lunch, excusing herself when Genny left to work on her studies. Hagan remained to talk business and ended up staying through dinner. He'd worked at Accelecom even before he'd graduated from university, and I'd always had the intention of training him to follow in my footsteps. It had been convenient having him around the past year when I'd made frequent trips to Amelie to visit Celia, and he'd handled the tasks I'd given him quite well.

That didn't mean he was privy to everything.

I had inherited the mistakes of my father, but I would not pass them onto my progeny. Thus Hagan was involved with my company, but he was not involved with my revenge. And right now that was the business that was front and center in my mind so his visit had walked the line between tedium and productivity.

"Young Mr. Fasbender is gone?" Jeremy asked from the doorway of my office, likely wanting to lock the house up and prepare for the night.

"He is." I shut my computer down and stood. "My wife has already gone up. I'm headed now as well."

"Don't forget you promised Master Freddie you'd check in on him."

My nephew was often more attached to me when I'd been away. He'd come into my office, despite the rule that it was an off-limits space, begging for a bedtime story. It had been tempting to give in. *The Little Engine That Could* was more entertaining than discussing television market opportunities of the Czech Republic, if only barely, but Hagan needed my attention. Freddie wasn't the only one more attached when I'd been away.

I'd managed to mollify the little boy by promising to peek in on him before I retired.

"Thank you for the reminder," I said, though I hadn't forgotten. "I'll head up there first."

I took the stairs two at a time, continuing past the floor that held my bedroom space to go to the top level of the house. These rooms had belonged to Hagan and Genevieve when they were younger, but for the past several years, Camilla had resided in them, and now I thought of them as her apartments. As such, I rarely ventured up there, and it felt somewhat like trespassing as I stepped onto the landing.

Quietly, so as not to disturb my sister, I walked through the playroom to the door ajar on the far end. Ghosts of the past hovered in the corners of the space, bidding me to remember other trips to the nursery, long ago, when I'd had a different wife and a different life. Then, the days had remained hectic, even after I'd left the office, the energy of corporate doings replaced with the energy of small children. There had been no such thing as downtime, and when I looked back on it now, it seemed like they must have been the primary occupation of my existence.

But I didn't have any evidence to back that up.

In fact, the evidence that I did have—the business I'd built, the instances of justice I'd carried out, the woman I'd chosen when I'd remarried—all pointed to an existence that was quite the contrary. Had my children been as frontmost in my life as they should have been? Had I given them the time and attention they deserved?

They certainly were smart, competent, well-adjusted young adults, but the plaguing doubt that I'd been a subpar parent might have been what drove me now to be so attentive to Freddie, even though he wasn't my own.

The boy was fast asleep, as I'd known he would be. I retrieved his ragged bunny from the floor and tucked it under his arm before pulling the covers up. Then, after sweeping two fingers gently across his forehead, I switched off the bedside lamp and crept back out, shutting the door behind me.

"Oh, good. I caught you." Camilla stood in the doorway on the other side of the playroom, where the hallway led to her bedroom suite.

I cursed under my breath. Eventually, I knew I'd have to talk to her, but I'd hoped to put it off, at least until I'd had a good night's rest.

Perhaps I still could. "Shh," I said, using Freddie as my excuse. "You'll wake him."

She shook her head. "He sleeps like the dead, and you know it. You can't use him to get out of talking to me."

The problem with being close to my sister was that it was very hard to get away with anything.

"Would you prefer to come into my sitting room for this?" she asked, knowing she had me completely where she wanted me.

I preferred not to be doing this at all.

"Here will be fine." Standing would be easier to insure it was quick.

"Have it your way." She folded her arms over her chest, clearly not pleased with my choice. "Now, don't get cross with me for asking, because I'm only looking out for you…"

I'd found that the most irritating conversations began with "Don't get cross," and I had to take a beat before urging her on. "Go ahead."

"So it wasn't Warren Werner who brought down father's company. If you're certain of that, then I can be too. But how can you be certain that Celia isn't in this marriage to help him take you down now?"

It was a reasonable question, and one that had merit considering how little Camilla knew about the situation and my relationship with my wife. "Her father is no longer in control of Werner Media," I explained. Even though he was no longer my target, this fact still stung. "He's acting CEO, but his power is limited. He doesn't have the ability to make a move on me in his current position."

"Okay," Camilla processed the information faster than I had. "Then what about the uncle? How can you be sure she isn't going to warn him of any of your plans?"

"I can be certain." It could have been enough. Camilla would drop it with my assurances, but I wanted her to know more. I wanted her to understand, not just the predicament but Celia.

So, at the risk of betraying my wife's confidence, I gave Camilla what she needed to put the pieces together. "Let's just say she feels about him the way you felt about Mitch."

Mitch Ferris, the man who'd physically abused my sister when she was in his care through the foster system.

"Ah." Her features softened as her body wrapped more tightly. "I thought I recognized...something..."

It had been nearly impossible to see the effects of Celia's abuse when I'd first met her, but the woman she was now was much more transparent. She would hate it if she realized she no longer masked those secrets as she once had, but I was glad that she'd revealed enough of herself to possibly start a bond with Camilla.

Now my sister just needed to be decent about it. "Then you'll be nice?" I prodded.

"I'll be nice." She took a deep breath and exhaled slowly. "I should move out."

My reaction was immediate. "No. This is your home. This is Freddie's home."

"It's your home. And now it's her home, and we're only intruders."

"You are not." But even as I insisted, I knew she was right. If I had any intention of making a marriage with Celia—and I did—then it had to be a real marriage. There wasn't any place for in-laws in the home of a real newlywed couple.

"It's for the best to do this sooner rather than later," Camilla continued. "Easier on Freddie when he's young."

I looked behind me at the closed door, thinking of the child beyond it. Thinking of his mother and the circumstances that had brought her pregnant and alone to my house.

Hideous circumstances. Circumstances that tended to have a long-lasting effect.

"It's too soon," I said, suddenly intent on protecting her, no matter the cost.

"Too soon after Frank?" Her tone said she thought the idea was rubbish. "It's been four years. Do you really think me that fragile?"

"I didn't mean that." I didn't know what I meant. It wasn't as though she still needed protecting. We were long past that.

She smiled slightly. Knowingly. As though she understood my meaning even if I didn't. "There's a bond between people who share a secret, Eddie. We won't lose ours just because I have a different address."

Was that all this was? Me, afraid that we'd somehow grow apart?

Perhaps that was some of it. But there was more, and she seemed to sense that as well.

She crossed the room midway then stopped. "I'm all right with it. With what we did, okay? I've never said that, I realize, and I should have way before now. Honestly, I try not to think about it very often because I hate to think of myself as someone who has ambiguous morals, but I'm all right with it. I don't regret that it happened, and I know you don't either. So let's put it behind us, once and for all. All right?"

I had already put her husband and the details of his death behind me. It had been easy. But I was a man who'd built an identity on seeking justice. I'd lost my soul to that devil long ago. Camilla still had hers, and I feared that if she actually did put Frank behind her, that would be the day that she lost it.

Then again, that might be the cost of learning to live again.

It wasn't my road to walk, and as much as I wanted to preside over her journey, I could see it was time to let those reins go. "Do what you feel you need to do," I said, finally. "But let it go on record that I didn't push you out."

"What, Edward Fasbender? Push his little sister out of his life? Never." She laughed and so I chuckled too, despite the painful reminder of what I'd done to her in the name of vengeance in the past.

The worst part? I'd do it again. Every time.

———

THE BEDROOM WAS empty when I got there. Even though the lights were off, I checked the closet and the bathroom before opening the door that adjoined mine and the one Celia had slept in before we'd married. Marion's old room.

I found her sitting on the bed, rubbing lotion onto her long limbs. Instantly, my trousers were uncomfortably tight.

"What are you doing?" I asked, wondering why she'd chosen to primp here instead of in our bedroom.

"I'm getting ready for bed."

"In here?"

"In my room, yes."

"No, no, no." I shook my head vehemently. We'd been sleeping together regularly for the last couple of months, whenever we were together anyway. It was possible she'd assumed that being in this house meant returning to the previous arrangement, but it was more likely that she knew that wasn't the case and just wanted to hear me say it. "You can keep this space as your sitting room, if you like. I honestly don't care, but you will sleep with me."

"That wasn't what was negotiated before we got married." Her smirk gave her away.

I hated being manipulated, particularly being manipulated into displays of affection, and I was tempted to leave her where she was and retire alone, simply so she'd understand that I wouldn't play her little game.

But the truth was, I would play her little game. I liked it, even. Playing her little games meant she'd play my much more significant games, and that was where the fun really happened between us.

I gave her a stern scowl instead. "Those terms are null and void, and you know it. Now, unless you prefer sleeping in here—in which case we'll have quite a row about it that I will win—"

"I don't prefer it."

"Then get your pretty little ass over there where it belongs. Speaking of, I believe I need to turn it red after the way you spoke to me in front of my sister earlier."

She stood and moved toward me and the door leading to our bedroom. "So the separate bedroom terms are null and void, but the respect you in all instances term is still valid? Who says I'm on board with that?"

My jaw clamped tight. There could still very well be a row in our future. Several, even. We'd come into our arrangement under false pretenses, but we'd shared a lot in our time on the island. I'd hoped that what we'd established in our time there would be easily transportable. Part of me had believed we might be able to come home and just be who we were together without any fuss.

But not only was that an overly optimistic scenario, it wasn't the one I honestly preferred. I enjoyed setting boundaries. I enjoyed even more when they were somewhat confining. Mostly, I enjoyed pushing them until she saw how much she appreciated that they'd been set up for her in the first place.

That's when things got interesting.

"Tomorrow night, we will set new terms," I said, allowing her the illusion that she would have room to negotiate. "That doesn't get you out of what happens tonight. No matter what you thought about the terms of our relationship, I know you were fully aware that I would be displeased when you voiced opposition to my method of handling Camilla."

"Was I fully aware?" she asked, her lips puckering into a taunt. "Hmm."

She sashayed past me into our bedroom, drawing my attention to the ass I meant to have under my palm soon. I followed with a stiff cock, half from anticipation and half from the sight of her. The night-shirt she wore invited the most improper thoughts. It was pink and girly and made her look young. So, so young. I felt indecent even looking at her.

Her sauciness only added to the need to dominate her.

"I guess I was being naughty then. The question is, what are you going to do about it?" She sat on the bed, her arms braced behind her.

Her flippancy was adorable and irritating both at once. Consequences for lack of respect was not something I ever treated lightly, and I didn't intend to now. It was possible to take advantage of the sex kitten while also reminding her of her place. I just had to get her ass bare and bend her over my knee.

But then she gasped, her face suddenly going pale.

She stood, her eyes wide and drawn to the far wall. As though she couldn't believe what she was looking at, she went closer, her expression more aghast with each step.

I kept my own gaze glued to her, not needing to see what she was looking at. I already knew. I'd been the one to put it there. I'd even known she'd likely have a reaction when she saw it, which was the reason I'd put it up in the first place.

What I hadn't known was what kind of reaction she'd have.

Yes, this was where things got interesting.

"It was with your belongings when I had them sent from the States," I said, my eyes never leaving her. This painting had been wrapped differently than any of her others with more care and attention. The assumption could be that it was important to her, but when I opened it up and discovered what the painting depicted, I guessed it was more complicated than just being important.

"Blanche Martin gave it to me," she said, her voice raw. "I'd been trying to convince her that I was going to get her art in some rich guy's house. It was a stupid scheme, and anyway... She brought this one to show me personally. I didn't want it, but I could hardly give it back to her. I should have thrown it out. I don't know why I didn't."

I glanced at the country garden scene, at the path that wandered off into the distance, at the swing that hung from the branches of the centermost tree.

"It makes you think of your uncle," I said. It wasn't a question.

She nodded, her chin trembling.

I'd supposed as much. She'd told me that was how he'd begun his grooming of her at the age of seven. He'd built her a swing large enough for him to sit with her on it. He'd referred to it as their special place as he'd held her inappropriately on his lap.

"It's confusing, really. Because the memories of being on that swing were actually quite good ones. I was too young to understand what his end goal was or that the way he treated me wasn't right." She swallowed then turned her gaze to me. "It's only with what happened in later years that the garden memories soured, and they didn't sour in the way they should have. I should see this and feel nothing but rage and horror, but I don't. I see that swing..." She shifted to stare at the painting again. "And I remember what it felt like to fly, what it felt like to be free. And then I feel guilty and wrong because it's all associated with him and he made my life a mess."

My little bird was wounded. She had been for so long, her wings damaged and torn, but she'd kept it hidden until I forced her to let it be seen. Now, she needed to learn to fly again, and she would. I swore to it with every passing breath.

She turned all the way around, putting her back to the painting. "I know you couldn't have known. But could you please take it down?"

I paused, even though I knew my answer. I'd had the painting before she'd told me the story, but I hadn't opened it until I'd been preparing for her to move back with me. As soon as I'd seen it, the words of her story had come back to me, and while I didn't know why she had the painting, I couldn't imagine that she'd be able to look at it without similar thoughts.

But she'd still owned it. Which meant she wasn't ready to let it go.

And if she wasn't ready to let it go, then she was damn well going to look at it. Even if it made her uncomfortable. Especially if it made her uncomfortable.

"No," I said after several beats.

Her head jerked up in surprise. "What?"

"You heard me. I won't take it down."

"Then I can't sleep in here. You can't expect that." She started back toward the door to the adjoining room.

But I was in her way, and I caught her as she tried to pass. Bending her arms behind her, I held her wrists at the small of her back. "I do expect you to sleep here, and you will."

"Like hell I will." She struggled to escape which only led me to tighten my grip.

"Celia, Celia. My little bird." I trailed kisses along her jawline, and though she was hesitant at first, she began to melt into my caress. "You remember what you are to me, right?"

Her brows creased as she tried to figure out what I was after.

"Everything. You're everything to me. And I will do anything to protect you, to keep you safe from the monsters in your past. Whatever needs to be done."

"But..."

"No buts. I will take care of you. You're mine, no one else's." The words wouldn't be enough to change her memories alone, but right now they served to distract her. I took her mouth with mine, reminding her physically how much I felt for her with my lips and tongue.

After a bit of coaxing, her resistance fell away, and she gave into my kiss completely. I devoured her then, swallowing her raspy mewls and bracing her body as it shuddered with pleasure. I let go of her wrists and her hands flew to clutch onto my sweater, fistfuls of cashmere twisting in her grip. My own hand snaked underneath the hem of her nightshirt and into her pants where I found her wet and swollen.

It only took a few rough swipes of my thumb at her clit before I could easily slide two fingers inside her, bending them to stroke without mercy against her sensitive inner wall. Her whimpers turned into ragged moans as I continued the assault, pushing as far inside her as I could, urging her toward her climax.

Good girl, I thought when she erupted, unwilling to break the kiss to reward her with the praise directly. *Be with me. Stay with me.*

It was manipulative, yes, because I had an agenda, but it was also sincere. My desire for Celia reached epic proportions. It filled me like a reservoir in the midst of a heavy rainstorm, the water pushing unforgivably at the walls of the dam. The only thing that kept me upright in its wake was the secure foundation I'd built out of control and rage.

I wanted her, wanted to touch her and fuck her. Wanted to hear her gasp my name while she came all over my hand.

I also wanted her strong and whole and resilient and mine, and I knew how to have it all. If that made me greedy, so be it. It was greed that served her best.

So when she was still spent and pliant in my arms, I acted on that greed.

I walked her backward until she hit the upholstered accent chair. Then I spun her around and bent her over the arm. She was still getting her balance as I swiftly removed her pants, kicking her legs apart when they were gone so that I had plenty of room to step between her thighs. A handful of seconds later, my cock was out and lined up at her hole, ready to drive in with one aggressive thrust.

But first, I gathered my hands in her hair and pulled back, lifting her head so that she would see the painting on the wall as I shoved into her.

"No," she cried out even as her body pressed back into me, meeting each controlled stroke.

To the side of us, the dressing mirror caught her reflection. Her profile showed her face was screwed up in an expression of pleasure/pain, her eyes closed tight against her view.

"Open your eyes, Celia," I demanded, pulling her hair so hard her back arched in my direction. "Look at it."

"I don't want to look," she begged.

"Look!" I said sharply, feeling her grow wetter at the strength of my demand.

Her eyes flew open, despite the deepening of her frown, as though she couldn't help but obey. She always responded when I got a bit mean, whether she liked that about herself or not, it was who she was, and I understood that.

I rewarded her with more thrusts of my cock and praised her with my approval. "Here you are, bird. Good girl. Keep looking. Do you know why I want you to look? Do you know what I want you to see?"

"No," she whimpered. "I don't."

In the mirror, I could see a tear running down the side of her cheek, caused by her approaching orgasm or emotional strain, I couldn't be sure, but my cock thickened at the sight, turning into a rod of pure steel. My balls tightened, too, signalling the nearness of my own release.

This was going to be over soon. I had to hurry on with it.

Pushing my free hand underneath her bent upper half, I found her clit and pressed on it slightly. "I want you to see where you are and where you are not. You're not in that place. You are not in that garden. You are not with that disgusting excuse of a human being. You are here, in my bedroom. In *our* bedroom. I'm the one who is with you. It's me who is touching you. My cock inside you. No one else's, do you hear me?"

Her eyes widened and her mouth opened, but all that came out was a single grunt of acknowledgment.

It wasn't enough. I needed more. She needed to be convinced.

"Who's fucking you?" I demanded, plowing into her so hard my thighs slapped audibly against the back of her legs.

"You," she whispered.

"Say my name."

"Edward."

Fuck, the sound of my name on her lips nearly undid me. My rhythm stuttered, and I had to fight not to lose my load right then.

With a growl, I took hold of myself, increasing the pressure of my thumb on her nub. "Who owns this cunt?"

"Edward."

"Who makes you come?"

"Edward." Her voice tightened as she clenched down around my cock, her body trying to push me out as she came explosively.

I forced my way through her grip, determined to ride her until the very end. "That's right. It's me, and I'm not going anywhere. I'm here with you now, and it doesn't matter what's on our wall or what memories are lurking in the shadows, they can't own you. You belong to me. Only me."

My words strained with the last of my declaration as my release overtook me. With my hand still wrapped in her hair, I jerked into her, shooting every last drop of my climax into the tight sheath of her cunt.

I stayed inside her while my breathing slowed, running a firm hand up and down the length of her spine, reassuring her of my presence. I watched her still in the mirror. She'd laid her cheek on the opposite armrest, her eyes once again closed. Her features were soft, her expression sated. Or tired. Perhaps, resigned.

Was this really going to work between us?

This was who I was, a man who would keep pushing her comfort levels because it bettered her, yes, but also because I liked it. Could she accept that?

Could she accept it without losing everything she was?

I pulled out of her, and she let out a soft sound of protest.

"Shh," I soothed her. "I'm not going anywhere." I reached over to the wall and turned off the switch for the light on this side of the room. The painting disappeared into darkness.

Then I gathered her into my arms, kissing her temple as I carried her to the bed. She was half asleep by the time I tucked her in, but she reached for me before I could leave her side to get cleaned up.

"I get it," she said. "And I'll try. I'll try to be here more than I'm there with him." She nodded her head toward the now unseen painting.

I brushed the hair from her forehead. "You can ask Jeremy to have it taken down in the morning," I told her. "It's your choice."

She nodded.

But she knew as well as I did that the garden and its swing was still there, whether it was on our wall or not.

THREE

CELIA

I SAT UP WITH A START, panting in the dark. My hand went automatically to my chest where I could feel my heart pounding. It felt like I'd been running, but the images in the nightmare I'd just had showed me in a confined space.

Just trying to recall more made my skin crawl. I shook the thoughts off of me with a shudder.

"Another one?" Edward's voice graveled from behind me.

My shoulders tensed. This was half the reason I hadn't felt ready to come back to London. He knew about the occasional bad dreams, but since he'd been away so much, he hadn't been aware of the recent uptick in frequency.

"I'm fine," I said, swallowing the truth. It was bad enough that I'd become so fragile in my waking hours. He didn't need to know the extent of my weaknesses.

As always, though, he could see me, even when I tried to hide.

His palm slid heavy and comforting along my bare back, massaging the rock of a muscle lodged beneath my shoulder blade. "You won't be able to go back to sleep until you tell me."

I wanted to snap back at that, inform him that it wasn't true. I'd woken from recurrent bad dreams for years without him and been just fine.

But the truth was that I hadn't been fine. I'd been suppressing a lifetime of experiences that I'd never fully dealt with. Traumas that left me emotionless. Wounds so deeply buried in my subconscious, that most of them didn't even haunt me when I closed my eyes. In fact, the only dream I'd remembered having for the past several years had been a recurring one of a faceless man and a tightly bundled baby that I could never quite see.

Then Edward came along with his "sessions" and his constant probing into my psyche that compelled me to examine events in my life that I had wanted to never look at again, and now, along with having all sorts of feelings, I had all sorts of dreams. Terrible dreams. Fragments of memories, mostly, or variations on things that had happened to me in the past. He'd opened a gate inside of me, and everything that had been secreted away behind it refused to be shut up any longer. He'd forced me to deal, whether I wanted to or not, and now that I'd started, I couldn't stop. Even when I was sleeping, the thoughts would come, begging to be processed. Pushing them away was impossible. The only way to be rid of them was to face them head-on.

"It's a blur," I said, unable to recall any of the pieces to describe them. "But I know what I was remembering. I can see that clearly."

The bed lurched as he reached for the bedside lamp.

"Keep it off," I snapped. As if remaining in the dark would help me be able to hide. "Please," I added, softer.

He paused, and I could feel him deciding whether or not to comply before he sat up, the lamp untouched. "Something new?"

"Yes." A lot of the memories I'd been dreaming lately had been things I'd blocked out, if that was the right term. At least they were things I hadn't thought about in so long that I'd forgotten them.

"Something worse?"

I turned toward him, studying the outline of his features as if they could tell me the answer. The bulk of the pain that Uncle Ron inflicted had been cumulative. So many of his individual acts only became vile when added to the others.

But there were still moments that were singularly horrific. Auctioning parts of my innocence off to his friends had been the one that I'd considered the worst. As I began to remember more of what he'd done, other instances rallied for the title.

"I don't know if it's worse," I answered, finally. "Just...different."

"Different how?"

I groaned. I didn't want to talk about it. It was easier to explain a bad dream than to share something terrible that had actually occurred. Nightmares came without my free agency, and yes, it could be argued that I hadn't had agency when I'd been under Ron's care, because I'd been too young to understand, which was the truth. But I'd been in those moments, and they hadn't felt manipulative. It had felt like I'd actively participated. I'd let him hug me and fondle me. I'd let him bathe me and pamper me. How was I not to blame at least in part?

"Celia..." Edward pressed, his voice as hard as the force his hand was currently applying on the knot at my neck.

"Is this a session?"

"It is now." His hand dropped, and the mattress shifted again as he started to get out.

I reached out and grabbed his thigh through the covers, stopping him. "Okay, but stay, please? I'll talk but I want you here." Next to me, instead of across the room. Where I didn't have to face him. Where I didn't have to see what he thought about me written all over his expression.

"If you think that will be easier," he agreed, settling back into the bed. But he leaned against the headboard distancing himself from me even while remaining close.

His game, his rules.

Best just to get it over with.

"It was the summer I was ten, I think." Then I knew. "Yes. I was definitely ten because Uncle Ron had made a big deal about me being finally a lady which meant I was old enough to have a 'proper date' and go to the ballet."

The taste in my mouth soured as the words crossed my lips, not only because of the sick way my uncle had referred to an outing with a child, but because of how excited the pronouncement had made me. There had been so many things I'd been left out of then because I was too young—parties and events that my parents had told me weren't appropriate for a child. It had been maddening being left with a sitter when I'd felt grown-up and independent. I'd wanted nothing more than to be treated like the adult that I knew I was.

Ron had fed on that desire. And I'd eagerly given him more of myself to devour.

"He bought me a pretty formal dress. Which had been one of the best moments of my life to that point because he'd taken me to a fancy private boutique, and I'd had all this personal attention from him and the attendants when I modeled each of the items." I shifted toward Edward. "It's disgusting when I say it now, I know, but for a ten-year-old girl, it had been the best day imaginable."

"Don't make apologies for how you felt. Those feelings were honest. The disgust is in how he manipulated them."

Right.

My therapist said that a lot too. It was sometimes hard to remember.

I turned forward again, lowering my eyes to my hands gripped tightly in my lap. I could almost picture them back then, newly manicured with bright pink polish, innocent in their movements.

I was getting ahead of myself. "Anyway, he took me to a salon too and had my hair curled and my nails painted princess pink. The whole shebang. Then he took me to the ballet. *Romeo and Juliet*. He'd told me he'd chosen it just for us. That Romeo and Juliet had a love that people didn't understand, the way that people would never understand how he and I loved each other."

"He was a monster," Edward muttered. "That wasn't love."

"He was a monster," I agreed. "And it wasn't love. But it sure felt like it at the time. The *Romeo and Juliet* references went over my head, of course. I didn't really understand the story, and I'd been a little bored because it was so long, but it was hard to really be irritable when I was dressed so pretty.

"He told me how pretty I looked too. Over and over. Every time I started to get restless, he smoothed his palm over my hair and whispered in my ear. 'Pretty girls sit still and don't fidget so other people can truly enjoy looking at them.'" I swallowed the bad taste back. "I think he probably watched me more than he watched that performance. And I loved it. I felt like I was glowing from all the attention."

Edward's fingers pressed lightly on my lower back. "It wasn't your fault," he said, guessing where this was going, and I suddenly realized why he usually sat away from me during these sessions. Across the room, it was easier for him to listen objectively instead of consoling me.

It was also easier for me to go on without the endearment.

Right now, though, I was grateful for it.

I swiveled my head in his direction. "Let me tell the story, would you?"

His lips pursed, but he nodded, letting his touch linger for another beat before folding his arms tightly across his chest.

"We didn't go to the city often, but when we did, there'd be a driver. Charles was the name of the guy who drove us that day. He was new, and I'm not entirely sure he was even really a driver. I never saw him before or after, but I liked him instantly. He'd made the outing feel special as much as anything else. The way he called me 'Ms. Werner' and held the door for me like I was important. He let me tell him all of my terrible knock-knock jokes on the drive too, which made him a pretty cool guy in my book. He joined us for dinner too at this fancy restaurant that was famous for their ice cream concoctions, and then I had both of them talking and laughing and fawning over me. I had never been given so much attention in my life, and I remember thinking, 'This is what it must feel like to be grown-up, all the time.' It was the best."

"Then what happened?"

He was rushing me, and I almost turned to glare at him for it.

But all the expositional parts of the story had been shared now, and I was at the part he was pushing me to get to, so might as well just go there. "We drove back home. I slept most of the drive, and the Bentley was already pulled up in the driveway when Ron woke me to say we were back. I waited for Charles to open the door for me, like I'd been taught to do, but instead of stepping aside for me to get out, he got in. The backseat was spacious, but it was weird—all three of us sitting there in the driveway in the dark, me sandwiched between the two of them. I got nervous then. I remember worrying I did something wrong. I don't know why I immediately thought that after the rest of the day had been so fun. There was just a shift in the energy somehow.

"Ron asked me if I loved having Charles around, and when I told him I did, he said that was really good because Charles loved being around me too. He said that I should call him 'Sir,' because that's what grown-up girls called the men who loved them. He said I should call them both that, that it would be a special code between all of us. A fun way to express our love without anyone knowing.

"And then his voice got really sharp and he told me again how pretty I was. But that there were consequences for being so pretty, and it was time for me to address my responsibilities since I was such a grown-up girl." I swallowed, embarrassed at how much the memory affected me, at how believable his proclamation still felt.

"What did they force you to do?" Edward's tone had changed. It was softer, no longer pressing but reassuring. As though he suspected the words were stuck in my throat and needed a hook to pull them out. He would be that hook.

"They didn't force me," I said, feeling my cheeks heat. "Convinced me, is more accurate. Ron pointed to Charles's lap. I'd always been taught not to look at men's crotches, and I knew nothing about erections, but I did know that the bulge in his pants wasn't right. I'd felt Ron's pants get stiff a lot of the time when he held me on his lap, though, so maybe that clicked for me. I'm not sure what I thought, really, except that I shouldn't be looking at where Ron was telling me to look.

"But he told me I needed to look, because I'd done that to him. He said that pretty girls made men hurt there, and that I needed to fix it." The exact thing he said came to me suddenly. "He said it wasn't nice to leave men hurting, and that I could make him feel better. With my hand."

I could remember it distinctly. The sound of his zipper coming down, the sight of the red ugly baton of flesh Charles had hidden beneath. The way Ron showed me to spit on my palm before taking the other man in my hand. I could remember how his skin felt and how my fingers looked curled around his hot length. How my arm got tired, and how it smelled when the white ooze finally spurted over my fist.

The memory was so strong, I didn't notice Edward had leaned up beside me until his hand was turning my chin toward him. "Look at me, Celia," he said sternly.

I couldn't do it. I couldn't lift my eyes to meet his. "I know," I said, hoping it would be enough to acknowledge the point he surely wanted to drill into me. "It's not my fault."

"It's not. Now look at me." It took a beat before I managed to find his gaze. His eyes were intense and piercing, even in the dark, but they were also deep and warm. "Say it again."

"It's not my fault," I repeated.

"Whose fault is it?"

"Ron's."

"And this Charles guy. You don't have more of a name than that?"

"I don't." If there was more about the man buried in my head, I didn't want to go searching for it, though I could tell that was exactly what Edward wanted me to do.

I leaned away from him so I could get a better view of his expression. "You look like you're planning things. I don't like that look."

A beat passed before he smirked, a beat that confirmed he was definitely planning something. "Are my plans really that objectionable?"

In the past his sessions had inspired torturous oral sex and pretending to auction me off to a room full of strange men. "Uh, yeah, they kind of are. They're terrifying."

"You like that about them. About me. And my methods work." His smile widened.

That egotistical bastard.

Admittedly, I hadn't had nightmares about the auction my uncle had put me through. Edward had successfully "replaced" that trauma with his version, where he told me I was worth more than all the money in the world and that no price could be put on any part of me.

So, yeah, his methods did work. "It doesn't mean they're easy to endure."

"You can handle it." He reached for me.

But I leaned away. "What if I can't? What if you fucked me up forever?"

"Me?!"

He wasn't the one I was mad at, yet I suddenly felt angry, and he was there. "Yes, you. I was fine before you came along. I might not have been a decent person, but at least I wasn't visibly fucked up. You're the one who brought all this to the surface."

"And I'm going to be the one who helps you sort through it so it doesn't destroy you," he said, soothingly. He reached his hand out to rub his knuckles across my cheek. "I have a plan, bird. I'll take care of you. Trust me."

I wanted to trust him. I loved him, and I was smart enough to know that the two went hand in hand.

But the thing about him forcing me to look at myself meant that now I saw everything. I saw the ways I'd been taught to manipulate others. I saw what it looked like when people manipulated me. I recognized patterns of behavior in my relationships I'd never noticed before.

And what I saw scared me.

"There's something else," Edward said, reading me with his astute ability. "Something else you remember?"

"No." It sounded like a lie, even to my ears.

"Tell me."

I didn't want to voice it, because if I did, and if his response wasn't good enough, I'd have to reevaluate our marriage and what we could be to each other.

But if I didn't voice it, our relationship would suffer just the same. He required authenticity and honesty from me, and if I couldn't give him that, we had nothing.

I shifted toward him, holding the covers tightly against my chest like they could hide the vulnerability that my question posed. "How are we different?"

His forehead wrinkled as he worked out what I was asking. "You mean besides the fact that I have not and would never share you with another man, how is our relationship different than the one you had with your uncle?"

I nodded, once, feeling guilty that the question even crossed my mind. But also feeling bold because another Celia, the one who had been the victim of her doting uncle, would have accepted that a man's love meant blindly submitting.

I couldn't be her anymore. I was fragile from my recent break-throughs, but I was strong enough to take this stand. I would not be groomed and molded into something someone else wanted, for his pleasure only. Not anymore.

And where did that leave me with Edward? A man who wanted to dictate my life. A man who wanted me to yield to his will.

His knuckles unwrapped to cradle around my jaw. "You want this," he said, holding me with his fierce gaze. "You want me to take charge of you. You want to belong to me. And the minute you stop wanting this is the minute I step away."

It was the right answer, and though I still held on to a fair amount of trepidation about what a healthy marriage would look like between us, I sank into his arms and submitted to his kiss, because he was right—I wanted it.

FOUR

THEN: EDWARD

"I CAN DO IT," Kofi said, decidedly. "It will take a while to make it look believable, but I can definitely do it."

"You'll do it little by little? Make it almost unnoticeable at first. There can't be red flags going off with the first transaction." There was no way this could be easily detected if it was going to be convincing.

"Sure thing. I'll spread the embezzlements over time. Then a larger one when you want him to be caught.

I nodded.

"I can't guarantee a long prison sentence," he warned.

"That's fine. I do want him in prison, but the more important thing is that he won't be able to qualify to foster anymore."

"He won't be able to be anywhere near kids after prison time," Kofi promised. "Depending on where he's sent, I can throw in a couple of prison beatings too if you like."

I thought about Camilla, about the burn marks she hid under her clothes, about the scars that weren't visible that took longer to heal. "I'd like," I said. "Make it hurt."

Kofi grinned. "Can do. I could start this as soon as you send your payment. Half upfront."

I took a beat, as though considering, but I'd already made up my mind. I would have paid twice the price he'd quoted, now that I had money. It was well worth it.

"I'll transfer the funds first thing when I get back to London," I said, extending my hand out to shake on the deal we'd apparently just made.

"Fanfuckingtastic," Kofi said, leaning back in his chair. He pulled a joint out of his front pocket, lit it, and took a drag.

"I told you this was a place of business," Roman said, with a wink.

I hadn't believed him when we'd first arrived. He'd told me I'd find the sorts of people I needed on the island, but when we'd landed, and I'd discovered Exceso was a place of pleasure and debauchery, I'd been skeptical.

After several hours spent in a building known as The Base, he'd proven he was right. Yes, sex was the main transaction on the island, but there were other deals that were made as well. Not only had I made the arrangement with Kofi to take down Camilla's abuser, but I'd also met with a group of bounty hunters who'd assured me they could help track down many of the family items that had been sold off after my parents' deaths. It was bound to be an expensive project, but I was completely invested.

I sank back in my armchair and took a sip of my brandy. There was still a long road ahead of me to get all the justice I sought, but today had been one of progress.

"And you doubted me," Roman said, throwing back the rest of his scotch. "Have I ever let you down?"

I should have known better than to doubt Roman Moore. He'd proven himself time and time again over the last two years. The man had been waiting for me after my graduation from grammar school.

"I was friends with your father," he had said. "Let's go get back his money, shall we?"

I'd been skeptical then too. I'd already tried to talk to the authorities about the money my cousins had stolen from us and been told adamantly that there was no case. The funds were gone, according to the investigation they'd conducted. Therefore there was nothing to pursue.

But Roman Moore knew differently.

"Your cousins hid the money in offshore accounts," he had said. *"They've spent some of it, and there's not an exorbitant amount left, but it's enough to get you started."*

"How do you know?" He was a stranger telling me about family money that I'd never heard of. I had no reason to believe him.

But he had a compelling answer. *"I'm the one who set them up."*

Roman Moore wasn't exactly the most ethical person, it turned out. When he'd discovered the cousins who had been entrusted to raise us and watch over our money had filed bankruptcy and turned my sister and I over to foster care, Roman had weaseled his way into their good graces, offering to help them hide the money only so he'd be able to lead me to it when it came time.

That wasn't all he had to share. He also told me in detail how my father's company had been taken over and disassembled, sharing information I never would have been able to glean without someone who had been on the inside. It was only with his help that I was able to add the most important name to my revenge list—Werner Media.

"You did leave Camilla and I in foster care for six years," I reminded him now. "I'd say that was a bit of a letdown."

"Pshaw." He rolled his eyes. "I've told you time and time again—I'm not fond of children."

That was Roman. Willing to help out the son of a former friend, but only if it didn't inconvenience him too much.

Though his version of loyalty was skewed, I'd grown to be quite dependent on him. He'd helped me get access to the money that should have always been mine, then he'd helped me destroy the cousins who'd stolen it, leaving them even more destitute than before my parents had died. Now, along with supporting my goals for vengeance, he was helping me build my own media company.

Three decades my senior, he'd become a sort of father figure, and I appreciated him more than I could ever express.

"Business is done for the night, got it?" Roman gestured to Stefania, the heavyset woman he'd chosen as "his" when we'd arrived. At the snap of his fingers, she came over and sat on his lap, flaunting her generous bosom in his face. "Now we enjoy the benefits of the island. The very voluptuous benefits."

I scoffed, realizing I should have kept my disinterest to myself only after I'd made the sound.

"Look, Ed..." Somehow I managed not to cringe at the nickname he sometimes used for me. "You can't be fed on revenge alone. You need to search for other things to feed you as well. Like women." Roman peeled down one cup of Stefania's bikini top. "Women taste much better than fury."

I wasn't fortunate enough to have found that to be true.

"I think I'll stick to my brandy," I said, watching as he trailed his tongue over her nipple, teasing her until it grew taut. Something hard and hot spiked in my chest. A sort of envy that didn't wash down easily with my drink.

Roman turned from his current feast to give me his full attention. "Whatever you're into, Ed, there are women here for that. I promise you."

I wasn't sure about that. I wasn't naive enough to believe that my tastes were singular, but I was experienced enough to know they were somewhat unique.

If there were ever a time that I was tempted to challenge that notion, however, it was now. We'd spent the day distracted with business, but I hadn't been immune to the abundance of beautiful women in our midst nor the sexual acts that had been performed with high frequency around us.

Still, fooling around wasn't my priority. There were more items on my list to be addressed.

"I'm good. Thank you." I finished off the contents of my tumbler in a single swallow.

"Can I refill your drink?" The words were said before I'd even lowered my empty glass, spoken perfectly but with a fairly thick French accent.

I looked up to scrutinize the woman who had asked. She wasn't even that—she was a girl. Fully developed in a dress that revealed as much as it hid, but very young. Her plump lips were lined in blood red, the color bringing out her brown eyes and olive skin.

"Are you even legal?" I asked before I could fully consider the question.

"Are you?" she tossed back, her hip thrown to the side, tauntingly. It begged to be touched, to be gripped with firm fingers while being fucked from behind.

Yes, she was young—too young for most of the men in the room. But I was young too. Age-appropriate, in fact.

I slanted my eyes, considering it. Considering taking Roman's advice, forgetting my schemes and losing myself in a woman instead, at least for the night.

Not this one, though. She was tempting, but as I'd hinted to my friend, I needed a woman who could handle me. Not a child, no matter how luscious her mouth.

"I'm closer than you," I said back, turning my gaze from her in obvious dismissal.

"Everyone's legal here. International waters in the middle of the Caribbean. What kind of talk is this?" Roman was intent on merriment and was determined that I join in.

I gave a halfhearted shrug. "I guess I forgot where we were. I'll have another cognac." I'd only recently discovered the brandy, and it was quickly becoming a favorite.

"Coming right away. Sir," she added with enough sarcasm to suggest I didn't deserve the title and enough challenge in her tone to dare that I try.

She was right—I didn't deserve the title. Compared to the others in the room, I was merely a boy. I had big confidence and even bigger plans, but I was still only an intern and grateful to those who would teach me how to carry them out.

Yet the unearned title ignited something in me, something low and primal that had my dick stirring with curiosity, and try as I might, I couldn't keep myself from watching her as she walked away. She still had baby-fat that many of the more mature women on the island had long lost. It made her appear curvy and lush, and the back view highlighted this as well as the front. Her short dress hugged her indecently, showing off the definition of her round behind, and I could suddenly imagine my face buried there, my teeth tearing at her juicy flesh.

No, no. She was too young for that. Too innocent for the likes of me.

But what was an innocent girl doing in a place like this?

A dark thought jarred my stare. I swung my head sharply back to the men. "Are the women here of their own volition?"

Stefania let out an uninterpretable laugh.

"Fuck, man!" Kofi scanned nervously around. "You shouldn't even be asking something like that."

Roman seemed less concerned with the implications of my question. "It's fine," he said, reassuring the other man. "You certainly don't want to be asking Maximillian about the women he's with, and anyone who comes with Abdul Bagher is most likely owned. But if you're wondering about our little waitress—she's definitely here because she wants to be."

I focused on the last part of what he'd said, which was somehow the most shocking. "How do you know that? She can't even have finished grammar school."

"That don't mean nothing," Kofi said. "She's obviously flirting with you, man. You should bang her."

"I know because she came with Claudette." Roman nodded to a woman across the room, kneeling at the feet of an older man who was sitting at one of the conference tables. "Claudette often brings friends. This is the first time I've seen this particular girl, but they're all the same."

"Wannabe subs," Kofi spelled out.

"Wannabe, exactly." Stefania smirked in agreement.

"Well, they come because they believe they want the submissive lifestyle," Roman asserted. "Most just find that they don't once they've truly experienced it. Claudette loves it, though, so I think she keeps spreading the gospel, so to say, hoping to find other disciples."

I studied Claudette. She was fully naked, her eyes cast down. Her arms were twisted behind her, and the spread of her thighs looked like it had to be uncomfortable. Yet she sat motionless, even when the man reached down to stroke her head, like she was a pet.

Her discomfort was an admitted turn-on.

Except I didn't imagine myself a typical dominant. A sadist, perhaps, but I enjoyed psychological pain more than physical. I'd learned that about myself early on. I'd fucked quite a lot, despite my young age. I also fucked quite mean, and I couldn't bring myself to believe that any woman would truly seek that sort of treatment, not for more than the occasional novelty, anyway. I certainly hadn't encountered any that found it particularly enjoyable, which was why I'd come to practice a one-time-only rule with my partners. That way it was my choice not to get involved and I never had to endure the inevitable conversation about changing my behavior if a relationship were to continue.

Because changing wasn't ever going to happen. I was who I was, and I was definitely not nice.

Seeing dominance in action, though, I wondered if maybe there were ways that I could adapt. Maybe I could be satisfied with rigid rules and doling out punishments. Maybe there would be room to manipulate sex into a game that fed my sadistic needs as well as the masochistic desires of another.

Shit, what was I thinking? That wasn't where my energy belonged. I had too much on my plate to worry about managing a complicated relationship as well.

"I need some air," I said, suddenly finding the environment stifling. Without waiting for anyone to acknowledge my pronouncement, I took off toward the main doors, swiping one of Roman's cigars from the side table on my way.

Outside, the air was heavy and thick, but it felt less suffocating than the impenetrable fog of sex and desire that hung inside The Base. I walked far enough up the path to be out of the sightline of the security guard outside the building, then, when I was truly alone, I bit off the tip of the cigar and lit the end.

I puffed on the end, reveling in the flavor of the Belicoso. I'd managed to successfully kick the cigarette habit, but Roman had turned me on to these in the process, and I doubted this form of smoking was a vice I'd ever be able to abandon. Besides revenging, I considered it my favorite hobby, an enjoyable way to draw out the flavor of my thoughts along with the taste of the cigar.

The sound of heels on the stones tugged my head to look behind me. I nearly groaned when I saw her, so irritated at having my solace interrupted, the girl from inside. The friend of Claudette's.

The twitch of my cock only aggravated me more.

"You're stalking me," I said, not bothering to hide my annoyance.

"You left without your drink."

"And so I did."

She came close enough to hand me the tumbler, and I took it from her, my fingers brushing hers as I did, purposefully. I wasn't quite sure what I intended with her, but the fact that she'd followed after me had me pissed off enough to want to harass her, at least a little.

She jolted at the touch, her eyes growing darker, the dilation of her pupils noticeable even in the moonlight.

She thought she wanted this? From me? Well, we'd see about that.

"How old are you?" I demanded.

"Old enough."

"That's not what I asked."

"Twenty," she said, sticking out her chin with the obvious lie.

"Try again."

She licked her lips. "Eighteen."

I turned my back to her, dismissing her. I didn't do bullshit. I'd had enough of it in my lifetime. I only cared to deal in honesty now.

"Merde," she muttered. "Seventeen."

I gave her only the rotation of my head. "Is that the truth?"

"Oui."

There were only two years between us. I'd fucked plenty of women with a greater separation, both older and younger.

Why then did my attraction to this one strike me as so depraved?

It was because of what I wanted to do to her. The obscenity of which was so vivid in my head, I'd be able to use it as wanking material for months.

My pants stiffened as I thought about acting those images out.

"You're seventeen and you're so sure you want this? To be ordered around by a man who knows better than you what will bring you pleasure?" I was incredulous.

But, also, hopeful.

She tilted her head, assessing the subtext of my question. "I'm good at being told what to do. I like it. I'm old enough to know that."

That was fair. Hadn't I known for myself when I was still younger than she was?

I wasn't ready to trust it. "To be treated like a pet? Like a dog?"

She nodded definitively. "Completely cared for."

It wasn't an unappealing idea, caring for another creature, though I'd so far neglected doing so in any form. My flat was animal free. No matter how much she pleaded, I still insisted Camilla stay at boarding school. The only thing that truly had my care was the list of people who had wronged me. It was all I had room to commit to.

Yet, there was so much opportunity in what this girl seemed to want. I could see it. Could see the ways I could enjoy her, enjoy manipulating her life this way and that. The question was, could she really enjoy it as well?

On a whim, I tapped the growing ash off my cigar and threw it slightly down the path. "There, dog. Go. Fetch."

She was on her knees in a flash, crawling along the rough stones, marring the smooth skin of her knees.

And I was instantly hard.

When she reached the cigar, she bent and picked it up in her mouth, before turning to crawl back to me, her breasts swinging and straining against the light fabric of her dress. Once at my feet, she knelt back and thrust her neck forward in offering, extending her hands up my thighs like a dog pawing its master.

There was no way she could miss the rigidity of my cock. It was at eye level.

Yet, she kept her gaze on me, laser focused, and in that moment, an intoxicating kind of power that I'd never felt before surged through me like a lightning bolt.

I took the cigar from her mouth and brought it to mine, puffing on it to rekindle the cherry as I appraised her. "Do your knees hurt," I asked, knowing she wouldn't move from her position until I allowed her.

"Yes, sir." This time the title was given with respect, and the bolt of power surged through me once again.

Good. She was uncomfortable, and I was in control of that discomfort, and it wasn't exactly the way I liked to fuck with my women, and it didn't taste quite as succulent as fury, but it was bloody delicious all the same.

"What's your name?"

Her eyes stayed pinned to mine. "Marion Barbier."

I took one of her hands with mine and moved it from my leg to the pulsing rod above it. She was fumbling and inexperienced, but so willing to be instructed.

This could fit into my life, couldn't it? There had to be enough space for this. Roman was right—a man needed more than the hobby of cigars to escape the business of retribution. This could be a very agreeable hobby.

As I guided my crown between her ready lips, I already felt the beginnings of our attachment, an invisible leash from the core of my being to the core of hers.

"Marion," I said, shoving deep into her tight throat with a grunt. "I think we're going to get along just fine."

FIVE

NOW: CELIA

I'D KNOWN before I woke that it would be to an empty space beside me. Even while sharing a bed in Amelie, Edward often was up before I was. We were still new at so much of our relationship, but I'd already learned he slept very little and was an early riser, and now that we were back in the real world—the world that was supposed to be our real home—he had responsibilities and obligations that he hadn't on the island.

He was the CEO of a major media company, after all. I knew what that job entailed. Long hours at the office, rising early, late arrival home from work. I'd grown up with an absent father. I expected an absent husband as well.

The knowledge didn't curb the stab of loneliness that pierced through me as I lay with my eyes still closed, wondering about what my day would be. It had been easy in the Caribbean. Much of my time had been dictated by Edward, and as much as I'd fought it at first, I'd liked the rhythm of the routine he'd given to my days. Yoga and chess games and beauty appointments and books—not all of my time had been planned for me, but the moments that had were pillars that helped form the structure of my life around them.

Where were the pillars here in London?

I had no job, no friends, no family but Edward. What was I supposed to *do*?

Lying around in bed certainly wasn't an option. The staff would talk. The employees that worked here weren't warm and affable the way the staff had been on the island. They ran the house with formality and decorum and would likely look down on a mistress who spent the day lounging around.

With a weary sigh, I opened my eyes, planning to head to the room that had been mine. Whether or not Edward meant for me to move into his suite or just *sleep* there remained to be discussed, but for now, my belongings were still next door, including my clothes. Finding something to wear would probably occupy a portion of my morning. I'd had some seasonally appropriate items from before I'd left for my honeymoon, but that had been more than a year ago, and my body had become trimmer while on the island. I wasn't sure anything would still fit.

Conscious of the painting on the wall—the painting I would definitely deal with before the day was over—I climbed out of the warm bed, and immediately halted, my eyes caught by the armchair that my husband had bent me over the night before. My lower belly hummed involuntarily, but it wasn't the memory of the thorough fucking that had me frozen in place. It was the white and black colorblock jumpsuit draped over the back that had me riveted, along with the lacy white bra and panty set. The black pointy-toed pumps on the floor in front were nothing to blink at either.

A smile crept up on my lips as I walked over to pick up the single piece of paper laid out on top of the clothing. Sure it was possible that the outfit had been borrowed from Camilla—the long sleeves were certainly her style—or that a staff member had been instructed to set the items out, but I recognized the paper before I touched it. Edward had written me dozens of personal notes when he'd sent me clothing in the past, and the cards had looked just like this, embossed with his initials in the bottom corner.

Bird,

Wear what I've laid out and nothing more. Put your hair up and light makeup, if you wish.

I expect you to get reacquainted with the staff. You are the lady of the house now and they'll look to you for guidance. Meet with the chef early to plan dinner. I'll want it ready to be served when I get home at seven-thirty. Then speak to Jeremy about having your belongings moved to our suite. There is plenty of room in my closet for the both of us, but if you like, you may keep off-season items in the closet next door.

After dinner, we'll meet in the den to discuss our marriage going forward.

Taking care of the household should occupy a good deal of your day. You also have a manicure appointment at one. The manicurist will come here. She has been instructed to paint your nails pink. If you have time left over, I invite you to try out the pool downstairs. Or there is space in the exercise room for a yoga session if you prefer. You are also welcome to take any book from my library. I've had it stocked with several titles I think you will enjoy since the last time you were living here.

Last, but not least—call your mother.

Edward

THE SMILE VANISHED and reappeared as I read through the letter. Frankly, I didn't know how to feel about it. I was irritated at being ordered around, especially in such detail. So irritated that I was ready to crumple up his note and ignore every word of it.

But I was grateful for it as well.

Thrilled about it, even.

How could I not be? I had longed for structure, and he'd known, without me ever saying a word. Not only had he known, but he'd gone out of his way to give me what I needed. He'd taken time out of his busy life to attend to me. It made me feel special in a way that I hadn't felt since Ron had doted on me all those years ago.

The comparison sent a chill down my spine.

I shook it off remembering what Edward had pointed out the night before—I chose this.

I chose him.

I hadn't chosen Ron. And the reason Ron had so easily wormed his way into my graces was because I had so badly wanted to be treated the way he'd treated me. Like I was meant to be cared for. Like I deserved it. Like I was worthy of a person's time and attention.

I still relished that sort of care. And if Edward wanted to care for me like that, without the nefarious expectations that had been attached to Ron's care, then why not let him?

Because you don't entirely trust it, I reminded myself.

Or rather, I didn't entirely trust myself. I didn't trust that I knew what was best for myself. Was this it? Or was this falling into an unhealthy pattern because I was too lazy or too weak to work out a better one?

I didn't know the answer.

And I wasn't going to figure it out standing here naked. With that decided, I scooped up the clothing and carried them with me to the bathroom, the smile back on my lips. I could accept what was given. For today, anyway. I could allow myself to find comfort in Edward's care. I could follow the orders he'd given this one time, if for no other reason than it was easier than finding any other way to approach the day.

FALLING into the role of lady of the house was easier than I'd anticipated. I'd watched my mother perform the duties for all of my life, never with any particular interest in following in her footsteps, but once the job was laid out in front of me and handed to me as my own, I found it unexpectedly satisfying.

The clothing Edward had selected helped, if I was being honest. The jumpsuit was a power outfit. After having worn sundresses for so long, the pants were noticeably different than what had become my norm. I couldn't help but feel like a different person wearing it, a person who was meant to be taken seriously. A person who commanded authority.

Then underneath, the underwear, though virginal in its white color, was see-through and sexy and fit the situation so perfectly, it could only be considered what it was—a personal message from Edward. He wanted me to remember that he knew who I was, remember that I was new at the tasks I'd been given. Innocent and yet not. Without stating it out loud to everyone else, he wanted to remind me of my place. *You are in charge of this household, but I am in charge of you.*

It was strange to realize he'd given me power in my submission. I wasn't sure how to process that fact, but I couldn't deny that I liked the way it made me feel. Maybe not quite as fierce as a dragon, but definitely stronger than a wounded little bird.

As instructed, I met with the chef as soon as I'd dressed. Solene was nowhere near as approachable as Joette had been, but she was organized and polite. She made our meeting simple, giving me options rather than requiring me to come up with a menu out of thin air.

When we'd finished planning the meals, she'd sent me to Jeremy to confirm which dinnerware to set out (I chose the fancy china) and go over the calendar. There wasn't much on the schedule for the day, but there were several parties and social obligations that Edward expected me to attend with him in the near future as well as a bunch of items that were left for me to decide. I said yes to Handel's *Messiah* and no to *The Nutcracker* and held off on deciding about the revival of *My Fair Lady* in the West End until the reviews came out next week.

After that, I instructed him on moving my belongings from my suite to Edward's, and by the time we got to discussing the removal of Blanche Martin's country garden painting I was sure that I was making the decision from a place of strength. I didn't want to look at reminders of the past on a daily basis. That didn't mean I was overly vulnerable. It meant I was capable of knowing what was best for me, at least as far as what environment I spent my time in.

Besides, the whimsical feel of the landscape portrait didn't fit the rest of the masculine decor, and even if it was no longer my job, I was still a designer at heart.

With the house taken care of, it was time to call my mother. Surprisingly, this was the hardest of the tasks that I'd been assigned. It wasn't as though I hadn't communicated with her at all in the last year —I had written her letters that Edward had passed on, though not all of them had been quite intact. He'd shown me all the emails she'd sent in reply so I was caught up on her life as well.

But I hadn't actually *talked* to her. Hadn't heard her voice. Hadn't had to wonder if she could detect the secrets that I kept in my tone.

Not that she'd ever figured out my secrets in the past.

I was making too much of a big deal about it. Straightening my spine, I sat at Edward's desk in the library, picked up the receiver from the cradle and dialed my home number.

"Edward," my mother said in lieu of hello. "I was wondering if I'd hear from you soon. It's been a few weeks."

My chest pinched at the sound of her voice in my ear. It had been so long. I hadn't realized how much I'd missed it.

I would have probably said something to that effect, but her greeting had me stunned speechless. Quickly, I tried to assign meaning to what she'd said and came up empty-handed.

"Edward?" she prompted.

"Mom?" It was the best I could manage.

"Celia? Darling, is this you? I saw the number and naturally expected your husband. Why isn't this a surprise. Does this mean you're finally back from the middle of nowhere?"

I pulled myself together. "Yes, it's me. I arrived back in London yesterday."

"Thank God. Sending letters via email is sweet and quaint and all that, but it's such a pain to have to sit down in front of the computer and go through all the nonsense of composing my thoughts."

That was my mother. She had a smartphone but I was fairly certain the only thing she used it for was playing solitaire and calling her friends immediately when fresh gossip crossed her path. She was glad I was back to civilization because my absence inconvenienced her, not because she'd missed hearing my voice. Not because she'd wondered how I sounded.

Really, had I expected anything different?

But I was still caught on what she'd said first. "Why did you think I was Edward?" Sure his name probably came up on the caller ID, but wouldn't she assume that was me? And she'd said something about it having been a few weeks. Had he...?

No. He couldn't have.

Could he?

"Because it's usually Edward calling from this number," she said like the question was ridiculous.

Damn. He really had.

"It's been a little while since his last call," she went on. "I figured he'd be ringing soon."

"He's called more than once?" I was having a hard time processing any of what she was saying.

"Well, yes. Every time after he visited you, I think. At least it seemed that was the pattern. He always said he'd just been to see you, so I presumed—"

"Mom, wait," I said, cutting her off. "He called you after his visits to the island?"

"Like I said, I never asked specifically. Why is this so surprising to you? Did he not tell you he was calling?"

No, he most certainly did not tell me he'd called my mother. Another incredible idea shot to mind. "Did he talk to Dad, too?"

"Oh, no, no. Definitely not. After the idea had been proposed at your wedding, your father has been hounding Edward to do some sort of corporate deal and, well, you know your husband. He wanted to wait to get past the newlywed stage before getting tangled with business. Smart man you married, honey, though your father wouldn't under-stand. So I haven't mentioned the phone calls to him at all. You shouldn't either."

"No, of course not." I was blown away. Not only because Edward had called my mother—on more than one occasion—but because of how he'd handled my father. Even if he hadn't decided whether to keep me alive or not, he could have certainly weaseled his way into Werner Media through my parents if he'd wanted to. Which, I would have assumed he'd want to.

I really *didn't* know my husband.

So why had he called my mother, if not for some sort of gain? "What did he say when he called you, Mom?"

"Just told me how you were doing, what you were working on. Since you couldn't call yourself. It was really sort of sweet, reaching out on your behalf. Told me how you were getting really into yoga and about all that work you did to the house there. Edward said you fell in love with the island. You must have to have stayed away from your new husband for so long. I told him I didn't raise my daughter to be so negligent of her husband's needs, but he insisted he was happy if you were happy. Not only is he a smart man, he's a good man. Amazing you were able to find him after you managed to let go of Hudson. Those men don't usually come twice in a lifetime. You better hold on to that one. You'll be a fool if you don't."

With that, my mother burst into the latest society gossip, unable to continue a conversation not focused on things that interested her.

I sat back in Edward's chair and half listened to her, my mind so caught up in her revelation I was even able to ignore her dig about Hudson. My husband *was* a smart man. He'd endeared my mother to him, which was one of the smartest moves he could make.

But what if he hadn't made the move because he was smart? What if he'd actually called because he'd cared about me and thereby cared about her? What if he'd cared about me for longer than I'd realized? For longer than he'd like to admit?

There was no question that Edward Fasbender was a smart man.

But a good man? I was still trying to figure that one out.

I MANAGED a swim in the afternoon. The pool on the lower level was a good size and was heated, but couldn't compare to swimming outdoors in the Caribbean. Still, it was a familiar activity and put a sense of routine to my day.

Afterward, when I'd donned the jumpsuit again and fashioned my hair the way Edward had commanded, I came downstairs to await his homecoming and ran into my first household management snag.

"They're for special occasions only, Jeremy," Camilla was stating sternly. "They always have been. You're well aware of this. So why would you suddenly pull them out for a Monday in December? It's not even a saint day."

Curious, I walked into the dining room and realized right away what they were discussing—the china set I'd selected to be used for the evening's meal.

I hadn't been spotted yet, so I considered for a handful of seconds which way to approach this. I could assert my authority, which I was sure that Edward would insist that I do.

Or I could try to make friends with the only woman currently in my life who wasn't paid to be there.

"It was my faux pas," I said, drawing both eyes to me. "I selected them because they were the most beautiful set, and I thought it was a shame to hide their beauty away. I didn't realize they were special. I sincerely apologize."

Jeremy had the good sense to stay quiet.

Camilla opened her mouth twice to say something then shut it again. It was only then that it dawned on me what an odd position this must be for her. Before I'd married Edward, I'd lived in the house for a couple of months, never considering who it was who oversaw the house. Never considering that it was Camilla.

Now that I'd returned and was Edward's wife, I certainly hadn't thought about what that might mean for his sister's role in the household. It couldn't have been easy, watching someone she'd thought of as her enemy usurp her throne.

It didn't mean I should cower to her, but I could make the situation more bearable. "Jeremy, please do as Ms. Dougherty suggests. We'll save this set for Christmas dinner."

Before he could begin to gather the dishes, Camilla stopped him. "No, that's not necessary. It didn't occur to me that you'd requested them. I apologize for interfering." Swiftly, she stepped past me and out into the hall.

I nodded to Jeremy to leave the place settings as is and then followed after my sister-in-law.

"Camilla," I said, catching her before she charged up the stairs. She paused, her shoulders rising with a visible inhale before she turned to face me. "I really am sorry. I didn't mean to step on your toes."

"I was the one stepping on toes." While she wasn't quite warm, she was direct. "They were my parents' wedding china, is all, but they are Edward's now and therefore yours to use as you see fit. And perhaps you're right—their beauty is wasted all locked up."

"Maybe we could carve out some time later this week and figure out how we can manage things together?"

She studied me with incredulous eyes. "You're joking, right?"

"Not at all. You've lived here longer than I have. You know how things work best. It doesn't make sense for me to change things that aren't broken."

She blinked in disbelief. "I'm sorry. It's just so unexpected. I had you pegged as...well. I suppose that's what Edward's been trying to tell me. That you aren't at all the woman we believed you were. It might take some time before I truly understand what that means."

"If it helps, I'm not quite the woman I believed I was either. And it's definitely going to take some time before I figure out who that is."

Her features softened, her jaw relaxing. She moved down the steps until we were on the same level. "I know I've been cold and, at times, cruel. I hope you understand that it's out of a sense of protection. For a long time, Edward was all I had in the world. In all fairness, he's been equally as protective of me."

"I'm sure he has," I said, barely above a whisper, too afraid to break the honest moment between us.

"He believes in you, though. So I shall too." She swallowed, her throat swelling with the action. "I want you to know, I contacted an estate agent this morning. I'll be moving out as soon as I find something suitable for me and Freddie."

My gasp was audible. "No! Edward would never want that! I'm sure of it. Please, please don't leave on my account."

"I've already told him," she insisted. "You are correct that he wasn't happy about it, but let me assure you that it's not because I feel threatened by you or because I have lingering animosity but because I want this relationship of yours to be successful. For his sake. And marriages never work when there is a third party present. Trust me, I know."

My brow quirked, intrigued by her insinuation. Was she speaking about her own marriage? I didn't know enough about her relationship with her husband before he'd left her a widow, only that he'd died in a house fire several months before Freddie was born.

Before I could even consider prying, however, two members of the staff came around the corner of the stairs, the country garden painting carried between them.

"Excuse me, madam," one of them said. "The canvas was too large to fit in the lift."

Not that the canvas was all that large. European elevators tended to be quite compact.

"No problem," she said, shuffling out of their way. "May I ask why it's being removed? It was only put up just last week."

She looked at me with her question, the subtext clear—*Eddie put that painting up, does he know you're taking it down?*

"I know," I said, trying to figure out how I was going to step around this response. "Edward was very sweet to hang it, thinking that it was special to me, but it's not, and it doesn't go with the room. I told him I'd have it removed today."

Rather, he gave me permission to have it removed. I didn't want to be that specific, possibly because I was embarrassed to admit that I believed I needed his consent, though Camilla already seemed to understand what kind of man her brother was.

"It's such a lovely piece, though," she said, peering at it with awe.

I was half afraid she'd suggest we display it elsewhere, and after just inviting her to help make household decisions, I knew I needed to cut the possibility off at the head. "Honestly? It brings up bad memories. When I see the swing, I'm back in a place I don't want to visit again, if that makes sense."

I didn't know what Edward had told her about me or if she knew that I knew anything that had happened to her, but as one abused girl to another, I hoped it was enough of a response to resonate without further explanation.

Again she studied me, her eyes as focused as her brother's often were, and without ever having seen any of her art, I suddenly knew she was probably a very good photographer. "I think I understand," she said after several heavy seconds had passed. "Objects as well as locations can be haunted."

"Yes," I agreed.

"Every time I see a fire poker, I'm reminded of my dead husband. Best to move it on out or at least out of sight. If you've noticed, all the pokers in the house are well hidden."

Like the thread of conversation that had been cut off by the arrival of the painting, this thread was cut by the arrival of my husband coming home from work. He greeted me with a kiss that curled my toes and made me blush since his sister was present.

Then Jeremy announced that dinner was served and the moment was long past reviving the topic.

But all through dinner—which was unexpectedly convivial, Edward at the head of the table, me at one side, his sister on the other with Freddie in a booster seat next to her—I wondered about the odd statement and the hint she'd given to an unhappy marriage. Frank Dougherty had died in a fire, and perhaps it wasn't a stretch then to believe that fire pokers upset his widow because of the association. But why didn't the fireplace itself bother her? Or candles, several of which were lit up on the dining table as we ate?

My husband was still a mystery to me, so it made sense that his sister was as well. It was only surprising that her mystery was starting to seem equally intriguing.

SIX

EDWARD

CELIA REACHED into the side table drawer and pulled out a coaster, setting it down pointedly before taking the cognac I offered. "There. In case I need to put my glass down momentarily," she said, referencing the last time we'd been in this room negotiating, when she'd set her tumbler on unprotected seventeenth century rosewood.

My blood hummed as it circulated lower. She learned fast and she learned well, which pleased me more than she could possibly know. "I would have thought you would be as keen to preserve old furniture as I am, considering your interests."

"Yeah, but last time the furniture wasn't mine." A smirk grazed her lips briefly, disappearing as she brought the glass up for a sip. When she lowered it again, her expression was serious. "Last night, you said you wouldn't share me."

I almost laughed, surprised by the lead she'd taken. I used the two steps it took to get to the armchair to gather myself, unbuttoning my jacket on the way. When I sat, facing her, I was composed.

"Is that where you want to start?" I asked, crossing one leg over the other then perching my own tumbler-clutching hand on my thigh.

The setting was exactly the same as the first time we'd negotiated the terms to our marriage—after dinner in my den, Celia on the sofa and I seated across from her. Both of us drinking one of my favorite three-star cognacs.

The only difference from that other night and this was that I no longer hated her as much as I wanted her, and the things that I intended to ask for would be genuine instead of passive-aggressive attempts to scare her away from our union.

Her brows turned inward as she considered how to respond. The topic made her noticeably nervous—her jaw was tight, her breaths shallow. She was beautiful like that, her agitation sending a charge to the air, causing her to fidget and buzz. I had the power to quell that anxiety, and I would.

But I'd let her linger in it first.

"It's just a complete one-eighty from the first time we were in this room," she said finally, the strength of her tone belying the lack of confidence underneath. "When you told me you'd help me find other lovers if necessary."

She took another sip then set the glass down on the coaster, the tremble in her hand barely apparent before she stroked both down her pant legs, likely to wipe clammy palms.

Breathtaking.

But she'd suffered enough on this point, especially when there were still things to discuss that would make her sweat more. "I was trying to find ways to keep you at a distance. You can see how well that turned out."

"Then you don't want other women." This time her pitch was higher and thin, almost more of a whispered prayer than a statement of confirmation.

"There will not be other women." There hadn't been since I'd slipped the ring on her finger, and the few I'd been with in the months before had all taken her face as I'd pushed them and prodded them and fucked them, only to be left wanting the real thing.

It had been the first sign that I'd fallen for her, when no other woman could come close to leaving me satisfied. When her name repeatedly fell from my mouth, ragged and angry, as I jerked myself raw.

Her shoulders loosened somewhat at my response, but her body remained mostly tight. "Didn't quite answer the question, but okay. Good." She reached again for her glass, as though she needed a point of focus that wasn't me. As though she thought she could disguise her turmoil.

As if I'd let her get away with hiding.

I could make her say it, could make her beg for the words she needed. I would have her begging for something or other before the evening was finished.

But we were only at the beginning of a conversation that mattered. So I wouldn't press. Not yet. "I do not want other women, bird. Is that better?"

Her relief was palpable. "Much."

A surge of unfounded jealousy raged through me, prompting the next commandment I issued, even more important than the first. "And there will be no other men. Which is non-negotiable."

"I suppose I can live with that." She was teasing, and it was obvious, but I couldn't help wanting to bend her over my knee and leave palm prints on her ass.

I managed to restrain myself. Barely. "How very noble of you."

Her eyes met mine and her grin widened, and as sure as I was that she rarely could fathom my thoughts, I was sure this time that she could. We held this gaze for several thick seconds, each one more taut and wanting than the last, until I moved my attention to the drink in my hand.

She took the cue to move the discussion along with it. "Then everything you said last time was just to turn me off?"

"No. Some of it I very much meant."

She knew I'd tell her eventually—that was entirely what this evening was about, after all—but she still hadn't shed her constant need to try to stay a step ahead of me, and she tried again now. "The traditionalist, man-of-the-house stuff. You don't want me to have a job."

I gave her a beat to second-guess before confirming her doubt. "Not true. I think work would be good for you. Part-time, anyway." She'd become a different person on Amelie when she'd begun her redesign projects. More alive and vibrant, and there was no way in hell I was letting her lose that. "In fact, I insist on it."

"*Insist.*" She said the word like it tasted bad. "Interesting."

She was a funny bird, quick-witted and wise but still completely clueless when it came to understanding herself. She was disgusted by the idea of yielding to me, recoiling any time it came up, and yet she submitted to me so naturally in other ways. Here she was wearing the clothes I'd dictated she wear, drinking the beverage I'd chosen for her, discussing the topics I'd planned, subconsciously following my cues to bring up the subjects herself. And she did it all happily, with a flush in her cheeks and a glow to her eyes that shone only when she surrendered.

And yet, she still believed it wasn't what she wanted.

That ended tonight. There would be no more insinuation on my part. My command would be acknowledged. "Yes, insist. As the man of the house, I have that authority."

Her arms folded over herself defensively. "So the whole subservient wife role is still something you're clinging to. I thought you didn't want me to be like Marion."

"You aren't like Marion."

"As you keep reminding me."

Again, she was ignorant. Acting as if she'd be better favored if she *was* like Marion.

How could I make her realize that wasn't what I wanted with her at all?

Marion had been precisely what I needed at the time. She'd been uncomplicated, never distracting or competing with the goals that had taken precedence above her. It had been easy to command her, and I'd liked that. She'd handed me the reins without any struggle, and that had made me powerful. Powerful enough to dominate the other areas of my life with similar ease.

But she'd been so willing. Too trusting. I couldn't count the number of times I'd wished she put up more of a struggle. Wished that submission was hard for her.

It was hard for Celia. And that was a very big turn-on, in more ways than just sexually.

I threw back the last of my brandy, rid myself of the glass, then steepled my hands over my knee. "I do not want you to be my submissive in all things, Celia. I don't want you to wear a collar, and I don't expect you to be kneeling naked at the door when I arrive home from work. I want—"

"Were those things you expected of Marion?"

I couldn't decide if I was more irritated by her interruption or by her continued mention of a woman who was solidly no longer a part of my life. My overall annoyance was plain in my answer. "My arrangement with Marion has no bearing on the arrangement I'd like to have with you. May I go on?"

"Yes, Edward."

Her smart mouth and saucy tone was going to get her in trouble soon. My cock roused in anticipation.

We aren't there yet, I silently instructed the swelling organ in my pants. There was too much still to be made clear before bringing sex into the equation.

I lowered my crossed leg to the floor and switched it for the other, subtly adjusting myself in the process. When I spoke again, my tone was softer but resolute. "I want you to let me take care of you. I want you to let me look after your well-being. I want authority over your free time, over your income. Over your body."

Heat simmered in her eyes, which she quickly blinked away. "Why?"

"Because I think you'll like it."

She let that settle. I could imagine the argument she was having over it in her head. She knew she'd like it, but could she let herself? What would that mean about her as a woman if she did? As a person? All logical questions yet irrelevant if she simply gave away the responsibility of answering. If she gave the decision-making to me.

After a dozen or more seconds had passed, she sank back into the couch. "That's it? You want to tell me what to do because you think I'll like having you pick out my clothes and tell me what I'm allowed to spend."

It wasn't quite a question, but I affirmed all the same. "And because I think it will be hard for you. And I know I will like that."

The heat returned to her eyes, and this time she let herself hold it. She was considering it. Really considering what it could be like, it was evident in her expression.

And thank God, because now we could have a real conversation about it.

"That sets me up to be very vulnerable," she said, finally understanding what I wanted from her.

"That isn't new."

"I thought we were past that."

"Did you think we were past it because you wanted to be? Because you didn't like it?"

She didn't hesitate. "I didn't say that."

That's right, she didn't say that. Because she couldn't say that and mean it. She'd very much enjoyed the ways I'd broken her down, even though the process had been difficult. She couldn't deny that.

"It's the dynamic between us that has brought us the closest," I pointed out, in case she hadn't connected that.

She swallowed. The next breath she took in shuddered through her. "It's made me weak."

"Not at all. It's made you strong."

"It's made me unstable."

"It's made you irresistible."

A smile flickered on her lips, her cheeks turning the lightest shade of red.

A beat passed.

"It makes me have to trust you."

She delivered this last statement as though she were giving confession, so I knew the answer before I asked it. "That's still a problem for you?"

She responded with silence, her eyes unable to meet mine.

One of the reasons I was so attracted to her was because she was one of the few people who could still surprise me. Though this partic-ular subject was not one I enjoyed being surprised by.

I wanted her to trust me. I *needed* her to trust me. All of my rules about honesty and transparency had been set specifically to build up trust between us. It would be impossible for me to care for her the way she needed without it. Our relationship required it.

After the panic subsided, I could see the situation for what it was more clearly. She *did* trust me. We never would have gotten this far if she didn't. She just didn't realize that she did.

"You say you love me," I challenged.

"I do." The response must have come more sharply than she meant it to because she repeated it with effusiveness. "I do, Edward."

"Doesn't love require trust?"

She opened her mouth to answer, then shut it again. Then repeated the opening and shutting, and I wondered how much of this argument had been given to her before from the shitstain of a human that was her uncle.

"I'm not him," I reminded her. "We aren't that."

She nodded, affirming that she had indeed been thinking about him. "I think I'm beginning to know that," she said. Then, after a pause, "Maybe it's myself I don't trust."

"And that's why you want me to take care of you."

Her nose wrinkled. "I *want* you to take care of me?"

"Mm."

I could feel her temptation to argue, but she knew as well as I did how much she wanted to be cared for. The thought of it alone made her eyes shine and her body press forward with eagerness. "What would...?" She licked her lips, gathering courage to explore the desire. "What would that look like exactly?"

And now we were at the heart of the discussion, the part I'd been waiting for, where I'd lay it all out for her to accept and embrace. I took a breath, ready to explain on the exhale, but she cut me off.

"You know, it's hard to consider any of this talk different from last time when it still feels like we're negotiating a business deal."

I'd purposefully set up the seating arrangement, keeping us apart. It was the same positioning I used in our sessions, the positioning I'd always used when I played with a woman's mind. It was more of a challenge to manipulate without touch, but I'd learned from experience that it brought the most authentic results.

Then, with Celia, when physical manipulation might have given me a hand up, I'd sat away from her because I'd needed the barrier. Because I hadn't been able to trust myself if she were within reach.

That concern had obviously been invalid. I hadn't needed to be touching her to lose myself to her. Distance hadn't had any benefit in the least.

Tonight, though, I had assumed the boundaries would help her keep a clear head. The decisions she needed to make about our relationship required it.

But I'd forgotten that she also needed reassurance. That, more than anything, she needed to feel loved.

"Come here," I said, the command abrasive with my self-displeasure.

She didn't need to be told twice. Within the space of a few seconds, she'd risen from her spot on the couch and crossed to me, where I pulled her into my lap. The chair was wide enough for her to sink down on the cushion next to me, her legs thrown over one of mine. It constantly amazed me how well we fit together like this, how her body seemed made to be melded to mine. How still my thoughts went when she was in my arms, like she was a meditative mantra that brought my focus laser sharp.

I stroked her cheek with the tips of my fingertips, glad that she'd kept her makeup light so I could feel the true softness of her skin. "There are things that you need," I said, my voice as much a caress as my hand. "And I will give them to you, but I will be the one who decides what those things are."

"What things do I need?" She looked back at me with an adoration I didn't feel worthy of, but gladly accepted all the same.

"There are your basic needs, for starters. You need to feel pampered yet important. You need to be admired for your intellect more than your beauty. You need structure to your day, but you prefer not to organize it. You need to have boundaries but you need to feel free."

"Yes," she whispered.

"I want to be in charge of your schedule so that you don't have to worry for yourself if you're taking on more than you should. I want to ensure you have the tools you need to stay healthy—physically and mentally—because you won't consider those things important on your own. You need me to do that for you. You need me to make sure you are getting appropriate exercise and brain stimulation. You need me to tell you how to prioritize your interests, because you have too many and they overwhelm you on your own.

I brought my thumb to trace the edge of her bottom lip. "You need me to care for your appearance—to dictate how to wear your hair and what to dress and how to groom your pussy so that you aren't tempted to use your body as a weapon as you have in the past. You won't be able to play games with something that doesn't belong to you. You need me to remind you that you belong to me. You need me to be sure there are consequences when you don't."

She gasp-laughed, apparently shocked that I'd called her out so bluntly but unable to refute it as truth.

I took the opportunity to slide my thumb past her lips and teeth into the recesses of her hot mouth. "Suck," I demanded, feeling my pants tighten when she did, imagining it was my cock between her lips instead of my thumb. "You need me to turn you on," I said, my voice low. "You need me to get into your head and understand the way you need to be fucked."

She hummed her agreement, sending a sharp jolt to the rigid bulge that was quickly growing beneath her.

And then, because sex was so connected with psychology where I was concerned, "You need me to force you to face your demons. You need me to put you through sessions and ensure you see your psychiatrist and that you write in your diary regularly. You need me to be sure you don't bury your hurt inside, turning you into a shell of a person. You need me to keep you present, and trust me, everything that I demand from you—every pain I press from your body, every rule I require you to adhere to—it will all be with that goal in mind. I will keep you a full person. I won't let you be anything less."

I drew my thumb out, resting it on her chin, my fingers curling around her jaw. She swallowed, and I could feel it against my knuckles. "I would expect you to respect me, because that's what a master deserves. My demands here haven't changed. You will support me publicly in all things, and if you do decide to argue with me privately, you accept that there may be punishment. This is a tough one for you, I know, but I believe you've had enough experience with me now to understand you can manage. Am I wrong?"

She blinked, doe-eyed and nervous, her lids heavy with lust. "Are you wrong about the last thing or all of it? Because you aren't wrong about the last thing. I know I can manage it."

I chuckled. "And the rest?"

Her shoulders rose with her breath. "If that's everything...I think I could manage it all too."

"I know you can." My subtext was clear, prompting a more sincere agreement.

"I want to. I want to try."

I leaned in to brush my lips against hers. "Good girl." I kissed her lightly, wrapping my hand around the back of her neck to hold her how I wanted her. I only pulled back briefly to issue my last stipulation for her care. "There is one more thing you need, one more thing I am prepared to give you as soon as you agree."

"What's that?" Her eyes were dilated and focused on my mouth, begging for more than the chaste kiss I'd delivered. It was tempting to give in to her desire.

But I was in charge of her well-being, and the last thing she needed to accept from me was likely the most important.

So I resisted and gave her the one word that would be the key to her healing. "Revenge."

SEVEN

CELIA

"REVENGE," I repeated, cautiously, pulling back to look at Edward. "On who?"

Asking the question was a stall tactic, perhaps. I knew the answer already. He'd spent years going after my father, going to absurd lengths in pursuit of justice. He'd abandoned that quest because I'd pointed him in another direction, not because he'd suddenly decided he didn't need retribution.

Sensing that my true question was why, he answered that instead. "You can't understand the benefits of closure until you've experienced it. It may feel like life goes on. You may feel yourself get better and stronger as you accept the things that have happened to you in the past. But you can't ever truly move on until you find resolution."

A moment ago I'd felt warm in his lap, my body keening for more of him physically. Now I suddenly felt cold and guarded.

I rubbed my hands over my sleeves, trying to heat the skin underneath. "How can you know that? Since you haven't found your own resolution yet yourself. What if you finally close that door and it doesn't change anything?"

He settled back in his chair, his head tilted as he examined me. "I haven't felt resolution where Werner Media is, no. But I have experienced the rewards in other areas of my life. Trust me when I say they were worth the effort."

The hair stood up along the back of my neck.

Edward had gone to dark places trying to make my father pay for something, it turned out, he hadn't done. He'd not only married me but had also wanted to kill me, all so he could get his hands on my father's company shares. It was still hard for me to believe I'd fallen in love with a man who could be so sinister, but in the end, he hadn't murdered me, and maybe that made it easier to overlook his thwarted plans.

I smirked thinking about that. My husband, the man I was in love with, had only *almost* killed me. That was still a serious crime, and I'd forgiven him. It was quite possible I was a lunatic.

Maybe the craziest part was that I'd never considered there may have been other plans of his that hadn't been thwarted. Other revenge schemes just as ruthless and sinister that he'd gone through with. My skin tingled with curiosity. My gut churned with revulsion.

Did I want to know?

"Let's not think about it," he said, reading my expression correctly. He ran the back of a single finger across my jawline, tenderly. Soothing my unease. "Focus instead on your own lack of closure. How much easier would it be to press forward if you knew that Ron had atoned for the things he's done?"

"You mean how much easier would it be for you to know that he'd paid."

He dropped his hand at my acidic tone. "Yes, he owes me a debt, and I plan to collect, but in this moment, I'm thinking only about you."

His own words were stern but genuine. He really did mean to help. The least I could do was discuss it with him. "I can't try to prosecute him. My parents would never back me, and without them on my side, I'd have no chance of winning. He's a rich, powerful man. I'm sure you know as well as I do that rich men never pay for their crimes." Besides, I was sure that revealing all the horrible secrets of my past to the world would do more harm to my psyche than good.

"There are other ways besides the legal system to seek out justice."

I breathed through the shiver that threatened to crawl down my spine. Of course he wasn't just thinking of the legal system. Had any of the ways he'd gone after Werner involved authorities? Even if there had been something illegal to nail them on, I had a feeling Edward would have avoided that route.

And if the methods he wanted to pursue weren't legal, I didn't want any part of it. I should just say no and move on.

But Ron had hurt me deeply and permanently, and as I'd begun to feel again, I'd only skimmed the surface of the well of rage that existed inside me.

Did I want him to pay? Fuck yes.

Only, at what cost?

"What exactly *are* you suggesting?" I asked, unable to tamp down my interest.

His lips puckered with a shrug, as if he didn't have a long list of ideas already waiting to execute. Before I could call him on it, though, he said, "I thought I should leave that up to you."

Oh.

I hadn't been expecting that.

He took advantage of my surprise to press on. "What would you like to do with him, my little bird? You can't tell me you haven't thought about it."

I *hadn't* thought about it for a long time. I'd pushed down all the memories and the feelings associated with them until they'd formed a cement chrysalis, holding them in and away from my conscious mind.

Edward had broken through that shell, though, and now thoughts of vengeance did occupy more of my time than I liked to admit. But mostly they were rough and unformed ideas. The fantasies that had taken better shape were impossible to carry out or, at least, impossible for *me* to carry out. While I'd certainly love to parade Ron naked in a room full of rapists and sell him to the highest bidder, for example, I wouldn't begin to know how to go about making the scenario take place.

Edward might, however.

That thought scared me as much as it excited me.

"I've thought about hurting him," I admitted, vigilant that anything and everything I said to my husband was collected and stored for later use. "And yes, I want him to pay. But short of killing him—which I refuse to do—I wouldn't even know where to begin that sort of take-down effort. I'm not that diabolical, I suppose."

God, the topic nauseated me. That I'd had to specify that I was against murder because I didn't know my husband's limits, doubly so.

His caress was back, the hand he had wrapped around my waist stroking along my ribs. "Sure you are," he said, and it took a moment to get past my indignation before realizing he had every reason to believe that was true.

That wasn't who I was anymore, though.

Was I?

"You know how to manipulate people," he continued. "You've prac-ticed these games for years. Same thing now. Only, this time, your victim is deserving."

"You mean use my powers for good?" I asked, scornfully.

He chuckled. "Something like that."

I jumped out of his lap, the action so sudden he didn't have time to try to tighten his hold before I was up. I had to put some space between us—not between me and him, but between me and the lure of being someone I didn't want to be anymore.

I crossed to grab the brandy I'd left on the table by the couch and took a long sip, my back turned to the man behind me. It was tempting. It really was. To be our kind of superheroes. To play the game that had invigorated me for so long. To finally give Ron a taste of what he deserved. Me with the devil at my side—what could possibly get in our way?

"I don't know, Edward," I said, finally, setting the tumbler down and turning back toward him. "I did those things before, thinking it would help, and it left me cold and unfeeling and terrible. I don't want to go back to that. I don't want to live that way anymore."

He nodded once, patiently. "It wouldn't be that way, you under-stand. Not with the right motive."

I threw my hands up. "And *vengeance* is the right motive? 'A man who desires revenge should dig two graves.' 'Neglect kills injuries, revenge increases them.' There's a reason why there are hundreds of quips about the futility of revenge, Edward. It's not a healthy aspiration, and I'm trying to thrive here."

"'It's every man's business to see justice done.'"

I couldn't help but smile at his comeback. I hadn't forgotten he was a worthy rival, still, sometimes he surprised me with the reminder.

"How about this?" I leaned back to perch on the arm of the sofa. "I don't care what you want to do to Ron. Have at it. He's yours. I'm not going to stop you from doing whatever you need to do to get closure on what he did to your family. But it's for you, not for me. I don't want this. I don't need this. I want to focus on healing in other ways, if you don't mind."

There. It was a solid compromise, as far as I was concerned.

He leaned forward, his elbows propped on his thighs, his hands clasped together. "What if I do mind?"

I blinked. "What?"

He stood up and stalked over until he was standing right above me, making me feel caged in without actually surrounding me. "You heard me."

Hearing him hadn't been the problem. "I don't understand why it matters if I'm involved."

"Because I believe you do need this, that you will never be able to fully heal without it, and being a passive observer is not going to deliver the same results as being an active participant. And I care about your well-being very much. In fact, it's one of my main responsibilities as your husband, as we've discussed tonight."

I bit the inside of my upper lip. Something bloomed deep in my belly, something wild and beautiful and satisfying. It was unfamiliar to feel so looked after, so protected. As frightening as it was to imagine Edward with blood on his hands, I couldn't deny how good it felt to believe he'd likely kill for me if he believed it necessary.

It was the most loved I'd ever felt in my life.

I reached up and placed my hand on his lapel, over the place where his heart drummed in his chest, and even though I couldn't feel it through the layers of material in the way, I knew the beat was steady and driven. "I'm grateful. I truly am. But we're going to have to agree to disagree. It's still a no from me."

The smile that inched onto his lips was ominous. "I could insist, you know. I have that right."

My own heart tripped, and while I felt a rush of endorphins at his exertion of alpha attitude, there was also a notable flood of panic. "I don't like that. Maybe I'm not ready for this whole submission thing after all."

He let a heavy span of silence pass before his features softened. "Settle down, bird," he said, tucking a stray hair behind my ear. "You don't need to get your feathers ruffled over this. I can drop it—for now—if you agree to at least think more about it."

My answer wouldn't change, but I could give him that. "Okay. I'll think about it. No promises."

"Thank you."

But, even with the conversation tabled, he'd made me anxious. "We should still probably talk more in detail about the submitting stuff."

"You're nervous about what I may decide is best for you."

"Uh, to put it bluntly—yes." I dropped my hand to my lap, but he stayed where he was, hovering over me.

"Let me ask you this—how did it feel today, to wear the clothes I'd picked for you? Performing the tasks I'd instructed you to perform?"

"I liked it," I said, honestly. "But—"

"More specific, please," he demanded, cutting me off.

I gave a beat to thinking about exactly what I'd liked about it, then gave up, sticking to the original addendum that he'd interrupted. "But they weren't important things. If you chose something I didn't want to wear, it won't really have bothered me to wear it anyway. The tasks were fine, too, but what happens when you want me to do something I am strongly against?" Like participating in his schemes for justice.

His arms came around me now, settling on my hips. "Then we discuss it, privately, just as we have tonight. I'm not entirely impossible, as I believe I've proven here."

That wasn't any different from any other healthy marriage. I should be able to do that.

Still, I wanted to be absolutely clear that I was not giving up my autonomy entirely. "I just wouldn't want to mislead you into thinking I'm easy to boss around. I'm not. I'm probably going to argue a lot."

"Oh, I'm well aware." The low rumble of his voice was panty-drenching. "We'll get through our disputes as we have so far. Though, I will remind you, there may be repercussions for disagreeing."

Again, my heart skipped. "Is there going to be a repercussion for disagreeing with you tonight?"

He bent in to whisper at my ear. "Oh, yes, Celia. There will be." His breath on my skin made my own breath quicken. "And you're going to like it. In fact, I think it will prove just exactly how much you enjoy submitting to me, if you'll let it."

Oh, fuck.

That feeling of fear/excitement flooded over me in a single wave. It was a dual emotion I was becoming quite familiar with. Edward always summoned the two ingredients in equal measure, had since the first time I'd met him, and it wasn't worth even trying to lie and say that I didn't find the hybrid as addictive as any drug.

"Tell me what to do, Edward," I said, surrendering to him.

With my capitulation, he took the role of dominant, immediately releasing his hold on me and stepping back. "Turn around."

I straightened then turned. The sound of my pantsuit's zipper accompanied the parting of the material along my backside.

"Take this off," he commanded. "Fold it nicely and set it on the sofa. Leave your shoes and underthings on. Come stand before me when you're done."

"Yes, Edward." I started working myself out of my outfit while he took his empty glass to the wetbar. This wasn't bad. His punishments in the past had always ended in orgasms. It was like a game, really. Like Simon Says with sexy stuff involved. What wasn't there to enjoy about that?

"One more thing," he said as he poured the cognac. "Tonight, you will call me 'sir.'"

I froze. He knew I didn't like that term. He knew why now, too. "But you said before—"

"I know what I said. Need I remind you tonight is a punishment? You will do as I ask."

My jaw tensed. I'd forgotten somehow that he also had to dole out a certain amount of discomfort in these games.

I liked that too, in some ways. But that was harder to admit, even to myself.

"Celia?" he prompted when I hadn't responded.

It took a second before I realized what he was waiting for. "Yes, *sir*," I said, unable to control the acerbic tone that came when the single syllable crossed my lips.

He didn't seem to mind the abrasive response. "Good. Carry on."

By the time I'd finished stripping and folding, he'd taken his drink and crossed the room to stand where the hardwood flooring turned into rough tile stone in front of the fireplace.

I walked over to him, feeling both sexy and oddly bashful wearing only heels and lingerie. This was the moment I'd thought of as I'd put the white lace items on—the moment when he'd be seeing me in them. Was this what he'd thought of as well when he'd set them out?

His eyes were dark as he studied me over the rim of his glass. He took a swallow and set it on the mantle. "Turn around for me."

I complied, spinning slowly so he could see me from every angle. He let out an appraising hiss that shot lust through my blood, made my skin flush, and almost made me forgive him for requiring me to address him as "sir."

Almost.

"YOU'RE BEAUTIFUL, CELIA," he said when I was facing him again. "All covered up, too—you looked quite regal in that suit—but especially like this, in nothing but the bra and pants I chose for you."

Okay, maybe he was forgiven entirely.

He kept his hands to himself, crossed over his chest, much farther from my body then I would have liked them. Whatever punishment he planned for me, I had a feeling it would also hold rewards, and I was more than ready to discover both.

My heart sped up with excitement when he suddenly dropped his hands to his sides, but instead of touching me, all he did was remove his jacket. "Hang this over the arm of the sofa," he instructed. "Give me a show when you do."

I did as he asked, practically prancing back to where I'd been, bending with exaggeration to drape the jacket on the couch and giving my hips a little sway as I straightened again. When I strutted back to him, the bashfulness was gone. All I felt was pure seduction.

"You feel beautiful right now, too, don't you?" he asked, never missing a beat. "Is it because of what I'm saying to you or because you're wearing items I picked for you to wear?"

"Both, sir."

"You felt beautiful all day, didn't you? Wearing items that I'd laid out."

"Especially the underwear," I confessed. "Sir," I remembered to add a beat late.

Disapproval knitted his features at my mistake, but it passed quickly. "You enjoyed wearing my underwear because you knew that only I'd see you like this, your nipples peaked and rosy for me."

My nipples went even harder at his acknowledgment. "Yes, sir. And also because I knew you chose them for me because you would like seeing me in them."

"That's right. I very much do," he rasped. "They're naughty, but you don't have to take responsibility for that, do you? Because I was the one who picked them."

I swallowed, realizing I did like that only as he pointed it out. In the past, when I wore risque underwear, it had usually been because I meant to use them manipulatively later. All the women who wore pretty panties for themselves—I'd never been that girl. I'd been taught early on that everything I did and wore had an effect on the men around me, and that it was my job to be conscientious of that.

I was so sick of dressing for other people. For thinking of all of my actions as moves in a chess game. It could be argued that this was more of the same because I'd dressed for Edward, but it didn't feel that way. He had chosen the items that would make the day easiest for me.

The naughty items underneath were like the compensation he got for taking on that responsibility. I didn't mind giving that to him in the least.

And when, with hungry eyes, he said, "Kneel down in front of me," I didn't mind that either. Even when my knees hit the hard stone tiles and I understood the reason he'd moved over here.

Beautiful bastard.

Reaching around, he pulled my hair from the knot at my nape. "You're gorgeous like this. On your knees. I should have had you in this position sooner."

"You did once, sir," I said, reminding him of our first session, when he'd very nearly had me go down on him then went down on me instead. "You decided it wasn't demeaning enough, if I remember correctly."

"I decided it wasn't a fitting punishment at the time, and I was right. You were much too eager. Tonight, I think it will do just fine."

I was eager now too. My mouth watered at the opportunity to finally suck him off.

With my hair down, he threaded his fingers through the strands. "Now, look in front of you. What do you see?"

I'd already been staring at the bulge currently tenting his trousers. "You're hard," I said sounding more thrilled than I'd meant to let on.

He pulled firmly at the hair in his hand. "What did you say?"

"Fuck. Sorry, I forgot. You're hard, *sir.*"

"You did that. You made that happen." He let his words sink in, but I recognized them immediately.

And I understood what he meant by this now. What this was.

This was his redo of my first hand job with the chauffeur.

I'd known this was coming, somewhere inside of me I'd known. Yet somehow I was still surprised. I also discovered it was possible to feel both dread and excitement at the same time because that's what I was feeling. Like I had both butterflies and stones in my stomach.

I didn't want to relive this.

I also very much wanted to have the memory replaced with Edward.

"You're going to take care of it, the way I want you to, aren't you?" he asked, and I knew what *this* was too—my chance to back out.

Not that there was ever really backing out where Edward was concerned. If I refused to face this now, he'd make me face it again sometime else, in some other way.

There was probably a lesson in that for me about our current disagreement, but I wasn't able to focus on that at the moment. I had a hard cock to take care of.

"Yes, sir," I said, with the trepidation of the child I once was. "Tell me how, please, sir."

Anxiety threatened to seize me, but the accompanying bolt of lust was stronger.

"Undo my buckle and my pants."

I did as he said, my pride swelling with his head as it poked out over the band of his boxer briefs.

"Take out my cock."

When it was out, standing stiff and boastful at eye level, I couldn't help myself. I wanted it in my mouth, and putting it in my mouth differentiated this moment from the one that had preceded it all those years ago. At ten, I hadn't even conceived of blowjobs, let alone wanted to give one.

Immediately, Edward flicked the side of my cheek with two fingers. I released him with a gasp at the sting.

"I didn't tell you to suck on it. I'm the teacher here." Just like Ron had been then. And Charles. Teaching me things a child should never need to know.

The memory sat heavy at the sidelines, refusing to disappear from the present. "What do you want me to do, sir?" I echoed the girl I'd been.

Like Charles and Ron had been, Edward seemed pleased with my willingness. It was confusing to recognize. As confusing now as it had been in the past. I'd hated what they wanted me to do then, but I'd still glowed in their praise.

Just as I glowed in Edward's praise now. "Thank you for asking. I want you to spit on your pretty hand." He waited for me to do it before going on with his instruction. "Now grab it, just like this."

The sight of him holding his cock made me wet. The scent of my arousal drifted up, and I swore Edward caught it, his mouth twitching as though trying to hide a grin.

I brought my hand up to wrap around his length, stacking it on top of his. The bright pink of my nails against his flesh looked so eerily similar to that day so long ago, I had to close my eyes momentarily to recenter myself.

I'm here in the present. With Edward. No one else.

When I opened my eyes again, I recognized the adult size of my hand and how differently it fit around the cock before me than my child hands had fit around Charles. Another gush of arousal pooled between my thighs. "Like this, sir?"

"Two hands," he said, letting go to make room for mine. "Yes. Just like that."

It made me dizzy, the way my head flipped from past to present to past to present again. One minute I was still barely clinging on to my innocence, the next I was desperate to be further debased. There was something cathartic about the merging of the memory with the moment. It made me have to choose between who I was then and who I was now. There wasn't room for me to be both, and there was no way I was going back to that other me.

Edward wouldn't let me.

"Good girl. Such a pretty, good girl." He anchored me like that, his encouraging tone bringing me back to him every time I started to disappear into another time. "You keep on rubbing it just like that, keep treating it real nice. Because you're the one who did this to me, didn't you?"

You did this to him, Ron's voice pierced through the fog of lust.

I shook him away, looking up at Edward's eyes to remind me where I was. "Yes, sir."

"And it's not nice to leave me hurting, is it?"

"No, sir."

As though sensing the ghosts of other men crowding the space with us, Edward acknowledged them. "I'm the only man you need to worry about, Celia. Anyone else who tells you that you make them hard, that's not your problem. Do you understand?"

My hands stuttered at the change in script. "Yes, sir," I said, absorbing his words.

"It's not your job to take care of the men who you make hurt. Say it."

I took a breath in then let it out. "It's not my job to take care of the men who I make hurt."

His dick twitched, and my gaze went back to the job in front of me. I put more vigor in the churn of my hands, sensing he was getting close. My pussy throbbed with the anticipation as though it was the genitalia being rubbed. I wanted him to release, not just because I wanted to get past this scene but because I was also fully into it.

Edward seemed not to be as concerned with coming right away. He grabbed my chin and tilted it up, roughly, to look at him. "And even though I'm hard for you, Celia, even though looking at your gorgeous body and watching you twist and writhe through our discussions tonight made me need to fuck your pretty hands, there's only one reason you are responsible for taking care of me. Can you tell me what that is?"

"Because you're my husband, sir." I swiped my palm over his crown, earning me a growl.

"Try again."

I paused, unsure what he wanted.

Then I knew. "Because I choose this."

"Say it again."

"Because I choose this, sir."

"That's right, Celia. You aren't a victim here. You choose to let me dress you like my doll. You choose to let me degrade you on your knees like this, with the stone scraping against your skin." My hands picked up vigor with the raw grate of his words. "You're going to have bruises, later, aren't you?"

"Yes, sir."

"You choose to let me do that to you, don't you?"

"Yes, sir." *Yes, yes.* And I loved it.

"You choose to let me do what's best for you, too," he said, his hips shoving forward. "Because you trust that I know how to care for you. That I'll build you up to who you want to be. That I will protect and honor and love you in every way that I know how."

My throat felt suddenly tight, like his cock was lodged inside it instead of thrusting in my hand. I couldn't speak. So I just nodded, instead.

"All right, my turn." He stepped back taking his cock into his fist. My arms dropped to my sides, but I could barely feel their exhaustion, I was so mesmerized by the rapid tug of his hand back and forth over his steel length. "Pull out your tits for me, pretty bird. I'm going to decorate them with my cum."

I grabbed the bra cups and pulled them down, thrusting my chest forward, a willing canvas.

"Yes, yes, fuck." His words disappeared into a groan as hot liquid spurted from his tip, shooting ribbons of sticky white across the peaks of my breasts.

Yes, yes, fuck was right.

It was dirty and filthy and debasing, and I was soaring. How was it possible to be both claimed and liberated all at once? To be treasured *and* defiled? To be taken *and* given back?

I didn't realize there were tears falling down my cheeks until Edward's thumb swiped them away. After tucking his still semi-hard cock into his briefs, he pulled me to my feet and into his arms, not seeming to care that his semen was now pressed up against his chest.

He kissed me thoroughly, his tongue slinking predatorily deep into my mouth, promising there would be more generous rounds of love-making before the night was through.

When he pulled away, it was abrupt, and I had to cling onto his shoulders for balance, even though his arms were still wrapped tightly around my waist.

"You didn't answer me earlier—how do you feel when you submit to me? How does it feel wearing my clothes and doing what I ask and jerking off my cock and wearing my cum? How does that make you feel?"

I could sense the importance of the answer he was looking for, and I paused to make sure I found it too, repeating his questions again in my head. I'd felt powerful. I'd felt important. I'd felt cared for. I'd felt desirable. I'd felt strong. I'd felt worthy. I'd felt horny. I'd felt new. I'd felt...

Then, there it was. The truth clicking into place. By submitting to him, I gave up all the baggage that I'd carried all these years. That peace I'd searched for in The Game with Hudson had been false, but this peace was real. With Edward, I no longer had to pretend the chains around me weren't there. They'd actually gone, because he'd picked them up for me, he'd taken them as his own like reins.

How did I feel without that burden?

My voice was sure with my answer. "Free."

EIGHT

EDWARD

"WELL?"

At the sound of her voice, I turned to find Camilla leaning on the doorframe behind me. I swept my eyes once more around the guest room then gave an approving nod. "It's nice."

"That's all?"

It wasn't fair, and I knew it. I'd been a giant ass, actually. She'd started her search for a new flat as soon as Christmas passed, and while she'd given me many opportunities to be part of the process, I'd declined every step of the way, too busy nursing the wounds of her impending departure.

Of course I'd had my advisors look at the property before she made her official bid, just to make sure she wasn't making a mistake. It had been without her knowledge, which I felt no guilt about. She insisted she was ready to be on her own, and she probably was, but she was still my sister. Still the girl I'd had a hand in raising. Parental instincts didn't just turn off.

Now the deed was in her name, and she was already moved in, and the London rags were already gossiping about a family dispute between us. I couldn't delay a visit any longer without creating a great deal of animosity.

Besides, we had other things that needed to be discussed.

"I think you chose well," I said as I crossed to stand at the door beside her. From here I could see across the hall into the playroom where Anwar was tending to my nephew who was currently occupied with the Lego set I'd brought for him just this morning. It was a smaller space than the one he'd had, but brighter, giant latticed windows bringing in an abundance of natural light. "Freddie seems to like it. The courtyard is nice. Warwick Gardens is a respectable neighborhood. Not too far from the park or the office."

Not too far from my residence, either, though it might as well have been across the ocean as far as I was concerned.

"But...?"

I blew out a sigh, letting go of my stubbornness along with it. "But nothing, Camilla. I would rather have you at home is all. I hadn't realized how quiet the house is without the two of you around."

Her body sank with relief, and for the first time since I'd arrived ten minutes ago, she smiled. "It's not me, you miss. It's him. He's the noisy one."

"Mm." True, but I wasn't about to admit it.

"You could have a child of your own."

I laughed, stepping out into the hallway to head toward the stairs. "I have children of my own."

Camilla's footsteps echoed on the floor behind me. "I meant with Celia."

A strange weight of yearning pressed against my chest, imagining the family we might have had, if I'd met her as a younger man. If my path had taken a different route. "I'm passed that time in my life."

"You're only forty-three. A lot of men aren't even starting their families until now."

"But I did start young, and now I'm done. I'm not about to start the whole process over again." I stepped off the landing onto the stairs that led to the main floor. They weren't carpeted, but there was a runner, and they were less steep than the ones on Cornwall Terrace. That was a benefit of the move, at least. Safer for the boy.

"Genny and Hagan were easy for you," Camilla said, continuing the conversation I'd thought I'd closed. "You got to be the typical man who left the childrearing to your wife. What are you complaining about?"

Ouch.

We were generally honest with each other, no matter the expense. Unfortunately, that sometimes resulted in blatant truths that I would have preferred been left unsaid.

This one had been said now, though. I turned at the bottom of the stairs to face her. "Perhaps that was exactly the problem—I wasn't the best of fathers the first time around." Not with Genny or Hagan, and certainly not with Camilla.

She reached her hand out to rest on my arm, an unusually affectionate gesture from my sister. "You were a fine father, Eddie. A bit preoccupied, perhaps. You had an empire to build. Your children understand. They weren't neglected. But if you truly think you weren't as good as you could have been, then all the more reason to give it another go."

I frowned at her logic. "All the more reason *not* to give it another go."

It was her turn to frown. For a moment I thought she meant to push the issue, but then her expression shifted. She dropped her arm and crossed it with the other over her chest, putting up the familiar wall. "Why are you here?"

I narrowed my eyes. "What do you mean? I came to see the place, now that you're settled."

"That's your excuse, but it's not the reason you came. If that were all, you would have brought your wife along. I called to see if you had left yet. She didn't even know you were coming here. She said you'd gone out shopping for Valentine's Day."

"That was what I told her," I admitted.

"See, then? Secrets and subterfuge. Are you going to at least tell *me* what you're up to?"

I glanced around the house again, wishing this hadn't been the way we'd reached the subject I'd been aiming for eventually. "I really did want to see your new place."

"I know. I'm glad you did." The wall didn't come down all the way, but it was less fortified. Which was good, for what we had to discuss.

"Shall we sit?" I asked, gesturing toward her living room.

"I'll tell Perry to put on the kettle."

Thirty minutes later, we'd drained the pot of tea between us, and I'd finished telling her the major points of my plan to go after Ron Werner. This scheme was much different from any I'd had for his brother. With Warren, I'd wanted to steal his corporation, let him experience what I thought he'd done to my father.

Ron, I wanted to ruin. Entirely. His reputation, his fortune. His life.

Since he'd sold his shares of Werner years ago, the different tactic was somewhat out of practicality. Mostly, though, it was because of Celia. Whether she wanted to be part of his ruin or not, she remained a large part of my motivation.

For the most part, Camilla had sat quietly, letting me tell her my ideas without interruption. Now it was my turn to ask, "Well?"

She set her teacup on the ottoman before her and folded her hands in her lap. "That's quite a plot, Edward. A long game. And not like you to use the justice system."

"It has to be a long game, I think. There's no way around that." I was familiar with long games. In fact, I considered myself quite good at them.

"Likely true," she said.

"And I'm only using the justice system because I think, in this case, it's the best way to completely ruin him."

"Agreed." I could see the gears shifting behind her eyes. "If you can get him to go to Exceso, why don't you just arrest him at that point?"

That was one of the early stages of my plan. Get him to the island where all sorts of debauchery played out. It would help earn his trust. Make him think that those of us who were members there were men of the same ilk, or at least were willing to look the other way.

"That would be easiest," I agreed. "But international waters. There's no jurisdiction there. It will have to be here or the US."

"It will be more devastating for him in the US, I'd think."

"I agree." I studied her, looking for any clues as to what she thought about the idea on the whole.

There were none to be found, though. She'd learned to guard her emotions as much as I had.

She clicked her tongue, a habit she'd had for as long as I could remember, and then pursed her lips together. "You usually don't tell me this much about your plans. You rarely care about my opinion. Why are you involving me this time?"

Either I was losing my touch or she could read beyond my mask better than I realized. "I think you should be the one to make the first connection," I said, realizing that trying to hold it back any longer was futile.

Her eyes widened. "You're kidding me."

"You're well-bred and polished. There's nothing that screams undercover agent with your pedigree. He'll be in town in a couple of weeks, staying at the Savoy. You could casually meet him at the bar—I'm told he'll likely spend his evenings there. You could leave Freddie with us, check in a couple of nights. It's the perfect opportunity."

She barked out a laugh. "Casually meet him and say what? 'Would you like to come to an island with me in the Caribbean where you can rape little girls without getting caught?' That's not something strangers just bring up over a drink."

"No, of course not. But I do think directness is key. You would approach him purposefully. Tell him you know who he is and what his interests are. Assure him not to worry, that you're discreet, and then inform him you have a client who is looking for a particular sort of hookup and then ask him if he might have any leads."

"And you expect him to just hand over that sort of information to someone he's never met before?"

"No. He won't give you anything." Only a fool would, and there was no way Ron Werner was a fool. He'd managed to remain untouched by gossip or speculation for at least twenty years. "He'll pretend he has no idea what you're talking about. You'll thank him for his time, give him your card, and tell him to contact you if anything changes. As you're leaving, as almost a throwaway, you'll mention that you'll reach out to him if you find another lead yourself. Then we let a few months pass before you call him and invite him to Exceso."

"You want me to be Ghislane Maxwell to his Jeffrey Epstein," she said, correctly identifying the type of role I envisioned for her.

"Only, if this works—and it will work—you'll be saving girls. Not destroying them."

She crossed her legs and clasped her hands around the top knee. "Why me? Why don't you make that connection yourself?"

"I'm married to one of his victims. He might see right through it."

"How am I any different? I'm her sister-in-law."

"Exactly. Close enough to the family to have learned about her uncle's proclivities, but not necessarily close enough to feel obligated to her in any way." I let that her absorb that before continuing. "It wouldn't be ridiculous to let him believe you aren't fond of your brother's choice in wife. You've already got the rags talking about a possible family dispute. Ride with it."

It only took a beat before her mouth opened in a silent gasp. "You planted the gossip."

I shrugged then thought better of it. She deserved honesty. "It was the perfect opportunity to set up the scene," I admitted.

"Again, why me?" She leaned forward now, as if to press me physically as well as with words. "It could be just as believable with one of your hired men. Or women, if you prefer. A real agent of the law, preferably. Someone who knows what they're doing."

"You know why."

"Because you think I need this."

"Yes. As much, if not more, than I do." Also, I didn't trust anyone who wasn't blood or on my payroll. Fewer people than that, actually.

Her tongue clicked again, the wheels turning. With a sigh, she sat back and draped her arm over the back of the sofa. "What else are you working on?"

The question took me aback. "What do you mean?"

"I heard you on the phone when you got here. I didn't mean to eavesdrop, but this is my house. You were talking about someone in prison, from what I gathered. Definitely not talking about Ron Werner."

I'd already been on her doorstep when the call had come in, and while I would normally have sent it to voicemail, I'd been waiting for weeks for Kofi to call with the information I'd requested.

There was no reason to try to hide this from my sister either. "There were more men involved in Celia's assaults than just her uncle."

Her skin paled as she digested my meaning. "Jesus," she said with a shudder.

I understood the feeling. My stomach was constantly on the brink of heaving, thoughts of what she'd endured never far from the forefront of my mind. "I'm working on tracking down the ones I'm aware of. One of them, a Charles Endcott, worked briefly as a personal chauffeur for Ron. He's currently serving time for child abuse, rape, and molestation as well as several counts of possession of child pornography."

"Look at that. Justice somehow managing to get done without the intervention of Edward Fasbender." Her teasing held a bite, but it was lighthearted all the same.

I, on the other hand, was deadly serious. "He's one man, Camilla. I can't find any others either currently serving time or with records who are connected to this monster. They're smart and they cover their tracks. There are dozens of men with close ties to Ron, but none I can be certain are part of his pedophilia ring."

She sobered at that. "And Celia isn't able to help point you in the right direction?"

"She doesn't know I'm looking for them," I said, my throat tightening at the admission.

Of everything I'd said, this seemed to alarm her most of all. "She doesn't know about any of this?"

"She's given her blessing on going after Ron in whichever way I choose, but she declined to take any part in it. She doesn't know I've expanded my quest for vengeance beyond that."

"Ah. I understand now why you kept this visit from her."

The accusation in her tone was warranted, but unnecessary. I already felt guilty about it. Not about my actions, but about the lack of honesty. I'd promised truth to her, and I intended to keep that promise. I'd share this with her, eventually. Perhaps even before I actually did anything to those arseholes who had hurt her.

For now, at least, all I was doing was gathering information.

But my sister could see my long game here as well. And apparently, she didn't approve. "Are you sure this is necessary? Why is this so important to you?"

"These are bad men, Camilla. I'd think you, of all people, would support this."

"And I do, for the most part. But not at the expense of your relationship. If this isn't important to Celia..."

She didn't have to finish her sentence. I could guess the ending. If this wasn't important to my wife, why put so much energy behind it? Why make it such a priority? Camilla knew firsthand what my pursuit of revenge had done to my first marriage.

But Celia wasn't Marion, and this quest was *for* her, not in spite of her. "It is. It will be," I insisted, "She just hasn't realized it yet."

Camilla considered me, her skepticism evident. Her support was slipping away, and I didn't know how I'd go about getting it again if I lost her now.

"I'll do it, Edward," she said, to my surprise. "Because these are bad men, and there are other young girls who need to be protected, and I would very much like to be a part of that. Not because I need any closure where our father is concerned, but for them. Is that clear?"

"Whatever you say. And thank you." I didn't appreciate the high-handed attitude, but I had her on my side. That was all that was important.

Except, I couldn't let it lie there. "Have you truly never felt any relief from the other times I've sought justice on your behalf?"

Her expression pinched with frustration. "That's an unfair way to frame the question. Of course I've slept better knowing Mitch can't foster children anymore. And I'm much happier having our family money back in our pockets instead of in our cousins'. And how you helped with Frank...I'm always going to be grateful for that, and you know it. But am I a better person knowing that the people who have wronged me have also suffered? I can't say that I am."

"Well, I can say that I am."

"Good for you then. I hope that's really true." She held my stare for brief tense seconds. Then she released me, standing up, an obvious dismissal before she'd even spoken. "You better get out of here if you're going to get shopping done as well."

"I already picked up her present earlier this week." But I stood as well.

"Oh? What did you get her?"

Her curiosity seemed genuine, and I hated leaving on such a fraught note. I pulled my phone from my trouser pocket and flipped through my gallery until I found the picture that had been taken for insurance purposes then handed it over.

Her eyes went immediately wide as she studied the ruby drop pendant. It was a top quality Burmese stone surrounded by twenty-five diamonds and just the thought of what my wife would look like wearing it was worth the small fortune I'd spent.

"It's absolutely stunning," Camilla said, her expression telling me she finally understood why I had to do what I was doing where Celia was concerned. That she finally understood what the woman meant to me.

I expected her to say something to that effect, but instead, she asked, "Do you know how rubies are formed?"

Surely I'd known at some point. At the moment, I couldn't recall the exact chemical process, so I shook my head.

"They're from the mineral corundum, which is usually colorless, a combination of oxygen and aluminium atoms. But when the substance is exposed to intense heat and pressure, some of the aluminium atoms may be replaced by other substances and then the stone takes on other colors. Chromium is what makes the deep red of a ruby. They're rare, though, because the presence of iron or silica prevents the formation, and the earth is abundant with those minerals.

"You've had bad things happen to you, Eddie. You've survived the heat and the pressure, and trust me, I know what that does to a person.

It can destroy us, if we let it. But it can turn us into gemstones too. Beautiful and solid and undestroyable.

"But you can't reach the splendor of the ruby if you let the iron in."

It was a pretty analogy, one she was too proud of for me to feel good about tearing apart. Thankfully, Freddie ran in then, distracting us from more serious conversation.

Still, I knew the truth. I'd accepted it a long time ago. I would never be the ruby in her story. There was no fear of ruining my color. There was no possibility of letting in too much iron.

I'd survived, though, solid and undestroyable all the same.

Because I *was* the iron.

NINE

CELIA

I GASPED, my knees buckling as Edward added a third finger to the ones already thrusting in and out of me. I'd already had two orgasms and my nerves were highly sensitized. My skin felt like fire and if he weren't holding me up at the waist, I was sure I wouldn't be able to stand.

"One more," he commanded, his thumb skimming over my clit.

"I can't." Despite my protests, my insides were clenching, preparing to go wherever he led.

"You can. You'll do it for me."

I clutched onto his stationary arm, needing more support. "I didn't realize this was supposed to be a punishment."

His chuckle was low, making his beard tickle against my cheek. "It's not. But I enjoy that you can't tell the difference."

He was savage, and my love and hatred for that aspect of him mingled until I was in miserable bliss.

"Open your eyes," he urged. "Look at us."

I did as he said, my breath hitching at the sight.

We were standing in our en-suite in front of the full-length mirror. I'd been watching, until the last wave of pleasure had forced my eyes to clamp shut, but seeing our image anew sent me spiraling higher. He'd brought me directly in here after spending the evening at the opera. Though he'd stripped me to nothing but my heels and my jewelry as soon as we'd walked in the bedroom, he was still fully clothed in his tux, his undone bow tie the only thing to suggest he was in for the night.

It was an overwhelmingly erotic sight—him fully dressed, his head resting on my shoulder as his hand snaked between my naked thighs, the brilliant ruby pendant at my neck catching the light in our reflection.

We were sinfully beautiful together.

Was this how the serpent had looked tempting Eve? Was this how he'd enticed her to eat his fruit? In moments like this, he owned me completely, and it was hard to fathom anything I wouldn't do for my ruthless devil.

My focus shifted to his face. His expression said he knew the power he had over me. It should have been frightening, but instead, it only fueled my arousal. Only strengthened my desire to please him, and when his brutal smile appeared and he ordered me to "Come," I happily went over the edge, spiraling into the abyss of my surrender.

He continued to hold me, coaxing the last of my release from my body until I was completely spent. Then he shifted me in his arms just enough that he could take my mouth with a vicious kiss. "Happy Valentine's Day, my little bird."

"I love you," I said.

He responded with another kiss, sweeter though just as deep as the last. After he relinquished my lips, he brought his pussy-soaked fingers up to feed me instead. I sucked each one thoroughly, cleaning off every drop of my wetness.

"Now to clean *you*," he said, his eyes dilated with want. After making sure I was able to stand by myself, he moved to the oversized clawfoot tub behind us and turned on the faucet.

"We're taking a bath?" This night just got better and better.

"*You're* taking a bath," he corrected.

I frowned in disappointment. It was a large enough tub, and I was eager to make him feel as good as he'd just made me feel—repeatedly.

He was yielding a pretty stiff erection, from what I'd felt poking at me as he'd made me come. Surely, he couldn't ignore that.

But he was my master, and he decided my life for me now. It was hard, but I was learning to trust his decisions more than question them. I tried not to argue unless it really mattered, and this wasn't one of those times.

I let out a breath as I gave the reins over to him, and focused on the sight of his tight backside, bent over to adjust the water temperature. A wave of euphoria spiked through me. He was so good-looking. And I was so lucky.

This was my life, this was my man, and I was in awe.

I had demons. I always would. Their hold on me diminished every day, though, thanks to therapy, diary-writing, and constant vigilance to mindfulness. And more than all that, thanks to Edward. In the two months since we'd been back in London, he'd pushed me and challenged me, ensuring I remained in the land of the feeling instead of sinking into the void of nothingness. He'd continued his sessions with me on occasion, which were tough and cathartic and helpful beyond expression.

But perhaps what had helped even more had been giving him my submission.

God, it was hard sometimes. Not to fight and buck against his control. It was my default to protest.

But it also felt natural to give in.

And when I did, when I truly gave myself over to him, I felt more alive and whole and powerful than I ever had.

Satisfied that the water was hot enough, he returned to me. His eyes scanned hungrily up my body, halting at the necklace he'd given me earlier in the evening. He raised his hand to trace the pear-shaped diamonds that enclosed around the ruby. "I don't think I can stand taking this off of you. You're too stunning wearing nothing but my jewels."

Submission be damned, I had to put my foot down. "I'm not wearing anything this valuable in the tub." I hadn't seen the price tag, but I knew luxury when I saw it.

He smirked, as though he were considering overruling. But then he moved behind me. His fingers paused at the clasp, the tips skating across my skin and making me shiver. "I feel like I've collared you."

Goosebumps skated down my arms. I liked being claimed by him, in every way that he wanted to claim me. Be it with his words or his cum or his jewels, they all expressed the same thing—that I was his.

I swerved my head toward him. "I don't need the necklace to feel the same."

Content with my response, he undid the clasp. Then he handed it to me to hold while he took off his jacket, which he traded me for the pendent. "Hang this up, please, while I put these away."

He turned toward my vanity where I'd left the box earlier in the night when he'd presented me with the gift. I went the other direction, to the closet. I hung up his jacket and took off my shoes before returning.

When I got back, he was ready for me, sitting beside the tub on my vanity stool. He'd removed his cufflinks and rolled up the sleeves of his tuxedo shirt.

Seeing him like that, from the back, hit me solidly with its familiarity. My stomach quivered with both unease and want. The two feelings often traveled in tandem, Edward frequently inspiring both in equal doses.

He looked up, noticing I'd paused. "Come get in."

"You're really not joining me?" I asked, hoping I was wrong about where this was going.

"Just you, bird."

The unease turned into dread, my belly dropping. "I know what you're doing."

"Then get over here and let me do it." He poured a dollop of body wash onto the oversized bath sponge, the vanilla fragrance taking me back to another time, to another man sitting by a bathtub waiting for me to get in.

I'd told Edward about the baths when I'd first told him about Ron, but only recently had he dug into that in one of our sessions, getting me to give him the details. They'd occurred nightly when I visited him, and began innocently enough. I'd always enjoyed the way it felt to be rubbed down and washed, loved the feel of hands scrubbing through my hair from a very young age. As I'd gotten older, he'd added sensual bath beads that made my skin feel like silk. The bathing became more drawn out then, his touch lingering when he washed the tiny buds of flesh on my chest, his fingers more exploratory between my legs.

The first time he'd brought me to orgasm, I'd thought he must be magic. There'd been colors across my vision and the sweetest burst of elation. With that one little trick, I'd been spellbound.

All these years later, I'd told Edward, the thing I found most shameful about those baths were that they'd been my favorite part of my relationship with my uncle.

And now Edward was recreating the experience. Like he always did.

"Sometimes he joined me in the tub," I said, reluctant to spend the rest of our evening on an activity that would require a great deal of mental energy on my part.

Edward raised a skeptical brow. "Did he?"

"No."

"Come on," he said with a gesturing jerk of his head. "It will just be a bath. It will be nice, if you let it be."

If he were going to wash me, as it seemed he most certainly intended to do, then it didn't matter what else happened—it would already be more than just a bath. I'd be caught between what he was doing to me and what it reminded me of, warring internally for one to win out as more significant than the other.

That's what all his redos were, though, weren't they? And in the end, as exhausting as the mental battle was for me, he always ended up turning something bad into something nice.

I continued over to him, giving him my hand so he could help me into the tub.

"You even added the bath beads," I said sinking into the extraordinarily soft water. At least he'd made it a decent temperature. Ron had preferred that baths be more on the warm side than the hot. This one was scalding, the way I liked it.

Edward smiled slyly as he brought the sponge up to scrub along my neck. "Shh, now. Let me pamper you."

So I did.

He took his time, washing every inch of my skin with thorough deliberateness. He talked to me the whole time, as I'd told him Ron would do, but the words were all his own. He told me how attractive I was, which was perhaps generic, then told me how my attraction affected him. How he got dizzy from my scent. How his blood felt thick in his veins when he was around me. How he had to constantly remind himself that he was a civilized human and not a primitive being who was motivated only by his lust.

The very nature of the situation pulled me to the past, settling around me with eerie familiarity, but every time I thought the memories threatened to overwhelm me, Edward's soothing praise and declarations of affection would anchor me to the present.

It was nice.

And weird.

And my emotions were all over the place, but mostly it was nice.

"It might take more than one go to erase this," I said when he moved on to soap up my hair, teasing.

"Greedy girl."

God, though, his fingers kneading into my scalp did all sorts of crazy things to my insides. Melted me and built me up, all at once.

Then the conversation took a turn.

"Have you thought anymore about joining me in going after him?" Edward asked, threading his hands through my hair.

"No," I said instantly.

"Liar."

He pulled the extendable nozzle from its holder and turned it on to rinse out my hair. I tilted my head back and let the water wash out the soap, the sound of the steady spray accompanying the thoughts his last words had stirred up in my head.

I had spent a lot of time thinking about Edward's revenge on Ron. Of course I had. I still had no interest in participating, but I desperately wanted to know what he was planning, how soon it would happen, how badly it would disrupt my parents' lives.

I worried too for Edward. That his actions would go too far and get him in trouble. That he'd be caught.

That concern always led me to the worst of my fears—how far would Edward go? What was he capable of? What had he already done?

"You said you've gotten revenge on people before..." I said, as he applied conditioner to the ends of my hair. I closed my eyes, pretending I didn't want soap in my eyes but really not able to look at him while I asked my question. "Did you ever kill anyone?"

Behind the dark of my lids, the silence that followed was ominous.

"Death is far too forgiving for many people's sins," he said eventually.

I wanted to be relieved about his answer—murder was something I absolutely couldn't get behind. But did that mean he tortured them instead? Because that was intolerable as well.

But also, he hadn't denied killing anyone.

"What does that mean?" I pressed.

He sat back to let the conditioner sit and met my eyes. "There are other ways to bring people pain, bird. Generally, the punishment should fit the crime. But I do prefer ruin."

"Okay. You ruin people." I nodded. Then I shook my head because I still had no idea what that looked like. "Ruin people how?"

"Well. Mitch, the foster parent who abused Camilla, for example. No one believed her claims were strong enough to pursue in court, despite the scars she wears. So instead, I framed him for embezzlement. He spent only three years in prison when he should have spent a lifetime, but he lost his wife, custody of his children, and the ability to foster any other kids, so I called that a win."

"Oh." I let it sink in. Framing a man for a crime he hadn't committed wasn't technically a good thing, but was it really that bad when the guy deserved some sort of punishment?

I hated myself because I actually didn't think it was bad at all.

"Then the cousins who'd stolen our money," Edward said. "I

drained them of every penny they had, including taking away the restaurant they'd opened up with our funds as the seed. They should have gone to jail. Instead they went bankrupt and had to live off government handouts. Seemed fitting that they experience what Camilla and I had to, if you ask me."

Sure. I could get behind that.

"When Hagan was still a teenager, he was approached by some men who pretended to run a modeling agency. Said he had a look that would sell. He believed it, and unbeknownst to me or his mother, he drained a good portion of his savings account to pay for bogus talent agency fees. There were other victims as well, but the men left town in a hurry and were able to dodge any attempts at prosecution.

"I had the means to track them down. My people gave them the opportunity to pay everyone back and turn themselves in. When they didn't, they beat them within an inch of their lives."

My breath caught. I'd been a terrible person with questionable ethics for a long time, but violence was a different kind of terrible altogether. It was disgusting and vile.

Then why did I feel almost proud?

And a little bit turned on?

Edward picked up the nozzle again to wash out the conditioner. As soon as he was done and the water was turned off, he had more. "There's another man I want to tell you about. A man I discovered recently who has been serving a life sentence for several accounts of rape and assault of a minor. He seemed to have a predilection for prepubescent girls. Some of the accounts were limited to just fingering and oral sex, but other girls he raped, brutally."

I shuddered, a bitter taste forming in my mouth. As awful as my assaults had been, they'd never been that. I'd been lucky in comparison.

"He was beaten severely in prison, as many child sex offenders are. Sent to the infirmary with several broken ribs and damage to his testicles. I imagine he's also been raped."

"Hopefully several times," I said, feeling more malicious than I liked. "He sounds like he deserved it."

Edward nodded. "He did, didn't he? Oh, I should also tell you his name. Charles Endcott. He spent time as a private chauffeur a couple of decades ago before going on to become a school bus driver."

Charles.

Ron's chauffeur. The man who I'd gotten off in the back of the limo at the age of ten. I felt like I wanted to throw up.

I also felt something else, something stronger than my revulsion.

I felt validated.

I felt relief.

I felt like fucking cheering.

"How do you feel hearing that?" Edward asked, his eyes studying me.

I didn't have to tell him. He could see it on my face, surely.

"But you didn't make that happen." It was almost a question. It had only been a couple of months since I'd told him about Charles, not enough time to track down the man and put him on trial. Still, it wouldn't surprise me to find Edward had a hand in his prison beatings. How had he even tracked the guy down?

"No, I didn't," he admitted. "It feels just as good when I do."

I swallowed. It was despicable how good I felt about someone being beaten and raped. Even someone who deserved it. But I really did feel a rush from it, especially knowing that he was no longer able to hurt other girls.

No one had believed me when I was young. I hadn't been able to go after him the legal way, but if I'd spent my adult years trying to go after his ass instead of playing Hudson's silly game, how much better the world would have been for it.

Once again, Edward was the serpent and I was tempted. It would have made me feel powerful to be part of something like that. I still could be now. It wasn't too late. The two of us working together, badass heroes, of a sort.

But even if the world would be better for that sort of vigilantism, would I be better for it?

I looked over at my husband, a devil who had promised to take care of his own. A thought occurred to me. "Did you ever seek revenge on Marion's behalf?"

He shook his head once, then said, "That doesn't matter.

"But I want to know."

"And I don't want to talk about it." He began cleaning up the bottles of body wash and shampoo to put on the side table where the items were usually kept, his actions as well as his tone shutting down the topic.

My jaw went rigid. He always closed down when I tried to talk about Marion. It infuriated me, but more than that, it hurt.

And I couldn't help but make up a slew of awful ideas about why he wouldn't talk about her. What had happened between them? Had his determination for revenge been part of it? Had he gone too far on her behalf? On her behest?

Or were his reasons simpler and more devastating to imagine. He'd told me before that she'd been the one to leave him. Was he still in love with her? Did he love her more than he loved me?

If I submitted to him as fully as she had submitted to him, would his feelings change? Could I win him over completely?

When he was done cleaning up, he sat down again and sighed. Reaching out, he traced my tense jawline with a gentle stroke. "You don't have to change your mind about Ron. He'll go down no matter what. But there are other men, men who should be dealt with. Men who are dangerous to others."

He wanted me on board, and I wanted to be his. I opened my mouth to agree to whatever he wanted from me.

Then I shut it again.

No. I couldn't try to earn a man's love. Not anymore. Not ever again.

I loved Edward, but I had to stay true to me, above all.

"You're right. They should be dealt with. And I hope they are. But it can't be by me. It's a path that leads too closely to the person I was, and I'm not going back there again."

He sat silent, his fingers moving down my neck and across my collar, tracing the bone with a delicate caress. Did he think this would persuade me to his point of view? Or had he moved onto something else?

I kind of liked the something else. A hunger was blooming at his touch, despite the three orgasms he'd given me earlier.

On the verge of giving into his seduction, I pulled myself together and turned to him, reaching my wet hand up to cup his cheek. "And not by you, either, Edward. You don't need to do this for me. I don't want you to, okay? Please don't go revenging on my behalf. Promise me you won't."

His eyes locked with mine, steady and dark. He held them there for a heavy beat.

Then his gaze moved down. To my lips. Then to my arm where his fingers now danced across my bicep. "You know, I understand why he'd bathe you," he said, his voice a rumble of need. "Touching you like this is a drug."

My stomach flipped, setting off a storm of butterflies. Somewhere in the last several minutes, he'd managed to make me forget about the baths of the past, about their predatory nature. Even talking about Ron, tonight had been about me and Edward in the present.

His words now should have been a reminder that I'd once been a sexual object to a man who should have loved me like a parent, should have made me cringe and feel the shame I'd always felt for being cast in the role. And they did, in a way, but they also made me remember I'd come out the other side. That I could be sexy and sexual and it would be appropriate. That I could be desirable and it not be indecent.

I felt very desirable in this moment. And full of desire.

As if connected to my thoughts, Edward stood with me as I stood, his mouth latching with mine. I threw my arms around his neck and, when he lifted me from the water, wrapped my legs around his waist, neither of us caring that he was still in his tux and I was dripping wet.

He carried me to the bedroom and made love to me until I was drowning in ecstasy, until I was sated and boneless, until the conversations of the night became flecks of pigment instead of the whole picture and I was completely lost to being his.

TEN

EDWARD

CAMILLA PEERED at me from the other side of my desk and nervously fidgeted with the cuff of her blouse. "What will my excuse be for staying at the hotel? I live in London. Why would I need someplace to stay?"

She was stalling her departure, anxious about her mission to intercept Ron Werner at the Savoy. She wasn't as good at improvising as I was, so these last minute details were important to her. I reminded myself of that, resisting the urge to rush her out.

While she was on edge, I was eager. I'd been waiting almost my entire life to bring down the man who'd ruined my father. I'd thought I'd been close to triumph when I'd married Celia, but though the taste of victory should have been on my tongue it had been bitter, knowing what I'd have to do to my wife in order to obtain it.

Thank God that hadn't worked out the way I'd planned.

Now, my enemy wasn't mine alone. My motives for taking down Ron Werner were as much for her as for me, and that made the nearness of his demise all the sweeter.

"You just purchased your new flat," I said, with more patience than I thought I had in me. "Say you're having your kitchen redone."

"You live in town too. Why wouldn't I just stay with you?"

"Because we're on the outs. The papers are still talking about it. You left your son with us for the weekend, because he missed his uncle so." I ignored her eye roll. "But you couldn't stand to stay in the house with *her*."

"Celia, you mean." She sighed. "You really want me to play up this family feud with her?"

"I think it makes sense, yes. From what she tells me, his abuse has gone unmentioned for decades. He may not even consider she holds animosity toward him—who knows what a monster like that believes about his actions—but in case he does, it would be good that he doesn't think you have any reason to be sympathetic toward her."

"I suppose you're right," she agreed. "I just want it all to be believable. I don't want to be the reason this messes up."

"You won't be. You'll be—"

A knock on my office door interrupted my train of thought, the rap too light to be Jeremy. "Come in," I instructed, sure I knew who would enter.

"Sorry to disturb you." As I'd guessed, Celia sauntered in, a small package in her hand. She carried it directly to me. "You said to bring this up right away when it arrived. Jeremy was in the middle of changing a bulb in the reception room, so I offered to take it."

"Thank you." I took the box, my eyes reluctant to leave her. She'd begun taking on design work recently, which meant leaving the house and meeting with clients, so I'd taken to dressing her in clothing that wrapped her up completely. I was possessive by nature and preferred others saw as little of her body as possible unless I was on her arm.

Not that it made a difference. She was still delectable wearing wide-leg gold studded black trousers and a long-sleeved sweater, not an inch of skin showing below her neck. Maybe even more so.

With effort, I pulled my gaze to the package, tearing into it as I half listened to the conversation between the women.

"I really appreciate you letting Freddie stay here. I hope it's not too inconvenient."

"Not inconvenient at all. We love having him here."

"He won't be a bother with your work?"

"Of course not. Anwar's here and the staff. And it gives me an excuse not to hyperfocus on my projects."

The box opened now, I pulled out one of the matte business cards and looked it over. It was clean, simple. Only her name, email, and phone number.

"It looks good," I said, handing it over to my sister.

She took it, twisting her lips as she admired it. "It does. It should do."

Celia gestured at the card. "May I?"

Camilla passed the item over to my wife who examined it, her brows knit together as she did. She had to have plenty of questions— why it was so stark. Why it didn't say that she was the Consulting Art Director at Accelecom or, if it was for her photography hobby, why it didn't list her website.

The question she voiced, however, surprised me. "Fasbender?" she asked, referring to the fact that Camilla had chosen to drop the Dougherty.

"I've officially gone back to my maiden name," she said in explanation. "It's a new era. New home. New name. New me."

She looked better for it, too. Her eyes were less sullen, her face more filled out. I hated to admit it, but being on her own was doing wonders for her.

Or maybe it was her own thirst for vengeance that was bringing her to life. It was the first time I'd involved her. I should have considered doing so long before.

Celia gave a teasing grin. "Am I to assume this long weekend means there might be a man involved? Edward said you were staying in town."

Camilla gaped as she looked wide-eyed from my wife to me.

Celia followed her gaze, her smile disappearing when she realized she wasn't going to get an answer. "It's okay," she said, her voice tight. "You don't have to say anything. It's really none of my business."

She handed the card back toward Camilla who refused to take it. "Edward," she spit sharply, and though that was all she said, I knew what she wanted from me.

"It's not a secret from you, Celia," I said. "We'll tell you. It's just a matter of whether or not you *want* to know."

"Is this about Ron?" Celia's voice was steady, but I could see the card shaking in her hand.

I reached out to take it from her, and she immediately wiped her palms down her trousers, as though they were sweating. "He's staying at the Savoy through Sunday."

She swallowed. "I didn't realize he was in town. Do you know why he's here?"

"He seems to be attending a party this weekend. An acquaintance. I'm not sure the relationship."

Seeming to be dissatisfied with the rate at which information was being exchanged, Camilla jumped in. "I'm going to try to meet up with him at the hotel bar. Accidentally."

"And then what?"

I studied Celia's expression, but she'd put up her mask, her emotions tightly guarded.

Either she didn't care in the least or she didn't want me to know how much she cared. Since she was still standing there, since she'd asked for more information, I had to think it was the latter.

Which meant this was the time to convince her that she should be involved in going after her uncle, not just because it would please me, but because it would be deeply satisfying to her.

"Camilla is going to try to pique his interest, that's all," I said. "Casually let him know she's aware of his interests. Give him her card. Later, she'll reach out and invite him to Exceso. He should feel safe in that environment, no matter whether he trusts the person inviting him or not. There he'll connect with plenty of the type of men he's interested in knowing. I won't even have to interfere. That's how relationships work there.

"But I do have some friends there who will be looking out for him. One is an undercover FBI agent who will be there at the same time. He'll get close to Ron and hopefully, either through Camilla or directly, he gets an invitation to whatever Ron has planned next in the States.

Once we get him on his own soil, at an event he's hosting, we should be able to take him down for good."

Again I watched for a reaction and found nothing.

"Well?" I prodded.

"It's a noble plan and all. I admire the amount of thought you've put into it. But it's not going to work."

"Why is that?" Camilla asked, concern evident in her tone. "Did we miss something? What part won't work?"

"All of it, really. You're going after him as if he's a serial pedophile, trying to appeal to some attraction he has for little girls in general. There was only just me."

I *had* missed something. I'd missed *this*. It had been apparent to me from the first time she'd told me about him that Ron was a predator. Men didn't get that good at that kind of grooming without having practiced before. And when they were done with one victim, they moved on.

It had never occurred to me that Celia wouldn't realize the same thing.

"You're sure about that?" I asked gently, hoping I didn't have to be mean to make her see the truth.

She paused to consider for only half a second. "Pretty sure. He's dated many women since then. Long-term relationships. And who else would he have had access to? Who's letting their daughters stay over at his house? I was a singular situation."

"You were *special*."

"Right." But she hesitated, not as sure as before.

"You were his Lolita," I pressed. "His girlfriend. He loved you because you were you, not because you were a child, is that what you're trying to tell me?"

She scowled, her arms crossing over her chest defensively. If my sister hadn't been present, I was certain she would have pressed back.

But she was trying to be respectful, because I demanded that from her, and I took advantage of her silence to push on. "I know you aren't that naive, Celia. Are you willfully ignoring the truth here?"

"Are you willfully being an arse?" Camilla asked, not bound to the mandates of respect that my wife was bound to.

It gave Celia enough time to come up with her own response. "I'm being honest, Edward," she said firmly. "I want to get him as much as anyone."

"Do you?" It was a fair question since she'd told me before that she wanted nothing to do with my revenge schemes.

She answered with tightly pursed lips.

I changed tactics. "There have been other girls," I said softly. "It wasn't just you."

"How do you know that?" Her voice was thinner now, her guard finally coming down.

I opened a desk drawer and pulled out the file I'd been collecting. I threw it on the edge of my desk, facing her, and opened it up, spreading the items out so she could see the photos, police reports, and copies of cleared checks I'd managed to obtain through my investigators. "He has a circle of friends who are rumored to have been involved with illegal sexual activities. Some have even faced charges, nothing that has stuck. There have been several undisclosed payouts over the years, however, including two from Ron. One made to the daughter of one of those long-term girlfriends you mentioned. I'm guessing that's where he's gotten his access."

The color drained from Celia's cheeks. "What?"

"And he got access through his friends. He and the lot of them hold regular events. Semi-annually, it seems. The location varies, always at one of their country houses. Based on the few accounts that have made it to my sources, I believe they're parties like the one where your uncle auctioned you off at."

"He auctioned you off?" Camilla asked, horrified.

I hadn't told her the details. They hadn't been necessary. Now, though, it seemed important to remind them both why Ron Werner deserved to be destroyed.

"I think I need to sit down." Celia looked for the closest seat.

I was up out of mine before she took a step. I helped her to the chair against the wall, then knelt in front of her.

"There have really been others? Besides me?"

I reached out to stroke her cheek with the back of a single finger. "I'm afraid so, bird."

"Oh, God. I didn't know." Her tone was broken and weary, and yet it sliced through me. If I could have taken the pain from her, I would have. I would have siphoned every terrible ache, adding them to my own until I couldn't tell the difference between hers and mine. I was a blackhole, yet despite the gravity of my emotions, I couldn't draw hers to me without taking her with them.

And I was devil enough to do that. To take her along with all the poison she felt. To drag her into my schemes with me.

"I didn't want to believe it. I knew it was a possibility, but I didn't want to be responsible." She put her hands together and propped her elbows on her lap.

"You aren't. It's not your fault." I leaned up to kiss her forehead. "You tried to tell."

"I didn't try hard enough."

I tilted her chin up forcefully. "Stop. I won't hear that from you." My eyes darted between both of hers. "We're doing this now. You got that? We'll stop him now."

She nodded. Then, after thinking about it for another few seconds, she shook her head. "I just don't understand. How could he be involved in something this big for so long and not have been stopped?"

"Powerful men with lots of money," Camilla said, reminding us of her presence. "They're above the law."

If Celia realized I was included in that group, she didn't acknowledge it. "Can't your FBI friend just show up at one of Ron's events and catch him in the act? Why does it have to be the two of you?"

It had to be me because of her. How could she not realize that? I had to be the one to do this for her because it was my job. Because I was her husband. Because, when I'd said I would love and care for her, I'd made those vows with utmost sincerity.

"The parties are all kept very hush hush," I said instead. "Only people on the invite list know the time and location. Also, the authorities can't go in without a warrant, and they don't have enough reason to get one, legally. They need an undercover operation for something like this, and going after Ron Werner is not on the priority list."

"Wasn't on my father's either."

And that was why Warren Werner was still on my vengeance list as well.

But I wasn't about to get ahead of myself.

I pulled the handkerchief from my front pocket and handed it to her. "He might have someone he's paying off to keep his activities on the down low. It's possible he's just too big of an entity to even consider going after. I'm guessing they all are."

"I guess that shouldn't surprise me." She dabbed at her eyes, then, with one last sniffle, pulled herself together. "Can I see those pictures?" She nodded to the open file on my desk.

I grabbed the few on top and handed them to her.

"This man," she said pointing to one in a group shot. "And this one. And this one. Those men were there that night. They were...they..."

They'd been the men who'd "bought" her. She didn't have to say it. I knew. There had been five of them in total. I'd been hoping that I'd found at least a few of them.

I'd hoped I'd found them all.

"I'll get them too," I promised, leaning against the edge of the desk.

"Me too." Camilla reached out to take Celia's hand. "I want to get them too."

Celia smiled faintly, and my chest tightened. I hadn't realized how much I wanted them to like each other until that moment. It had been silly to think otherwise, to believe I could keep my world compartmentalized, especially when I so wanted Celia to be a part of all of it.

It hadn't been that way with Marion. But then Marion had wanted to be kept separate.

"What can I do to help?" Celia asked, drawing me from my thoughts.

Camilla responded before I could. "You don't need to do anything."

I didn't quite agree with her answer. "You can help me try to identify the other two who were there that night. To make sure I have them on my radar."

"Okay. I will." Celia grew serious, her eyes piercing. "What about with Ron? What can I do to help get Ron?"

The exhilaration that rushed through me was nearly blinding. I'd done it. I'd brought her to my side, and hell if we weren't going to be formidable together.

"Can you feed a little gossip to your parents?" I asked. "I think it would help if Madge Werner thinks you and your sister-in-law are not friendly."

"Yes. I'll call now," she said, rising from her chair.

It wasn't far to the door, but I hurried to walk her there. "Are you all right?" I asked quietly, when we were at the threshold. Camilla was still close enough that she could likely hear our whispered conversation, but I didn't care about that. I cared about my wife.

"I'm fine," she insisted. "I should have gotten involved sooner."

I cupped her face with my hands. "There was no need. I told you I'd take care of you, of this, and that's what I'm doing."

"I know, and I appreciate it. But you were right—I need to do this." She brushed her lips against mine in a soft kiss. "You were right about something else, too, you know."

"What?"

"When we get him? It's going to feel real, real good."

ELEVEN

CELIA

"THE SOFA GOES THERE. The chair goes there."

Freddie moved the furniture pieces on my model, adjusting them the way a three-and-a-half-year-old boy thought they should go rather than what was functional. It was fortunate I even had the thing. These days, most designers rendered their designs on computer. I was one of those people, though, who had a better vision when I saw the thing in 3D. Real 3D, not a flat-screen version.

I handed him the fireplace, giving up on my work. "And where should this go?"

He thought about it for a minute then moved the piece to be in front of the windows.

"That's an unusual place for a fireplace," Edward said as he came into the space I'd once used as a bedroom. It had been completely transformed to be a cozy work area, and while I was glad for the space and for the work, I couldn't help but think it might be better suited as a nursery.

It wasn't a thought I had too often, but Freddie's visit over the last couple of days had settled the idea more firmly in my mind. I hadn't had a lot of experience with children before him and had always assumed I would be terrible with miniature humans. Turned out I actually had a knack.

At least I had a knack for Freddie.

"I don't know," I said, defending the kid's choice in fireplace placement. "The smoke can go right out the window now. No need for a chimney. Quite convenient."

Freddie's eyes suddenly went wide with panic. "Father Christmas comes down the chimney!"

"He has a point, Celia. There has to be a chimney for Father Christmas."

I laughed. "I'll work on adding that to the design then."

"You do that. Meanwhile, it's time for this one to get to bed." Edward swooped Freddie from his chair and flew him like an airplane to Anwar who was waiting in the doorway. Once the boy had been deposited in his caretaker's arms, Edward ruffled his hair. "Sleep well, you monster."

"I'm not a monster," Freddie said.

Edward feigned surprise. "You're not? What are you then?"

"I'm a little boy!"

"Maybe you'll be more recognizable after your bath. Now get to it. No more delays. Blow your auntie a kiss first."

Freddie kissed his hand and opened it with what was supposed to be a blow of air but came out more like spitting. I pretended to catch the kiss and placed my palm to my cheek. "Got it," I said.

Edward walked the pair out the door and as far as the stairs, then returned to stand in my doorway, his hands thrust in his pockets.

"You're good with him. I bet you were an amazing father." I focused on rearranging the model pieces instead of looking at him. So he wouldn't think the statement was significant. Because it wasn't. Not really. I knew where he stood on having more children.

"I wasn't," he said, surprising me into looking up. "I was much too young. Too impatient. Too preoccupied. I never had time to play with them like I should have."

Part of me longed to know what had preoccupied him, if it had been his relationship with his wife or simply the details of building a wildly successful business.

But another part of me—a stupid, hopeful, optimistic part of me—wanted to grab onto the thread he'd so casually thrown out. "Maybe you should try again, then. Now that you're older and more settled."

His expression became stony. "No."

That was it, nothing more. One syllable, and the subject was officially closed.

I sighed, wondering if this was a battle I wanted to try to wage. I'd gone into our marriage knowing his thoughts on the matter, I'd stayed when our relationship became real knowing he hadn't changed his mind. I hadn't wanted them, so it hadn't been an issue, except that maybe that had been a lie. Maybe I had wanted them. Maybe I'd always wanted them. Maybe that want had just been one more of the feelings I'd buried deep in numbness.

But did I want a child more than I wanted Edward?

I didn't. So there was no battle to wage.

"Besides," Edward said, as though sensing where my head was. "I'd much rather play with you." As easily as he'd scooped up Freddie, he bent and swept me up from my chair. "Work is done now. Let's play."

I tilted my head wondering what he was up to. Then when he set me down in front of the white side of the chess board he'd given me for Christmas, it was evident.

"This wasn't exactly what I hoped you had in mind." But I moved my pawn.

He sat across from me and pushed his pawn out to meet mine. "I'm sure I have more in mind than this. Just, this first."

That was promising. I moved a knight. He moved a bishop. I moved my other knight. He moved one of his.

The rhythm of our game should have focused me entirely, but my head was elsewhere, had been since I'd interrupted his conversation with his sister a couple of days prior. It had been a heavy revelation, realizing that Ron had other girls. I was disgusted, of course. And sad—sad that I hadn't done more to stop him. Sad that he had other victims.

The worst part, though, was that I also felt jealous.

It was stupid that I could feel that way and gross and shameful. It showed how deeply he still affected me. Ron had groomed me to care that I was special, and even after everything, after the auction and therapy and finding real love, I still was programmed to care.

That had shocked me.

But Edward had known. He'd understood that there was closure needed where my uncle was concerned, and he'd been certain that vengeance was the road to achieving it, even when I'd insisted that it wasn't. That I was fine.

I hadn't been fine. Not if Ron still had the power to make me feel those kinds of things. I could see that now, could see what Edward had seen all along, and except for encouraging me to journal and schedule an impromptu session with my doctor, he hadn't pushed the topic since I'd left his office. He'd given me space, and I was grateful.

But now I was ready to talk.

"Have you heard from Camilla? Was she able to meet with Ron?" That was an easy place to start. I moved a pawn.

Edward's other knight came out. "Yes."

I picked up a pawn and stared at him, dying for more. "And...?"

"Make your play."

I set the piece on the board, not even looking to see how wise of a move it had been. "Did it go as planned?"

He moved a knight before he responded. "It went as expected. He played dumb, but he took her card. He did ask who had told her he might have knowledge on the subject."

I played my bishop, knowing no questions would be answered until I did. "What did she say?"

His knight took mine. "You aren't paying attention."

I scowled and tried to focus on the board. I took his knight with my queen. "I'm not?"

"Not the wisest move."

I wasn't exposed. I'd taken one of his pieces. I couldn't see any flaw in the thought process. He was just trying to rile me. "Keep your commentary to yourself, please. And tell me about Camilla."

With a sly smile, he castled. "She didn't exactly answer. Just said that she'd recently become a sort of relative, by marriage. Left him with that."

My stomach felt queasy. It felt dangerous knowing that Camilla had interacted with him, that she'd referenced me in any way. *This will always be just between us*, Ron had said to me, over and over and over. It was cruel how I could still worry he'd be mad.

It made *me* mad.

I moved my other bishop. "I want you to get him," I said as he moved his own bishop in response. "I want you to get all his friends." I took his bishop with mine.

Then, seeing my opportunity, I made a move of another sort. "And I want to talk about who else you think deserves my wrath."

He paused, his fingers on his rook, his eyes on me. He studied me for a beat before sliding it to the next space. "Who says I think anything?"

I glared at him. "Don't even pretend you don't have thoughts. You've been hinting that there are others you think I should go after, and I know you meant those five assholes, but I think you have more people in mind than that. I haven't wanted to discuss it, but I'm giving you a chance now. Talk."

He gestured at the board.

"Goddammit." I castled, "Now talk."

He slid a pawn out with a chuckle. "How about we both talk?"

I moved a pawn. "Fine. Let me state for the record that we are just talking. You won't do anything based on this conversation. You hear me?"

He chuckled. "Giving me orders, are you?"

"I'm serious, Edward."

His face grew somber. "We're just talking," he agreed.

"Good. Now you."

Another black pawn came out. "Your father."

My breath lodged in my chest. That was why we needed to have this conversation. Not because I thought he might be right and that I should seek justice from other people who had wronged me, but because he thought I should, and the unspeaking of it was like a silent wedge between us. If it wasn't addressed, it would eventually drive us apart.

With great determination, I moved my piece and found my voice. "My father didn't have anything to do with ruining your father's company. I told you. Ron had autonomy."

He played a pawn. "We aren't talking about your father wronging me. We're talking about how he's wronged you."

I looked at the board, but all I could see was my father's face the day I'd told him what his little brother had done to me. "You think I should get back at him for not listening to me about Ron." I made my move absentmindedly.

Miraculously, I didn't lose any pieces with Edward's next play. "I think he deserves to pay for that. Yes."

I moved my queen. "He made a mistake. I was a little girl."

"You were his little girl, and he should have protected you. That's a father's job." He slid his bishop diagonally across the board. "Not only did he not protect you, but he used you to protect himself, putting his shares in your name to evade taxes. Those are not acts of a good father. You yourself said that your relationship with him is strained."

"Which is why I should probably do as my therapist suggests and talk to him." I had no plans to at the moment, but the idea made more sense than whatever Edward thought I should do.

"Talking doesn't pay back what you're owed."

"I don't know that he owes me anything. Besides an apology. He didn't make me go back to Ron's after that, at least." I wondered what his reaction would be when Ron was finally arrested, if he'd apologize then or pretend I'd never said anything. "Anyway, he's going to get blowback when all of this goes down with my uncle. That will make me feel better."

"But it won't make *me* feel better."

I stared at my husband, dumbfounded. Was this still somehow about what Werner Media did to his family or was Edward that upset for me? I'd explained that my father wasn't responsible for Ron's actions, so it shouldn't be that. But the other option was more unbelievable.

Did he really love me that much?

"Take your turn," he said, not giving me any insight.

I made a thoughtless move and lost a pawn on his next turn. After I played again, I opened my mouth to ask about his motives with my father, but he spoke first. "There are others besides your father. John. The man who took your virginity. That was statutory rape."

"Technically, yes, but I asked for it."

"It doesn't matter. It was illegal. He should pay."

"Like you should pay for all of your illegal activities?"

He took my bishop. "We aren't talking about me."

Right. Because he was the devil. He doled out the punishments, he didn't ever pay for his own.

We made our next several moves in silence, mostly because I was beginning to think there was no reasoning with my husband, and worrying what that meant for our marriage.

It meant that I had to try harder, was what it meant. I wasn't accepting any other option.

"Who else?" I asked after he took another of my pieces from the board.

"I have mixed feelings about the boy who tricked you into dumping your boyfriend for him. He broke your heart, and he did it maliciously, but you paid him back already by sleeping with his father, didn't you? And he did step up when you got pregnant by claiming to be the father. That seems like retribution in its own right."

I took one of his pawns. "I agree. He should be off the hook. You would have a hard time taking Hudson Pierce down anyway."

His fingers froze on his queen. "That was Hudson Pierce?"

Shit. I'd forgotten I'd kept that from him.

Maybe it was good to come clean about this, though. "Yep. That was Hudson."

"So the father you seduced was Jack Pierce."

I shrugged, guiltily. "It wasn't one of my finer moments."

Edward blinked several times, and pride jolted through me. It was rare that I surprised the man. It made me feel like a worthy opponent when I did.

Even though he did take two of my pieces with each of his next two moves.

"So when Hudson bought out the majority in your father's company, it wasn't just because he didn't want you interfering with his relationship. It was more like the endgame in a long chess match."

"Actually, it was exactly like that. He won, obviously. And I have no desire for a rematch."

Edward's eyes narrowed, calculating, and I had a feeling that it wasn't the current game he was assessing.

"I mean it, Edward. I'm not going after Hudson for anything. He and I are done. If he hadn't won, it's very unlikely I would be with you here now. And don't forget, he has those shares. He could hurt us if we tried to hurt him. Which I do not want to do." I was bordering on pleading, but this was important. Not only had I accepted the status of my relationship with Hudson, but also I'd played the man before. I'd seen what he could do, how devious he could be. I did not want to be on the other side of that again.

"Fine," Edward said, his accompanying exhale proving his sincerity.

I relaxed, letting out tension I hadn't realized I'd been holding. Then his bishop took mine.

I swiped his bishop with my king in response, which wasn't that brag-worthy considering the state of the board, but it made me feel good all the same. "Is that all? Are we done?"

"With this game? Practically." He moved his queen down the length of the board. "Check."

"No way. I still have a fighting chance." I didn't. I'd only ever beaten him twice, and we played quite regularly. For now, though, I could move my king out of play. "But I meant with your list."

He moved his queen again. "Just one more person to add—the man who introduced you to your games."

My stomach dropped. *Checkmate.*

And not because of anything on the board.

The man who introduced me to The Game was also Hudson, another fact I'd refrained from telling my husband. And thank God I had, because if Hudson had that stacked against him, there was no way Edward would let him off without some sort of recompense.

Except, this was only a conversation. This was *my* list we were discussing. Edward wasn't doing anything to anyone. We were only talking about possibilities, and there was none where Hudson was concerned. Period.

"No," I said. Now to see if my one-word decrees were as effective as Edward's.

"No? I think very much yes. He was the reason you were such a cold-hearted bitch when we met."

"Dragon," I corrected, moving my castle. "Cold-hearted *dragon*."

He moved his queen, and again I was in check. "You can't say he doesn't have sins to pay for."

"He has to pay for his own sins just like I have to pay for mine. Personally, I'm not holding anything against him." I scrutinized the board for long seconds, trying to get the shaking of my hands under control. What if he found out it was Hudson? Would that make him retreat or double down? It could go either way. I didn't like the lie, and I wanted to tell him the truth, but I wasn't sure how far my husband would go in his search for justice.

One thing was certain—I could not let him take on Hudson Pierce.

I could feel him studying me the way I studied the board. "What happened between you?" he asked, in the cold detached voice he used in our sessions.

No. This would not become a session. I would not pour out my heart over this. "I've already told you all that matters," I lied, moving my king to safety once again. "He knew how to be cut off from the world, emotionally, and I begged him to teach me how he did it. Like with John, I was the one who asked for it."

It took him a bit to find his next move. "Like with John, your wishes were irrelevant. He taught you how to hurt people. He made you a weapon. That's wrong whether you asked for it or not."

"You're exaggerating. He didn't make me a weapon. He helped me become mean, but I wasn't dangerous." I brought my queen nearer to my king, hoping it would be enough protection.

"What you planned to do to me wasn't dangerous? I beg to differ."

Edward's tone had grown sharp, bringing my gaze up to his.

His expression was serious. Deadly serious. "Maybe it's you who want revenge on him because of what I set out to do to you. Maybe this has nothing to do with him at all."

"Possibly." His eyes took on that mischievous gleam that was present throughout our earliest meetings.

A chill traveled down my spine. Or a thrill. It was hard to tell the difference between the two where Edward was concerned.

"I'm pretty sure you and I are even, darling, considering what *you* planned to do to *me*."

He smiled, and if I hadn't won the round, I'd at least gotten a point.

The game resumed. He moved his knight. I took it with my bishop. He took my bishop with his queen. I moved my king. He moved his.

"You called him A," Edward said, breaking the silence. "In your journals. Was that his initial?"

The hard, heavy dread returned to my stomach. I'd thought the subject had been dropped. Silly me.

"I'm not answering that," I said firmly. And I was in check again.

"Why won't you tell me about him?" The sharp edge had returned, demanding I give answers.

It wasn't fair. He pushed and pushed and pushed and expected me to always capitulate. And yet he never once yielded to me. Was that always to be our roles?

No. I could submit, but there had to be a limit. He had to give back. "Why won't you tell me about Marion?" I challenged.

His eye twitched but he otherwise ignored the question, the same way he was now ignoring the board. "Did you love A?"

A beat passed. "No."

"You paused."

"I wanted to be sure of my answer. And I'm sure the answer is no." I hadn't always been sure. There'd been a time when I'd thought I loved him, but if I admitted that, would he figure out he was also the boy who tricked me into falling for him? Had he already figured it out? Was that why he was asking?

But I was wrong about his angle entirely. "Then Marion and I are different."

"That makes no sense. You should be telling me about Marion *because* you loved her. She was a significant part of your life. Why won't you share that with me?" I was frustrated, and it showed.

"You want to know about Marion because you want to compare yourself to her." With only a glance at the board, he took my rook with his. "I'm not feeding your tendency to try to be something other than who you are."

I winced. "That wasn't very nice."

"Was it untrue?"

God, he could be cruel. So brutally cruel.

Brutally cruel and honest. "No, it wasn't." I was insanely jealous of Marion, mostly because I knew nothing about her except that she'd once owned Edward's heart. It was possible she still did, and that hurt.

If Edward thought the man who taught me The Game owned my heart, would he be jealous too?

"I didn't love him, but if you must know, he did break my heart." I could be cruel too, in case he'd forgotten.

His nostrils seemed to flare, but beyond that, he remained stoic. "Even more reason why you owe him this. You'll never get over him otherwise."

Oh, for fuck's sake. "How will *you* ever get over *Marion?*" I threw back, wondering if we'd crossed from discussion to argument.

"Stop worrying about Marion."

"Stop worrying about A!"

He held my gaze, his fists curled on the sides of the chessboard, his lip curled downward.

Then suddenly, with one dramatic sweep of his arms, he brushed the chess pieces off the board, scattering them all over the floor.

I stared, taken aback. As angry as the move had been, he seemed calmer now, as though he'd only needed to let out his temper and then he'd be fine.

Still, I asked, "I guess this is a fight now?"

His mouth quirked up into a half-grin. "How about we skip the rest of the arguing and get straight to the punishment for disagreeing with me?"

I felt the impulse to argue more for half a second.

And then I recognized it for what it was—an attempt at conciliation, and I was all for that. Being "punished" by Edward was better than fighting any day.

"Yes, sir," I said, for once not bothered by the term of address.

His pupils darkened as he began undoing his belt. "Crawl over the table and put your head in my lap. If you're such a dragon, prove it to my cock."

I did as he said, climbing across the board then, with my legs still on the table, bracing my arms on his thighs so I could take his fat, steel rod into my mouth. Sometime between the first spurt of pre-cum on my tongue and the moment when he released down the back of my throat, his hips bucking with wild abandon, his hands wrapped firmly in my hair, I let our quibble go, dismissing it as a simple lover's spat.

But deep down, in the place inside me that I used to bury my feelings, I knew the truth—this conversation was far from over.

TWELVE

THEN: EDWARD

"HOLD THIS, WILL YOU?"

Before I'd answered, Roman thrust his whiskey tumbler into my hand so he could pull a lighter and cigar out of his inside jacket pocket.

"Is that a good idea?" I asked, as he bit off the end. It was his house and his party, so he knew I wasn't asking because I questioned if it were the right environment.

"I'm already dying, Edward. Smoking a cigar seems like a splendid idea." He winked as though it wasn't macabre to speak of his approaching death so casually.

Stage four colon cancer, spread to the liver and stomach. And he'd chosen not to pursue treatment. There wasn't any point, he'd said.

Instead, he was throwing a party.

"You're making it hard to not enjoy this," I said, because I knew it was what he'd want to hear, but I most certainly was not having a good time. I didn't have many friends, mostly because I didn't like the bother of relationships. Roman had become more than that, though. He was family. Practically a father, and I'd already lost one of those. I wasn't ready to go through the pain of that loss again. No amount of drinking or celebrating would ease the storm of gloom gathering inside.

"It's a phenomenal evening," Marion said, her French accent faded from so many years in the UK. "It's a beautiful way to honor this season of your life. Much better to have the festivities now instead of later."

Instead of after his funeral, she meant. She was more tactful than I, though, always able to be charming, no matter the circumstances.

"That's exactly what I was going for." Roman took his tumbler from my hand and clinked it against my own filled with cognac. "May we never go to hell but always be on our way."

I grimaced and chuckled at the same time.

Then he turned to Marion to clink her wine glass. "Sante, my dear."

"Somehow it seems gauche to say it in return." Her smile was lovely, both demure and reassuring at once.

"Cheers will do just fine," he said, his gaze warm.

"Cheers then, Roman."

When the older man's focus moved again to me, he had the expression of a stern mentor. "Your wife knows how to play along. Take a cue from her, my boy."

I forced my lips upward, or at least less down. "Here's to friends and family who know us well but love us all the same."

"That's better. Not great, but better." He tipped his drink back, finishing it off before setting it down on the tray of a passing waiter.

I sipped my drink more slowly, taking the burn in measured doses, wishing I could do the same with the news of Roman's health. It was too fast, all of it. He was too young, and I needed him. A selfish reason to want him to live, but wasn't all affection selfish?

"Camilla has a new boyfriend, I see."

I shook myself from my thoughts and followed Roman's gaze across the ballroom. Camilla was there on the arm of her latest beau—Frank Dougherty. She'd been through a string of men over the past several years, none of them any good for her. Most of them had disappeared before I'd been able to discern just how not good for her they were. Frank was the first in a long time to stick around.

"What do you think of him?" Roman asked.

Like the others, he didn't deserve her, that was certain. He was bred well enough, but he was entitled and impulsive. He had no job, and with the way he splurged, he was sure to reach the end of his trust fund before he turned thirty.

But money didn't buy happiness, as well I knew, and if Camilla was happy with the lazy prick, then I could support the relationship.

I just wasn't yet sure she actually was happy.

Once upon a time I would have discussed my concerns with Roman in full. Now, it seemed unkind to burden him with such trivial affairs. "I don't know yet," I said, trying to be honest without going into it.

"Edward's worried he's a brute," Marion said, wrapping her free arm around mine. It was subtle, but I read the subtext of the gesture clearly. She was goading me, challenging me publicly. Not that it was much of a challenge. She liked to get in trouble, knew that I liked catching her in it, but she was submissive through and through. She liked to please way more than she liked to get in trouble for defying.

Roman studied me. "That's fine criticism, coming from him."

"He's a different breed of brute," I said with a defensive scowl. "He's pushy and controlling and indulgent. With Camilla, specifically. I'm not sure he knows when to rein it in."

Roman stared at me, his gaze so pointed it was impossible to miss the meaning.

Fuck, he had a point. I might as well be describing myself and my relationship with Marion.

But Marion was into what I offered her. I hated to think about what Camilla might want in a sexual relationship, but I was worldly enough to know she might be into it as well.

"I'm sure you'll step in when needed," Roman said, seeming to understand my concerns.

"Yes, I will."

At my side, Marion let out a sigh, small but noticeable. If she had more to say about my methods of interference, she should say it. Not now, but later, when it was just the two of us.

She wouldn't, though. She never did.

"How are the kids?" Roman asked. "Hagan's...what? Seven now?"

Marion brightened at the turn of conversation. "Nine. Genevieve is seven."

"That's right. What are they up to now?"

I rolled my eyes. This was as bad as pretending to enjoy his death party, only this time he was the one acting disingenuously. "Don't answer that, Marion. He doesn't care for anything to do with kids."

"I don't," he agreed. "I was being polite."

"Excuse me, may I steal you momentarily?" A man I was only somewhat acquainted with ushered Roman away to introduce him to his companion. As though he had any reason to want to meet new people now.

God, I was an arse.

Marion shifted next to me, the kind of movement that said she'd likely been uncomfortable for some time and had been holding it in. Only now that we were alone could she let her poise go.

I smiled, realizing I was the source of her discomfort. Pulling her into me, I positioned my mouth near her ear. "Are you feeling the reminder of yesterday's punishment?"

"Yes, sir."

She'd asked for it, essentially, when she stayed in my bed after we'd fucked the night before. Separate bedrooms had been her decision, a space she said she needed due to the intense nature of our relationship. Choosing to not sleep there was one of the not-so-subtle ways she used to indicate she wanted some physical discipline.

The irony was that I would have preferred for her to sleep at my side. Every night.

I resented her for that, if I was being honest. It was that resentment that I'd clung to when I'd doled out her punishment. "Perhaps I was a little vicious with the belt."

"That's not what's feeling sore."

I pulled back to look at her and saw the color rise in her cheeks.

I had been vicious with more than the belt. After leaving her with red welts along her backside, I'd taken her ass. And I hadn't been gentle.

Still feeling cross today, probably more because of the event we had to attend than because of anything that had to do with us, I'd found a way to torture her further.

"I suppose you've been a good girl today. You can remove the plug." I reached in my pocket and took out the drawstring bag the toy was kept in. I exchanged it for her wine. "Bring that back to me immediately. I'll hold your drink while you're gone. Oh, and Marion," I grabbed her arm, drawing her back so that she could hear me when I whispered. "I'll know if you touched yourself."

"Yes, sir."

I watched her walk away, admiring the tight fit of the white gown I'd selected for her to wear. It was a style she wasn't comfortable in, one that showed her curves and didn't allow much room for movement, but when I'd set it out for her, she'd put it on without batting an eye.

I loved that about her, that she would bend and yield to my every command.

But sometimes it wasn't enough. Sometimes I longed for the struggle, and though she'd give me that too, when I asked for it, it was never real. It was a game we played with very specific moves. She'd go against me on something with no meaning. I'd pretend to be angry. She'd pretend to beg for my forgiveness. I'd punish her. Then she'd go back to submitting to my every wish.

It had been satisfying for a while.

Lately, I yearned for it to be more authentic.

"Ten years and two kids, and she's still a perfect little doll. You lucked out with that one, didn't you?"

I looked over to see Roman had returned, another whiskey in his hand, still puffing his cigar.

"Yes, I suppose I did." No marriage was perfect, after all. No one person could ever be exactly what another needed. I should be satisfied with what I had.

And I was.

Mostly.

"You have the rings back now, I assume. Will you give them to your wife?"

I'd spent much of our friendship hunting down my parents'

wedding rings. My cousin had kept them, claiming they'd been lost. After I'd bankrupted her and her husband, she'd pawned them. Then they'd been sold, even though I'd had a description of the items sent out to every pawn shop within a hundred miles. It had taken me years to track them down and had only just recently acquired them.

The relief I felt at having them in my possession was impossible to describe. It was akin to the way I used to feel when I was little, when my parents would stay out late, and I'd wait with the silly worries of a small child, afraid they wouldn't return and then finally my mother would slip into my room to place a kiss on my forehead, and the world would suddenly feel right again.

"I haven't decided yet. They would need to be resized."

"What does she want?"

"Marion doesn't seem to have a preference." *Whatever you think is best,* she'd said. "She's fine with what she's currently wearing. I'll likely save my parents' set for Hagan."

"Did you have to pay too high a price for them in the end?"

The new owners had been very reluctant to sell. They'd used them for their own marriage, so, of course, the rings had sentimental value.

I'd had to pay out more than I'd paid for Marion's three-carat princess cut. "It wasn't above my limits, though I shouldn't have had to pay at all."

"I didn't realize you had limits." Roman's smile was teasing, but his tone said differently.

I turned to face him straight on, but I couldn't think of a comeback. He had every right to suggest that I acted without restraint. I'd never shown him otherwise.

The question was out there now, though—*did* I have limits?

I wasn't sure that I did.

And that was terrifying.

"What about the pawn shop owner?" he asked.

I'd wanted to destroy him. I'd wanted to take his entire business down, wanted to ruin his reputation, wanted to make it impossible to work another day in his life. He'd ignored the requests I'd sent asking dealers to be on the lookout for the items. I'd promised a reward in exchange.

This particular owner must have thought one in the hand was worth more than two in the bush. He'd sold them for less than what I would have offered.

Roman had been the one to talk me down. *He was just trying to make his living,* he'd said. *He hadn't intended malice on you directly.*

"I didn't touch him." It had been hard, but I'd staved off the desire. For Roman.

He grinned, the smile reaching his eyes this time. "Ah, you *can* listen to reason. Good thing I was around."

But he wouldn't be for much longer. The truth sat heavy on me, a suffocating boulder on my chest.

And the other words unspoken between us: *Who would reason with me when he was gone?*

Roman was pulled away once again, a weepy niece this time with fond memories she insisted on sharing.

I was grateful she'd chosen to share them with him alone. I was already feeling overwhelmed with emotions, and the storm that had been brewing inside me was threatening to become a hurricane.

"Here you go." Marion returned to my side and discreetly slipped the drawstring bag with the butt plug into my pocket before taking her wine from my hand.

"Feeling better?"

"Feeling empty," she said, probably trying to soothe my obvious bad mood with the promise of dalliances to come. "Maybe we can—"

Whatever she'd come up with to distract me from my melancholy went unheard, when someone hurrying through the room bumped into her, sending her wine spilling.

She gasped, her eyes wide with horror as the red stained the front of her white Oscar de la Renta gown.

"What the hell?" I looked around for the offender and saw it was a waiter, rushing toward the kitchen. He hadn't even stopped.

I ran after him, irate. "Excuse me!"

"Edward, it's fine," Marion said, at my heels. "I'm sure it was an accident."

I stopped to level a glare at her. "Even if it was an accident he should have apologized."

It would have been a simple thing for her to stand her ground, to say it didn't really matter all that much, that it was just a dress and accidents happen.

That opinion was clearly written all over the lines of her face.

But when she opened her mouth to speak, she said, "Yes, sir. He should have."

Her refusal to push only fueled my indignation.

I spun in the direction of the kitchen and found the waiter as he was exiting, a tray of desserts on his shoulder.

"Excuse me," I said with gritted teeth. "Yes, you."

He was genuinely surprised at my aggressive tone. He truly was unaware of his careless behavior.

Well, I was here to enlighten him.

"You bulldozed your way through here moments ago and bumped into my wife, making her spill merlot all down her dress." I gestured toward Marion who still carried the empty glass, her skin and dress sticky with the wine.

The kid—he couldn't have been older than twenty-one—went nearly as red as the stain my wife wore. "I...I didn't realize. I'm so very sorry, sir."

"It's not me you should be apologizing to, it's my wife."

He shifted toward her, his posture bent with the full tray still on his shoulder. "I'm so sorry, ma'am. I guess I wasn't paying attention. Please give me the drycleaning bill. I'll take care of it."

"Marion?" I looked to her, giving her an opportunity once again to let the boy off the hook.

Without giving him a second glance, she met my eyes. "Thank you, sir."

Jesus. Even now? Even in this moment she was still at it? Still playing the faithful sub?

"I'm not sure that will be enough," I said, flatly.

"Sir?" The color now drained from the waiter's face.

"I don't believe your apology is enough to mollify my wife. She may require more."

"Is there a problem over here?" Roman asked.

I hadn't noticed his approach. If I had, I might have backed down sooner, because I already knew he would step in when needed. He would reason and rein.

But would she?

It wasn't what she'd signed up for. She'd promised to stand by me, to honor and obey. She'd never promised to save me from myself.

He was here now, though, and I'd already started this, so might as well finish. "Yes, there's a problem. This irresponsible young man here plowed into Marion, spilling her wine all over her outfit, then ran off without even so much as an acknowledgment. He's offered to pay the drycleaning bill, but only after I tracked him down. And clearly this is stained. I highly doubt it can be removed and this is a designer gown."

Roman regarded us, taking in the ruined outfit, the boy's frightened expression, and my obvious rage. "I can have the amount for the dress taken from his wages."

"I doubt his wages could cover it." I stared directly at my wife as I spoke. "I think he should be fired."

Roman's eyes narrowed, but perhaps realizing I had some point to prove, he didn't argue. "If you insist."

I didn't insist. I didn't *care*. It was a fucking dress, it was a fucking accident.

But the hurricane inside me had taken hold. My friend was dying, my sister was preoccupied, and I was out of control. My wife was the only one left, the only possible hope of bringing me back to a place of calm.

"Marion?" I asked, knowing it wasn't fair. Knowing no matter how she answered, she'd fail.

She didn't even glance at Roman. Didn't even pause to consider. "Whatever you think is best, sir," she said, surrendering to my wishes as beautifully as ever.

I pulled her in, kissing her more aggressively than was appropriate in front of company.

"Yes," I said when I broke away. "I insist. Fire him."

I could have kept going. I could have fired the entire crew, and still my rage would have barrelled on. Still, no one would have intervened. Roman was right—I had no limits. And Marion, the woman who counted on me to be her master, would stand by my side no matter what.

It was a frighteningly powerful realization—with my ambitious aims for revenge and ruin, there was no one to stop me but myself.

THIRTEEN

NOW: CELIA

I SAT down at my vanity and switched my phone to speaker so that I could do something productive while my mother spilled her gossip.

Until I'd moved to London, I'd lived my whole life in close vicinity to her. We saw each other so often, the only thing to talk about was the goings-on of others. I'd thought with an ocean between us we'd share more of our own lives, that she'd tell me about herself. That she'd ask about what was happening with me.

Turned out that wasn't the case.

"You should have seen it, Ceeley. She had the tackiest hairpins, in the shape of bumble bees. She might have well been one of the children at the event instead of the organizer. It was so embarrassing. I refused to even let the paper take my picture with her."

"Good call," I said, setting the phone on the counter. I had no idea who she was talking about. I'd only been half listening, and as long as I made a comment or a sound every now and then, my mother wasn't any wiser.

As she started into another story, I opened the jar of my moisturizer and applied it over my face and neck. There was a reason why calling home first thing in the morning was a bad idea—it made for an awfully late start to my day. At least I hadn't planned to do any design work.

Genevieve was graduating from university the next day, though, and we had a party planned afterward at the country house, a party I was completely in charge of.

Thank goodness for a competent staff. It meant I didn't have to do most of the heavy lifting. I wasn't even planning to go out to the house until the morning, but there were still a lot of details to oversee.

"Who else is there to tell you about? I know I'm missing something."

"Hmm," I said, as though I were trying to be helpful. I didn't care about anyone in her social circle. Not a one. The only person she could tell me about that interested me was Uncle Ron, and there was no way I was going to be the one to bring him up.

It had been three months since Camilla had met up with him at the Savoy, and while it hadn't been expected that he would reach out to her, there was always a hope that he might. The next step to the long game wasn't supposed to take place for another couple of months, when Camilla planned to invite him to Exceso. I'd wanted it to be sooner—now that I was part of the scheme, I was eager to get it going—but Edward felt we'd have a better chance at earning his trust if the "right" people were on the island when Ron was there. Apparently some men with questionable sexual interests would be visiting in the fall, so the invitation would be extended at the end of summer.

Still, I wished there was something that could be done now. Was he currently planning his own event? Would he be attending one soon? Those were the things I wished my mother might tell me. If we could find out about one of his soirees, we could skip the island all together and inform Edward's FBI friend of the gathering.

But my mother never had anything to say about my uncle at all. She didn't know much about what was happening in Ron's world, or she didn't find it interesting to share. Either way, he never came up, and it would be too suspicious for me to ask.

All I could do was continue to press my supposed animosity with Camilla and hope that she'd tell Ron, in case her relationship with me was an obstacle to trusting her.

"While you're thinking," I said, flipping the cap of my foundation open, "can I just vent for a minute? I've managed to avoid having to see Edward's sister for the last several months, but with Genny's graduation, I'm going to have to see her."

She picked up on the cue perfectly. "You're in charge of the seating at the dinner, correct? Make sure she's assigned a place far from you. And be sure to tell that husband of yours not to invite her to drive with you to the ceremony."

"Oh, good thought about separate cars." My mother was experienced with snubbing people. It was nice to know she was helpful in something. "Seating isn't going to matter. It's all stand-up buffet so people can mingle. That means she's easier to ignore, but also easier for her to infect others with her hateful ideas about my relationship with Edward. If I can keep her near me, however, she'll be a pain, but at least we can control the drama."

None of it was true, of course, and perhaps the drama was a little more than necessary, but since there might be photos released to the media, I wanted there to be an explanation of why Camilla was included front and center.

"That's really a shame. Circumstances are what they are, though. You'll have to play nice. It will be hard, but I raised you for just this kind of thing."

No shit, she had.

"Oh! I just remembered a bit of interesting news!" She spouted into some new scandal, and I went back to my face.

I finished applying my foundation and had picked up my bronzer brush, having tuned out, when something she said caught my attention. "Wait a second...say that again?"

"You know the Holcombs," she said, in a way that suggested she wasn't actually telling me what she'd said before but inferring what it was she thought I'd missed from her original story. "They've owned those stables near the country club for forever. John owns them now, or I guess he did own them. Malachi passed them on to him when he died. You might remember John. He's been working there in one form or another since you were a teenager."

Yes, I very much remembered John. He'd been in his late twenties, and I'd given my virginity to him when I'd still been underage.

The hair at the back of my neck stood up, my insides tightening with a knowing kind of dread. "What did you say happened to the stables, Mom?"

"They were repossessed by the bank. I'd thought the Holcombs owned them outright, but apparently they'd gotten another mortgage, and I don't know. They had some financial difficulties a few years back and must have gotten behind. I didn't realize they were still struggling."

I put down my makeup brush and picked up the phone, turning the speaker off. "You're saying that they lost the stables? That the bank foreclosed?" I had to be sure I had this right.

"Outrageous, isn't it? It seems they were in default and the bank was working with them, but then the title got sold to an investment company and they foreclosed. John and his family were living on the site. They had to move in with his little brother. Not sure what he's going to do now for work. Such a shame to no longer have those stables available. They were so close for families in the city. They're for sale now. Hopefully someone else will buy them and open them up for business again."

Yeah, that was the shame of the situation. That privileged rich folk no longer had a convenient place to keep their expensive thoroughbreds.

God, this was terrible.

Terrible because the situation was terrible, but also terrible because I had a deep-sinking feeling that Edward was involved. It couldn't be a coincidence, could it? He'd said he thought John deserved to be punished for having sex with a minor.

But I'd told him not to do anything. And he'd agreed.

Fuck.

Maybe I was wrong.

"Mom," I said, interrupting whatever she'd been saying. "Something's come up. I'm going to have to let you go. Talk soon."

I hung up without waiting for her to say goodbye.

Tying my robe around me as I stood up, I left our suite and went to my office space. It took a minute to find where I'd last put my laptop, but once I found it, I booted it up and did a search for stables for sale in that area of New York. It was easy enough to find the Holcombs'. There were only two other properties available, and the Holcombs' was the only one listed as having been foreclosed.

And right there, in the foreclosure information, the current owner was listed as EMF Enterprises.

EMF. Edward Michael Fasbender.

I wasn't familiar with the company, but there couldn't be any question about who owned them.

I printed the page and slammed my laptop shut. Party preparations be damned. My day's agenda had just changed.

I'D BEEN to Edward's office on numerous occasions, but since the first time when I weaseled my way past security, none of those visits had been unannounced. Usually, when I was asked to present my pass, I was able to give my name and the security guard could check the list that had all of the day's approved visitors and see I was on it.

Today, Edward hadn't known I was coming, so I wasn't sure what would happen, if the guard would let me up or have to call for permission. Fortunately, it turned out I'd been put on the permanently approved list, which would have been satisfying to discover if I hadn't been so mad.

But I *was* mad. Fuming mad. Which was why I hadn't called ahead. I was the kind of mad that couldn't be put off or dealt with over the phone. I needed to see my husband in person.

Before the elevator doors opened on his floor, I took a centering breath and threw my shoulders back. Edward's secretary wasn't fond of me, and I didn't have the patience for a battle with her today. Besides, I was saving all my energy for Edward.

Charlotte spotted me as soon as I got off the elevator, her eyebrows furrowed in confusion. She clicked a few keys on her computer as I approached her, likely checking to see if she'd missed my name on Edward's schedule.

I took advantage of her momentary distraction to plow right on past her. "I'm going in," I called over my shoulder. His door was open, which meant he wasn't with anyone, thankfully. I took care to slam it shut behind me before marching toward his desk.

He was on the phone and was undoubtedly surprised at my arrival, but he had practiced skill at containing his emotion, and he managed to keep a solemn face and steady tone as I approached him.

I slapped the printed paper from the real estate site on his desk in front of him. "You promised," I said, not caring that he was otherwise engaged or that my voice could likely be heard on the other end of his call.

He hadn't shown respect for me in this matter. Why should I show any for him?

Edward only had to glance at the paper to know what it was, a final confirmation that he was indeed behind the bank repossession of the stables. "I'm going to have to call you back," he said into the receiver then immediately hung up.

Before he could launch into denials or excuses, I attacked again. "You promised not to interfere, and then you went ahead and did this!" I pointed my finger forcefully at the proof.

He sat back in his chair, cool as a cucumber except for the darkness in his eyes. "I didn't promise."

"You did! You said..." I trailed off, trying to remember exactly what had transpired in our conversations. The last time we'd talked about it, we'd argued. The time before that, when we'd bathed, I'd asked him to promise not to strike out on my behalf...

And he'd changed the subject.

He read my realization in my features. "See? Never promised."

His juvenile behavior only fueled my anger. "Fuck you, Edward. This is bullshit. That man has a family! John Holcomb didn't do anything except succumb to the wiles of a horny young girl. He doesn't deserve to be punished."

He shrugged dismissively. "That's where we disagree."

God, his nonchalance was maddening.

And I was all anger and rage. I wanted to pound my fists against him. Wanted to bring out my claws.

I braced both of my hands against his desk so I wouldn't strike. "How is this justice? He doesn't even know what he's being punished for!"

"He committed a crime."

"And how many crimes have you committed?" I leaned toward him, daring him to name them, to recognize his hypocrisy.

He sat forward, his gaze piercing. "It's a dog eat dog world, Celia. I'm on top for a reason."

He didn't care. He knew he was a hypocrite, and he didn't even care.

"You are narcissistic and self-righteous," I seethed. A devastatingly attractive devil who cared first and foremost for himself. Was his heart even attainable? I was insane to ever believe it might be mine.

"Narcissistic and self-righteous? To want to stand up for my wife?" His tone had an edge now, his composure slipping.

Somehow that felt like progress.

"I didn't ask you to. In fact, I expressly asked you not to." I searched his features to see if I'd gotten through to him at all. But the expression etched there was as determined and unyielding as ever.

I shook my head, mystified, and stepped away from his desk, suddenly feeling like I needed the space between us, as though my bewilderment needed room. "You know what I don't understand, Edward, is why. Why did this insignificant stablehand mean anything to you? Was it jealousy?"

"You can't seriously need me to explain this to you."

I studied his smug expression, trying to figure out what I wasn't getting, and finding nothing but this answer. Why else did he care enough to invest the energy to go after a nobody in the suburbs of New York? "That's the only reason I can come up with. You're so possessive and entitled that you can't stand that another man was the first to fuck me, is that it?"

God, if that was really what this was about...

A horrifying thought occurred to me. "Was that why you recreated that whole 'pretend-you're-a-virgin' night?"

Edward shot up from his chair and leveled a stern glare in my direction. "You're trying me now, Celia."

He'd reacted too quickly, too defensively. Had I hit the nail on the head?

It hurt, but I explored the idea further. "It had nothing to do with making my memories better for me. It was all about you claiming a part of me that didn't belong to you."

He stepped out from behind his desk, and automatically, I took a step back.

He stopped and pinned me in place instead with his gaze. "That wasn't the reason I did that, and you fucking know it."

"Do I?" I searched my feelings, and yes, in my gut, I did know that. He'd done what he'd done because he'd wanted to erase the bad and replace it with his good. He may have had personal reasons for doing it —he did enjoy breaking people down, after all—but he could have left me like that, broken and ruined, and he hadn't.

He took advantage of my pause, traveling several steps in my direction before I noticed. When I did, I put my hand up, as if to stop him. "If not that, then *why*? Why are you obsessed with being a vigilante with people in my past? It's over and done. I've moved on. You forced me to move on."

"And this is the next step in your healing process." With confident caution, as though he were a lion trying to coax his scared prey, he took another step toward me so that my palm was almost touching his chest.

He was magnificent like that, when he was a predator. When he was single-minded and primitive. When it felt like he could devour me with a single bite.

Even angry, I was strongly aware of my heartbeat. It quickened when he was like this. Tripped over itself with anticipation.

"How the hell is this healing?" I asked, dropping my hand and shaking my head of the wanton thoughts. "It's unproductive. It's petty."

His jaw set firmly. "It isn't unproductive at all. Nor is it petty.

Taking out your anger on someone who deserves it is a very useful coping method."

"This isn't coping. *You* aren't coping. You're just as fucked up as I ever was." I threw up my hands, frustration agitating me so completely I couldn't stay still.

"Because I still haven't gotten the vengeance I need to move on." He leaned forward as he prowled toward me.

I hadn't realized I'd backed up with him until my legs hit the couch, bending me over the backside. Immediately, I straightened, determined not to bow in his wind. "Oh, is that how it works? Anytime you're mad, anytime you feel slighted, you have to strike back in order to get past it?"

"Why not?" He was feral, his eyes dilated, his lip curled.

Ugh, he was so attractive. And so arrogant. And such an asshole.

What kind of world did he think we lived in? How would anyone be civilized if they were constantly lashing out at every insult? Was that how he expected me to be with everyone? With *him*?

"How about this?" I asked, my breaths coming out hard and shallow. "I'm angry at you right now."

I hadn't meant it as a challenge, or maybe I had. Either way, that's how he took it, and one beat later, his arms were around me, his face angled above me. "Good," he said, his lips whispering over my lips. "Then it won't just be me who's taking out my wrath on you."

His mouth crashed against mine, and he kissed me with a forceful and tempestuous kiss. He was greedy and aggressive, his tongue possessing my mouth, the length of him pressing tightly against me so that every inch of my body met with firm, hard Edward Fasbender. It was difficult to think when he invaded me like that. Difficult to remember that I was anything besides blood and lust and hormones, that I was a person who could think for myself rather than just bend and submit.

Difficult, but not impossible.

I wrestled my mouth free and leaned away.

He raised a brow, as though daring me to defy him, and so I did. I raised my palm to push him away, but he grabbed my arm and wrenched it behind my back, which for some stupid reason made my pussy throb.

I brought my free hand up, not even sure what I meant to do with it, but he caught it in midair.

"No?" he asked, his eyes dark, the blue rims like thin rings around a planet of black.

No, of course no.

But my body said differently. My back arched toward him, my skin flushed, my skin broke out in goosebumps.

And when he shifted to grip my wrists with just one hand and the other ventured under my skirt to rub against the crotch panel of my panties, he found them wet.

"Tell me to stop, and I'll stop," he said, his fingers working beneath my material.

I gasped as his skin made contact with mine, and though I hadn't yet decided that I wanted this, my legs widened to give him room.

"You don't want me to stop, do you?" He traced along my wet seam. "You want to want to, but you don't actually."

"If you're talking about the shit you pulled on John, you're wrong. I do want you to stop."

"I'm talking about ruling you. You wish that you didn't love it. You wish that you didn't need it."

I wanted to argue, but just then, he shoved two long fingers inside me, and even if his thrusts hadn't taken my voice away, I wouldn't have told him to stop.

Because he was right. I did love it. I did need it.

I tilted my chin up, my mouth reaching for his.

Again, our lips collided. This kiss was bold and ruthless, his fingers mirroring the fervor as they fucked in and out of me with shameless strokes, until I was writhing, until I was a rush of heat and euphoria, until he'd swallowed every last one of my whimpers of pleasure.

Then we were a flurry of movement, both of us desperate to be connected, to remove anything that stood in the way. My panties were pulled off and tossed to the floor, his jacket joined soon after. His pants were unbuckled and undone and pushed down just far enough to get his cock out. My skirt was pushed up and when I threw my arms around his neck, he lifted me, setting me down on the back of the sofa.

As he lined himself up at my entrance, I silently congratulated myself for having chosen a low-back couch when I'd redesigned his office before we'd gotten married, and then he was there, inside me, pushing so deeply into my body that I felt more than penetrated. I felt conquered. I felt owned.

I let my dangling shoe fall off, then bent my knee and brought my foot up to rest on the back beside me, opening myself wider to him, giving him more access. With one arm wrapped firmly around my waist to hold me up, he rammed into me, over and over at a dizzying speed. His pelvis hit against my clit, sending delightful shocks through my body that had me gasping in rhythm to his jabs.

I was already halfway to an orgasm, already too blissed out to form words when he started talking.

"You want to know why?" His voice was strained, but he could still speak coherently.

I could barely remember my name, let alone form an answer, especially not to a question that I didn't fully understand.

Thankfully, he clarified. "You want to know why this man? Why righting this wrong was important to me?"

He didn't expect me to respond. It was obvious when he cupped his hand around my neck, his thumb stretching across my pulse point, pressing just enough to make speech difficult.

No, he didn't need me to say anything.

He needed me to listen.

"Because I love you, bird," he said, his thrusts somehow reaching even deeper. "I fucking love you so much that I can't separate myself from you anymore. Your pains are my pains. I feel them as if they happened to me, and I can't let them go unpunished, not because I care about how much these sins hurt me, but because I understand how much they hurt you."

Exhilaration shuddered through me, and my pussy tightened around him. He lowered his arm from my waist to my hips, drawing me closer, refusing to let my body push him out.

He pressed his forehead against mine. "You are mine to care for and protect and fight for. You gave that honor to me. Let me own that. Let me love you right."

I was overtaken with rapture, rapture that exploded from my center, up through my belly and my chest until it was everywhere in my body, until I was shaking and sobbing and moaning out Edward's name. Until I was shattered by the euphoria. Until I was nothing but blissful radiating energy.

And then immediately, as the spots before my eyes disappeared, while he was still plunging into me, chasing his own release, my thoughts cleared and awareness seeped in.

This had been a valid argument, a subject that we clearly needed to resolve, and instead of fighting it to the end, I'd let him distract me with sex.

Again.

If this was how every disagreement was going to end up, I was literally fucked.

Which meant I had to find another way to fight.

But how could I fight him on this? When he truly believed that he was right. When he wouldn't listen to reason.

When he was this obsessed with his end goal.

My husband was like an addict, addicted to the rush of dispensing retribution. He said he sought justice, but his motives were wrong. Justice was best doled out with impartiality. There shouldn't be emotions involved, and he was completely wrapped up in his feelings. That made him dangerous. How far had he gone? How far would he go?

How far would I let him go?

A voice of reason chirped in the back of my head, warning me to walk away. Take what he'd given me, the new person that I was, and leave. Find a better way in the world without him.

But I fucking loved him too.

And I was selfish with that love. With *his* love. I wanted to be cared for and protected and fought for. No one had taken that role before. Hudson had come the closest, teaching me how to be what I'd thought I needed to be to survive. Edward had been and done so much more, and I didn't know how to give it up.

If he *was* addicted to vengeance, I was addicted to him. Walking away was not an option I could choose easily. I had to stay. I wanted to stay.

But that didn't mean I had to give in.

He wanted my submission, and I could give him that to an extent. I could still push back when I needed to. I could stand up for what I believed was right. I could fight for my own wants.

Yes, that's what I'd do.

If this marriage had any chance at all, it was time I made my own demands.

FOURTEEN

EDWARD

I TUCKED myself inside my pants and glanced over at my wife as she straightened her skirt. "Nice outfit. I'd rather it was the dress I picked out, but this one proved easy to work around."

Honestly, I didn't care what she was wearing at the moment. She was ruffled and flushed from fucking, and as far as I was concerned, she'd never been more beautiful.

She bent to retrieve her underwear. "I was making a statement."

Her voice was terse. Apparently the physical activity had done little to alleviate her rancor. It had sure helped relieve mine.

Not that her ire wasn't justified. I would have expected her to be angry about my actions with the Holcomb estate. I just had never expected her to find out.

There was nothing to do now but tread lightly. "Message received," I said, an attempt to smooth her feathers.

She paused, her pants halfway up one leg. "Was it?"

This wasn't going to be as easy as I'd hoped. Dealing with her was certainly different than dealing with Marion. When she protested to something I'd done, she most often didn't voice it, and on the rare occasion that she did, she was generally soothed with domination and a round of rough sex.

My old tactics weren't going to work, and I had yet to figure out what would.

I sighed, sitting on the arm of one of the chairs she'd chosen for my office. "I am who I am, Celia. You might not have known who that was when you married me, but you certainly have learned since then. You chose to stay."

Her rigid stance eased. She finished dressing then came around the couch to face me. "You're right. I did. I didn't expect that you'd change, but I also didn't expect you'd be completely unreasonable. Marriage is supposed to be about compromise."

"You've been married before, then?" It was a knee-jerk reaction. Definitely a dick statement.

"I've never been divorced," she countered.

I couldn't hold back a smile at that. "Touché."

Perhaps neither of us were an expert in marriage, but I had both success and experience in business and negotiation. She and I had negotiated our partnership. We had our roles.

I stood to retrieve my jacket that had ended up on the floor in our earlier haste. "It certainly would be easier to navigate this relationship if you would just submit to my authority, like you agreed that you would."

"You knew who I was when you married me. You chose to stay." She was infuriatingly smug, having thrown my own words back at me.

"I thought I'd broken you down after that."

"I agreed to elements of submission. I never said I'd be docile." Her brow creased, and her voice softened. "Is that really what you want from me?"

I already knew the answer, but I thought about it for a moment anyway, remembering what life had been like with Marion, how unfulfilling her obedience became over time.

"No," I said, as I buttoned my jacket. "I much prefer you like this." Challenging, perhaps, but never boring.

She crossed to me. "This isn't fair either, though," she said, straightening my tie. "You like me to fight you because it turns you on, or whatever, but you still expect to always win. I'm only supposed to think I have a chance at getting what I want. Eventually, I'm going to realize it's futile, and I'll..." Her palm smoothed down my chest, pausing above my heart, which pounded against my rib cage, anxious about where her train of thought had been headed.

"You'll...what? You'll leave?"

She shook her head and smiled. "I was going to say I'd stop fighting. Because what would be the point?"

I wasn't sure that would be any better than her leaving.

"I don't always expect to win," I said, taking her hands in mine.

"Really? Tell me one time that you haven't." I hadn't gone after her mystery partner in crime, but I wasn't writing that off as a battle lost yet. When I couldn't come up with any other response, she pulled away. "One time, Edward."

This was ridiculous. Of course I didn't always win. Because I couldn't think of any instance that I hadn't didn't mean that it had never happened. It simply meant I wasn't holding a grudge about it.

I circled around behind my desk and looked at her, still staring at me waiting for an answer. "You're wearing the wrong dress," I said, suddenly. "And I haven't even hinted at a punishment."

"That's not going to cut it. I need to be given wins about things that matter."

"You're working now." I unbuttoned my jacket and sat down, relieved that I'd been able to come up with something meaningful.

Except, once again she shook her head. "Not because I asked to. *You* decided I'd work. You oversee my clientele and how much time I put into it."

"I haven't gone after your father."

"You're going after his brother. I'm not sure that isn't the same thing."

I ran my fingers over my forehead, feeling the beginnings of a headache. "Fine. You want to win sometimes. I hear you. I'll make an effort in the future to be more conscientious of not dominating every aspect of our lives."

"Nope. That's not enough. I want some things now. I deserve some things now, especially after the bullshit you pulled, going behind my back like this with John."

"I should have known you already had something in mind. Go ahead. Let me hear it."

I gestured for her to take a seat, but instead of sitting in the chair in front of me, she came around to my side and perched on the corner of my desk.

I swiveled my chair to better face her. I wasn't sure I liked her there, sitting over me like that. It felt like the balance of power had shifted, and that made me uneasy.

"First," she began, and I definitely didn't like that there was a "first," suggesting that a list was about to follow. "I want you to pull the sale of the stables and offer them back to John. He was behind on his mortgage, I know. Go back and work out something he can manage."

"I can't do that."

"You can't? Or you won't?"

I considered. "To be honest, a bit of both."

"I understand that you have some deep need to do these things you do, Edward, that seeking vengeance fulfills something in you that nothing else can. Well, you got your vengeance in this situation. Vengeance that I consider to be completely out of line, but it's done. Now you can move on. Which means you shouldn't have any lingering emotional attachment to getting the stables back to John."

It wasn't that simple. As though I could trick my brain into not realizing that a settled matter was being unsettled.

But there was merit to her argument. I'd played it out. I should feel satisfied. It should be enough to be able to move past it.

If it wasn't enough, what would be? Would I still be unfulfilled after Ron?

I ignored that thought and concentrated on the practicalities. "Look, business doesn't work like that. I bought out the Holcombs' existing bank note, but I never planned to continue to carry it. That hasn't been budgeted for."

"Then I'll pay you what he's behind. I have money."

"It's a good chunk of money."

"Then I'll sell some of my Werner shares. They are in my name now."

My jaw tightened. "You definitely won't do that."

"You'll get John back his stables, or I will do that." She folded her arms across her chest with stubborn determination.

It ignited something primal in me. Something that made me want to roar and take her down. Make her surrender. Make her yield.

She was right—I did always have to win.

Old tactics aren't going to work.

She had me. Much as it hurt to do so, I had to give her this. *Zugzwang* was the term for it in chess, when a player was forced to make a move that put him at a disadvantage. I was extremely good at putting others in that position. I didn't like it so much being on the other side.

I leaned back in my chair and lifted my ankle to rest on my opposite knee. "Look at you, getting better at chess all the time. I'll speak to my loan officer and work out something by the end of the week."

"Thank you."

The satisfied gleam in her eyes made my chest warm. Losing didn't have to be so bad, I supposed. "Feel better?"

"Yes, but that wasn't really a victory. That was righting a wrong. Even though everything will work out for John in the end, I'm sure you caused him a lot of stress in the meantime. Not to mention public scandal."

So that was how she'd caught on. Her mother must have included his woes in her latest round of gossip.

"It still feels like a loss to me."

She shrugged and stood. "That's the recipe for a perfect compromise. Neither party walks away feeling satisfied."

"If that's what marriage is supposed to be, I'm glad I've been doing it wrong."

"I'm sure you are. Not so fun when you have to be a team player, is it?" Finally, she circled around and sat in the chair in front of me.

"What else? I know you have something more." I had a feeling this wasn't going to be as easy of a loss to take.

"I do." She straightened her back, as if gathering courage. "I want a baby."

"Absolutely not." There were other ways she could win. I'd give her the moon. I'd give her a million different things. This would not be one of them.

She didn't cower, though, as she usually did when the subject was broached, and I cut it off. "No, you don't get to decide, and that's it. This isn't a dictatorship. You have set the foundations for every part of this relationship, and in the end, I have bent to your will, each and every time, whether I wanted to or not. Now I'm putting my foot down. I'm telling you what I need, and what I need is a baby."

It was strange how her request pulled at something in me, deep and buried. Some lizard part of my brain that was programmed to spread his seed, ignited. Wanted to stand on the desk and pound my chest and ravage her again with the intent to impregnate her right that minute.

Fortunately, I was a civilized man, and the more civilized parts of my brain could overrule the caveman with saner rationale. I'd already had my children. I'd been a mediocre father at best. There was no wisdom in putting another child through that, and frankly, I had no desire to battle with the constant pressure associated with parenting.

The answer had to be no.

"I *don't* need a baby, Celia. In fact, I very much need to *not* have a baby. I understand your desire to have a win, but it can't be at the cost of my needs."

Her lips turned downward. "That's funny. You don't seem to consider my needs when you make any of your decisions."

I put my leg down and leaned forward. "That's practically all I consider anymore. All the time. What's best for you in every situation. You still may not see it, but going after John Holcomb was for *you*."

I'd never been like this with Marion. Everything was always about me. I was the self-centered star of the universe. With Celia, even my need to ruin the man who had destroyed my father was outweighed by the need to destroy the man who had destroyed *her*. She might not have expected me to change when she married me, but I had, maybe not for the better, but for her.

And she didn't see it. "I know you think it was for me, that you've convinced yourself it was, but when you outright ignore my wishes, you are not actually acting in my best interest. I am a fully capable human being. I may like being pampered and cared for, and I may kind of love it when you make decisions for me, but I am not incompetent. When I feel strongly enough to make a stand, that should matter."

She was passionate, but the anger from earlier had dissipated. It made it easier to listen, and because I knew she was really making an effort, I tried harder to hear her.

"I am well aware of your capabilities," I said, recognizing she needed me to acknowledge her competence. "You are very intelligent and quick-witted and resourceful, as well as independent. I don't desire to take care of you because I don't think you can't take care of yourself. It's because I long to take that burden from you."

"And I love that about you."

"Capable as you are, however, sometimes your scope of vision is limited."

"And, sometimes, so is yours!" she exclaimed, with evident frustration. "You know what a loss I felt when I had my miscarriage. You know how it was devastating enough to send me to dark places, how it made me do bad things. It seems fairly obvious that having a baby would do the exact opposite. It would bring me to good places and good things. You say that you love me and that you want to care and provide for me above all else. If giving me this one thing that I truly want isn't part of that, then it's kind of hard to believe that you really feel the way you say you do."

"You know how I feel." My tone was as raw as my insides. "You *know*."

"And now you know how I feel."

We sat in silence for several heavy seconds, our gazes locked. I wasn't a man who gave in. I wasn't a man who resigned. I wasn't a man who didn't win.

And that's who she claimed she needed me to be now. Someone who I wasn't.

I took in a deep breath and let it out. "Is this going to be a deal-breaker if I refuse?"

I could hear my heart thumping in my chest, could feel the milliseconds crawl in her pause as if they were hours.

"It might be," she said after what felt like an eternity.

My chest tightened, like it were being squeezed together with a vice-grip. I'd never understood the saying about losing a battle to win the war in quite the way I did at this moment. Fucking zugzwang.

"Come here." I opened my arms, needing them to no longer be empty. Needing them filled with her.

She sank into my lap and clutched onto me as though she felt the same.

I buried my head in her hair, inhaling the scent of her shampoo before kissing her temple. "I don't want to lose you, bird."

"Then don't."

Anxiety about the prospect of her leaving morphed into concern about the thing she needed in order to stay. "I can't be the father I was before. I was distracted and unavailable."

"You won't be."

Fuck, was I really considering this? Was I really agreeing?

Concern rose to borderline panic. My mind fought to order it, to give the crazy idea structure.

I pulled back so I could see her. "I need to make sure that I'm able to focus this time. I need to wrap up these...outstanding debts, so to say. Ron, specifically. It may be another year or so. Can you wait that long?"

She searched my face, bringing her hand to cup my cheek. "Are you saying yes, then?"

It was hard to get a deep breath, but I tried. "If you can wait."

"I want you to be able to focus on us, too, and I know how important finishing up these plans are to you. You've been working toward this for a long time, and I wouldn't dream of interfering with that. So, yes. I can wait. Not forever, but a year or so isn't that bad. Gives us more time to be ready."

"All right." It still felt hard to breathe. "All right," I said again. For her. I could do this for her.

I kissed her, sealing the deal.

But as sweet as her lips were, my mind couldn't stop spinning. A hundred possible addendums fought for my attention. Only one made its way through the fog.

"One more thing," I said, breaking away suddenly. This was important. "Besides Ron, I need to go after A."

Her body went stiff as she pulled back. "No. I said no, Edward, and I meant it. I still mean it."

"He deserves to pay retribution even more than John Holcomb. You can't let that go."

"Actually, I can."

"*I* can't," I said, more firmly. "You said you understood my need to do this."

"I said I understand that you have the need, not that I understand the need itself. And I will support you as best as I can with it, but this man has nothing to do with you. He has nothing to do with *us*. And there has to be a limit somewhere, Edward. I will support you, but I won't enable you, and going after A is going too far."

How long had I yearned for someone to give me these boundaries? It had seemed like forever since Roman had died. Since someone cared enough, was strong enough to insist that I needed to stop.

But I was like a heroin addict who needed one last fix before going to rehab. "*He* would be the limit. *That* would be the end. Ron, the men associated with him, and A." She moved as though she wanted out of my arms, but I only tightened my grip. "And then you get your baby, bird."

Her expression remained steadfast. She opened her mouth, but before she could speak, Charlotte's voice came through the intercom.

"Mr. Fasbender, sorry to interrupt you, but you have yet another unannounced visitor."

She enunciated the "unannounced visitor," an obvious jab at Celia's surprise visit.

As disruptive as her arrival had been, I didn't appreciate Charlotte having an opinion about when Celia showed up. "Tell whoever it is to make an appointment, like everyone who isn't my wife is supposed to do."

"That's just it, sir," she said, and already dread was filling in my stomach. "She isn't everyone else. It's Marion."

FIFTEEN

CELIA

MY MOUTH WENT DRY, and even though I was still sitting securely in Edward's arms, the room started to sway. I'd expected to meet Marion the next day, at Genny's graduation. I hadn't expected to come face to face with her here, in Edward's office, without the formalities of the event to hide behind.

And, especially, after the conversation we'd just had and the tense way it had ended, I wasn't ready for this.

I wasn't ready for this at all.

Edward looked just as taken aback, but his surprise was only momentary. Then his features smoothed, and his expression turned stoic. "Give us a few minutes," he told Charlotte, before clicking off the intercom.

He stood, taking me with him, then set me aside as though I were something inanimate that had been on his lap rather than his wife. He turned to glance in the mirror behind his desk, and adjusted his dress shirt and tie before running his hand over his mouth and beard, removing the bit of gloss I'd left on his lips.

"Edward..." There were so many things I wanted to say, wanted to ask. *What is she doing here? Were you expecting her? Why are you primping for your ex-wife?*

The most pressing issue at the moment, however, was my own appearance. We'd fucked and we'd fought, and I was doubtful I looked anything what I'd like to look like when meeting the woman who my husband might very well still be in love with.

"I can't..." I searched the room, as if somehow a secret escape door would pop up.

His forehead pinched, and he stared at me, stared *through* me, as though he'd forgotten I was there. Then he shook his head, and his eyes cleared. "You can clean up in my en-suite."

It was what I needed, but it wasn't reassuring. Reassuring would have been, *You look perfect, just the way you are.* Reassuring would have been, *I'll get rid of her.* Reassuring would have been, *You're the one I want, only you.*

Instead, he'd sent me on my way, then instantly turned his attention from me to his phone. He picked up the receiver and dialed three numbers, obviously an inter-office call. "I need you to do something," he said to whoever was on the other line. "Come to my office and interrupt me in ten minutes. Remind me that someone's waiting for me in the conference room."

He didn't want to spend time with her any more than I did.

That, at least, made me feel better enough to grab my purse and make my way across to the bathroom that was tucked into a nook at the opposite end of the office. Once inside, I shut the door and pressed my back to it, trying to catch my breath.

This wasn't a big deal, I told myself.

They'd been divorced for ten years. Even if Edward had still had feelings for her when she'd left, he had to have gotten over her by now. There was no way he could have been harboring a broken heart all that time.

Right?

Whatever the answer, it didn't change the situation. Forcing myself to focus, I went to the sink and fixed my face and hair as best I could in the mirror there. I applied my lipstick then threw it in my bag, my eyes pausing on the stack of washcloths on the counter. I'd just been fucked and should probably clean between my legs.

But I was jealous and petty and the notion that Marion might be able to smell sex on me was pretty damn satisfying. So I skipped that bit of freshening, took a deep breath, then put on my best fake smile.

Showtime.

I opened the door and immediately froze when I heard voices. I'd expected Edward to wait for me to invite Marion in, for some reason, but he hadn't.

"...thought we might do best to see each other privately before tomorrow," Marion said, her slight French accent giving her away.

"I'm not sure why you thought that was necessary."

"We've seen each other so few times since the divorce." Her voice was tentative and demure. "And after the last time..."

"That was a mistake," Edward said sharply, and my stomach dropped.

What had happened? *What* was a mistake?

"Which is exactly why I thought we should talk. I'm sorry if I assumed incorrectly, sir."

I had to brace my hand against the wall to steady myself. I'd known she was submissive, that she'd been submissive to Edward, but he'd told me so little about their relationship and I hadn't been able to picture what it must have been like.

Now, I could envision more than I wanted to. Enough to make me sick with envy. I hadn't even officially met her yet, and I already knew she was so much better for him than I ever could be.

Tears threatened at the corners of my eyes.

It felt like forever before Edward responded. When he did, his words were warm but firm. "I am not your sir, Marion. Not anymore."

That felt as good of a cue as any. Blinking back the urge to cry, I came around the corner of the nook with gusto.

Both Edward and Marion turned toward me at my entrance. They stood several feet apart from each other, and while I was glad for that, I was disappointed that I couldn't look at both of them at once.

I chose to focus on her. She was notably surprised they weren't alone, but she covered quickly, and when she did, it was impossible not to stare. She was beguiling with her dark hair, her olive skin, her bright eyes. Much more beautiful than I'd gleaned from her pictures. They hadn't been able to capture her presence, which was breathtaking in its unpretentiousness.

It was terrible how strong the urge was to claw her eyes out.

Maybe I hadn't changed as a person after all.

"Marion, this is Celia," Edward said. "My wife." My jaw tightened at the way he'd amended my title, as though it were an afterthought. "Celia, this is Marion."

I crossed the room to stand next to him, hoping he'd put an arm around me or take my hand. Something to claim me as his.

But his hands remained at his sides.

"Yes, I'd heard you'd remarried." Her eyes darted from Edward toward me, then back to him, as though she were seeking his permission to look somewhere other than at him.

Only then did he put his hand at the small of my back, automatically almost, as though sensing what she needed from him.

"It's a pleasure to meet you," she said, her gaze firmly on mine now. "I have heard good things of you from my children."

I wondered exactly what they'd said. I'd become a little closer to them over the past six months, but before that, I'd spent the entire first year of my marriage to their father on an island in the Caribbean. I could only imagine the awful impression it had given them, let alone their mother.

"Likewise," I said. I could feel an old familiar mask falling into place. One that I hadn't worn in a while but had once been second nature. "I must say, though, they never told me how beautiful you are. I see where Genny gets it."

She flushed, seemingly thrown by my compliment, which had been the intention. She was gorgeous, but she was also a decade older than I was. There was likely some insecurity about her ex having married younger, whether she admitted it to herself or not.

"Merci beaucoup," she said, flustered. "But I can say the same for you. Edward has chosen well for himself."

Edward's hand fell from my back, and with it, Marion's gaze fell from mine.

"I must admit," she continued, looking at him. "I'm surprised to find he married a Werner."

My stomach clenched. Of course she would have known about his having it out for my father. It hadn't occurred to me until just then. She might even think our marriage was part of his revenge schemes. Which, it had been, but not now. I couldn't stand the idea of her thinking we weren't real. But how the hell was I going to correct it?

I glanced toward Edward, hoping he'd step in.

"Well...yes," he said returning her gaze. "That's a complicated story, actually. Too long to get into at the moment."

Was it really? I was sure it could have been simplified if he tried.

"Ah, well. Another time, then." Marion's smile was small but sweet. I would have pushed him for more info right then. I was too curious about shit like that to let it slide.

Her eyes said she might be curious as well, but she didn't press. She was so serene. So demure.

And he'd loved her.

Why the hell had he ever stayed married to me?

An awkward beat past, long enough to make me too unsettled to stay silent or behaved. "So Marion," I said, threading my arm around Edward's. "What brings you by the office today? I thought you'd be staying closer to Genevieve. I didn't expect to see you in London."

She went pale, her mouth falling slack.

"Marion was in town to see friends. She stopped by to see if there was anything last minute she could help with before she headed up to Cambridge." He patted my hand. "I assured her you had everything taken care of."

I wanted to kick him for stepping in for her. Then I wanted to kick myself for being so bothered by it.

"Exactly that," she confirmed, obviously grateful for the excuse. "I didn't feel comfortable just stopping by your house since you and I had never met. And I was in the neighborhood, so I thought why not. Thankfully, my name was still on the security list here, and I was able to come up."

Dizziness swept through me again, making me glad that I had

Edward to clutch onto. Her name was still on the security list. Sure, it could have been an oversight, but after ten fucking years? Edward wasn't the type of man to overlook those things, and I highly doubted he tolerated employees who did either.

If her name was on there, it was because he wanted it to be. Because he wanted her to stop by. Because he hoped.

I couldn't decide if I were more jealous or hurt. The emotions felt too similar, and both felt like shit.

I smooshed the feelings down, way down inside and put the mask back on. "That was so nice of you to offer. Everything's handled, though. Since I have a job as well as a house to run, I made sure to delegate those tasks early on. I find it's the only way to balance it all."

Edward stiffened beside me.

Sure, it was catty. Marion had only ever been a housewife, a job that I admitted was incredibly difficult, but she had also had a full staff to assist her, and I was desperate to make myself feel better, *seem* better, in whatever way I could.

"That's very wise. It was especially hard when the children were little. Nothing got done around the house without delegation."

Unlike when I'd spoken, there was no spitefulness in Marion's tone. She was just being honest, and that hurt somehow more than if she'd been malicious. She was the mother of Edward's children, and that was something I was not. While he'd agreed to having one with me, his last addendum was a no-go for me. I wouldn't give him Hudson's name. Not for a baby. Not for anything.

And since I'd yet to find something Edward truly yielded to, there was a chance I'd never have his child.

Standing in front of Marion, it was an even more bitter pill to swallow.

Thankfully, the office door swung open, and Camilla peeked in. "Eddie, Barry is waiting for you in conference room three."

"Thank you, Camilla. I'd lost track of time." Edward stepped away from me, moving around his desk and straightening it as I'm sure he always did before he left his office.

Camilla's brows lifted in surprise when she saw who else was in the room. "Marion! I didn't know you'd arrived yet. How are you?"

Of course Camilla and Marion would have had a good relationship. Fuck me with a side of ranch. Could this situation get any more mortifying?

I tuned out their reunion and focused on Edward. He was as unreadable as ever, his jaw hard, his expression guarded.

I wished I could get inside his head. Even more, I wished he was inside mine, wished that he saw how I was hurting. Wished he would say what I needed to hear to make it better. I didn't know what that was, but he should know. He usually did.

But he wasn't aware of me at all. He busied himself with his desk, then, once satisfied, he nodded toward the door, silently ushering all of us out.

I lingered and ended up being the last one out, following even him, which meant I had a bird's-eye view of his hand resting at Marion's back as he escorted her out. It was probably automatic. He likely didn't even realize he'd done it.

That didn't lessen the sting.

"Sorry to cut this short," he said to her. "There's even more to do today than usual since I'm taking tomorrow off."

"An empire doesn't run itself," Marion said in a tone that suggested she was merely repeating something that he'd said to her before.

"No, it never has." He glanced down at his hand on her back then quickly dropped it, as though he'd only then realized it was there. "See you tomorrow."

Then he went down the hallway leading away from the elevators toward the conference room. He walked three steps then, just when I was convinced he'd forgotten me altogether, he turned around.

"Oh, Charlotte. Can you please call for Celia's car?"

Maybe I should have been glad he was taking care of me, the way he said he always would.

It wasn't close to being enough.

But then he turned to me. "Celia," he said, his voice summoning.

I was in his arms instantly, relief flooding over me as his warmth surrounded me. I was overthinking all of this. I was over-*feeling* it. As usual. He'd probably call me out on it later, when we were alone. He'd remind me that I was the one he loved then, when it was just the two of us. When it mattered.

He kissed me chastely on the cheek then tilted up my chin so he could look at me. "I know what that was back there," he said softly. "You're past catty behavior, and I most certainly won't tolerate it in my wife."

Adrenaline rushed through my body, a combination of rage and heartbreak.

To anyone else, it would look like he was simply telling me good-bye, not reprimanding me like I was a child. Like I was his doormat. Like I was Marion.

I had a feeling that was how he'd behaved with her all the time when they'd been married. She'd probably liked it.

I, however, did not.

Especially when what I needed was reassurance of his love. Not reassurance of his ownership.

But we were on display, and I had as much reason as he did, if not more, to want Marion to believe we were as happy in our relationship as they'd ever been.

So I cupped his cheek and made sure to smile when I whispered my reply. "Then perhaps you should exchange your current wife for an older model."

More loudly I said, "See you tonight." To remind Marion that I was the one he was going home to. Because *I* was his wife, and I *was* that catty.

Before he could say anything else, I pulled away and crossed to the women, leaving him to go to his pretend meeting. I didn't know if he lingered in the hall. I didn't look back.

The elevator had arrived by the time I reached the others.

"Marion and I are going to grab some coffee and catch up in the downstairs cafe, if you'd like to join us," Camilla said as we walked into the elevator.

"No, thank you. I have to be getting back." There was no way I could stomach sitting with the two of them feeling like a third wheel.

Though, if Marion was staying in the building, there was a chance she might see Edward again. He'd clearly been the one to get out of visiting with her, which meant I shouldn't worry, but maybe that had been because he hadn't wanted to be with her *and me*.

I almost told her I'd changed my mind.

But if Edward wanted to see Marion alone, he'd see her alone eventually. Me hanging around trying to prevent it wasn't going to change anything.

Camilla and Marion continued to chat as we rode down. I pulled out my phone, just to have something to busy myself with so I wouldn't have to talk with them.

"I was sorry to hear about Frank," Marion said, somberly.

"Were you really? I know how you and my brother felt about my marriage."

I couldn't help looking up. I hadn't had any idea that Edward hadn't approved of his sister's relationship with her dead husband.

"It was a terrible situation, nonetheless." Marion paused. "I saw Edward around then, and I wondered if he..." She broke off, her gaze fleeing to me, as though she'd forgotten for a moment that I was there.

"Wondered if he...what?" I asked.

But then we'd arrived at the lobby, and the elevator doors opened, and the security guard was waiting for me with a message to meet my car down the block.

"See you tomorrow, Celia," Camilla said, then she and Marion headed to the cafe without a second glance.

I cycled through several emotions as we made the drive home, replaying the entire office visit in my head. By the time I shifted myself through the hurt and confusion, I found I was angry.

Fuming.

Because he'd never told me anything about him and Marion. Because he was a closed book most of the time no matter how open I'd been with him. Because he demanded I share every last secret, including Hudson, when he'd shared so little with me. Because of the asshole thing he'd said when I was leaving.

If he hadn't been such a major prick, maybe I wouldn't have had to act catty. Did he think of that?

Well, I had no qualms about telling him. In fact, when he got home that night, he and I were going to be talking about a lot of things, whether he wanted to or not.

I spent most of the afternoon working on the finishing details for Genevieve's graduation party. Then I arranged with the cook for dinner to be light so Edward and I could have plenty of time for the arguing that was very likely to follow. And after a late afternoon swim, I changed into the dress he'd laid out for me, to show that I could be what he wanted, even when I was so very often not.

And when Jeremy came to me with the message that something had come up and Edward wouldn't be home for the night, that he'd meet me at the graduation tomorrow, my rage disappeared inside the pain of betrayal. I somehow managed to keep my tears in until I had reached my bedroom and was alone.

SIXTEEN

EDWARD

I PARKED the car on the pavement at the side of the house and used my key to go in the side door. It was immediately apparent that preparations for Genny's party had already begun. The mudroom was stuffed with odds and ends, knickknacks and such that usually adorned furniture but had been moved to accommodate trays of food and glasses for wine.

The kitchen, on the other hand, was immaculate, every surface having been cleared so that the caterers could unload their goods in the morning. If it weren't for the smell of pasta baking in the oven, I'd have wondered if I'd mistaken the invitation for dinner.

I pulled out my mobile to check my earlier texts and saw three missed calls from Celia. I'd had it on silent as I'd driven to Bluntisham, which had taken me nearly two hours. I was debating about calling her back when the house manager of the country estate appeared.

"Good evening, Edward. You're looking well," she said, her voice cheery despite the late hour.

"Thank you, Iba. The same to you. The little one keeping you young?"

She beamed at the mention of her newest grandchild. "Keeping me busy, anyway."

"Good busy, I hope." When she nodded, I changed gears. "I was supposed to meet—"

She cut me off, our relationship informal enough to disregard the strictest rules of polite conversation. "Already outside waiting for you. I pushed her to start without you. Told her you wouldn't mind."

I put my phone back in my pocket. "Of course not. Thank you for looking out for her."

"No worries. Get on out there, and I'll follow with a plate for you shortly."

I made my way through the kitchen door to the solarium. Before continuing out onto the patio, I paused to gaze at the woman sitting outside while she didn't know she was being watched. Her profile was to me, her mobile in one hand, her fork in another. She seemed older than I usually thought of her—something about her posture or her facial expressions as she swiped the screen of her device. And she was breathtaking. More so than ever.

As if she could feel my eyes on her, she looked up, her face breaking into a grin when she saw me.

I took the cue to push open the door and join her outside.

She set down her phone and stood as I approached her. "You're late."

"I am. I didn't get out of the office until seven, and traffic was horrendous." I embraced her, placing a kiss on her temple.

"I suppose I'm lucky I got you here at all. Frankly, I'm surprised you said you'd come. Especially on such short notice."

Genny's casual tone didn't match the implications of her statement. How many times over her lifetime had I been too busy for her, too involved with business or schemes to give her the attention she desired?

The reality sat like a hard lump of coal in the pit of my stomach. Especially, when the truth was, if I hadn't already been feeling guilty about my relationship with my children when she'd texted, I would likely have blown her off this time as well.

I forced a smile. "I'm glad I could make it work, princess."

"Me too. Thank you." She gestured for me to sit. "I'm sorry. I've already started, as you can see. I'll get Iba—"

On cue, the sprite older woman appeared with a plate of food and an uncorked bottle of wine. "Pinot, good?"

"Is that what you're drinking?" I asked my daughter as I took the wine bottle and examined it. It was a decent choice paired with the tomato-based pasta. I wondered if she'd selected it herself. It was funny to realize that I didn't know her preferences for alcohol or whether she drank much at all.

"I was a bit overwhelmed with the wine cellar," Genny admitted. "Hope I didn't choose poorly."

"You didn't." She glowed when I praised her, and for the millionth time in my life, I told myself I needed to do it more often. What was it about me that made it so hard to love my children openly? Was it because I'd lost my own parents when I was still young? Was it because my father hadn't been that affectionate when he'd been alive? Was it because expressing emotion made me feel vulnerable?

Most likely it was all of those combined. It set me up to be a mediocre parent at best.

And Celia wanted me to go through all of it again.

I poured the wine and took a long swallow. The day had been one that deserved something harder than this at its end. For now, this would have to do.

"The house looks nice," Genny said after Iba had left us to dine alone. "The garden's already set up, and the menu looks lovely. Celia has done an amazing job."

"I'll let her know you appreciate it."

"I wasn't sure about the two of you at first. I'd wanted to see you dating for years, but you sprang that marriage on us out of nowhere, and you have to understand that I wondered a bit if you'd gone off your rocker. I can see now why you chose her. She's very good for you."

"She is." I took a bite of my pasta, hoping it would loosen the tightness at the back of my throat that accompanied the subject of my wife. It had been a tumultuous afternoon, mostly revolving around her. It bothered me that Celia believed I could never let her win, that I could never choose something that was both right for her and wrong for me.

It scared me more that she might be right. Was having a child with her really the only way I could prove otherwise?

And then there'd been Marion...

"Have you seen your mother yet?" I asked, wondering if Genevieve could provide some clue as to why Marion had stopped by the office.

"No." She swallowed her food with a sip of wine. "Talked to her, though. She's coming in tomorrow morning from London and flying out again the same night. I'm gutted she didn't bring Enzo or Sante with her. I haven't seen either of them since they were still in nappies."

I had to fight not to scowl. I didn't like to show judgment in front of my children where Marion was concerned, but it was hard not to express obvious distaste when it came to her parenting skills. I had been subpar at the job myself, but at least I hadn't deserted them. When Marion had left, Genevieve had only been twelve, Hagan only two years older, and I could count on both hands the number of times she'd seen them since.

Then, on top of denying them her presence, she kept her youngest sons from them as well.

The only thing stopping me from saying something nasty was the awareness that much of her behavior was due to me. If I'd been better to Marion, if I had been what she'd needed, if I hadn't compartmentalized her place in my life, she wouldn't have left, and she could have been there for her children. It was my fault, in the end.

Always my fault.

"Sante and Enzo are still young. They'd easily bore at commencement ceremonies, and your mother would have to constantly find ways to entertain them. Perhaps she didn't want to draw attention away from you."

"Perhaps." Her pursed lips said she didn't buy it for a second.

She had understandable resentment for her mother. Was that why she'd wanted to meet tonight? Her text hadn't exactly sounded urgent, but the fact that she'd reached out at all was unusual enough to garner concern.

I studied her for several seconds, noting the tense furrow in her brow and the way she kept tracing the collar of her shirt with her fingers. She was nervous. Marion couldn't be the reason I was here. Her mother didn't make her nervous.

"As much as I enjoy a random dinner with my daughter—soon-to-be-graduated, top-of-her-class daugher—I feel fairly certain you have something you want to discuss."

"I do." She wiped her mouth with her napkin then draped it over her plate. Then she rolled her shoulders back, preparing herself to dive in. "There will be a lot of people asking tomorrow what I plan to do next."

"Yes, that is the way with graduations."

"I didn't want to tell anyone else before discussing it with you."

But we *had* discussed this. She planned to move back to London and take her time finding a position that utilized her skills. She didn't need a job right away. I was more than happy to provide for her. "Go on."

"I'm declining the flat you offered to pay for."

I had meant it to be a graduation present. I raised a brow. "Have you found somewhere else you prefer to live? Get me in contact with the flat owner, and I'll sign the lease. Or would you prefer we purchase something outright?"

"Actually, I have found somewhere else. In Lambeth. And I've already signed the lease."

I sat back. A flat in Lambeth was definitely not where I wanted my daughter living. Too Bohemian. Too cheap. "You already signed? Without my approval?"

"I don't need your approval because I'm paying for it on my own."

"I see." And this was why she'd been nervous. She knew how I felt about her dipping into her trust fund. I'd thought she felt the same.

"Not with my inheritance," she clarified, as though reading my mind. "I got a place I can afford on my salary."

"Salary?" Now I was nervous as well.

She swallowed. "Yes. Uh, I've accepted a position with Mills and Varga on their content development team."

I knew what the right thing to say was. Even behind her anxiousness, her excitement was evident. The right thing would be to acknowledge that. To congratulate her. To support her in her decisions.

Except that her decision was wrong, and I couldn't temper myself to pretending otherwise. "M&V?" The disgust was evident in my tone. "The cable network? Why on God's green earth would you do a thing like that?"

"I know they're bottom of the barrel, as far as you're concerned. I know I said I'd wait to accept any offers until I was sure. But they're media, and that's where I want to be working, and it's a job I not only got without you, I got it in spite of you." She spoke rapidly, reminding me of similar speeches when she was still a teen, ones where she begged to go on weekend trips with friends or to take a break from playing cello. It had been difficult to let her make her own choices then, when the outcomes of her decisions weren't so critical.

Now her future depended on her choices, and even though she was an adult, I very much wanted to pull the father card and put my foot down and say no.

I forced myself to count to five before speaking. "What happened to pursuing PR work? You've always wanted to work in public relations. With your class rank, there are plenty of good jobs available in that area."

She rolled her eyes, making her momentarily look like the little girl she'd been. "I've never wanted to work in PR. *You* wanted me to work in PR because you thought it was a field more suited for a girl. Your words, not mine."

I winced at the reminder of the sexist remark. "Yes, I might have said that."

"I can't believe you still have such traditional values," she huffed. "Women are as capable as men, you know. They've proven it. Even more so, in some cases."

"Definitely in your case. I have no doubt you are more capable than every last man in your class." There. I *could* be supportive. It wasn't even a lie.

"But...?" She left space for me to fill in the rest.

"There is no but."

She threw her forearms down dramatically on the table, her palms up. "Then why have you encouraged Hagan to follow in your footsteps and not me? Why haven't you once suggested that I come on board at Accelecom? You have to know it's the field I'm interested in. I've said so numerous times."

I put my fork down, my appetite gone.

She was right—I had known. She'd said as much for several years, even before university. There were several good positions at the company she was already qualified for. I could offer her one. Start her Monday morning.

But I wouldn't.

Because, as much as Accelecom would benefit from her being on the team, I couldn't have her working there. The company I'd built was a media empire, but the truth was, the only reason it had been built was so I could eventually take down Warren Werner.

And even though Ron was now the man I wanted to ruin, I wasn't done with Warren's company. He was on the eve of retiring, and the stocks were in my wife's name. While I didn't plan on talking to her about it anytime soon, there were opportunities there that I refused to overlook.

It took a certain kind of man to have that vision. A man that was ruthless and relentless. A man that would behave cruelly and without ethics.

I didn't want my daughter to know that man.

Maybe it *was* sexist to want to exclude her and not my son, but Hagan was a different sort of breed than Genevieve, having nothing to do with his gender. He was detached. He was ignorant. Even working at my side, he didn't see the truth about who I was, and if he ever did, it wouldn't faze him.

Genny was too smart to miss anything, too earnest to not have serious objections to my questionable morals, and too ambitious to expect that I could hide my truth from her by placing her in a remote role of the company. It wasn't only that I feared what she'd think of me, which was an honest concern, it was also that I feared what it might make her become.

I refused to be a father who put her down that path.

And if she had to believe that I thought less of her because of her gender in order to keep her from following in my footsteps, then so be it.

"You aren't suited for Accelecom, princess." The words sounded as cruel and patronizing out of my mouth as they had in my head.

Good.

It was what she needed to stay away.

Hurt flashed across her features, but she quickly recovered. She'd learned that well from me, how to pretend to be unfeeling. How to turn to stone.

"That's what I thought." Her tone was even and sure. "Hence the reason I took the job at M&V. It's better this way. No one can accuse me of nepotism."

Yes, it was better this way. Outside my arena. Safe.

But that left Mills and Varga.

I groaned. Did she really have to choose to work at a company so beneath her? A network that I could easily buy out if it were decent enough to add to my portfolio. "You're so much better than M&V. There has to be someplace with a better offer."

"Not in media."

"What about Winton Globe? I could talk to Sheldon—"

"I don't want to work in print. That's so archaic, Dad. And I really don't want your help. I want to do this on my own. So don't think about giving me a big check for a graduation present, because I won't be cashing it." She'd started our conversation with more maturity than I'd ever seen from her.

Now though, she was bordering on a temper tantrum.

In turn, I slipped deeper into the father role. "It's my job as a parent to look after you. You should be grateful that you come from a family who is able to provide for you at this level. Most of your fellow graduates would be envious of your options."

"I *am* grateful. Of course I am. *But I do not want to be Mom.* I do not want to be a woman who relies on her husband to guide her in life or give her an identity or pay for her living, and if I rely on you for those things now, I'm only teaching myself to be reliant on someone else forever. I can't go down that path. It won't make me happy."

I suddenly understood so much about my daughter I never had, about what my relationship with her mother must have looked like. About all the ways my marriage had been a fucked-up model for my children.

Even leaving sex aside, Marion had clung to the submissive life. It had consumed her. How could I explain her need for dominance? Or my need to dominate her? How could Genny see it as anything other than misogynistic? How could she ever understand that about her parents?

This wasn't something a father could tell a daughter, and Genny, being as intelligent and independent as she was, had already figured out she needed to navigate this area on her own.

God, she would be such a firecracker to work with. She could help me take Accelecom to the next level. I could see it clearly. I could even find a way to let her remain independent, since she seemed to so badly want that.

For a moment, I second-guessed my decision not to invite her to come on board.

Then I remembered who I was, and what I didn't want her to be, and that was more important than giving her an opportunity she dreamed of.

Celia was right. I did always have to win.

"It's a good thing I'm not offering you a job at Accelecom then," I said, doubling down on my stance, "since according to your own guidelines, you couldn't accept it."

Her mouth opened and closed, her eyes blinking as she forced herself not to make an exception. She pulled herself together, though, like the champ she was. "Then we're on the same page."

"We're not, but I don't think there's anything I can do but respect your decisions, is there?" I swore under my breath. "M&V? Really? Do not even think of giving me one of those silly sweaters with their logo. I will not wear it, no matter how proud of you I am."

She chuckled at that. "You guessed your birthday present. I had thought about throwing in the socks as well, but they wouldn't be so noticeably embarrassing when you wore them."

That earned her a smile. "Well. This dinner has been delightful. Is there any other bomb you'd like to drop on me this evening, Genny, before I retire for the night?"

"Only one more—I'd like to be called Genevieve from now on. It's more professional. Genny is so girlish."

She was trying to kill me. She really was.

This, at least, I could give without debate. "I always did like the name Genevieve."

"Go figure." She stood, and I with her. "I should probably get back to my flat. Long day tomorrow. You're staying the night?"

I nodded. "It doesn't make sense to drive the two hours back only to turn around and come here again in the morning. You could stay here as well. I'm sure Iba wouldn't mind preparing your room." It was only half an hour to Cambridge, but as always, I worried.

She shook her head. "I didn't bring my cap or gown and that would be an added hassle in the morning."

I nodded then reached out to hug her good night.

"Thank you for listening," she said. "And for trying to understand."

My throat burned, so I didn't speak. I just squeezed her a little harder. Then, as difficult as it was, I let her go.

Upstairs in the estate's master bedroom, I took off my jacket and sat down on the bed with a sigh. I'd brought a glass of brandy up with me, and though I'd already drunk half of it, I still felt just as restless as I had before my first swallow.

It had been an endless day.

A day revolved around the most important women in my life. They each fought for individual attention in my mind. Would Genevieve be better for pushing her away? I'd tried that tactic with Camilla, and years of additional scars and therapy later I wasn't sure I wasn't to blame for a good portion of her pain.

And Celia trusted me enough to bring another human into my universe.

Did she not understand what sort of mistake that would be? Was there any way to keep her without paying that cost?

And then there was Marion.

I'd have to deal with her tomorrow. I couldn't think about her now. Not in the state I was in.

I took another long swallow then looked at my cell phone, the missed call notification still at the top of my screen. It was well after ten. Celia should be asleep, considering she had to be up early the next day.

I cleared the notification then plugged my phone into the charger we kept beside the bed. Even if she was still awake, I wasn't sure I could find the words she'd need from me. The explanations she would surely expect. The promises she'd want me to make. Not tonight.

It was probably better that we not talk until I could.

SEVENTEEN

CELIA

I MADE it to Bluntisham a little after nine in the morning. Thank goodness that I had a driver so I could spend most of the ride with an ice pack over my swollen eyes. Then, the last fifteen minutes, I did my makeup, hoping the heavy layer of foundation would hide the dark bags. It was an important day for Genny, which made it an important day for Edward, and even though I was still stewing and fretting about his absence and what it meant, I intended to give them the event she deserved.

Though, the thought of seeing Marion again, of having to watch her and Edward interact amongst friends who probably knew her better than me, made me nauseated.

It was time to bring out the old Celia, the one who could fake her way through anything.

The façade fell immediately when I walked into the kitchen of the country house and found Edward standing at the island, a mug in his hand, the local newspaper spread out in front of him, a half-eaten omelet at its side. He was already in his trousers and white dress shirt. His tie was still open at his neck, but his suspenders were on, and damn did that man look good eating breakfast. It was insane how good.

"You're here," I said, stunned. I'd expected I wouldn't see him until

I was surrounded by others. If I'd known I would have had a chance to talk to him alone before that, I would have prepared my anger. Instead, all I could do was blink at him in surprise.

He looked up, a smile lighting his face at the sight of me. "Of course I'm here. Where else would I be?"

All casual like. As if he hadn't just up and disappeared the evening before.

Not sure where the staff was, having come in through the side door, I paused a beat before I spoke so that I wouldn't make a scene. Still, my words came out terse. "You didn't come home last night. I had no idea where else you might be."

He set down his mug and stuck his hands in his pockets. "I didn't come home because I was already here. It seemed a waste of a drive."

That was all the explanation he planned to give? He was maddening.

"Why were you already here? Was I supposed to know you were here? Why didn't you answer my calls? Were you alone?"

He smirked as he came around the island and walked toward me. I was too angry for whatever he had in mind, but I couldn't seem to move, his eyes pinning me in place.

"You're cute when you're suspicious," he said, wrapping his arms around me.

I tried to squirm free with no luck against his firm grip. "You're an asshole when..." The ways I could finish that sentence were endless. "Well, most of the time, actually."

Refusing to look at him, I stared at his neck, at the skin that would be covered up when he buttoned his collar. It was astounding how hypnotic a man's throat could be.

He brought his hand up to my chin and tipped it until I was forced to look up and my gaze crashed into baby blues. "Yes, I was alone," he said. "When I slept, anyway, since that's what you're really asking. I was not alone before that."

My mouth fell open, but before I could react further, he went on.

"Genevieve was here. She asked me spur of the moment to have dinner with her."

"Oh," I said, processing. And then when I'd processed, I said it again, this time in relief. "Ohhh."

His daughter. That's what would take him away so urgently. Not Marion. Everything was fine.

Unless, Genny wasn't fine. "Anything wrong?" I asked, suddenly concerned.

"Nope. She just wanted to talk to me before the big day."

She'd needed him, and he'd been there for her. Came running at the drop of a hat, even. And he thought he wasn't a good father.

A different kind of jealousy pinged in my chest.

"Anything important?" I buttoned his collar and began working on his tie.

"She got a job. I'll leave her to tell you the details. Well beneath her, but she's happy about it."

I tightened the knot and patted it down. "So you will be too."

"I'm trying to be." He grimaced. "And she'd prefer we call her Genevieve from now on."

"Got it." I completely understood the girl, remembering exactly what it felt like to be that age, wanting to be taken seriously.

Still it had to be hard on Edward to realize his daughter was a grown-up. I rubbed my hand against the stubble at his jaw.

He gave a small smile that quickly turned right back into a frown. "You've been crying. Your eyes are puffy."

"Oh, God. Do I look terrible?" I pulled away and scanned for something I might be able to see my reflection in.

But he pulled me instantly back into his arms. "You look stunning, bird. I would have said so first thing if you hadn't directed the conversation elsewhere. I promise that no one will notice your eyes unless they looked hard and long at you every day, and I better be the only person who does that. So, tell me, why were you crying?"

Remnants of my fury returned. "My husband didn't come home after discussing a subject that was very important to me. Why do you think I was crying?"

His reasons for not coming home may have been warranted, but the way he had treated me was unacceptable. Marion might have let that kind of behavior slide. There was no way his current wife would.

He let out a sigh and pressed his forehead to mine. "You're right. I'm an arsehole."

"I'm glad you agree. Unfortunately, I doubt that acknowledgment alone will change how you behave."

"You're probably right there too." His candor was both charming and irritating.

I stretched my arms around his neck, allowing myself to hold him for the first time that morning. "You could try though, maybe? To be a little more considerate to what I might be thinking in situations like that? To show me the respect you expect me to show you?"

He considered. "Yes. I can try."

Well. That had gone better than expected.

He sealed the agreement with a kiss that wasn't at all chaste. He tasted like coffee and, faintly, like toothpaste, and if it hadn't been for the long list of items on my to-do list, I would have been happy to stay right there and continue kissing him for much longer.

"I better..." I said, pushing away.

This time he let me go.

I started out of the kitchen, the knot in my stomach considerably looser than when I'd awoken. The day was still young, and there were still a lot of things to be anxious about, but at least where Edward had spent the night wasn't one of them.

Or was I being too trusting?

I stopped at the doorway and looked back toward him. "You really only came out to see Genny. Er, Genevieve? There's nothing else I should know?"

"I really only came for Genevieve." He sounded genuine, and I was sure it was the truth. It would be easy enough to prove otherwise. He wasn't the type to tell disputable lies.

Still, not everything was settled between us. Whether it was just the conversation from the day before that remained unfinished or something else stirring in the air, I didn't know. Either way, I was going to have to try to ignore it for now.

THE REST of the morning flew by with preparations for the party. Camilla arrived soon after I did, Freddie's sitter in tow, so she could help out, which I hadn't thought I'd need but was grateful for in the end. Edward hid away in his office during most of the hubbub, but he came out near the end and helped with the finishing details. Then we all drove together to Cambridge for the graduation.

Marion arrived with Hagan who had brought a date, putting one more person between where she sat and where Edward sat, which was definitely a plus in my book. At least she was out of my eyesight, and while I could still feel her presence most of the time, I managed to forget about her for long stretches of time during the commencement ceremony.

Afterward was a different story.

Though Camilla was an excellent photographer, Edward had hired a professional as well so that she didn't have to work a family event. That meant lots of pictures—several of which had the star of the day posing between her beaming parents. Pictures that I was mostly not a part of since I had to head back right away to greet early guests.

The arrangement made sense—me going early with Camilla, and Edward, Marion, Hagan, and Genevieve following later—but that didn't mean I had to like it. I lingered after the last big group shot before leaving, my chest tight with envy as I watched them take a few immediate family shots.

They looked good like that, the four of them. Hagan tall and chiseled like his father. Genevieve a perfect blend of both her parents. Edward dominating each setup without even trying. Marion always posed just a little too close.

"They won't be too long after us," Camilla said, misreading my hesitation. "And if we hurry, we can have a glass of champagne before anyone else arrives."

That was all I needed to prod me away. "Count me in."

Everything after that moved in a whirlwind. Guests began arriving almost as soon as we got to the house, people I didn't know and had only heard of when filling out the guest lists with Edward and Genevieve. Fortunately, Camilla knew most of them and was able to play hostess while I took deep breaths, smiled a bunch, and tried not to hyperventilate.

When Edward showed up, I felt much calmer, even though his presence meant Marion's as well. She quickly found some friends from the past that occupied her, though, which was a relief. By that time, most of my party-planning assignment was completed. Iba managed the caterers and took care of any hiccups that occurred while Edward paraded me around the party introducing me to more people than I'd possibly be able to remember. It was busy and I constantly had to be "on," but being at my husband's side made it sort of fun. I liked the attention he gave me, the way his voice intoned when he said my name, with similar pride that he bestowed on Genny.

It was more than an hour into the event when Edward finally let me slip away while he talked boring financials with someone from the company. I still hadn't had a chance to congratulate his daughter, and it felt like the perfect opening.

She was gathered with a small group of women, but she didn't seem to be that engaged with the current conversation, so I tapped her on the shoulder to get her attention.

"You did it!" I exclaimed, embracing her when she turned around. "I can't imagine the kind of hard work it took to get top honors. Your father is proud of you. I am, too, for that matter."

She was beaming when we separated. "Thank you. And thank you so much for the party. It's exactly what I wanted. High class but laid back. It's very..." She searched for the word to describe it.

"Mature," I said, helping her out.

"Yes. Exactly," she laughed.

"I'm glad to be a part of it. It's all my pleasure." It was an honest statement. Edward was traditional and bossy with my time, but being in charge of the party planning had been my idea. The project felt similar to design work. There was an esthetic and a mood that Genevieve had wanted to capture, and I approached it in the same way I would have if she'd asked me to redo her apartment.

Plus, she was Edward's daughter, and I'd had very little opportunity to get to know her since she had been at school, and that bothered me for selfish reasons. She was a part of my husband's life that I wasn't a part of, a part of his life that I envied. Right now she and Hagan were as close as I had to having a child of my own.

"Well, good on you then," she said. "I wouldn't know where to begin to do something like this, let alone want to. Believe me when I say that your skills are much appreciated."

"I second that," came a voice from the group behind her. "Thank you for this."

My stomach dropped, recognizing who it was. Genevieve stepped to the side inviting me into the circle of women, and exposing the one particular one I'd missed. "Marion, I didn't see you there. Sorry to steal your daughter away like that."

Something flashed across her eyes making me reexamine what I'd just said. Realizing the statement had been an unintended threat to her motherhood, I didn't feel any regrets. If she had insecurities about her parenting skills, that wasn't my problem. No, my problem was my own insecurities, both about parenting and wifing.

She got me back with a jab of her own, whether she realized it or not. "No problem. We were only talking about her as a baby. Difficult pregnancy. Very easy birth."

People had spoken about their pregnancies in front of me numerous times, and it had never bothered me in the slightest. Hearing about it from Edward's ex-wife was a different story. She'd owned his heart. I was certain of that, even though he'd never said as much. He loved me too, but I didn't know if I owned his heart.

On top of owning his heart, she'd mothered his children. He'd *wanted* her to mother his children. I was equally certain about that fact. Edward didn't let even insignificant details occur in his life without his direction. There was no way he hadn't been one hundred percent on board with her getting pregnant.

And I wanted to be pregnant with his child. And I wanted to own his heart. And suddenly in that moment, despite all the evidence to the contrary, I was convinced I would never have either.

I was soaking in envy, and it was hard to pretend otherwise.

There was nothing to do but lean into it. "Was that why you stopped at two? Because of the difficult pregnancy?"

She shook her head. "The pregnancy was hard because she was a girl. I'm convinced." She laughed, making light of the superstition. "And because Genny was stubborn, even in the womb."

Her daughter winced. Apparently Marion hadn't gotten the memo about the name change.

"But it was a fluke," she continued. "I didn't have problems before or after with my boys. No, it wasn't for the pregnancy. Edward would have had more, I believe, but two was a good number to have. Easy to manage when they're small. It worked out well, I think." She gave a loving yet distant smile to Genevieve.

And I tried not to hyperfocus on the five words that stung like a million bee stings at once. *Edward would have had more.*

More with Marion, not with me. Not unless I gave up every last shred of my control. Not unless I gave up Hudson.

I was well aware that his thoughts on more children could have changed over the twenty plus years since Genny was born, but I was overwhelmingly vulnerable when it came to this woman. I was ridiculous and insecure.

I was so wrapped up in my inner misery, I almost missed Marion's question, only the sound of my name caught my attention.

"...Celia? Do you want children?"

I could feel the color drain from my face. The rest of the women— wives of businessmen, ladies I'd only been introduced to as a second thought, socialites and trophies like my mother had been—looked eagerly at me, waiting for an answer. This was exactly the kind of gossip Madge Werner's type lived for. Even if I had a solid answer, I wouldn't want to share it with them.

Yet, I really wanted to share it with Marion. Wanted to be on her level, if only for a moment. Wanted to lie to get it if I had to.

"Oh, wow," Genevieve said while I debated how to respond. "I hadn't thought of father having more children. Are you going to?"

My mouth felt like cotton. "Uh. I..."

Surprise of all surprises, Marion was the one who came to my rescue. "I'm sorry," she said. "That was very rude of me to ask."

I looked across the garden to Edward who caught my eye and winked. The lie wouldn't come. "No. It's fine. We haven't quite decided."

"Edward's probably against it," one of the others said quietly. Did she think I couldn't hear her?

"Yes, probably," Marion agreed.

"No," I protested. "We just haven't quite figured it out yet is all. I have a job and all that." *Take that, Marion, Mrs. Stay-At-Home-Perfect-Wife.*

"You're young still. You have time." Whatever her goal had been, it felt patronizing.

"Well, not a *lot* of time," another woman pointed out.

Just what I needed to hear.

I forced a smile. "If you ladies would please excuse me, I see another bottle of red needs to be opened."

Restraining myself so that I didn't break into a run, I crossed the garden and slipped into the solarium. The room was practically made of glass, but even with the unobstructed view, being inside versus outside made it feel like I was hidden.

I turned around to stare at the group I'd just left. They were laughing together, probably at a joke told at my expense, none of them looking in my direction.

I don't care about your opinion, I told her in my head. *You don't mean anything to me. You're not a threat. I can have a baby whenever I want to, Edward on board or not. It's not like he controls my birth control.*

He'd probably controlled hers.

That made me smile, as though I'd won some imaginary battle when in reality her submission likely earned her more devotion than he'd ever give me.

"Is it hard having her here?"

I glanced at Camilla who'd sidled up beside me. She must have followed my gaze. For half a second, I considered pretending otherwise, then the impulse was gone. "If I'm being polite? Yes."

"And if you aren't being polite?"

"Fuck yes." I laughed with her, feeling better now that this tension had somewhere to go. "She's just..." There were so many things I wanted to say about Marion, most of which were completely unfounded. "So accommodating, which shouldn't be irritating, but somehow it is, especially because of how accommodating she is to Edward. And have you noticed how she looks to him all the time? When someone asks her a question or she wants to fill up her wine glass or, Jesus, when she wants to go to the bathroom. She always looks to him as though she's asking for permission."

Even now as I watched, she was looking at him. He'd come to join them, seeming to have something to say to Genevieve, and there was Marion, gazing at him like he ruled the roost.

I mean, I probably did too, but it was our roost, not hers.

Camilla let out a sigh. "They were always like that."

"But she's married now to somebody else. She can be like that with her own husband. Leave mine alone." I glanced at my sister-in-law, gauging her reaction. "Petty, isn't it?"

"Not at all."

Taking that as permission to vent, I continued. "Like...it feels like she's still with him. Or like she still wants to be with him. And if that's the case, then why did she leave him?" Suddenly I wondered if I had my facts wrong. "She *did* leave him, right?"

"Yes," she said hesitantly. "Edward hasn't told you about it?"

The question brushed up against one of my vulnerable spots, making me flinch internally as though she'd smashed against a bruise. He hadn't told me. No matter how many times I'd asked.

And that hurt. And felt suspicious. And was too embarrassing to admit.

"Is there something to tell besides Marion left him for another man?" If I couldn't hear it from Edward, maybe I could get it from her.

She gave a half shrug. "Aren't those stories always more complicated than they seem on the surface?"

If "those stories" referred to any type of relationship breakup then the answer was yes. I hadn't had many of my own, but the ones that I'd been involved with—Dirk, Hudson, the ones I'd made happen for other people—all of them had been complex.

Camilla nudged me with her shoulder. "Ask him. I could tell you some, but there are missing pieces in my version. He should be the one to tell you."

Right. Like it was that easy.

As though reading my thoughts she added, "And if he doesn't want to, *make* him tell you. That's something a wife should know."

I nodded in agreement, wondering exactly how I could make Edward do anything.

I had to figure it out, though. Immediately. Not only because it was destroying me to be left in the dark, but also because he'd just walked off into the private hedged gardens with Marion. Alone.

And I'd be damned if he didn't plan on telling me what the fuck that was all about.

EIGHTEEN

EDWARD

IT WAS my idea to explore the garden. Marion needed time alone with me, I could see it in her gaze, constantly tugging at me throughout the day. Old habits being what they were between us, she would never bring herself to ask. I had to be the one to care for her. As always.

I hated that I could still know how. A decade since our divorce, and I could still govern her with very little effort. It was like riding a bicycle. My body did it naturally, such as when my hand pressed at the small of her back to guide her out of my office the day before. There was no thought behind these movements. It was in my bones.

I'd said I was no longer her sir, and I wasn't, but I also was and always would be.

Which meant I could have denied her the private conversation, and we would go on with our lives, the words that needed to be said between us remaining unspoken. It was my call. She'd made as big of an effort as she would, stopping by Accelecom like she did. Everything that happened next was up to me.

It was tempting to let it go and move on. For Celia more than anyone else.

But to move on, I needed there not to be anything between us anymore.

And so I suggested a walk through the garden.

"This reminds me of the hedge garden at Brayhill," she said as we entered through the arch. The garden here wasn't very big, a little more than fifty square meters enclosed with hedges that reached eight meters high. More hedges divided the space into rows, but it wasn't a maze. There were a couple of resting spots with benches, a fountain along the back stretch, and an array of florals, most of which I couldn't identify if I wanted to.

The garden she referred to at Brayhill, the country home I'd owned when we'd been married, had been much larger, a thousand square meters in size or more, and it had very much been a labyrinth. The kind that made old English country houses charming but also a lot of work to maintain.

I supposed this garden was similar since both were enclosed by hedges, but their functions were completely different. "You can't get lost here."

"That's a plus, if you ask me. Do you know how much time I spent chasing after Hagan there?"

Her statement felt pointed. I *didn't* know how much she'd chased Hagan there, mainly because I'd rarely gone on family weekends to Brayhill, and when I had, I'd spent most of the time in my office. I missed out on a lot, too busy with my work.

But Marion wasn't the kind to make passive-aggressive remarks. Or aggressive remarks, for that matter. If she judged me for that, she'd keep it to herself.

"I'm pretty sure he would have made you chase him with or without the garden. But I see how it would be harder to find him in the maze. I liked it for that very reason. It was a good spot to wander." Particularly in the early morning, when the house was still asleep and the fog settled on the land. More than a handful of problems were sorted on those walks.

She looked up from the plant she'd been admiring, one *she* could likely name. "Why did you sell?"

"After Frank..." I trailed off, not sure what I'd meant to say. It wasn't necessary, anyway. She knew where that sentence went, that his death would have been etched into the environment of that house as firmly as the initials the kids had drawn into the cement at the end of the driveway. "Camilla would never have visited again. Honestly, I'm not sure I could have either."

She moved on along the path. "It seems fitting that it's gone."

"Yes. Selling it marked the end of..." Again I found myself at a loss for words. I let out a breath. "A lot of things." It had been the end of Marion and me, too, in many ways. Except for the island, which had always been more my place than ours, the sale of Brayhill had removed the last property that we'd made memories in together from my life. There was a melancholiness about that.

But it had also been the end of Camilla and Frank. And the feeling surrounding that was much different.

Marion pursed her lips and nodded, understanding more than almost anyone else could.

We came to an opening in the hedges, a sort of window where the plants had been trimmed back. There was one on each side of the garden. This one had a view of the back of the house.

She paused there to look out over the party. I followed her gaze and landed on Genevieve who was still in the spot we'd left her in.

"We did well with that one," Marion said. "Somehow. Despite everything. *You* did well with her."

I appreciated that she recognized her absence from our children's lives. But she was wrong to give me any credit. Marion hadn't left until Genevieve was twelve. I'd been aloof long before that. Neither of us had been there as we should have been. "She did it all on her own, I think."

Marion made a sound of disagreement, a two-syllable rumble in the back of her throat. "She's you, Edward. You should be proud."

"Oh, I am. Whether I deserve to be or not." My stare glided from my daughter to Celia, who had joined the circle along with Camilla sometime after we'd left. It was odd to think that my wife was as close to Genny's age as she was to mine, and I wondered if that was why she'd leaned into a more friendly role with my children than parental.

Or maybe that was simply because they'd already been grown and out of the house by the time she'd moved in.

What kind of mother would she be? Attentive and regimented like Marion had been before she'd disappeared, or something else altogether?

It startled me to realize that I wanted to know.

"Is it real?" Marion asked, seeing who I was focused on.

"Yes. It wasn't at first, but that changed." It had to be confusing for her to see me with a Werner when Warren had been my enemy the entire time I'd known her. It didn't make me feel the need to disclose any more than that, though. It wasn't her business, and Celia was mine. I didn't want to share her with anyone, especially with Marion.

"It seemed as much." Marion turned away from the window to continue along the path. "The way you look at her. The way she defers to you."

I laughed. "She's not really very submissive."

"She is. I see it. But she makes you work for it."

"She does." There was something quite satisfying about my ex realizing that I loved someone other than her. That another woman fit my preferences in a way she never could. I supposed it was like that for most people who had once been part of a couple, but it was particularly delicious in my case, after the way that Marion had left. It was karma. Or, at least, things had come full circle.

And if things had come full circle...did that mean we were finally done with each other?

It was almost too much to believe. The chains binding me to her had been there so long, I'd become used to their weight. What would it feel like to have them gone?

I spun toward her, suddenly needing answers. "Why did you come to the office yesterday?"

Her cheeks flushed, her eyes cast down. "I don't know."

"Were you hoping something would happen?"

Her shoulders rose and fell with her breath.

"Look at me, Marion." I used the tone she'd never been able to ignore, and as I predicted, she looked up. "What were you hoping would happen between us?"

"I didn't think that far ahead, uh, Edward. I was anxious about how it would be with you, and I wanted it dealt with before all this." She swallowed. "I love Renato. You know that."

I took a step back, needing distance. The fact that she needed to clarify her feelings meant she'd considered the possibilities.

It made me unreasonably angry. I wouldn't have touched her, I wouldn't have wanted to, but she had to stop this. She had to stop being available for me. She had to take responsibility for her actions instead of always leaving them to someone else's whim.

She loves Renato.

Bullshit if she thought that meant anything. "Your feelings didn't stop you last time."

"That's not fair. You needed me, and I don't know how not to respond to that."

"I took advantage."

"I don't blame you."

"You *should*." I fisted a hand at my hip and walked in a circle, memories of the night four years ago unwittingly filling my mind. I'd been a wreck, holding it together as best as I could for my sister's sake. Then Marion had called to check on Camilla, but I'd been the one to answer, and instead of passing on the phone, I'd latched onto the familiar source of comfort.

"*I need you,*" I'd said.

And she'd come.

She shouldn't have. She had a husband and a family, and she shouldn't have come running, but that was what Marion did, and I knew better. I was the one who should never have asked.

That had always been our problem, though, hadn't it? I never knew the limits, and she never made me find them.

"The circumstances around Frank's death were difficult," she said, stupidly defending me. "You needed someone to take that out on. Who else could you have turned to?"

No one. There had been no one who knew the truth about Frank except for Camilla, and she certainly wasn't someone I could have leaned on.

It didn't change the fact that I'd made a mistake. My weakness didn't excuse anything.

"I told Renato after the fact," she added after a beat.

That shouldn't have been surprising. "And he was okay with it?"

"He wasn't exactly. But we sorted it out."

I could imagine just how they sorted it out. She likely hadn't been able to sit comfortably for a week.

That wouldn't have been enough for me. If my wife had cheated...

I was such an idiot. "I was about to say I wouldn't have been so understanding, but I suppose we both know that's not true."

She and I and Renato...it was a fucked-up situation all around.

And it wasn't my problem anymore. *She* wasn't my problem anymore. She was his. And that was exactly how it should be.

With that realization, my anger dissipated. "Anyway. I was grateful. But it won't happen again."

"I know. You have her now, and you've always been faithful, at least as far as women go."

Then it was settled. We were over, and she understood.

I shoved my hands in my pockets and started leading us back toward the exit, thinking about her last words as we walked. She was right that I would always be faithful to my wife. But even if I didn't have Celia, I wanted to say that I wouldn't let Marion and me happen again. The truth was, I didn't know that for sure. Because I couldn't imagine myself without Celia anymore. Whoever I'd be without her would be too unrecognizable for me to attach certainties to.

Celia. My little bird.

There were things I should tell her, things about Marion and Frank, things I wanted her to know. But how could I let her know those parts of me and still expect her to stay?

Marion hadn't stayed.

That was a piss-ant excuse, and I knew it. The reason Marion had left had nothing to do with who I was and very much to do with who I wasn't.

It was time I faced that once and for all.

I stopped abruptly and faced my ex. "When you left, I never asked why."

"Are you asking me now?" She straightened her spine, girding herself for an uncomfortable exchange.

"I'm not. I know why. I didn't want to admit it for a very long time, but I know."

"Thank you for telling me," she said, and even if there was some chance I was wrong and my reason differed from hers, it didn't matter. The point was that I'd accepted it, and that she knew.

I thought that would be the end of it, but just as I started to walk on, she asked, "Will things change with that understanding?"

"Between us?"

"Between you and her."

That was a question I didn't have an answer for. On the one hand, Celia wasn't Marion. Our problems would never look like the problems that had broken up my first marriage. On the other hand, I understood the things that might come up between us, I understood the traits of my personality that were divisive, and I understood that understanding did not necessarily equate change.

"Do you care?" I asked, finding deflection easier.

"I want you to be happy," she said, and the rawness of her voice as she said it made me believe it was true.

It occurred to me that I wanted that for her too. I'd wished misery on her for a long time after she left. I didn't know when that had changed.

"Are *you* happy?" I asked now.

"I am. There are things I regret losing—Hagan and Genevieve, to be specific."

"You could still win them back if you decided to try."

"Maybe." She focused somewhere in the distance and sighed. "Or maybe things are best as they are. Because I *am* happy."

I was surprised to realize I envied that.

Not that I wasn't happy—I was, for the most part. But I was well aware that the rage that drove my desires for vengeance were toxic.

They were iron, according to Camilla. It tainted every other emotion I had. It shaped all my relationships. It prevented the ruby from forming.

I understood that.

Understanding didn't mean I could change.

It was better with Celia, though. The fury inside me was reshaping, and for the first time in my life, here with Marion, I felt closure without having to first destroy her.

And so when Celia's incensed gaze pinned me coming out of the garden with Marion, I smiled. She was jealous, and I'd have to do some explaining, but she loved me, and it was the closest to pure happiness I'd ever felt.

NINETEEN

CELIA

AFTER THE PARTY had ended and everyone, including the caterers and the clean-up crew, had finally left, I filled two glasses with cognac and took them with me to the solarium.

Edward had offered to help Iba to her car, her arms full of leftover food that would go to waste at the house since we were leaving the next day. I hadn't told him where I would be waiting when he got back, but I was confident he'd find me.

Inside the windowed room, I set one of the glasses on a table next to the loveseat then dimmed the overhead before taking the other glass to the armchair across from it. The string of lights that had been put up outside for the party were still lit, creating a romantic mood. Not exactly what I was going for, but it would do. In my experience, the darker setting made confessions easier.

I stretched my neck, easing the knots there as I looked out over the yard. The day had been busy and full, and the party had been, by all accounts, successful, but I'd spent the entire time preoccupied with Edward. Even when entertaining strangers or running around trying to find Iba to tell her we were out of toilet paper, I'd been aware of my husband. He was a magnetic force, always pulling my thoughts and my body in his direction. Like gravity holding me in his orbit.

I'd never felt that way about anyone before. Not just that in love but also that attached. I was still reeling from the newness of it, eighteen months after we'd wed.

I was also still adjusting to the way he affected me. How he'd brought me peace yet could stir up levels of jealousy within me that I'd never thought possible. His trip to the garden with Marion was innocent—it had to be considering the way he grinned at me when he'd returned. The devil himself wouldn't flaunt his discretions so openly.

Would he?

No. I couldn't believe he would. But innocent as his visit with her may have been, there was still a divide between us where his ex-wife was concerned. As near as he drew me, as forceful as his pull was, I could never close that final gap, and I was sure it was because of her. They were over, their relationship was done, but whatever had happened between them still mattered. She'd left him feeling so defenseless that he seemed to think he had to protect himself, had to shut part of himself off. Had she broken him so severely that he couldn't bear to love that hard again?

Or had he withheld those parts of his heart because they couldn't belong to me when they still belonged to her?

"I'd expected you'd already have gone up to bed."

My head jerked up to find him standing in the doorway. "I thought we'd sit a while first." I nodded toward the loveseat. "I got you a drink."

His smile was bright but suspicious as he sat down where I'd indicated. "How attentive, and after everything you've already done today." He took a swallow of his brandy and stared at me, his gaze hot and inviting. "Might be nicer if you weren't so far away."

It would have been a lie to say I wasn't tempted. We'd only spent one evening apart, but it felt like weeks since I'd been in his arms. Been underneath him.

But it was past time for this to be addressed. "I had something else in mind, actually."

"Oh? Do tell."

I cleared my throat. "This is how this will work," I said, trying my best to mimic the words he'd once told me. "We will sit here, and when you're ready, you will tell me about Marion, why she left you. It won't be pleasant, as I'm sure it affected you deeply. You will tell me everything relevant surrounding your breakup. I may ask questions. I'll expect answers. And all of it, every single word, will be true."

"Are you trying to lead a session?" He tried to glower at me, but I could tell he was fighting off a laugh.

"I *am* leading a session."

This time he did laugh. "You're cute when you think you can play my part."

"You're charming when you're patronizing. It won't work. I'm committed."

He narrowed his eyes and sat back against the cushion, considering. Calculating. "What if I'm not interested in participating?"

"I wasn't interested either when these began, and look at us now."

"I didn't leave you much choice. You had to comply."

"Believe me when I say I'm not leaving you much choice either." I wasn't exactly sure what my threat was, because there *had* to be a threat if the statement was to hold any weight. If he asked I'd have to be ready to say the worst. Ready to *do* the worst. And as important as this was to me, I wasn't sure that I was ready to go that far.

Thankfully, just the hint was enough.

"Ballsy," he said, swirling the contents of his glass.

"I learned from the best."

He brought the glass up to his lips and took a decent sized swallow. "I suppose it is time we discuss this. For the record, after the last couple of days, I have realized we should. I just hadn't expected to dive into it tonight."

The tightness in my chest loosened ever so slightly.

He took another swallow of his drink then settled in, crossing one leg over the other, ankle on the knee. "But you must be exhausted, bird. Are you sure you're up for this?"

"You're stalling."

"Since you're playing me, it's only fair that I play you. You went down this road kicking and screaming, if you'll recall."

"You fought back with patience. I can be patient."

"Yes, you can be. You have been." Acknowledging how long I'd waited for him to open up was already significant progress. An eager anticipation fluttered inside me. Was this what these sessions had been like for him?

God, if so, that man could handle his angst like a statue. As for me, I had to cross my ankles to keep my foot from wanting to bounce.

"All right," he said, earnestly. "Let me decide where this should begin."

"If you aren't honest, I'll know," I teased. Though I wasn't sure that was true.

"It will be authentic, bird. You might not like what you hear, but it will be authentic." His reassurance was typical Edward—soothing but not soothing enough to get comfortable.

Typical Edward, though, was something I was quite used to. So in *my* typical fashion, I challenged him right back. "I'm sure I can handle it. If you can."

He smirked.

Then he grew solemn. "Marion was quite submissive, as I've told you. As you've seen now. It wasn't just a bedroom game for her. It was a lifestyle choice. It wasn't just about being subservient. In every area of her life, she wanted to be molded and instructed and commanded and dominated."

"And you liked that." It was impossible to keep the bite out of my tone.

"I...did," he admitted. "And then I didn't."

"You didn't like being in charge? I call bullshit." Apparently, reading him was easier than I'd expected.

"Oh, I did like that. I'll never grow tired of that." He didn't wink, but it felt like he had. "I didn't even really mind the time and energy it required to live like that, though, at the time, I thought I did. I had things that were more important that needed my focus."

"Your business," I guessed.

"Yes. And other things."

Other things. Like planning a takedown of my father.

His revenging certainly had a life of its own. With our different opinions on the subject, I thought it best to avoid that topic. "You were busy. I got it. Making a schedule for her and setting out her clothes got tedious."

"We are not making this about you," he said, correctly assuming my subtext. "If I thought it were *tedious* to do those things for you, I wouldn't have insisted that you let me."

"What's the difference? How can you be so sure you won't resent it for me when you did for her? I'm sure she didn't even argue with you about it like I did."

"That was exactly it."

"She liked it, and *that's* what irritated you?"

He let out a rather hefty sigh. "The problem wasn't that she accepted those things. It was that she accepted *everything*. She didn't ever argue, except when she wanted to bait me into a punishment. She didn't stand up to me. She didn't speak her mind. She wanted me to decide all of it, and so I did."

"How boring."

He pierced me with an unapproving glare. "You're being catty, but yes. It was boring after a while. And not always very safe."

"You mean sex? Did she not have boundaries or something? Did you go too far?" I wasn't just being catty—I was being petty. I felt like my mother, greedy for the triflest of gossip because, if Marion and Edward had problems in the bedroom, I was going to feel a thousand times more secure in our marriage since our sex was fanfuckingtastic.

"The sex was just fine, thank you." Ouch. "Brilliant, to be truthful." Double ouch. "I do appreciate being the boss in that arena."

"Really? I couldn't tell." Add snide to my list of faults. *Way to be an adult, Celia.*

Fortunately, Edward was grown-up enough for the both of us in the moment. "The problem wasn't her boundaries. I knew them—better than she did even—and I respected them. The problem was that with no one to challenge me, *I* was the one with no boundaries."

My breath lodged in my chest. "I'm surprised to hear you admit that."

"You're starting to see why this story isn't a favorite of mine." He slid his ankle farther down the supporting leg, fully crossing them now. With his brows knit, he spent silent seconds smoothing away an invisible wrinkle, seemingly lost in a self-analysis.

Then, after a dismissive shake of his head, he went on. "Anyway, believing that you are unstoppable is fun for a while, but it gets lonely. Especially when the other aspects of our life were added in. She didn't want to share a bed to maintain the separation of master and servant. She didn't help with family decisions except to praise whatever I'd decided. I rarely knew what she was really thinking about anything. I had a sub, not a wife, and for that reason, I began to resent those parts of our marriage specifically. I no longer enjoyed picking out her clothes, and deciding what she was going to do with her day was, as you said, tedious, and I stopped putting as much effort into it as I should. It put a strain on our relationship, naturally. Those things were important to her. She needed them to be happy. And I wasn't there for her."

Something began to shift within me as he spoke, and I stopped listening for things to boost my esteem and started hearing him. Started hearing the story of two complicated people who began down a path together. Started to understand how it must have hurt when those pathways diverged.

"Did she complain?" I asked, quietly.

"No. But I knew. It was my job to know, and I knew. It didn't change my behavior, but it weighed on me. It was a vicious cycle. The guilt was another distraction that took my time away from focusing on her."

"Yeah. That guilt shit can be a mighty energy sucker."

"Yes. You understand." His smile was brief, lost behind another tip of his glass to his lips. "We'd been married about twelve years, three of them particularly tense, when I decided something needed to be done about it. Actually, that's not true. I had decided that several times before then, each time promising to myself and to her that I'd do better, I'd *be* better. I just was never able to follow through for whatever reason. Different reasons. All poor excuses, but I clung to them and went out of my way to validate them. Which didn't help things. So twelve years in, our marriage on the rocks and knowing she needed to be dominated, believing I couldn't be the one to do it sufficiently, I took her to Exceso for a week. And I introduced her to a dominant I knew there, Renato Fernandez."

My eyes widened. "You introduced her to the man she ran away with?"

"Yes."

"Did you...?" I tried to picture it. *Hi, here's my wife, I can't fulfill her needs so she's all yours.*

That wasn't how marriages worked. No matter how subservient she was, she wasn't property. That couldn't be how it happened. "I don't understand. You *wanted* her to leave you?"

"That hadn't been my intention, no. That was just how it turned out in the end."

So if he hadn't *given* her away...

Comprehension clicked in. "You *shared* her."

"Yes."

I blinked at him, my mouth gaping. "And she just went along?"

He shrugged. "She didn't say one way or another. She never did. She trusted me to make those decisions for her and when I did she simply said, 'Yes, sir,' and complied."

"I don't know what to say." I didn't know what to *feel*. I couldn't decide if it was sick or wrong. Was it even consensual? If she didn't speak up to stop it, then...yes?

But if I had been in her place, if I had been Marion...

Edward uncrossed his legs and sat sharply forward. "These were different circumstances, Celia. She was a different woman, with different needs. I would never—*never*—share you with anyone."

"Let's not make this about me, remember." But that was exactly the lens I was looking at this through. If he ever told me to go to one of his buddies willingly, we'd be over. Immediately.

"I need you to understand that before I go on." His gaze was heavy and insistent. Pleading.

I swallowed down the bad taste in my mouth and tried to focus on what he said. I was not Marion. "I would never go for it, and you know it. You wouldn't even try."

"No, you wouldn't go for it, but that night you and I were on Exceso, you wouldn't have had much choice. If I had really meant to give you to one of those men, you better believe they wouldn't have cared if you consented. It's vital to me that you trust that I would never have gone through with it. You are mine, and no one else's, is that clear?"

"Yes." It came out clipped and tight.

"I need you to say that you understand definitively. That you know I would not do that to you."

He'd told me this that night too, and since, and I did believe him. He hadn't shared me then, and like he'd said, he could have. For that matter, except for when we were wrapped up in hating each other before we'd married, everything he'd ever said and done backed up what he was saying now. In fact, he was almost overly possessive of me.

Well, not *overly* possessive. Since I liked it.

"I believe you, Edward. I'm yours and no one else's."

"You are," he confirmed. Satisfied, he sat back. "Besides, with Marion, sharing wasn't about sex. Or, it wasn't just about sex. There was that too, which I was part of when it was happening. At least, in the beginning."

"Wait, wait, wait." I pressed my palms together and brought my fingertips to my lips. I was still trying to process that the Edward I knew and loved was not the Edward that Marion had known and loved. "You had a threesome?"

That was it. There was no way I was ever going to compare with her in the bedroom.

He shook his head. "I didn't participate. I watched."

"Oh." Still processing. "Was it hot?"

He chuckled. "Some of it was very hot. When I could get past the seething jealousy."

"Fuck. Why is that just as hard to hear?"

"Because you believe my jealousy says something about how I must have felt about her. It doesn't say any more than the fact that I let it happen in the first place. She was my wife. I loved her. I didn't want her in another man's bed, but I was willing to allow it because I knew it was the only thing that might help me keep her."

"Quit topping from the bottom." This was supposed to be *his* session, not mine, and yet *he* was still analyzing *me*. And still saying things that made it impossible to stop thinking about *us*. "So you're saying that you wouldn't share *me* with anyone, even if it was the only way to keep *me*?"

"Bloody hell, Celia, you're impossible." He growled with frustration. "That would never be the way to keep you, so it's a moot point. It seems you may have other similarly arduous demands, though, so if you want my love for you tested, I'm willing to bet you'll have your way soon enough."

Because I wanted a baby, and he didn't.

I wasn't ready for that conversation again. Not yet. "Okay. You did what you needed to do to keep her. What happened then?"

"It helped, actually," he said. "Renato helped our marriage, I mean. Not because of what occurred that week on the island, but because afterward I urged them to continue their relationship online, and he overtook the tasks I'd grown to resent. He managed her day. He gave her assignments. He gave her what she needed.

"And, I thought, that would be enough for her. She was happier, and I felt...well, free. We made it through two more years together that way. Then, one day—it seemed like it was out of the blue at the time, but in retrospect, I see that it was little by little that she fell for him. That he became more of her master than I was. That she was less and less mine. She wasn't even the one who announced that she was leaving. Renato flew in from Turin and told me with her at his side. He helped her pack her bags, told her what to bring, and she left."

"And you just let her?"

"I was barely in command of her anymore at that point. I should have seen it coming. I wondered for a long time after what would have happened if I'd told her to stay. For the kids, maybe I should have. But asking her to stay would have meant offering to be someone I wasn't, and I couldn't bring myself to say the words."

"Oh, Edward." I slumped in my chair, the reality of what he'd been through finally hitting me. I ached for him, for the man who had loved and tried. For the man who had been forced to fix his marriage on his own. For the weight he must have felt with that burden, and the greater weight he must have felt for having to make a painful choice, one that ended up only bringing him more pain in the end. One that had repercussions on his children.

His guilt had to be endless.

"It's not your fault," I said, realizing that was the reason he'd kept this from me. I leaned forward, my body reaching toward him even as I stayed seated. I wanted to go to him, but also wanted to respect his space. "You couldn't have known. You did your best. You can't blame yourself."

"I know," he said, softly.

"Do you?"

We'd had this conversation in reverse, him assuring me my role in blame, me saying I understood, but not really. It had been horrendous sitting where he was now.

He studied me, as though checking my expression for wounds, as if I were the one who had been confessing my heartache, because he knew what it felt like listening to a loved one's pain.

Then, he came to me. Kneeling in front of me, he wrapped his arms around my calves and kissed the inside of my knee. "She didn't break me, Celia. I know you think she did, but she didn't."

"It's okay if she did. I'll understand."

"I know you will, but she didn't." His hands slid up, over my knees and glided over the skirt of my dress. "I was devastated when she left, not because of her—not because I missed her more than I should, but because I had failed. I had failed at being the husband she wanted me to be."

I ran my hands through his hair, wanting to give him reassurance.

"That stayed with me a long time. I was convinced I didn't know how to do this—this love thing. This commitment thing. Because I hadn't been what Marion needed." He looked up at me, his blue eyes bright. "It wasn't until I met you that I was able to see that she wasn't who I needed her to be either."

My eyes pricked. I spread my thighs wider, inviting him closer.

He came, stopping only when he hit the chair. Reaching up, he brushed his knuckles against my cheek. "I don't want to win all the time, Celia. I don't want to always be the one who decides. I don't want to be alone in this marriage. I want you to challenge me. I want you to step up and stand in my way. I want to boss you around and dominate you, but that can't be everything there is between us. I need you to be with me too. *Beside* me."

Tears spilled out over my cheeks. "I am with you, Edward. Beside you all the way."

He didn't let me say more. His mouth captured mine, tugging me forward. I slid down to my knees in front of him, pushing the chair back with my body as I did. His kiss grew savage. He devoured me like a hungry man, like he had been too long without affection, without understanding, without love, and now he was starving for it.

Fuck, I was starving too, ravenous for what only he could give me. Together, our hands worked fast, removing clothes at lightning speeds until we were both naked and sprawled out on the floor.

He paused as he perched above me, the head of his cock notched at my pussy, while he traced my swollen lips with a single finger.

"Don't tease," I begged. "Fuck me, Edward. Fuck me hard."

He pushed inside me then, slowly, ignoring my pleas for speed. Even after he was deeply seated, he didn't move faster. He took his time, making sure I felt every inch of his cock on each one of his strokes. It was maddening how it prolonged the build of my orgasm, stretching it out like the anticipation of a dawdling sneeze. Coupled with the way he gazed at me, his eyes spearing me with equal intensity, I felt more filled by him than I ever had.

He spoke to me as he fucked me without ever using words, whispering kisses along my jawline, murmuring his hands along my skin, articulating his love through each thrust of his cock, until I was overcome by his discourse, my entire being shivering and trembling with sensation.

I love you, I said without uttering a single syllable, as I arched up, my back bent with the atomic force of pleasure ripping through me. My pussy clamped around him, and he stilled, rooting firmly inside me until my climax had finished. Then, when he resumed his thrusts, he relaxed his tempo further, threatening to drive me even more insane as he leisurely drew another orgasm from my body.

Minutes might have passed. Or hours. I lost all sense of time and space, my focus anchored only on him and the infinite joy that existed in that singular moment. I'd meant what I'd said to him—I was one hundred percent committed to be with him through this marriage, to be by his side, but right now I was perfectly content being underneath.

Later, when we were in our bed, my cheek pressed against his chest, I began to remember the issues that existed beyond the here and now. We'd entered a new phase of our relationship. We'd leveled up, and I didn't want to ruin the mood when I felt so deeply connected to him, but there was no real progress in our new position if we didn't face it all.

"What about the other stuff, Edward? The things we talked about yesterday." The baby I wanted, the revenge he wanted. I was grateful for the dark and that I couldn't see his expression from where I lay in his arms.

"Well," he said, his arms tightening around me. "First, we deal with Ron."

"Okay."

He placed a kiss on the top of my head. "Then, when that's done, we'll fight. And one of us will win. But we have a while before we have to think about that, so let's leave that for the future."

And, for once, I didn't challenge him. I didn't push him or make a stink. I simply agreed and clung onto the truth that we'd both acknowl-edged now—that I wasn't Marion, that he didn't want me to be—and hoped that meant he understood I wouldn't fight fair.

TWENTY

EDWARD

I STUDIED the prospective report in front of me, zeroing in on required labor. The last report on this subject hadn't been as favorable. That had been a year ago, shortly before Genevieve graduated.

"We need someone else on the development team," I said to Hagan, who sat on the other side of my desk. "Do you have someone who's capable?"

"I have some possibilities."

When he didn't say more right away, I sensed he was reluctant to air his suggestion. I looked up from the report to him. "Whoever it is, tell me."

"Just...are you sure you don't want to move Genevieve over? She's really got a unique viewpoint and could be an incredible asset."

I had to force myself not to growl. When I'd broken down and hired her before the holidays, I'd made sure Hagan understood that she wouldn't work anywhere near my department. I'd drilled it into him. "We've been over this."

"We have, but we haven't. I don't get why you hired her if you don't want to actually use her skills."

I set the report down and folded my hands together on my desk so that I wouldn't be tempted to punch it. "I hired her because she wouldn't accept a handout any other way. And because that pathetic excuse for a network made a poor line on her resume."

When she continued to reject all my attempts to give her assistance, I'd reluctantly offered her a position in outreach, a department I rarely worked with, and given her an annual salary that provided her a comfortable cushion. After a couple of years, she could move on to something worthwhile. Accelecom would look good under her belt. There was no one in the industry who could deny her with that experience.

She'd only accepted because she was eager for good work in the field. Once she did, I felt a mammoth relief, despite knowing I was bringing her to the fringes of my world. It was the right thing to do, in the end, though I was still irked that she refused to move from the miserable dump of a neighborhood that she'd selected.

Maybe I could negotiate that in exchange for bringing her to the development team...

No. That was too close to me. Too close to her discovering the person I didn't want her to realize I was.

Without any warning, my office door flung open.

"My father is retiring," Celia declared as she strode in. It had been nearly a year since the last time she burst past my assistant, the day she'd yelled at me for acting on her behalf behind her back before asking for a baby. I was grateful that she didn't use the tactic often, but my wife did indeed know how to make an entrance.

On the heels of her announcement, Charlotte's voice rang over the intercom. "Your wife is here."

"Thank you, Charlotte. I'm well aware." A second glance at Celia's expression inspired me to add an addendum before I released the button on the intercom. "Please make sure we aren't disturbed."

"Will do."

Hagan spun around in his chair to face Celia. "Warren is stepping down from Werner Media? Who is he naming as his replacement?"

He'd beat me to the burning question. I looked back to her, eager for her response.

"He hasn't named anyone yet. He isn't planning to make a formal announcement for several weeks. My mother told me this morning that he's only just definitively decided." Her voice tightened, and only then, I realized she was on the verge of tears. "He's going to find out. He's going to name someone, and if Hudson doesn't vote in his favor, he's going to find out he doesn't own the majority shares anymore."

Technically, Warren already knew he didn't own the majority shares because he gave all of his to his daughter. But even if Celia hadn't signed over her voting power to him, she would never vote against his wishes.

None of that was the point.

I stood up from my desk and came around to embrace her. "Shh. No need to worry down that route. You have no idea how this will play out."

She pulled out of my arms. "I know that Hudson wants to have the upper hand, and without my father at the helm, he doesn't have that anymore. He loses his ace. Trust me when I say he's not going to just hand that over."

My head was at least five steps ahead of her, my pulse racing from the possibilities that this change in situation might bring.

I forced myself to slow down until I'd brought her up to speed. "If Pierce still believes he needs to put pressure on you after all this time—"

"He will," she insisted. "Trust me on this. He will."

I wasn't so sure. Few people had the doggedness to intimidate a foe for long periods of time. If Hudson Pierce truly was one with such tenacity, well, then he was a man after my own heart. One to be admired.

Either way, it was best to plan for the worst. "Then he'll want to keep that card as long as possible. He'll let the position go to the person your father chooses so that he can remind you that he's only allowing it as long as you behave."

That was how I would play it, anyway. His threat over Celia only worked as long as his ownership of the shares remained secret. Once that was out, he had no more leverage.

She frowned as she considered my logic.

"I feel like this is an appropriate time to ask what you're talking about. Are you saying Hudson Pierce owns more shares of Werner than your father?" Hagan had no issues inserting himself into conversations that might not concern him. It made him a good businessman. It also made him an annoying son.

I opened my mouth to tell him to get out of my office, but Celia spoke first. "It's a long, complicated story, but the short answer is yes. Hudson secretly owns more shares and has promised to let my father continue running the company as though he's in charge as long as I..." She sighed. "As long as I leave him alone, really."

"Ah." His expression said he understood clearly. "Dad's usually on the other side of those arrangements. Listen to him on this one."

I grimaced, not sure I liked how well my son knew me. It shouldn't have come as a surprise, really, considering how long we'd been working together. He was a bright fellow after all.

But Hagan's knowledge of my less ethical dealings wasn't where my focus needed to be at the moment. "Think it through," I said to Celia. "Like you said, there is no advantage to Pierce letting the upper hand go."

She nudged a tear away from the corner of her eye with her knuckle. "Hudson will want to have a say in who my father chooses, though. He has a lot of money wrapped up in Werner. He won't just care about keeping a thumb on me. It's also in his best interest if the company succeeds."

Now she was thinking logically. "He's trusted Warren so far. There's no reason Pierce won't trust him to pick his replacement." I thrust my hand in my pocket so she wouldn't see it twitching from my anxiousness to get to the next part of this scenario.

She brought her hands together and rested them against her lips. "You're right," she said with a nod. "You're right. I don't need to worry about this. It's not a problem."

"Precisely." I gave it a single beat before I launched her in a new direction. "There is an opportunity here, though. Do you see it?"

Her nose wrinkled in confusion.

"You could take his spot," Hagan said, excitedly. "Accelecom and Werner could merge, and you could run them both."

He really was my son. With, perhaps, a little less tact.

Celia chortled. "That wasn't what you were going to suggest, was it? Because if it was, you've clearly gone mad."

"I don't think it's all that insane of an idea," I protested. "We've done that joint deal in India recently. Your father keeps pushing me to do more joint ventures. He already likes the idea of our companies working together." The only reason I'd refrained from doing more was out of spite. Warren Werner might not have been the person who brought down my father's company, but he'd been the man who hadn't believed his daughter when she'd told him about her uncle's assaults. It was a subtle form of punishment. One I could dole out without Celia's wrath.

But merging after Warren stepped down? Me at the helm? That was even better than vengeance. That was providence.

Hagan jumped up from his chair. "I think it's absolutely brilliant."

This time I turned to glare at my son. Helpful as he thought he was being, he was not.

"I'm already leaving. Don't worry." He picked his briefcase off the floor and hustled out of the room.

As soon as the door shut behind him, I turned back to my wife who was staring at me in disbelief, all signs of amusement wiped from her face. "How can you possibly think that would be a good idea? Even if you can win my father over to it, there is no way Hudson will stand for it."

I shrugged. "Why not? You said yourself that you believe he wants the company to succeed."

"He wants power over me, Edward. If he let control of Werner go to my husband, he'd be giving me power, not holding it over me."

"Not true. It wouldn't be any different than when your father had control. Pierce would still have the upper hand. He could still overrule any one of my decisions."

She continued to gape. "You wouldn't ever really be in charge. Why would you even want that?"

Because I wanted Werner Media. I had for a long time. While my initial reasons for wanting it were no longer valid, the desire was still there, a bad habit I couldn't kick.

And now, it was possible I didn't have to.

"I would be in charge," I said. "As much in charge as your father has been for the past handful of years, and as everyone in the world besides you, me, and Hudson Pierce—including your father—believe that Warren is running the company, I think it's fair to say he *is* running the company."

"I don't believe this." She turned away from me to pace. "I've spent the last couple of years trying to rid myself of the hold Hudson had on me, and you want to take me right back to where I was. This is my chance to extricate myself from that completely."

I was about to give her another reason that this idea was, as Hagan said, indeed brilliant, but her latest statement tripped me up. "What do you mean by that? You'd played a game on Hudson, and he bought into Werner to prevent you from doing that again. Was there more to the situation? Why did he have more hold on you than any of the other people you played?"

She stopped mid-stride, her back to me. Then she shook her head and turned to face me. "He didn't. I meant that I've been trying to distance myself from everything from that time."

There was something off about her excuse, something not quite the truth. But I was pretty sure I could figure it out without her admission. Likely, the reason Pierce bothered her more than the others was because he was, as far as I knew, the one person who had played her back. I had a feeling she rarely had anyone pull one over on her. Before me, anyway.

I took a conciliatory step toward her. "That's understandable. I know you aren't the person you once were, and I'm sure it's hard to accept that there are others who will never realize that. But I assure you, the situation won't be any different from what it is now. In fact, if he's as smart as I think he is, Pierce should prefer that the person who takes over for your father be one that is close to you. His ace has higher value then."

Her mouth twisted as she thought it over, obviously torn. "What if Hudson doesn't see it your way? He might want to be done with me as much as I want to be done with him. He might not agree with your reasoning."

"Then we convince him." It was the wrong thing to say, and I knew it even before her shoulders went rigid and her brow tensed.

I reached out for her hand and tugged her into my arms. "*I'll* convince him," I corrected. I kissed her temple. "You won't have to have any part of it. I'm fairly confident I can point out the wisdom of having me in the position on both a business and personal level. And I'm *absolutely* confident that I can persuade your father to name me as his successor. He'll never know the decision wasn't his."

Celia remained stiff, yet she didn't pull away. She clearly wasn't convinced, but I had a feeling she wouldn't stand in my way if I pursued this plan. And I *would* pursue this plan.

But I wanted more than reluctant acquiescence. I'd spent the last year trying to live up to my word, encouraging her to be my partner. I wanted her on my side on this.

And, for the life of me, I couldn't understand why she was against it.

I massaged the small of her back with the flat of my hand. "Don't you want to see Werner stay in your family? Don't you want to pass it on down the line?"

I wasn't playing nice, baiting her like this. We hadn't spoken again about a possible child in the last eleven months, but it was always there between us, the thing we both knew she wanted.

Soon, we'd discuss it again. Camilla had made significant progress with Ron. He'd initially accepted her invitation to Exceso last September, but then pushed off actually going until January.

The delay had made me more anxious. I needed to feel more in control of the setup. So, despite the worries that my marriage to Celia might make it hard for Ron to trust me, I went to the island in January as well, just to be sure the introduction to Leroy Jones, my FBI contact, happened as it should.

Once we were all there, the pieces fell into place. Though I didn't much interact with Ron personally while I was there, he saw the unorthodox sexual acts that took place on the island, realized I was more than open to the majority of them, and any doubt he might have had about me was seemingly erased.

Camilla was the linchpin of it all. She introduced Ron to Leroy who did his part by sharing child pornography with Ron that he'd borrowed from the bureau and talking up the young girls he'd supposedly taken advantage of, all in the hopes of gaining Ron's trust. They hadn't shared contact info when they parted—Leroy insisted it was too suspicious, that these men kept private details to themselves as much as possible—but Ron did promise to contact Camilla when he next had an "event" so that she could forward the invitation.

That had been five months ago with no word since. Still, I was sure that he'd reach out soon. That he'd be arrested and put away. That I'd finally be free of the burden of revenge, and Celia and I could move on to figuring out the rest of our lives.

If that future could include a baby for her, why not also Werner Media for me?

"Yes, I do want that, but..." She tilted her head up toward me. "But I don't care who runs the company. That's not lasting. I'd rather have the shares back. That's what I really want, and all of this just reminds me that the reason they're gone is because of me. And I can't change that."

The weight of her guilt was so heavy, it felt like I carried it too. God, I wanted that gone for her. I wanted her pain erased. I wanted the man who'd encouraged her to play these games in the first place to have to pay for these mistakes the way she did.

He would, eventually. I was determined.

I was also determined to get her company back for her, in whatever way I could.

I cupped the sides of her face. "It won't be like this forever, bird. I'll take over the company, I'll show Pierce he can trust me. Then, when it's time, he'll sell those shares to us. I promise you."

"No, Edward. Don't worry about that, please. Don't go head to head with Hudson. I don't want that."

"It won't be like that. Trust me. It will be friendly." Unless Pierce refused to keep it that way.

Before she could respond, Charlotte's voice sounded over the intercom. "Sorry to interrupt but Camilla is on the line. She insisted it was urgent."

I exchanged a glance with Celia before I pulled away and crossed to my desk. "Put her through," I said, my finger pressed on the intercom button. A split second later, the phone rang. I hit speaker. "What's up?"

"We have a problem," she said. "I'm in the elevator. Be there soon."

She hung up. Immediately, I buzzed Charlotte, telling her to send Camilla in when she arrived.

"Is it Ron?" Celia asked, her voice thin.

"I don't know what else would be urgent." If it were something at Accelecom, she would have brought her issues to me through different methods. If it were something to do with Freddie, she'd be with him, not coming into my office.

The tension built as we waited in silence, the seconds passing like years before Camilla knocked once and burst in.

"Is it Ron?" Celia asked at the same time I said, "What happened with Ron?"

My sister paused, taken aback by the barrage of questions. "Good. You're both here. This makes things easier." She tossed her purse on the sofa and crossed to my minibar where she took out a bottle of tequila and poured herself a shot, arguably a better means of coping than her usual means. She threw it back before turning to address us. "I heard from Ron."

Instinctively, Celia and I stepped toward her in unison, as if being nearer would encourage her to deliver her information more quickly.

"And...?" I prodded her.

"And it's all a big fuck-up," she said with despair. "He's having a 'party,' and he invited me and Leroy, which is all good. But the party isn't in the States. It's here. On Saturday night."

"Fuck. That's in two days," Celia said, aghast.

"Right. There wasn't a contingency for this. And it's not enough time to make one." She ran a hand through her hair. "I stuck to the plan, though. I told him that Leroy was interested and that I was sure he'd be there. I'm supposed to call back by five to tell him for sure."

I was already moving back around my desk to retrieve my cell phone from the top drawer. I pulled up Leroy's contact number and hit the call button, glancing at my watch as I did. It was half past one here, and Albuquerque was seven hours behind us. That made it...

"It's six-goddamned-thirty in the morning," Leroy said when he answered. "This better be good. I was just about to go for my run."

"It's not good, but it's important." I turned away from the women so I could focus on my conversation instead of theirs. "Ron reached out to Camilla. Party's on Saturday. Problem is it's here, in London. You can make that happen, can't you?"

I wasn't honestly sure that he could. Sure, Leroy could get on a plane and arrive in time, but Britain wasn't his jurisdiction. He couldn't make any arrests without coordinating with the local police, and with the short notice, an operation of that size could very well be out of the question.

But I wasn't ready to acknowledge the improbability. We'd worked too hard, invested too much time. This had to work.

"Jesus Christ," Leroy swore loudly in my ear. "This guy is good. He did this purposefully. He never said one word that this might take place off of U.S. grounds. He knew this would pose a problem."

"He is good, and that's why we have to take the bloody arse down. Tell me you can make it happen."

He groaned. "Fuck. Yes. I think so. I have to... Fuck." I waited as patiently as possible while he thought through the process. "Okay. I know some people at MI6. I'll contact them, see what we can do. This isn't their arena, but hopefully they can get us in touch with someone local. I'll give them your name and contact info, since I'll be on the soonest flight I can book. They may need to arrange some of this shit with you while I'm up in the air."

I could hear typing in the background, Leroy on his computer, likely pulling up the contacts he needed as we spoke.

"That's good. That's all good." If I said it enough, maybe it would decrease the size of the boulder in my stomach. "You'll get on a plane, I'll wait for the cops to call. What else do you need me to do?"

"I'm going to be honest, Edward. This is going to be tough. There might not be time for warrants. I don't have authority. I might not even be given permission to go to this shindig with immunity."

Panic crept into my voice. "You have to be here, Leroy. It's your name on that invite list. You're the one he trusts."

"I know, man. And I'm going to be there. I'll deal with the red tape afterward. Meanwhile, I need to get things rolling. I'll call you back when I have some more news."

"All right," I said, calmer now that he'd assured me he was seeing this through. "Talk later."

I hung up and turned around to find both my sister and my wife looking expectantly toward me.

"Call Ron back," I said, sounding more calm than I felt. "Tell him Leroy will be there."

She started to cross to the couch, reaching for her purse, but I wasn't done. Leroy had me worried. If he couldn't get permission to put this together, if he didn't have authority, there was a good chance he'd call everything off.

Even if he didn't, I didn't feel good about having all our eggs in one basket. Leroy was the one who had developed trust with Ron, but so had Camilla. Like hell was I letting her walk into that party, but she might be able to add another name to the invitation list, if the name was someone that Ron knew for absolute certain wasn't an undercover agent of some sort.

"And one more thing," I said as Camilla brought her mobile to her ear. "See if you can get me on that list as well."

TWENTY-ONE

CELIA

I STOOD in front of the door to the library for several seconds, my hand on the knob. Then changed my mind and headed back down the hallway toward the stairs. Once I reached them, I changed my mind again. I'd tried to hold my tongue, but this was too important, and if I didn't speak now, it would be too late.

Determined, this time I didn't pause at all. I threw the door open and marched in.

"Don't do this," I said, my eyes pinned on Edward.

He was standing in front of his desk, one hip leaning against it. From his open mouth and the position of his hands, I guessed he'd been mid-sentence when I interrupted.

He looked at me for a solid two seconds before turning his focus back to the others—Leroy who was perched on the arm of a chair, Camilla who was pacing by the fireplace, Dominic and Felisha, two police officers, seated on the sofa.

"—send the signal for the bust to take place?" Edward continued with whatever question he'd begun before I entered.

Following his lead, the others ignored me as well. "The situation has to progress far enough that they'll be 'caught in the act' when we arrive," Felisha said.

"I can give the signal," Leroy said. "But if I'm unable to, for any reason, I'll ask you what time it is. You can naturally look at your watch and hit the button then."

I'd been in the room earlier, not for long because it made me anxious, but long enough to hear about the watch that they'd given Edward with a button that would send an alarm to the police. Leroy and Edward wouldn't be allowed to bring their phones in, and they might even be screened for a wire. The watch, though, should pass inspection.

Should being the key word.

Should being the reason I had anxiety.

Should wasn't definite, and with all the talk of how sophisticated Ron's operation was, there was no telling how he'd handle someone found to be operating undercover. What would happen if Edward and Leroy got caught?

"Edward, don't do this," I pleaded. "Leroy already offered to do it alone. It doesn't have to be you."

Except for a glance at me before Dominic spoke, I was again ignored. "Fortunately, since we were already watching Garrick Till, we know the best ways to approach. We'll be inside within minutes after you send the alarm."

Garrick was a long-time friend of my uncle's, apparently, and though Ron was the official host, the party tonight was taking place at his house. I'd never heard his name until this week, but unbeknownst to Till, he was well-known by the local authorities as a possible sex offender. They'd been trying for months to nail him with something but hadn't been able to infiltrate his circle. Their investigation was the only reason this sting was able to come together on such short notice. They'd already had the primary evidence gathered when Leroy had reached out. Getting the needed warrants hadn't been a problem at all.

I'd been flabbergasted as the details about Ron's circle had unfolded over the last two days. I'd always believed the man who had groomed me and abused me had only been able to do so because he'd had access to me. When I was no longer sent to spend time alone with him, I was convinced his behavior had come to a forced end.

Instead, it seemed I'd only been a small part of his sick network. I likely wasn't even the beginning. His methods had been too exact. He'd become an expert well before I came into his life.

Every new thing I learned confirmed one thing—Ron Werner needed to be taken down.

But that didn't mean that Edward had to be the one to do it.

I changed my tactic. "Leroy, tell him. Tell him this is stupid. What if Ron already suspects Edward? What if he discovers the watch before they get in?"

"It's seven twenty-three," Leroy said, disregarding me. "We should get going soon."

"I'll go up and get changed." Edward strode past me and out of the room.

Felisha, most likely pitying me, stood and walked to me. "There's no way anyone will suspect the watch signals the police to come, but if they do, the worst that will happen is they'll confiscate it before he goes in. In which case, Leroy or Edward will flash the lights. We'll be watching, and we'll see it."

Her words didn't comfort me. It only brought up a whole new slew of what-ifs, but I had no interest in discussing them with her. I turned away from her only to find Camilla waiting at my side.

"Ron didn't flinch at all when I asked to put Edward on the guest list," she said. "He doesn't suspect. After getting him to Exceso, he trusts me. I understand why this might be hard for you. I don't know if Edward ever mentioned, but Frank, my husband, was abusive. I knew I needed to leave him, but I stayed eleven years because I believed I loved him. What I'm saying is it's okay to have complicated feelings about your abuser. It's natural."

I was sure my expression was one of horror. There was too much to process. Her husband had abused her? She thought I wanted to stop Edward because I had "complicated feelings" for Ron?

"That's not—" I shook my head and left it at that. I didn't have time for this. Turning again, I hurried out after Edward.

In our bedroom, I found his shoes kicked off by the door and his jacket thrown on the bed. I headed toward the closet and found him in his boxer briefs, about to put his leg into his tuxedo pants. He glanced up at my arrival, then, like downstairs, went back to what he'd been doing.

"Don't go tonight. Please," I begged. When he didn't look up again, I snapped. "Do not just ignore me, Edward. That's not fair."

He finished fastening his pants then put his fists on his hips and sighed. "You should consider going to Amelie for a while. There will most likely be press clamoring to talk to anyone related to your family. Might do you good to stay away from the chaos."

Ordinarily, I liked the way he looked out for me. Tonight, when he refused to let me look out for him, it just pissed me off. "Don't treat me like I'm a fragile fucking flower."

His eyes flashed with anger. "Then stop acting like a fragile fucking flower."

Oh, it was on now. I took it as progress. Fighting was definitely a step up from being ignored. "It's not fragile to want my husband to stay safe. It's smart. Usually I don't have to explain intelligent behavior to you."

He pulled a white dress shirt out of his drawer, shaking it out before shoving an arm in the sleeve. He was calmer when he spoke. "There's nothing unsafe about what we're doing tonight. Our plan is solid. We've worked hard to gain Ron's trust, and it's paid off. I promise you."

"You can't promise that when you don't know. You can't have any idea what you're getting into. What if they take the watch? What if you don't have access to the lights? What if you can't get word to anyone?" My throat burned, I was so worked up. "Don't do this. It's too risky. Let the experts take care of it. It doesn't have to be you."

"You're really asking me to walk away from this? After everything that I've done to get here? After all the time and energy and years I've put into avenging my family?" He took a step toward me, his voice sharper. "After what he did to *you*? You're lucky I don't insist on murdering him with my bare hands. If you're worried about the risk, that's the biggest one I'll be facing, because believe me when I say that it will take a lot of restraint not to do just that."

He fumed, his nostrils flaring. "And you're worried about me being safe? I guarantee you that I'll be a whole hell of a lot safer than the little girls he plans on parading out tonight to a room full of predators. Little girls as innocent as you once were. How safe are they?"

I wanted to be strong.

But I couldn't help it—I burst into tears.

In an instant, his arms were around me. He hadn't gotten to buttoning up his shirt yet, so I pressed my cheek against his warm skin and let all the anxiety, all the fear, all the tension come out through my tears.

He rocked me, his voice soft and soothing. "We're so close to having this be over, bird. I want to be there when it is. I *need* to be there. I need this motherfucker to know that I'm behind this. That this is for us. That this is for you."

I hated it, but I got it. How many times had I imagined doing horrible things to my uncle? Or my father for not believing me? I'd even started to fantasize what my father would say when this all went down. It was sure as shit I'd tell him that Ron was in jail because of me. I suspected that would be the best part of all this.

Could I ask Edward to give up the best part for him? When he'd emphasized so many times that he was sure this would be the only way he'd truly be able to heal?

The tears fell faster. "You're going to see things, Edward, shocking things, and you're going to know how it happened for me. I don't want you to see that. I don't want you to know."

"Oh, bird." He forced my chin up so he could look into my eyes. "It doesn't matter what I see. Nothing that happens tonight will change that terrible things have already happened to you. If I know more of the details of that, or if I don't, it doesn't change that I am bloody deep in love with the woman those terrible things turned you into. Let me prove that love to you. Let me be there to see his face when they nail the bastard."

My breath shuddered as I drew it in. "Okay."

He swiped a tear from my cheek with his thumb then kissed my forehead. "Thank you." Then his lips found mine, and he kissed me with his gratitude.

He pulled away reluctantly. "I have to finish dressing now."

I nodded, then left him in the closet. The outburst having drained me of all my energy, I only made it to the armchair in the bedroom before I had to sit. As Edward said, all of this was almost over. After all the years I'd spent believing Ron would never be punished, he was finally going to have to face his wrongs.

It was exciting, in a way. And overwhelming. Was this really part of the healing process? Was this a necessary step? Would I be free of his hold on me once and for all after tonight?

I closed my eyes, trying to imagine that relief. Instantly, I was taken over by a memory from the distant past. The first party that Ron had brought me to, not the one where he'd auctioned parts of me off to the highest bidder, but one that had occurred the year before. He'd dressed me in a fancy gown, one much too mature for a girl of twelve. My breasts had only started to come in, and the bodice of the dress gaped, showing my nipples if I wasn't careful. I remembered being self-conscious about it, constantly trying to pull the dress up while Ron swatted my hands away.

"Leave it," he'd said. "You're breathtaking. Let all my friends see how gorgeous you are."

Then he'd paraded me through the den filled with men in tuxes who gave me similar compliments as I passed. I was instructed to address each one as sir, told to thank them for their praise. Told to not look away when someone pulled out his cock and stroked it in my presence or when one of the scantily clad women put it in her mouth while the man stared at me with a heavily lidded gaze.

I opened my eyes and shook the memory from me, swallowing the bile that had formed in the back of my mouth. These thoughts still haunted me. Less than they once had, but they still popped up now and again, when I least expected it. I was pretty sure that no matter what happened tonight, even if Ron was put away for the rest of his life, the past would still linger. I wouldn't be magically healed. Vengeance couldn't undo what had been done.

But Edward believed it could. Maybe believing would be enough to make it true for him.

So when he came out of the closet looking crisp and dashing in his tux, I ignored the knot in my stomach, ignored how he reminded me of the men from that party in the past, and smiled appraisingly up at him. "Good luck," I said. "I hope it's all that you need it to be."

And if it wasn't, I wondered what it would take, what he'd have to do. Wondered how far he'd go to reach the ending he desired.

I stayed sitting there for a while after he left, not thinking about anything while the sun set out the window, spreading orange and pink rays across the wall. It was almost dark when I finally stirred from my daze. I stood and flipped on the overhead light then picked up Edward's shoes and jacket and carried them to the closet. After putting the shoes on their space on the shelf, I took the jacket to the bag designated for drycleaning, remembering to check the pockets before I dumped it in. There were only a few items this time—a pen, a small stack of business cards, a piece of stationary folded into a square.

Being nosy, I unfolded the paper, and when my eyes found Camilla's signature at the bottom, I decided to read the entire thing.

Eddie,

I haven't always been enthusiastic about your schemes, even when they've been orchestrated for my benefit. I want you to know that I do support you, that I appreciate what you're doing in the name of our parents, and that I'm forever grateful for what you've done for me. After what we did to Frank, I didn't think that I'd ever be able to say that, but you were right—his death was the best thing to happen to me. I'm lucky to have you on my side.

Camilla

With my heart in my throat, I read it again. And a third time. I thought about what Camilla had said earlier, that Frank had been abusive. I thought about the odd ways she'd talked about her husband's death in the past. Thought about Edward's admission to having no boundaries.

Then I sank to the floor in shock.

Because I was pretty certain that I'd just learned that Edward killed Camilla's husband.

TWENTY-TWO

EDWARD

LEROY and I arrived separately to the party. My driver had taken him and dropped him off while I'd driven myself, leaving about ten minutes after he had. It was likely an insignificant detail that few people would pick up on, but we decided it was better to take every precaution.

"No cameras or recording equipment of any kind are permitted," the security guard at the door said. He gestured to a row of containers laid out on a long table behind him. "You can leave your phone in one of the boxes."

I retrieved my mobile from my jacket pocket and set it in an empty container. It wasn't secured the way belongings were at The Open Door in the States, but I imagined the trust level at these things was already high. Guests in attendance were confident that others weren't going to turn them in for illegal activity. Stolen devices seemed a trivial concern under the circumstances.

No one realized that all of these items would be confiscated before the night was over.

Leroy had warned me about that prior, so the mobile I checked in was a dummy. Mine was tucked safely in the glove box of my BMW.

"Spread your arms, please," the guard said next then waved a wand metal detector across my body. When nothing set it off, I was allowed past the entry. All of this before even giving anyone my name.

Two men in tuxes greeted me as soon as I stepped into the hall. One asked for my ID and then scanned a copy with his mobile when I handed it over.

"He's on the list," the other confirmed before making eye contact with me. "Follow me, Mr. Fasbender."

He led me down the hall, stopping when the walls opened up to a game room on our left. "The bar is self-serve," he said. "You can make yourself a drink and mingle with the others in the billiards room. We won't escort anyone into the ballroom until everyone has arrived."

I nodded and stepped over the threshold, scanning my surroundings. Immediately, I spotted Leroy, gathered with a trio of men by the liquor. Across the room from him, I saw another man I knew, Jeffrey Varga, one of the owners of Mills and Varga, the pathetic little network that had briefly employed my daughter.

Thank God I'd rescued her from that establishment. I'd thought Jeffrey was smarmy because of his pathetic business practices. I never would have guessed his wretchedness extended to his sexual behavior as well.

He lifted his glass when he saw me, and I forced myself to return a smile. He likely wasn't the only prominent man I would encounter this evening. It gave me a strange sort of high realizing I would be the downfall of these nasty predators.

At that thought, my smile turned genuine.

"I don't believe we've met." A portly man, old enough to be my father, extended a clammy hand in my direction. "Garrick Till. This is my house. You haven't been here before. May I ask who vouched for you?"

I wasn't sure whose name to give. Camilla's? Leroy's? And while the answer would be just as baffling if I'd come as a true guest, not knowing made my pulse speed up.

Before I could form a response, a hand clapped at my back. "Leave him alone, Garrick," a male voice said beside me. "I vouch for him. He's family."

"Ron," I said, somehow managing to keep the tightness from my voice. "I'm glad to know you consider me family, as we've had so little time to get acquainted." My skin crawled under the flat of his palm, and it took everything in me not to shudder.

"Nonsense. What else would you be? Though, if I'd known we shared the same interests, I would have made it a priority to get to know you sooner. I'm surprised our paths hadn't crossed before Exceso."

"My interests aren't quite so narrow in focus," I said. "All sorts of taboo catch my attention. This particular arena hasn't been one I've been able to delve into before now, I'm afraid."

"You're in for a real treat, I'll tell you. Hope you brought your checkbook." He dropped his hand and nudged Garrick. "Edward Fasbender. Owns Accelecom, and guess who he married. Celia."

Garrick's brows rose. "*Your* Celia?"

No, not his fucking Celia. Possessiveness boiled up inside me like lava.

"Yes, *my* Celia," Ron said with a disgusting chuckle. "I think you remember her fondly."

Garrick's eyes sparked. "That I do. Tightest virgin I've ever had around my fingers, that one. I'm sure you don't mind me telling you that. We're all accustomed to sharing here."

My vision went red. Garrick Till had to be one of the five who had bought my wife when Ron had auctioned her off to the highest bidders, and I wanted him dead. Fuck the mission for the evening. I was three seconds from lacerating his carotid artery with my fingernail.

Fortunately, an almost imperceptible jab at my side stopped me before I attacked. "Ed Fasbender," Leroy said, a warning in his tone only I would be able to detect. "I thought I saw you come in."

"That's right, you two already know each other," Ron said. "Camilla introduce you?"

I shook my head, remembering our story. We'd decided beforehand it would be easiest to keep details straight if they were close to the truth. "I'm the one who introduced my sister to Leroy. Met him on Exceso. When was that, 'Roy? Eight years ago now?"

Leroy pretended to think about it. "Sounds about right."

"He had the best damn collection of porn I'd ever seen at the time, and it's only gotten better since."

"I've seen it," Ron said excitedly. "Mine isn't quite as extensive, but I encourage you to check it out." He pointed at a bunch of photo albums strewn across the farthest billiard table. "That wife of yours used to be a good little model. Hope she's still rewarding you with what I taught her."

I was going to be ill. Not only was he a bloody sick bastard, but he was proud of it. If I could ensure he got raped in prison, it still wouldn't be what he deserved.

"Has he seen our star of the night yet?" Garrick was an equally despicable monster.

"Ah, let me show you." The rule banning recording equipment obviously didn't extend to Ron who pulled a mobile phone from inside his tux jacket. After a few taps, he tilted the screen toward us. "Aster. She's as much of a flower as her name. Absolutely stunning girl."

The picture had three figures dressed for a night out—Ron, a dark-haired woman around the age of forty, and a young girl, the mirror image of the woman, who couldn't be more than twelve.

I could hear the blood rushing in my ears as anger flushed through my body. What horrors had that girl already been through at his hands? Did the mother have any idea what he was doing? How the fuck did she allow Ron to be alone with her daughter?

Leroy, trained to be better at this than I was, had the appropriate response. "Nice. The mother a friend of yours?"

"I've been seeing her casually," Ron said. "She's good enough at the role play, but obviously the highlight of dating her is Aster."

"Lucky asshole," Leroy said conjovially. "Mother isn't going to be a problem tonight, is she?"

"Definitely not. Roofied her up about an hour ago. She'll be out until morning."

Again, Ron sounded like he was boasting. He fit right in with some of the depraved men I'd met on Exceso, but none had ever been so revolting. I knew it was because of Celia, that I cared more because I loved her and knew what he'd done to her. That knowledge made me disgusted with myself as well. After this, I vowed, when I was sure all the men here had thoroughly paid for these crimes, I'd be sure to invest in going after more of the evil fucktards that I dealt with. That was a promise.

Garrick flicked his wrist to look at his watch. "'Bout time to start, Ron."

Ron looked at the time on his mobile before tucking it away. "I'll go up and get her ready. Meanwhile, men, I hope you get some time with my albums. Oh, and Edward, there are some women of the night waiting in the ballroom, all of them paid to do whatever you're up for, no matter how taboo. Be sure to know that anything you do with them, as everything that happens here, will stay confidential."

He winked, alluding to the secrets he expected I was keeping from my wife, then merrily left the room. Garrick wandered on as well, needing to refill his drink.

I exchanged a glance with Leroy. Were we monsters for letting any of this happen at all? The police had emphasized the need to catch Ron and Garrick in the act, meaning we needed to not only let Aster be presented before signaling the raid, but we also had to let her be violated. Could I really do that? How much could I stand? Could the collection of porn be enough to nail Ron right now? Hell only knew what would be found on the guests' mobiles.

My gaze shifted toward the albums.

"Ten year max," Leroy whispered, reading my mind. "Not nearly enough. I'm going to go check them out, see what we have." He paused, and I knew we were both thinking about the pictures that he'd see, the ones that were very possibly of Celia. "Don't look at them, okay? You know enough. This doesn't need to haunt you too."

If it happened to Celia, I wanted it to haunt me too. She was certainly haunted. It wasn't fair that she had to endure that alone.

But she wouldn't want me seeing that like this, surrounded by men who got aroused by her young image. If there were indeed pics of her, she'd find out when the images were sorted and documented in the future. I couldn't protect her from that, but I could protect her from the crude things that were said by those viewing them if I wasn't there to hear them myself.

"I'll make myself a drink," I said, deciding that was a better way to spend the next few minutes. Maybe the alcohol would burn away the rotten taste in my mouth.

It was almost ten minutes later when Garrick gathered the guests together. There were twenty-six in all, twenty-four men who would be charged at least with indecency of a minor before the night was through. Some would be hit with more depending on how the rest of the evening played out.

The thrill of that knowledge—along with the cognac—was the only thing propelling me out of the game room and into the room that was set up to look more like a pleasure den than a ballroom. Comfortable sofas and chaise lounges were scattered throughout the space, beautiful women perched on several. Baskets littered the room, filled with what looked like lube and condoms. A table hugged the back wall with a variety of pleasure toys laid out, including two child-size sex dolls. The lights were on, but dim, and in the middle of the entire room was a makeshift stage, circular with a red sex chair positioned front and center.

The entire scene could have come out of a really good sex party, one that I would have been glad to attend, if it weren't all focused around a prepubescent child.

A fucking sex chair for an eleven-year-old. The girl wasn't old enough to know they existed, let alone how they were used. I bit down to keep myself from vomiting and ended up tasting blood when I snagged my tongue.

"Can I help you with something, sir?" A topless woman who looked too young to be legal wrapped her arm around my bicep. "We could find a cozy spot to sit. Up near the front, maybe?"

I couldn't do this. I couldn't be in here, casually flirting with a possibly unwilling sex worker so that no one would question my desire to be at the party. I needed a few minutes. Or thirty. Needed to get my head in the game.

"You could help me find a WC," I said. "I should freshen up before the evening gets more fun."

"Right this way, sir." She led me to a bathroom set just outside the ballroom. "Come and find me when you're back. I'd love to help with that fun you talked about."

She licked her red lips and batted her long lashes, an expert at both, making me wonder if she'd been superbly groomed or if she was a very skilled call girl. God, I hoped it was the latter.

I also hoped she'd been paid well, and in advance, and if she was here voluntarily, I hoped she didn't get in too much trouble for her part in the evening. Prostitution might be illegal, but in this pedophiliac environment, her profession felt as innocent as church.

Not that churches were necessarily innocent these days. But that was a crusade for another day.

Inside the bathroom, the door shut and locked behind me, I let out a long breath of tension. When my lungs were completely empty, I drew the next breath in with a measured inhale, counting each meditative in and out until I got to ten. I felt better when I got to the end, more focused. Centered. My reasons for being at this den of evil were sharply pinned in my mind. This was for my family, for the father I lost, for the life I could have known, for the sister who bore the brunt of the fallout.

And this was for Celia, heart of my heart, the child that Ron ruined and the woman I loved so much I'd ruined her more. Tonight would be a victory in her name. I could practically taste it.

As I returned to the ballroom, I gripped her name in my mind, holding it like a talisman. She was my motive and my drive and I could endure all of this and a hell of a lot more for her.

The room had settled in my absence, electric anticipation charging the room as Ron made his way up to the stage, Aster at his side. She wore a button-down white satin nightgown, her chestnut hair braided to the side and resting over one shoulder. She clearly felt intimidated by the crowd, and the way she clung to Ron suggested she considered him her safety, as though she trusted that he would protect her from any harm.

I had thought I understood his relationship with Celia, but until then, until I saw the way Aster looked at the predator at her side, I hadn't really seen the whole picture. He hadn't just violated her in unimaginable ways, he'd also fucked with her mind. He'd convinced her that exploitation was what love looked like. Fuck him for everything he'd done, but fuck him most of all for that.

And fuck him for whatever he was planning to do to Aster.

He introduced her to the crowd, interviewing her with questions that seemed almost innocent until viewed through a predator's lense. Questions about what toys she liked to sleep with and what her favorite sweets were to lick.

I hung at the back of the room, near the wall, unable to force myself in closer. I was antsy, my eyes drifting repeatedly to my watch, not looking at the time, but at the button that would bring this whole circus to a close. Reminding myself over and over that the charges against these arseholes needed to stick, that whatever would happen to this girl, it would have been a whole hell of a lot worse if Leroy and I weren't there.

After what seemed like a year, after Ron paraded Aster through the crowd then back to the stage, he finally got to what he called the "good stuff." "Aster, sweet flower, come hop up on this seat so all my friends can see how beautiful you are. We're going to show them the most beautiful parts of you, the parts that are our special secret, remember? These are my bestest friends, so it's okay if we share with them."

I tensed, my breath no longer moving evenly through my lungs. I wanted to look away, but my eyes were locked on the child's, part of me willing her to fight him off, part of me hoping she would cooperate so that we could hurry up to the part where she was rescued.

Apparently groomed well enough beforehand, Aster got up on the sex chair, putting a foot in each stirrup, her legs barely long enough to reach. The position would open her up, expose her innocent private parts to the men once she was undressed.

And there was no way Ron wasn't going to undress her.

When my hand reached toward the watch, Leroy caught my eye. With one sharp shake of his head, he warned me it was too soon.

Fuck. I couldn't stand it. I couldn't stand it for Aster, and I couldn't stand it for Celia. The two wrapped themselves as one in my head, though they looked nothing alike. Each thing Ron said to this girl, I heard the imaginary child voice of my wife in response. Each errant caress, each overly fond stroke of her skin, I saw the stain his touch had left on Celia, invisible bruises that could be seen decades later.

Ron stood in front of Aster and began unbuttoning her gown, coaxing Aster too quietly for me to hear in the back. When he was finished, he pushed the nightie off her shoulders and stood aside to reveal the girl's undeveloped chest and white cotton panties.

I stared at the side of Leroy's head, willing him to push the button. It was supposed to be his call, and I trusted him, but after his years in this line of work, he was immune to this shit. He could tolerate it longer than I could. For too long, in my opinion, considering Aster was almost naked.

Leroy didn't flinch, didn't make a move to even check the time.

"Aster, I'm going to share a secret with my friends tonight, and then they're going to share a secret with you," Ron said. "Would you like that? Do you like our secrets?"

"Yes, sir," she said, her voice too small and high pitched to be thought sexy.

Yet, as I looked around the room, several men were already reaching for their cocks.

"I knew you would enjoy this, my sweet girl. First, let me give you a hint about the secret they're going to share with you. Remember that feeling I told you about the other day? The one that takes hold of your body with a rush and makes you feel so so good, the best you've ever felt? Remember how I told you I sometimes have that feeling about you when I'm touching myself and you said you wanted me to show you that feeling too one day?"

The girl's cheeks went red as she gave a single nod. I could feel my own face going red with anger, hot and potent and ready to destroy.

"That's not how you respond to me, young lady," he said, his tone suddenly sharp as he flicked the skin on the inside of her thigh.

She flinched at the pain then corrected herself. "Yes, sir. I remember."

"That's a good girl," he purred. "You're about to get your reward."

He turned again to speak to the crowd. "Gentlemen, Aster has never experienced an orgasm. Never been stroked by a grown man's hand. Never been tasted." He let his words sink in, the declaration causing an excited stir in the room. "Who here would like to be the first to show her the ecstasy of pleasure?"

Hands raised, voices shouted out starting bids.

And I pressed the button on the watch.

It had to be enough, with the testimony of myself and Leroy and the girl, and there was no way I could let any of those men touch her like that. No way in hell. I'd do whatever I had to in order to keep their dirty paws off of her.

Anxiously, I tapped my foot as the bids increased, willing the police to hurry up and bust in. I'd been warned it would take them a few minutes to approach, but I hadn't realized the minutes would crawl by at an excruciatingly slow speed.

"Aster, love," Ron said when the bidding stalled out. "I need you to take off your panties so my friends can see your pretty pussy. Can you do that?"

"Yes, sir," she said, then began to shimmy out of her pants.

I lurched forward, wanting to stop her, wanting to stand in front and hide her from lecherous eyes.

An arm shot forward, barring me from going any closer.

"I hit the button," Leroy whispered. I hadn't even noticed him come over.

"I did too," I admitted. But the cops still weren't here and Aster was now naked with the auction at a stall.

"Going once," Ron said. "Twice."

I did the only thing I could do. "Seventy-five thousand," I shouted, not sure if we were bidding in dollars or pounds. It didn't matter. The money would never be paid. This was a stall tactic and nothing more.

"Eighty," came the man with the previous high bid.

"Eighty-five," I said.

"Ninety."

"One hundred." The two of us were in a bidding war, which was fine with me. I'd match him as high as he'd go.

"Gentlemen, please remember," Ron said. "If you don't get to go first, you can certainly be second. Do I hear higher than one hundred thousand?"

The other man was silent.

"Going once, twice." The obligatory pause. "Sold to Edward Fasbender."

"Keep stalling," Leroy whispered with a smile, clapping his hand across my back as though to congratulate me.

Jesus, where were they?

Somehow refraining from looking over my shoulder, I walked forward, taking my time to engage with each debauched man who had a lewd comment to share as I approached the stage. It took everything in my power not to cover Aster up when I got there. I did manage to stand in front of her, blocking the crowd's view while I spoke to Ron.

"Should I write the check first?" I reached into my jacket pocket, looking for my billfold.

"I think you're good for it," Ron said, his face flushed with exhilaration. "Let's not waste time with the housekeeping. I'm ready for the show."

All the ways I wanted to hurt him flashed through my mind in the space of a few seconds. I wanted to take his eyes out with my teeth. I wanted to rip his intestines out through his arsehole. I wanted to break his erect cock with my hands then press on his balls with the heel of my foot.

I smiled at him. There was a commotion out in the hallway, and I knew what was coming next. "I'm ready for the show, too," I said. "I think it's going to be a good one."

Then, right on cue, the task force was upon us, shouting out commands, guns pointed. I turned to Aster, handing her the discarded pants and helping her cover up before passing her off to Felisha who was designated to take her away.

By the time my attention went back to Ron, he was on the floor, his hands pinned behind his back while an officer cuffed him. I was seconds from being cuffed as well—I'd been warned that Leroy and I might even be booked before Dominic could get to us. I could spend the night in jail, for all I cared. Nothing would take away the glory of this moment, of watching Ron's horrified face while he was read his rights.

It was over.

It was finally over, and I was higher than I'd ever been. This moment was karma and justice and, yes, it was revenge, but it was the most deserved of any I'd ever administered, and the power that stirred in me was beyond intoxicating. I was no longer human—I was a god, doling out Ron's reckoning as though I were sitting on a throne on Judgment Day.

"This is for what you did to my father's company," I told Ron, making sure that he knew without a doubt that this came from me. "But most of all, this is for Celia."

His horror turned to outrage, the look of murder sharp in his eyes.

And I laughed, amusement bubbling up through me like champagne despite my arms being wrenched behind my back and slapped with metal cuffs. I was untouchable. I was without bounds. I was on cloud nine.

It was over, and deep in the marrow of my bones, I knew it had only just begun.

TWENTY-THREE

CELIA

"YOU'RE STILL UP?" Edward asked as he walked into the bedroom just after four in the morning. He'd entered the house so stealthily, I hadn't even heard him moving around downstairs.

I sprang up from the armchair I'd been sitting in. "Of course I'm still up! Did you think I'd be able to sleep?"

Honestly, I hadn't even tried. I'd taken a shower and changed into loungewear simply so that I could appear to have made the effort, knowing Edward wouldn't want me staying up all night, but I never even made it under the covers. There was every chance he'd want to punish me for it, and I didn't care one bit.

It wasn't punishment on his mind, though, when he strode to me and wrapped me in his arms. He held me like that, his face pressed into the crook of my neck, his embrace so tight it was almost uncomfortable.

I tolerated it for about fifteen seconds.

Then I couldn't stand it. "What happened?" I asked impatiently, needing to know everything.

I tried to push him away so I could see his face when he answered, but he only gripped me harder. "I'll tell you. Just...give me a minute. I need to hold you first."

Understanding rippled through my chest sending goosebumps

down my arms. Whatever had occurred, it had been awful. Of course it had been. I lived with the memories all the time. I was used to them. They were second skin, so embedded in the fabric of my being that I sometimes forgot how brutal they were to look at head-on.

I reached my arms around Edward's back to hold him closer. "Okay," I said soothingly. "I'm here. It's okay."

Time passed without measure while we clung to each other. What he'd witnessed, what I'd discovered about him earlier—none of it meant anything in the moment. It only mattered that we loved each other—in good and bad, in dark and light, within boundaries and beyond. Everything outside of that was insignificant.

But moments only last so long.

And eventually, his grasp loosened, his breathing steadied, and slowly, he untangled himself from my arms.

Then, we were no longer alone, our recent discoveries about each other as present as though they were beings in the room with us.

I hugged my arms over my chest, suddenly cold. "If you can't talk about it right now, I understand. But I need to know—did we get him?"

His chest lifted and fell before he answered. "We got him."

I wanted to believe it too badly. I needed to be sure. "He can't talk his way out of this? You're certain the charge will stick?"

"There are several he'll be facing after tonight. Too many witnesses and evidence against him. He won't get bail. He'll serve time. No doubt in my mind."

Relief threaded through me, overwhelming and euphoric. Not the relief I'd imagined, like a tight muscle suddenly becoming unknit or a heavy weight being taken off my shoulders. More like a release from a tether, like the flight of a butterfly bursting out of its cocoon or the rising of a phoenix from a fire.

Tears sprang to my eyes, the ecstasy so unbelievably potent. I'd never realized how captive I was to my uncle, after all these years. After all the work I'd done to break loose. His freedom had been my tether. Now, with him behind bars, I was finally unleashed. I wouldn't have believed it could make such a difference to my existence.

Edward had known, though. He'd said this would matter, and he was right.

Did that justify all his acts of vengeance?

The thought threatened to ruin the glory of my liberation, and I shoved it away.

"Thank you," I said, focusing on the good. "Thank you for doing this, Edward. I know it was for you, too, but I'm grateful beyond words."

Hands in his pockets, he leaned against the wall, looking so tired that he needed the structure to keep him standing up. "It was primarily for you, bird. Especially after tonight. After what I saw, after knowing what it must have been like..."

He trailed off, and what he didn't say—what he was *unable* to say was more telling than if he'd used words. The party had to be agonizing. Whatever those men had done, whatever Ron had done...

"You don't need to say," I told him. "I know."

"You do. You know."

His gaze locked with mine, so full of sympathy for what I'd gone through in my past. So full of compassion. So intense, I had to look away.

I perched on the arm of the chair, thinking about the terrible things Ron had done that hadn't been done to me. "This was meant to heal you as well. Did it do that? Is it what you wanted it to be?"

"Yes." He nodded. "It's more than I wanted it to be."

This relief was almost as intense as the first. "I'm so glad, Edward. Now we can move on and put all these schemes behind us." Yes, I was grateful he'd done this, but I was equally grateful that his distractions could be done.

But his response put me back on edge. "I don't know about that."

"What do you mean?" I asked, digging my fingernails into the upholstery because I was afraid of the answer.

He smiled suddenly. "We found the fifth man, Celia. All of them were there. The ones who were still alive. We have them all now."

Over the past year, with my help, Edward had discovered the

fourth man who had purchased me at auction had passed away. The fifth we had yet to identify.

Those men were the sources of my nightmares as much as Ron was, if not more. He'd given me whiplash with this change of subject, but I was happy for the turn. "Thank God for that. I can't begin to express how that makes me feel. *Thrilled* isn't the right word. *Relieved* isn't good enough either."

"I understand." He ran a hand over the scruff of his jaw. "To think how long they've been doing this...all those girls who will feel the same way you did when they find out about this bust. This will bring them so much peace."

"And all the girls you've saved from future harm."

"Yes, that." His smile slipped away into solemnness, his gaze laser sharp. "I realized a lot tonight. I realized that these schemes are important. That they make a difference. And I realized that I have power. Because of my class, because I'm a man, because I have the stomach to fight the fights others can't fight. I can't retire from this work now, just because my own list has been completed. There are more battles, and I have a responsibility to wage them."

My mouth went dry as unease settled again on me.

"Okay. That's good. That can be...good." I didn't want to jump to conclusions, but I was sure I knew where he was headed. All I could do was try to steer him another way. "There are others who need help. People who need a social justice warrior. Our resources could be extremely valuable. We can reach out to different organizations, see who needs money and advocates and..."

There were so many ways we could contribute. My mind was spinning with possibilities.

"Yes, we can do those things too. But there are personal battles we still need to get through."

My heart sank. "I don't like where this is going."

He pushed off the wall and crossed to his dresser, undoing a cufflink as he did. "One of the men there tonight—I knew him. He's one of the owners of the company that Genevieve worked for before coming to Accelecom. I can't stomach how close he was to my daughter."

"I don't mean to minimize how that must have made you feel, but I'm sure he wouldn't have done anything to her. If he was there tonight, I'm guessing he has another type."

He set the cufflink down and started on the other. "Yes, I'm sure you're right. But other people's daughters aren't so lucky. It takes the people who are close to the predators to call them out. The reason we don't catch them in their horrible acts is that their friends keep their secrets. We can't be bound to those sorts of obligations. To be better, we have to be willing to expose what needs to be exposed."

"Edward..." Silently, I willed him not to do this, not to turn tonight into a crusade.

"Tell me his name, Celia."

My eyes closed briefly, and in that tiny space of time, I allowed myself to be disappointed. I'd hoped beyond hope that tonight would have taken him another direction. I'd allowed myself to believe he'd drop his pursuit of A's real name, that he'd let it go, that a change of heart might be possible. Finding that it hadn't happened was devastating.

But as soon as I opened my eyes again, I let that emotion pass so I could focus on the one that was necessary, the one that would give me fuel—anger.

"No," I said sharply. Then I stood and brushed past him to go to the closet.

Edward followed on my heels. "He's a predator of a different kind, but he's still a predator. You are well aware of the harm a man like him can do."

I pulled a sundress off a hanger and haphazardly folded it as I spoke. "He's not like that anymore. He's changed, and this is not your responsibility."

"You thought you were the only one with Ron, too. Do you know how many victims he's had since you? You have journals upon journals of games you played with this shithead. You really believe he stopped when your friendship ended? You didn't stop."

I paused to glare at him. "Our friendship ended *because* he stopped. I was the bad guy in that scenario, Edward. *Me*. Not him."

"There's no way you can know that he really stopped." He took off his jacket and threw it on the closet island, ignoring my attempt to shift blame. "Even if he did stop, he has to take responsibility for what he did before. Not only his own victims, but yours as well, because he's the one who taught you. Tell me his name."

"I won't." I threw the dress into my open suitcase then reached for another off a hanger. I'd set the bag out earlier, when I'd realized what Edward had done to his brother-in-law, unsure how I should react to that knowledge.

All night, as I'd paced and waited for word, the luggage had sat untouched. The truth of it was that my husband scared me. But he'd always scared me. If I'd stuck with him before, there was no reason for that fear to suddenly drive me away.

Now, though, I was glad I'd set the case out for a different reason—because I was raging, and I needed space.

Apparently, Edward was too narrowed in on our fight to have noticed. "Stop stalling. You will tell me eventually. Get it over with and tell me now."

I spun toward him. "And then what? What will you do to him when you find out who he is?"

"Whatever is needed." He smirked like he was untouchable. Like he was omnipotent. Like he had every right to rule the universe, and if that meant taking extreme action, so be it.

It was too much power for a man to have. He believed in calling people out? Then, fuck if I didn't call *him* out. "Did you kill Frank?"

Something flashed across his eyes so fast I almost missed it. "What?"

"Don't play dumb. You killed Camilla's husband, didn't you? Do you want to tell me about that?"

"Not particularly," he said cooly, as though detached from the accusation.

His nonchalance flamed my fury. "I'm just supposed to give up A— a man who is a decent, respectable human, no matter what you think— when you still can't tell me all of your secrets?"

"The two aren't related in any way."

"Aren't they?" I threw the outfit I was holding in the suitcase. "Did Camilla know what you were going to do to her husband? I'll bet she didn't have a clue."

"You're guessing." But his tone wasn't so sure.

I pounced on his uncertainty. "She might be thanking you now, and that might justify your actions as far as you're concerned, but it doesn't justify them to me."

"Ah," understanding clicked on his expression. "You found her letter."

I'd given myself away, but it didn't mean I was wrong.

I doubled down. "It makes me sick, Edward. That you could take things that far. You said you had no boundaries, and I knew you didn't, and still I let myself believe you wouldn't do *that*. Now I'm facing the truth, and I'm horrified."

The corner of his mouth lifted into a sneer. "No you're not."

"Yes! I am!"

"You're telling yourself that you are, because you think that's what a decent person should think." He took an intimidating step toward me. "But deep down, you're not horrified at all." And another. "It excites you." He was right in front of me now, bending to my ear. "To know that I would go to those lengths for someone I love. To know the lengths I would go for *you*—you're turned on."

His breath was hot on my skin, and I shivered, not only from his nearness, but because he was right, as always. It did excite me. It did turn me on.

And because of how it made me feel, I was horrified.

This is where he usually won, where I backed down and admitted he knew me better than myself and his ego puffed up a little bit more because of his omniscience.

Not this time. He'd told me he needed me to give him limits, so this would be mine. I wouldn't fold.

"You're full of yourself." I pushed past him to go to the drawer where my underwear was kept.

He chuckled behind me. "Only the truth, Celia, remember?"

"The truth is that you're insane."

"Let's stop with the harsh words, can we?" His voice was softer but still patronizing. "Listen to me. You can't deny how tonight has changed things for you. It's given you an end that you so badly needed. You need this closure with A too. *We* need this closure. Then we can be free of the past, and we can have your baby—"

I cut him off sharply, my finger pointed at him. "You're just as manipulative as anyone else. Hanging a baby in front of me like bait. You think I'm thinking about a baby right now? When I know how dangerous you can be? I'd be just as crazy as you are to even consider it."

Now wasn't the time to tell him what I'd already done. I couldn't even think about it myself.

Edward was silent. I could feel his eyes on my back as I dropped the handful of panties in the suitcase then reached for my shoes.

"You're packing," he said, after a beat. "Where are you going?"

"I'm going to New York. My parents are going to wake up to a scandal. I should be there." I didn't look at him, set more than ever on what I was doing.

"I'd feel better if you were here or Amelie. *Because* of the scandal. You don't need to be wrapped up in this, and you will be if you're with your father."

I slammed my pajama drawer shut, feeling a flicker of satisfaction when it banged. "What I need is to not be told what to do for half a minute. What if what I need is to be away from you?"

"Are you leaving me?" The question came out deep and provoking. Daring me to say that I was.

I didn't want to answer. It wasn't my intention to leave him, but I certainly wanted him to think it was a possibility. I wanted him to be scared that I could. I wanted him to have consequences that would mean something. I wanted him to have to fight—wanted him to *want* to fight—wanted him to want to *change* in order to keep me.

The truth wouldn't push him to that.

"I'm leaving this house," I said, trying to talk my way around it. I pulled two more dresses off hangers and tossed them in my bag. "And I'm leaving without you, so I suppose I am."

"You know that's not what I was asking. You aren't leaving me, Celia." His declaration came out as a growl. "I won't allow that. Especially not over this."

His possessiveness usually made me melt.

Not this time. "Well, I'm not staying. And if you try to keep me hostage again, I can tell you sure as shit that that will be the end of us." I zipped up the suitcase. I didn't have everything I needed, but I was making a statement. Anything I'd missed, I could buy in the States.

I could feel Edward's brain calculating as I grabbed a jacket and slipped on a pair of shoes. I was calculating as well. It was best to leave now and not give him time to find ways to keep me. I didn't have a ticket yet, but I could buy the next flight out at the airport. If he didn't let me have a car, I could call a cab.

When I went to lift the suitcase off the luggage rack, Edward was suddenly there, taking it from me. "Perhaps you're right," he said, his tone even. "Perhaps facing this with your parents will be good for you. But you will come home to me."

I took in a shaky breath and wrenched the suitcase away from him. I was too upset, too pissed, too determined to let him do anything for me at the moment.

When I had it in my hand again, I felt emboldened. "We'll have to see how that goes, won't we?"

Then I spun my back to my husband and marched out of the closet, leaving him, not forever, but for now.

TWENTY-FOUR

EDWARD

THE DOORMAN HUNG up the phone and handed my passport back to me. "You're cleared to go up, Mr. Fasbender. Second elevator. Top floor."

I had held my breath while he'd called up to the Werner penthouse, half afraid I'd be turned away. After four weeks of nothing more than curt texts from my wife, I wasn't sure I'd be welcome at her parents'. Especially showing up unannounced and uninvited.

If Celia would have answered any one of the fifty-plus calls I'd made over the past month, she would have known I was coming. Though, if she'd answered, I wouldn't have had to make the trip at all because I would have demanded she return home. A month apart was far too long to be away from her. God only knew how I'd managed longer absences when she'd been on Amelie.

I was honest enough with myself to realize that I'd been in control of our time apart back then, and that having the power made it easier to endure. The realization only made these last few weeks harder to bear, knowing I was most likely alone in my misery, and that Celia had probably faired the month better than I had.

All that would be behind us soon enough, though I was fully aware I could still be turned away at the door.

I was alone in the elevator. Once it was in motion, I turned to the mirror that lined the back of the car, surveyed my image, and frowned. I looked tired, like a man who had spent the last week in a plane rather than a handful of hours. My outfit was fresh, since I'd changed my clothes when I'd stopped by my hotel, but now I wished I'd chosen something more impressive than a T-shirt and jeans.

I sighed, and shoved a hand through my hair in a fruitless attempt to improve my appearance. When the car stopped, I looked no better than when I'd gotten in, but I took a deep breath to straighten my posture and took the few steps to the Werners' door with confidence.

My knock was answered by an apple-shaped woman dressed in clothes that suggested she was staff, but Madge was just behind her.

"It really is you, Edward," she said, blinking. "I couldn't believe it when the doorman gave me your name." She turned to the other woman. "Lupita, this is Celia's husband, all the way from London. Can you put on some coffee? Better yet, brew some tea."

I nodded in appreciation for the gesture, despite not having any interest in any type of beverage at the moment. Frankly, I was grateful for the hospitality simply because it meant I hadn't been banned from the family.

Lupita and I exchanged greetings, then, as she went off to her assigned task, Madge ushered me into the living room. "I apologize for the unprepared welcome. We should have had you on the door list. Celia didn't say anything about you coming."

My mother-in-law, though not overly warm in countenance, was much more congenial than the last time I'd seen her on my wedding day. The phone calls I had made to her while Celia had been on Amelie seemed to have earned her trust. That hadn't been my primary intention at the time, but it was a definite benefit.

"Celia didn't know I was coming, actually," I said, when she finally let me get a word in. "It's sort of a surprise visit." Having no idea what my wife had told her family about her stay or the state of our marriage, I decided the best move was to act as though everything was normal, avoiding the fact that I hadn't really spoken to her since she'd come to the States.

"How fun. I can't remember the last time Warren did something romantic. I keep telling Celia she snagged a good one. She best be treating you right." Her tone said she was fishing. Either she suspected a rift in our relationship or she just loved any sort of gossip, both seemed likely possibilities.

Whichever it was, I wouldn't give her the satisfaction of confirming anything. "I'm certainly lucky to have found her. Is she here?"

"Oh, yes. Lupita?" She caught the attention of the servant as Lupita set a tea tray on the sideboard. "Could you please tell Celia that Edward is here?"

"My pleasure."

I almost asked if I could just tag along, but I didn't get the chance.

"Edward Fasbender. In my own home. Who would have thought?" Warren Werner entered the room as Lupita left, his expression as smug as mine had likely been when he'd last been a guest at my house.

I bit back a grimace. "Warren. I hadn't expected to see you home this early in the day." I'd specifically chosen to come on a weekday, hoping my father-in-law would be at the office, not that he spent much time there in the last few years. Rumor was that he was running the company on a fifteen-hour work week. What I could do with that company...

The potential was endless.

"Been a bit chaotic at work. Get more done at home these days."

I hadn't failed to notice the reporters as I'd come in the building. I'd had my fair share in London as well. They'd been quite an annoyance back home, but I smiled when I encountered them today, knowing I had a hand in the irritation they must cause Warren.

"I am sorry to hear about your family troubles," I said, attempting sympathy that I hoped read sincere.

"It's been one helluva debacle, I'll tell you that. I got him a good lawyer. But if it turns out he's really done these things, there's nothing I'll be able to do to help him."

I wanted to punch the arsehole.

He was still trying to live in the dark. Had Celia even tried to talk to him again about her own history with Ron?

"It really is a surprise," Madge said, laying it on thick. "We had no idea. Celia used to be close to him when she was little. Never any problems at all."

I knew about the psychology of denial, but never had I seen it so blatantly displayed. I was angered by it, naturally, but some of that anger was directed at myself. I should have thought about what this environment might be like for Celia when she was very likely struggling with her emotions as Ron's crimes were shared all over the media. I should have been there for her. I should have come sooner.

I shouldn't have let her leave London in the first place. Not that she'd given me any choice in the matter.

"I'm sure it's been a difficult time for all of you," I said, resisting the urge to open their eyes to Celia's past horrors. She needed to be the one to talk to them, for her own healing.

"Excuse me," Lupita said, returning to the room. "Celia seems to be napping. Shall I wake her?"

Napping? My wife rarely slept during the day. "She's not unwell, is she?"

Madge made a dismissive gesture with her hand. "No, no. This whole nonsense has been exhausting is all. I think she's had trouble sleeping from it."

Again I kicked myself for having let her be away so long. Though, a small part of me hoped her lack of sleep might mean she'd been as miserable without me as I'd been without her.

Regardless of the cause, I couldn't disturb her, much as I was desperate to see her. I was just about to tell Lupita not to wake her when Warren answered for me.

"Let her sleep. Gives us time to talk."

Fanfuckingtastic.

"Should we go to my office?"

"I'm comfortable right here," I said. "Lupita's just served tea." As little interest I had in being caught in a conversation right now, I had even less interest in discussing business with Warren seated behind his desk. He already held dominion just by being on his turf.

"We can stay here then," he said, disappointment evident in his tone.

The women took that as a cue to disappear, leaving us alone.

Immediately, Warren headed to the minibar. "Can I make you a drink?"

I looked at my watch. It wasn't even two in the afternoon. "A tad early for me, I'm afraid." It was probably best to have a clear head around my former nemesis.

"Yes, I suppose it is," he said. He looked longingly at the tumbler in his hand then set it down. "I guess I don't need one either. Have a seat, will you?"

Another opportunity to hand over power that I refused to cede. "I'd rather stand, if you don't mind. Long flight and all."

"Right, right." He glanced at his armchair, considering. In the end, he stayed standing as well. "I imagine you're pleased with how our joint efforts are panning out in India. I'm quite pleased as well. I'm eager to see what else we can put together. Be a good chance to brainstorm face to face while you're here.

"Oh, and I know all this hullabaloo with my brother has put a damper on our stock prices, but they'll bounce back. I assure you. Ron hasn't worked with Werner in quite some years. We'll rise above his misdeeds, no problem."

I might have been impressed how he could be so laser focused on business despite his family turmoil if I weren't so disgusted with the way he spoke about his brother's sins. As though he'd simply been caught going a few miles over the speed limit. As if his crimes were only menial sins.

He defiled your daughter, I said to him silently as he spouted out potential ideas for future collaboration. *He violated her and assaulted her, and you don't have the balls to confront it.*

He was a coward and an opportunist and deserved to pay for those flaws. I'd hoped his brother's arrest would bring him sufficient turmoil, but seeing how minimally it had affected him, he would need to pay retribution in other ways.

Giving me control of his company would do just fine.

"I have another thought," I said, interrupting whatever he was saying—I hadn't been listening. "Instead of spending our time and energy on a trivial joint venture that ends up being quite meaningless in the big picture, why don't we do something that will have a significant positive effect on both our companies."

He frowned in annoyance, probably because he'd been quite proud of whatever idea he'd been presenting, but he took the bait. "You have something in mind?"

"I do. We should merge."

He visibly drew back. "You can't be serious." He studied me, looking for signs of my sincerity. Apparently finding it, he let out an affronted laugh. "Oh, hell no. You're family now, but you think that makes up for all the obstacles you put up for me in the past? It doesn't."

I smiled, imagining exactly how this would play out, which move I'd make, which move he'd counter with. I could see all the way to checkmate, and fuck if that wasn't thrilling.

"We've both done a quite many misdeeds in our rivalry," I said, using his word from earlier. "And yes, I do believe that should all be water under the bridge. Because we're family."

"That's a lot of nerve you got. This the real reason you married my daughter?"

"It is not." Eh, it was mostly true. "I love your daughter very much. Speaking of Celia, it's really her decision what happens next at Werner, isn't it? It's because of my respect for you that I'm going this route instead."

My wife had been right in her accusations—I was manipulative. Maybe even more so than any other man in her life. Warren still believed the majority shares were in the family, that Celia had them in her name, and though she'd signed over her voting power to him, that she had the potential to override any of his decisions if she took her vote back.

I was fully committed to exploiting that fact.

His face blanched, then he scowled. "Those shares aren't really hers. If I had to take it to court, I'd win."

I wasn't so sure of that. "No need to bring up talk of lawsuits. Celia has no plans to take advantage of those shares you gifted her, and neither am I planning to encourage it. If you took that as a threat, it's not what I intended."

No, it was exactly what I'd intended.

"I was merely reminding you the reasons you signed over those shares to Celia. Because you wanted to provide for your only child. Because you wanted the Werner legacy to remain in the family."

"Of course that's why I gave them to her," he said.

Which was an utter lie. He'd had thoughts of tax evasion in his mind when he'd done it, and nothing else, but I was purposefully playing to his sense of fatherly duty.

"You mentioned the current state of your stocks. I'm sure, as you said, they will recover, but what if they don't? Merging with a company that has a considerable share of markets Werner has no access to would give a meaningful boost to the bottom line. Not only will your stocks go up again, they'll skyrocket. Isn't that the legacy you want to leave your daughter?"

Warren glowered at me in silence. He was caught and he knew it. Zugzwang. Warren wasn't ready to trust me with his company, but it was the right move. Not only for his company, but for his daughter. To prove he cared about her. He'd failed her so completely in other ways. This was his chance to show she was his priority.

"Sorry to interrupt," Lupita said.

I waited until Warren's gaze moved to her before I moved mine. "What is it?" he snapped.

"Celia's awake now. I told her you were here, Mr. Fasbender, and she asked that you meet her in the conservatory. I can take you there when you're ready."

"Splendid. I'm ready now." I patted Warren on the arm, patronizing him purposefully. "No rush to decide right this minute. Sooner the better, though, probably, considering how far Werner has dropped. Thirteen points just today, wasn't it? Yikes."

Before he could say anything else I turned back to Lupita. "Where's the conservatory?"

It was tempting to feel self-righteous as I followed the servant down the hall. Warren would concede eventually. Unfortunately his motives were most definitely his own pocketbook and egotistical desire to have his company thrive, but he'd say it was for Celia, and that would mean something to her despite the lie.

Werner Media completely vanished from my mind, though, the minute I was out of Warren's sight. Celia was the only thing I was thinking about now. How close she was, how soon she'd be back in my arms.

My whole being vibrated in anticipation.

"Through there," Lupita said when we reached a set of open double doors.

I nodded appreciatively then stepped over the threshold, halting as soon as I did. Because there she was, standing at the window, looking out over Central Park, her hair tied in a messy knot, her skin pink from too much sun, her lips gripped in a straight line.

God, she was magnificent.

I could hardly breathe in the splendor of her presence.

She must have sensed my stare. I hadn't moved or made a sound when she turned and caught me looking at her.

Her eyes lit up—or I imagined they had, because I very much wished that she'd be excited to see me—and her chin quivered, as though she were about to speak, but she remained silent.

She remained on the opposite side of the room, as well, which was disheartening when I wanted so badly to touch her.

For that matter, I was still standing at the door. There was a chasm between us, wide and yawning, and I knew I had to be the one to find a way across.

But I was stubborn too. Stubborn in my belief that I knew what was best for her, and as much as I wanted us reunited, it couldn't be by surrendering my side of this fight.

Which left only the truth to close the gap.

"I am well aware that there are more than my feelings that matter in this, but for what it's worth, I've been a wreck without you." My chest shuddered with the act of being vulnerable, but I pushed on. "I don't sleep well without you in my bed. It's extremely hard to focus on anything at all, even the crossword, and my stomach is in constant knots when I'm not able to look after your care."

I took a timid step forward, approaching her as a hunter would approach his prey, despite not knowing who really held the power in the room. Was it her? Was it me? It was impossible to tell. "I know we both feel strongly about our current positions. You know who I am. You *know*, and I'm certain you don't expect me to be a different man. Likewise, I'm not asking you to lose any ground you've made by coming here. I'm simply asking if we might find a way to love each other past our differences. I'm better at your side, and I believe you're better at mine."

I waited for her to say something, ready to go to her as soon as she gave the sign. The seconds passed loudly, the ticking of the room's grandfather clock deafening in the silence. As I watched, her chest lifted, her mouth opened. Then it shut again without having said a word.

My pulse sped up as my heart plummeted in my chest. Was this it? Was it over between us? What would I have to do to keep her?

"Bird...say something. Please."

She did then, her voice carrying loud and clear across the invisible gorge, bringing me two words I'd never thought I'd hear a woman speak to me again. "I'm pregnant."

Celia and Edward's story concludes in
Rising: Slay Four. But before you go on, you should
consider pausing this story to make sure you're caught up
with Genevieve's situation first.

The Fasbenders are in the U.S.! And Celia and Edward aren't the only pair of lovebirds.

Chandler by Laurelin Paige
Available Now

I'm good in a boardroom, but I'm better in the bedroom. Much better. I can charm the skirt off any woman in one encounter. I'll even give her an orgasm before I put her in a cab. Or three. No more or she'll start making plans for the future and I'm not into that.

Or I wasn't until Genevieve Fasbender. She's the first woman in five years that I want to spend the whole night with. And she's the first woman who's told me I'm not what she wants in a lover, even after multiple O's. She's brash and bold and stubborn as hell, and she doesn't believe it's possible to satisfy her.

But I'm up for the challenge.

And after an incident in my brother's office closet—a downright dirty incident—I think I'm just the guy to deliver.

Genevieve Fasbender will never know what's coming.

"A sexy, wild, and red-hot romance. I LOVE this man!" - Lauren Blakely, #1 NYT Bestselling Author

"SPOILER: You're going to fall in love with him." - CD Reiss, NYT Bestselling Author

NOTE: Chandler overlaps with Rising, Slay Four. Now is a perfect time to read it if you can't wait for a glimpse of Edward and Celia.

Get Chandler now!

Need help recovering from Revenge?
Join the Recovery Room! See you there!

**Order signed copies of this book and merchandise
related to Slay on my website or listen to it on audio,
narrated by
Elena Wolfe and Shane East.**

*You can find a timeline of events related to the Fixed series at the back of
the book.*

RISING: SLAY FOUR

The stakes have never been higher, and she's full of the devil.

Edward Fasbender is my husband.

Together, we brought down powerful men.

Now we have a chance to start over. To be the family neither of us ever had, to leave the past in the past where it belongs. Edward has a choice to make.

It will decide if we fall into the flames--or rise together.

For Amy "Vox" Libris,
for always telling me my words are a blessing,
especially when I fear they're a burden.

PROLOGUE

FIVE MONTHS BEFORE THE END OF REVENGE, SLAY THREE: CELIA

EDWARD WRAPPED his arms around me from behind, complicating my attempt to tie the belt of my robe.

"For someone who's spent the better part of a week on a pleasure island, you're awfully handsy." I tilted my neck, encouraging him to nuzzle in.

He nibbled along the skin I'd exposed. "A week with sex happening all around me while I slept alone in my cabin. You better believe I came home greedy."

"Hurry up with your shower then so you can have your way with me."

"You sure you won't join me?" He was already undressed except for his boxer briefs, and the heat of his skin at my back as well as the hardness of his body made my belly curl low with desire.

But there was a buzz in my head, and I needed a few minutes to sort my thoughts before abandoning them entirely to wanton ways. "If I join you, you'll never get clean," I said, nudging him to the task with the promise of what would come after.

"That's very likely true, bird." He turned me into him and kissed me deeply, making his own promises before pulling away abruptly. "I'll hurry."

"I'll be here."

I wandered over to the sink to begin my nighttime routine of makeup removal and moisturizing, eyeing my husband in the mirror as he stripped from his underwear and stepped into the glass walk-in shower. He was magnificent to look at, and I admired the view with full attention until the whir of my thoughts grew too distracting, and I gave myself into them instead.

Edward had said he'd come home greedy. Considering how highly he prized honesty, it was almost strange to hear the lie cased in the statement. Not that it was a bold-faced falsehood, and not that I didn't understand his reasons. It was for me. He was romanticizing the trip on my account. He didn't want me to have to think too hard about why he'd really been there, about the perversions he'd had to interact with. Didn't want me to think about my uncle Ron and the sick things men like him were into.

Grateful as I was for Edward's desire to protect me, the shield only worked on the surface. It allowed me not to have to talk about it. I could avoid the questions that pressed like a heated iron at the edges of my mind, wanting to straighten the wrinkles of my imagination that were surely as terrible as the truth.

But not talking about it meant the acrid thoughts remained inside me, seeds of poison ivy that would grow if given the right soil.

Old habits dying hard, my instinct was to make that ground infertile, to close off. To become numb. I'd been working through the things my uncle had done to me, but as much as I trimmed and hacked at the memories, I could never cut them away completely. The pips remained inside me, sprouting unexpectedly in the sun, and the urge to withdraw would shiver through me.

It was a funny thing, the fight or flight response. Most people who knew me would probably say hands down that I was a fighter in every instance. I would have said the same before Edward. It was ironic that he showed me the error in that presumption considering how often he drew me to fight with him. I certainly did deal with many threats with a bulled head and sharp tongue.

The truth, though, was that when the threat was severe, when it brought on intense levels of emotional pain, I didn't fight at all. I flew. Like the bird that he'd always seen me to be, I abandoned feeling and took flight to a sky of gray and numb. It had been a practiced skill, one I hadn't been very good at on my own. I could still clearly remember the day I'd begged my friend to be my mentor, when the baby boy inside me had decided to make a much too early appearance to the world. I'd been nearly twenty weeks along, one day later and his death would have been called a stillbirth instead of a miscarriage. Whatever the appropriate term, the result had been the same—my womb had once been full of life and with that life gone, it was full of pain.

"*Teach me, Hudson,*" I'd said when I'd woken from sorrowful dreaming to find him at my hospital bedside. Even the burn of the IV at the back of my hand was intolerable, and his games—experiments, as he called them—beckoned to me like the whispered praise of a magic healing elixir. "*Experiment with me.*"

"*What? Why would you want me to...? I'm not experimenting on people I know anymore.*"

"*Not on me,*" I'd corrected. "*With me. I want to learn how you do it. Teach me.*"

"*No. That's absurd.*"

"*Please.*" It wasn't just in the wording that I begged. My entire body leaned forward in supplication, as though he were my messiah. The only one who could release me from my heartache.

"*No.*" But his features had furrowed as if he was thinking about it. "*Why?*"

"*Because I want to be like that.*"

"*Like what?*"

"*Like someone who doesn't feel.*"

He'd had mercy on me then, and he'd taught me. He'd taught me so well that not feeling had become second nature. And even after Edward had tethered me with an invisible collar, forcing me to stay grounded when the pain grew too great, the impulse still niggled inside me, and I had to take deep breaths and center myself so that I wouldn't thrash against my leash, longing for the gray, numb sky.

Tonight, the urge was especially strong, a driving beat pulsing in my blood, increasing in volume as if to drown out the myriad of memories accompanied with Ron's grooming. The swing, the baths, the first orgasms. The attention from strangers, their eyes, their hands, their mouths. The look of disgust and disbelief when I tried to tell my father. My wings fluttered. The wind called.

Deep breath in.

Deep breath out.

Feel the feeling, find the anchor, stay on the ground.

I dropped the dirty wet wipe and my hands went instinctively to my belly, ensuring my breaths were full and from my diaphragm. The pain washed in like the tide overtaking a dry stretch of land, but then it slowly began to pull out again, and a newly familiar desire was left on the shore. The desire to replace emotion with emotion. To relieve the fullness of anguish with the fullness of joy.

I wanted a baby.

And Edward would allow it, but only on his terms, terms that I was unable to concede to. He believed too deeply that unburdening my sorrow required balancing karma. I supposed I did too, in a way, we just had different ideas of how to go about that balancing. He wanted to make the people who'd hurt me in the past suffer for their sins. I wanted to look forward and replace the pains of the past with happiness in the future.

We'd fight about it again, he'd promised me that. After Ron was taken care of, which would happen soon if all went right. But Edward fought dirty. He fought dirty, and he always won, so this time I promised myself to fight just as dirty in return. I thought of it as an act of love, really. He needed the challenge from me, and I wanted to be able to deliver.

So when he got out of the shower and wrapped a towel around himself, I set the trap. "You have the nurse practitioner on the schedule to come by Tuesday for my birth control, but I have a meeting with a vendor at the same time that can't be changed."

Edward had been arranging my shots for me since I'd been living on Amelie, when I'd been his prisoner. He took care of me in many ways now as he did then, because he liked it and because I liked it, so I didn't automatically believe that he continued this particular arrangement because he didn't trust me.

I was about to find out for sure.

"No problem. I'll have Charlotte get it rescheduled."

"Thank you." I waited a beat then turned toward him. "On second thought, could Charlotte make me an appointment for a full gynecological exam in the office instead? I'm due for a pap smear and all of that. The doctor can renew my birth control at the same time."

He raised an eyebrow, and for half a second, I thought he suspected. "I didn't realize the time had flown so quickly. Of course you're due for your yearly. I'll get that scheduled immediately. Sorry I hadn't thought of it myself."

I turned back to the mirror and smiled at his reflection behind me. "You would have," I assured him. "Don't beat yourself up. Let me have the rare victory of thinking of it before you."

Again he wrapped himself around me, the scent of his body wash making me weak in the knees. "Yes. Have your victory. I do know how you need those wins."

I appreciated that he could laugh at himself, and I chuckled with him, but the humor I felt was for an entirely different win. Because, while I had every intention of going to that doctor's visit, I knew that changing the scope of the visit would make it much easier to hide the fact that I had no intention of getting that shot.

I'd have my baby just as Edward had had his revenge. It would be on my terms. No obstacle too great to overcome, even if the obstacle was my husband. I knew that once I was pregnant, he'd come around. The same way he'd ruined me, I'd ruin him and we'd both be better for it.

This time when I met his eyes in the mirror, the urge to fly felt different, as though my wings were unfurling and readying to fly *toward* something, not away. The sky above me wasn't gray or numb—it was sunlit and cloud-free. I was no longer Edward's little bird. I was a phoenix, and I was rising.

ONE

EDWARD

A SUIT-CLAD arm shot out to hold the lift doors open as I approached.

"Thank you," I said in earnest as I slid inside the crowded car, the words out of my mouth before I had time to assess who the saintly gentleman had been. "Ah, Pierce. Edward Fasbender. It's a pleasure to finally have a real meeting."

I held out my hand to Hudson Pierce, the CEO of Pierce Industries. We'd seen each other in passing before, maybe even shaken hands once or twice, but we'd never really spoken. We had plenty to speak about, though, which was why I'd made the four o'clock appointment with him.

Subtly, I glanced at my wristwatch. Was I running early?

Three forty-seven. Perhaps he was just returning from lunch.

Hudson smiled as he took my hand, an expression that didn't reach his eyes. Not because he was cold, necessarily, but because he was guarded. The way men in his position had to be in order to survive the dog-eat-dog environment they existed in. I imagined my own expression was as severe as his.

"Yes, I'm glad for this opportunity as well," he said. "I must admit, though, if I'd known it were you I was holding the elevator for, I might have let the doors close. By the time you arrived upstairs I would have been safely in my office, and you would have had no idea how late I was running this afternoon."

Stoic but had the ability to laugh at himself. I appreciated that in a rival, if that's what he was to be. Hopefully, I'd know by the time I left his office later this afternoon.

"I'll make a stop at the little boy's room, if you'd like. Pretend I never saw you."

"Ah, but that would never do. You and I would both know the truth. I have to accept that my first impression has already been made. Excuse me for a moment." He pulled out his mobile and hit a contact that must be called frequently since it was at the top of the list. "Patricia, it's me. I'm headed up now. Edward Fasbender is with me. Would you make sure the coffee is fresh and…" He looked to me, an eyebrow lifted in question. "That there's water for tea?"

I shook my head. "Coffee's fine."

"Nevermind the tea. See you shortly."

The doors opened and half the people in the car emptied out before they shut again.

"It hasn't been a bad impression," I said when Hudson had pocketed his mobile again, moving to occupy the space that had opened up. "You did hold the door to the lift for a stranger."

"I'm surprised I had enough sense about me for even that." Hudson's features relaxed, and now I glimpsed the man underneath the mask. There were shadows under his eyes, his lids appeared heavy. "Twins," he said in explanation. "I went home for lunch, hoping to sneak in a nap. They're only a month old, and I haven't timed it for sure, but I don't think a full hour passes that they both stay asleep. It's why I sent my brother in my place to your gala on Friday. I would have been a zombie if I'd gone myself."

Being a parent with a newborn brought an exhaustion like no other. I'd been spared much with Hagan and Genevieve. Because I'd been the type of asshole father who left the upbringing to my wife and the children's nurse. Marion's insistence on separate rooms only helped feed into my detached style of parenting—I didn't have to be disturbed by the sound of a baby's cries over a monitor.

Still, I hadn't been immune to the fatigue. It had spread through the household like a contagion. I remembered it vividly, lethargy setting into my body at the thought like muscle memory.

"You didn't miss anything at the gala." The charity auction had been merely a diversion for Celia, something to keep her mind off the press about her uncle's arrest as well as something that would show her name in a good light. "I did see Chandler at a distance. I didn't get a chance to speak with him directly, but my daughter connected with him. I suspect it was more of a social conversation than anything pertinent."

"Knowing my brother, I'd suspect that as well."

I wasn't sure how I felt about Genevieve hitting it off with a Pierce, but at least it was something to keep her preoccupied. Hagan had pressured me to bring her to the States as we aggressively pursued Werner, and though I'd conceded, it had been reluctantly. Perhaps she'd be focused on this boy now instead of trying to involve herself in what would likely eventually become cutthroat business.

"As for the lack of sleep, I can only imagine what that must be like," I offered in sincere sympathy. "Congratulations and consolation. My wife is pregnant, and I've been dreading the coming exhaustion since she told me of her condition. I'm much relieved at the moment that we only have a single baby on the way. I don't think I have the stamina for more."

"You find it when you need it. Even if it has you running late to the office on a Wednesday." His back straightened and the weariness disappeared from his features, tucked behind his mask of professionalism once again. "Please accept my congratulations to you as well. I'd only just heard that Celia was expecting."

I surmised what that news must have meant to Hudson. He'd claimed to be the father the first time she'd conceived, hiding that it had actually been *his* father who'd knocked up my wife. He'd likely been relieved when she'd lost the baby since it had alleviated him of his duty, but if he was a decent man—as I supposed he was—he'd probably felt guilty for feeling that way when the loss had hurt Celia so terribly.

The news that she was now pregnant must have lessened that guilt if not eliminated it all together.

It would have been better for negotiation if he still carried that shame, but there was nothing I could do about that. "Yes, she's four months along now."

"She must be thrilled."

"We both are," I lied. Because that's what people were supposed to say in these situations. It was uncouth to grumble about the coming of a baby. And it showed weakness to allow anyone to believe I wasn't on board with it. Men with power such as I had didn't have unwanted children. They got rid of them, or they got rid of the women who conceived them.

Truthfully, I didn't want to get rid of either.

Celia was mine for all of eternity, despite the contention that wound around us concerning her pregnancy.

And it wasn't her baby that was unwanted, really. It was all the rest of it. The trickery. The deceit. The secrets she refused to share. The clipped conversations between us. The sliver of cold space that separated our bodies every night in our bed at the Park Hyatt.

The discord in my marriage leaked into every aspect of my being. I'd become meaner over the weeks. Brutal. Defiant. She argued to go home to London as soon as the charity was over. I insisted we stay in the States. She refused to give me what I needed to continue seeking vengeance for the past. I refused to drop the pursuit. She wanted to let control of her father's company go to whomever Hudson Pierce chose to lead it. I wanted to be the one he chose.

She'd got to have her baby. I should get to have what I desired as well. I was determined that I would.

Another stop of the lift and when the doors shut this time, it was only me and Hudson in the car. Fueled by thoughts of Celia, by the dissension coursing through my veins, I turned to my would-be nemesis. "I'm not going to waste either of our time here, Hudson. You know from my emails what I'm after. It should be an obvious choice to put the company in my hands."

He opened his mouth and then closed it, and I could practically see the gears spinning in his head, trying to decide what excuse to give me, perhaps. Trying to guess what I knew about his possession of the majority stocks.

He was aware that I knew he owned them and that Warren Werner was in the dark. I'd made that clear in my correspondence so far. I hadn't yet admitted that I knew *why* he owned them. I was curious whether or not he'd bring it up himself. Throwing accusations at a man's wife took guts, but it was also a dirty move. If he chose to expose my wife's manipulative past, I might be impressed. I'd be equally impressed if he continued to step around it. Whichever choice he made would tell me a lot about the man. Would tell me what I was up against. Would help me prepare my own weapons.

"I have great respect for Warren and the company he ran," Hudson said finally, all traces of informality gone from his tone. He was pure businessman now. Focused and sharp. "It would be quite desirable to see Werner Media continue in that direction, and I understand the attraction of keeping it in the hands of family. I am not, however, yet convinced that your motives are as noble."

Impressive. Without mentioning Celia at all, he'd managed to hint at her possible intentions while throwing the accusations at me instead. He was smooth, that was certain.

"Then I need to do a better job of persuading you of my business plan." The business plan wasn't the problem. In our previous communications, I'd given him a five-year and ten-year prospective. He'd returned with a number of aims he wanted to see added. Some of them had been ridiculous asks, but I'd implemented them all. It was a solid plan.

What Hudson needed would have to be given off-page. Behind closed doors. Just between the two of us.

The lift opened, and I followed him across the hallway to a waiting area with frosted glass walls. He paused to greet the woman behind the desk.

"Coffee's still brewing," she said. "I'll bring it in shortly."

"Thank you, Patricia." He turned back to me, gesturing for me to follow as he opened the solid wood doors revealing a luxurious office space behind. "It's not what you intend to do with Werner Media that I'm concerned with," he said over his shoulder. "It's how that will affect Pierce Industries."

Rather than lead me to the comfy seating area, he sat in the over-sized chair behind a magnificent wooden desk, staking a clear position as king. He held all the power here, and he wanted to be certain I knew it.

It made my insides seethe with envy. I rarely encountered a situation where I wasn't the one sitting on the throne. Even if he gave me the reins to Werner, we still wouldn't be on equal footing. He'd still have the majority shares.

But I'd get those too. One day. Somehow. I had patience.

For now, I'd have to accept the inferior role. I sat in the chair facing him. "I can assure you, Accelecom has no interest in taking any predatory action against your company. I've conceded to every one of your conditions, Hudson. Our position should be quite obvious."

He eyed a messy pile of papers on his desk and his brow creased, as if he were annoyed that any of his belongings would fall out of complete order. He straightened them, his gaze quickly scanning the room lingering on a spot behind me.

I followed his line of vision to land on an ordinary coat cupboard. When I turned back to him, his attention was focused on me, whatever had distracted him apparently gone from his mind.

I took that as a cue to press on. "What more can we do to prove good faith?"

He steepled his hands together, leaning back in his chair, and considered.

My jaw twitched, and I realized it was time to make a choice. I could sit here and listen to a list of unfounded demands, or I could cut to the chase.

"Let me be candid," I said, leaning forward. "I'm well aware of how the Werner shares ended up in your hands. Celia told me."

His eyes widened ever so slightly. "She told you everything?"

"She did." On the subject of Hudson Pierce, at least, she'd been forthright.

But there was someone else from her past that she'd kept secret, a mysterious man she'd referred to as A in her diaries. A man who had used her to play devious games on the innocent simply for entertainment. A man who had taught her to be manipulative and cold and unfeeling.

He wasn't convinced. "I'm curious what exactly she said."

He was being cautious, but I could understand if there was a bit of curiosity as well. I also was curious about his relationship with my wife. I would love to hear his version of events. Whether or not he'd justify the way he'd led her on before sleeping with her friend. If he'd take full blame for her running to his father's bed or if he'd pass that blame to her. I especially wondered how he'd discovered about the games she played, and wondered what specific reasons he had for thinking he needed insurance to keep her from coming after him and his family.

Honestly, I wouldn't have been surprised to find that his side of the story painted Celia in a much harsher light. I knew what kind of woman she'd been. I knew what kind of woman she still could be if not nurtured and cared for.

Guilt stabbed between my ribs. I hadn't done a good job of caring for her lately. There had been too much hostility between us, and the will to nurture her had been eaten in the flames of that fire.

I'd shirked some of my duties, it was true. But I was here because of her. For her. I focused on that, stepping carefully as I spoke of her past misdeeds. "She's told me about the ways she's preyed on innocent people around her. It's clear that she attempted to play you as well, and that you required leverage to protect yourself. It might not mean anything coming from me, but I can assure you that she isn't the same person she was when you had to make that move, and I'm certainly not a man who would allow his wife to behave like that in the future."

He scrutinized me with narrow eyes, his expression calculating the risk of trusting me. "You're sure that she isn't currently playing you?"

She had played me in the end, hadn't she? Though forcing a baby on me should hardly count. It was par for the way we negotiated with each other. The games between us would likely be deemed as sick to anyone on the outside.

None of that was relevant to the conversation. "I'm certain that any way she *is* playing me has been welcomed and deserved. Point being, she has no interest in playing *you*."

"But you see how I can't take that on blind faith. You could be in on the game along with her. Or you could be a man blinded by a pretty woman. The Celia I knew would never stand for a man 'allowing' her to do anything. It's suspicious that you believe you have such complete control of a woman I've always thought of as a dragon."

"Dragon?" I let out a gruff laugh. She'd tried to convince me of the same and failed. "Hardly. She's a little bird. Menacing only if you're an unearthed worm."

I sobered. "However, I do understand your plight. Which, I believe, gives you even more reason to want me in the lead position at Werner. You lose your power over her as soon as Warren steps down. If I were to replace him, your thumb would be on her once again."

He nodded an acknowledgment. "Or the two of you have figured out a way to ruin me from the inside out. I have a lot of money wrapped up in Werner. It behooves me to see it do well."

"Please. Even if I ran Werner into the ground, it wouldn't ruin you. Pierce Industries is as solid as they come."

"Unless you discover a way to bring both companies down."

It wasn't on my agenda, but if it were necessary, I would do just that. It was possible he might see that in my eyes, which I wasn't sure was a bad thing. If he thought I was against him, he had even more reason to keep me in his sights. *Keep your enemies closer* and all that.

I let silence be my response, allowing it to fully settle before I spoke again. "There's no way anything I can say will persuade you one way or another. All I can do is offer you a solid business plan and give you my assurance that I want to see Werner succeed, and that I am fully convinced that with the power of Accelecom behind it, I can take Werner to levels you've never even imagined."

It took a beat, but eventually he smiled. "I do like that sort of certainty in my CEOs," he admitted. "But I'm going to need more time to make a decision. You're not the only candidate I'm looking at."

I refused to let any disappointment show on my face. It was standard phrasing. It didn't mean that I hadn't gained any ground. It didn't mean I didn't have him exactly where I wanted him.

He confirmed my confidence a second later. "You do currently have a nice lead, however. So let's discuss next level. The prospects you've shown me are ambitious compared to the ones I've had drawn up myself. I'd like to look closer at the discrepancies."

"You can only reach as high as you dream," I said smugly. "I'd be happy to justify the differences. It would please me to show you where your team has been small-minded."

"I would find that quite interesting. Do you mind?" He stood, signaling me to stand as well. "My chief financial advisor can show you the projections she's put together. Her office is just down the hall. Let me walk you over."

I followed behind him like the moon in the shadow of the sun. On the surface, he may have appeared to have the superior position. But the sun only ruled the day. Everyone knew when the night dawned, the throne belonged to the moon.

TWO

CELIA

I STEPPED out of the sunk-in tub and grabbed a towel from the oversized bathroom counter. While I greatly missed the house in London, the Presidential suite at the Park Hyatt was nothing to frown at. We'd been here for more than two months, and I was already addicted to the luxury amenities and sleek modern design.

I'd give it all up, though, in a heartbeat, to have things go back to the way they'd been in England.

No, that wasn't true. I wouldn't give it *all* up.

I put my hand over the bump that had just begun to protrude noticeably from my abdomen. I couldn't feel my baby move yet, but I was always aware of her presence. She'd changed my body completely, high-jacked it like she was an alien invader. Besides the constant exhaustion and the intermittent nausea, nothing about who I was felt the same. Food tasted different. The taste *in my mouth* was different. The temperature of my body was different. My head spun differently. My muscles and joints ached differently.

I hated it, and I loved it. I'd already decided one would be enough because of how miserable the ordeal of pregnancy was. I also already knew without any doubt that she would be worth it.

"Totally worth it," I told my belly. I imagined she found the sound of my voice comforting, so I spoke to her often like this. Or maybe I spoke to her because I knew she couldn't respond, unlike my husband who had taken to spending long stretches of our time together in silence. There was a sexiness about the way he brooded, as there was about almost everything he did, but knowing I was to blame for his taciturnity put a damper on the visual benefits.

Would he be like this forever? Distant and withdrawn. He didn't pick out my clothes anymore, didn't dictate my days. Didn't command me or boss me around.

And I resented him for it, which was ridiculous since almost everything I did was meant to push him away. If he tried to care for me like he once had, I'd most likely argue or ignore him outright, and since he surely knew that—because didn't he always know everything?—why would he make an effort to connect?

I didn't even know why I pushed him away anymore. At first, I'd been angry. He demanded to know the identity of the man who'd taught me The Game, and if it were simply because he wanted me to share everything with him, I would have told him long ago. But it was because of his stupid quest for vengeance. A quest that had come to mean so much to him that he'd lost sight of the person he claimed to be looking after. Me.

And that felt worse than the anger. That hurt.

Add to that his secrets—what he'd done to Camilla's husband, the lengths he'd gone to for other acts of justice. I was scared on top of hurt. Not for what he'd do to me, but what he could do—what he *would* do—to Hudson. To my father. To himself.

But then I found out I was pregnant, and my anger and hurt and fear became centered around something else. Some*one* else. Around her, the child living inside me that I was certain was a girl despite not having confirmation yet. She was everything, and I'd hoped beyond hope that she would be everything to Edward too.

And for a moment, when he'd walked into my parents' apartment and declared his love to me in such beautiful words, I really believed it was possible everything would work out. *"I'm better at your side,"* he'd said, *"and I believe you're better at mine."*

But then I told him I was pregnant.

His response to that announcement stung so sharply it erased anything he'd said before that.

"How is that possible?" he'd asked.

"No birth control is infallible."

"You didn't get your shot."

I hadn't expected him to put the pieces together, but when he did, I couldn't lie. So I'd said nothing.

And he'd walked out of the room.

We hadn't recovered from that. Nine weeks later and we lived in a shell of the marriage we'd once occupied. I didn't know how to go back to what we were, and maybe he didn't either. Point was, neither of us made much effort to try. We'd fallen into a wretched cycle—he wouldn't reach out so I'd do something to make sure he didn't reach out the next time, and sure enough he wouldn't, and then I'd do something else to make sure he wouldn't again.

We'd been good lovers. I truly believed that. But we'd been even better rivals, and we fell easily into that well-worn groove.

"He'll come around," I said, as much for my sake as my baby's. "He loves us too much to stay away forever."

Please, oh, please let that be true.

With a sigh, I toweled off, staring at the pile of panties and tank I'd brought into the bathroom with me. It had become a standard bedtime outfit for me—not purposefully provocative, yet still revealing in a way that caught Edward's eye. He tried not to notice, I could visibly see him trying, but he always did. His eyes would skate over the bare skin of my legs, lingering at the V of white cotton at the top of my thighs.

It was a passive-aggressive move on my part, wearing what I knew would grab his attention when we were barely on speaking terms. It hadn't yet worked in my favor though. No matter that he couldn't resist looking, he somehow was still able to resist the need to touch.

He was fantastically good at self-denial. I'd learned that from the first time we were enemies. It put me at a disadvantage because I did not have that skill. And I was desperate for him. Desperate for his words and his care and his regard and his love, and definitely desperate for his touch.

But there was no way I'd beg for it.

Which meant my passive-aggressive behavior had to become decidedly more aggressive-aggressive.

Ignoring the clothing, I wrapped the towel around me and opened the door, planning to walk out to the living area where Edward had been working before I'd gotten in the bath in search of a bottle of water or acetaminophen or a nighttime snack. And if I dropped the towel when I reached for whatever item I was after, and Edward had to face me completely naked, well, whoops.

Except when I stepped out of the bathroom, I discovered Edward, still dressed in the suit and tie he'd worn for whatever business he'd done today, was in the bedroom. Which was unusual since he generally waited until I was asleep before he came to this part of the suite. Even stranger, he was standing at my side of the bed.

And any thought that he might be having the same ideas as I was were seemingly confirmed by what he was holding in his hand—my newly purchased pink Lelo vibrator.

"Really, Celia? You think this little thing is going to satisfy you?"

I forgot I'd left it on the nightstand before I'd taken my bath. I'd lain there for nearly half an hour, contemplating using it before I'd abandoned it for a soak instead. In fact, I hadn't used it even once since I'd bought it two weeks earlier. It wasn't that I thought sex toys were immoral or that masturbating was a form of cheating. The prospect of using it just increased my feeling of loneliness. I wanted to play with my husband, and the inanimate object was sure to be a poor substitute.

Forgetting to put it away suddenly seemed fortuitous.

While there was absolutely no hint of seduction in his tone when he'd spoken, he'd at least engaged. It was progress I intended to use to my advantage.

I nodded at the object in his hand. "I have a better bet at getting off from that than from a husband who refuses to touch me."

"I told you before I'd fuck you."

The offer had come in the middle of a terse conversation and had been so full of venom I'd ignored it. It pricked to hear it again, recognizing it as a weapon. A way of shifting blame. *The problems between us are you, obviously. I'm here. I offered.*

Well, fuck him and his "offer." I didn't need him cold and hard. I'd do better with the toy.

"No need to trouble yourself," I said. "I wouldn't want to put you out." I spun back to the bathroom to grab the lotion I'd left there on the counter.

When I returned, Edward was still where I'd left him, but now he had the vibrator pressed to his nose, sniffing.

I shivered, knowing what scent he was looking for. The indecency of the act caused arousal to pool between my legs.

I hated him for that. For having such an effect on me. Hated him almost as much as I loved him.

"Are you equally loathe to put this toy out? It hasn't been used." His smile was smug, and I hated him for that too.

I marched across the room and snatched the toy from his hand. "Maybe I washed it."

"Pussy scent doesn't wipe away that easily."

"I only just bought it. I had it out because I was planning to use it now." It was a challenge. An attempt to make him jealous. To make him plead, *please don't use it. Use me instead.*

What he actually said was nothing like that at all. "Good idea. Now that you're all nice and clean you can get yourself dirty."

I spun away from him and set the lotion on the nightstand, using that as an excuse so he wouldn't see my disappointment knit across my features. This was how every conversation went with him these days. Barbs and jabs back and forth. Never a winner. What did I have to do to make that change? What did I have to say?

I took a deep breath and tried to listen to the conversation objectively. Tried to hear what his goal was in this exchange. Edward was the last person on earth I'd call passive, but was that what this was? His version of walking in and dropping the towel? His way of saying he wanted me as much as I wanted him?

I turned back toward him, and with less hostility, I awkwardly held out an olive branch. "Would you rather it were you dirtying me up?"

He was three feet away, the closest he'd been for any real amount of time in weeks, and I was nearly naked, a fact I was very aware of as his eyes skimmed down my face, down my neck, to the top of my breasts. I held my breath and silently begged for him to make the next move.

He stepped a foot closer, the heat between us as thick and solid as a wall. "Would *you* rather it were me?"

My jaw tightened. Of course he would force me to be the vulnerable one. That was the true goal of these battles, wasn't it? Both of us intent on the other being the first to bend. The first to be exposed. The first to say something honest.

If there was ever going to be a chance for us, a chance to be the family I knew we could be, then one of us would eventually have to take that risk. It could be me. Maybe even it should be.

"You can," I whispered. "If you want." It wasn't the complete surrender that was needed, and I knew it. I was chickenshit, too scared to say what I really felt. *Yes, I want it to be you. Make me dirty, Edward. Love me like you used to.*

My heart pounded with anticipation as his heated gaze drifted once more over my face, lingering on my lips before dropping lower to my abdomen. I saw the change in his expression as he remembered what lay hidden behind the towel, underneath the expanding stretch of flesh. The last victory taken in our war, and it had been mine.

He stepped back, cold sweeping in between us like an arctic front. "You've already made the purchase. It would be a shame to waste the money." He glanced at the vibrator still in my hand. "No matter how disappointing the experience might be. Two of my fingers are wider than that, and you're not usually satisfied until you have at least three."

There he was, the devil I'd married. In full-blown splendor. Taunting me with what he wouldn't let me have.

It brought out the devil in me as well. "Size is less important than what's done with it. This should do just fine."

"Since you're so good at knowing what you need, yes, I'm sure it shall." The words dripped with sarcasm as he turned away from me, removing his jacket as he walked to the closet. As though he were done with me and my "needs."

"It will," I said, wanting his attention back, as cruel as it had been.

He hung up his jacket then shifted back to face me. Undoing his tie, he threw me a challenging stare. "What are you waiting for then? Go on."

"I'm waiting for you to leave."

"Leave? I'm done with my work. I thought I'd retire early tonight."

God, he was infuriating. He'd probably only come in the room to get his reading glasses, or some report that he'd left on his nightstand the evening before. The only reason he was staying was to prove I had no real intention of getting myself off.

But I'd bought the damn vibrator, so I did have the intention, even if I hadn't used it as of yet. And if he wasn't going to give, I'd take care of myself. "Stay then. You can pretend I'm not here, like you always do. Turn the light off, will you?"

I dropped the towel, and somehow managed to stay standing tall underneath his gaze.

"I'd rather keep it on," he said, his voice deeper than it had been a moment before. It was barely noticeable, the change in timbre, but it was there, and it bolstered me.

I baited him. "So you can watch?"

"So I can judge."

The upward curl of his lip got me low in my belly, a tug of desire so strong that any inhibitions about masturbating fell away. Besides, I'd done this before. On our wedding night. I'd played with myself while he watched until he couldn't stand it anymore and he'd taken over. Then he'd fucked me, and nothing between us was ever the same.

Maybe that would happen again.

"Suit yourself," I said, laying on the bed, my shoulders propped up by the headboard. I pressed the button on the toy, increasing the power until the buzz was quite loud and strong. It was a steady vibration, the default out of twenty possible settings, and while I would have experimented more with which one I liked if I were alone, I left it as is and shoved the pulsing tip between my legs.

"Oh my God." I closed my eyes, the sensation against my clit more intense than Edward's fingers. Which wasn't necessarily a good thing. It was almost too intense, and if I weren't trying to prove some point, I would have turned the damn thing down.

But I *was* trying to prove a point, and beyond that, I had grasped something that I hadn't been able to get hold of for weeks—my husband's attention. I was desperate to keep it, even if it meant enduring the brutal buzz against my sensitive nerves.

I lasted all of ten seconds before I had to lift the toy ever so slightly to give myself a break. Fortunately, my knees up like they were, I was pretty sure Edward couldn't tell. Not that I was even sure he was actually watching since I wasn't about to look at him. It was enough to imagine that he might be.

I tried the tip against me again and had to immediately jerk it away.

"Too much for you?" Edward's voice cut through the haze of sensation.

So he *was* watching.

"Fuck you, it's perfect." I tried a new tactic—pressing the head of the toy to the spot next to my clit instead of directly on it. This, I could manage. This sent enough vibration to my hotspot without being overwhelming.

And now I could concentrate on the real source of my gathering pleasure—Edward. His eyes were more effective than a vibrator ever could be. It turned me on to be watched by him. It felt sexy and naughty and almost like cheating. Combined with the steady pulsation of the toy, an orgasm was building, slowly but surely. My back arched up off the bed as I let out a sigh.

"You're faking."

"I am not." I shot him a glare, which was a mistake because then I saw how hard he was, how the crotch of his pants tented with his cock at full mast. He couldn't be wearing underwear, and hell, that was hot.

I forced myself to look away, but I kept the image in my mind. Imagined more. Imagined him taking his cock out, about fisting it with one strong hand, about him crawling over me and sinking deep, deep...

"Open your knees."

No way. "Undo your pants."

"Already undone."

At that, my head swung back toward him. Sure enough, his pants were undone and his cock was in his hand, just as I'd imagined. There was no looking away from him now. He'd caught my gaze and trapped it.

"Open your knees," he demanded again.

I wanted to hold on to his eyes too much to deny him. So I opened my knees, showing him everything between them. Which meant I had to move the vibrator to my clit again so that he wouldn't know I hadn't been able to handle it.

Of course I jerked almost instantly.

He stepped closer. Closer still, his stare boring like a hot laser onto my pussy. "Turn down the vibration," he ordered when he was at my side. I clicked it down a notch. "More." Another notch. "One more."

I clicked the button again, and it was better now, but I handed the toy toward him anyway. "You could take over."

"I'm busy." He reached over to the lotion at my bedside and pumped a dab into his hand, then he spread it over his cock with the downward glide of his palm.

Yes, he was indeed busy.

"You could be busy with me," I purred, no longer able to restrain myself.

"I *am* busy with you." He stroked leisurely up his length. "Put it inside you."

For a fraction of a second I thought he meant his cock, and my breath hitched with anticipation. But before I could reach out and pull him to me, he nodded to the vibrator still in my hand.

"Oh." I brought it down to my entrance and worked the head inside the hole. He'd only been somewhat exaggerating when he'd made fun of the small size—it was a fairly innocuous vibrator—but it had been months since I'd had anything inside me at all, and I was tight.

I was also sensitive. The pregnancy alien that had invaded my body had done especially strange things to my lower regions, and the vibration of the toy against my inner walls made my entire pussy tighten and buzz, even with just the tip buried inside.

It was already enough for me, but it wasn't enough for Edward.

"Deeper," he ordered, and because I could rarely ignore this particular commanding tone of his voice, I pushed it in a little farther.

It still wasn't enough. "All the way," he said sharply.

I whimpered as I pressed it in as far as I could. I felt so full. So tight. So on fire.

"Good," he said, and I almost came right then I was so happy I'd pleased him. "Now fuck yourself with it."

I did as he told, shoving the object in and out while his dark hooded eyes watched in earnest.

"Harder," he said, and I complied. Then, "Pretend it's me," and I increased my tempo yet again, and let out a moan at the erotic sound my juices made as the toy slid in and out. "Fuck. Yes. Just like that." His own strokes quickened, matching mine. "Touch your clit with your other hand."

My fingers nudged against the sensitive bud, and my knees involuntarily pressed together, as if to push away the intensity of the sensation.

My husband wouldn't have that. "Keep your legs open wide so I can see."

I took a breath and eased them back down. I was panting now. So close to coming. So close to falling apart and breaking down and letting him have every last piece of me, even the parts I'd managed to withhold.

"Edward..." Tears pricked at my eyes.

"Say it."

"What?"

"Say what you want to say."

He knew. He knew everything that was inside of me, and he was determined to reel it out.

But it wasn't that easy. The words were lodged so far inside that I couldn't recognize their form. "I don't know what that is."

"You do."

I shook my head, trying to shake off the overwhelming feelings that pressed like high waters behind a dam. "I need to come," I said, focusing on the physical.

"That's not it." His voice was coarse and insistent.

"Edward..." I blinked up at him, my eyes darting from his to the brisk jerk of his hand. "I need..." *you. I need you inside me. I need to feel you driving hard and deep into my cunt. I need to feel your skin on mine. To taste your lips. To feel your body go rigid when you rut against me with your release.*

It was too much—the sensation, the sight, the emotions bottled up inside me, and I exploded like a firework on the Fourth of July. Color and light streaked across my field of vision as my body undulated against my hand. And any words that had been at the tip of my tongue, fell out of my mouth in a tangle of unintelligible grunts and gasps as pure bliss strangled through my limbs.

When I'd come back to myself enough to speak real words, I realized he was also at the brink. His face was as tight as his grip on his cock, his hand flying back and forth along its length.

I scooted quickly to the edge of the bed. "Put it on me," I begged. "Come on me. Please, Edward. Please!"

But even in the throes of pleasure, he had strength enough to resist. With a low groan, he stepped back just as white liquid spurted out over his hand.

I envied his hand. I wanted to be decorated in his cum. I wanted to be marked by him. To belong to him. To be so attached to him that he couldn't ever retreat.

I was still staring at the mess he'd made when he spoke. "You're starting to show."

My eyes moved to find his staring at my once-flat abdomen. Warmth spread through my chest. He never talked about the baby or the pregnancy unless I forced the subject, and then his responses were always clipped and dismissive.

I put my palm across my belly, as if I could hold his gaze there. As if

I could connect it to the child within. "I barely notice the change, but I guess I am. I don't fit in my pants anymore."

He continued to stare for another few seconds. Heavy, silent seconds where I wished more than anything to know what he was thinking. To be in his head.

"Edward?" I said when the weight of the silence became unbearable.

He snapped out of his reverie, tucking himself into his pants as he turned away from me. "An excuse for you to go shopping. You should enjoy that."

I preferred when he shopped for me, and he knew it.

The moment was broken. We were back to opposing sidelines, back to our distance and our war.

I sat up, wanting to pull him back. "Tomorrow's the ultrasound. Are you still coming?"

"I said I would when you asked last time." He disappeared into the bathroom.

"Just wanted to be sure you hadn't changed your mind," I called after him. The sound of the faucet running was my only response.

I sat for a second, trying to decide what I should do next, or if there was anything I *could* do. Maybe I should let the conversation lie. Let him get ready for bed then, once the lights were out, roll innocently into his space.

I stood and picked up the discarded towel from the floor and used it to wipe off the toy. When I looked up, Edward had returned from the bathroom, still dressed.

Without a word, he crossed the room toward the living area.

"Where are you going? I thought you were going to bed," I asked, sure I already knew the answer. Away from me was where.

He glanced at me but looked away quickly, as if looking at me for too long was painful. "I changed my mind," he said, then left the room without another word.

I sank back on the bed and brushed away a tear. Pregnancy made them fall at the drop of a hat these days, and while they were often justified, this was not an occasion to cry. We might have just had sex without any touching, but it *was* sex. And he'd brought up my preg-nancy. It was more than he'd allowed me in months.

I had to see it as a step forward. I refused to see it as anything else.

"We'll get there," I promised our baby. "One step at a time, I have to believe for your sake that we'll get there."

THREE

EDWARD

I RUBBED my lips with my thumb, watching the technician as she stuffed the edges of a paper blanket inside the waistband of my wife's pants. How long had it been since I'd been at one of these ultrasounds? Genevieve was twenty-three now, so about twenty-four years.

Nearly a quarter of a century ago. What was I doing here now at the age of forty-five?

Of course, I hadn't even been a quarter of a century old when Genevieve was born. I'd only been twenty with Hagan.

I remembered that first ultrasound now, sitting at Marion's side in a small office in Bordeaux. The technician had used a wand that time, one that was inserted inside, and within seconds the black and white screen filled with a tiny sac of cells that resembled a sea creature more than a human, with big black holes for eyes and a body that curled in on itself.

I'd been too shocked to register any other emotions. Marion and I had become extremely close over the previous months, but we didn't even live in the same country. Our time together had been measured in a handful of long weekends on Exceso and several sporadic weeks where I'd flown in to be with her in France. The bulk of our relationship had been over the phone and via email. I'd spend a few minutes every morning detailing a list of things I wanted her to do over the course of the day, then that evening she'd send an email with proof that she had. It had been more work for her—besides the tasks I'd given she had to set up a digital camera, load the photos to her computer, write a detailed message about how the assignments had made her feel. Or, if it were convenient for me, she'd call to tell me about it over the phone while I stroked myself to release.

It had been a one-sided relationship in many ways, and I had been aware of that. I'd been comfortable with that.

Until I saw the quick pulse at the center of the creature on the screen.

"*Heartbeat's strong,*" the tech had said. "*Measuring at seven weeks, two days.*"

I'd clutched Marion's hand with mine, and without thinking about it, without imagining what our lives would be, I turned to her and said, "*Marry me.*"

And as she responded to everything I ever asked, she said, "*Yes, sir.*"

That had been a lifetime ago, and my current wife, whom I loved so intensely that the emotions I'd felt for Marion seemed as small and alien as that embryo on the screen in comparison, was not so agreeable.

I surveyed her now, her shirt pulled up to her tits, her swelling belly bared. While I'd known there was a baby growing inside her, it hadn't been real for me until last night when I'd seen the protrusion of Celia's belly up close. Her body was changing. It *had* changed. Her breasts were fuller, her nipples darker and more pronounced, and buried underneath her expanding skin, my child was growing.

I was going to be a father.

Again, and yet it felt like the first time in so many ways.

And I was terrified.

Celia was too, I realized. If she was all the time, she'd done a good job of hiding it from me, but here and now, whatever masks she might have worn had been dropped, and I could see the fear etched on her features, her brows knit tightly above concerned eyes as she chewed on her bottom lip, much the way I was worrying my own with my thumb.

I dropped my hand and wondered if I could do anything to put her at ease.

But the barricade between us was thick, and gestures that had once come as naturally as breathing now took great effort. I glanced at her hand, resting on the table at her side, the rings on her wedding finger a blatant show of our commitment to each other. It should be easy to reach out and take that hand, thread my fingers through hers. I could do that. I *wanted* to do that.

Instead, my hands sat in my lap, as the technician put on latex gloves and then reached for the transducer. With her free hand, she picked up a white bottle with a top that resembled a mustard dispenser and shook it before turning it upside down above Celia's abdomen.

"This will be cold," she said, squeezing until a tiny drop of jelly plopped out. The tech shook the bottle then squeezed again with similar results. After glancing around the room for another, she said, "I'm sorry. I have to get more gel. I'll be right back."

She hung the instrument in its place on the machine then slipped out into the hall, her footsteps on the hard floor diminishing until the only sound in the room was the gentle hum of the equipment.

Celia's eyes darted to the blank screen where her name flashed at the top. *Fasbender, C.* She let out a heavy sigh.

And I reached out and took her hand.

She turned to me immediately, her usual hostility completely absent, and in its place, apprehension.

"What if she's not okay?" she asked quietly, as if speaking the words any louder might make them come true.

"This is a routine checkup," I assured her. "There's no reason to believe that everything we see today won't be perfectly normal."

"But the last time..." She shook her head and swallowed. "If I'd set my ultrasound a week earlier, we would have seen that he was already gone."

I was a bloody idiot. The miscarriage she'd had years before had happened right around this time in her pregnancy. That was why she'd insisted on making the appointment for her anatomy screening as early as possible, right at eighteen weeks. Of course she was worried about it.

I scooted to the edge of my chair and put my other palm over the hand that held hers, squeezing gently. "This isn't last time, bird. This is this time, and you are strong and stubborn, and there is no way that our baby hasn't inherited that from you." I considered what I'd just said. "From both of us," I corrected.

"Mostly you," she said with a smile so bright it cut straight to my heart.

I held her gaze like that for several long beats, and when the door opened, and the technician drew my focus, my hands remained clutched to Celia's.

"Let's try this again," the tech said. She squirted gel in zigzag lines across Celia's skin, then spread it out with the transducer and settled it down on a spot near her navel.

I glanced at Celia's face, her expression breaking into pure joy before I followed her eyes to the profile of a white figure filling the previously dark screen. Unlike the seahorse that had appeared that first time with Marion, this figure was recognizable as a baby. I could make out so much of it—the curve of the nose, the indent of the eyes, tiny limbs flapping near the head.

"I can make out the individual fingers," I said, astonished. Ultrasound had come a long way in the last twenty-four years. The pictures hadn't been nearly this clear.

"Ten total by my count." The technician clicked a few things on her keyboard, drawing lines and inputting numbers. "Length is right on track for eighteen weeks."

"She's growing like she should?" Celia asked tentatively.

"So far so good. Still a lot to see." The technician made a few more measurements, this time near the skull. "The head is the right size. Nothing concerning there." She moved the transducer to the torso then tapped a key and a whoosh, whoosh, whoosh sound came over the speakers. "That's the heartbeat. Sounds nice and strong."

"Told you." I squeezed her hand again. This time she squeezed back.

"What are we looking at now? Is that her foot?"

My throat felt tight. I'd never seen her so excited. I'd never seen her this aglow.

"Yep," the tech affirmed. "And I count ten toes."

As if on cue, one set of toes stretched wide. "It knows you're watching," I said, absolutely charmed by all of it.

"She's moving so much." Celia's voice was thick with emotion. I didn't have to look to know she was crying. "Is that what that flutter feeling is?"

The technician nodded. "Possibly. First-time mothers often don't feel anything for another month or so, but it's not uncommon to feel it by now."

"And she's okay? Everything looks okay?" Even though she could see that the baby was moving around, though she'd heard the heartbeat, Celia still needed reassurance.

"She looks great." The tech met Celia's eyes this time, briefly, before going back to her keyboard. "A few more things I need to see to be absolutely certain. You already know the gender?"

"No," I said.

At the same time, Celia said sheepishly, "We think it's a girl."

I appreciated being included in that "we," even though we'd never discussed it. It felt hopeful. Like proof that we still were a "we," despite all that was going on between us.

I hadn't realized until that moment how much I'd worried that we weren't.

"Well, you're right," the tech said. She drew an arrow on the screen. "Right there. That's the labia. She's showing off for you. I don't always get such a clear shot."

I chuckled. "Definitely your daughter." The words said out loud brought levity to the situation. *A daughter.* I was having another daughter. *We* were having a daughter. Together.

My breath got stuck somewhere in my throat, and I had to blink several times before I could see clearly.

The rest of the ultrasound went by in a haze. Every new view brought another wave of elation from Celia immediately followed by another request for reassurance about the baby's health.

I smiled and nodded and smiled and nodded, the whole time trying to ignore the screaming voice in my head that said, *This is really happening. You're a fuck for a father, and currently not any better as a husband, and this is really happening.*

No matter what happened between me and Celia, we were now bonded forever. And I wanted that. I wanted her—both hers. The mother *and* the child. Why had it felt so much more like being collared than when Marion had gotten pregnant?

Because then I'd known my place. I'd known who was in charge. I'd known how to be the husband Marion had needed, and I'd been that for her. Until I couldn't anymore, and she slipped away.

This time it was Celia who wouldn't take what she needed from me, and it felt so much like being on the other side, like clinging to the side of a crumbling mountain, my hands clawing in the dirt.

I had to get a better grasp. I had to hold on to her, the only way I knew how.

I didn't come out of my trance until the technician went to print pictures for us to take home and hit another snag. "Out of photo paper. I apologize. The room was obviously not stocked after the last shift. I'll be quick."

The door shut, and I looked down to see I was still holding Celia's hand in both of mine. Then I slid my eyes up to her face. She was watching me. Studying me.

She stroked her thumb along the back of mine, and warmth flooded through my veins. "She was beautiful. Wasn't she?"

She held her breath after the question, and I could see it like I always could—what she needed from me along with what she thought she needed. They were less often the same thing than she would have liked. It would be easier between us if I could just be a man willing to provide the latter.

I'd almost tried the day before. I'd gone into the bedroom, meaning to tell her about my meeting with Hudson Pierce. I'd thought briefly that maybe that could be enough—Werner Media, under our control. We could go after it together, she and I, and that would be enough to repair the damage between us.

But then I'd seen the sex toy, and her—naked and newly clean—and something primal roared up inside me, and I remembered who I was. I wasn't *that* man, the one who could step aside or stand back. I was a man who stayed the course. I was a man who didn't back down, and I had to believe she loved me for that.

I shifted my hands, halting the gentle caress of her thumb, and looked at her sternly. "She needs a better home than the one we're giving her, bird."

Her forehead wrinkled. "What do you mean?"

"She needs a solid foundation. She needs her parents to have plowed down the obstacles that could prevent her from having the best life. A rich life. She needs that from her father."

"What are you saying, Edward?"

She understood, I knew she did. Still, she was forcing me to be clear.

"Tell me who he is." There was no need to say who he was. A, the nameless manipulator. The man who'd come between us.

She jerked her hand away from mine, and I instantly missed its warmth. "Oh my God. *This* today? Right *now*? I can't believe you. Seeing our baby didn't show you what's really important?"

Her volume rose, and her tone had grown sharp. I forced mine to remain low and calm in contrast. "It absolutely did show me what was important. Putting a clear end to the past. Tying up loose ends. Sharing the last secrets between us."

"So that you can go after someone who doesn't deserve it." She rolled her eyes and wiped a wayward tear from her cheek. "You have secrets too."

There was only one important secret that I'd withheld—the circumstances surrounding the death of my brother-in-law. I thought it hadn't mattered, and it hadn't, until she'd stumbled onto it, and now she was sorely due an explanation.

But keeping it to myself gave me an advantage at the moment, and I loved her enough to take any advantage that I could. "I'll tell you mine as soon as you tell me yours."

Her frown deepened, and she turned her head away. This was how many of our arguments ended, with one of us retreating into silence.

This time I kept pushing. "You don't want our baby girl to come into our family with those things between us."

Her head shot back to me. "That's not fair, using her as leverage."

"It seems only fitting since you used her as leverage first."

"Not on purpose."

That got me, and my composure shattered. "Stopping your birth control wasn't on purpose?"

Of course it was that moment that the technician chose to return to the room. From the way her eyes flit from Celia to me back to Celia, it was evident that she'd heard our arguing from the hall.

Thank God, she had the decency to pretend she hadn't.

"Almost got it," she said as she loaded the paper into the printer. She tapped at the keyboard again and the printer came to life, shooting out a bunch of screenshots she'd captured during the visit.

Seconds passed as they continued to spit out, tense seconds that felt years long before she ripped the scans from the roll and handed them to Celia. "Here's a few of the best ones." She spoke directly to my wife, ignoring me completely as if I weren't there. "Just a few standard reminders—make sure you're taking your prenatal vitamins daily, getting enough water, as well as exercise and rest.

"And keep in mind that any undue stress at this time should be avoided." Her eyes whisked momentarily to me, just in case the message wasn't received from her words alone.

"Got it," I snapped. "Are we done now?"

Celia scowled, then quickly shook it off. "I'll keep that in mind. Thank you so much for all of this."

"My pleasure. You can use that paper blanket to clean up. Just dispose of it in the trash can in the corner." Leaving Celia to wipe the jelly from her skin, she handed the routing slip to me. "You can give this to the man at checkout."

She was out of the room before either of us could say another word, likely eager to get away from the oppressive tension, feeling good that she'd passively delivered a warning to a wife who might be suffering from abuse at the hands of her husband.

Good thing I wasn't a real threat. If I had been the type of man that she seemed to fear I might be, Celia could have been beaten for the stranger's poorly subtexted message. Didn't she understand how domestic violence worked?

I glowered at the door where she'd gone, simultaneously wondering if I should go after her to kindly educate her about her mistake and despising her for interfering where she had no business.

I didn't even notice when Celia came to stand beside me. "You heard the woman. Undue stress should be avoided."

And then I felt like an arse. Because obviously abuse didn't always come in the form of physical violence, and it was true that I had a tendency to bully my wife. It was one thing when she welcomed it. It was safe to say that these days she did not.

I breathed out deeply and turned to her, wrapping my arms around her, my forehead pressed to hers. "Let me take your stress from you," I said softly. "Let me carry your burdens. Let me do what should be done for you. For both of you." *Give in to me. I know what's best.*

She shook her head, extricating herself from my arms. "You wouldn't want that from me, Edward. I'd be Marion, and you'd be unrestrained. I am who I am, and either that's good enough, or she is. Maybe neither of our ways are, but it can't be both."

She had a point, didn't she? There was no pleasing me. I wanted her to challenge me, and I wanted her to bend. I wanted her to have her own thoughts and opinions, and I wanted her to accept when I was right without question.

She couldn't be all of those things. No one could, and by that logic, that meant that the someone who had to change in our marriage was me.

Except it wasn't that simple. Our dynamic wasn't that black and white. I could let her win. It just couldn't be this.

But she was already gone. Without waiting for me to reply, she had grabbed the route slip from my hand, and I was once again staring at a closing door.

FOUR

CELIA

"I'M GOING to name Edward as CEO of Werner."

My father's words startled me more than his presence in the kitchen, which was unusual. He was a conventional type man who, though he firmly said otherwise, believed that there were duties best-suited for women, as well as the rooms associated with those jobs.

In my parents' house, the kitchen belonged to Lupita. She was the only one who spent any real amount of time in this area of the penthouse. Undocumented and paid under the table when she'd first begun to work for them nearly twenty years before, she was now not only a citizen (with the help of my father's lawyer), but also practically "family," according to my mother anyway. I would echo her sentiments if I thought that paying someone a low-end salary to clean toilets and scrape dinner plates was how a person treated family. I supposed, in some ways, it wasn't any more humane than the way some members of my family treated blood—throw some token gestures of love and then put the rest of the person in a neglected box and you had a Werner daughter. Shower her with affection and then misuse her trust and her body and you had a Werner niece.

I often thought I might prefer the measly salary and a scrub brush.

Whatever she was to my parents, Lupita had always been one of the realest people in my life, and I frequently found myself huddled in her spaces when I visited. Even when we didn't speak, I enjoyed her mutterings, half English, half Spanish, as she dusted and straightened and brought order to the luxurious life Madge and Warren led.

I'd officially moved to the Park Hyatt when Edward came from London, and while he spent his days in the rented-out event space he used for his office, the suite would become small and unbearably quiet. Not that we spoke much when he was there with me. In some ways it was a worse form of captivity than when I'd been on his island. I had free rein here, but on Amelie I'd had care, and the only reason I didn't run back to that paradise prison now was because of the lack of prenatal care.

So instead, I found myself coming regularly to the apartment under the guise of wanting time with my mother, but more truthfully, it was for Lupita's companionship. Today, Mom had her weekly mahjong. Dad had been at work, presumably, and with no need to pretend to be there for them, I'd gathered my newly purchased stationery and set up a spot at the kitchen high top while Lupita organized the grocery delivery. My task was to write thank-you letters for the charity gala Accelecom had sponsored the week before. Hosting the event wasn't my favorite of assignments that Edward had given me, but it had done its job to distract me, as I was sure its real purpose was, and writing the obligatory notes now was strangely engaging.

Until my father's unexpected pronouncement, anyway.

I set down the Montblanc rollerball pen I'd borrowed from his desk and spun on the stool to face him. "What?"

"When I retire. I'm giving it to Edward. My position." He leaned against the side of the table, propping himself with his elbow, and waited for my response, which he obviously expected to be gratitude or praise or some combination of the two.

I glanced at Lupita, wishing for help that she couldn't possibly give me. She wasn't even looking my way. As if the mention of business was her cue—or perhaps just the presence of my father in general—Lupita shoved the last of the groceries in the pantry and disappeared from the kitchen, leaving us alone in her space.

I let out a slow breath, my heart pounding at my insides as I tried to manage my panic. There was no way I could let my father try to hand over his command to my husband. Hudson would never allow it, and the secret I'd managed to keep for years would come barreling to light— my father no longer owned the majority shares of his own company. Hudson did.

Changing my father's mind about anything, though, was something I'd never been good at.

Nevertheless, I had to try.

I attempted a smile. "That's so very thoughtful. But is that really what you want to do?"

"I know this business stuff is all over your head." He reached over to steal some fruit from the plate Lupita had put out for me earlier. "Trust me. It's a power move," he said around a mouth full of berries. "Merging the two companies. Werner will be bigger than ever. I'll go out with a bang."

My neck tightened as I swallowed back a bitter response to his patronizing tone. "I see why combining efforts with Accelecom can be attractive. And there are many ways to do that without a formal merger."

"I'm surprised at this reaction. You don't want Werner to stay with the family?"

"You still own the same stocks, whoever is at the helm, and Edward is not a Werner."

"He's your husband and the father of my grandchild. That's close enough. I don't understand why you'd be opposed to building a bigger and better Werner Media." His tone was stern now. He was losing patience with what he considered ignorant thinking on my part.

I leaned forward, trying not to lose *my* patience with *his* ignorance. "I'm being practical, Dad. Not letting my emotions get involved. For decades, Accelecom has been your enemy. This is a real turnaround from that. It's one thing to drop your rivalry but quite another to get in bed with him simply because he's married to your daughter. What if something happens to us? If we broke up or something."

"Are you saying there's trouble between you?" The way he looked at me I understood clearly that it wasn't going to be my side he took if there was. Ironic considering he'd been opposed to our marriage in the first place.

"I didn't say that."

Before I could expand, he jumped in with a lecture. "You have a baby on the way, Ceeley. This isn't the time to get wishy-washy about your vows. Be the daughter I raised and act responsibly. Hold on to your man no matter what the cost."

I was so infuriated I almost told him right then and there the real reason he couldn't give the company to Edward.

But then the slightest flutter happened in my belly, a feeling similar to what I'd felt when we'd seen our daughter moving on the ultrasound a week before, and I paused to let the joy of the moment sink in.

In that pause, I remembered that it wasn't just my father's ego that would be harmed from knowing the truth. It could be the first tile knocked down in a line of dominoes, exposing Hudson and forcing him to take more of a leadership role. There could be good at the end of that road, but it was too much of an unknown to want to risk finding out.

"I'm not having trouble with Edward," I lied. Divorce wasn't on my radar. I didn't want to get rid of my husband, I wanted to win him back. "I am very much in love with him, but that doesn't mean things don't happen. He's been divorced before. What if he loses interest in me?"

I shook my head, not wanting to hear whatever chauvinistic response my father had to that. "My point is that marriages are not always permanent, and with the previous bad blood you've had with Accelecom, I doubt you'll get support from your board for deciding to go all in with them now."

"I hold the majority. It doesn't matter if—"

I cut him off. "*Edward and I* hold the majority. Don't forget they're in my name now. And it's only forty percent. If the other stockholders got together to go against you—"

It was his turn to interrupt. "Glamplay holds thirty percent, and they're legally bound to vote with me. Er, you."

They weren't bound anymore. That agreement became null and void when Hudson purchased them.

Since I couldn't tell him that had already happened, I decided to hint that it might. "Those kinds of deals aren't permanent. Something could happen to Glamplay in the future, a competitor could buy them out or something, and you'd lose that guarantee."

My father astonished me by smiling. "You must be learning from your husband. That's indeed true, and he's right to worry about those risks. But he and I have already discussed that possibility, and we've found a way to get around it."

"You and who? You and *Edward*? You and Edward have found a way around it?" I didn't know why it was a surprise that my father had spoken about all of this with my husband before telling me. Of course he had. In fact, it probably had been Edward who had brought it up. What did I think he was working on every day in his temporary office space? Sure he could connect with London and still effectively run Accelecom from the States, but I knew he wanted Werner. Why would I think for even a second that he wasn't pursuing it just because he hadn't said anything to me?

"Yes, me and Edward. I'll admit, he's the one who brought up this particular scenario. I was quite impressed at his foresight. He's quite an intelligent man. The right man to run Werner."

Foresight, *right*. I had to agree with my father, though, about Edward's intelligence. It had been a brilliant idea to get my father involved like this. Without exposing the truth, he'd gained an ally in his quest to get the CEO spot.

I almost didn't want to ask, but I had to know. "How are you getting around it?"

"Glamplay's thirty percent only becomes an issue if it's combined with other stockholders, as you said. So we need to be sure that we have another stockholder on our side from the beginning. Then, even if the others gang up, we'll still have a majority. Edward's already reached out and met with the guy whose partnership would give us the most power."

My stomach sank. There was only one other stockholder who had enough shares to mean anything, even before he'd acquired Glamplay's thirty percent.

"What did Hudson say when Edward met with him?" What I really wanted to know was what Edward had said to Hudson, but there was no way my husband would have told my father the truth about that.

"Oh, good. You know it's Hudson. I didn't want to say his name in case that brought up any hard feelings from the past. I have to say, Ceeley, it might have been a big disappointment when you lost him to that Alayna woman, but you snagged a more savvy man with Edward. Hudson doesn't have the vision your husband does. He can't see the potential with a merger quite yet, but we're working on him."

I almost laughed. Hudson's vision was beyond what my father could even fathom. Edward was sharp too. Maybe even sharp enough to go head-to-head with my old friend, but Edward was used to having the upper hand in these kinds of dealings, and he did not have it this time.

I'd been stupid, ignoring my father's looming retirement and my husband's pattern of going behind my back to get what he wanted. I'd been too focused on my pregnancy and Edward's anger and protecting Hudson's identity, I'd forgotten to be mindful that Edward desired more than just the name of the man who'd taught me The Game.

Well, I wasn't going to sit back and let him outwit me now. Admittedly, there wasn't much I could do to interfere, but there was one move I could make.

I glanced at my watch. I couldn't make it downtown before five, especially not if I changed, and since I was wearing baggy shorts and a tank, I'd definitely have to change.

Tomorrow. First thing so I'd beat the summer heat that turned people into melting wax by the end of the day. I could go to Bergdorf Goodman now and find something that fit and was flattering, which was important. I might not have the influence I needed for the task, but I intended to use whatever tools I had. And that meant, when I walked into Hudson's office tomorrow, I needed to look good.

I TURNED to face my reflection in the steel wall at the back of the elevator. My hair was perfect, my eye makeup subtle, a severe shade of red on my lips. I looked exactly like the woman I once was, the dragon that used to frequently make this trip to Hudson's office.

Well, except for the change at my midriff. Seemingly overnight, my belly had popped, displaying to the world the baby growing inside me. Thank goodness I'd bought a sundress. My pre-pregnancy clothes officially did not fit.

I put a hand on the bump and felt immediately both centered and chaotic. This wasn't who I was anymore. The countenance I'd adorned for this occasion was a mask that no longer sat well on my face. It made me itch and fidget. My shoulders had to fight to stay lifted, and focusing my scattered thoughts was a chore.

But my baby was gravity. She rooted me to my purpose. What happened to me mattered in a way that hadn't before. What happened to her father, an equal concern. If it weren't for her, I could maybe let this whole Edward/Hudson thing play out on its own, even if it meant I had to face the consequences of what I'd done in the past. I'd done it before, and I could do it now if it were only my skin in the game.

So, for her, I would play this part. I would be the woman I needed to be.

When the elevator dinged at a floor near the top, it was a composed version of myself that stepped into the familiar waiting area and greeted Hudson's secretary.

"It's been a while, Trish," I said cooly, practicing the tone and the confidence required for the man beyond the double doors behind her. "Could you buzz me in? I need to see him."

"Uh..." I'd made her flustered, which I took as a good sign. "Did you have an appointment?"

"It's twenty past nine. If he keeps a schedule anything like he used to, he should be free right now." I meant it as a reminder that I had once been very familiar with her boss and his routines. Hudson being the methodical kind of man he was, I doubted they'd changed much. Early meetings then a break at nine for coffee and conferring with his secretary before more meetings tied up the rest of the day.

Of course, he had children now. Word on the street was that they changed everything.

Trish frowned, her expression hardening, the kind of look that preceded a dismissal.

I cut in before she tried. "Just ring him. Tell him it's me. Tell him I need to see him now. Tell him I insist." I stared at her then her phone, willing her to pick it up.

She hesitated for only a beat before she did. "Mr. Pierce, I'm sorry to interrupt, but you have a visitor that insists on seeing you right away."

I strained to hear his response but the receiver was too tight against her ear and I heard nothing.

"It's not a him," Trish said, eyeing me up and down. "It's Celia Werner-Fasbender."

The next few seconds passed like they'd been dipped in molasses. I held my breath. I tried not to move. If he turned me away, there was a very good chance I could cry, my hormones being what they were these days. In fact, if he made me wait a second longer—

"Yes, sir." She hung up the phone and pasted on her too-friendly smile, the one that said there was a whole lot going on behind it that no one in the world was privy to. "He's with someone. It will be just a moment, if you'd like to take a seat."

Every cell in my body seemed to sigh in relief as I let out the air I'd been holding. I gave her a matching fake smile, raising her a sugary tone. "I'd rather stand, thank you."

"Suit yourself."

A handful of seconds later, I wondered if that had been the right choice. Sitting was never a powerful position, and I wanted to present as strong. But if he made me wait, like he very well might, I wasn't sure my swollen feet could handle it. My fault for wearing a pointed-toe stiletto instead of choosing a more sensible pump.

But only a couple of minutes passed before the doors opened, and instead of being faced with whomever Hudson had been with, it was the man himself stepping into the lobby, as handsome and as formidable as he'd ever been with his imperious expression and his bespoke suit that brought out the gray of his eyes.

"Celia Werner. I didn't expect I'd ever see you step foot in my offices again." He didn't offer his hand, and the chilly timbre of his tone was more threatening than welcome.

What had I expected? A smile and a warm embrace? I'd been tormenting his future wife the last time we'd spoken.

I channeled the woman I'd been then and sneered. "Don't get your panties all twisted. This visit is harmless. And it's Werner-Fasbender now, which I'm sure you already know."

"Yes, I'd heard."

I felt a twinge of guilt at adding the hyphen in my name. I hadn't been using it, not just because it was Edward's preference, but because it felt right. I was more his than I'd ever been my father's.

Right now, though, as irritating and archaic as the surname construct was, it seemed useful to claim both, a subtle reminder that I had come from two powerful men, a suggestion that I had them both behind me, nevermind that it wasn't true.

He assessed me with calculating eyes, and I let him, taking a moment to study him in return. I was wrong, I realized now. He wasn't as formidable as he used to be, and while I could credit my newly found self-worth as the reason, it seemed there was something else as well. Something gentler in his gaze. Something gentler in his jaw. And the new lines at his mouth added a dose of friendly to his character. They said he was a man who could laugh. A man who *did* laugh. That hadn't been the Hudson who'd taught me The Game.

It seemed I wasn't the only one of us who'd changed.

My throat felt thick as melancholy rushed through me. I forced it down with a hard swallow before it took hold. "Are you going to keep me in your lobby all morning, or are you going to invite me in? I'll say what I have to say wherever. I just think you might prefer the privacy."

His eye twitched, a hint that my presence unnerved him more than he let on. "Very well. Come on in." He turned and I followed after him, halting when he did a few steps inside his office. He nodded to a young man I'd only just noticed. "Celia, I'm sure you remember my brother, Chandler."

"Of course I remember Chandler. My—" I blinked as I looked him over "—you sure grew up." He was a dozen years younger than me and Hudson. I'd always known him only as an irresponsible kid, but now he was a full-fledged adult, looking professional and serious in his designer suit.

He'd been graduating from high school the last time I'd seen him. Had that much time really gone by?

"It's good to see you again. It's been a while." His icy tone made it evident that he didn't remember me warmly, and I wondered if he'd learned about my part in his father's infidelity or if he was just following Hudson's lead.

It didn't really matter, I supposed. I hadn't expected this to be a friendly visit, though I'd thought I might have gotten a little credit for having stayed away as long as I had.

"Yes," I said, answering Chandler, my eyes pinned on his brother. "I've kept my distance. Haven't I, Hudson?" In case he needed a reminder.

That earned me a tight smile.

He glanced over at Chandler, and I assumed he was about to dismiss him, but when he spoke again, he said, "Whatever you have to say, Celia, I hope you're comfortable stating it in front of Chandler because I'd like him to stay."

Chandler gave a smug grin. "You won't even know I'm around."

"Afraid to be alone with me, Huds? I suppose that's fair." I smirked. He wouldn't be cruel with his brother in the room. So, really, the situation was a win for me.

Apparently, Hudson didn't appreciate my gloating. "Why are you here, Celia?"

"So we're jumping right in then. I suppose it was too much to expect we'd catch up first." It had been just something to say, but as I scanned the room, I wished for a moment we could be something else. Not friends, maybe, but something less guarded than whatever this was. We'd been close once. I'd designed his office. He'd been my first official client. We'd celebrated with champagne on the roof.

"You've changed the décor," I said, hoping I'd hid any trace of sadness from my tone. "Not what I would have done, but I like it. It suits you."

"Why are you here?" This time the question was emphatic, a warning that his patience was wearing thin.

I sighed. "Can we at least sit?"

He rubbed a hand over his chin. "Fine. Sit." He gestured toward the sofa, waiting until I sat before taking the armchair. Chandler perched on the arm of the loveseat, a silent bodyguard who, despite having grown, came across more poodle than rottweiler.

It was almost adorable how he wanted to protect his older brother. How he thought I had any power to hurt him. I had to bite back a laugh.

Then there was Hudson, keeping me to task. "Out with it, Celia. We don't have all day."

Well, here goes nothing.

I straightened my back and rested my hands on my belly like it was a talisman. "I have a favor to ask."

Hudson laughed. "That's ballsy of you."

"Perhaps. Or perhaps I just know what to say to get your attention."

"You have my attention. But it's waning quickly."

I nodded, acknowledging that he was already giving me a favor by letting me in the room with him at all, then got to the point. "I know you aren't going to go through with the Accelecom merger."

"Did your stepdaughter tell you that?"

My mask broke, and I could feel my brows rise in surprise. "Genevieve?" What the hell did she have to do with anything?

Chandler pounced. "You aren't the reason she's gotten close to me, then? That wasn't your idea?"

Hudson frowned, his gaze demanding I answer.

I was baffled. Though her room was next to ours, I'd barely seen Edward's daughter since she'd come to the States. "I didn't even realize you knew each other. Genevieve and I aren't particularly close. We definitely don't talk business. If you've already told her the merger was a no-go, she didn't pass it on to me or Edward."

That might have been a lie. It was very possible that she'd spoken to Edward, that he had her on some mission that I was unaware of, but if so, I didn't know about it. And considering how adamant he had been not to involve Genevieve in revenge-related activity, I was pretty confident what I'd said had been true.

Unless I didn't really know Edward anymore either.

I didn't want to think about that possibility.

Thankfully, Hudson distracted me from those thoughts. "If Genevieve didn't tell you, then how did you know?"

"I know there's no way you'd hand over the company to my husband." I flicked my eyes toward Chandler, wondering how much he knew, then deciding I didn't care. "It would contradict the reasons that you bought it in the first place."

"Let me guess—you're going to try to convince me to give him the job anyway."

His sardonic expression ruffled my feathers. "You really do have a bad taste in your mouth where I'm concerned, don't you? I hope you understand when I tell you I feel the same."

He took a beat, growing somber. "That's fair."

It felt like he'd given me some ground, and I did my best to stand on it, delivering the speech I'd prepared. "In answer to your question, no. I'm not here to convince you to give him the job. Frankly, I'm happy with our lives the way they are. I'm not interested in moving back to the States, and I'm especially not interested in that kind of move with a baby on the way." Nevermind that we were here indefinitely at the moment.

"Then the favor you want is for me *not* to give the job to Edward?"

Guilt wrenched my intestines. "I didn't say that."

I considered backpedaling, considered trying to fight the other side, considered begging on my knees. But as much as I was doing this for our baby, I was also doing this *for* Edward, even if he didn't see it that way.

I pushed on. "Let's be clear—I'd love for Werner Media to be back in the hands of my family. I simply know that isn't an option on the table."

"Then what is it that you're asking?"

I thought about what I really wanted, for Edward to come away from this unscathed. I wanted him to let this go on his own. I wanted him to walk away and focus his energy elsewhere. On Accelecom. On me. On his baby.

Hudson couldn't grant that, no matter how much power he had.

But there was one person I could try to protect, whether or not he deserved it. "My father," I said. "This company is his pride and joy. His legacy. He wants Edward to take his place because he thinks it will make me happy, yes, but mostly because he thinks it will be good for Werner Media. He hasn't even considered giving the job to anyone else. You and I both know that you will give the job to someone else. I'm willing to help convince him that's best."

"If...what?"

"If you let him believe it's his idea."

"I'm not sure I understand."

It was satisfying to find I could throw Hudson Pierce for a loop. It gave me confidence to plunge ahead with what I knew would be a near impossible request. "I'm saying go ahead and pick who you want to pick for the job—I know you have other names in mind. I'm confident that you'll select the best person to head Werner Media in the future— you'd never let a good business fail, no matter how you feel about me. It's not in you. I just want my father to believe the decision is still up to him. Let him leave his company in a dignified fashion. Let him think it's his creative vision he's implementing, not just yours."

"What a noble endeavor," he said, and he almost didn't sound like he was mocking me. "Unfortunately, I don't know how I would begin to convince your father of anything."

I didn't either. If anyone could, I'd hoped it would be him, that he'd have enough dignity to try to keep the ruse up, especially when I'd kept my end of our bargain and left his family alone.

I was seconds from saying just that when Chandler shot to his feet.

"I'll do it. I can do it," he said. "Get me a meeting with him, and I got this."

"Chandler?" Hudson was as surprised by this as I was.

"The proposal I was telling you about. I'm confident Warren will be interested in it. I just need to be able to present it to him. Thirty minutes. That's all."

I didn't know anything about Chandler's professional abilities, but he was eager, and he wanted to try, and I was so grateful, I almost fell to my knees. "I can arrange that. If Hudson agrees."

Hudson studied me intently. I knew what he was looking for, and even though I understood why, it still stung that he couldn't just see me for who I was now instead of who I'd been. Hadn't he said the same to me once upon a time? Implored me to see that he had changed when he'd given up The Game? I hadn't wanted to believe him then. Was this my karma? That he wouldn't believe me now?

See it. See me.

After what felt like a full minute, he gave up. "I can't figure out what game you're playing."

"Maybe I'm not playing any game," I said, my voice oddly raw.

"Wouldn't that be the most conniving scheme of all?"

"Wouldn't it?"

Our eyes locked, and something shifted. Not by much, but by enough that I could see glimpses of the man he must be now—a father, a husband. A person who did good in the world instead of harm.

Could he see something of the same about me?

"Random acts of compassion aren't like you. Thinking of anyone else's feelings isn't either." But he didn't seem to be accusing me, more he was puzzling. Then his eyes widened like he'd figured something out. "You fell in love."

Now Hudson had thrown me.

Because of course I had. Of course that was exactly the reason I was here. Because I'd met a man who had ruined me so completely that I would now care enough to ruin him in kind.

I'd loved Edward more for it. Could he love me more as well?

I couldn't think about it and not fall apart. "Do you want the meeting or not?" I asked stiffly.

"We'll take the meeting."

Relief blanketed me. My breath shuddered as I inhaled, my throat tight. "Thank you, Hudson."

Needing to get out of there before sentimentality took over, I stood. "I'll make arrangements with your secretary. No need for us to have any further contact, as far as I'm concerned."

"I appreciate that."

I beelined for the door and was halfway to escape when he called after me. "Celia." He waited until I turned back around, and it took a beat because I had to gather myself first. When I did, his eyes grazed my belly. "Congratulations on your pregnancy. I once thought you'd make a good mother."

Tears pricked at my eyes as the past slammed into me, bringing vivid memories to mind. We'd been friends. And he'd hurt me. So I'd hurt him. Then the pregnancy. And he'd claimed it. And I'd lost it. So I'd begged him for an escape. And he gave it while I'd given him companionship.

We'd been bad to the people around us. Really, really bad. Bad to each other, as well. But we'd been good to each other too. When both of us had needed it most.

No matter what else between us, we had that.

My vision blurred, I nodded toward the framed picture on his bookshelf of him, his wife, a baby in each of their arms, a little girl tucked into his side. "Congratulations on your own little family," I said, amazed my voice didn't crack. "I once thought you'd make a good dad."

I went straight from his office to the bathroom, planning to schedule the meeting with Trish on my way out, when I was composed.

Now, though, I needed a minute to myself. Locked in the privacy of a stall, I let the tears fall. Tears I couldn't quite explain. I wasn't sad. I was a bunch of other things all rolled into one, a muddy mess of too many emotions to name.

It felt good to let them out, the way it felt good to pull out a fresh clean sheet of paper. A blank slate. A place to start anew.

Edward had said I'd needed closure with the man who'd taught me how to play. It was why he was so determined to find out his identity, because he wanted to seek out that closure for me with hellfire and brimstone and revenge.

But this was what I'd needed. Just this. Just today.

My story with Hudson was over.

Now I could shut the book and move on.

FIVE

EDWARD

HAGAN LEANED over to whisper something to me.

Whatever he said, I couldn't hear it above the pounding in my ears. I was seething. Violent rage surged through my veins, my vision flashed with white hot anger, and there was absolutely nothing I could do about it but sit and continue to listen to the presentation being given to me in the conference room at Pierce Industries.

Pretend to listen, rather.

I'd stopped hearing much of the details after I'd got the general gist of the whole thing. In a nutshell, Pierce Industries proposed that Werner Media and Accelecom enter into a three-point alliance, and that, when Warren Werner stepped down, the CEO position should be handed to Nathan Murphy.

Nathan Fucking Murphy.

A man with credentials, yes, but not a man with *my* credentials. No matter what his experience, he was not the right man for the job. For the last twenty minutes he'd been sharing his plans for the company, and except for the idea of the alliance—which was clearly not his own—not a one was new or visionary. I'd given Pierce a missive with a dozen more innovative proposals. He knew that Murphy was the inferior choice, and still he chose to sell it to Warren, knowing the old man would jump on a Pierce-backed proposition in a heartbeat.

Hudson hadn't even had the nerve to introduce the idea himself. He'd left it to his brother, Chandler, a kid, fresh out of college, with less experience than Hagan.

Worse? Genevieve had a hand in it as well.

Not only did she hand over Accelecom numbers and strategies, but she'd assisted in leading the hour-long presentation that was just now coming to a conclusion. I'd known she was spending time with the younger Pierce and had even suspected they were growing close, but never had I imagined she was drumming up the idea of an alliance that would effectively kill the merger that Warren and I had discussed.

Again Hagan whispered something at my side.

I blinked, clearing my vision before I leaned in to better hear him.

"...not what we were after, but it's better than nothing. At least they didn't leave Accelecom in the dark. It's a rather good compromise."

What had Celia said was the recipe for a perfect compromise? None of the parties walked away satisfied, something to that effect. Well, from the look on the faces of those around me, the only one dissatisfied in this particular arrangement was me.

This didn't feel like a compromise. This felt like a giant *fuck you.*

Except, I was having a particularly difficult time figuring out just who had done the fucking.

I looked at my daughter, smiling confidently as she expertly answered a question from Pierce's financial analyst. A burst of pride swelled out of the midst of the cacophony of rage and betrayal inside me. She'd had a part in this, but I couldn't blame her for selling me out. I hadn't treated her any better, holding her at arm's length, refusing to let her really sink her teeth into the job I'd given her, forcing her to try to stand out on her own. In many ways, I'd given her no choice but to go prove herself elsewhere.

And, by God, had she proven herself, presenting an attractive strategy to men and women who had far more experience than her under the belt. She'd been bloody brilliant, and I couldn't take any of the credit for that.

Hagan nudged me again. "We could run this from London, even, which is a plus. Less manpower than a merger. Less risk, too. Merging with Werner while all this business is happening with Ron Werner isn't necessarily the wisest of moves."

I turned to face my son as I digested his words. There was logic in them, and from the point of view of the CEO and owner of Accelecom, a merger right now probably wasn't in the company's best interest.

It was from the point of view of Celia's husband that losing Werner mattered. That company belonged in her family. She may have done things that had forced Hudson to take control like he had, but he was well aware that he could still keep that control with me in charge. I'd made sure he understood.

"Look, Dad," Hagan said, his tone more direct. "Pierce could have shut us out all together. We could be going home empty-handed. We should look at this as a win."

I studied him, blinking again as I began to come to my senses. There was no betrayal. This was business. This strategy was sound. Had I been in Pierce's position, this was a move I likely would have made myself.

Honestly, I may not have even been this generous.

"I wonder if it was Genevieve who had a hand in looking out for us." I turned my attention back to her as I rubbed my thumb along my bottom lip. I'd failed her, hadn't I? She was smart and savvy and stunning, and even when I'd failed to lift her up, she'd made sure I was taken care of.

I didn't deserve her for a daughter.

And, Christ. I had another one on the way. How long before I failed that one too?

My thoughts were interrupted by the shuffle of chairs as those around me stood. The meeting was officially over. For a brief second, I imagined ducking out without having to speak to anyone, but before I could really begin to entertain the idea, Warren, still seated, nudged me with his elbow.

"Edward, this is a pretty appealing scenario."

I had to make a choice—show my true feelings about this bloody plan and risk losing the opportunity of the alliance altogether or play nice.

Being a smart man, I made the smart decision. "It is," I said. "One I'm happy to support if you're on board."

Warren grinned and turned his attention to the other proposed entity in our alliance. "Hudson, I've got to say, Pierce Industries as media players—quite a bold move. I like it."

"We try to be innovative whenever we can," Hudson said.

Right. Innovative. More like *safe*. His motivation had been protecting his personal best interests. Real innovation was about taking risks.

Fortunately for Hudson, Warren was easily impressed. "I'd like to study these numbers more closely, boys," he said, standing. "But if everything checks out, I think we have ourselves a solid strategy."

It was too much business for him for one day. He was obviously itching to get out of the building, probably headed for the golf course in the afternoon. Warren hadn't officially retired yet, but he'd been acting like he'd checked out for the last few years.

Sure enough, it was less than three minutes later when he'd gathered his team and was walking out the door.

"I'll walk you to the lift," I said, heading out with him.

"That went well," he said when we were in the hall and the conference room door had shut behind us. "Not at all what I was expecting. Love the idea of putting down our own digital cable. That will be very valuable to us. Nathan Murphy—have any qualms about him?"

I reminded myself I was playing nice before answering. "I hear good things about him. It's an interesting direction."

"It's not what we discussed, I know. You're still my first choice, but if Hudson's picked his horse to back, then we have a problem. Because of the risks involved with Glamplay, we really need to have more support across the stockholders."

I closed my fist and dug my fingernails into my palm. I'd been the one who had presented him with the risks of Glamplay, and now the man was acting as though he'd thought of it himself. It reminded me of another reason I wanted to be at the helm of Werner—because

Warren was a douche and deserved to see his age-old rival sitting in his place.

"Now, here's an idea—you could go after Glamplay, buy up those stocks, and then we'd definitely have the strength we need to push a merger."

It was hard not to laugh. Yes. Great idea. Too bad Hudson had already had it six years earlier.

"They've refused to sell," I said, implying I'd already approached them. It wasn't exactly a lie. Hudson had made it clear he wasn't going to hand those stocks over anytime soon.

"Really?" Warren considered. "If they're not open to selling, then they'd have to vote however I do. Maybe we would have a shot at a merger after all."

If only it were that easy.

"I think your first notion was right. It's better to have Pierce on our side. We should stay the course." God, it hurt saying it.

"Then this alliance is a good idea. Show Hudson what you're made of, build his trust. Later on down the line, when this fuss with Ron has quieted down and Werner doesn't have so much media attention, we come back to the idea of a merger then."

I hated to admit it, but he had a point. This alliance was an opportunity to win Hudson's trust. Show him Celia was no longer a threat. In the future, maybe a merger. Or, perhaps, he would be amenable to selling his shares.

Werner could still be mine.

One way or another, it *would* be mine.

Bolstered by the knowledge that this quest wasn't over, I gave him the reassurance I knew he was seeking. "Good points, Warren. Good plan."

He nodded, as though my approval didn't matter as much as I knew it did. "Celia will like this too. Always a good idea to keep the wife happy."

I frowned. "Celia? Has she said something?"

The lift dinged then and the doors opened. "Nothing we haven't already discussed," he said, following his assistants into the lift.

"Pointed out the risks. Said the timing was bad. Hey, we'll talk more. Come over for dinner, and we'll celebrate."

The doors shut, and I was left to wonder exactly what the conversation had been between my wife and her father.

I couldn't stand there for long, though. I had my own daughter to talk to.

Back in the room, I approached her while she was busy unhooking her laptop from the projector. "Genevieve. You had a hand in this proposal?"

Her face fell, guilt written across her expression. Stepping away from her task, she gave me her full attention. "I'm sorry, Daddy. I'm sure this feels like a betrayal. I know you wanted to run Werner Media yourself."

Playing nice worked with the men. With my daughter, I'd have to take it to a whole other level. There was no way I could live with myself if she had to carry this as a weight. I'd kept her away from my vengeful dealings so she wouldn't be poisoned by my rage. All the pushing away would have been in vain if I let her be poisoned by my feelings now.

Swallowing any traces of lingering emotion, I gave her the most laid-back, most unaffected version of her father I could muster.

In other words, I lied.

"I did want to run Werner Media. Until this morning when Celia broke into tears and told me she really wishes we could stay in London. I wasn't looking forward to telling her father that I wasn't going to take his position. This solves that dilemma." I smiled, hoping it was sincere enough to pull off the sham.

Her eyes shone bright with hope, and any doubts I had about deceiving her vanished. "Then you're not mad?"

"I'm not mad." Not at her, anyway. At myself, yes. And who else, I wasn't sure.

But there were other things I genuinely felt about her. "I'm surprised," I admitted. "I'm also quite impressed. A lot of work went into this. Lots of those ideas I recognize as yours. It's first-rate."

"You think so, even though you don't want me working in the business?" There was a catch in her voice, and for the first time I realized all the real damage I'd done in keeping her at a distance.

I moved closer, as if that one step could bridge all the steps away I'd taken over decades. "The only reason I haven't wanted you working in this business was because I truly thought you'd be happier elsewhere. You've had ambitious goals for Accelecom, and I feared you'd never be able to achieve what you wanted if you stayed with us, but it seems you've found a way to make them possible. I'm proud of you, princess."

Her eyes glistened, and I wasn't sure if it was me or her who reached first, but the next thing I knew, I was holding her. Clinging onto her in a way I hadn't since she was little. Something tightened in my chest and stretched up to the back of my throat, making it hard to swallow, and for a moment, I wasn't sure that I could stand anymore if she weren't in my arms, holding me up.

We held each other like that for long seconds. When she pulled away, she swiped a tear from her cheek before she spoke, her eyes cast down at my shoes. "I know you're bluffing, Dad. You're disappointed. I know you don't like me to see your feelings because...well, I don't really know why you hide so much from me. Because you think I won't see you as strong maybe. Or because you don't think a man should show his emotions."

She looked up at me then, bravely. "Whatever the reason, I want you to know that you'll always loom tall in my eyes. You're my hero, and that's all there is to it. I'm super proud to be your daughter, whether you run every company in the world or none at all."

She'd got me. Right in the heart.

"Genevieve." I pulled her back into my arms. She'd left me speechless, and I needed another moment to simply hold her tight before I could respond.

"It wasn't all a bluff," I said, when I had enough voice to manage a harsh rasp, her head still pressed against my shoulder. "I really do have higher hopes for you than Accelecom. There are better places, better people to align yourself with." I was positive she'd have a job working for Pierce Industries before the day was over, and as much as it pained me to think it, I knew they'd treat her better than I had.

I drew away from her so I could look her in the eyes, needing her to hear this next part—to really hear it. "And I am so proud of you. So very proud, which is entirely ridiculous because I can't take any credit for the woman you've become. I'm proud just to know you, I suppose. It's one of the greatest honors of my life."

With two straight fingers, she wiped at her eyes. "Daddy, stop. I'm working right now, and you're making me a blubbery mess." She swatted me playfully. "And shut up about not being able to take the credit. I'm all you, you prat. For good or bad, who I am is completely your fault."

"In that case, maybe you should be congratulating me." I cleared my throat, and eyed Hudson's younger brother, eager to move to a less sentimental subject. "This Pierce boy..."

"He's not a boy." She rolled her eyes, but it was her blush that gave her away. As I'd suspected, they'd gotten close.

Which made me really tempted to pull him away from his brother so I could break every bone in his body.

But I was a somewhat civilized man and reasonable enough to know that she was old enough to make decisions for herself—for good or bad, to use her words—and if this boy was one of the decisions she wanted to make, I had to let that be her choice.

There was one thing I needed to know, though. "He's good to you?"

"Mm." She peered over at him, her lips twisted. "He's trying to be. I think that's what counts. And I like him, a whole heap, so you can stop perusing him like he's prey."

A growl rumbled in the back of my throat. I expected better than "trying to be" good for my daughter.

"Please, Dad," she said, sounding a little more like she had when she'd been a teen than when she'd delivered her speech only thirty minutes before.

"Fine," I conceded. "But if he hurts you in any way—"

"I know, I know."

"You tell him that."

"Would you...?" She pushed at me with her shoulder, nudging me toward the door where Hagan was waiting with our things. "I'm good. Go. Meeting's over."

"I'm going," I said, chuckling. "I'm going."

The second walk down the hall was less tense. The episode with Genevieve had loosened something in me. Unwound me. My steps felt lighter. The weight of disappointment felt not so burdensome.

Hagan was business as usual, chattering at my side. "I set up a meeting for us next week with Pierce's chief finance officer and that Murphy guy, and I sent a text back to the London office. I'll brief them this afternoon, if you'd like. Or, if you'd rather. Oh, and I heard something."

"Heard what?"

"Gen mentioned that Celia was the one who arranged for Warren to be there today."

"Celia?" That didn't make sense. There were a dozen ways Pierce's office could contact Warren. Using Celia for a business arrangement was not the most effective method of communication.

Unless.

I stopped abruptly and looked back at the conference room just as Hudson walked out with his financial officer. With a handful of strides, I was standing in front of him. "I've a question for you, if you don't mind."

"Certainly." His tone said he was only surprised that I only had one.

There actually were several I would love to pose to him, if given the chance, but at the moment, there was only one that seemed important. "Would you have considered giving me the position if Celia hadn't intervened?"

It was a hunch. A gut feeling that I couldn't explain, but in my experience, my gut feelings very often paid out when I listened to them.

And sure enough, I was onto something. Hudson's usual austere expression had slipped into one of surprise, which might have indicated he had no idea what I was talking about, except for the way his eyes darted. That said he was hiding something. His surprise wasn't that I'd asked an odd question but that I'd known to ask it at all.

I held the higher card now, so I pressed on. "It's a fair question. After being denied a coveted position, a candidate has a right to know whether he even had a shot."

He took a slow breath in, his features composing as he did. "It *is* a fair question, and you deserve a truthful answer. I'm not sure whether she helped you or she hurt you. But she is the reason Warren thinks he has any say in this decision. I'd mark that as a victory, if I were you."

"Thank you. You've been very helpful." I ignored the outstretched hand he offered and turned back to Hagan, resuming my walk to the lift at a brisk pace, the earlier rage roaring over me in a gust.

I'd been right, then. I had been betrayed.

And the one who had betrayed me had been none other than my wife.

SIX

CELIA

I'D BEEN PACING the hotel suite for two hours, checking my phone every five minutes while I waited for news from my father. Not that he'd necessarily update me right away. It would probably be my mother who would call and only if what happened at his meeting was interesting enough for him to tell her, and then interesting enough to *her* to pass on to me.

It occurred to me I might have a better chance of getting the story if I waited at my parents' house, and I'd called to say I was headed over earlier only to be told that Dad was going straight to the club when he was done, and my mother was headed to lunch with "the girls," whoever her gossip buddies were this month.

"Call me right away if you hear anything from Dad, will you?" I'd begged earlier.

"Sure," she'd said, distracted. Then, "You want me to tell you about a business meeting of his?"

"It's regarding his replacement," I'd said impatiently, for the third time. Not wanting to explain more, I'd twisted the truth into a lie. "I want to know if he's changed his mind about working with Edward. So I can know if I need to prepare to comfort my husband or make reservations for celebrating."

"Oh, that's right," she'd said in a way that made me pretty sure she'd forget again as soon as I hung up. "I'll call if I hear anything."

Now, it was almost three hours later, and I hadn't heard a word.

Frustrated, I paused my pacing and texted her. **Any news yet?**

I hit send and then decided it was probably a good idea to clarify. **From Daddy?**

It took several minutes for her reply so I jumped when the notification pinged.

Mom: **Only talked briefly. He says things are good. Ask Edward for more details. He was there as well.**

Considering I'd asked her to give me the update so that I could be prepared for Edward, her text was not very helpful.

Except that she'd filled me in on something I hadn't even thought to consider—Edward had been at the meeting as well.

Fuck.

Why had Edward been there? Chandler had asked me to get a meeting with my father. When had that invitation been extended to Edward? Did that mean Hudson had changed his mind? Was he giving over the top spot to Edward after all?

After our last encounter, it was possible, but didn't seem likely.

Then Edward had to have been there because my father had taken him along. Which meant he probably argued any alternative CEO suggested. Which meant Hudson had very definitely argued back, and though there were a dozen different ways I could imagine the scenario going from there, I was pretty sure many of them ended in the same way—with Edward in a rage.

There was a chance he wouldn't come straight home after. He spent most of his days in his temporary office, and even if he did come home, he might not give any indication that he'd had a bad day, seeing how he barely gave me any indication of his days at all as of late.

But if things had gone very, very badly for him, if he had any reason to blame me...

Going to my parents' house was once again appealing. Very appealing.

I turned my pacing into a purposeful stride, slipping on a pair of flats, searching for where I'd left my purse, finding it at the far end of the living room next to the sofa. After checking to make sure my sunglasses were inside, I turned to head out, muttering to myself how ridiculous I was being since, even if the meeting had gone as I'd suspected, there was little chance that I'd be connected to it at all, only to stop abruptly when I looked up and saw Edward at the mouth of the room.

Though his expression gave away nothing, his eyes said everything. They burned into me with vehement, laser focus, radiating hatred and fury and murder, and he didn't have to say a single word. He knew. I didn't know how it was possible, but he *knew*.

And here I was, trapped. Two glass walls at my back, a wall of books and a wall of concrete before me, Edward blocking the only way in or out.

Trapped.

"Good. You're here." Despite the indignation in his gaze, his tone was cold.

Scary cold. Cold that lashed and bit and bore down to the bone.

I always found him irresistible like that, when he was menacing and mean. It sparked something in the lizard parts of my being, turned me into a baser version of myself. Made me feral and restless and aroused.

At a more civilized level, it made me wary.

I swallowed, taking a careful step around the cocktail ottoman, calculating my options. Could I make it past him if I ran? Did I need to try to escape?

Did I *want* to?

"I was on my way out." This step was less cautious, as were the next two that followed.

But then he took a step of his own, toward me. "It can wait."

"It..." I was on the verge of making up a lie, but where would I urgently need to be? The doctor was my only obligation these days, and Edward had been with me when I'd made my next appointment for a month out.

Maybe I was making this into more than it was anyway. "Okay. What's up?" I forced a casual inflection and urged the corners of my lips up, not quite a smile, but less not than before.

He moved again, toward me, stopping at the desk to deposit a small brown bag I only just noticed. The kind they used at the drugstore down the block. The shape the contents made wasn't quite discernible, but whatever it was, it stayed standing when he set it down.

"I had an interesting meeting this morning that I wanted to discuss with you," he said, and the bag was forgotten as I returned to panicking.

I pushed the strap of my purse up my shoulder, clutching to it with the need to clutch to something, and somehow managed to sound collected. "That's new. Since you don't usually talk to me about...well, anything."

"I probably wouldn't this time either, if you weren't so inextricably involved." He stalked toward me, circling round the ottoman like a lion on the hunt.

"Oh? What happened?" I reversed direction, which wasn't any better because now the couch was on the other side of me and the rest of the way around was narrow and more caged.

In a flash, he was right in front of me, heat emanating from his body now as well as his mood, and I dropped my purse and thought again of making a run for it, willed my legs to make the move, but something deeper willed me to stay still, not quite in surrender. More like in curiosity. In enthrallment.

"It's less of what happened that I'm apt to share at the moment," he said, backing me up toward his desk without laying a single hand on me. "And more of how it made me feel."

Shit. "Do you need to have a session?"

Not really the time to poke at the beast, but I never could help myself when it came to him.

And, as often happened when I poked, I was rewarded. I fought not to purr as his hands gripped my hips, his touch sending electric pulses to my core and warmth up through my chest.

God, it had been so long. I wanted to lean in. Wanted to cling. Wanted to urge him to touch more.

Turned out no urging was needed. "I believe a session isn't necessary." He pressed his body flush against mine. "I can already succinctly articulate the emotion."

Delicious chills ran through me as he slanted his mouth toward my ear. "It feels," he said in a husky baritone, "like I've been fucked in the arse. By my wife."

My mouth fell open, my body ready to protest before my mind had strung any defense together.

He pushed tighter against me, pinning me with his hips while also showing off an impressive erection hidden inside his Brioni suit. Vaguely, I was aware of him reaching across the desk for the bag he'd set down earlier, then fully aware when he dug inside and pulled out a bottle of generic lube.

"I thought it only fair to reciprocate," he said.

Adrenaline shot through my system, my heart palpitating as I understood his intent. "Now...Edward..."

No words came after that because I wasn't all too sure what it was I wanted to convey. I needed a second to think.

But he didn't give me any time at all.

"Turn around." He was already guiding my body to do as he'd commanded.

I was halfway turning, so used to surrendering when he took charge, then came to my senses. "Wait. I'm..."

I blinked up at him, unable to finish this sentence as well.

His eyes connected with mine, serious and seeking. "Are you telling me to stop?"

I should have.

I should have stood my ground, pushed him off of me, and said *This is not happening, no fucking way.*

But I was scared. Not because I thought he'd force himself on me, but because I was afraid that if I protested, he *would* stop, and while I was also very intimidated about what he apparently wanted to do to me, I was desperately wanting him, in any way he'd give himself.

Especially if he planned to give himself on his terms. That air of danger and dominance exuding from his every pore was not a detriment but, rather, a bonus.

Instead of responding with words, I simply finished turning around and leaned my palms down on the desk, readying myself for whatever he wanted to give, be it pain or pleasure or some cruel combination of the two.

"Good girl," he said, stroking from the collar of my dress down my spine, like he was petting a beloved animal.

I arched into it, seeking more as he continued over my ass, squeezing one cheek before gathering my skirt up at my waist. With one hand, he wriggled my panties down until they were stretched taut across my thighs then stepped back to admire the view.

He emitted a throaty, "Mm," a sound I echoed when he touched me, a single finger tracing my cunt. I was embarrassingly wet, dripping without any more stimulation than that. Eager, too, my hips pushing back, urging his finger inside me.

He granted me the smallest dip only to bring it back out almost immediately, trailing my wetness up to the hole above it, the rim that had never been breached, not in this direction anyway.

He worked himself in with his thumb, if I had to guess from the shape and curve of the rest of his hand on the flesh nearby. The tracing of this hole elicited a different reaction from me. It wasn't exactly unpleasurable. In fact, it felt kind of nice, though, also foreign, and while my body knew what it wanted from a finger at my cunt, it didn't quite know what to do with one in my ass. Should I lean in? Should I pull away?

Currently, I was frozen in place, and that wasn't doing much for me.

But then his hand was gone from my ass, and he was slanting over my body, his mouth at my neck. "Who do you belong to?" he asked.

And even though I'd heard him and knew exactly what he wanted to hear in return, I said, "What?"

His hand came up to collar my throat, firmly, but not threateningly. More possessive. "Who. Do you. Belong to?"

It was a thinly veiled request of consent, maybe because, while I hadn't told him to stop, I also hadn't told him to go on. I hadn't given him an outright "okay." It was admirable that he needed that from me, I supposed, though I didn't believe he would ever actually force himself on a woman, despite his tendency to dominate and control.

I also didn't suspect that was all this was about now.

He knew it would be easier for me to "let" it happen and maintain the right to resent him for it later. It gave me both my cake and the eating of it, and that was way too much for Edward to ever let me have.

If I wanted the cake, I had to *own* the cake.

And that meant answering his question with yielding honesty. "You."

I could feel the whoosh of hot air as he sighed into my nape. "Say it again."

"I belong to you, Edward."

I didn't have to say any more for us both to understand my meaning. I was his to do with as he pleased. Because I wanted to be his. Because I trusted what he'd give me. Because I needed it, too.

With my consent given, he went into action, moving his hand from my throat and standing straight up. I glanced over my shoulder to see what he was doing.

"Eyes forward," he ordered.

I lingered, watching as he undid his pants, pushing down his boxer briefs just far enough to bare his steel column of flesh. It was hot, as always, his cock impressive to look at as well as be fucked by, but knowing where it was going this time, it was also a bit intimidating.

Maybe that was why he'd wanted my eyes forward.

I shivered and turned back to the desk, leaning down on my forearms. I had a feeling I was going to need the support.

He reached for the lube next. I watched from the corner of my eye as he flipped open the lid with one hand and pulled it out of my view. A tickle of wet down my crack told me he'd poured some there. His thumb returned to push some liquid inside before his touch disappeared again.

Then I could hear the slick sound of moisture and skin as he applied it to himself. I remembered watching him the other day, staring at his hand gliding along his cock, and imagining it now behind me made a fresh pool between my legs.

Cold pressure against my tight rim snapped my thoughts back to the present, to the foreign sensation at my backend and the visitor who wanted in. My muscles stiffened, my breath caught in my lungs, as I waited for the part that came next. The shove forward, the pain that would undoubtedly accompany it.

But it didn't come.

His tip stayed poised at the entrance—the exit?—while, once again, his palm traced down my spine, soothing me. Settling me.

"Touch yourself," he said sharply.

"I can't."

"I'm not asking."

I shook my head and bit my lip. "I don't want it to feel good."

It wasn't as though I thought I deserved to be punished. I'd done what I'd done for good reason, and however it had turned out in the end, I had no regrets.

But I also knew that Edward wanted me punished, and I wanted to be *us* again, and if giving him this could pay for what he perceived I'd taken away, then I would give it absolutely, with complete capitulation and trust.

From the low groan he gave at my words, he not only understood but appreciated it.

"I'm not sure right now if I want it to feel good for you either, but the fact remains that I will tear you apart if you don't relax, and I certainly don't want that." This time he moved my hand down for me, using my fingers to caress the blazing bud of nerves, held them there until he felt confident about my finger strokes.

Then his fingers were inside me, in my cunt, pushing in from behind. He crooked them to massage against my G-spot in exactly the right way, the way only he'd ever discovered, and within several seconds, I relaxed into him, pushing my hips back, begging for more.

He took advantage of my ease, and slipped the tip of his cock inside me, stopping when he got to the tighter rim inside.

"Keep rubbing," he commanded.

I hadn't even noticed I'd stopped. I'd been too focused on the new sensation at my ass. His cock, it turned out, felt definitely bigger than his thumb. Like I-do-not-know-how-this-will-ever-fit big, and panic tensed my shoulders. Rubbing myself didn't seem to help. I was too busy concentrating, too distracted to feel anything good.

Edward's hand disappeared from my cunt, more liquid trickled in around the head stuffed in my ass, then his hand returned to mine, shoving it out of the way so he could swirl firm circles over my sensitive bud.

Yes. Just like that. Yes.

I'd forgotten how good he was at working my clit. Bodies couldn't remember sensation like that. Like pain. I could remember that I liked it, that it was really, really good, but I couldn't remember the exact feeling.

And the feeling was fucking fantastic. My back arched, and I moaned.

He leaned over me again, and sprinkled kisses at my neck while pushing his cock back and forth against the tight ring inside me. Wanting blatantly to be in.

Rather metaphorical, I thought abstractly.

"You spoke to him," he said, low and urging. This wasn't a question, but the next part was. "In person or on the phone?"

That's what this would be then? An interrogation? I was glad, at least, that he didn't say *his* name. It didn't belong in this act, though even keeping his name out of it, he was still here, between us. As he had been for so long.

I hung my head, resigning myself. "In person."

"Did you play the seductive role or the dragon?"

"They're not mutually exclusive."

"You know what I'm asking."

I did, but the question irritated me. "I didn't try to seduce him, Edward. His brother was there, and even if he hadn't been—"

My words cut off as he inched farther inside me. Not a lot, not the whole of him, but his crown had definitely breached that rim.

He stayed there, still, letting me get used to it as his fingers worked magic, going back and forth from my clit to my cunt. Discomfort morphed with pleasure, and pretty soon I couldn't tell if I loved his cock in my ass or I just tolerated it.

Just when I decided it was definitely more on the love side, he shoved in all the way, filling me completely.

Holy.

Mother.

Fuck.

I felt filled. Overwhelmed. Full of Edward in every possible way—in my ass, in my cunt, in my head. In my belly, where our baby reminded me of her presence with a gentle flutter. He was all-consuming, and I never felt closer to him or more taken over or more on the verge of...something...something unnamable, and all of it was so fantastic and thrilling and new and painful and it terrified me to tears.

"Play with your nipples. Breathe." He was insistent but reassuring, and without even thinking, I complied, brushing the flat of my palm across my clothing, which was enough to stimulate my breasts these days.

And I breathed. A deep in and out followed by another. And another.

Then everything knotted inside me relaxed, and he was still there—still so completely there and everywhere—but it was no longer unbearably oppressive. Now it was fascinating and tremendous and even a little comforting and a whole lot of wonderful.

"There you go. Like that. Just like that."

He started moving, slowly. With short, delicate thrusts that sent shivers down my spine, made me warm and flushed and disoriented. Spun me up toward orgasmic euphoria.

I was in this blissed-out stupor, dazed by feeling *so much* in *so many places* at once, when his interrogation resumed.

"You saw him, his brother was there." He nipped my ear before going on. "And you said, 'Please don't let my husband have your company. Give it to someone else. Anyone else just not him.'"

"No!" He shoved harder, or in my alarm, I'd pushed back on him, and now I wasn't responding just to his accusation but to the throbbing heat inside my rear. "Ohmygod, ohmygod, no." Then I worried he'd think I meant no to the action, which even at its most overwhelming, I didn't want to stop. I tried again. "Oh my God that's intense, and no, I didn't say anything close to that."

"What did you say?" His voice was hypnotic as was his rhythm, steady and pulsing, somehow hitting that tender spot deep inside me from the other side. Stars spread across my vision. A sonorous hum vibrated in the back of my throat.

"I said I knew." I had to close my eyes and take a second so I wouldn't explode. Once I caught my breath, I rushed on. "I knew he wouldn't give it to you. So I asked him to help make whatever he decided look like my father's idea."

Edward slowed ever so slightly. His hand tangled in my hair, smoothly before giving a rough pull. "You weren't out just to fuck me?"

Does he really think...?

I was on the verge of coming when I got it. Got why he was giving me this aching pleasure when he was so entirely incensed with what I'd done, not just now but the whole last six months—stopping my birth control, running away, refusing to give up A's name.

He wasn't *just* angry. He was also *impressed.*

He wanted me to submit to him, and I did, but he also wanted me to challenge him, and I did. And maybe it was like how I enjoyed being scared of him as much as I enjoyed being cared for, two opposing emotions that pulled and tugged and stretched and made him crazy and confused and basically fucked. No wonder we'd been at such an impasse—his battle was with himself as much as it was with me, and what was he supposed to do with that?

There wasn't much I could do for his personal wars.

That didn't stop me from wanting to acknowledge it. "No," I said, my syllables short. "But admit it." Heaving breath. "You kind of admire that I did."

"That's enough. That's enough. That's enough." A mantra repeated over and over as he pounded in, in, in, his pelvis slapping against my thighs, his words a hoarse string of *That's enough,* no breaks in between. One more time he tried to say it, his voice threadbare as he thrust harder, harder, harder. "That's e—

If he finished the end of his sentence, I didn't hear it. Sound muffled around me, as though I'd been plunged underwater, or like the aftereffect of a very loud boom. All I could hear was my heart in my ears underscored with a whir as an electric storm flashed across my vision and my muscles went completely rigid.

I cried out and spiraled and convulsed, taken by a full-body climax that was at least a 9.0 on the orgasm Richter scale. I couldn't remember ever being so devastated from pleasure, so completely wrecked that I didn't know up from down. Couldn't tell if I was standing upright or a puddle on the floor.

Distantly, I was aware of clenching around Edward's cock, of his dedicated commitment to keep thrusting, to the stuttered final jab before he roared with his own release, a jagged sort of groan that I was sure would make me hot every time I thought about it for years to come.

I sort of blacked out then. Several seconds went missing from my awareness. One moment I was braced on my forearms with Edward coming in my ass, the next thing I knew, my panties were up, my forehead was against the desk, and my husband was zipped up and put away behind me.

With gentle urgency, he pulled me up, gathered me into his arms and kissed me. Complete and thorough and all him because, even though I was grateful for his lips, I was too boneless and dazed to really do anything but take it.

When he'd seemed to get what he needed, he broke away, pressing his forehead to mine and sighed. "What am I supposed to do with you, bird?"

"Love me."

He let out a gruff chuckle. "I love you too much, I think, sometimes." Without moving our heads apart, he ran the back of his knuckles across my jaw. "I hurt you."

He had that pitch of regret, and the way he was holding me, I was certain he was talking about what we just did.

"Yes," I conceded. "But not how you think. And I hurt you too."

His eyes closed briefly then opened again. "Knowing that doesn't erase our argument."

"I know."

He brushed his nose lightly against mine, then untangled himself from me in degrees—first his forehead, then his hand from my jaw. Then his body was no longer pressed against mine. Then it was the desk that held me up entirely and not him at all.

He turned away to the windows to gaze out.

I wasn't ready to lose him again, and I wasn't sure that I even was losing him, but I needed to know some things regardless, and this seemed as good a time as any to ask. "Will you tell me how it played out?"

He didn't turn around. "A three-point alliance between Werner, Accelecom, and Pierce Industries. An opportunity to bring our assets to the US and for Werner to break into the foreign market while simultaneously developing hardware that can compete with Google Fiber. Nathan Murphy from Mirage is being offered Werner CEO."

"And no merger."

"No merger."

It was ambitious, but also totally doable with the financial strength of Pierce Industries. Hudson had that kind of power—gigantic power. The kind that was both awe-inspiring and ominous. It was a top-of-the-game privilege to be able to partner with him.

My ribs ached with realization. "He tied us more securely to him, didn't he? He doesn't just own the majority shares of Werner but now he's linked Accelecom as well." I thought I should probably tell Edward I was sorry, but there wasn't an apology I could give that would be worth the one deserved.

"If it makes you feel any better, I don't believe it was all Hudson's idea." After giving me time to react with shock and curiosity, he went on. "The younger brother presented the idea. You'll never guess who was at his side."

But I could guess because of what Chandler had said the other day. "Genevieve."

"You knew?"

I wished I had, simply because it was rare that I had the opportunity of surprising my husband. Except I didn't really wish that, because I hated that I knew it now. Hated how much her part in this had to have hurt him. How much it must have felt like a betrayal.

On top of my betrayal.

Yes, he'd had a very, very bad day indeed.

"I didn't know," I answered truthfully, aching to say something more comforting. "I'd heard a mention that they knew each other, and the pieces sort of fell into place."

"She sold the idea rather brilliantly. In other circumstances..." He turned back to look at me. "I couldn't bear to let her think she hadn't masterminded a good thing. I told her you were crying, begging to go back to London."

"You're as good at playing games as I ever was." I smiled weakly. He almost smiled back. A beat passed. "Then we're headed back to London?"

"Do you want to go?"

Our conversation was painfully stilted but vitally important, so I stuck with it in earnest. "Cornwall Terrace is my home now. I want to raise our baby there. Turn my office into a nursery. Redo the play-room." Imagining us in London made my sides ache with longing. "But I'm attached to my doctor here. And the trial is about to start there."

"We'll stay then," he said, resolutely. "I'll get us a connecting suite for when the baby comes. We'll go home when you're ready, after she's here."

After she's here. I couldn't bear to think we'd still be this awkward with each other when she arrived.

I had to keep him, had to pull him back before we lost this moment entirely, but I didn't know quite how. "Genevieve and Chandler, then," when I couldn't think of anything else.

"Genevieve and Chandler." He seemed less dismayed than I thought he would be.

"I'm sure that has Hudson mortified. Though, could you imagine? If they stayed together?" It was comical, so I laughed. Then reality sank in. "Even more tied together."

"Perhaps that will work out in our favor."

I gave him a stare that very blatantly said I just can't possibly see how.

"It's a wonder what being family can do to a business relationship. Your father would never have agreed to a joint venture let alone a merger before we married. Maybe Hudson would finally feel comfortable about selling us those shares."

"You still want Werner."

"I'll *have* Werner. Eventually."

Of course he wanted it. He always wanted, wanted, wanted. There was nothing ever enough to satisfy him. He would get it too, as he always did. I had no doubt. It was something I both admired and resented about him. His hunger and avarice made him powerful, powerful enough to succeed, and that was a major turn-on.

Just, it would be nice to believe he had all he needed in loving me.

Way to dream, Celia.

And since the dream couldn't be reality, I had to fight for what I could get, for our baby. "I'm guessing this will be a long game. May I propose a truce?"

He raised a brow, intrigued.

"You keep your secrets, I'll keep mine. Whatever you pursue in business is, no pun intended, your business." I wished he were closer, that I could reach out to him or that I had the nerve to go to him and throw myself in his arms. Since I didn't, I put my hand on my belly for reassurance instead. "Until she's born, at least."

His eyes went from mine to my hand resting over our child. A split second later, he was in front of me again, wrapping himself around me. "Yes. A truce. It would probably be best. For both your sakes."

I blinked back tears, wary of asking for too much, but wanting more all the same. "For your sake, too?" I asked, hopefully.

"Definitely for my sake, too."

I relaxed into him, feeling like we were finally on the same side, even if we weren't really. We were for now, united in our love for each other and our baby and our determination to stay together no matter what.

It would be hard, though, when the truce was over. When the secrets pushed their faces up against the windows, demanding to be let in.

He was thinking it as well, he had to be.

I knew for certain moments later, after he'd suggested a bath to clean us up and soothe my tail end and after I'd cooed about his desire to take care of me like he once had so routinely and after he'd promised he would again from now on. He cupped a dominating hand at my cheek and brushed his lips over mine, hot and possessive and open-mouthed.

"It's not just Werner I want," he said. "I'll want all of you, too. Eventually."

And like everything, he'd get all of me. Eventually.

I was a fool if I believed anything else.

SEVEN

EDWARD

NOTHING COULD HAVE PREPARED me for this moment.

Not the birth of my first two children, delivered so long ago in another country, when newborn practices varied in small but significant ways, when infants were immediately carted off to a nursery to be weighed and measured and cleansed instead of placed, all coated in white, waxy vernix, on the mother's bare torso to stretch and squint and whimper and root.

Not the childbirth class that Celia had requested I take with her, and I, in an attempt to honor the truce we'd made in good faith, had humbled myself to concede—a twelve-week course that had consisted of labor rehearsals and relaxation techniques and a thorough tour of our birthing facility and guidance on how to coach and instructions on how to give a good massage, that I, thank you very much, did not need.

Not the hours of late night talking when Celia should have been getting her rest but, instead, curled up next to me with a baby book on her e-reader as I caressed the expanding swell of flesh that housed a tiny human forming in our image.

Even through the preceding fourteen hours of labor—as my wife had, despite growing weary from contractions that squeezed and wrung her like she were a sponge, soldiered and triumphed while I'd made poor attempts to guide and support her—I hadn't quite grasped what we were headed for, what the end result would be. That I would eventually be looking through glassy eyes at the most beautiful scene witnessed in my forty-five years of life—my daughter in the arms of a tear-streaked goddess, a woman so evidently made to be a mother that I suddenly wondered what importance I could possibly be in her life.

How had I ever thought to keep this from her?

I was thoroughly convinced this child was more than just a blessing of joy. She'd been fated.

"Ten on the second apgar test." The nurse folded the blanket back over the baby then pulled the tiny hat farther down on her head. "Make sure she stays warm now. Skin-to-skin is best for that, but you'll want to keep that heat trapped around her."

Celia nuzzled our daughter closer. "She's doing okay, then?"

I didn't know if the nurse noted the hint of worry in her tone or not, but she was sufficiently reassuring all the same. "Her color's good, she's breathing well. She's perfect."

"Oh, thank God." More tears leaked from her eyes as she bent down to kiss our baby's head.

Without leaving her shoulder where I'd been firmly planted for the last ninety minutes, I peeked over at the hospital team still working down below. Knowing our daughter was in good health was a relief, to say the least, but I wouldn't be able to relax until I knew my wife was as well.

"Everything routine?" I asked, afraid I sounded far more on edge than Celia had.

"Placenta's just been delivered," the obstetrics doctor said, not the one we'd met with over the course of pregnancy, but the one that had been on call when Celia's contractions had begun in earnest the night before, sending us to the center with her packed bag. "There's been no tearing. Nothing to stitch. We should be out of here shortly."

That hadn't quite been an answer to my question, and I teetered between asking again and forcing myself to accept that all was fine.

Before I made up my mind, the baby nurse—or pediatrician or

delivery assistant, I didn't know who was whom anymore, the room having got crowded—called me over. "Would you like to cut the cord?"

"Uh." I blinked, having forgotten about that tradition. I'd assumed the job had already been done. "Sure. What do I...?"

A pair of scissors were placed in my hands, and a spot on the cord between two clamps offered up for me. I brought up the instrument and made the cut and the whole thing took a matter of seconds and, especially compared to everything Celia had done to deliver our baby, was nothing, yet I felt quite smug in that moment.

My wife called me. "Edward?"

Frankly, I'd thought she might have forgotten I was here in the midst of her elation, which was more a reflection on my feeling of insignificance than of her preoccupation with our child, and I returned to her side at once. "I'm here."

"Look at her. She's beautiful. Isn't she so beautiful?"

I picked up a miniature hand as it curled reflexively in the air. "She's exquisite."

"I know this pregnancy was uneventful for the most part, but I can't stop feeling like she's a miracle."

"She is," I agreed. "And meant to be."

Celia's head spun toward me. Her surprised eyes also held a question that she didn't have to voice to be understood. I'd been so vehemently resistant to conceiving. Of course she'd be confused about how much I wanted our child now that she was here.

I didn't get a chance to respond, though, before Talyse, the nurse who had been with us for the past several hours, put a comforting hand on Celia's shoulder. "We've done the immediate clean up needed. I'll be back within the hour to give her eye drops and Vitamin K. Meanwhile, we'll give you three a little bit of time to bond."

Panic registered on my wife's face. "You're just going to leave her with us?"

Talyse managed to hold her laugh. "She's yours now. You'll be just fine. I'll be a click of a button away, if you need me. Let her try to nurse if she wants to, or if that seems to not be happening, you can just hold her close. Let her hear your voice. She already knows you, and that will make her feel right at home." She paused to make sure Celia had really heard her before going on. "Does this precious little thing have a name yet?"

"Cleo." Celia glanced at me. I'd been charged with deciding on a middle name, which I had, but I'd yet to share it.

"Cleo Wren," I said now.

Celia's expression lit up as she put the meaning of our daughter's full name together. "Small bird of glory."

I suddenly worried it was the wrong choice. "Is it...okay?"

She nodded. "I love it."

"It's gorgeous," Talyse said. "And it fits her, as this small thing is definitely glorious." She ran her thumb across Cleo's cheek. "Now enjoy yourselves."

The door shut quietly behind her as she left, and we were left alone, a little family in awe.

My own alarm began to rise. It had been so long since I'd been around a child so small, and even when I had been, I hadn't done a whole lot of engaging. Mostly because I'd been a fuck of a father, and here we were with this sweet child, sure I was about to fuck up again.

Before the panic took hold of me entirely, Celia set down an anchor. "Sit by me?" She wriggled to the side to make me room, which wasn't much, but turned out to be just enough.

I sank onto the bed beside her, throwing an arm around her shoulders, then peered down along with her at the wiggling bundle pressed up against her chest. "You did it, bird. You did this. You grew a person and brought her into this world. I'm so unbelievably amazed by you."

"I know I complained a lot this last month about my feet and my back and my bladder and, well, everything, really, but it kind of feels like all that was nothing right now." She considered for a second. "Okay, that's not true. The last few hours were the worst. I honestly didn't think I was going to make it."

"I knew you would."

She looked up at me earnestly. "You did?"

I tightened my hold around her. "Never a doubt in my mind."

Her complaints about pregnancy hadn't been much either, to be honest. Marion had been quieter, of course, as I suspected she found a certain joy in her suffering. Celia, on the other hand, had been down-right miserable, and it showed, even without her saying a word. The way she moved like it took a lot of effort, the way she tossed and turned every night trying to find a comfortable position, the way her feet had swollen up to the size of logs—I'd been astonished she hadn't carped more.

I'd done what I could for her, taking care of her in the manner I had before we'd fought so terribly as well as in new ways, and none of it had seemed enough. Of everything I was able and willing to bear for her, this had been the one thing I simply could not, and it had infuriated me almost as much as not being allowed to seek vengeance in her honor.

It was funny how that had begun to mean both less and more to me.

I much preferred loving her to bickering. And the glow she carried throughout her pregnancy had made me truly doubt whether she needed the closure to her past that I believed she needed.

At the same time, as the weeks turned into months, as Celia carried the burden of pregnancy and our child became real and inevitable, my sense of purpose became more primal and fully rooted. Wasn't I supposed to be the caretaker? Wasn't I supposed to look out for her in everything? There existed a natural instinct for her to be a mother, a need that she had desperately required be met. Wasn't it natural that I possessed a similar instinct to protect and defend?

Her denial to let me be that for her, primitive as the notion might be, seemed as oppressive as I'd been in trying to keep her from having a child.

There.

I could admit it. I'd been wrong. It was impossible not to acknowl-edge it in the presence of the creature suckling at Celia's breast.

"Hi, Cleo. It's your mom. I've been waiting so long to meet you." She let out a giggle as the tiny mouth closed around her nipple. "Wow. That feels so weird."

"It can't be that odd," I teased. "I've sucked your tits on plenty of occasions."

She gave a glare that was hardly effective with the grin that accompanied it. "It's not the same. At all."

"I probably shouldn't find that so mollifying, but I do."

"You're such a man." Her smile lingered as she cooed again at Cleo. Then it disappeared entirely, her brow knitting ever so slightly. "Our truce has expired."

I winced. It shouldn't be the thing on her mind right now, and I felt entirely to blame that it was. "This isn't the time for that discussion."

"Actually, I think this is exactly the time for that discussion. Everything changes now, with her. We have to get used to a whole new rhythm of life, we have to develop new routines, and I can't do that if I don't know where you and I stand."

"We stand exactly where we've always stood, bird—I love you, you love me." I reached across her face to sweep a piece of hair behind her ear. "That should be all that matters."

My hand remained there, cupping her face, and I don't know if it was me or her that tilted her chin up, but soon her eyes were locked with mine. "If that's all that matters, then you don't ever need to know all my secrets."

The room felt suddenly colder, like the air had just kicked on, which was definitely not the case seeing as it was early in February with a snowstorm predicted in the coming days. What she'd said may have been a casual statement, one of her barbed jabs she was so fond of pointing in my direction, but it had the heaviness of an ultimatum.

I opened my mouth to respond, but nothing came out.

She shook her head against my palm. "You can't drop it, can you?"

"This does not need to be decided right now," I insisted, rubbing my thumb across her skin. "I'm certainly not going to begin efforts to find out what I want to know anytime soon."

"Then when?" Her voice was as sharp as her gaze. "Will you wait until she's a year old? Five years old? How about until she's eighteen?"

"Celia..."

"If you can't let this go permanently—"

I cut her off, dropping my hand from her face at the same time.

"You better not be headed where I think you are. Not ever, but certainly not right now, of all occasions."

She swallowed, her eyes dropping back to Cleo who had fallen asleep at her breast. When she looked up again at me, her expression was both softer and more resolved.

"Here's the thing, Edward—this isn't just about us anymore. Our battle doesn't just affect you and me. I could live with your distance and your resentment before, but not now. She doesn't deserve that. She deserves parents that are partners, not rivals. I won't be that for her."

"Then we won't be that for her. We are far from rivals. Just because we don't agree on everything doesn't mean we aren't a good pair."

Abruptly, she seemed to switch gears. "Do you love her?"

It gutted me that she had to ask. I had to take a moment before I could answer. "Of course I love her. How can you not know that?"

"You didn't want her."

"I wanted her. I just..." I sighed. I'd been scared, in truth. Also, I'd been a bully. "I shouldn't have leveraged a baby to try to get what I wanted. I know that. But you see, don't you, that you were also not fair in how you went around that?"

"I do see that. And I refuse to be like that anymore, a person who has to scheme to get what she needs. So if you can't give me what I need then—"

"Don't say it." She stopped at my command. Momentarily, anyway. Then was about to say more so I said it again. "Don't. Please. Please, don't." I couldn't bear to hear how the sentence ended because if it went where it so definitely seemed to be going, I didn't know if I could continue drawing air into my lungs. I'd been through one divorce, and it had nearly killed me. I couldn't imagine what it would do to me to lose Celia when the way I loved her was so much more than the way I'd loved Marion.

She nodded once, conceding. "I don't need to say it for you to know."

That confirmed it then. My worst fear.

My eyes fell to Cleo, the sun and all the stars combined. It was insane that we were talking about this right now when she was here, and she was glorious, and ours, and I loved her. More than I thought I would. More than I'd thought I was capable of loving anything.

"What is it you need?" I pushed the words out with quiet force, knowing the conversation wouldn't go away just because I wanted it gone.

It was an atomic bomb of a question, though. Because when she answered, as I was sure she would answer, demanding I give up the quest to avenge her wrongdoer, asking me to be a man that I was not and had never been, then everything between us would explode, impossible to ever put back together again.

But she didn't answer how I expected.

"It's not what I need, it's what she needs. And it's nonnegotiable." She bent to nuzzle her nose against Cleo's head, then, with her eyes still centered on her, she said, "You will be everything for our daughter. Everything. You will be present. You will be engaged. You will put her before any other pursuit—before your business, before your obsessions. You will care and provide for her. You will keep her safe. You will protect her from predators. You will believe her when she comes to you in a crisis. And when the world lets her down, and she needs to crawl into your lap and fall apart, you will listen to her and console her and build her up again, but you will not destroy her monsters for her, not even if she asks you to, unless we both agree it's the right thing to be done, and—" she lifted her eyes promptly to mine "—I'm telling you right now, Edward, it will very rarely, if ever, be the right thing to be done."

It was like slamming into a wall of bricks the way her words hit me, their impact was so forceful. I was supposed to take care of her, to see what was best for her. I knew the horrors of her past and her father's role in her pain. How had I not understood that what she'd need most for me to be was a father for her daughter that she wished she'd had for herself?

As sure as I had been that I had fucked up my older children and that I was doomed to repeat it with Cleo, I was suddenly sure that I wasn't. I could be those things she asked. For our daughter. Because

Celia believed I could be. Because she demanded it of me. Because I wouldn't be the man who repeated the sins of her father.

I once again brought my hand up to her cheek. Her face was wet with tears, her eyes full of more that had yet to be shed. Yet she was, at that moment, the strongest person I had ever known.

"I will," I said hoarsely, a ball stuck at the back of my throat. I cleared my throat. "I promise. I will. For both of you."

A tear leaked down my cheek as I kissed her forehead. Another fell as I bent to kiss Cleo. She stirred, her eyes squinting and relaxing several times, as though she were trying to open them. Then she gave up and gave her energy instead to suckling at her mother's breast.

"Good," Celia said, her own voice tight. "Thank you, that's...good."

We settled into silence, heavy but not burdensome. As though I was carrying a load that I very much wanted to be carrying. My emotions were a knot inside me, too tangled to pick out all of them individually.

One, though, stood out from the rest, one I was quite familiar with —the "almost" feeling. The one I'd experienced most frequently after Celia had come into my life. Before her, I'd always been insufferably far away from whatever it was that was the goal, the abstract completion that I longed for and could never actually achieve.

Then she'd appeared, and that "will-never-reach" feeling had grown more and more possible, and now it felt so close. Like trying to catch a string of a helium balloon just as it drifts out of my grasp. Like closing my hand around a fistful of fog or smoke and opening it again to find a bare palm.

I closed my hands now, one around Celia's shoulder and another around Cleo's tiny foot. I lay there, as long as I could, until a nurse came in to tend to my women, way beyond when my limbs had fallen asleep and my neck had got a crick, afraid if I opened my hands again I'd find them both empty.

EIGHT

CELIA

I GASPED and brought my hand to my chest, a cliched gesture that was both authentic and fitting for the moment. "Oh my, that's spectacular!"

Spectacular was actually an understatement. The Edwardian style jewel on Genevieve's finger, with its bead of diamonds around a larger stone, was genuinely one of the most gorgeous engagement rings I'd ever seen.

Also, possibly one of the most expensive. The center stone had to be at least two carats, and if I had to guess, I'd say the whole thing probably cost a hundred grand.

I supposed that was the kind of bauble you got when you hooked up with a Pierce. Once upon a time, I would have been seething with jealousy, despite having not an ounce of attraction for Chandler. It was his last name that I'd coveted. I could barely remember feeling that way now, as content as I was with a sleeping four-month-old baby in the next room and a husband that I loved madly at my side.

A husband who hadn't said a word since his older daughter stuck out her hand to share the good news.

"Daddy?" Her voice was cautious but hopeful. Understandably so. She was only twenty-four, and last she'd told us, she'd indicated marriage wasn't anywhere on their radar. She and Chandler hadn't even been together quite a year yet. Not to mention the bit about him being a Pierce. It was natural to assume that her overprotective father might have some reservations about their union.

I bit my lip as Edward remained silent, feeling the tension thickening around us. Just as I was about to put my hand out to touch his thigh so I could nudge him out of his stupor, he stood and without a word, walked out of the room.

Genevieve and I exchanged a glance, then she exchanged one with Chandler, who had her ringless hand clenched tight in his. The expression on her face was one of bewilderment. His, on the other hand, was tightening with what I could only imagine was rage.

Heat rushed up my neck in mortification. It was one thing to be skeptical about their relationship. It was quite another to be an ass about it.

I stretched my neck so I could look through one of the openings in the bookcase that separated the living room of our suite from the next. Edward hadn't gone far, apparently. He was in the dining room leaning over the wet bar.

"Edward? What are you doing?" Admittedly, there was a sharpness to my tone. Things had been so good between us, and I didn't want to start a fight, but I would if he didn't get his act together. She was still his daughter, and she deserved his support no matter what her choices. Weren't those words that had come out of his own mouth when she'd first decided to work for a company he abhorred after graduation?

And what was there not to support, anyway? He'd said he'd been happy when she'd taken the job at Pierce Industries. He already knew she wasn't returning to London anytime soon. She'd been dating Chandler for months. The only thing that had changed was she was now engaged to one of the wealthiest men in America. There was no way he could justify the cold shoulder.

"Coming." The clinking sound accompanied his response. A second later he was back in the room carrying four glass flutes and a bottle of Dom Perignon that had been put in the fridge a couple of days before in preparation for a celebration of our own that we had yet to make time for. "I thought the occasion called for champagne," he said, distributing the glasses. "It's not every day that your child gets engaged."

The rest of us sighed in unison, the tension immediately evaporated and replaced with smiles and hugs and congratulations.

Then Edward popped the champagne. "Shall I pour one for you, love?"

I mentally calculated how much breast milk I had stored in the fridge. Enough to get through the night, I was sure. Which meant I could express and dump if I had any alcohol now.

Still, I hesitated. Nursing was one of my greatest joys, a special time for me and Cleo to bond with each other. With Edward too, who was often at my side for feedings when he was home.

Seeming to read my mind, he said, "Let me feed her when she wakes. I rarely get the opportunity."

My devil had grown awfully princely over the years. It made my chest tight to think about. "In that case, fill mine to the top."

Everyone laughed as Edward poured each of us a full glass. When he'd finished serving, he set the bottle down and lifted his flute. "To a long and happy union. May you continue to love and bring out the best in each other for the rest of your days."

Simple, but sincere. Genevieve wiped her eye as she raised her glass to clink against each of ours.

"Honestly, Dad," she said when we'd all taken our first swallows and remarked on the quality. "I was scared there for a moment."

Edward arched a brow. "You were? Whatever for?"

She stared at him like the question was ludicrous. "You didn't say anything. Then you got up and Left. The. Room. That's not the behavior of a father who is about to give his blessing."

"Genny had already been nervous you wouldn't approve." Chandler gazed adoringly at his fiancée. "I'd even prepared a speech defending our decision in case..." His brows knit, and I could tell he was imagining himself standing up to Edward. "Well, thank God it didn't go that way."

I smiled to myself, feeling lucky that I was married to such an intimidating specimen.

An intimidating specimen who was at that very moment being especially intimidating. "You thought I wouldn't approve? Because you're both so young or because you've known each other less than ten months or because you're a Pierce?"

"Most people think the name is an advantage." Chandler, poor thing, managed to sound brave despite himself.

"Indeed, I'm sure they do."

"Dad," Genevieve chided. "You are being awfully *you* right now when I was just praising you for *not* being you."

My husband smirked, which his daughter responded to with an equally childish sigh.

"Fine, let's discuss this then." Edward crossed one arm over his chest, his flute held up with the other. "How could I possibly argue about your age? I married Genevieve's mother when I was younger than you both by a few years, even though perhaps that isn't a good example since we ended in divorce. On the other hand, Celia and I had known each other far less time than you when we got engaged, and whether she likes it or not, she's stuck with me."

His glance at me was playful with the hint of a wink without actually moving his eyelid. "As for the name..." Here Edward grew eerily sober. "Chandler knows full well it won't stop me from killing him with my bare hands if he ever hurts you. Don't you, Chandler?"

Chandler swallowed. "Uh. I do now."

A chill ran down my spine. Edward was considered formidable for a reason—he was as much bite as he was bark. Even now when I suspected he was pulling the kid's leg, I couldn't help remembering Camilla and her abusive husband. Edward had killed Frank, I was sure of it, and maybe it was justified, but was murder ever really justified?

I wished I knew the story. It was a secret he refused to tell since I had a secret of my own, and I'd gotten used to ignoring the burning want to know for the most part, but today, I desperately wished I had answers. It might calm the terrifying certainty that, though I was sure

Edward meant for his words to be taken in jest, he was actually being quite sincere.

"Dad!" Genevieve said with a laugh, breaking the tension knotting in my belly. "Stop it. Please. You're scaring my fiancé."

Finally, Edward caved, a grin breaking out on his face. "In all seriousness, blessings to you both. I'm very happy for you. And maybe sometime Chandler can tell me how he gets away with calling you Genny."

She nuzzled into Chandler. "It doesn't sound the same when he says it as when you do. Out of your lips, it makes me feel like I'm seven years old. Out of his..." She blushed, making it apparent the nickname had become special between them.

"It's very exciting," I said, stepping in so she wouldn't have to say more in front of her father. "And I'm so thrilled for both of you. Truly. Now tell us everything about how it happened. I'm dying to hear the details."

An hour later, after we'd finished the champagne and heard the story twice—once from Genevieve then almost entirely again from Chandler with Genevieve frequently interjecting to comment, the conversation began to die down and the couple made innuendos about calling it a night.

"Thanks again for the bubbles," Chandler said, setting down his empty glass. "They really stock the good stuff here, don't they?"

"No, actually, they don't," Edward laughed. "I'd purchased it Friday for other celebratory reasons."

"Oh. Did we...?" Chandler's ears went red, obviously afraid he'd made some gaffe. "I feel bad about taking your champagne. Not if you were saving it for something important."

"Stop it," I said, feeling pleasantly tipsy. "We'd rather share it with family. We can get another bottle, or better yet, we'll wrap that celebration into this one and call it good."

Genevieve was the one who thought to ask. "What was the occasion?"

Edward looked to me, giving me the opportunity to decide what I wanted said. I appreciated it. And I also didn't. There had been a time when he would have made these decisions for me, when he would have taken more of a dominant role in our relationship. He still cared for me in all the ways he once had, choosing my clothes and helping me with my agenda, just now he deferred more to me for my opinion. He didn't command anymore, he suggested.

Maybe he thought he was being a better man by giving me more space of my own. It was true that I'd grown stronger and more capable since the days after he'd broken me down. This might very well be the next step in building me up again, and I was forever grateful for that. But I missed the way we used to be and desperately hoped we would find our way back to some form of that eventually.

Meanwhile, it was up to me to answer. "My uncle's trial is over. Or, it's almost over. The Crown Court found him guilty on several charges on Friday. Now we're just waiting for sentencing."

God, it felt better to say than I'd realized it would. I hadn't had a reason to verbalize it since I'd found out since Edward had been with me when the verdict had come through. He'd been the only person I'd discussed it with at all so far, partially because I couldn't imagine who else I would talk to about it. I'd avoided my parents, not wanting to hear my father lament about injustice that I related to far better than he ever could. Edward had called Camilla, but I had let them talk alone rather than jumping in.

Beyond not having anyone to speak to about it, I hadn't quite known how it would come out if I did. It felt like a weight had been removed that I hadn't realized I was still carrying. I'd thought that I had unloaded everything Ron-related by now, so it was surprising to feel I still had more to set down. And as good as it felt to finally be free of that, it also made me strangely sad. I'd spent the better part of Saturday crying off and on about it, and Edward had been a saint, taking care of Cleo by himself since it was Elsa's day off, bringing her only when she needed to nurse, and I needed to cuddle.

Today, I felt much better. The grieving was over, and now there was only release in its place. It sort of felt like floating, like a feather in the wind, rising and falling with each gust, never touching the ground.

"Will the US extradite him?" Genevieve asked. We hadn't told her much about my past with Ron, but she was a smart cookie. She knew.

"Not unless the sentence he gets is minimal. Which it could be, and that would be a whole other nightmare, but there's also a real good chance it will be severe."

"Oh, Celia. What a relief!"

Chandler seemed still in the dark, but he was gracious all the same. "You must be grateful to have that media circus finally done with."

"I am. I am." Tears pricked at my eyes, much different than the ones that had overtook me the day before. I blinked them away. "But I'd much rather focus on your celebration instead. Have you picked a date yet? Please, say it isn't too soon. You have to leave time to let me throw an engagement party in your honor."

Her eyes widened in surprise. "You don't have to do that."

"Of course I don't have to. I *want* to."

"I'm so flattered." Her own eyes looked glossy. "And, after the amazing event you threw for my graduation, I would be a fool to turn you down. But don't you want to be getting back to London now that the trial is done? I don't want to keep you here any longer than need be. I know you've been quite homesick."

"It's true, I want to get home, and we will. Soon." I felt Edward's eyes on me, but I couldn't look at him without giving myself away, and I wasn't quite ready for that. "There's some other things we're tying up here first, and neither of us want to miss out on the fun surrounding a wedding. Please let me plan something. It would be my honor."

Another quarter of an hour later, with permission granted to throw a dinner party in their honor, the couple made their goodbyes. I slipped away to check on Cleo in the adjoining suite, then, finding her still asleep, I returned to the living room where Edward was settled on the couch, his legs crossed and his arm draped across the back of the sofa, waiting for me. "Would you come sit with me, bird?"

A sharp ache pierced between my ribs, a longing for the order rather than the request. The dominance had even been toned down in our sex after we'd come to our truce. I'd hoped it might spice up again after Cleo, but the handful of occasions we'd found time and energy to make love since her birth we'd done exactly that—made love. I wasn't complaining, I really wasn't. I enjoyed what we had, and if we kept the status quo for the rest of our lives, I would die a happy woman.

Still, I knew we could be more. That we *were* more. That the absence of his command was really an absence of my submission. I'd walled off a part of me from him and so he'd walled off a part of himself from me. Intentional or not, I wasn't sure, though I suspected it was the latter. Maybe he noticed it too, but I doubted he'd done it purposefully. And now that this was how we were with each other, perhaps he was as uncertain as I was how to return to what we'd been.

"If you'd rather not..." he said when I hadn't moved or responded.

I shook my head from my thoughts. "No, I want to. Sorry. I guess the champagne gave me a little bit of a buzz." I sat next to him on the sofa, curling my feet up underneath me as I burrowed into his side.

"Are you too buzzed for a serious discussion?"

"Nope. Just buzzed enough to feel good. Are you going to kill it?"

"I don't plan on it." He drew me tighter to him, stroking his fingers down my arm. "I'm only wondering why you want to delay going back to London. Have you changed your mind about living there?"

"I haven't. I'm dying to take Cleo home and settle in where there's more space. Even with the additional suite, this place is rather small and stifling."

He was silent a beat, and I sensed he was trying to figure me out. I liked his curiosity enough to not rush to giving him answers. It was rare that I had an upper hand with him, and I wanted to relish it a little longer before laying down my cards.

"I hope you didn't offer to throw the engagement party on my account," he said after a time. "I'm very appreciative, but it wasn't necessary."

I sat up so I could look at him. "Yes, it was for you, you silly. And for her. I'm not that close to Genevieve, but I do love her and want to be part of her life."

"I love that about you."

His declaration gave me the confidence to reveal more. "But also it was for me. It will give me something to do besides be cooped up in here all the time while we go after Werner."

The air turned electric. I could feel the charge emanating off his body as he studied me. "What are you saying?"

"I'm saying, I think it should stay in the family."

"And you have a plan for that? I doubt you would bring this up if you didn't."

It wasn't quite a plan that I had, but rather a desire. A desire to give my husband what he needed. A desire to lay my heart at his feet. A desire to show him that I was a strong woman, but not so strong that I couldn't also be sometimes mastered.

Just, how to turn that desire into action?

I turned my body so I was facing him completely. "I've been so stuck on making sure you didn't go head-to-head with Hudson, and I still feel that's the right choice, but I was too preoccupied to realize there are other ways to get what it is you're after. Not the CEO position —even if we could manage that, this isn't the time. Cleo needs a father who isn't working all the time, and that would definitely keep us in the States, which is not where I want to be in the long run.

"But majority shares—or at least equal shares with Hudson. That could be doable."

His eyes narrowed, considering. "You think Hudson might be amenable to selling us one percent now that Genevieve is marrying his brother?"

"Possibly. I think it's worth trying. But if he won't, there could be another way." I ran my teeth across my bottom lip. "I want to help you find a way."

"Go on." I could practically hear his pulse tick up.

My own heart was racing. "Hudson owns forty-two percent. We own forty percent. There are still those other eighteen percent shares."

It wasn't news to him how the shares had been distributed. Werner Media was still privately-owned—*family*-owned for the most part. The company had been started years ago by my grandfather and his brother, Chester. When Uncle Chester had died, his fifty percent had been distributed among his children, just as Grandpa Werner's shares had been passed to my father and Uncle Ron, but no one had had the ambition to run the company like my father had. So little by little, he'd bought family members out of most of their shares. A few relatives had since sold their remaining shares to outside parties who were unwilling to sell again, but there were four cousins that still owned two percent each.

Edward guessed where I was going and shook his head. "I've already approached the other shareholders. They've all said no to selling."

"You approached them when you were still an enemy of my father. Now you're part of an alliance with him. You'll have been validated in their eyes. Also, since the values of those shares have dropped recently with Ron's trial, some may be more interested in bailing now."

"Possibly." He wasn't convinced, but I hadn't expected he would be.

The real benefit of my involvement came with what I offered next. "If none of the outsiders are interested, I could talk to my cousins. None of us are particularly close, but I'm pretty sure I have some sway with two or three of them, especially if I leveraged some family secrets here and there. Buying out any one of them would make us equal with Hudson. Buying one percent off two of them would do the trick too."

His eyes sparked with something I hadn't seen in months. "Buying them all out would put us ahead of Hudson."

For half a second, I worried I'd made a mistake bringing this up. I didn't want to hold him back, but his ambition scared me at times. It was too monstrous. Too much a life of its own.

Instead of pulling back, though, as I would have done in the past, I gave him the chance to step up to the common ground as I had. "I don't think we need to be greedy. He still has power in unexpected ways. I'd prefer to strive for equality. For now."

Again he considered. Seconds passed, long and thick, until he reached his hand up to caress my cheek. "This isn't for you. This is for me, isn't it? You'd really help me go after those shares?"

"If it's still what you want, yes. I will."

In one swift move, he lifted me from his side, brought me to straddle his lap, and kissed me. Kissed me hard. Kissed me like he hadn't in months, with hunger and desperation and worship and control. His cock pressed intently at the space between my legs and my pussy wept with eagerness as finally, *finally*, his mouth took mine with rough authority, a reminder of how he'd fucked me once upon a time. A promise of how he planned to fuck me again.

And then the urgent wail of a hungry baby burst through the monitor. My breasts leaked in response, my nipples aching with the need to express.

Reluctantly we broke apart. "I'll heat her bottle," I offered.

He shook his head. "Go pump," he said, and I shivered at the emphatic tone in his voice. "I'll bring her to you when she's been fed."

I walked to the bedroom, wet and unsatisfied, but a smile curved boastfully on my lips. We'd had our bumps, but I could see a path for us now, a path that might not be easy, but one that I was confident we could walk together.

NINE

EDWARD

"'THE MARKET'S reaction to the alliance between Werner Media, Accelecom'—that's daddy's company, Cleo-Leo—'and Pierce Industries has been strong, despite the recent drama surrounding former Werner CEO Warren Werner's brother Ron. This support is likely due to the manufacturing giant Pierce Industries and their contribution of tech components enabling the partners to not only make plans to lay cable networks in the near future, but also to dominate the field.'" I frowned at the words I'd just read. "Well, that's bloody rubbish. As if Pierce is the reason for anything that's successful."

"You've bored her to sleep."

I peered up at the soft voice to see Celia standing in the doorway between our suite and the adjoining bedroom we'd been using for a nursery. She nodded toward the bundle in my left arm, and I looked down to find the baby that had been wriggling only a moment before was now fast asleep.

I chuckled. "I don't blame you, kiddo. Talk of Pierce Industries bores me too."

"I know they encourage reading to your child from an early age, but do you really think business magazines are the most appropriate choice of material?"

I shrugged. "She was fussy, and it needed to be read. Seemed like a two birds with one stone sort of situation."

Celia's smile was filled with adoration, and it warmed my chest recognizing it was meant for me as much as our daughter. "Better be careful. I'm at risk of being charmed."

"Oh, you're charmed all right." I tossed the iPad onto the ground so I could cradle Cleo with both arms as I stood from the rocking chair. We'd had it brought in only a few weeks before, and I couldn't for the life of me figure out how we'd got on without it. "She's charmed too, as you can tell."

Celia laughed, a sound that turned into a yawn as she stretched her arms overhead. "You should have woken me. I would have taken her." She glanced at the clock on the bedside table. "Oh, it's not even six. Where's Elsa?"

I set the baby down in her crib, careful not to disturb her slumber. "I sent her home early. And why would I wake you? You don't get nearly the amount of sleep as you should, and caring for our child isn't a job designated strictly to you and our nanny."

"Look at you win bonus points. You've been so good about being here for her, but I also appreciate that you have a full-time job on top of it."

I turned to study her, suspecting she needed validation for expecting me to participate in raising our baby. She wanted my involvement as much as I needed to be involved, but neither of us had experience with a household where the father shared in the child-rearing duties. It was new ground for both of us, and though it was often bumpy, I was grateful to be walking it with her at my side.

"It's hardly a hardship to cuddle with Cleo," I assured in a hushed voice, picking up the baby monitor as I crossed to my wife. "But it's also nice to have a break, so if we want her to stay sleeping, we best get out of here."

Once the door was closed behind us and Celia had taken the monitor so she could check the volume, I pulled her into my arms and kissed her. "Should we start thinking about dinner?"

She cocked her head, exposing her neck, and I suddenly regretted making our kiss so brief. Dinner, it seemed, was not what I was hungry for.

"I need a shower first," she said, pulling away. "I changed before I fell asleep on the couch, and I still smell like spit-up."

She smelled perfectly fine to me. I was tempted to tell her so or to offer to help her smell like something else, but I was conscientious of making sure my wife had time for the pleasures of ordinary things like bathing that were often foregone in the hustle and bustle of motherhood.

Recognizing that didn't mean I was noble enough to resist imposing. "I'll join you."

"Good." She threw a saucy look over her shoulder as I followed her through the bedroom into the bathroom where she set the monitor on the counter. "I can tell you about the phone call I had this morning."

I would have frowned if she hadn't chosen that moment to peel her shirt over her head. Men could say what they would about children killing all desire—they hadn't seen my wife in a nursing bra. Her breasts pushing full and plump against the lace cups turned my cock to stone.

"Talking wasn't exactly what I had in mind," I said, tossing my tie on the floor then quickly undoing my cufflinks.

"I think you'll be interested in this particular conversation." She shimmied out of her yoga pants, leaving them in a heap with the discarded top before reaching in the shower to turn on the water.

"Nothing is as interesting to me right now as you taking off your clothes. But go ahead and try to prove me wrong. Who was this phone call from?"

"Hudson." The name echoed against the tile, giving it more emphasis than it would have had if she'd said it while facing me instead of the faucet.

It was a suburb effect, intended or not.

I froze mid-unbuttoning my dress shirt. She was right—I *was* interested in this conversation. "Go on."

Seemingly happy with the water temperature, she turned back

toward me. "He wanted to talk about the engagement party we're throwing for Chandler and Genevieve."

"News travels fast." I continued the task of loosening my shirt, my pace slower than it was a moment before, distracted by the change in conversation as much as I was by the damp spot at the front of Celia's panties.

"It does always seem like Hudson is the first to know most everything." She stepped into me and grabbed my shirt, tugging it out of my pants as I finished unbuttoning, then helping me discard it.

I slipped my hand inside her panties to cup her cunt while the other played with the strap of her bra. "This needs to go."

She tried not to react, but I saw the flash of lust in her eyes at the command. Or perhaps she was merely responding to my fingers skating along her seam. Her breath caught when I skimmed higher, against the bud under the hood of skin. She clutched onto me, her eyes closed, as she shivered.

I loved her like this—playing strong while falling apart. A beautiful dichotomy orchestrated with the touch of my hand.

"You're distracting me," she moaned.

"That's the point."

"Two can play this game." She stroked her hand up the length of my cock, still buried inside my trousers. "Now that I have your attention, I can go on. Hudson is concerned about everyone's 'comfort'—his word, not mine. Wants to be sure there won't be much reason for me to interact with his precious wife."

The scratch of her nails up my length made me hiss. "He really is scared of you, isn't he?"

"Eh, he's protective. His efforts to look after his own would rival yours."

"I doubt it." I tugged again at her bra, reminding her she was not as naked as I wanted her then shooed her hand away so I could be rid of my own clothes. Talking was fine and I appreciated the tales of her days, but if all her Pierce news amounted to was talk of upcoming nuptials, I was of the mind to postpone it.

Celia, though she got the hint about stripping, wasn't ready to give up the conversation. "Anyway, I agreed to let him approve the seating chart—"

"—That was generous—"

"—and then I told him we weren't leaving the States without a bigger share in Werner."

Nearly completely undressed, I paused in the midst of tugging off my sock. While I normally didn't find talk of business very erotic, I was suddenly extremely aroused. "And what did he say?"

"That he wouldn't sell, of course." She stepped out of her panties and tossed them aside with her toe. "But I also reminded him there were other ways for us to get what we wanted, that we were serious about going after them, and that the only way we could ever truly move on from this outdated feud was to give us equal stakes in the company."

As much as I loved Celia shattering because of me, I equally loved her dominating others. Especially when it was on my behalf.

I prowled toward her, backing her into the walk-in shower. "I don't think I've ever been more attracted to you than I am right now."

She smiled coyly but with pride. "He said he'd think about it."

"He won't."

"He might."

Her back hit the wall, and I caged her in with my forearms pressed against the tile on either side of her head. I stared at her lips, plump and inviting. "Bloody greedy." I didn't know anymore if I was speaking about Pierce or myself.

"I don't think this is about money."

I forced myself to focus, lifting my eyes up to meet hers. This really was a significant turn of events. It had been one day since she'd told me she would join me in the pursuit of Werner, and if there had been any question as to whether or not it was simply lip service, I couldn't doubt her now. She'd thrown the gauntlet.

And Pierce had stood his ground.

It was such a ridiculous business move. He had no reason to keep that controlling interest when he didn't ever exercise any authority in the company. With our alliance, it was possible he could face monopoly accusations if his investment ever became public, a risk that didn't concern me since Accelecom was foreign-owned. Pierce knew I'd pay well over the market value. So why was he so obstinate?

"He *is* scared of you," I said, finally seeing the situation with clarity. My wife hadn't just been a nuisance to him as I'd previously suspected —she'd been an outright threat.

Fuck, that was hot.

I cupped my hand over her breast, letting the weight of it settle in my hand. "To think you're a dragon after all."

"You've reminded me plenty of times that I'm not."

"That's how a man dominates a woman, don't you know?" She gasped as I pinched her nipple, rivulets of milk running down her skin as it mixed with the streaming water. "Tells her she's something other than she is enough times that eventually she believes it."

"You mean they gaslight? Who knew?"

I bent to tug at her peaked nipple with my teeth, despite knowing it would cause more letdown. Her breasts had been more or less off-limits because of the mess it made, a mess only she cared about. In the shower, though, she didn't have that excuse, and I took full advantage, expecting still to be scolded.

When she pushed me off of her a second later, however, it wasn't the nipple play that earned the scolding. "Are you admitting you gaslit me? I was a dragon this whole time and you made me believe I was only a little bird?"

"You'll always be my little bird, bird," I said, chuckling. I ran my knuckles down the side of her cheek, my smile fading. "But you were also always a dragon."

"You *did* gaslight me!" Rather than being angry, her expression seemed victorious.

It was a victory that I wasn't ready to let her have. "Perhaps it wasn't about you. Did you think of that? It was about *me* not wanting to believe you were a dragon. For my own sake."

"As if I scared you." It was bravado, though.

"Are you sure you didn't?" I fisted my cock, stroking it up and down once, twice before rubbing the tip against her seam.

"*You* scared *me*."

"You liked being scared."

"I still do."

I let a beat pass, let my head dip between her folds, then let myself say the thing that had been between us for weeks now. For months, even. "You like being loved more."

It shouldn't have been such a pronouncement, but it was. The shift that had occurred when she'd stood up to me had been named. She was no longer afraid of me like she had been, and fear was what had brought us together. It had been our glue, hadn't it?

Then I'd fallen in love with her, and that was what she required now from me. My love. And that should have been better. That should have been more than enough. It shouldn't matter that she no longer bowed to me, that I could no longer bend her to my will. At my side was what I'd wanted, too.

Or so I'd thought.

Celia understood the significance of the statement. Her brow cinched. "Can't I like both?"

I flipped her around to face the wall, unable to look at her while she asked for what I didn't know how to give. Lifting her thigh so her foot rested on the bench, I spread her open and notched my crown at her entrance.

My method of distraction wasn't working. She twisted her head over her shoulder. "Can't I *have* both?"

For a split second, it seemed possible, and I tried to imagine myself in that role—the husband that both ruled and equaled. A man who could let his wife win and still be in charge. How did that work?

Even if I thought I could fill that position, Celia would have to yield, and she didn't do that now. She stood her ground. She fought like a dragon, and a dragon didn't need a master.

As the possibility flickered away, I shoved into her with one blunt stroke. "I don't scare you anymore."

"You still have secrets." Her words came out choppy as I drove into her with staccato jabs.

Fucking her should have taken my mind off the rest. It didn't. "Is that why you insist we keep them secret? So that we can have some-thing mysterious between us?"

"I shouldn't have brought it up."

No, she shouldn't have. Because now I was mad, and it was stupid and petty to feel so, and also it wasn't. The truce between us had calmed the conflict but it hadn't erased it. The secrets still stood between us like a clear barricade of teflon. There was no getting through them no matter how transparent they appeared, and still the illusion that it was possible kept me beating my hands against the walls.

"There's good reasoning to it," I said, pushing her with my words as well as my brutal thrusts. "Because if you don't know, you can always assume the worst. Then you can still pretend I scare you whenever you want." I reached around her body to pinch her clit. "Or is it not my secrets that scare you the most, but rather what I'd do with yours?"

She cried out, on the verge of orgasm, I suspected, but she managed to hang on, and a moment later she was collected enough to speak. "Even without the secrets, you scare me." It was quiet, a confession of sorts. "You're the only person who has ever loved me exactly like I am. The only person I've ever trusted entirely. That means you are more capable of hurting me than anyone who has hurt me before, and that's the most frightening thing I've ever imagined."

My tempo stuttered as I digested her words. Knowing everyone who had hurt her, knowing the *ways* they'd hurt her—that was a mighty declaration. It rocked me at my core. Made me off balance. That was a form of submission, wasn't it? Being vulnerable like that. Making me aware of my power.

Then if the problem between us wasn't her inability to submit to her equal then it was me who couldn't dominate mine. All that time ago when she'd said I always had to win? She'd been more right than either of us had known. Because when I'd given in, when I'd dropped my pursuit of her past, and committed to loving our child as she'd demanded, I lost hold of something I'd taken for granted as permanently mine. I'd lost hold of my authority, and I didn't know how to get it back.

Taking advantage of my slowed pace, she turned around again to face me. She cupped my cheek with her palm and wrapped her leg around my hip, guiding me back into her heat. I pressed into her, all the way, as far as she could take me.

Sighing, she pressed her forehead against mine. "So good," she said. "You feel so good." Then, "We're good too, aren't we?"

Once again, I turned her around, this time pivoting so I could bend her, and she could brace herself against the bench. I shoved inside her, moving in and out with increasing speed.

"How can you ask that?" I gritted out. "How can you even ask?"

Then I fucked her with savage stabs, over and over and over, until her question was long lost to the friction and the frenzy and the orgasms that shuddered through us both. Until even I could believe that I'd ignored responding because the answer should have been obvious and not because I didn't know what it was.

TEN

CELIA

HUDSON: **I need to see you.**

THE TEXT POPPED up at the top of the Atlantic article I was reading while feeding Cleo. It was early, still. Just after six, and it was a Saturday. But Hudson was always up at the crack of dawn so that wasn't the surprising part of the message. The surprising part was that he'd sent it at all.

Of course I'd see him. I'd told him what we wanted, and if he was reaching out, it meant he wanted to negotiate. What else could he want? And he wouldn't want Edward there. I knew that as sure as anything, so meeting when Edward was at work was my best option.

Before I could overthink it, I typed a one-handed response.

My Monday is open. Where?

His next text came almost immediately.

Hudson: **It needs to be sooner. Today. At my office.**

"He thinks he's out of The Game, but he still tries to control every situation," I said, mostly to myself, though Cleo looked up at me with her bright blue eyes and smiled around my nipple. "Right? We won't let him do that, will we?"

Tomorrow, I typed, just to hold some ground. **In the restaurant at my hotel. Five pm.**

The baby was usually sleeping then. A good time to slip away.

Hudson: **The Sky Launch. At six.**

"Oh, please." I was not meeting at his nightclub. I didn't usually care about his turf or mine, but since it so obviously mattered to him, I was reluctant to give in. Though, maybe being amiable was the way to go. I was the one who wasn't in the position that he was. He was the one with the stocks we wanted, not the other way around.

But if I'd learned anything from the men in my life—my father, Edward, Hudson himself—it was to never take the weaker stance. If anything, that was when to be even more firm. Besides, Hudson didn't hold all the cards here. I'd meant it when I told him we'd pursue purchasing stocks elsewhere. I didn't have to be as amiable as he demanded.

I pulled up WhatsHalfway, an app that found a middle location between two spots, and entered in the hotel and Hudson's office address.

Randall's, I texted back. **It's a bar halfway between you and me. Six pm will be fine.**

His response didn't come as quickly, which meant he was thinking it through. And if he was thinking it through, it meant he'd come to the same conclusion as I did—we'd have to compromise.

Sure enough, his next text settled the matter.

Hudson: **See you then.**

I dropped my phone in my lap with a sigh. It had been almost two weeks since I'd talked to him about letting Edward and me buy those stocks. Hudson did like to think things through, and it had been enough time for him to have done that, but it wasn't like him to have a total one-eighty without much prodding. Had something—or someone—changed his mind?

Or was this meeting about something else entirely?

No. It had to be about the shares. I wouldn't know any more than that until we talked. But there was still one issue I had to deal with before then. I rubbed my hand over Cleo's fuzzy head. "Now we just have to figure out what we're going to tell Daddy."

She broke away from my breast so she could smile again. "You're not really interested in eating anymore, are you?" I pulled her away and reattached the cup on my bra then sat her up on my lap. She was getting strong. Soon she'd be sitting on her own. It felt suddenly like it was all moving too fast, that any second she'd be asking for her own phone and locking herself in her room with her music blaring. I hugged her to me, as though that could somehow hold the moment, as though it might slow time down and keep her *mine* for longer.

The door between our two suites creaked open, pulling my focus.

"If that's not an adorable sight," Edward said from the doorway, wearing nothing but his pajama bottoms. "We need to get a photographer in here. Before she's too wiggly to pose."

"I was just thinking she was growing up too fast." I brushed my lips across her forehead, making her grunt with frustration since the action had blocked her from tugging at the open drawstring on my nursing nightgown.

"That's how it happens. One minute they're crawling, the next they're engaged and moving permanently to the States."

It was the first time he'd said something suggesting any melancholy at all about his older daughter's upcoming nuptials, but I'd suspected he felt it. "Good thing you have this one to help lessen the blow of losing that one."

He came toward me with a smirk. "Yes. Good thing." He reached for Cleo, and I passed her over, then had to take a second to catch my breath. The sight of a bare-chested man holding a baby had never done things to my insides until it was *my* bare-chested man holding *my* baby.

Whoa. It was the definition of breathtaking.

Edward rocked her as he stepped away, running his nose along her forehead. "Good morning, birdie," he said, the variation on my nickname one he'd adopted for her recently. "It's too bad you can't talk yet. You could tell me what it is that Mommy's trying to hide from Daddy."

I froze midway from standing up from the rocker, color draining from my face. How did he know?

Dammit, I was an idiot. "The baby monitor," I said as it dawned on me.

"The baby monitor," he repeated.

He held out his hand to help me up the rest of the way then used it to pull me into him, wrapping his arm around my waist when I was there. I didn't mistake it for affection, though it was clearly that too. No, this move was about asserting himself on me. "Do you have something you'd like to tell me?" he asked, pressing his lips to my temple.

I didn't even consider lying. We were on the same side when it came to the Werner shares, even if we weren't on the same side when it came to Hudson, but there was no reason for that to be an issue, as far as I could tell. "Hudson wants to meet up. He texted a little bit ago."

"That's great," he said, surprising me. "Did you tell him yes?"

"I did."

"Good. When are we seeing him?"

I pushed gently out of his arms. "Well. Tomorrow night. But he didn't invite *us*. He invited *me*."

"I'm okay with showing up without an invitation." He said it casually, his focus seemingly on Cleo who was suddenly very interested in his beard.

"Edward..." I tried to decide if this was worth battling.

Yes, it was. For several reasons, not the least of which was that the fewer personal interactions that occurred between my husband and Hudson, the more likely I was to keep my secret about him.

Not that I could tell that to Edward.

"If we both show up, then he'll feel outnumbered," I said instead. "He won't likely be willing to negotiate if he doesn't feel like we're coming to this on equal ground."

He knew I was right, but he still considered. "I could go in your place."

"If he wanted to talk to you he would have reached out to you." I forced myself not to take a defensive posture. "Look. He didn't have to ask to meet at all, and he did. I don't think this is the time to try to turn the tables. I should go and see what he has to say, and if that doesn't turn out to our benefit, we can change the game plan."

A beat passed. Then two. I was just preparing to double down on my argument when he surprised me once again. "I suppose I can agree to that."

"Really? Awesome." I stood up on my tiptoes and gave him a chaste kiss. "Now, since you're up...want to make the coffee or change the diaper?"

He pretended to think about it. "Hazelnut or Colombian blend?"

TURNED out Edward's agreement had caveats—he wouldn't come in with me, but he insisted on waiting in the car.

"It's not like there's any parking here," I said as the driver neared Randall's bar. "Are you just going to have Bert circle the block until I text you, or what?"

"Works for me." He called to the front seat. "How about you, Bert?"

Bert shrugged. "Whatever you want, Mr. Fasbender. Doesn't matter to me."

I folded my arms over my chest knowing anything I said would be dismissed. We'd already argued about it all afternoon as I'd gotten ready, donning a fitted red dress that I only just barely fit into post-pregnancy and taking extra care with my makeup. All I'd accomplished with the bickering was that I was arriving for my meeting almost fifteen minutes late. Edward wasn't budging.

Still, I couldn't drop it. "What's even the point? I'd call you and tell you everything just as easily."

"Call me eager," he said as the car pulled up in front of the bar.

If it were only that, I wouldn't be concerned. The problem was that I didn't trust him. There was one reason he'd insist on coming with and one reason only.

I hesitated before opening the door. "Give me at least half an hour before showing up, if that's what you're planning. Please?"

The driver behind us laid on his horn, but Edward took his time answering. "Fine. Half an hour." He looked at his watch. "Starting now."

I couldn't decide if I should take that as a victory or a loss. Since I was on the clock, I didn't have time to ruminate. I opened the door and began to step out when Edward grabbed my arm to halt me.

"You're a dragon, Celia. Go in breathing fire."

It shouldn't have boosted my confidence as much as it did, but I walked into the bar with courage and composure, my spine straight, my wits together.

Until I realized Hudson wasn't alone—his wife was with him.

I knew right then, whatever I'd thought this meeting was about, I'd been wrong. This was something else entirely. Something I had not been prepared for. Hudson saw me as a threat to his marriage, to his wife. It was why he still held those shares over me. He'd never put us in the same room without good reason.

Unless I was wrong. Unless her presence signaled things had changed.

It was too much to hope for, and a knot tightened in my belly, weighing me down. To counter it, I rounded my shoulders. Lifted my chin. Put on my mask.

My eyes met Alayna's before I got to the table, and I saw a flicker of insecurity. Should I take that as some sort of victory? Or should I admit that it hurt that she still didn't trust me?

I stuffed the competing emotions down inside me and activated the safety switch, the one Hudson had shown me—I went numb.

"Hudson, Laynie," I said, injecting a smile into my tone. They sat at a circular booth, Hudson on one end, his wife pressed so closely to him it was almost as though they were one person. Without being invited, I scooted in at the opposite end and addressed Hudson, mostly because he was the only one of the two of them I really knew how to talk to. I'd only ever been fake with Laynie. Attempting to be genuine now seemed futile.

But also, he'd been the one who set me up in this arrangement, and my complaint was meant specifically for him. "I didn't know we were bringing our significant others," I said curtly. "Should I call Edward? He doesn't have any plans."

He's just down the block, I added, silently wondering now if that was a good thing or an even worse thing than I'd originally thought.

"That won't be necessary." Hudson was cool, his words clipped. "This conversation doesn't involve him. It does, however, involve Alayna."

The hair raised at the back of my neck, some strange sense of foreboding that I couldn't shake.

It was silly, honestly. Probably just PTSD from the last time I'd seen Alayna, when she was still Withers instead of Pierce. When she'd broken my nose with one jab of her fist.

I'd deserved it. But that was ages ago. Why were we all together now?

"I'm intrigued," I said, studying the woman who had once been my foe. She still hated me. It was evident in her expression, and a few recent remarks from Genevieve had indicated the same. "How are you, Laynie? It's been so long since we've seen each other face-to-face. You look..." Like a woman with one-year-old twins. *"Tired."*

It was childish and petty. Mean, even, and I wasn't quite sure exactly what I meant by saying it when, honestly, I could relate. Maybe that's what I resented most about our relationship—there could be so much to like about the woman, so much to bond over. I could imagine the friendship that would never be, and it made me ache in strange places. Made me more bitter than I should have been.

Because wasn't all of this supposed to be over? For me, it was. I thought it was for Hudson too.

His face gave nothing away, his expression stone, still I could feel the glare behind the facade. "What can we get you to drink, Celia?" A tumbler of scotch already sat in front of him, but he raised his hand to signal the waiter.

"Nothing. Water, I suppose." I crossed one leg over the other.

"Really?" He sounded irritated, which meant the situation was getting to him too. "You were the one who suggested we meet at a bar, and you're not even having a drink?"

I hadn't chosen it, the app had.

But I was irritated with his irritation. And with being set up. And with all the distrust around me, whether I'd earned it or not. "I'm nursing. I can't drink, unless I'm going to dump it all after, and I'm not." I nudged his drink closer to him. "But we all know you're in a much more agreeable mood when you've had one of these. Hence, the bar."

Yeah, again it was petty, suggesting he might have an alcohol problem. I couldn't help myself. He'd ganged up on me. Ironically, I realized I was probably reacting exactly the same way I'd told Edward that Hudson would react if we'd ganged up on him.

"I changed my mind," Hudson said abruptly. "We don't need to meet with you. This isn't going to get us anywhere. Alayna, grab your purse. We are leaving." He pulled out his wallet and began flipping through the bills inside.

"Hudson," his wife said, placing her hand on his arm. "We should stay."

He hesitated then threw some money on the table, but when he pocketed his wallet, he didn't stand to leave.

I had to concentrate to keep my jaw from dropping. Whatever they needed to discuss with me had to be important. Important to *them,* anyway. Which meant it could be useful to me.

For the first time since I walked in, I felt a flicker of hope.

"Thank you," I said. "I would hate to have wasted this trip." Conscious that the clock was ticking, I pressed the conversation. "Now, since Edward is not involved in this matter and Alayna is, I am assuming that we are not here to speak about the three-point alliance?"

"That is—"

Alayna interrupted her husband. "Like Pierce Industries is going to sell you shares. Did you forget that we have the majority for a reason? Hudson needed to have something to hold—ow!"

She cut off sharply, throwing a scowl in Hudson's direction.

"That is correct," he finished, his teeth gritted. "We are here to ask you for..." He paused. "*Assistance.*"

I tilted my head, evaluating. "This is interesting. You must be mighty desperate if you're asking me for help. You have to know that's going to indenture you to me."

"Why don't you hear the situation out before you start bartering about payment? At one time, you and I helped each other with no strings attached. Especially when we found the outcome benefitted both of us. You might find this is one of those times."

A welcome stab of warmth penetrated my numb cocoon. Whether he meant it to be manipulative or not, his words acknowledged the friendship we once had. That friendship had been real. With all the poison we created in the world, we'd also soothed each other's aches. For a time, anyway. And even if he wanted to use that against me, he couldn't deny that we'd been what we were.

That cost him to admit that. I could set down my weapons for a moment, though I kept my shield up as I gestured for him to continue. "Go on then. I'm listening."

He glanced at Alayna, to assure her or be reassured, I didn't know. Then his focus came back to me. "We have received a series of threats recently. Letters, addressed to me, containing menacing language toward my family."

The momentary warmth vanished. "And you think I did it?" Of course they did. Of course the past could never be forgotten. Of course I would live with my sins for the rest of my life. How had Hudson managed to escape the same curse?

"No, we didn't—" he began.

"Well..." Alayna said softly.

Hudson shut her up with a glare. "We didn't come here to accuse you. But the threats reference the past. The time when you and I were..." Another glance toward his wife, and I realized that he was as uncomfortable about who he'd been as I ever was.

"Playing together," I finished for him. His gaze dropped, weighted with guilt. "I see."

I also saw I'd been wrong with my earlier assessment—Hudson *hadn't* escaped his past, though there was every chance the worst was just now catching up to him.

I could empathize with that. More than I wanted to admit. In fact, with my husband currently circling the block with every intention of busting in soon, I understood Hudson completely.

"Do you have these letters with you?" I asked, despite feeling the pressure of time. "May I read them?"

He reached into his jacket pocket and pulled out a stack of photo-copied papers then slid them across the table toward me. Then he threw back the rest of his drink, finishing it in one swallow.

It had taken all my courage to go to him that day in his office, to ask him to help keep my father in the dark about the ownership of his company. I'd had to set down a lot of anger and shame and regret in order to walk through his door. It was evident that he was now doing the same.

I know, Hudson. I fucking know.

I blinked away the sting in my eyes and focused on the papers in front of me. Quickly, the words I read replaced any notion toward sentimentality with something else—fear. The letters were clearly threats, the most haunting phrases sticking out as though they'd been written in bold.

"...should have counted on your past coming back to haunt you."

"You can't buy your way out of paying for your sins."

"...don't deserve your happy life."

"The safety of your tower is an illusion."

"You weren't always perfect. Your past is filled with misdeeds."

"The people you hurt remember."

I tried to ignore the sick feeling in my stomach to see the clues peppered in, references, as Hudson had said, to games we'd played. A mention of an affair. Of a marriage charade. "This reference about the mask you wear," I said, thinking out loud, "could be referring to that masquerade party we went to." Whom had we messed with that time? Whomever it was, it was a different game than the one with the fake marriage license that was mentioned in the next letter. And another game entirely from the one with the sick dog.

I shook my head, confused. "But none of the rest fits." I flipped to the last page of the five he'd handed me.

"That one contained a picture of Alayna in the park with the twins. She hadn't known she'd been photographed."

A chill ran down my spine. If I'd discovered that Cleo and I had been secretly followed...

Then a more chilling thought—had Edward found out about Hudson? Was this his doing?

I swallowed down another wave of nausea with a, "Hm."

I didn't want to think about it, but I forced myself to really consider. It wasn't impossible that this was Edward. He had access to my journals. He could have made these references based on what he'd read there.

But was this really Edward's M.O.? Threatening children? And why would he keep trying to press me for my secrets if he already knew?

Maybe I was jumping to conclusions. Please, God, let me be jumping to conclusions.

But a glance at my watch said more than twenty minutes had

passed since I'd sat down, and if I didn't get out of there soon, Edward would walk in and discover who Hudson really was, whether he already knew or not, and then Hudson would have a whole hell of a lot more trouble than just a stalker.

I gathered all the letters together and passed them back to Hudson. "I do think you're right, that it's someone from the past," I said, throwing the suspicion off of Edward for myself if not for anyone else. "But it's like a scavenger hunt. You have to do a lot of digging before you can figure out what these vague clues mean."

Hudson didn't take the letters. "We were hoping that you would help us put those clues together."

If I helped them, I'd be able to rule out Edward for sure.

And if it wasn't Edward, would that be better or worse? Knowing that there was a real threat to Hudson and his family. Or, rather, an *unknown* threat, because Edward was as real a danger as any.

But if it wasn't Edward, he'd find out about Hudson and all the time I'd spent protecting him would be in vain.

And, if it was Edward...

I wasn't sure I wanted to know.

"I can't do that. I can't take these." He still refused to take the letters so I set them down on the table. "I'm sorry that I can't be more helpful, I just can't."

Alayna leaned desperately toward me. "You can't? Or you won't?"

I wanted to help her then, genuinely. From one mother to another, I wanted to figure out who was behind the threats to her family. Threats that I'd helped cause, one way or another.

"We don't have to take up much of your time, Ceeley," Hudson said. "If you even just allowed us access to the journals so we could piece together—"

"The journals?" It shouldn't have startled me that he would remember the journals or even that he'd ask for them, but it did, only because, I realized then, how easy it would be for Hudson to put things together and suspect Edward might be involved.

And now twenty-five minutes had passed. "I don't have them here. They're in London. I'm sorry. It's not going to work. I can't help you.

Now, if you'll excuse me, I really must be going." I grabbed my purse, slid out of the booth, and without looking back, headed swiftly toward the exit.

"Celia, wait."

Against my better judgement, I stopped just feet away from the door and turned back toward Hudson.

"This person could come after you, too," he said. "I might only be victim number one. You aren't innocent here. Your past is as tainted as mine."

If it wasn't Edward sending these letters, having Hudson on my side would be a real benefit.

But getting involved wasn't worth the risk. The risk to *him*.

"And I understand I'll be on my own if and when that happens. I can't help you, Hudson."

He looked at me incredulously. And with utter disappointment, like I'd let him down more now than at any other time in the course of our relationship.

"I really thought you'd softened," he said, and the words hurt most because I had and because he couldn't understand how much I'd fought to protect him.

"You know nothing about me, Hudson," I said as Alayna walked up to us. "Not anymore." I was out the door before he could say anything more.

...and three steps later I plowed right into Edward. "What's going on? The meeting's over already?"

Fuck.

"There was no meeting," I said, then realizing that Hudson and Alayna might be seconds from leaving the bar themselves, I corrected myself. "It was a bust. Nothing useful."

I started walking down the block, wanting distance from Randall's, but Edward snatched my elbow, stopping me. "What does that mean? He refused to sell again? Why did he want to meet?"

His questions sounded genuine, not like the kind meant to throw a woman off his tracks. But was I blinding myself about Edward?

Suddenly, I felt like crying.

All of it was too much. Either my husband was an unhinged psychopath or there was someone with a real grudge going after Hudson, and whichever it was, I couldn't explain it to Edward without making matters worse.

Which meant I needed to lie, and I didn't want to lie to the man I loved.

So I stuck as much to the truth as possible. "It was a setup," I said. "Hudson brought his wife. They have no intention of selling. They made that very clear."

Edward's brows furrowed. "Then why did they call this meeting? Just to rile you up?"

I shrugged, a tear escaping despite my attempts to hold it back. "Yeah. Something like that."

Immediately, he was fuming. "He brought you here to bloody bully you? Fuck that. Fuck that man. I'm going in there and telling him exactly what I think about that."

He'd already turned toward the bar so I had to quicken my steps to grab him. "You can't!"

"I'm not letting him get away with this, Celia. We've been reasonable. Terrorizing you is indecent and uncalled for and like hell will he do that to my wife without paying."

"He didn't terrorize me! I promise. He didn't. Can you please let it go?"

He calmed down, but only slightly. "Obviously he did *something*. Tell me what happened."

I shook my head, at a loss for what to say.

He turned toward the bar door again, and once more I pulled him back. "Please, Edward. Please, let it go. I'm upset because he reminded me of who I'd been in the past. That's all. There's nothing you need to say to him. I promise. Please, just take me home."

He looked unconvinced, his body still slightly poised in the direction I'd just come from.

"Please!" I begged, more desperate than I'd ever remembered being with him, and it felt like I was pleading for so much more than just to stop him from going in that bar. I was pleading for him to choose me, for once, instead of his wrath. For him to listen to what I needed and not what he thought I needed, a battle I'd lost over and over and over in our marriage. "Please, Edward! Please!"

He paused.

With a labored sigh, he put one arm around me and pulled out his phone from his pocket with the other. "Bert, we're ready," he said.

He held me until Bert came, neither of us speaking, and even when we got into the car, I clung to him, grateful that he'd listened, relieved that he'd chosen me.

But also fully aware that the clock was still ticking, and that eventually—soon, even—the time bomb would explode.

ELEVEN

EDWARD

"SECOND QUARTER REPORTS aren't ready yet, but I guarantee you the earnings are well above predicted. Now is the time to double down on investment, not back out."

I tapped my pen against my chin and stared out the suite's living room window at the sun setting over the park. The rep from Sonovision continued his spiel through my mobile, but I was barely paying attention. The phone call had been on my agenda for days, and as it was Sunday evening (after nine in the morning in Tokyo), I hadn't thought to cancel it until it had been upon me.

I had no real cause to cancel, anyway, except that I was distracted. Celia's reaction to her meeting with Pierce unnerved me for several reasons. I very much wanted to hang up on Sonovision and call him instead. Whatever he'd said or done to cause my wife's distress deserved following up, and I was eager to do so for her sake.

And I was still very much interested in negotiating for the Werner shares. That battle wasn't anywhere near over, and if Pierce had expected his little scene tonight to dissuade me, he obviously didn't know who he was dealing with.

But as much as I was ready and willing to attack Pierce, I was very aware that Celia was keeping me in the dark. She'd shut down entirely on the ride back to the hotel. Once in our suite, she'd occupied herself with the baby and ordering dinner. When the meal arrived, I'd hoped to have a chance to talk with her, but she'd spent the entire time on a phone call with her mother who was lamenting about the likelihood that Ron's sentence would be announced the following day. The bits and pieces I'd gleaned from that conversation riled me up in their own way. How the woman's concerns about her brother-in-law could still be so self-centered and trivial with no regard to Celia baffled me. Though Madge's ignorance to what happened to her daughter might have been understandable before Ron's arrest, it certainly seemed she should ask the question after his past was revealed. Her husband, for sure, was practicing willful denial, and so I spent my own dinner alternating between fantasies of putting Pierce in his place and fantasies of putting the Werners in theirs.

As soon as Celia hung up with her parents, my alarm went off reminding me of my scheduled phone call with Sonovision, forcing any discussion to wait even longer. All that to say, negotiating a new anime streaming service for distribution in the UK was the least of my current concerns.

"We could be ready to send a contract over in an hour," Toshiro said, calling my attention back to him. "You could be ready to stream by August."

He allowed me to consider. In the silence, I realized the water had stopped running in the next room, which meant Celia was done with her shower, and frankly she was the only situation I could truly invest in at the moment.

"I'm going to need to discuss this more with my team, Toshiro," I said, hoping he wouldn't realize the conversation had been the waste of time that it had. "And we'll want to wait for your second quarter reports before deciding anything. Get those sent over when you have them, and we'll talk again."

I hung up before he had a chance to refute, just in time for Celia to come out of the bedroom to grab something from the kitchen fridge.

"Feel better?" I called from my desk. It took all I had not to jump up and corner her, demand answers, force her into breaking down her walls and telling me everything.

We weren't like that anymore, though. We hadn't been for quite some time.

She crossed to stand by the bookcase, a bottled water in her hand. "A bit," she said, unscrewing the cap and bringing it up to her lips. When she lowered it, she kept her eyes out the window. "I'm sorry tonight wasn't more helpful. We just need to change our course of action, is all. I'll start reaching out to my cousins with shares available to sell tomorrow."

"Mm," I said, taking a deep breath before commenting with something more substantial. "You realize that it would be helpful if you talked about what happened tonight. Not just for me, but for you."

"I'm not so sure about that."

"I am. Sit down. Let's talk."

Her gaze swung to meet mine, and I caught a flash of panic in her eyes. "Are you suggesting a session?"

"Why not?" Immediately, I chastised myself for not being more commanding about it. "Yes, I am suggesting a session."

She swallowed, then ran her tongue tentatively across her bottom lip as she looked toward the couch then me at the desk. I could sense her thoughts whirring as she contemplated giving in.

Once upon a time, she wouldn't have deliberated at all.

Once upon a time before that, I wouldn't have given her a choice.

Eventually, she shook her head. "It's really not necessary. Nothing needs to be rehashed. I just..." She trailed off, her brow creasing deeply.

Whatever was bothering her, it was pressing at her. I could feel her anxiety in the air, like it was a live thing with energy. It ripped at my insides, making me feel both like fire and mush. I burned to do something for her, to fix it, to figure it out, and I ached that she wouldn't allow it, that she stood so far out of reach.

"What is it?" I asked, standing from the desk. My mobile buzzed with a call, but I ignored it and took a step toward Celia, stopping when she shook her head.

"Go ahead. Take your call."

I silenced it. "It's not important. What are you worrying about? Tell me."

"Nothing," she said too quickly. She paused. "Just...you haven't done anything...have you? With Hudson?"

"I don't know what you're asking."

"Like...you haven't tried to bully him or, I don't know. Terrorize him? In some way?"

"No." It rankled that she had to ask, despite knowing that I wasn't forthcoming about a good deal of my agendas. "I'm trying to earn his trust right now, not destroy it. Why? Did he suggest that I had?"

My mobile started to ring again. A quick glance said it was Hagan, likely wanting to know if he needed to follow up on my call with Sonovision.

At the same time, the bell to the suite rang. "Take it," Celia said, nodding to my phone. "I'll get the door. It's probably turndown service." She headed down the hall.

Cursing under my breath, I answered the call without saying hello. "There's nothing to follow up on. I postponed negotiations until their next quarter reports come in."

"I heard. Toshiro's assistant pinged me. They're threatening to try to sell elsewhere."

"Fuck." The deal was a good one, not one I wanted to lose.

But the heated conversation that drifted from the front of the suite suggested it had not been turndown service.

"Do you want me to call them back?" Hagan pressed.

I tried to concentrate on the question. "They aren't going to attract other buyers without the latest quarter reports," I reasoned. "If they're pushing so hard, especially. It looks like they're hiding numbers."

"I can arrange some sort of temporary agreement based on quarter finals," Hagan suggested.

The tone of the voices in the background escalated.

"Do that," I said, knowing the decision was rushed. "I have to go." I had already started toward the door, pocketing my mobile as soon as I hung up.

I hadn't expected the sight I came across when I turned the corner into the entry hall. Hudson Pierce holding back an angry brunette who was screaming at my wife and looking like she would tear out Celia's throat if let to do so. "It was you!" she shouted. "You're so fucking sick. Hudson said you'd changed, but you will never change. You have no heart. Manipulating and conniving. Does your husband know what... what a...*dragon* he married?"

Celia protested defiantly, and knowing her as I did, I was positive that whatever she'd been accused of, she was innocent.

False accusations thrown at *my* wife? In *my* hotel suite?

I was immediately livid.

"What the hell is going on here?" I roared, not so loudly that the baby would hear me in the next room, but forceful enough to be given notice.

The room went abruptly silent, all eyes turned to me. Hudson loosened his grip on the rabid woman who I could only assume was his wife.

And Celia, the woman who had been only strong and defiant in her interactions with me for more than a year now, went white, her eyes wide with fear.

It would have been one thing if it seemed that her fear was directed at our guests. It was quite a different thing realizing that her fear was directed at *me*.

"Edward," she said, taking a cautious step toward me. "It's nothing. Hudson and Alayna are...old friends."

"Old friends, my ass," the woman blurted out.

I knew the relationship between these women was rocky at best. Pierce's insistence that he needed insurance against Celia from going after his wife was proof that their past had been highly complicated.

But except for Celia's apprehension toward me, it seemed more like she was the one needing protection. Mrs. Pierce had both her claws and teeth out.

I felt suddenly feral, ready to take her on. "Is there a problem?" I asked, coming farther into the space.

Of course, the other issue was that my wife very obviously wanted me calm. "I didn't realize that you and Hudson Pierce had been *friends*, darling," I said, because why the fuck was she using that term to describe him now?

Celia's shoulders sagged, her eyes lowering to the ground, an act of submission I hadn't seen from her in months.

"Actually, there *is* a problem," Hudson's wife said defiantly.

"Alayna," Hudson hissed, seeming to want her tempered. Cordially he addressed me. "Edward, you haven't met my wife."

"No, I haven't. And I hear we are about to be family." I studied her in a way meant to put her in her place. "It's a pleasure to meet you, Alayna."

"It's really just a misunderstanding," Celia said quickly, her eyes imploring.

I knew what she wanted from me. She wanted me to turn around, let it go, walk away, the same way she'd wanted me to do so at Randall's earlier in the night.

I'd walked away then, against my better judgment. Because I loved her, and she'd begged, and I was trying to be the man she wanted me to be, one who listened and respected and yielded.

I couldn't be that man now.

Not when it was clear that there was a battle that Celia was fighting alone. Not when I had every reason to doubt she was leaving me out of it for motives other than my own good.

"I'd like to hear what Alayna has to say, if you don't mind?" I stared at Celia intensely, willing her to defy me. As often as she'd fought me in our marriage, she'd always obeyed my demand to heed me in public. For half a second, I wondered if that would change now.

Then her eyes lowered, giving in, which was both a relief and emboldening. "Alayna?" I said, encouraging her to speak.

She lifted her chin like a star student proud to have been called. "Hudson and I are being terrorized. We have reason to suspect the threats may be coming from your wife."

"That's not necessarily true," Hudson said immediately.

Simultaneously, Celia piled on. "I haven't done anything to you. I didn't send a single one of those threats."

I put my hand up to silence her, noting her choice of words.

Threats. She'd asked if I'd threatened Hudson. What the fuck was going on?

"If she didn't do it," Alayna continued, "She could prove it, and help us find out who is threatening us, at the same time. It would be easy, if she'd let us see the journals that she kept from the time that she and Hudson..." She trailed off, but she'd said enough to start the pieces coming together.

Celia's journals documented the "games" she'd played on other people. With her partner. Did that mean her partner was—?

Alayna plowed ahead suddenly, answering my unspoken question. "Hudson and Celia had a working relationship in the past. I don't mean to butt into your marriage. It would be truly cruel and devious to interfere with your relationship." She threw a glare toward Celia. "And so I apologize if this is the first you are hearing about their former partnership. But my family's safety is on the line, and this is truly important."

And there the picture locked in place, a second's worth of time sharpening the image until it was crystal clear—Hudson Pierce was the man who taught her. Hudson Pierce was the man she'd been protecting. Hudson bloody Pierce.

My mind wanted to follow each of the threads this discovery highlighted all at once, wanted to try to analyze whether I felt victorious or validated or irate or goddamned relieved, but of course, I couldn't react at all. I had to keep it together for the moment. Protect my family. Stand up for my wife.

"I see," I said, careful to hide any trace of surprise. "I *do* know about Hudson and Celia's working relationship, of course."

"You do?" Alayna sagged with disappointment, as though she'd hoped the news would put a riff in my relationship with my wife.

She had no idea.

"I do. Celia tells me everything. Don't you, darling?" I sidled up to my wife, putting my arm around her. Protectively? Threateningly? "Well, almost everything." Admittedly, my clutch around her waist might have been tighter than necessary.

Celia's head lowered with guilt.

Or fear.

Fear that I now understood.

Fear that was justifiable.

First, there was the matter of threats that the Pierces had been receiving, not altogether surprising considering the shit I'd read they'd done. I could imagine there were plenty of people who wanted to see him hurting. Celia, too, which was why it was important to help find the bugger.

"I can guarantee you that Celia is not behind this," I said, intent on clearing up any thoughts to the contrary. "And to prove it, we will have the journals flown here from London. They can arrive here by Tuesday. You may come back then. Now, if you don't mind, Celia needs to get some sleep. Our baby will be waking up in about five hours for her feeding, and you are correct, Celia really is a dragon when she hasn't gotten enough sleep."

Alayna appeared both shocked and relieved as I ushered her out the door. Hudson managed to hide any emotion, but I sensed his gratitude.

Good. He'd best remember that feeling when I talked to him next, and I would talk to him again. Soon, in fact. Very soon.

Tonight, though, I had my wife to deal with.

TWELVE

CELIA

I'D BEEN afraid of my husband on many occasions. Many times it was even a turn-on, as he'd so often pointed out.

Tonight, though, as he closed the door behind Hudson and Alayna, the quiet that filled the space between us was thick with dread that I'd never felt before. A kind of foreboding that made my bones feel cold and my stomach feel like it was carrying a cannonball.

After the door had shut all the way he still didn't turn around. He just stood there, one hand braced firmly against the wall, the other on the knob of the door.

"Edward..." I said tentatively.

"Don't." His voice was tight but controlled.

I gave it a beat, watching the muscles in his back expand as he breathed in deep then let it out. Then breathed in deep again.

Apprehension got the best of me. "What are you going—?"

He whipped around to face me, his eyes blazing. "I mean it, Celia. I'm not ready for you to talk yet."

I clammed up. While I was desperate to know what he planned to do to Hudson now that he knew who he was, I sensed it was probably best not to push him right now. I had no doubt I'd find out soon enough anyway.

I just had to hope that, whatever he planned, it wouldn't be devastating. Or that I'd be able to talk him down.

My silence seemed to settle him somewhat. His next breath came easier. Then he said,

"Living room. I need you to be sitting down for this conversation."

He also appeared to need a drink for it because he stopped at the minibar on the way and filled a tumbler of cognac before following into the living space where I'd perched myself on the edge of the couch.

I'd left plenty of room on both sides of me, thinking he'd sit as well or take the armchair or his desk, but instead he stayed standing. It made me feel small, and perhaps that was his intention. It also made me irritated because it was obvious he was going to handle this with a heavy hand instead of like a reasonable adult.

That meant I had to be the grown-up. "Look," I said as soothingly as possible, "I can imagine what you're thinking—"

"You cannot possibly imagine what I'm thinking. If you could, you would be scared to utter a single word until I asked you to."

A chill ran down my spine. I shut up and waited as he paced the room, back and forth, taking small sips of his brandy, each second adding to my growing apprehension.

He's processing, I told myself. Instead of acting rashly, he was actually thinking it through. That was a good thing.

Wasn't it?

"I think it's safe to say we're clear now about who A was," he said, finally. "Who A is. Is that correct?"

"That's correct." I added "Sir" as an afterthought, hoping a show of deference would help my cause.

"Oh, that's cute. Thinking you can earn points now with subservience. It's too little too late, I think, don't you?"

So much for that idea.

I thought the question was rhetorical, but when he waited, his eyes stabbing into me, I felt compelled to respond. "I'm not sure if you want me to actually answer that or not."

"No. I don't." He took one more swallow of his drink before setting it on the desk. He clapped his hands together. "So. Hudson Pierce."

I nodded once.

"Hudson bloody Pierce." His fist pounded against the desk, causing me and the liquid left in the tumbler to jump.

Automatically, my mouth opened in an anxious need to try to clear up whatever needed clearing, but the warning look he gave me caused it to close again just as fast.

I wasn't just scared of him, though. My irritation had escalated to pissed. Because shouldn't he be happy now? He'd finally gotten what he wanted. Finally discovered my secret. Shouldn't he be gloating? Why was *he* angry?

Yet he definitely was. I could feel the anger radiating off him hotter than the fireplace burning in winter.

"Let's go through this," he said curtly. "If you don't mind, just so I can have a clear picture."

"Sure."

He glared at me, as though my speaking had been out of turn.

"You asked if I minded," I said with hostile bravado. "If you expect to get anything from me at all, you better treat this like a civil conversation, Edward. I am not your property. I am a human being, and whether you feel like I deserve it or not, I will not sit here if you're going to do nothing but belittle and terrorize me."

His gaze narrowed. "If you'd rather be treated like I would treat any rival who had crossed me, then I can do that. Granted, I don't think you realize the privileges you gain from your status as my wife."

You're being an asshole right now.

It was what I wanted to say, but his threat reminded me that although I knew without a doubt that Edward would never do anything to really harm me, that wasn't the case with someone he wasn't married to. Someone like Hudson.

And so my capitulation was about protecting my one-time friend, nothing else. I lowered my eyes to my lap, signaling my submission.

"Good. We're on the same page here, at least. How about you help me confirm the rest." It wasn't a question. "You grew up with Hudson, your mothers were friends. You developed a bit of a crush on him that he proceeded to take advantage of. Correct so far?"

It had been more than a crush but less romantic than he suggested. I'd been in the aftermath of Uncle Ron, needing some assurance of my value as a woman. As a person. Hudson had been the one I'd turned to.

But Edward wasn't interested in any of that right now, and honestly, he already knew. And the ending was accurate. Hudson *had* taken advantage of my feelings. So I answered simply. "Yes."

"He played you, then you took the betrayal badly—"

"Is that really necessary?"

He ignored my interruption. "—and got back at him by sleeping with his father. Honestly, did you need Pierce to teach you anything? You seemed to already have retribution down pat."

He was being mean, and it hurt.

But I could handle betrayal better these days, and I knew how to be mean back. "If you're going to look at it that way, then the person I didn't need to teach me was you. Hudson never aimed for retribution. That was always your angle."

He smirked, as though I'd shot him with an arrow that had long missed its mark. "Right. Because the people Hudson taught you to manipulate were innocent whereas the ones I've encouraged you to go after were not."

"This is pointless." I stood up, ready to walk out of the room when his sharp tone cut through the air like a whip.

"Sit. Back. Down."

That rage would have to find an outlet somewhere. I'd come this far making sure Hudson didn't receive it. I couldn't stop now.

I sat back down.

"So. The score was settled." Was that what he was doing? Keeping tally, back and forth? Trying to decide who deserved to punish whom? "Until you got pregnant with a child that, had the true father been implicated, would have potentially destroyed Pierce's family."

"I didn't get pregnant on purpose," I said when I could see him mentally adding that as a point against me. Though, after I said it, I realized it was helpful to Hudson if the marks weighed in my favor.

His expression grew colder. "Forgive me for not jumping to believe that's true. You should understand why I might have trouble believing your conception had been unintentional."

My anger heated like molten lava nearing eruption. "I didn't try to get pregnant. Believe it or not, it's the truth. And fuck you for comparing that situation to Cleo who was very much wanted and conceived in a marriage after my husband had outright said that we could have a child together at some point."

The mention of Cleo, whom I knew full well that he loved, did nothing to settle him. "Regardless, you got pregnant. Then you bullied Hudson into taking responsibility? Showed up and threatened to disrupt his life unless he did?"

"He offered! I hadn't expected anything." I was mad enough at the insinuation, madder still when I realized it might not just be something he was considering now. "Have you thought that all along?"

"He clearly despises you, as does his wife. I'm trying to understand his motivation. Why did you even go to him first if you didn't want him to fix it?"

"Oh. Because you assume I always need someone to fix things for me. That I can't take care of anything myself."

He didn't deny it.

My hands clenched into fists in my lap. "I'm so fucking mad at you right now, I can't even begin to express it."

"That makes two of us."

We'd been mad at each other before and worked it out through some rough sex, but this was different. This couldn't be solved by his cock.

I wasn't even sure it could be solved by words, and yet, I took a deep breath, and tried. "I went to Hudson because he'd been my friend. And after I'd involved his family like I had in our fucked-up battle, it seemed only fair that he be the person who knew first."

"So it was out of compassion that you went to him. Not exploitation."

He was taking my confessions, things he'd suggested he thought I should put behind me, and using them against me. Spinning my words to show me in my worst light.

My chest ached, like my heart was splitting in two.

But maybe this was my due. We'd never fully addressed The Games with Hudson. Maybe there were still demons for me to exorcise here, and maybe these were things Edward needed cleared up too.

I sighed. "Compassion is probably giving me too much credit. I went to him because I needed him. And I think it was because of his own guilt about the situation, that he stepped up and offered to claim it as his."

"Not because he cared for you."

This was harder to admit for some reason. "Maybe that, too."

"He would have married you?"

"I don't know. It was assumed that we would."

Edward's jaw tensed. He picked up his drink again and threw the rest back. "But he was looking for a different kind of partner. Not a wife. One who would participate in his cruel games."

"He wasn't looking for a partner at all," I insisted. "He hadn't even told me about his experiments. I had to guess. And none of that came up until I lost the baby. He never intended to invite me into that, whether we'd gotten married or not. Whether I'd had the baby or not."

"Except that he *did* invite you into it."

"I invited myself. You know this. I've told you this." My frustration was growing, despite my best intentions. "I was sad and distraught and tired of feeling things, tired of not knowing how to cope, and I just wanted it all to end. Can you try to understand that? And there was Hudson, stone cold and stoic, and I desperately wanted to be like that. So I asked him to teach me. I *begged* him! It wasn't him at all. It was me. All me."

"Was it *all* you? You're sure he didn't manipulate you into that position?"

I hadn't ever considered that before, and the question gave me pause. When I thought about it, though, I was certain I knew the truth. "I'm sure."

Edward was determined to see the worst. "But he knew you were hurting. Agreeing to anything with a woman who is in that state of mind is irresponsible."

"Seriously?" I stared at him incredulously. "Because a woman can't know what she wants for herself? I knew, and I went after it, and we became a team, and those terrible things we did? They made me better."

"They made you an emotionless dragon."

"Is that any worse than being a vengeful devil?"

My words hung in the air, and I regretted them almost immediately. They were honest, but they weren't productive, and I didn't want to be fighting, I wanted to be fixing.

"You're right that it didn't help long-term," I conceded, not entirely withholding my anger from my tone. "I get that now. It was a survival technique, and you already knew this about me when you decided to love me, so don't act like I'm suddenly not good enough because I had a rocky past."

"I never said that." It was the softest he'd spoken since the discussion began.

I matched his mild tone. "It feels like you're saying that."

For a moment, he looked like he might yield. Like he might set down his fury and wrap me in his arms instead.

Then the moment was over, and he went hard again. "You're displacing. That's how you feel about yourself, not me. I don't have a problem with your past. My problem is with your present."

The accusation surprised me. "What bothers you specifically? That I don't want my husband to go to war with someone who got me through a terrible time? That I want to put the bad parts of my life behind me?"

Without answering, he changed gears. "Why did you and Pierce fall out?"

I looked away and shook my head, frustrated that this whole conversation, like every conversation, was on Edward's terms.

But I'd known who he was when I'd fallen in love with him, too. "He didn't want to play anymore. And I did."

"He quit his own game?"

"His sister intervened, I think. Because he had someone who could see he had fallen down a hole, someone who loved him, and she pulled him back out. I didn't have that someone, though Hudson tried to get me to quit too, but I couldn't. It was all I had. I didn't know how to *be* without it."

I looked back at Edward, the man who had been my confessor through so much of my past sins. Once again, I confided my wrong-doings. "I was lonely without him. I tried to rope him back in a few times. He'd taught me well, you see, and I used it against him. Or I tried. Nothing worked until Alayna. I was there when he first saw her, and I'd never seen him like that—lit up and interested. Over someone that wasn't a potential pawn. He'd gotten better enough to be able to start feeling like that, which I couldn't understand, but I could observe.

"I took advantage of that." My voice cracked suddenly, the gravity of what I'd put Hudson through hitting me squarely. "It makes me sick, what I did. Makes me literally taste bile. I used his attraction to Laynie to bring him back into The Game. I coerced him into hurting her. And when that wasn't enough, I tried to unravel them in other ways, and part of it was simply because I didn't know how to give up on an objective. Hudson had taught me that too. But a bigger part of it was me trying to hold onto something that had never really been mine. Had never really been real, even."

I swiped at the tear on my cheek with the back of my hand. Crying always had an effect on Edward, which made me more conscientious of trying to hold the tears back. I didn't want to manipulate him. I wanted to come together honestly.

Turned out I needn't have worried. My tears didn't faze him in the slightest. "So you kept at him, kept pecking away at their relationship, and in order to get you to stop, he got Glamplay to sell him their Werner shares."

There was no amusement in my chuckle. "It's funny, isn't it? I got his father involved when I slept with him. He got mine involved when he bought those shares. Karma, man."

Edward's brows raised as I stood slightly in order to reach the tissue box on the ottoman then settled when I was back in place. After dabbing my eyes, I went on. "It worked, of course. Not just because I didn't want my family's business to fall apart, but because that was when I finally got it. Hudson had gone to extremes to put me in my place, and from everything I'd learned from human behavior in our years together, I realized he'd done it. He'd truly fallen in love.

"That was a big deal, you see. I'd wanted in on The Game because Hudson didn't have feelings about anyone. When he fell in love, it made everything that we did seem futile."

Whoa.

I huffed out a long breath. I'd never articulated that before, not out loud. Not in my head. But that had truly been what had ended us, hadn't it? Hudson had shown me that The Game didn't work. It was still possible to feel things while playing them, and so what was even the point?

Still, like a hamster on a wheel, I'd kept on, praying he was wrong, hoping to one day play my way out of feeling any guilt for everything I'd done.

It had all been in vain.

The only reason I eventually changed and rebuilt and learned to accept myself was because I'd met Edward.

I wanted to tell him that, and I started to, but he spoke first. "He fell in love with Alayna and that was devastating. Because you were in love with him."

"What? No." I was appalled. "Where did you get that? Are you actually listening to me?"

"I am. Very intently, and what I hear is that you were so in love with him, this man that was all you had, that you tried to break up his relationship, and when that didn't work, when he went to extremes to get rid of you, you still held onto him by continuing with his games."

"*The Game* was all I had. Not *him.* I still played because it was all I was good at. It was all I knew."

"And then, years later, when you're supposedly in love with me, you still choose him. Choose to protect *him* instead of opening up to *me.*"

I shot up off the couch. "Because you said you were going to go after him! I didn't choose him over you."

"Choose to keep me in the dark about someone who might be after both of you because of things you'd done," he continued, his tone rising. "Someone who might be a threat to the mother of my daughter, because you still are more concerned about his safety than our family."

The lightbulb finally went on. "Is that what this is? You're jealous?" In another situation I might have been flattered. Right now, I was livid. "Are you fucking kidding me?"

"This isn't jealousy, Celia. This is rage. This is betrayal. This is me questioning every vow we made to each other and doubting the very foundation of our marriage. It was one thing when A was a distant ghost in your past, but to discover he is in your life now, that you are still interacting with him, that you are continually choosing him—"

Cleo's wail broke Edward off mid-sentence. Honestly, I was surprised she hadn't woken up sooner. Our voices had certainly risen in volume. It was a good thing that it was only her wall against ours, or we might have had management knocking as well.

"I'll get her," I said, unsure if it was the worst or the best time to put the conversation on pause. On the one hand, there was so much left to be worked through. On the other hand, upset as we both were, it was probably a good idea to take a breather.

I left the door slightly ajar when I went to Cleo's room, hoping Edward might follow. Her presence was always calming. Even when she was upset, she put things in perspective. Forced us to recognize what really mattered.

But Edward didn't follow.

I wiped my own tears before I picked Cleo up and hugged her to me, tight. "I'm sorry, baby," I said, kissing her head. "Mommy and Daddy just got a little mad at each other. It's going to be all right."

I didn't know that, though. I doubted things would be all right tonight, anyway. And when I heard the heavy slam of the door in the suite next door, and I realized that Edward had left, I worried it might never be all right between us again.

THIRTEEN

EDWARD

I LEFT because I needed to think.

Problem with thinking was that it meant feeling as well. The hotel bartender was helping with that.

Or, he was until he announced last call and left me with a tab that could have bought an entire bottle of cognac.

"One more," I said, handing him back the bill so he could adjust the total. "And I'll charge it to my room. Twenty-seven-oh-five."

"Got it, Mr. Fasbender."

I threw back the remains of the glass he'd poured the last time he'd been by, and tried once more to organize my thoughts.

Hudson Pierce was the enemy.

Hudson Pierce had been the enemy all along.

What should I do about Hudson bloody Pierce?

Ruin him, was the usual answer to questions like these, and it did keep returning as an option, but I could never hold onto the thought long enough to conceive of a viable plan because every time I tried to imagine what he *deserved*, I had to consider, not only what he'd done, but what had been done to him, and that brought me time and time again back to focusing on Celia.

And with Celia came the emotions, bleak and drenching like a torrential downpour. She'd deserved what he'd done to her, hadn't she? Why did that make me so enraged?

I'd known about her past. I'd overlooked her sins even if I hadn't forgiven them. I'd destroyed the woman she'd once been and had paved the way for her rebirth. Her history hadn't mattered.

It still didn't.

So why was I so utterly shattered?

Nothing had changed, really. Hudson owned as many shares of Werner now as he had yesterday. He still owned them for the same reason. Celia had still had a partner in her crimes. The anger I'd felt about her secrecy regarding that partner had already been dealt with. It shouldn't matter that the man she'd protected had a name that I already knew or that it had been a man who shared such an extensive history with her. It shouldn't matter that the man had been the first that she'd loved.

Except that it did matter.

It mattered very much.

Because, as I'd said so blatantly to her before I'd left the room, she'd chosen to honor her bond with that arsehole above the bond she had with me. Because not only had she once had feelings for Hudson, but it was also quite evident that she still felt something for him, be it romantic in nature or something more complex, and that feeling had obviously meant more to her than complete transparency in our marriage.

Because no matter what I did to Hudson, even if I ruined him completely, it wouldn't make Celia any more *mine*. Which was what I wanted more than anything, if I was honest—to own her heart completely. To be her one and only master, the man she not only loved above all others but at all.

That felt outrageously juvenile to admit.

I drowned the emotion with a long swallow from my newly filled glass. Then, I pushed it away and signed the tab before standing. Too quickly, it seemed, since the floor teetered as I did.

"You need help to your suite, Mr. Fasbender?"

The bartender was trying to be helpful, but it took all I had not to snap his head off for the inquiry. "I'm fine," I said tightly.

Besides, I wasn't going to my suite. Too much alcohol had left my head—and my heart—more muddled than when I'd first come down. When the room finally stopped spinning, I headed instead to the front desk.

"Do you have any rooms available?" I asked.

"We do. How long will you be needing it, sir?"

I gave him the most honest answer I could. "I don't know."

I WOKE to my mobile ringing, the volume seeming much louder than usual as the normally gentle chirp sounded like a gunshot next to my head. With bleary eyes, I looked at the screen, half expecting to see Celia's name before I silenced it. She'd texted the evening before, several times, and each one I'd ignored. The only reason I even looked was to be sure it wasn't Jeremy asking questions about her journals since I'd texted him last night to have them shipped overnight.

It wasn't his name on the ID, though, or Celia's. I glanced at the time before I answered. Why the hell was Leroy Jones calling me at eight in the blasted morning?

"It's early," I said instead of hello. It was even earlier in Albuquerque where Leroy worked for the FBI.

"It's not early in London," he said, decidedly more chipper than I was. "From the tone of your voice I'm guessing you've forgotten what day it is?"

It was Monday. Beyond that I was having a hard time even remembering where I was. A few more blinks, and my head cleared although the pounding throb at my temple remained.

I sat upright, regretting it as soon as I did. "Ron's sentence has been announced?"

"Yep. Ready for this? Twenty-six years."

"Twenty-six years," I repeated, dumbfounded.

"Twenty-six years. It's more than we'd hoped for."

"What does that mean as far as the US is concerned?" There'd been talk of extradition to face charges in the States, but that decision had been put on hold until the trial in the UK was over.

"It's more than we could get on the evidence we have here," Leroy said. "Statute of limitations has long passed for Celia, and the couple of leads we have with recent victims don't hold a lot of weight."

"So it's a closed case."

Leroy misread my subtext. "He's going to be locked up for the rest of his life," he said. "Does it matter if it's in your jails or in ours?"

"No, it's good," I said, meaning it. "Celia will be happy about this. I'd be happier if he'd gotten life, but I'm not displeased with the outcome."

"Think you can put this behind you now?"

"Not sure I'm good at putting anything behind me." It was a little more honest than I'd meant to be. "As for Celia, I'm not sure this is something you ever get over, whether justice is served or not."

"No, I'm sure that's true. I'm not going to hear some mysterious account of the douchewad hanging himself in prison, am I, or getting taken out with a shiv?"

I chuckled, then winced as the sound echoed too loudly through my skull. "If you do, I won't be behind it. Man deserves to spend the rest of his years suffering. Death would be too merciful."

"Tell you what, Fasbender. You ever want a side job taking down motherfuckers like Werner on the down low—aka, outside government jurisdiction—let's just say I can make that happen."

I managed to smile. "Good to know I have the right kind of friends. I'll even honestly consider it before telling you no. Thank you for the news."

I hung up just as my mobile beeped with a low battery warning. Tossing it down, I lay back down and covered my face with my arm. I hadn't bothered to close the curtains before falling asleep—I hadn't even made it under the covers—and the sunlight streaming in felt like shards of glass in my eyes. It had been quite a many years since I'd had a hangover, and now I remembered why I was very strict about limiting my drinking. I needed a bottle of water and two Advil, but both required getting out of bed and one possibly required leaving my hotel room.

I sat for a few minutes contemplating going back to sleep, but despite my misery, my head was awake now and that meant the thoughts were back, a tangled web of what to do and how to feel. I'd never understood Celia's desire to escape her emotions so distinctly as I did right then.

And now there wasn't just The Problem with Pierce on my mind, but the news about Ron. I should be there for Celia when she found out. We'd done our celebrating when he was found guilty and the sentencing was a relief, but every announcement about the man stirred her up in some way or another, as was to be expected.

News of Ron stirred me up as well. He was one of the sources of my anger. He was such a vile, despicable excuse for a human being. He was Satan himself, as far as I was concerned. What he'd done to Celia was unfathomable and unforgivable. If I'd been around when it was happening, if I'd known, I would have murdered him on the spot.

And her father!

Warren had been around, had known and he'd turned a blind eye. He'd chosen the easy path instead of the right one. He'd ignored the signs and her confession and chose to stand by his brother...for what? For the sake of his company? For the sake of convenience? Was that where Celia learned to protect her tormentors? From the man who'd chosen Ron over her?

I sat up again, ignoring the pounding in my head as I swung my feet over the side of the bed and stood up. I couldn't be there for Celia right now—I wasn't up for it physically or in the right frame of mind—but my temper raged on through the repercussions of last night's overdrinking, strong and bold and unrelenting.

And while I had yet to decide what to do with Hudson Pierce, I now, at least, had somewhere to focus my anger.

THIRTY MINUTES LATER, still wearing the clothes I'd slept in, Madge Werner opened the door of her penthouse apartment to greet me. "Edward, what a surprise to see you so early." Then, she got a good look at me. "Oh, goodness, you look terrible. What's wrong? Is it the baby?"

"Cleo's fine. Where's your husband?" I pushed past her, leaving the foyer in pursuit of the son of a bitch. "Warren?"

I found him in the hall wearing a robe and pajama bottoms. "Morning, Ed." If he was startled to see me, he didn't show it, barely giving me a nod before heading toward his office. "Phone's ringing off the hook, people wanting a statement. We'll want to coordinate with Murphy on the company's official stance, but my lawyer's already on it. Nothing to worry about on this end." He paused at the door so he could give me his full attention. "And we can still appeal, you know. Be sure we'll appeal."

"You most certainly will *not* appeal," I snapped.

Madge gasped behind me.

Warren frowned slightly, his expression perplexed, as though he hadn't heard me right. "What was that?"

I pinched the bridge of my nose. The two Advil I'd found in the hotel minibar were not working as well as I would have liked, the terribleness of my headache adding fuel to the volcano churning inside me.

There were things I needed to say. Important things that needed to be heard. While I was desperately close to just "blowing," it wouldn't be productive.

I took a breath to calm myself. "Warren, sit down." I nodded at the couch in his office.

His frown became more severe. "Can this wait? I know you have concerns about this whole Ron debacle, but—"

"Sit. The fuck. Down." So much for being calm.

He was so stunned, he did without further objection. I pivoted to find his wife sneaking off toward the kitchen.

She gave a fake smile. "I figured I'd just leave you two to—"

"You should sit down as well, Madge, since this also involves you." I managed to be softer with her, but only barely.

"Oh. Okay." She went dutifully to the couch, folding her hands in her lap. Celia had definitely not inherited her need to buck authority from her mother. Her father then?

Actually, she'd probably developed it as a survival technique since Warren wasn't really an authoritarian either. He was entitled, which was entirely different and more annoying as far as I was concerned.

I moved to lean my backside against Warren's desk, taking the place of command in the room. By that time, Warren's irritation at being ordered around in his own office caught up with him, and he stood back up. "What's going on with you, Edward? Whatever this is, it can't be so important that it needs to happen now. In case you haven't heard the news from London, I have things I need to be doing."

I gave him an intense glare that sent him sinking back into his seat. "Yes. You do have things you need to do. Defending your good-for-nothing brother is not one of them."

His irritation escalated to frustration. "Hey, now, that's uncalled for."

"Is it, Warren?" I folded my arms across my chest, my gaze piercing into him. I'd come here with an agenda, but I hadn't quite worked out this part of the confrontation. Despite the current disagreement with my wife, spilling the details of her abuse felt disloyal. But I didn't need to spill anything, did I? Warren already knew. "Think about it before you answer because you know exactly what I'm talking about."

Madge looked from me to her husband. "What's going on?"

"I think you should leave," he said coldly, his eyes pinned on me.

I gave him a quick smile that held no warmth. "I bet you do. But I'll assure you that I am not leaving. It's past time that we had this conversation. The only reason I didn't confront you sooner was out of courtesy to Celia, hoping she'd eventually deal with you herself, or that, miracle of miracles, you'd behave like a decent father and reach out to her on your own, but you aren't a decent father, are you, Warren? And it isn't really fair to expect her to approach you considering the reaction she got from you the last time."

His jaw tightened. "I don't have to listen to this. In my own home. Madge, call security."

She stood immediately, as though it were a habit to do as her husband bid, but she stopped just as quickly when I said, "Madge, you need to hear this, and I believe, you are ready to hear it."

"Leave her out of this," Warren said with as much hostility as fear in his tone.

It was understandable, really. I couldn't imagine the terror of having to admit how he'd betrayed Celia to anyone, let alone her mother.

Madge hesitated, deliberating. When she spoke, she looked at me. "Is this about Ron? Ron and...Celia?"

"No," Warren said.

"Yes," I said simultaneously.

She swung to face her husband. "Warren, you told me that nothing happened. You promised me that nothing happened."

So she'd guessed. It was reassuring, at least, to find out the woman wasn't as clueless as she'd seemed. Though she should have had the balls to ask her daughter about it, not her worthless, cowardly husband.

"I said...well." Warren was flustered. "I'm sure I didn't promise anything."

"You did," she insisted, her tone growing shrill. "When I asked you if it was possible if anything happened, you said there was no way. That all of the charges were a fabricated lie from a money-grabbing ex-girlfriend. And when I brought up how odd it was that Celia had wanted to stop seeing him so abruptly as a teen, when I said I had a bad feeling about it, you said..."

She trailed off, but I didn't have to hear the rest of the conversation recapped to know the basic premise. "He lied."

"I didn't lie," Warren barked. "I didn't know anything, honey. I still don't."

Lying piece of dirt. "You did. He did, Madge. He knew because Celia came to him as a teenager and told him that her uncle, a man she had trusted and looked up to, had been grooming and abusing her for years."

"No," Madge half gasped, half cried. "Oh God. No." She sank back to the couch, her face ashen.

"And then," I continued, "after all the courage it took to tell her father, the man who was supposed to love and protect her above all else, he accused her of lying."

"She told you?" she asked, incredulous and horrified.

Warren shifted toward his wife. "It was so long ago now. I can't remember exactly what she said. You know how kids are. The things they say to get out of spending time with family."

Madge heard past the bullshit. "Why didn't you tell me? Why didn't *she* tell me?"

"Would you have let yourself hear her?" I asked, happy to stir the pot. "Your husband certainly couldn't be bothered."

"That's not how it happened. She came to—"

I stood up straight, cutting him off. "You know what, Warren? I don't fucking care about your side of the story. The only version of events that matters to me is Celia's, and thank God after more than twenty years, she's finally seeing justice and that shitty piece of human garbage is behind bars. Countless lives that man destroyed, and you could have prevented all of it."

I was well aware that Ron had ruined my family long before he'd ever set a finger on Celia, but it still felt good to pin it on Warren. If he had been more involved in his brother's hand in his business back in those days, he could have prevented what happened to my father's company too, though I suspected he would have turned the same blind eye to his business practices as he had to Celia's confession.

Strangely, after all the years I'd wanted to destroy Warren for the demise of my family, it was only anger for Celia that incited me today. "Your brother is in jail for the rest of his life, but you still have amends to make. I came here today to be sure that happens."

Warren stood, his full height still several inches below mine. "I don't owe anyone anything, and I'm not giving out explanations or apologies for something that happened—"

I took a threatening step toward him. "You don't want to finish that sentence. Because if it ends with you dismissing all of this as something that's ancient history, then I will not be responsible for my actions, and

I promise you, you do not want to find out what happens when I'm this mad."

I let that sink in, not just to menace him, but also because I needed some composure before going on. As much as I wanted to break every bone in his body, it wasn't the goal.

"I already think your daughter is too good for you," I said when I was the tiniest bit calmer, "and if she walked away from you completely, I would be elated. But she loves you, both of you, for some unimaginable reason, and because I'm devoted to that woman with my entire being, you *will* fix this. You *will* do right by her. You *will* step up—years too fucking late, mind you—but you will finally step up and show her that she is more important to you than you've ever led her to believe. Do you understand?"

Madge shook her head. "I don't feel well. I need to lie down."

I watched her leave the room with disappointment. From what I knew about my mother-in-law, I expected she would spend the next week in bed. No wonder Celia hadn't gone to her as a child. She would have had to coddle and soothe her mother when it should have been the other way around.

Madge was a lost cause.

Warren, though, the man whose amends mattered most, still stood in front of me, silent, half cowering, half ready to do combat. I watched the bob of his Adam's apple as he swallowed and the way his eyes darted, calculating his next move.

I could have punched him in the throat for even considering anything other than what I demanded. "Do you understand?" I asked again, my voice practically a growl.

His shoulders sank then, as though he finally felt the weight of his betrayal. "I'm not sure how to do that."

I nodded, because I'd assumed a response like that, an unwilling-ness to even try to figure out what his daughter might want or need from him. Even knowing it was coming, it made me want to remove his balls with my bare hands.

With gritted teeth, I forced myself not to launch myself on him. "Good thing I figured it out for you already." I pulled my mobile from my jacket pocket, opened up my email app and hit send on the message I'd drafted on the ride over, the device plugged into the car charger as I'd typed. "I've sent you a statement. I recommend releasing it word for word since I don't trust any of your alterations would be suitable. Of course it's your decision whether you decide to release it or not, and if you can find a better way to make amends with Celia, then go ahead. If you can't, I recommend you stick to this script."

He scowled as he circled around me to his desk. A few clicks later, I watched his eyes scan the screen as he read what I'd sent, his skin going pale. "I can't just release this. Not without coordinating with Murphy and the board. There could be financial repercussions from saying something like this. It isn't just about our family here."

"Atonement isn't supposed to be easy," I said, coldly. "In my experience, it only means something when it comes at a price."

"I don't know," he said, rubbing his fingers over his brow.

I'd had enough, my patience completely worn out. "Take the time you need to make it real, Warren," I said, putting the discussion to a close. "Difficult as this may be, you and I both know this is the least you can do to make things right."

I left without a glance back, and only when I was in the lift did I finally sigh with relief. I felt good. Well, better than I had. Adrenaline surged through my veins and for the first time in the last twenty-four hours, I remembered an emotion that wasn't based solely in rage.

But I was still angry. And still a wreck. Still not in any sort to be around my wife, so when I got back to the hotel, I grabbed the dry cleaning waiting for me at the front desk and changed for my work day in my new hotel room instead of going back to the one I shared with Celia.

FOURTEEN

CELIA

AS SOON AS Elsa arrived in the morning, I handed off Cleo and set off for Midtown. I was frustrated and paranoid, worried Edward would follow me and think the worst so I took a cab instead of calling for Bert, and I left my cell at the hotel.

The phone was a source of distress, anyway, and it felt good to be unleashed from it. I'd spent most of the night texting and checking for replies from my husband. He didn't answer any. He hadn't even read any after midnight, which increased both my anxiety and my anger.

Because what was he planning to do?

What had he already done?

Was Edward the one harassing Hudson? It was still possible. Based on his reaction, I was certain that Edward hadn't known Hudson had been the man I'd been protecting before last night, but that didn't mean Edward hadn't gone after him for another reason.

I comforted myself with the fact that the threats I'd read hadn't been in Edward's handwriting. That got him off the hook, didn't it?

Whether it did or not, I clung to it as truth.

But then I couldn't stop playing out other worst-case scenarios in my head, imagining what Edward would do to Hudson if he hadn't done this. Imagining what he'd do in return. God, it was awful. They were both so powerful, and while I'd seen the best of each of them, I also knew how diabolical they could be at their worst.

It made my stomach hurt to think about.

When I could distract myself from ruminating, I didn't feel any better. In some ways, I felt worse. Fuck Edward for putting me through this. Fuck him for disappearing on me. Fuck him for being so rigid and domineering and manipulative.

And fuck me for loving him as desperately as I did.

Needless to say, I probably wasn't in the most ideal frame of mind when I showed up at Pierce Industries just before nine in the morning, but there I was, pissed and ready to lash out.

"He's on his way up," Trish said when I demanded to see Hudson.

Not bothering to sit down, I waited, my stare pinned on the elevator across the hall.

He saw me immediately. Our eyes met, and whatever spark of life had been in his before he'd seen me vanished, leaving his gaze cold and stony.

Without saying anything, he unlocked his office and gestured for me to go in. He followed closely, shutting the door behind him.

I'd told myself on the ride over I'd be civil. I'd told myself I'd be restrained.

Both promises went up in smoke as soon as I was alone with him in the office. "You really fucked up, Hudson," I said before he'd even made it to his desk. "And you can't blame that on me. This was your doing. *You're* the one who brought this to my house."

I hadn't realized how much guilt I was feeling until the words came out. I didn't want to be the person harassing Hudson and his family. I didn't like that version of me. I was a different person now, but if Edward wreaked havoc on his life, it would be my fault. Hudson would point the finger at me.

But I'd tried to prevent it! I'd tried and risked my relationship doing so. It was Hudson and his busybody wife that had fucked everything up, and I was here to make sure he got the record straight.

Unfortunately, Hudson wasn't in a mood to listen, which probably stemmed in part from my hostile approach. He slammed his fist down on his desk. "Did you do it? Are you behind this? Yes or no? Once and for all."

I flinched, the accusation hurting more coming from Hudson than when his wife had only alluded to it. "No! I told you, I didn't—"

He cut me off. "Then I *didn't* fuck up. We need those journals. We need them to solve this. Whatever it took to get them, I don't regret it."

He was curt and dismissive, and I knew in my bones that this entire interaction was unproductive, but I was now not just angry and worked up and worried but also I was goddamned hurt. By both Hudson and Edward. And while I was still learning how to deal with strong emotions, these were some of the most potent I'd had in a long time. They spun in my belly and pressed upward, demanding to be let out. They ruled me.

So instead of leaving, I spewed on. "I have *always* been real with you," I told him with raw sincerity. "No matter what I've done, what schemes I've pulled. I have still always been honest with you, when we were face-to-face. So when I say I didn't do this, you should know I'm telling the truth."

Hudson sank into his chair and looked up at me with disdain. "How could I know anything?" he asked with feigned innocence. "I don't know you anymore. Remember?"

The sharp pain in my chest made it impossible to speak, impossible to even breathe. All I could do was nod and stare and nod some more. What had I even expected? That Hudson would just intuitively understand all I'd done to protect him? That he would apologize or acquiesce or that he'd console me and tell me not to worry about a thing?

Even if it were possible for him to set aside everything that had happened after he met Alayna, even if he knew that I'd tried my damndest to keep him out of this, he was still going through a crisis of his own. Someone was threatening his family. His focus was there, as it should be, on the drama that was already happening to him. He couldn't be expected to be concerned about drama that was yet to come. He couldn't be expected to be concerned about me.

Then why was *I* concerned about *him*?

Without another word, I spun around and left Hudson's office. It was time I got my own priorities straight. Hopefully both of those priorities would be waiting for me when I got back to our suite.

EDWARD WASN'T at the hotel when I got back. He didn't return that evening either. My messages remained unanswered, as did my calls. By bedtime I'd stopped reaching out all together. He'd come back when he was ready, no sooner, and that was that.

I'd done this to him once. I'd taken off from London and hid away at my parents', refusing to talk to my husband except for short yes or no texts.

Reminding myself of that fact did nothing to calm the intense storm inside me, but at least it helped my head keep it together.

Thankfully, once I put away my phone, I had a task to keep me preoccupied. The diaries had arrived in a box from London by special delivery just after eight pm. While Cleo gnashed at baby cereal in her high chair, I spread out the books across the dining table, eleven black leather-bound journals containing the record of my cruel past.

I picked one up and leafed through it, my stomach churning as my eyes scanned familiar names and places. There was a lot written in them that I'd forgotten. Much more that I didn't want to remember. Going through them with Hudson was going to be tough, and for the first time since he'd disappeared, I wished Edward was back specifically to guide me through the task. I still wanted to fight with him, but I wanted him to comfort me, too. Wanted him to wrap me in his arms and let me feel my feelings and tell me what to do.

I can take care of myself.

With a sigh, I put the book back down and worked out a plan for how to get through them. Then I put in an order for breakfast room service and left the journals for the next day.

When I woke up the following morning, my priority was firm in my mind—put our differences aside and find the person who was terrorizing Hudson and Alayna. I'd been too wrapped up in myself to realize how serious the situation was. There was someone angry with things

Hudson and I had done in the past. Someone who very much wanted to even the score. His family's lives were in jeopardy. If it wasn't Edward behind it, there was a very good chance that my family would be threatened next.

And if it was Edward...well, I needed to know that too.

"Come on in," I said cheerfully when the Pierces appeared at my door. I nodded to the room service cart that had arrived only minutes before they had. "I've already ordered tea and coffee." I assumed Hudson still drank black coffee, but his wife...? I directed my next words to her. "I didn't know which you preferred in the morning. I also have an assortment of fruits and breakfast pastries, in case you haven't eaten yet. I know sometimes it's hard to remember to take care of yourself in times of stress."

"I've already eaten," Alayna said without feeling. Then, warmer, she added, "Thank you."

I refused to be anything but a perfect host. "They're here if you change your mind."

"How about we just get started?" Hudson said, as efficient as ever. "Where are the journals?"

"Since you're obviously not hungry either, Hudson, they're in here. Follow me." I walked them down the hall and around the corner to the dining room.

"Is Edward working with us as well?" Hudson asked as they followed behind.

I was glad I wasn't facing them when I answered. "No. He went into work." It could have been true for all I knew. Point was, my marital troubles were not of interest to Hudson, nor were they important today. "It's just us and the nanny."

When we reached the table, I turned to face them. As composed as Hudson usually was, I was surprised to see him viscerally react to the sight of the journals, as if their mere existence churned his stomach.

I know the feeling, bud.

It felt oddly reassuring to have that in common.

"I don't know if you had a plan about how to attack this," I said, suddenly nervous. I tucked a stray hair behind my ear. "But I was thinking that you and I, Hudson, could each grab a journal and start reading through it. When we come to a name of someone involved in an experiment, we could record the name as well as any other details that may be important regarding the subject. Such as whether or not we believe they might still have hostile feelings toward you or me. Most of those references in the letters seemed vague, but if we come across anything that seems to possibly be referenced, then we can note that as well."

It was a pretty straight-forward plan, one that removed Alayna from reading the journals, which was selfish on my part.

But they were, in fact, journals. They were private and terrible and not the kind of thing I ever wanted anyone reading. It had been bad enough when Edward had read them. He'd been enraged and disgusted. I couldn't imagine the contempt Alayna would feel reading them, especially when she already hated me so intensely.

I would have thought Hudson would feel the same way, but when no one spoke, I wondered if I'd thought wrong. "If you have another plan..."

"No," Hudson said. "This is good." He removed his jacket and sat down to work.

I followed suit, taking a chair across from him.

"What should I do?" Alayna asked.

It wasn't my place to keep her away from the journals. I looked to Hudson for that.

Thankfully, he seemed to be on the same page. "You can do the recording, Alayna. As Celia and I read, we will call out information. If you could track it and sort it, I think that would be the best use of your time."

I worried momentarily that she might object to being kept on the sidelines. From what I knew of Alayna, she had always been head-strong and ready to buck against anyone who tried to hold her down.

But she surprised me, taking to the job enthusiastically and even setting up a shared spreadsheet on the laptop she'd brought.

We dug in then, working throughout the morning. It was difficult reading, as I'd expected it would be, but I concentrated on detaching myself from the stories I read, and that helped the process go smoother. We developed a sort of rhythm between the three of us, Hudson and I shouting out details, Alayna confirming them before entering them into her computer. It was a good process.

That wasn't to say there wasn't tension amongst us because there definitely was. It wove around us like the tight weave of a spiderweb, keeping us trapped in its sticky silk-like thread. The only time it broke was when Elsa brought Cleo. Alayna was a sucker for a baby, it turned out, and no one could remain somber around mine.

It was only a momentary reprieve. As soon as Cleo was burped and back with the nanny, the contention was back, worse than before. It didn't just surround me, either. Alayna and Hudson bickered as well and eventually they excused themselves to take their clipped conversation to the hall.

Admittedly, I was pleased that, for once, their argument couldn't be blamed on me since I'd been on my best behavior, which was probably petty, but also it was a big thing. I hadn't ever spent time in a room with the two of them without scheming and plotting to turn them against one another. It was new for me, and as silly as it was, I took it as evidence of how far I'd come.

When Hudson returned, he came back alone. "It's a little much for Alayna," he said, vaguely. "We're on our own for the afternoon."

I held back a dozen snarky comments that came to mind. "Probably for the best. No one should have to deal with our shit except us."

"Amen."

If only my husband felt the same.

Reminding myself of my agenda for the day, I pushed the thought away. "I'll call down and tell room service one less dish for lunch."

When that was done, we resumed working, only breaking when our food arrived then quickly resuming when we'd finished. Our process had altered with Alayna's absence. Now we took turns reading, the other recording on Hudson's laptop. It was easier than it had been, despite being down one person. We both knew our stories so well that we could fill in the details that the other had read almost at the same time as they were recited out loud.

The tension was far less noticeable as well. In fact, there was almost a sense of camaraderie. Whatever our past sins, Hudson and I had committed them together. That created a bond between us that could never be broken, no matter what changed about us as individuals.

Maybe that's why I'd been so quick to keep Hudson a secret, because we'd been linked like that. I was bound to protect him. Whatever Edward thought, he was wrong—I hadn't chosen Hudson over him. I hadn't made a choice at all.

Eventually, Hudson closed his laptop. "I think that's enough for today."

I looked at my phone. Almost five o'clock. Where had the time gone? "Did we figure anything out?"

He hesitated. "Not really. Did you?"

"No," I answered honestly. Nothing we'd read connected to any of the letters Hudson had received, and I still was no closer to figuring out if Edward was involved. "We still have a few journals to go through."

"Back at it tomorrow?"

"Of course." He was about to stand when I stopped him. "Are you scared?"

"Of the person sending the letters?" He settled back in his chair. "Yes. I am. Someone is very angry, rightly so, I presume. Valid anger is one of the most dangerous weapons I've encountered."

I'd seen my husband use valid anger as a weapon. It had almost gotten me killed. I'd lived, but what about Camilla's husband? I was sure Edward had killed him. Would he go that far with Hudson?

A chill ran down my spine. "I feel like I should tell you I'm sorry."

Hudson seemed to assume my apology was for the past since his eyes scanned the journals laid out in front of us. "I was as much a part of this as you were." He waited a beat. "Sometimes I'm not so sure I shouldn't be apologizing to you."

It was peculiar how the cold I'd felt a second ago could so quickly turn to warmth. I didn't want an apology from Hudson, never had, but he'd considered it, and that meant something. Small that it might be, it was still something.

I flashed a brief smile. "It won't do any good, for either of us, at this point."

"No, I don't believe it will."

I stood as he did, planning to walk him to the door, but my thoughts were still tied up in the journals. "Should we be doing something? For all those people that we..." I couldn't find the right words.

Hudson didn't have that problem. "For our victims?"

"Yeah."

He sighed, a heavy sigh that practically thudded with its weight. "I've tried, you know. I still try, when I find the opportunity. Try to make it up. Try to pay it back. Every token of retribution is selfishly a way to ease my own heart. It's impossible to make up for those kinds of hurts. There's no price that can be paid to fix someone that you've so utterly broken."

An immense grief wrapped around me. Not just for my own wrongs that could never be fixed, but also for all the wrongs Edward felt had been done to him. He sought justice at every turn, trying to mend wounds that would never close.

"How are we ever supposed to move on?" I asked, my voice small.

Hudson shook his head, as though he didn't have that answer, but his words said differently. "We do just that. We move on. If we can't fix it, it doesn't do any good to dwell on the guilt. All we can do is forgive ourselves, try to be better in the future. And we can love the people in our lives wholly. We can believe in and fight for their goodness as strongly as we once worked to tear people apart."

"Use our powers for good." I'd said it once before to Edward when he'd wanted me to go after everyone who'd hurt me in the past. I'd hated the idea then, but now, framed like this, I could envision it as something different. Something beautiful and kind and right.

"Use our powers for good," Hudson agreed. "I like that."

Yeah. I really liked it too.

Suddenly I knew exactly what to say to Edward and what needed to be done in order to heal the rift between us.

Now he just needed to come home.

FIFTEEN

EDWARD

THE INCOMING NOTIFICATION sounded on my mobile, a different tone than a normal call indicating it was FaceTime. Only one person communicated with me through this app, and only for one reason.

I glanced at the time then lowered my cigarette out of screen's view before I answered. Freddie's face filled the screen. "It's nearly eleven there. Isn't it past your bedtime?"

My sister leaned into the screen. "He had a nightmare about you. Couldn't go to sleep until he made sure you were alive and well."

"There was a monster with fire coming out of its mouth and a big swamp thing, too," my nephew said excitedly. "And both of them were trying to eat you and I couldn't see your eyes and I thought you were gone forever!"

Freddie's dream felt eerily like a metaphor for my current life.

"No monsters here," I said, twisting my phone so he could see the expanse of the hotel room balcony. "No swamp things either. And if you can see, I still have my eyes."

He laughed as I brought the phone up close to one eye then the other.

"See?" Camilla said from the sideline. "Uncle's fine. You're probably just having dreams because you miss him."

"Will you come home soon?" he asked me.

He wasn't the only one wanting an answer to that question. Though the texts from Celia the day before had referred to our shared hotel suite as home and not London as Freddie meant.

I didn't have an answer for either of them, unfortunately.

"You'll be the first one I tell as soon as I know," I promised.

"I hope it's soon," the six-year-old said with a yawn.

Camilla kissed Freddie on the forehead. "Think you can sleep now?"

"I'll try."

Camilla took the mobile. "Hold on for a second while I tuck him in?"

"Sure." It wasn't like I was doing anything other than brooding.

The screen went dark as she held her mobile against her body, the sounds of good night and the shifting of bed blankets coming through muffled. I took the opportunity to flick the growing ash of my cigarette into the glass I'd brought out with me to use as a makeshift ashtray, then brought it up to my lips for a drag.

Just in time for Camilla to return to the screen. "Please tell me that's a joint and not a cigarette."

I blew out a stream of smoke. "I could tell you that, but I'd be lying."

"What the hell, Eddie?" The image bobbed as she walked down the hall to another part of her house. "You haven't smoked in years. Have you taken it up again?"

Her concern was both annoying and oddly comforting. "It's the first one of the pack so I can't say that I've taken it up again. I suppose that's something I won't really know until I do or don't buy a second pack."

She frowned, a frown that grew deeper when I took another drag. "I kept you on because I wanted to ask how Celia was doing after Ron's sentencing, but now I wonder if I should be asking after you instead."

I ignored the inquiry about me, which was an answer in itself. "I couldn't tell you how Celia is doing. I haven't seen her in two days."

The bouncing image subsided as Camilla settled into her bed. "Ah. Must be quite a row if you're both avoiding her *and* smoking."

"I'm not avoiding her, exactly." I took another puff then crushed the butt into the glass. "I'm relieving her of having to spend time with my temper. It's a courtesy, really."

"Yes, that is a courtesy. The Edward Fasbender Temper is quite terrifying, speaking from experience. Congratulations on having the sense of mind to stay away."

I let out a humorless chuckle. "It would be funny if it weren't so true."

"Perhaps."

A beat passed, and I thought seriously about lighting another cigarette.

"You know, Eddie, speaking again from experience, when you sent me away to school, I would rather have had your rage than your distance. Your anger blazes like an inferno, but your silence is colder than any winter I've known. Personally, I'd rather be warm."

"Thank you for that, Camilla. I didn't feel bad enough already." I pulled another cigarette from the pack.

"It wasn't said to make you feel bad. It was said to give you some perspective."

I tapped the unlit fag on my knee. "Should we talk about you now? I think that will be a lot more productive."

She sighed. Then she launched eagerly into telling me about the new man that she was seeing, and I lit the cigarette and listened and was happy for her, but also I thought about what she'd said, really thought about it, and by the time we hung up, I'd decided.

It was time to go home.

I FOUND Celia bent over the desk in the living room, scrawling something onto a piece of hotel stationery. She must not have heard me come in because when she looked up, she startled.

The flash of surprise on her face quickly vanished, though, and was replaced with a genuine smile. "You're here."

"I'm here."

"Thank God." She ran to me, throwing her arms around my neck.

Without hesitation, I hugged her tightly, burying my head in her hair. There were so many ways she could have greeted me—with accusations or resentment or the silent treatment—and she'd chosen joy. I couldn't have felt more cherished. I couldn't have been more relieved.

We held each other like that, neither of us willing to let go. I could have done without words for longer, content to be wrapped in Celia's warmth, except that there was something missing. Some*one* missing. "Is Cleo sleeping?"

I felt her head shake against my shoulder. She leaned back so she could look up at me. "She's with Genevieve and Chandler. They picked her up a few minutes ago. I'm surprised you didn't see them in the hall."

"I didn't. Are they sitting for us?"

"I asked them to take her for the night." Celia's expression grew serious. "So I could go look for you. I was just writing you a note."

The mention of my disappearance brought our argument back into view. We couldn't ignore the elephant. Might as well address it straight on.

I pulled away, slowly. Reluctantly. "Probably wouldn't have found me. I booked another room."

"You've been in the hotel all this time?" She tried to sound like it was funny but failed.

"Most of it." I took her hand in mine, running my thumb across the knuckle above her wedding ring. I'd never get tired of seeing it on her finger. "Can we talk?"

"I'd like that." She let me lead her to the sofa and set her down. As soon as I sat next to her, she turned her body toward mine. "I'm sure you have plenty to say, and I want to hear all of it, but I have something I need to say to you first."

Before I could respond, she'd moved to kneel on the floor at my feet.

My suit suddenly felt too warm. "Well, this is an interesting way to open up a dialogue."

"Does it get your attention?" She waggled her eyebrows as she nudged my knees apart so she could crawl between my legs.

"You definitely have my attention, though you had it when you were sitting at my side as well."

"Good." She flattened her hands and ran them up my thighs.

Naturally, my cock reacted. God, I loved her on her knees. I especially loved her on her knees for me.

The timing, however, was not necessarily appropriate. "Conversation is becoming less and less appealing, bird. I'm not complaining, but I think you'll agree that there is a lot that should be said between us, and my rehearsed script is suddenly leaving my mind."

"Then you can just listen because this has to be said before anything else." With her hands still on my thighs, she sat back on her haunches and peered up at me. "I choose you, Edward."

I didn't think I could breathe. I didn't dare.

Celia's hands slid so they were closer to my knees. "Above everything, Edward, I choose you and Cleo and what the three of us have together. There isn't anything else that matters. I trust you to love us and care for us. I trust you to keep us safe and protected. And I trust you to consult with and treat me as a partner on the matters that affect us all.

"I've said most of this before, I know, and I meant it when I did. But I realize now that it wasn't fair to say that and then keep parts of me from you. I've been entirely focused on what I needed—a say in the big decisions. But why should you give me what I need when I haven't given you what you need? So here I am giving you what you need— trust and honesty. Take it from me. It's yours. No strings. I know you'll give me everything I need in return."

Something dislodged in my chest, a loosening of something I didn't realize had been tight. Had I never believed that before? That she'd chosen me?

I *hadn't* believed it.

I'd chosen *her*. I'd gone after her for my own reasons, and when I fell in love with her, it was me who decided I'd keep her. She was with me because I'd made her mine, the same way that Marion had been with me because I'd made her mine. And when I'd lost Marion it had been because I'd lost interest in keeping her. There had never been any need for or benefit to being chosen. I'd believed with all my heart it hadn't mattered.

Yet, hearing Celia declare it now, I realized how very wrong I'd been. Being chosen made all the difference. It mattered more than her love. More than her submission. It was the greatest gift anyone had ever given me, and while I'd never worried about my merit, I suddenly felt very unworthy.

I cradled her face in my hand. She leaned into my touch, her gaze still on mine, her blue eyes intense as she waited for me to speak.

But what could I say after that? Everything in my head felt small and banal. And what was in my heart couldn't be expressed. There was no sequence of words that could relay the mass of emotions within me. I felt unleashed. Reborn. Aroused.

I moved my hand from her cheek to the back of her neck where her blonde locks were gathered in a low bun. Gripping my fingers through the hair underneath, I tilted her head toward mine as I leaned in. "I hope you understand that I'm going to have to fuck you now."

"Do what you want with me," she said just before my mouth crashed with hers. "I'm yours."

My teeth nipped on her upper lip, and she opened up to me, her mouth taking my tongue as it licked and stroked and tasted and devoured. Kissing her felt as intimate as fucking, and I kissed her for long, heavy minutes before the throbbing of my cock forced my attention elsewhere.

"Take me out," I said when I broke away. I bit the shell of her ear before leaning back to give her room. "Hurry up about it. My cock is lead."

I shimmied out of my jacket while she made quick work of my belt. Next it was the button, then the zipper. I was so hard that my crown popped over the band of my boxer briefs, red and leaking. I lifted my hips so she could pull my clothing down, but as soon as my erection sprung free, I sat back down.

My hand returned to grip her neck, messing up what was left of her bun. "Do you choose me even like this?" I asked, pulling her face toward my aching cock.

She couldn't answer since, the moment she opened her mouth, I thrust inside.

I plunged inside, over and over, deeper, until my head tickled the back of her throat and made her gag. When I pulled out, it was only meant to give her some air but she took the brief reprieve to cry out, "God, yes."

I'd made her choose like this before, but then I was asking her to choose the things I liked doing to her. It was so much different hearing her choose the man who did them.

I pushed her head back over my cock and held her down, her nose pressed up against my skin so tight there was no way she could breathe. "Do you choose me, angry and possessive and mean? Do you still choose me?"

This time when I let her up, she was gasping, tears running from the corners of her eyes. "Yes," she said, her voice raw. "I still choose you."

Her mouth was suddenly not enough.

I stood, pulling her up roughly with me. After a vicious kiss, I tore open her blouse, sending buttons flying through the air. Then I took advantage of her nursing bra, pulling down one of the cups so I could fondle her breast with my bare hand.

She whimpered when I squeezed her nipple, which only caused me to tighten my pinch. "And now? When I hurt you and make you cry, do you still choose me?"

"Always. I choose you always."

My need was a living beast. With a roar, I swept the accessory tray off the ottoman and shoved her down in its place. I wasn't gentle as I peeled down her knickers and trousers, grateful they were wide-leg so I didn't have to remove her shoes to get them off of her. Just as roughly, I hitched one of her legs over my shoulder and stretched out over her, pushing her thigh flat against her chest so she was open wide.

I grunted as I shoved inside her. "You choose me, good or bad, whatever I've done, whomever I've hurt. Whatever my sins, you choose me."

"Yes, yes, yes," she panted in rhythm to my thrusts.

Whether she was agreeing with me or begging for more, I didn't know, but I chose to believe it was the former while also giving her the latter. I continued my assault with one driving effort—in, in, in, in, knocking against her clit with each thrust. In, in, in. As far inside her as I could go. As far inside her as I could be. Until we were no longer she and I, each with our own history and baggage, but one entity, our pasts both part of the same story, one with a complicated but very happy ending.

She climaxed first, her cunt clenching tight like it didn't bear to let me go. I pressed through her snug opening, meaning to just stay inside her while she came. But she felt too good, and she was too beautiful beneath me, all wrung out and tortured, and I came too, the pleasure starting at the base of my spine and igniting every neural pathway as fast as a lightning strike.

I hovered over her, spent and unmoored. It felt like I'd released much more than my cum inside her. Like I'd been relieved of the weight of something much heavier and burdensome.

Fuck. She wasn't supposed to be like this.

But she was, and I loved her, and I would do everything in my power to keep her mine. Even if it meant setting down my ego and trying something new. Like partnership. Without resentment. Without any barriers between us.

I pushed off her, tucked myself away, then dropped onto the couch behind me and watched Celia's chest rise and fall as her breaths slowed and she pulled herself together. When she was steady, she propped herself up on her elbows and looked at me.

She was a mess—her hair all over the place, her mascara smudged, her lipstick smeared. She was gorgeous.

"It wasn't fair to expect your trust when I have betrayed it on more than one occasion." I was the one wearing the most clothing, but I felt strangely the more naked of us both.

She nodded once, taking it in. Accepting.

Then she peeled herself off the ottoman and climbed on top of me, straddling my lap. "So now we try to do better," she said. Plain and simple. So easy it would be impossible to screw up.

I grabbed her face with both hands and pressed my mouth to hers. It wasn't as erotic as our earlier kisses had been, but it was somehow just as intense.

The sun was streaking its last rays across the sky when our lips finally parted. "You taste tobacco-y," she said. "Have you been puffing cigars?"

"I took up smoking, actually. Don't worry, I've already quit." I'd tossed the pack as soon as I'd hung up with Camilla.

"Damn right you've already quit."

I smiled at her reprimand. "Oh, but I do happen to have two cigars in the inside pocket of my jacket for later. I bought some high-quality Cubans today thinking we might celebrate Ron's sentencing. I should have been here when you got the news. Are you happy?"

"Happy is a strange word for it." She shifted from my lap to sit beside me, leaning back into my arms when I angled toward her. "I'm glad, yes, but I don't know that his sentencing changes where I am with what he did to me. I'm only better because of you."

"I'm not taking all of that credit. It was you, too." I stroked my hand up and down her bare arm, enjoying the weight of her at my side so much that I hesitated before bringing up the delicate subject. "How did today go? With the journals."

She tensed, sitting up more. "It went okay. It was probably best you weren't around, even though I could have used your support."

"I'm here now."

"You are, and I have to ask...You knew I would eventually."

"What am I going to do about Pierce?" I was sure that was the question without confirming, but I needed her to know I was on the same page.

Being on the same page didn't make the question any easier to answer. I felt oddly less concerned with Hudson Pierce than I had in days, but he was still there at the back of my mind, waiting to be dealt with.

Right now, though, I was still more concerned about Celia's part in the equation. "Well," I removed my arm from around her. "Since we're trying to be better about discussing these things, what are you afraid that I'll do?"

I studied her profile as she took a deep breath in, then let it out. She kept her eyes straight ahead, not looking at me as she spoke. "You could try to ruin his business, which scares me because of what he might do to you in return. Or you could try to go after his family, and that scares me for the same reasons. But also it scares me because I don't want you to be the type of man who would do that. I'm afraid you already have done that."

I reached out and turned her face toward me so she could see my eyes. "I'm not the person who's terrorizing the Pierces. I promise on Cleo's life."

"I'm sorry," she said.

"Don't." I shook my head, not wanting her to feel guilty no matter how much the accusation stung. "I hate that you had to ask. But I also understand why you did."

"That makes me feel a lot better."

"Good." I swept my thumb across her bottom lip before I let her face go. "Do you believe me?"

"I do." And I believed her. She kept her gaze on mine. "I'm also scared of what you might do to Hudson personally."

"You mean you're worried I might hurt him physically."

Her nod was barely perceptible. "You told me you had those men beat up, the ones who scammed Hagan when he was a teenager."

"I did do that. That was a unique situation." Violence was generally not my preferred method. It was too easy. Over too quickly. It didn't hurt the way real ruin did.

"Okay," she said, and I could feel her gathering courage, could see the steely resolve in her eyes when she finally had as much as she needed. "But you killed Camilla's husband. Didn't you?"

We were in this now, both of us, honest and open and trusting, no more secrets, no more lies.

So I answered with the truth. "Yes. I did."

SIXTEEN

CELIA

I TRIED to swallow and couldn't.

I tried again as I wiped my clammy hands on my open shirt. "Okay," I finally managed to say.

And then nothing because what was there to say after that? I was still grappling with what to *feel*. On the one hand, Edward had shared something with me that I thought he never would share. On the other hand, what he'd shared wasn't something I necessarily wanted to know.

But I wanted to know all of Edward, didn't I?

Then why did I have the sudden urge to run? It warred with my instinct to stay.

"Hey," he said, taking my hand in his. I watched as he ran his thumb over my knuckles, his touch both warm and heavy despite the light strokes. If he knew the battle going on in my head, he didn't address it. "If I'm going to tell you this—and I am—we're going to need a drink."

"Like a session, but for you? That's serious." As if the fact he'd murdered his brother-in-law wasn't serious enough.

"More like it's a story that's hard to tell and alcohol makes things easier."

"Exactly. A session."

He stood, and somehow I stood with him. My legs still worked even though they felt numb. I was able to walk, one step in front of the other, like I always did, but I didn't follow him to the minibar. Instead I went to the bathroom to get cleaned up. I washed quickly at the sink then threw the tattered blouse in the trash, took off my bra, and put on a robe. Routine, normal things. Everything was good. Everything was fine.

In the bedroom, I paused to catch my breath.

My husband was about to tell me how he killed a man. A terrible man, perhaps, but did that justify murder?

This wasn't exactly new information. I'd guessed that Edward had a hand in Frank's death before now, but not knowing the details, I'd been able to push it away and ignore it. Once he told me this story, I wouldn't be able to pretend anymore. I'd have to decide if it mattered. I'd chosen Edward, but I'd have to choose again. Could I stand behind a cold-blooded killer?

I shouldn't have brought it up.

"Am I pouring you a glass?" Edward called from the other room.

Too late for regrets. For better or worse, I needed to know. Edward needed to tell me. And I needed to be there for him as he did, the same way he'd been by me when I'd confessed my worst sins.

Besides, against all reason, I wasn't really all that worried about it. Whatever he said, it wasn't going to change who he was, and I already knew who that was. I already loved him.

Nevertheless, wine would help.

"Sure," I said, meeting him in the dining room. "I have to pump later anyway since Cleo isn't here. I'll just throw it out instead of storing it."

He handed me a glass filled with some dark red with a bitter bouquet. *Fitting.* "The cabernet franc," I said, after I tasted it. "You'd bought that for a special occasion."

"Special doesn't always mean celebratory." He took a sip from his own glass, his mouth puckering as the flavor hit his tongue. "I think this will do just fine. Shall we?"

I walked with him back to the living room and took a place on the couch, curling my feet up under me. Edward looked from the chair to the bench. It was our pattern to sit apart during sessions, and I was sure he was deciding which he would find most comfortable.

"If this is your session, that means I'm in charge, right?"

He laughed. "Whatever you say."

I glowered momentarily then relaxed into a smile. Edward's way through these was to be stoic and controlled, which I appreciated, because I needed that from him. But he didn't need rigidity and distance from me. He needed warmth.

"Then, since I'm in charge, I say we change things up." I patted a spot on the sofa next to me. "Come sit by me."

His lips twitched with what might have been disapproval, but after a slight pause, he strolled over. "You know why I required the space between us in your sessions?"

I peered up at him standing above me. "Because you're cruel and cold and you like to be able to watch while I squirm?"

He scowled at my response. "Because I thought it would help me not accidentally fuck you."

Huh. It was odd how an unknown detail like that from our past could make me swoony, even under the circumstances. "Funny then how all of your responses involved fucking me on purpose."

"Funny indeed."

I grinned. "Well, I can't guarantee you won't accidentally fuck me if you sit by me. But since you've already just had your way with me, you might be safe for a bit."

"I suppose I'll have to take my chances." He sat down, not close enough so that we touched, but close enough to be cozy. "Whenever I'm ready?" he said, making fun of himself since those were the words he always said to start my sessions.

It struck me as surreal—the wine, the intimacy, the lighthearted vibe between us. It felt as though he were preparing to tell a story about "that one time" he went fishing or some other jovial reminiscence. Did that make him a worse person? To not only be capable of murder but to also behave like it was no big deal?

Or was the carefree act for me? His way of making his tale easier to hear.

Both thoughts sobered me. I took a long sip of my wine.

Then, I buckled in for the ride. "Yes. Whenever you're ready."

"Very well." He cleared his throat and began. "I've told you before that Frank Dougherty wasn't a good guy. I should have known it from the start because Camilla only ever found herself with the worst of men —a pattern, I'm told, that stems from the abuse at the hands of her foster father. But Frank wasn't like the others. He was from a good family, and though he was privileged and reckless as many trust-fund heirs are, he was the first man to make my sister happy.

"Or, he did in the beginning, anyway. By the time he stopped making her happy, she was too involved with him to let on. And when they married, which was a little after a year of dating, they moved to Berkshire where Frank's family house was located, and though I bought a country house near Bray to be near her, I didn't see her as often as I would have liked. I was busy with work and kids and. Well. I was preoccupied.

"So I'm not sure exactly when it was that he started hitting her. Let alone when hitting turned to full-on beatings." He paused to drink some of his wine, medication to follow the wounding words. "She had bruises when I'd see her, but I didn't come to the country enough to notice the frequency, and she always had an excuse. Fell while hiking. Tripped over the dog. Everyday injuries. Red flags, but she never made a big deal and so I didn't either. I believed the perfect marriage image was real. He worshipped her in my presence, and at a time when I was very uninterested in my own marriage, I envied what they had."

He finished off the rest of his glass in several gulps, and I was grateful for the break, brief as it was. It gave me a moment to absorb what he'd said. Gave me a moment to feel for the sister-in-law that I'd begun to feel close to during the effort to snare Ron. I'd known she'd suffered abuse in the past. Beyond what Edward had told me, it was evident in her carriage, in the way she dressed, in the reclusive manner in which she lived.

Hearing her abuse confirmed, though, made it real, as real as the ending we were heading toward. The words that my husband had used to explain that reality took up the space of a minute when the acts they conveyed had taken far more of Camilla's life.

I hurt for that life she'd led. The ache burrowed in between my ribs, a twisting constant sort of pain. I imagined those years she'd spent in secret, enduring abuse she most likely thought she deserved, walking on eggshells all the time in order to not incur more. Ron had hurt me too, similarly and not at all the same, and there was an intense part of me that felt her pain like it was a memory, yet I was sure I understood only a fraction of what she'd gone through.

More important at the moment was Edward's pain. His love for his sister was very fatherly. It was evident he felt responsible for what she'd gone through, so much so that years later the telling of her story still required a good amount of alcoholic lubrication.

When he set his glass down on the nearby stand, I passed him the rest of my wine. He smiled appreciatively. "Needless to say—" he swirled the liquid, watching it coat the sides of the glass "—I had no idea what was wrong when she called one day at the office and begged me to come to Berkshire to get her. Said she needed to leave and that she'd explain when I got there. Very vague. I tried to get more information from her on the phone, but she insisted it wait and that it was urgent. Camilla wasn't one to cry wolf. I dropped everything and went."

I smiled. "Of course you did."

He shrugged like it was no big deal, but it was. He wasn't a knight in shining armor, perhaps, but he was a hero all the same, and I loved him for that, even when his methods of protection were on the dark side.

My smile faded as I remembered we were headed to a grim ending. "Then what?"

"Not knowing what I was walking into, I drove myself instead of taking a driver. It was late afternoon when I got to her house. She was waiting at the gates with an overnight bag, wouldn't even let me pull into the driveway. She got in, urged me to drive, and refused to say anything more until we were somewhere 'safe.' I didn't know what safe meant, of course. I should have taken her to London, and I would have if I'd understood, but I didn't. So I took her to Brayhill, which was nearby, and flat out told her I'd take her nowhere else until she explained."

He took a sip of my wine then set the unfinished glass down beside him. Sitting forward, he rested his elbows on his thighs and clasped his hands together in front of his face. "I didn't believe her at first. Which I regret very much. But she'd put on that show for so long. They'd been married for ten years, and I'd never had any clue. I'd even forgotten about the times I'd seen bruises until I really thought about it later on. In the end, she had to peel off her shirt and show me the scars. Camilla's always stayed covered up. She's self-conscious about the marks her foster father left, and I'd known about those, of course, as well as other scars, but I hadn't seen so much of her skin in nearly a decade."

His torso expanded as he took a long breath in. "It's not my place or my story to comment much on what I saw," he said, breathing out. "Let's just say it convinced me."

I ran my hand up and down his back, not sure if it was meant to comfort him or me. He accepted it for longer than I thought he would. Then, when he glanced over his shoulder at me, I pulled my hand back into my lap.

"What happened that finally pushed her to call you? Something worse than usual?" It probably wasn't relevant, but the question came out anyway. A sick sort of curiosity, and I braced myself for details of an altercation that had to be horrendous. Being beaten at all was appalling. Yet my mind ran away with all the possibilities that would make it worse—did he burn her like her foster father had? Cut her? Break her bones?

In the profiled position, I could easily see Edward's jaw tense, mirroring the dread that I imagined. "She'd tried to leave him before, apparently. Without success. He always tracked her down, made her feel like it was impossible to get away. She'd been too embarrassed to involve me, she said. Can you believe that? Embarrassed."

Yes, I could believe that. I'd felt the same about Ron.

"As for the fight that day, she didn't say much about the details except that it had been a typical row. Apparently his violent streaks came in cycles, and there'd been a fairly good reprieve before that morning. The reprieves always ended eventually, according to what she told me, and she'd been half prepared for it this time, but was hoping beyond hope that he'd meant it this time when he'd said he'd changed. She thought if there was any chance that he would, this would be it."

Putting together what I already knew about Camilla at the time of her husband's death, I realized why she'd put so much stock in him. She'd been six months pregnant. "She wanted to protect Freddie."

"She did." Retrieving the glass of wine, he stood and paced over to the window. "Freddie was the only reason she called me," he said, looking out into the night. "She didn't care enough about herself on her own, but for him..."

He washed the thought away with a swallow of wine, then turned back to me. "To be fair, Frank had really made it difficult for her to see any other path. He'd ostracized her from her friends. He'd taken complete control of her life—her accounts, her daily schedule. She couldn't even get access to her car without going to him, which was why she'd needed me that day. She had no money, no vehicle. She'd only been able to phone because he'd been in the shower. She managed to call me and take her bag down to hide by the side of the road during that time. Then she spent the next hour placating his every whim and praying he wouldn't check her call log, which he often did. She got away to meet me by telling him she was going for the mail."

It sounded similar to every account of domestic abuse I'd ever heard, which made it no less horrifying. I pulled my feet up to the sofa and hugged my knees to my chest, needing the support to hear more.

Edward's support was the wine. He finished it off and set it down on the side table. "Obviously, once I was convinced, I was ready to tear the man apart with my bare hands. I fantasized doing so for much of the evening, in fact. Planning all the ways I'd destroy him when we should have been headed back to London. They were brutal, believe me. Ways in which he truly suffered. Who knows what I would have done. I would have started legally, though. I called my lawyer that night to request a meeting the next day when we got into town. I believed we had time, see. I didn't think that he would come after her so quickly or know to come looking for her at Brayhill. Stupid, right? Where else would she go? I suspect things would have gone quite differently if I hadn't thought I was so invincible."

He sank down in the armchair. "I never did figure out how he got past security. She'd left her mobile behind. My best guess is that he found where she kept the system code saved in her contacts, but he may also have lured her to let him in some other way. I'd given her my laptop when she'd gone to bed. He might have emailed her there or messaged her through a social app. I didn't want her to ever think I blamed her, so I never asked. All I knew was that, in the middle of the night, I was woken with shouting from the guest wing. I didn't even think about it—I grabbed my gun."

My skin prickled with foreboding, but I tried to remain expression-less as he went on, the way he always was when he listened in my sessions. It was harder than I'd imagined.

Whatever my face said, he went on. "Camilla and I were the only ones in the house. I was ninety-nine percent sure that Frank was our intruder, but I had no plan. I just went to the safe, took it out, loaded it with a full cartridge, and went to her room. The door was open when I got there, and I must have arrived just after it happened because they were both by the fireplace, Camilla standing with the poker in her hand, Frank swaggering as blood gushed from a wound at his head. Whatever threat he'd been, he was outnumbered now. We could have dialed 999, had him arrested and taken to hospital. He may have survived. Though she'd hit him pretty hard. There was a good chance the injury was fatal on its own. Either way, I didn't let us find out. As soon as I registered what I was seeing, I aimed my gun and shot. Three times, to be sure."

There it was. The terrible truth, not quite as terrible as I'd imag-ined, gruesome as it was. No premeditation. Self-defense, most likely, according to the law. Potentially hard to prove, but with Edward being who he was...

Except.

"Frank died in a fire," I said, remembering the accounts I'd read. The entire estate had burned down.

Though, of course that had been a cover, I realized now. As likely as it was that he could have walked away unscathed, there was also the chance that he wouldn't. It was only Camilla's word that her husband was a danger. If Frank had entered without breaking in, it made it harder to claim self-defense. It might have been different if it were only himself, but since Camilla had hit Frank first with the poker, Edward would never have risked going to the authorities. His only choice was to cover up what happened, which had to have involved a whole new level of risk.

Confirming my thoughts, Edward leveled his gaze on me. "Do not underestimate the power of a rich white man, Celia. It was nothing to get his body taken back to the Dougherty home, to have the estate burned to ashes, to have the fire service call it an accident, to have the coroner cite asphyxiation as the cause of death."

It was Ron's similar position that had kept him from being arrested for years. It was how so many men got away with evil deeds.

I rubbed my palm across my forehead. "That's terrifying," I said without thinking.

"Which part?" Edward asked sharply. "Because all of it terrified me. I'd killed a man in cold blood. I covered it up without any inquiries from authorities. I got away with it scot-free. It disturbed me so much that, needing comfort, I ended up calling the one person I knew that wouldn't care what I'd done."

"Marion." She'd referenced the last time they'd been together when she'd seen him that day in the office. This had to be the time she'd been talking about.

"She came straight away," he said, though I hadn't needed the confirmation to know I was right. "She let me take out my horror on her. When she left, she was as black and blue as Camilla ever was, I guarantee it."

Edward was a sadist, but he tended to prefer psychological pain to physical. For him to lean on the latter said what sort of place his head had been in.

I rubbed both hands over my face. There was a lot to process. It was outright murder. No denying that. But if he'd lived, it was unlikely he would have gone to jail for any real time. Frank had money on his side too, and rich men rarely got punished for their sins. He might always have been after Camilla. They'd definitely have always been connected through their child. What worse things could Frank have done to Camilla and Freddie if Edward hadn't done what he had?

It was complicated, and I would probably need to take some time before I completely understood what I thought about it.

None of that mattered right now. Strangely, my concerns at the moment were less about what Edward had done in the past and more about how he viewed himself now because of them. From his bitter tone, it was evident he was carrying a shit load of blame for things that, in my humble opinion, he didn't deserve to be blamed for.

Especially when the only one blaming him was himself.

I dropped my hands from my face, set my feet on the floor, and leaned toward him. "Okay, hold up. This is a terrible story—I'm not going to deny that at all—but there are a number of things you've said that seem to lack perspective."

"Oh, really," he said patronizingly.

"Yes, really. Number one—" I held up my index finger "—the things you did to Marion within a consensual sexual relationship are nothing at all like what Frank did to Camilla. You know that. My God, out of everyone in the world *you* know that. You were the one who forced me to see that the relationship I had with Ron was different from the relationship I had with you. You not seeing it now is shortsighted and, frankly, it's martyrdom. You are neither short-sighted nor a martyr, so what the fuck?"

His frown eased ever so slightly. "I didn't feel good about it, regardless."

"Of course you didn't. You were dealing with other shit, and you weren't behaving like yourself, but was Marion upset?"

He paused before he shook his head. "She was not. In fact, she was rather into all of it."

I held my hand up in the air to stop him. "More than I need to know, thank you, and let's just be clear that I'm not ever going to be into the pain stuff no matter what shit you're dealing with."

"Duly noted." This time his frown was almost a smile.

Feeling bolder, I moved to the ottoman in front of him and put up two fingers. "Number two, it was not your fault that you didn't take Camilla to London. It was not your fault that you didn't know what Frank was doing to Camilla all those years. Is it my mother's fault that she didn't know what Ron was doing to me?"

"Yes, actually, I think it really is."

I shook my head. "You're wrong, but bad example. The point is, you couldn't have known because she didn't want you to know. And I think, deep down, you know that. You know it, and you hate it, because it means you don't have control. It's probably one of the reasons you push so hard to maintain truth in your relationships now, because you don't ever want to be blindsided like that again. I understand, and I'm going to try to be better about meeting that need with you, but you also need to let yourself off that hook. It was not your fault."

His expression had grown unreadable, and I had no way to know if I was reaching him, but I sure liked what I was saying. It was making sense as I spoke it, and I was seeing him clearer than I ever had.

He must not have thought I was too far off base, because he was still sitting there, and he still appeared to be listening and he hadn't tried to win the conversation for himself, which was surprising. And validating. I knew what I was talking about, and he couldn't deny it.

Now for the most complicated part. "Number three." I put up three fingers then waited a beat to be sure I had his full attention. "You shot Frank to protect your sister and her unborn child. It was clearly self-defense. Was it lawful? No. Was it ethical? I think philosophers might argue about that one. Whatever. You may not have even been the reason he died."

He interrupted me. "Oh, no. I killed Frank Dougherty. It will never be thought for one moment that it was at Camilla's hands. I will not let that be on her shoulders."

And yet another reason why I loved him. Even at his darkest, he was always motivated by the ones he cared for.

"Okay. It was definitely you," I granted. "You killed a man. In cold blood. And you covered it up. I get it. It's not pretty. I'm not going to lie and say it is. It happened, you can't change it, and you probably should feel...I don't know, *something* about that for the rest of your life."

"I don't regret it, Celia. At all. And if I'd have been around when Ron..." He didn't have to finish that sentence. We both knew what Ron had done. "I wouldn't have waited for him to come into my house. I would have gone after him. I would have done worse."

"I know." I'd already had a feeling he'd only gone after my uncle legally because he'd wanted me on his side. "And maybe you would have done worse to Frank, too, if that night hadn't happened like it had. Maybe it would have made you hard and terrible. Maybe it would have turned you down a dark road that you could never come back from.

"But it did happen like it did. And you obviously do feel something about it. Whatever that feeling is, it's not a feeling that you like, and you can't let that go. So listen to me now—don't believe that this is your one and only defining act. It's not even in the top five. You are a man who took on the care of his sister as soon as he could when they'd both been orphaned. A man who gave his sister a job and a home again when she was pregnant and alone and needed it most. A man who rebuilt his father's business into something bigger than it had been before. A man who raised two children, a good portion of which he did alone, into two amazing, brilliant adults. A man who gave an entire family a job and a place to live on his paradise island. A man who spent more than a year of his life trying to put a predator behind bars.

"And you're a man who would kill for the ones he loves most. Not just a man who will say the words, but a man who will go the distance if need be. There's no one else I'd rather have my life in his care. There's no one else I'd rather have my heart."

I'd rushed through my declaration to be sure he wouldn't interrupt, and now my heart beat so fast it felt like I'd been running. I took a breath, waiting for him to speak.

In a flash, I was pushed on my back on the ottoman for a second time. Edward hovered over me, his mouth inches from mine. "How is it you see so much good in a man who is clearly a devil?"

"Oh, I see the devil, too," I assured him. "I like him just as much."

"Are you sure I haven't just groomed you to respond this way?"

"I might be who I am right now because of you, but it's exactly who I want to be."

He kissed me at that, a long, luxurious kind of kiss that ended with him sweeping me in his arms and carrying me to the bedroom where he peeled off my robe and kissed my entire body, taking his time to be sure there wasn't an inch of me that hadn't been covered with his lips.

Then, with his clothes deserted on the floor, he covered my naked body with his and made love to me with a sweet attentiveness that I'd never seen from him before. I loved this side of him, like I loved all his sides, like I loved the man who controlled and the man who would kill. I especially loved that, for the first time ever, I was pretty sure I was seeing all the sides of him there was. No holds barred. Bare and vulnerable and mine.

After, he held me tight around the waist as we lay facing each other, our eyes level. We didn't talk for a long time. We'd said so much already, and there was a lot that could be said like this—silent, our gazes locked as we stroked each other's skin.

But there was still something unresolved, and eventually he addressed it. "You have to let me do what I need to do with Pierce. It's my war now. I can't let it go unsettled."

My muscles tensed automatically. Then I took a breath in, and relaxed as I blew it out. This was what all of this had been coming to. If I'd thought it was going anywhere else, I was fooling myself. I'd told him I trusted him, and now I had to prove it.

"Okay," I said.

It was his chance, too, to prove what he would do when it wasn't a gun in his hand in the middle of the night. When the threat wasn't imminent. When there wasn't so much to lose. When it was only his pride versus his foe.

"Let me just ask you one thing," I added, careful not to undo all the progress we'd made. "With what happened with Frank, with what happened with Ron—which situation feels more resolved to you now that they're both said and done?"

He didn't get a chance to answer before the buzzer rang. It was late. I didn't know what time exactly, but it had to be late.

"I put the do not disturb up when I came in," Edward said, erasing any chance that it might be turndown service.

The buzzer rang again. I jumped out of bed and grabbed my robe, tying it as I rushed to the door in case it was Genevieve and the baby. The buzzer rang once again before I got there, followed by heavy pounding.

I didn't even bother looking through the peephole before opening the door, and was thoroughly surprised to see it wasn't my stepdaughter, but Hudson, alone, exasperation written all over his face.

Without an invitation, he pushed inside, clinging to me so desperately as he did, we almost both tipped over. "Find her," he begged, his voice threadbare. "Find my wife."

SEVENTEEN

EDWARD

CELIA GREETED me at the door as soon as I came up from work the next day. "They found Alayna," she said. "She's fine. A bit bruised up, but overall fine."

My wife was relieved, and so I was too. It had been Celia I'd been most concerned about when Hudson had shown up at our room the night before. His wife was missing. Presumably, she'd been taken by the person who'd been threatening them, and since all signs pointed to that person being someone from Hudson and Celia's past, I was rightfully worried that Celia was next.

Not one of us had gotten any sleep. While the two of them had stayed up scouring the journals for clues, I'd been on the phone arranging bodyguards and extra security for Celia as well as her parents, my children, and Camilla. When the sun came up, I showered and dressed and left for my makeshift office on the conference level of the hotel, but I cancelled all my appointments for the day and spent it instead investigating Pierce. He'd been looking for the perpetrator from the inside out. I thought there was benefit from changing the angle and searching from the outside in. Even after Celia called to tell me it looked like the abductor hadn't been someone they'd played at all, I kept on with my mission. Just in case.

"And the man who took her?" I barely dared to breathe.

"He's in jail. And anyway, he wouldn't have come after me, so don't be worrying about him making bail." It was like she could read my mind.

Still, I was wary. "You're absolutely sure? He acted alone? There's no one else in on the scheme?"

She wrapped her arms around my waist. "It was just him, and yes. I'm sure. Hudson and I never played him. His motives had nothing to do with me."

"Good." I kissed her before I released her. "I might just keep the bodyguards for a little while, though."

"If it makes you feel better, I understand. Besides, if you're going to tangle with Hudson, you'll need them."

"Celia," I warned. I knew what she was doing—trying to bait me into discussing my plans with Pierce.

She put her hands up in the air in surrender position. "I'm not interfering. Doesn't mean I can't still have opinions."

If I hadn't been so tired, I'd likely have spanked her ass red for her opinion. It would have been for fun, though. Not punishment.

"Are you hungry?" she asked, changing gears as she helped me out of my suit jacket. "There's a sandwich in the fridge, if you are. Otherwise, I'm ordering you to bed. I slept most of the day, so I can handle Cleo. You, on the other hand, haven't slept since yesterday, so don't try to tell me you aren't exhausted."

I peered at her over my shoulder. "Ordering me?"

She handed me my jacket with a sigh then dropped to her knees to bow dramatically at my feet. "Oh, master," she teased, "I know I am not worthy to command you. I beg of you to please have favor on me and allow me to care for you for once by feeding you and sending you to bed."

I laughed. "Get up, you temptress."

She took my hand as I bent to help her up. "Am I turning you on?"

"Always." I kissed her again, because she was there and because I wanted her. But she was right that I needed sleep, so I cut it off before it went anywhere interesting. "No food, thank you. And I'll sleep. Shortly." Now that I knew the Pierce threat wasn't a danger to my own family, there were other things that needed to be sorted out.

Cleo's cry came over the baby monitor, waking up from her late afternoon nap on schedule. "I'll feed her in her room so she won't be a distraction. Get to bed, soon."

She crossed toward the adjoining suite, and I headed to the desk.

"I mean it, Edward," she scolded.

"I will. I promise. Give me ten minutes." I smiled at her until she'd disappeared into the next room, the door shut behind her.

Then I hung my jacket on the back of the chair and sat down at the desk. I pulled the pad of hotel stationery from the top drawer, centered it in front of me, and stared at the blank page.

The day spent researching Hudson Pierce hadn't been a waste. I'd learned a lot about the man in relatively few hours, quite a bit I'd already known from previous investigations—I never did business with anyone without a thorough background check. Still, a good deal of what I'd discovered had been new, details that shed new light on the man I very much wanted to confront.

So much had changed in the past few days. New information had been revealed. My beliefs had been challenged. It was a different man who sat in my skin today than the one who'd worn it a week before. I wasn't even the same man as the one I'd been the night I'd learned Hudson's real role in my wife's life.

Change was inevitable. Of course it was. I expected it. I took pride in being someone who could pivot when needed, and I'd done it successfully in both my business life and personal life on many occasions. But through the years, as far back as I could remember, my core had been rooted in a well-proven tradition of eye for an eye, tooth for a tooth. Entire civilizations had thrived on that principal. It was simple. Justice in the most base form.

For me, it had been a compass as well as an anchor. Vengeance had dictated my direction and had held me together through the roughest of storms. Who would I have been without a place to put the mass of rage and spite and jealousy that lived inside of me? How could I have functioned? How could I have built my business or provided for my loved ones or even gotten out of bed day after day after day without the inspiration of a mission that I believed in?

But I'd heard Celia as she'd questioned me the night before. *With what happened with Frank, with what happened with Ron—which situation feels more resolved to you now that they're both said and done?*

All day it had been in the back of my mind, popping to the front whenever I let it. I wished it had been harder to answer. I wished it had been easier to dismiss with excuses. I wished it wasn't so obvious what I had to do next.

Wishing did nothing for progress. Only action mattered, and stalling wouldn't get me what I wanted or what my family needed.

Now was the time.

With my decision made, I reached into the inside pocket of my jacket hanging behind me and retrieved my pen, then scrawled out a note on the paper in front of me.

I'm grateful to hear your wife is back in your arms.
You and I have unfinished business.
Edward Fasbender

I tore the sheet from the pad, folded it in thirds, and tucked it in an envelope that I addressed with Hudson's name. In the morning, it would go out in the post and be received in the coming days. Then we'd officially be in the endgame. There would be a winner, and one or both of us could move on.

Now, though, with the course finally settled, I did as my wife commanded and went to bed.

A LITTLE MORE THAN a week later, I met with Hudson at an investor appreciation dinner that both Accelecom and Pierce Industries had been invited to. "Neutral territory," he'd said, which wasn't quite true since the whole of New York City seemed to belong to the man.

To be honest, whose territory was whose didn't concern me, as long as we had the opportunity to speak in private and at length. Hudson had assured me he could make that happen, even though the event had a forecasted attendance of two-hundred-fifty people.

It wasn't until we were at the top of the stairs to the roof and Hudson pulled out a personal set of keys that I understood how he could make the guarantee.

"You own the building," I said as we walked away from the door out onto the private terrace. "Seems like that should have been disclosed beforehand." I reached inside my tuxedo and pulled a lighter and the two cigars I'd bought the week before from my inside pocket. They'd been meant for me and Celia, but this felt more apropos.

Hudson took the cigar I offered and shrugged. "My building, your cigar. Seems an equal amount of trust is required from both of us."

"Are you so sure about that? Seems a lot easier to lace an item with poison than to push another man off a building."

He studied me, as though trying to discern how much of a threat I posed. While I'd told him on more than one occasion that I wanted Werner Media, I'd given him no reason to believe I felt any real loathing toward him.

After a beat, he bit the cap off his cigar and spit it on the ground. "Lucky for both of us, neither of us stands to gain by the demise of the other."

"Perhaps not." I held my lighter out to him. "Though that theorizing underestimates the value of pure satisfaction."

He laughed. "Touché." He toasted the foot, then lit the filler, puffing a bit before drawing the cigar away to study the label. "Gurka? These are high quality. Nice flavor. What'd they run? Twelve k a box?"

"Fifteen."

"Impressive." He handed me back the lighter.

I prepared my own cigar, making sure I had a strong cherry before pocketing my lighter. We puffed in silence, both of us looking out over the New York City skyline, the summer night bright with artificial light. It was astonishing how calm I felt. In my head—as I'd planned this approach, what I'd say, what I'd do—I'd expected more adrenaline. Instead, there was a quiet peace, so foreign to my nature it would have alarmed me if I let it.

Instead, I embraced it. Held it like it was my wife. Let it be my foundation, a firmer bedrock than any I'd planted on before.

I wondered in those moments what Hudson must think about this meeting I'd called. He hadn't asked its purpose, clearly believing my goal was the shares, a natural assumption. Would he bring it up? Or would he wait for me? It was a fun little game trying to guess.

But I wasn't here for games. The time for those was long over, for both of us.

The past seemed to be on his mind as well, because, after a long brooding silence, it was he who brought it up. "Did you read them?"

I didn't have to ask to know he meant the journals. "I did. Cover to cover. Every one."

He tried to hide his wince, but I saw it. "I didn't want Alayna reading them. I've tried to keep her from that as much as I could."

"Oh, Celia would have liked to keep me from them as well, I'm sure." I drew again on my cigar, letting him make of that what he would.

He considered. "While I'd like to say that I respect my wife's privacy, I'm not so sure I wouldn't have done the same thing in your position."

I didn't know enough about Hudson Pierce to make any assumptions, so I asked outright. "And had you been in my position, if you'd read that log of cruel manipulation, what would have been your reaction?"

He answered quickly. "I would have run. As far as possible."

"But Alayna knows, however much you've tried to spare her, and she's still with you."

"Alayna's a better person than I am."

"Mm." I didn't doubt that. I did, however, doubt his perspective. "And if it had been Alayna who had done those things, you still would have run?"

"She wouldn't have. She isn't capable." But he'd paused, and while I imagined he was right about what his wife was or wasn't capable of, I also sensed that he'd realized there was nothing he wouldn't have forgiven her if she were.

The point was made, anyway.

And it created a convenient segue to my next point. "There was one victim those journals never detailed. A game played on a naive young girl who never considered her childhood friend would betray her."

He remained stoic, but the accusation hit its mark. "It's true that I hurt Celia first. I don't deny that."

"And do you regret it?"

"Some days more than others." To his credit, he looked guilty. "Less so when I remember what she's done to me. What she's done to Alayna."

The reminder of Celia's sins felt pale next to all that I knew were Hudson's. The all too familiar call to vengeance beckoned at my ear. "I know all too well how easy it is to hold a grudge."

"Calling it a grudge is simplifying the matter. She caused real harm to people I love."

"Just like you caused real harm to people that others loved." I matched his defensiveness with my own. "To someone that I love."

For a moment, he held his stance. Then his shoulders relaxed. "It's different when you're on the other side," he admitted.

"That it is." I held up my cigar, non-verbally questioning what he'd prefer I do with the growing ash.

He nodded to a gold cylinder bin that I only realized was an ashtray when I crossed to it and saw the basin of sand at the top. I set the cigar down to allow the excess ash to shed naturally and turned back to face the man I'd considered my rival. "I investigated you, you know. Looked into more than just your business background. Dug into the charities you support—autism, mental health, addiction treatment. Plus there are a great deal of college and business grants you fund, most started in recent years. A few of those recipients seem to have familiar profiles." Having read those journals gave me an advantage. No one else would have connected Hudson's benefactors to the wrongdoings of his past.

His face turned to stone, but the slightest shade of color topped his cheeks. "Celia isn't the only game I regret."

"Right. You've changed. From what I can see, it seems genuine. Though, one might argue that guilt doesn't make for noble motivation."

"I never claimed I was noble."

"I find that respectable. You don't flaunt your philanthropic acts. There's actually a lot about you that reminds me of myself. I go out of my way to contribute to causes that represent what I consider to be my greatest failings. I also believe firmly that karma doesn't happen on its own. It requires time and attention that must be carried out by those with the ability to dedicate themselves to the cause.

"You are exactly the kind of cause I find myself most drawn to." I let that sink in, let the threat penetrate, let him understand precisely what I was implying before I went on. "Even if I hadn't known Celia, I would have wanted to ruin you after reading those journals. You think I should have wanted to run? No, I wanted a reckoning. You were a powerful man who took advantage of people who were vulnerable. For your entertainment. You preyed on the weak. You deserve to pay retribution for every heart you broke, every marriage you destroyed, every dream you crushed, every soul you wrecked. You deserve to have everything taken from you."

He turned to face me head-on, but while his posture was offensive, his words were not. "I'm not going to defend myself. I can't."

I hadn't realized how much I'd hoped he'd try until that moment. If he had, I might not have been able to go through with this. My anger would have been too fueled to smother.

But his refusal to fight made it impossible to change my course. Which was for the best.

"You don't have to defend yourself," I told him. "You already have a defendant. Celia has done nothing but defend you since the first time you came up. She's protected your name. She's justified your actions. She's stood by you. She's pleaded your case. At first, I thought you had her brainwashed. I've since learned that she's a smart, sane woman who is more than capable of thinking for herself, and she does. All the time. Sometimes to my detriment, which I admire more than I care to admit. So then I thought she was in love with you."

He perked up at that insinuation.

"She's not," I said quickly, unwilling to let him consider the notion for any length of time. "She never really was, from what I gather. You made her think maybe she could be once upon a time, but I'm sure you know as well as anyone the quality of manipulated emotions."

"Unfortunately, I do."

"The reason she defended you, I finally realized, is because she genuinely believes you are a good person. That you've changed. And I think the only reason she's able to believe it as she does is because she's changed too. It takes one to know one, etcetera, etcetera."

"And what do you think?"

I appreciated the question and answered gladly. "I'm less prone to believe it. Because if it were true, you'd know it was possible she's changed too. You would recognize the signs. You wouldn't be campaigning so hard to keep the upper hand. You wouldn't be so afraid." I chuckled. "Ironic that she's the one you fear. It should be me. I should frighten the hell out of you."

This was the kind of threat I was used to delivering, and a part of me expected the usual fawning and backtracking from Hudson that I had heard from countless other foes.

But Celia had warned me about the man for a reason—he was legitimately formidable, with his own threatening countenance. A man who wouldn't back down.

"Do you want to know why I don't?" he asked, sure of himself as ever.

"Please. Tell me."

"Because you love her."

I did love her. I wouldn't deny it. Yet, it felt almost like he was reading *my* journal the way he announced it, as though this piece of knowledge gave him insight into all of me.

I picked up my cigar to distract from how vulnerable it made me feel.

But he'd spotted my weak spot, and he pressed on it further. "Speaking from one man who is very like another, you'd move heaven and earth for the woman you love. You'd protect and defend her, no doubt in my mind. But you'd also honor her. From what you've just told me, hurting me would mean disregarding her wishes."

He did understand me. Because he was the same kind of man. Younger and more vain, perhaps, but still a king who bowed only to the woman he adored.

"You're smarter than I gave you credit for. Celia said that about you, too." I puffed thoughtfully on my cigar. "You're right. She doesn't want me to go to war with you, and that should be reason enough not to. I'm sad to say that it wasn't enough. She begged and bartered, and..." I shook my head, thinking about how painfully stubborn I'd been. "Didn't matter. I didn't care. I was determined. Because I knew what was best for her. Better than she knew for herself."

He nodded his head, knowingly. Then his brow creased. "Are we at war, then?"

"No. We aren't." I had to take a breath after I said it. It was like laying a heavy weapon down, and the effort of carrying it lingered after it was on the ground. "The thing is, she finally got through to me, and when she did, it wasn't her conviction in your character that made me change my mind. It was just her. It was realizing that she's everything, and anything that isn't her isn't worth my time."

I'd been wrong. My love for Celia wasn't a vulnerability. It was my strength. It was my bastion. It was my greatest weapon.

"I don't care who you are," I said, emboldened by my epiphany, "or what you've done to repay your debts. I only care about her and our child and what she's done for me. She hasn't changed me, but she's accepted me for who I am, and with that acceptance, my focus has shifted. I no longer see you or the battle I meant to wage. All I see is her."

He let a smile slip, but quickly tucked it away. "So you didn't meet with me to discuss the shares?"

I shook my head. "I don't bloody care about the shares. Whoever owns them, I already have what I need. Celia does too."

He pressed me with a quizzical expression.

"Then why are we here, you're wondering." I sighed. "I probably didn't need to meet with you at all since you weren't aware of my vendetta. Honestly, I'm here for selfish reasons. Closure, somewhat. Mostly, I'm here for Celia. She doesn't need me to stick up for her or fight any of her wars, nor would she appreciate it if she knew that's why I was here. If she knew I was here at all, that is. Regardless, I didn't think it was right that you didn't know what she's done for you, and my place or not, I needed to make it known. If she's what one of your enemies looks like, I'd advise you to get more of them."

The man was unreadable, another admirable quality, but I sensed he'd heard me. He gave the impression that he heard everything, including much that wasn't actually said. Rolling his cigar between his fingers, he stared vaguely into the distance. "It's funny, after everything that's occurred between us, I still think of her first as friend rather than foe. And what she did to help find Alayna...I know she was reluctant to help at first, for whatever reason—"

"That was my fault," I interjected. "She would have been helpful from the beginning if it weren't for me, guaranteed."

He took a second to digest that. "I wouldn't have found my wife without Celia. I know that. I have nightmares every time I sleep about it, thinking what might have happened. Knowing how close I was to losing...everything." Emotion shuddered through him, but he recovered quickly. "Celia was there when I needed her most, and maybe that doesn't make up for everything in the past, but as you seemed to suggest, there's not much value in holding a grudge."

Reaching into his tuxedo jacket, he pulled out an envelope, bent from being stuffed inside his pocket, and handed it to me. "It's not what you're here for, but it's what I'm here for. Both my lawyer and financial advisor have already approved the language. Take all the time you need looking it over. Whenever, if ever, you're interested, call my office, and we'll schedule a time to make it final."

I tucked it in my own pocket without looking at it. I knew what it was, and though it was a nice gesture, it didn't matter. It didn't change anything.

It was, however, a good note to end on.

I set my cigar back in the sand so it would extinguish naturally, then I held my hand out. "I think we're done here."

He accepted my hand and gave it a firm shake. "I'd say we are."

A vivid memory flashed in my mind of that night with Frank, of the way the fire licked against the night sky, the smoke rising above the flames. I'd stood watching as long as I'd dared, hoping for the finality to sink in. It never did.

It was different walking away from Hudson. The world might have been ablaze behind me. I never looked back to see.

EIGHTEEN

CELIA

I WALKED into the Werner Media lobby and checked the time on my phone. Twelve after nine. I was cutting it close.

I hurried past reception, flashing my ID to the security guard who knew me by sight, and down the hall to the press room located at the heart of the first floor. It took twice as long to get there because of the clothes I was wearing. A tight pencil skirt and sky-high heels were not conducive to speed.

But hey, I looked good.

I always looked good when Edward dressed me, which had become routine again. Usually, though, since my days generally consisted of mothering, the outfits he chose were simple summer dresses or rompers with easy access to my breasts for feedings. When I'd seen today's selection laid out for me when I woke for Cleo's six o'clock feeding, I'd been surprised he'd chosen something so businesslike. Then I'd seen the note from Edward who'd come in after I was asleep the night before.

Nine-fifteen today. Werner Media press room.

It had struck me as odd right off the bat. I hadn't been to the building at all since my father retired. Even with the three-point alliance, Edward had little interaction with Werner Media.

Strange as the request was, I'd also been immediately excited. Which might have been unjustified considering how many times Edward had led me into uncomfortable situations without any warning. As distressing as those occasions were, though, they always paid off in the end. If that's what I was walking into, so be it.

Too bad I was walking into it late.

With the handicap of the outfit plus another check-in point outside the press room, I didn't walk in until almost nine-twenty. The room was packed, standing room only. Flash bulbs were going off, cameras pointed toward the front of the room. After weaseling my way to a place where I could actually see, I saw it was Nathan Murphy, the Werner Media CEO, behind the podium. And at his side, waiting to be introduced, was my father.

For whatever reason, seeing my father made my stomach knot. I'd heard him speak at hundreds of pressers and events over my lifetime. It was an ordinary part of his job. So mundane, I hadn't tuned in to one in years.

But he was retired now and had less reason to be representing Werner Media in a conference. His presence suggested an important announcement was to be made. And if Edward had wanted me here for it, I could only guess what it would be in reference to, especially considering what else was going on in the Werner world.

Sure enough, after a short speech from Nate that said pretty much nothing, my father approached the podium with a digital reader in his hand.

A *prepared* speech. This was real serious coming from a man who liked to wing it.

He had my full attention, along with forty other people crowded around me. We all watched, a strange silence blanketing the press room while he took his reading glasses out of his jacket pocket and adjusted the microphone.

"I appreciate you all coming out today. So many familiar faces." His eyes roved around the room, greeting old friends with a nod. He paused when he came to me, the jovial expression he'd had a moment before slipping away instantly.

Somberly, he turned his gaze back to his device. "'Recent events have brought focus to my brother, Ronald Werner,'" he said, and I forced myself to breathe, to not go numb, to stay in the moment. "'While he hasn't had a position at Werner Media nor vested interest in the company for years, we feel it is appropriate to make a statement regarding his criminal charges and the sentence of twenty-six years that was announced last week in the Crown Court of London. It is our understanding that he is in the process of appealing these charges.' That's right, right?" He looked to the men gathered behind him. "That's what we hear anyway," he said after the man that I recognized as his lawyer nodded in confirmation. "'Many of his friends and colleagues have already come forward to testify on his behalf and more will likely show up in the coming days. My wife and I as well, as representatives for Werner Media, have been urged time and again to make our own statement, which we have refused to issue until now.'"

It was hard to not check out. Hard to not pay attention to his words when I was certain I knew where they were going. *These charges are false and egregious. I'll stand behind my brother no matter what.* A whole bunch of horseshit I didn't want to hear. Why did Edward want me here for this? To show that my father was the bastard he'd always purported he was?

Yeah, like I needed proof.

Fuck that. I didn't need to be here for this.

I turned, intending to push my way out of the crowd as he went on. "'Today, I am standing here to formally say that neither I nor my family nor any part of Werner Media Corporation stand behind Ron in any way.'"

I froze, sure I'd heard wrong. But the murmur of reporters across the room suggested they'd been shocked by what they heard too. I wiggled back into my place, attentive now.

"'The acts that Ron has been accused of are abhorrent and inexcusable. He's been found guilty of these terrible acts in a court of law.

Anyone wishing to believe him innocent hasn't taken a look at the proof, which is irrefutable. There is no doubt in my mind that he has committed these heinous crimes and that he has been willfully abusing and assaulting children for decades.'"

He took a beat to remove his readers and look at his audience. "I wish I could have understood earlier," he said, with more heartfelt sincerity than I'd ever seen from him. His eyes found mine again. "With all my heart, I wish I could have understood his nature and the danger he posed to those around him so that I might have intervened. So that I might have confronted his predatory behavior and rescued countless little girls from harm. I wish I could have prevented him from ever laying a hand on..." For a moment, I thought he was going to say *you,* but he caught himself. "Laying a hand on a child. It is a regret I will take to my deathbed."

My eyes pricked, and even several blinks weren't enough to stop the tears from falling. How long had I waited for this? Not even for an apology, but just an acknowledgment that it happened. That I hadn't lied.

It was validation that I hadn't believed my father capable of giving.

It repaired something broken between us. Not everything because it was still too little and oh so late, and because I knew this would be all I got from him. There would be no more talk of Ron after this. I knew that as well as I knew anything.

But it was something, and I could appreciate it for what it was. I gave him a tight smile, and his shoulders relaxed as he put his glasses on again and continued reading. "'While I can't undo my brother's actions, and while Werner Media assumes no responsibility for his crimes, we are committed to looking after those he has victimized. I am honored to unveil "For Our Children," a twenty-million-dollar fund dedicated to directly serving boys and girls who have been abused and assaulted by Ron or other predators.'"

I slipped out after that. There would be questions and accusations and details of Ron's crimes would come up, and I didn't want to be there for any of that. I'd gotten what I'd come for.

Everything else I needed was waiting for me back at the hotel with Edward.

I WALKED into the living room of our suite to find the ottoman upended against the window, the desk moved back against the wall, and the sofa pushed out of the way to make room for all three of the baby gyms we'd had folded up and stored under the crib in Cleo's room to be laid out and fully assembled. Various farm animals and nature figures were strewn across the floor under fabric-covered arches. Cleo lay on her back under the one nearest me, her legs kicking excitedly at the plush stars above her head.

The best part, though, was that Edward was stretched out on the floor with her, dressed only in a pair of pajama bottoms, his back to me, and God what a gorgeous back it was. He hadn't seen me, yet, so I took the opportunity first to ogle, and then to swoon as he played out a nursery rhyme using a stuffed animal and the plush moon hanging from the arch.

"The cow jumped over the mooooooooon," he said, elongating the last vowel as he jumped a stuffed horse through the air, over the crescent shape, and onto Cleo's belly.

She erupted in giggles and Edward did it again. "The cow jumped over the mooooooooon. The little dog laughed to see such fun and the dish ran away with the spooooooooon."

This time she squealed with glee.

My heart. It felt like it was twisting and bursting all at the same time. How did I get so lucky? It was a profound thought after where I'd just been. My father's statement at the press conference had been moving and much appreciated, but it was a reminder of where I'd come from. Of the disjointed family that barely related. Of my shadowed past where a father placed convenience and ease above the word of his daughter.

From that to this.

From the outside, I was sure my life with Edward didn't look so different from the one my mother had with my father. Living in it, though, the difference was night and day, and as much as it had destroyed me to go through what I had growing up, I'd live through that night a thousand times over if just once it brought me to this beautiful day.

Edward and Cleo. Life didn't get any better than this.

The simple moment was much bigger than one that could be captured, still I pulled out my phone from my purse and clicked a photo. The fake shutter sound wasn't loud, but foreign enough to be noticed. Edward looked up quickly, his expression saying he might have been just a tad embarrassed at being caught playing something so silly.

"I'm weak in the knees," I said, determined to not let him get out of being adored.

He gave me a bashful smile. "You probably should have had more than coffee for breakfast."

"From you, you goof. You're making me swoon." I frowned at the horse in his hand. "Though, that is definitely not a cow."

"If there is one in the bunch, I couldn't find the bloody thing."

My cheeks hurt from grinning. "So when her preschool teacher says she doesn't know her animals, we'll know who to blame."

"Elsa, definitely."

I laughed and sat down on the upholstered bench. "What have you done to this room?"

"The reason we've never had these out is because there wasn't enough room."

"You mean the reason we've never had all three out at one time was because there wasn't enough room. Which was fine since we don't need all of them at once." The space was tight, though. Not for the first time, I longed for our home in London.

"Pish posh. Everything's better in threes." He gave the horse to Cleo who immediately put it in her mouth, then he scooted closer and sat with his back against the bench, his legs stretched out in front of him. "She thinks the setup is brilliant. You can't tell so much when she's obsessing over the taste of that horse's mane, but trust me, she loves it."

He leaned over to kiss my thigh, his eyes skimming down the bare skin below the hem of my skirt. "And I love how long your legs look in these heels. Remind me to have you wear them later when I have my face between your thighs."

"Behave," I scolded as I nudged him with my knee.

He responded by reaching out to remove the shoe closest to him before rubbing the arch of my foot. I sighed into his massage. "The heels are a bitch, but I loved being in my old clothes today. It felt good just being out in the world, interacting with adults."

"Which is why you need to get back to work soon."

"Should I? I keep thinking about it, but does that make me a bad mother?"

"It does not. It makes you a woman who knows that her own mental health and well-being is essential to being a good mother." He looked toward my other foot. "Give me that one."

I slipped my shoe off then stretched my foot toward him. "You make it sound like such a simple decision. I don't want to miss anything important."

"You only work part-time. You'll miss some things, but you won't miss everything, and that's called balance."

Like he knew about balancing home and career.

Except, that was the old Edward. This Edward was trying. Doing better than just trying, so far. Proving it was possible to have it all.

"I'll think about it," I conceded.

Then I gasped as the foot rub was interrupted by a sharp slap across my sole.

"I wasn't giving you an option," he said with a stern look. The kind of stern look that wasn't to be argued with. The kind of stern look that made my lower regions tingle.

I'd forgotten that look. It had been missing for so long, since before Cleo was born. Now he wore it like it had never left his face.

This is my king, I thought. This is the man who cares for me and rules me and knows just what I need. And here he was rubbing my feet when I should have been bowing at his.

I gave him the next best thing. "Okay," I said. "I'll get back to work." That earned me a calf rub as well.

"Where is Elsa, anyway?" I asked when his hands were tired, and it finally occurred to me she wasn't around.

"I sent her home. Daddy's taken the day off to spend with his girls."

"I like the sound of that." The words turned into a surprised "eek" when he tugged me by the leg to the floor with him, my skirt riding up in the process.

I didn't have time to adjust it before he was climbing over me, his body stretched over mine. He studied my face, looking for what, I didn't know, but I found something in his as I stared back—a serenity I normally only saw on his features when he was sleeping. His jaw was relaxed, his smile loose. Maybe it was me seeing what I wanted to see, or projecting my own feelings, but he looked at peace for the first time since I'd known him.

Eventually, he gave me a brief kiss then rolled to his side next to me. "How did it go?" he asked, twirling a loose strand of my hair.

He meant the press conference. I couldn't believe it had taken this long for it to come up, but that was the way with things that weren't that important.

I glanced up at the TV, which was playing a news channel on mute. "You watched it. There's no way you didn't."

"Of course I watched it. I want to know how it went from your perspective."

But that wasn't as interesting as how he'd gotten my father to say it in the first place. "It was your doing, wasn't it? You wrote that statement for him."

"I didn't put a gun to his head to get him to read it out loud. To the entire world, no less." He traced his thumb across my bottom lip.

"You didn't push him to do it at all?"

He shrugged. "Merely suggested that he should."

I let out a sigh, trying to decide how that made me feel. I'd known Edward had been involved with the Werner Media statement. He'd sent me there, after all. To what extent, though? I'd probably never know exactly what he'd said or done to get my father to read it. I supposed it was enough that he'd read it at all.

It was more than enough that Edward had made it happen. "Thank you," I said, sincerely. "It was...as good as I'll get from him, I think. And that's okay. It's more than I expected."

"Much less than you deserve."

I'd spent years playing games where I made people fall in love with me. I was good at it. My uncle had taught me well. I'd never had a shortage of men willing to give anything, give everything, to be with me.

But the earnest way Edward looked at me felt brand new. Maybe because he was the first one who saw who I really was inside, and he still wanted to keep looking.

"You're besotted," I said, rolling to my side to face him.

"You're bewitching."

"You're super hot." I trailed my fingertips across his pecs. But it wasn't just his body that turned me on. I peered over Edward's shoulder at Cleo, who was now mesmerized with a hanging mirror sunflower, and the expansive baby playground he'd been inspired to set up all on his own. "Especially with this whole dad thing going on. I thought you were attractive before, but this is next level shit. Father-hood looks so good on you, in fact, we really should consider having more."

I had to bite my cheek not to laugh, even though I was only half teasing.

Teasing or not, Edward did not take kindly to it. "I should punish you for the mere suggestion."

"That's not a no."

"Oh, you asked for it." He swept his hand up the back of my thigh.

I flipped to my back, a desperate attempt to protect my ass. "You cannot spank me in front of Cleo," I warned. "You'll traumatize her."

"Spanking is not what I had in mind."

"Oh?" But then his hand was under my skirt and inside my panties. "Ohhhh." The man could ignite my pussy with just a brush of his thumb. A second brush, and I was molten. By the time he settled into a steady rhythm across my clit, I was halfway to orgasm. "Fuck."

"Shhh. You'll traumatize the baby."

I giggled. "It's your fault for making me..." Whatever I was saying got lost to the intense wave of pleasure. "God, I never realized how hard it was not to scream when you're doing this."

"Terribly hard?"

"Terribly hard." I bit my lip to suppress a gasp as he slid a finger inside me. Holy shit, it felt so naughty. Like we were teenagers fucking around when we were supposed to be babysitting.

Except we weren't babysitters. We were parents. We were supposed to be responsible.

I lifted my head to look behind Edward. "Is she watching us? I swear she's watching us." Really, she was still captivated with her reflection.

"Of course she is," he said, not bothering to look. "She adores us. We're the most absolutely fabulous people in her world."

He added two fingers on his next thrust, and I had to grip my nails into Edward's shoulder to keep from crying out. "Is it bad, though? If she sees this?"

"Do you want me to stop?"

"No! No." She couldn't really see anything anyway. His body blocked her view, and she wasn't even looking, and if she did, she wouldn't possibly understand, and with all that self-reassurance, I was able to relax and let the orgasm wind itself up, tighter, tighter. "I'm almost there," I panted, my eyes closed. "Almost—"

With no warning, the pleasure cut off abruptly. Edward pulled his hand from my panties and sat back against the bench, a smirk on his face.

I sat up, propping myself on my elbows. "Why did you stop?"

"Seriously, Celia. The baby is right there." When I glared, he said, "It was supposed to be a punishment." Then he smugly brought a finger to his mouth—a finger that had just been inside me—and sucked it clean.

I was wound up and blue-balled and I'd never been so happy. "I hate you a little bit right now."

"I always love you best when you hate me a little bit." He missed my scowl because he stood then and walked over to the desk. When he returned, he had an unmarked envelope in his hand. "I have something for you."

"What is it?"

"Open it."

I took the envelope from him, and sat up to open it while Edward attended to Cleo, who had started to fuss intermittently between her coos. It wasn't sealed, so all I had to do was lift up the flap to pull out the folded document. It was several pages of legalese. A contract of sorts. Or an option to buy, I realized as I skimmed through it, my pulse ticking up when I saw Hudson's name and my name and Werner Media mentioned.

"Edward!" I looked up at him, a magnificent god with the most beautiful baby cuddled against his chest. "He's selling us the shares?"

"He's selling us the shares."

"Oh, my God. He's selling us the shares." I read on, scanning for a catch, and finding none.

Then suspicion kicked in. "What did you do?"

"Nothing. This was all you. Hudson had it prepared before I met with him." He took his place again on the floor, propping Cleo up in his lap.

My ovaries would have burst if I wasn't so distracted by the document in my hand and the man who undoubtedly coerced Hudson in some terrible way to get it.

"You met with him—?"

"Last night," he said, misinterpreting what I was after, though I hadn't known that bit either.

"...and?"

"And he gave me that envelope. Which I have now given to you."

"You didn't...?" I shook my head in frustration, trying to fit the picture together. "I don't understand. Are you saying it's over?"

"We could counter, if you like. Demand the majority instead of just one percent."

I stared at him, then stared at the paper in my hand. Then stared again at him who was too preoccupied with playing peekaboo with Cleo to notice how intensely I was staring.

I just...

I was shocked, to say the least. Edward had put Hudson on his Revenge list at least three years before. That was when he'd mentioned it to me, anyway. He'd likely wanted to go after him the minute he'd first read my journals, which had been at least six months before that. We'd fought over his desire for vengeance. I'd nearly given up a chance at having Cleo because of it. It was so much a part of our marriage, it was almost a foundation stone.

Which was a shitty way to look at it. I wondered what our relationship might be like without this battle between us. We'd still find something to fight about, I wasn't worried about that. But maybe there'd be more of the good. Less of the jealousy. Less of the spite.

I looked again at the document. Hudson had offered to sell us enough shares to make us equal. We could probably announce it publicly, even, without the detail that Hudson had owned the majority before instead of the other way around. We could once again be partners, on equal ground.

Like Edward and I were partners, but also not like that at all.

"I'm happy with this," I said, setting the document down on the bench out of Cleo's reach.

"Then I am too."

"Okay," I said as I scooted up next to him so our shoulders touched. It was time to feed Cleo. She wasn't complaining too much, but she was rooting around on Edward's chest.

Except I was still stuck on my husband's beef with Hudson. I couldn't believe Edward was able to let it go. He never let anything go. Maybe he was still planning to ruin him behind my back. Or maybe he'd already done something he didn't want to tell me, which, in either case, would mean I was the one who should let it go, because I definitely didn't want to keep fighting about Hudson Pierce for the rest of our lives, and whether it was true or not, it was a gift to believe it was done.

But I could never do what I should. "And nothing else?" I asked. "You really aren't going after him?"

"I'm really not. I realized it wouldn't get me what I want."

"What's that?"

"You."

My breath caught in my ribs. "You already have me."

"Exactly." He shifted Cleo to me so I could breastfeed, but he stayed sitting next to us, his brows furrowed.

I let him be alone with his thoughts and focused on the hungry baby in my arms. When she was settled and latched on, I had my own thoughts to parse through. Edward had basically told me he'd felt second place to Hudson. I, too, had felt second place. Edward tunneled in on his schemes, always seeking retribution from this person or that, looking for something to fill some sort of aching need inside him.

So many times I'd wished I could fill that need. Wished that I was enough. Was that what he was telling me? That I was as much to him as he was to me?

"I'VE BEEN BURNING for a long time, bird," he said, breaking the silence. The somber tone immediately grabbed my attention, and before he'd said more I already knew it was something he vitally needed me to hear. "I've been completely consumed with rage and spite, these twin fires that ate everything in their pathway. No matter what I fed them, they continued to burn, burn, burn. Everything was fuel, and there I was, throwing flames at whatever I deemed deserving to be burned down.

"Then you came. And while I'd always been facing backward, always looking to the past, you beckoned me toward the future. It took a while to get me to turn all the way around, but now that I am, my back's to the inferno. If it's still burning, I don't see it. All I see in this direction is you. And Cleo. And whomever else you end up forcing me to love.

Everything that seemed to matter so much before is just smoke, rising in the distance."

"Edward..." A multitude of emotions pressed inside me—complicated, enormous emotions that were too multi-shaded to be named. There was love, of course. Overwhelming and boisterous, but saying I loved him didn't feel big enough. "I've never felt like this before," I said when I couldn't find the right words.

"I know," he said, cupping my cheek in his hand. "I feel it too."

He leaned down to kiss me, more lips than tongue. Appropriate with Cleo lodged between us, and also probably it was exactly the kiss he would have given if she hadn't been there. It was a kiss that made me feel cherished and adored and wanted and all those other unnameable emotions that I was feeling about him.

"God, I love you," he said when he broke away.

"Me too," I said, determined not to cry. "And I think you just said we get to have another baby."

"I said no such thing."

"Whomever else I end up forcing you to love? That was definitely a reference to another baby."

"You are definitely getting spanked when she goes down for her nap."

My belly fluttered in anticipation. "Any other surprises I should know about?"

"Just one."

I raised a brow. I didn't think there was anything else he could say to make me feel more content at the moment or more complete.

It turned out I was wrong because his last surprise, announced in his no-nonsense alpha way of his that I'd missed for so long, was maybe the best surprise of all.

"We're going home."

EPILOGUE

SIX YEARS LATER: EDWARD

"IT'S BEAUTIFUL, Edward. I don't know what to say."

I look at Camilla's reflection in front of us as I fasten the choker around her neck. It's an odd match with the silk black robe she's wearing, but it looks fantastic on her. The alternating ruby and diamond jewels catch the sunlight streaming through the window and sparkle in the mirror and somehow bring out the specks of green in her eyes. It reminds me of the pendant I bought Celia years ago for Valentine's Day.

This one is even more valuable, though, since it had belonged to our mother.

"She would have wanted you to have it today," I tell her.

Camilla turns to look at me directly. "You can tell me the truth, Eddy. Did you get this recently?"

I know what she's asking—she wants to know if I've been hunting down family relics again. More specifically, she wants to know if I've been bullying wrongdoers in the process.

"I've had it for a long time, which is embarrassing to admit because I should have given it to you sooner." I'd been saving it for Genevieve, but now I see the selfishness in keeping this piece from my sister. "As for what you really want to know, I am not involved in that sort of business anymore. I'm far too busy with the present to preoccupy myself with the past."

It's not a lie. My life is full on many levels. Celia and my children take up the majority of my energy, but there's also Accelecom and the three-point alliance and while Nathan Murphy is doing a fine job as CEO of Werner, I have a lot of input as a major stockholder, which means Hudson Pierce is more in my life than ever. It's not a complaint. There's much to admire about the man and much from him to learn. I reckon he'd say the same in return.

Then there's the work I do with Leroy. I don't share the details with anyone other than Celia. A good deal of it is illegal, and I prefer not to involve anyone who doesn't need to be involved, but Camilla is aware of my contributions. Turns out there is a lot of good that can be done by a man with deep pockets and a skill at wheedling into the private affairs of other rich men. There are far too many predators amongst my class, and my obsessive behaviors have found a noble repurposing in tracking them down. *Using my powers for good*, as Celia likes to say.

Since she's the purest of the good in my life, and since she's both the one who put me on the path of bringing down bad men and the reason I do it at all, I'd say she's exactly right.

Camilla turns back to the mirror, her hand fondling the jewels at her neck. "I'm glad you saved it. My wedding day is the perfect occasion to bring it out."

She blinks back tears, and I frown. "It's much too early for the waterworks. I'm going to have a hard enough time seeing where I'm going when I walk you down the aisle."

"Good thing it's a short aisle, isn't it?"

Short it is. Only three rows of chairs are set up in the backyard of Bluntisham House. The only guests invited are family and the closest of friends.

"My best wedding was intimate," I say, sensing she needs validation.

"The first one wasn't so bad," she defends. "But you did come out with a more compatible bride the second time, so I'll give you that.

Frank insisted on all the bells and whistles and to-do with my first one, you know. Look where that ended up. I would have preferred small."

"And now that's what you've got." I hope that brings her back to the present, though I appreciate that she may be compelled to talk about Frank today. It's human nature to compare and contrast. When I'd married Celia, my thoughts constantly measured the occasion to my wedding with Marion. Which ceremony did which part better. Who'd been in attendance. How I felt.

My situation had been different, of course, considering I hadn't expected to stay married to my current bride, but even as I planned her demise—a plan I'm convinced now that I could never have carried out —I'd given myself permission to live the fantasy that day. I meant the words when I spoke my vows. I sealed myself to her, til death do we part.

But I'd said those words to Marion as well, and I'd thought I'd meant them then. I *had* meant that. If she hadn't had the courage to leave, I'd likely still be married to her, both of us stuck in an unfulfilling marriage. It shows a great deal of progress for me to be able to look back on our divorce now and be grateful. Another lesson where the moral is keep moving forward and believe the best is yet to come.

All that said, I can't imagine what Camilla must be going through today. She wears a lot of scars from her relationship with Frank, some more visible than others. She learns better how to live with them every day. The short-sleeve, low-back wedding dress hanging on the closet door is proof in point.

Still, moving forward isn't always easy.

"Am I doing the right thing?" she asks now. She worries her hands together, her expression anxious. "Maybe I'm not cut out for marriage. Am I rushing into it, do you think?"

"After six years and two children together, yes, rushing it seems to be an accurate description of the situation."

She laughs, which was the point. "You're right. I must seem crazy. Most people are likely criticizing me for dragging my feet."

"Most people's opinions don't matter. Only mine. And since I only want you to be happy, and since I believe you're the happiest I've ever known you to be right now, then I believe your wedding is happening exactly when it was meant to happen." I pull my handkerchief from my suit pocket and dab at her eyes. "Not that you asked, but I also think you were quite efficient in the order of events. This way, you didn't have to rope other people's kids into being your flower girls. You have two beautiful daughters already lined up."

"If they do what they're supposed to. A three-year-old and a four-year-old are hardly reliable."

"Which is why you still had to recruit a child wrangler. I'm sure Cleo will keep them all to task just fine."

"Thank you for that," she says, and I know she's not just talking about Cleo's help with her daughters in today's ceremony, but she clarifies anyway. "Thank you for all of it, Eddie. You've been the best big brother a woman could ask for, and I'm so honored that it's you who will give me away."

I'm not given time to respond, which is likely for the best since my throat feels extraordinarily tight all of a sudden, before the door to the guest suite bursts open and Genevieve comes bounding in with Freddie on her heels, each of them carrying an assortment of cosmetic bags and beauty accessories.

"I'm late!" she says, scurrying to set her items out on the vanity. "I'm sorry. I should have stayed here last night as Dad suggested. I don't know why I thought it would be easier to come in this morning, but lesson's learned. I'm here now. I hope you're not terribly cross with me."

While I recognize there're more important matters at hand, I'm admittedly self-absorbed. "Where's Abigail?"

My daughter gives me a vexed look. "Chandler has her downstairs. Hello to you too."

I shrug. I'm not going to apologize for wanting to see my granddaughter whenever possible. I see her so little since Genevieve's life is across the pond.

Camilla clears her throat, reminding us she's supposed to be the woman in the spotlight.

"You're perfectly on time. It's meant to be a laid-back occasion," she says, the bride ironically soothing her matron of honor. "If I'd wanted something more formal I would have hired someone to do my hair and makeup. I asked you for exactly this reason—I wanted all of today to be real and authentic, and I hope it wasn't too much of a hassle. I'm so thankful to get to spend this time with you."

Genevieve settles, her aunt's words being what she needed to calm her nerves. "I'm honored to be part of this day. Let's get you sparkled up, shall we?"

"That's our cue to leave," I say to my nephew who I assume isn't needed now that he's done being my daughter's bellhop.

"Unless you'd like to stay. I could always use some help testing out blush tones."

Genevieve is teasing, but Freddie's expression says he's not so sure.

I jump in to rescue him. "He'd love to, but I need him downstairs for something. I haven't decided what yet."

Camilla laughs. "Get out of here, boys."

As soon as the door shuts behind us, Freddie sighs in relief.

"It's okay, kid," I say, ruffling his hair. "We men have to stick together."

"We do." He fist bumps me then disappears, likely off to lose himself in one of the books he's always carrying around or to latch onto Chandler. Between Camilla's daughters and Genevieve's and mine, there are a lot of women around. I understand the boy's need for any male companionship he can get.

I, on the other hand, couldn't be more content with those that surround me on a daily basis. Peering out the hall window to the back-yard, I see them now, three of the people I love most in the world. They're gathered round the maple tree near the hedged garden, and a momentary flash of regret cuts through me as I remember all the times I missed with my older children, days spent in the country where I stayed locked inside.

Instead of holding the regret, though, I let it go. I can do nothing for the moments I lost to distraction in the past. But it means everything that I choose to be present in the now.

CELIA

"Higher," Cleo pleads from the tree swing. "Higher."

"Mmhmm." But I don't push her any harder. I don't think of myself as overprotective in general, but since Freddie broke his arm last summer from jumping off this exact swing, I'm perhaps more cautious than I need to be.

Besides, I'm a bit distracted. "Stella," I scold. "Leave those alone. I mean it."

"Mummy," the four-year-old protests. "You said the balloons would fly!"

The strings of the helium balloons are gathered and loosely tied around the fence for later. We'll release them as part of the ceremony, which is still an hour away. "Later. I promise."

Stella's expression says there's no way she's dropping her fascination. She's willful and persistent and never takes no for an answer. A lot like her mother, in other words.

Fortunately, my dark knight has come to my rescue.

"Listen to your mother," he says, scooping her up in his arms. It may have been irresponsible getting her dressed up so early—there's every chance she'll be stained and wrecked by the time the ceremony starts—but seeing her bundled in tulle and lace in Edward's arms, I regret nothing.

"You look particularly dashing," I say as he comes over. I've completely abandoned pushing Cleo now, so when my husband leans down to kiss me, I'm there for it.

"Mummy!" Cleo complains while Stella giggles.

"You're breathtaking, as always." He picks at a leaf that has found its way into the bun at the back of my nape.

I pose dramatically to show off my floral embroidered strapless filcoupe dress. "You think so? My husband picked it out."

"Your husband has good taste."

"That he does. It has pockets." I shove my hands inside the hidden pockets to demonstrate.

"Because a woman can't be carrying a handbag all the time, and where is she supposed to put a binkie or her lipstick?"

He's practically quoting me, and I love it. I've obviously been complaining about it for long enough since both our daughters are long past using a binkie, but the sentiment remains, and my husband, as always, listens. Always looks out for me. Always puts my needs first.

What more could a woman want?

Stella wriggles in Edward's arms. "Flutterflies! Cleo! Flutterflies!"

I look where she's pointing and see a swarm of butterflies over the bluebells. Edward puts her down so she can chase them, and Cleo, not wanting to miss out on the fun, jumps off the swing to join her.

"Care—" I wince as she lands on the ground, my warning coming too late. "Ful." But she bounces after her sister, obviously unharmed.

Edward puts his arm around my waist. "You can't protect her from everything. Eventually, they're going to be hurt by something. Our job is to be here for them when they do."

"I know." I hug him back. I know it's just as hard for him to accept that as it is for me. Neither of us want our girls to ever feel pain, and if they are ever hurt maliciously, I am certain that Edward wouldn't let their abuser get off without serious maiming.

And I'm okay with that. I know who I married. While I'm grateful that he's set aside revenging for the most part, I also find peace knowing the lengths he'd go to if provoked. He's not an angel, and I'd never pretend otherwise.

What he is, though, is everything I ever needed. A man who challenges me and puts me in my place. A man who sees the real me and lives to make that me well and whole. He's not just that for myself, but for the children we have together. I hadn't wanted children before him; even after I'd lost my first baby, I'd put the notion out of my mind. After what I'd been through, knowing that there were men who preyed on the innocent waiting around every bend, why would I want to bring a child into this world?

Then, with Edward, I'd felt safe. I knew that he'd never let the things that happened to me happen to our girls. I knew that, if somehow something terrible did happen, he wouldn't turn his back on them. I knew he would be the father I'd wished I had, and every day watching him with them, that void inside me fills a little bit more, my heart is a little more healed.

"Want a go?" Edward asks.

I move my focus from our girls to the swing dangling in front of us. I hesitate, but then I'm climbing onto the seat that was purposefully made wide enough for an adult. For me, specifically. A response to a session, years ago now. Therapy I hadn't known I'd needed.

"Not too high, though," I warn, in contrast to my daughter's earlier pleas.

I know I'll be ignored, that Edward will push me exactly as high as he wants me to go, but I don't worry about it. I trust him completely.

As I sail through the air, I close my eyes, relishing the freedom of flying. When I open them, Stella's obviously been back to her agenda because there's a single red balloon rising in front of me.

Beyond that, all I see is miles and miles of sky.

**Need help recovering from Rising?
Join the Recovery Room! See you there!**

If you liked this story, consider leaving a review on one of your favorite vendors. Reviews help other readers find books they'll love, which helps authors too!

Also, be sure to **sign up for my newsletter** where you'll receive **a FREE book every month** from bestselling authors, only available to my subscribers, as well as up-to-date information on my latest releases.

**Order signed copies of this book and merchandise
related to Slay on my website or listen to it on audio,
narrated by
Elena Wolfe and Shane East.**

---

*You can find a timeline of events related to the Fixed series at the back of
the book.*

*Keep reading to see my author's note about how Celia's story came
about.*

PAIGE PRESS

Paige Press isn't just Laurelin Paige anymore...

Laurelin Paige has expanded her publishing company to bring readers even more hot romances.

Sign up for our newsletter to get the latest news about our releases and receive a free book from one of our amazing authors:

Stella Gray
CD Reiss
Jenna Scott
Raven Jayne
JD Hawkins
Poppy Dunne
Lia Hunt

ACKNOWLEDGMENTS AND AUTHOR'S NOTE

When I said I wanted to write a series for Celia, I got more than a few people complaining. Why on earth would I want to take my most hated character from my most popular series (a very popular series, at that) and make her the heroine? It didn't make sense to most readers, and from a business stand point, it was probably even more of a risk. To be honest, I didn't know if I could afford to devote a year to a project that might very well get skipped by most readers.

So why did I choose to pursue this silly, insane idea?

In answer, I'd like to share the bulk of a blog post I wrote earlier this year:

When I first started talking about writing the Slay books, people told me I was crazy.

Not just one or two people, mind you. Dozens and dozens of comments, emails, private messages. My agent questioned whether it was a good idea. One of my closest beta readers said she'd read anything I wrote, but did it have to be her?

I was pretty sure, based on feedback, that if it had been a man I wanted to redeem, I would have had much less backlash. A good deal of romance is based on a not-so-good hero becoming a better man. There are far fewer stories where a not-so-good heroine is redeemed.

I put off the idea for several years because of the blatant display of disinterest, but all the while the story brewed in my head. Partly because I'm that type of person that when you tell me I'm crazy to do something, I just want to do it more. I'm a challenge-authority kind of gal. The writer who likes to flip tropes on their head. The woman who consistently responds with, "Let's just see about that."

If it had just been my stubborn streak, though, I would have abandoned the project. I'm the sole provider for my family, and I'm smart enough to realize that writing a story that my readers don't want is not the wisest business decision.

But it was more than being stubborn that brought me back time and time again to Celia Werner's story. She fascinated me as a character. She'd done mean things to good people, things that I see play out in less dramatic ways in the real world, and I couldn't stop wondering why she would do that. What compelled her? What drives people—what drives women—to hurt others?

Lots of reasons came up as I continued to mull over it, but one answer spoke loudest from the crowd—she was broken. People hurt others because they are broken. Women hurt others because they've been broken.

So very often, those women have been broken by men.

In today's culture, that felt like a very important topic for me to explore. Especially when I tend to write alpha men with qualities that are often associated with toxic masculinity in the real world. It seemed relevant to differentiate masculine from machismo. In other words, differentiate men who are strong, courageous, and assertive from men who use their strength, courage and assertiveness to hold power over women.

Besides the aptness, Celia's story was completely on brand. Because broken people finding love—specifically dangerously broken people finding love—is exactly what Laurelin Paige books are all about.

And so I got brave.

I focused in on what it would take to tell such a complicated story. I decided to make it possible to read this series and enjoy it without ever reading any of my other books. I freaked out a little when I realized it would need to be four books (oh-my-goodness-four-books-is-a-ton-of-books!), but when I talked myself off that ledge, I carved out time in my schedule, and put book one up for preorder.

Then I took a deep breath and dove in.

It wasn't easy. The writing itself flowed well enough, but facing the terrible and dark places that Celia has been was much harder. I spent significant time researching and talking to a couple of close friends who were sensitive to the subject matter. I put my blinders on to the many readers who said they would never read this book (which is a decision I support completely—not every book is for every reader). I reminded myself this was a story I believed in, a story I needed to tell. I focused. I meditated.

And when I was done with book one, no matter what the critical response was, I decided I'd be proud of it. And I am.

Now, with the series completed, I'm over-the-moon grateful for the support readers have given me. It's beyond what I expected, and I'm very lucky for that. But even if I hadn't received such great reviews and comments, I would still believe in this story. I wouldn't want to write romance books that didn't include some aspect of redemption in them. To me, that's the truest form of love.

The idea that people can recover, that we can heal, that we can atone, that we can change and become someone better than what we once were, *that no matter what we've done we are still worthy of being loved—that notion is essential to the progress of humanity. I can't imagine living in a world where we didn't believe growth was possible. I certainly wouldn't want to.*

At the end of this journey, I have to take a moment to thank everyone who helped get me down this road. Take a breath, there's quite a few.

First off, my team is fucking awesome. I couldn't wish for a better one. Candi Kane, Melissa Gaston, and Roxie Madar are as much a part of Laurelin Paige as I am. I depend on them more than is probably healthy, and I love them more than I ever let on. Thank you for being my people, ladies.

Then there's Kayti McGee. She's half team member, half co-conspirator, and one hundred percent best friend. I may not be singing you Phantom of the Opera, but I'm definitely singing you A-Ha. (I'll be coming for you anyway.)

Next, my soul sister and agent, Rebecca Friedman. Even when there are long periods where I don't see you (I miss your face right now! Stupid Coronatine.), we always pick up right where we left off. You're a great friend and one of the few people who gets my neuroses (as well as my family's). Love you to the moon and back.

This series definitely couldn't have happened without Liz Berry. Even when she wasn't sure she wanted a Celia story, she spent a weekend with me trying to sort out my vision. I mean, she really went there, into the trenches, helping me discover what the story really was and the dark places it would go. Very few people have that kind of stamina and even less take the task on with such enthusiasm. I'm so lucky to have such a genuine, compassionate, intelligent woman on my side. Thank you for letting me into your family. You've definitely found your way into my heart.

My betas, editors, and proofers - Erica Russikoff, Amy "Vox" Libris, and Michele Ficht. Without these women, my words would be riddled with errors, but they contribute much more than that to my process. Their notes and ideas and, more than anything, their cheerleading are what keeps me going most days. I appreciate you ladies for everything you are. Thank you for letting me invade your lives like I do.

Marni Coleman at Lyric Audio and Elena Wolfe and Shane East—what a fucking audio team! I am so pleased with how you've made my characters come to life. I couldn't have asked for anything more, and as always, I'm so appreciative of your patience with my sometimes lack of organization. You all are saints.

Tom Barnes and Melissa Gaston for making my stunning paperbacks and Alyssa Garcia at Uplifting Designs for giving me such gorgeous insides.

I couldn't do anything without running it by Lauren Blakely. She's my sounding board and my mentor, and one of my best friends. It's so refreshing to have someone who never tires of talking business. Our chats and marketing sessions are the highlight of my day.

My LARCS and my Instagram team—you ladies are gold. I don't know what I did to deserve such treasure in my life. I hope you know I'm always grateful, even when I'm absent from the interwebz.

The Sky Launchers—I will never not be amazed that there are people who, don't only want to hear the stories I have to tell, but also love them with such devotion and enthusiasm. Thank you for your unfettered joy. I endeavor to be more like you.

And to all my readers all around the world—thank you for giving me this crazy, fantastic life. It's the best job possible.

To the friends who weren't before mentioned — Melanie Harlow, CD

Reiss, Jana Aston, ShopTalkers and all the other authors who share advice and knowledge and just life on the regular without any expectations in return. I can't imagine having better peers. You make the worst parts of the job bearable and you teach me how to celebrate the best parts in style.

To my mom, husband, and daughters—we bicker and we fuss but we sure do love each other too. Even after more than a month of being quarantined with y'all, I still look forward to popping the popcorn and going to the theater room to watch Magicians with you. What would my life be without you? Spoiler: not much.

Finally, to Open Cathedral for teaching me a new way to worship, and to my God. In this crazy, strange, surreal time, you've been my touchstone. You give my life meaning and direction and help me remember myself when it would easier to be lost.

For fans of the Fixed Series, here's a timeline to show how the books fit in together.

Year 0

May ——— FIXED TRILOGY begins

Year 1

April ——— Alayna & Hudson get married

Year 2

Year 3 ——— Alayna gets pregnant

June ——— SLAY ONE: RIVALRY begins

November ——— SLAY TWO: RUIN begins
Year 4

November ——— SLAY TWO: RUIN ends
Year 5

Year 6

August ——— CHANDLER begins

Year 7

June ——— FIXED FOREVER begins

ABOUT LAURELIN PAIGE

With millions of books sold, Laurelin Paige is the NY Times, Wall Street Journal, and USA Today Bestselling Author of the Fixed Trilogy. She's a sucker for a good romance and gets giddy anytime there's kissing, much to the embarrassment of her three daughters. Her husband doesn't seem to complain, however. When she isn't reading or writing sexy stories, she's probably singing, watching shows like Killing Eve, Letterkenny, and Discovery of Witches, or dreaming of Michael Fassbender. She's also a proud member of Mensa International though she doesn't do anything with the organization except use it as material for her bio.

www.laurelinpaige.com
laurelinpaigeauthor@gmail.com